SHADOW
and
LIGHT

SHADOW and LIGHT

PETER SARTUCCI

SHADOW AND LIGHT

Coming of Age

ISBN: 978-1-7335745-0-1

Edited by Kier Salmon.

Cover Art copyright by Claire Peacey, used by permission.

Book design by Kate Morin.

TABLE OF CONTENTS

ACKNOWLEDGEMENTS

No writer works in a vacuum. I want to thank some of the many people who helped me with the long process of creating this book.

First, to my wife Elizabeth, for the support and love that made it even possible.

To my workout buddies Brandon Slaten and Bill Cowern, who gave me much useful feedback in between sets. We might have exercised a little harder if I hadn't kept telling you snippets of stories, but we wouldn't have had as much fun.

To the members of the Northern Colorado Writers Workshop, especially Marie Desjardin, Rob Chansky, Vivian Cathe, Eneasz Brodski, Rick Friesen, Ronnie Seagren, Pat Smythe, Ron Hosler, and our beloved mentor the late Ed Bryant, who were with me on critiquing the book all the way through. I learned so much from you all!

To Kier Salmon, my copy editor and good friend, who made many good suggestions and caught several embarrassing goofs. (If I managed to sneak any others past her, that's my own nefarious fault.)

To Steven Michael Stirling, for encouragement when I really needed it. Nothing is more encouraging to a newbie author than having an expereinced old-timer tell him to get back up on that horse and try again!

To Claire Peacey, for a gorgeous cover that went so far above and beyond my expectation that I am still in awe.

To Kate Morin, for assembling it all into this volume that you are reading now.

And to the reading public, on which I and every other author depend; this one's for all of you.

AUTHOR'S NOTE

What do you do when your world turns upside down? When the foundations on which you built your life melt like ice and flow like water? When you lose—but find that you won, and the prize is entirely different from the one you thought you wanted?

This is the beginning of a set of tales that stretches across several novels. Each tries to be self-contained, but if you really want to know these characters and their world, here is where it starts. Welcome to the land of silver and sulfur, wealth and dearth, love and hate. Welcome to Silbar.

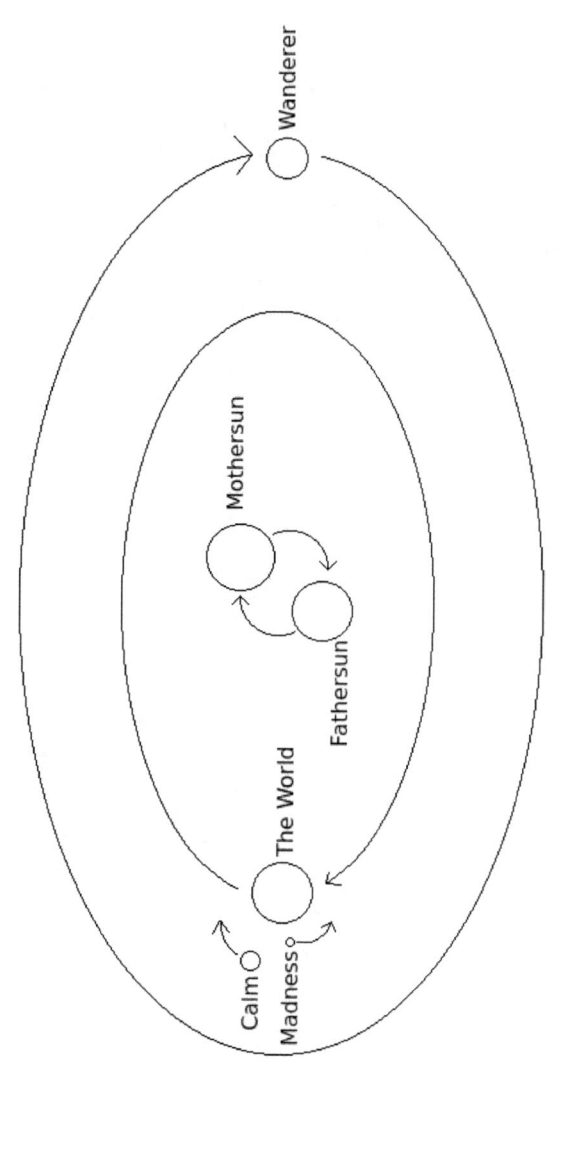

CHAPTER 1: KIRIN

May I tell your fortune?"

Startled, Kirin DiUmbra let the outhouse door bang shut. The woman's voice had an odd lilt that should have sounded happy but came out solemn. She blocked his way out from the narrow space between the theater wall and the troupe's wagons. A wool hood covered her hair and a coarse veil concealed the lower half of her face. The lively gray eyes that stared into his black ones from barely an arm's length away were set in a copper skinned face under a single joined eyebrow. The combination marked her as a Duermu tribeswoman from the eastern deserts. Her exotic scent hit his nose, desert incense and goats and sweat.

He recoiled in embarrassment at being taken so completely by surprise. How had she gotten inside the rear courtyard of this tiny rural theater? The wall rose a yard taller than he and its only gate stood high, massive, and closed.

Kirin breathed the scents of horses, goats, and the fetid outhouse behind him, and wished for more distance between himself and this unwelcome intruder. He put his hands on his hips and stared challengingly at her in the warm spring sunshine. In his most discouraging voice he told her, "I don't have any money on me."

Which should have been obvious. He wore nothing but the patched tightknit hose he used for the DiUmbra Acrobatic Troupe's rehearsals. In the midday heat of Silbar's vast central valley he'd even left off a shirt. Perspiration trickled down the pale golden skin of his bare chest and stuck bits of his curly black hair to his forehead.

"You didn't hear me ask for money, did you?" she answered in that same odd lilted accent. "I only ask to be allowed to tell your fortune, young sir. Surely a peerless star among acrobats can allow a desert woman that." She held out a preemptory hand, thankfully clean, and waited.

She stood several fingerwidths shorter than Kirin but blocked his path back to the theater as immovably as a tree. He couldn't bring himself to push her aside, though outcastes like her were even lower in social rank than a halfbreed acrobat. He'd seen Duermus tell fortunes in the bazaars and market places of Silbar. Grandfather DiUmbra claimed they were all frauds with no real powers of prophecy. Kirin's adoptive father Pieter wasn't so sure.

Agreeing might make her go away. He gave her his right hand.

She took it firmly, turned his palm up toward the doubled light of the Two Suns, and traced the lines with a surprisingly delicate touch. Her hands

PETER SARTUCCI

were as seamed with work as any peasant woman's but still youthful. She couldn't be much older than his seventeen-plus years. Without thinking he used his magesight to see if she had cast a spell on him. He had heard tales of Duermu witches doing such things. No swirl of power poured out of her fingers, though he could see she had plenty of magic in her. She might not be a complete fraud.

She gave him an ironic glance. "Have no fear, young sir. I cast no spell without consent. A courtesy that I hope you will return."

He flushed, hating the way it heated his face. The skin that marked his half-Silbari-half-Gwythlo ancestry always betrayed his feelings. Under his heart his Shadow stirred, and he hastily quelled it. Rural towns were bad places to be suspected of illicit sorcery or, far worse, demon summoning. He had no wish to be burned at a stake in the public square.

"A strong life line," she commented as she stared at his palm, oblivious to his brief internal struggle. An absorbed expression had taken over what he could see of her face. "Healthy. You will sire children, perhaps more than a few."

"Only not yet," Kirin muttered, pleased and worried at the same time. His wife Maia starred in the show that the DiUmbra Troupe had taken on the road for fame and profit. The family couldn't afford to lose her to motherhood right now. Her mother had bought her a pregnancy protection spell and they had been careful, but the thought still worried him.

"Strength and dexterity will be yours for many years, more so than most mortals," she continued. "So long as you do not make utterly foolish choices in the risks you take. Your wisdom line is less strong; you will need guidance."

Since every adult in the family shared that opinion, and said so frequently and with embellishment, Kirin snorted derision and rolled his eyes.

"One such moment is approaching, with several more following it like wolves." She frowned. "Beware. You shall be tested with fear and loss. Powerful people will help you, if you allow them, while others will endanger you. Remember always who you are, even as you discover what you are. That grounding can serve you well."

Those obscure remarks sounded like the kind of drivel he'd expected. He took back his hand and rubbed it as she bowed to him in an oddly flattering gesture.

"Are you done?' he barked, trying to summon a righteous outrage. "Will you get out of my way now?"

"No and yes, young sir," she answered. "We will meet again." She turned and darted away.

Maia called his name.

"Coming!" Kirin answered and hurried to the theater's back door.

"Who was that?" she asked, gazing at the rear gate in the courtyard's high adobe wall.

"Some Duermu fortune teller. Wouldn't get out of my way until I let her read my palm."

Maia frowned. "I hope you didn't give her money. That only makes them pester you more."

"She didn't ask for any, and besides," he gestured at his barely clothed state. "I've got nothing on me."

"And you sure look good that way." Maia smiled at him, which made his face heat again. "Hopefully she won't bother you again."

Kirin said nothing as he uneasily remembered the woman's parting words. *I asked her if she was done with me, and she said 'No.'*

* * *

Hours later he peeked through a knothole in the back wall of the crude stage. "That's a rough-looking crowd. You suppose they'll throw things?"

"Let's hope they throw money," his brother-in-law Sevan the Younger answered while Maia made a last-minute adjustment to his costume.

"There's a priestess out there." Maia noted when she finished and let her brother take his position. "Nobody would dare behave badly in front of her."

Kirin thought but did not say aloud, *unless she behaves badly first.* The fortune teller's words about 'powerful people' stirred his unease. Priestesses wielded power over life and death. He swallowed his worry as Maia kissed him, careful of his makeup, and said, "It'll all go fine, love. See you in Act Two!"

At that moment Grandfather signaled for the DiUmbra Troupe's presentation of *Malik and Mercia* to begin and Kirin had no time to worry.

* × *

At the end of the show when Maia's Mercia led Kirin's Malik out of the Tormentor's Hell, the audience rose as one and cheered.

"I'd say that went better than fine," Maia said to Kirin over the crowd's roar as the troupe gathered behind the stage wall.

"You're the reason why, love," he answered, hugging her.

Pieter Ille DiUmbra, Kirin's adoptive father and Maia and Sevan's uncle, smiled at the couple while the crowd's cheers continued. "You infants had better go take another bow before they riot."

"Everybody with us!" Kirin called, and the whole DiUmbra troupe lined up. They paraded back onto the stage amidst doubled roars. Maia flicked a long white scarf into the air and levitated it above them. Kirin sent his Shadow out to dance with it as they had done during the play. The audience, thinking they saw the clever stage illusions that accompanied the family's fame, roared even louder. Kirin gripped her hand and raised it between them, then he and Maia waved their free hands at the assembled troupe—Pieter still dressed as Salim the Tormentor, Sevan as his lackey Fear, all the rest of the extended DiUmbra family as the other roles. They bowed to the audience as one. A rain of coins hit the stage and the family's little kids scampered to gather them up. At a signal from Grandfather, Kirin and Maia blew kisses to the crowd and lead the others offstage as even more metal clattered onto the boards. Kirin glanced back in time to see a bulging pouch nearly thump one of the kids. The lad scooped it up and ran it backstage to Kirin, who triumphantly pressed it into the old man's hands.

"Feels like a profit," Maia's grandfather, Grigor Ille DiUmbra, murmured as he weighed the pouch in one hand and listened to the slowly fading cheers.

"Told you it would be, Father," Pieter said.

Grandfather only grunted. Kirin failed to hide his satisfaction at that grunt.

The old man glanced at him and narrowed his eyes. He waved to two of the teenage cousins. "Go out and help the little ones gather it up. Don't miss a single coin."

The cousins nodded and ran. The cheers were fading, and the rain of coins had stopped. Pieter, his face proud, clapped Kirin on the shoulder before the older men of the troupe went around to the front of the stage to discourage anyone tempted to raid the family's pay.

"Good work, Maia," her grandfather said. "As for you, Kirin, put that damned thing away!" He pointed at the lingering Shadow and glared.

Kirin wiped the grin off his face and mentally slapped himself for forgetting. He knew perfectly well that Maia's grandfather still suspected him of being an imp, possibly even a demon, not merely playing one on stage. He drew his Shadow back inside him and pushed it down under his heart, locking it away where the troupe's leader could forget about it for a while. The audience thought it a clever stage illusion; the family knew better.

Maia lost her smile and gave her grandfather a cool look. She let the white silk scarf fall into her hands and pointedly took Kirin's arm.

He let her lead him away, her silence a rebuke to her grandfather.

Not that the old man seemed to notice. "Get out of your costumes and get to work," he bellowed after them. "Maia, I want the backstage packed up before the next bell rings! And Kirin, get back in trousers and help my grandsons pull down the ropes and the traps. Make sure it's all packed correctly!"

"Yes, Grandfather," Kirin called back over his shoulder. He knew he packed the trapeze set as flawlessly as he performed on it, but the cranky old bastard would never admit it—or call him grandson.

"Ignore Grandfather; he's just in a mood," Maia whispered as they wended their way through the cramped backstage area.

"Hard to do," Kirin muttered back. "He's like a thunderstorm."

In the even-more-cramped dressing room, other family members congratulated the two stars while the troupe peeled off costumes and wiped paint off each other. Kirin untied his hair and shook his head. That let his black curls bush out again to cover his pale pointed ears. He hated the way they set him apart from the rest of his round-eared, brown-skinned family.

Carmella told Maia and Kirin to turn their backs to each other before he stripped out of his fancy black silk tights.

"Moth-er," Maia grumbled, disobeying while she peeled off her white costume, "Kirin and I have been married for half a season! I know what he has under his tights!"

This time Kirin blushed like a beet root. Maia giggled. She loved to embarrass him in little ways. He got her back by swiftly kissing her, which made her face shift from teak to mahogany even as her eyes grew misty.

"Show some modesty, both of you," her mother scolded. "You two can pillow like rabbits when you're alone, but we have a reputation to maintain and there are Purist priestesses about. I'll not have one accuse the DiUmbra clan of lascivious behavior!"

"Yes, Mama Carmella," Kirin answered in pretend meekness as he pulled on a battered pair of canvas trousers, ragged shirt and rope sandals. Even the prospect of facing down some terrifying old priestess couldn't spoil his elation as he got to work.

Grandfather had designed the DiUmbra troupe's travelling set for *Malik and Mercia* so that it both went up and came down quickly. Sevan and Maia's younger brother Attir pitched in for the takedown, and Pieter joined them as soon as he got his own makeup off.

"Grandpa says our take topped a hundred dohba again!" Sevan said triumphantly. "And it's because of you and Maia, Kirin."

"More because of Maia," Kirin corrected, grinning fondly at his wife as she carried a sack of costumes to the wagons. She blew him a kiss as she passed her father, Sevan the elder, and her grandfather. The two leaders of the troupe had paid off the stage owner from the day's take while the man quarreled over details.

People still milled around the audience space. Kirin paid them no mind until he glimpsed the yellow robes of a priestess in the severe, simple cut favored by the Purist sect. He retreated behind the stage wall where the woman wouldn't see him. He never knew how any of the Temple Hierarchy would react to him, an obvious halfblood. Most of the ordinary priestesses of the Orthodox sect, like Dona Zella at home, were sympathetic, seeing the flesh and blood man under the pale skin. The Dissenting sect, less so, and the Purist sect didn't see anyone with pale skin as human at all.

He tossed the last bundle of rope up to Sevan atop the second wagon, and nearly jumped when someone spoke right behind him.

"I thought it might be makeup, but no," a female voice growled. "You really are a halfbreed."

Kirin turned to find plain yellow robes and a cold pair of brown eyes above a gauze veil. The Purist. His heart beat faster.

He felt a wave of relief when he saw that there were only four silver stars on her starched wimple. She might be the ranking priestess of a rural temple, maybe even an abbess of a small convent, but no more than that. Two more stars and she'd have had the rank to force him into a trial for demon possession, which could end with him burned at the stake. But he ought to be safe, if he took care not to provoke her.

The Purist stared at him like something nasty stuck on her shoe. His fear faded while anger grew.

"Dona Quartissima." Kirin addressed her by title and rank, put his hands together and bowed. "I am loyal to the faith and a good Silbari, Dona." He knew he should stop there, but bitterness provoked him to add, "I had no more say in my birth than any other man does."

Her gaze hardened. Sevan blanched. Kirin wanted to bite his tongue. For all that he knew it was a bad idea to anger the pureblood faction, he'd just had to poke back.

"Dona." Pieter inserted himself between them and bowed low, using the move to shove Kirin away.

His father's shaved head with its central scalp lock bent right in front of the woman's face. The double silver rings that held Pieter's elaborate hair knot announced his affiliation with the former Sons of the Defender monastic order, and the torture scars showed that he'd been a survivor of the Battle of Black Pass. Everyone knew the heroic story of that desperate, doomed action. Kirin hoped the priestess would respect it.

"I am Pieter Ille DiUmbra, this young one's adoptive father."

Her eyes flickered over his father and Kirin saw how she forced herself to return the appropriate head bow. Good; he breathed a little easier until she spoke.

"Adoptive?" The woman's voice was incredulous. "What possessed you to take in such a viper, Monk? It should have been stilled in the womb."

That last was perilously close to blasphemy, for the Orthodox Hierarchy did not approve of abortion—for humans. But the Purists didn't believe folk like him even were human.

Pieter looked her in the eye and answered. "Mother Seraph Umana's charity *possessed* me, Dona Quartissima. Nothing more—nothing less."

Kirin saw her face tighten and her eyes squint. Plainly this Purist hated to be reminded that not all the Scholars of the Holy Writ agreed with her. At that moment voices cried for a healer's aid. Before the Purist could say any more, an acolyte called her away to help some old woman who had collapsed. The Quartissima spared Kirin a cold glance before she turned to answer the call.

Pieter's father came over and growled at Pieter. "When are you going to learn to keep your mouth shut, boy?" Turning to Kirin, he ordered, "Tidy up the stage and let's get out of here before you start more trouble, brat!"

Pieter bowed exaggerated obedience, his way of defying his father, and dragged Kirin away with him.

"I'm sorry, Father," Kirin whispered while they made sure the local stage had been stripped of everything the DiUmbra Troupe owned.

"I'm not," his father answered quietly. "The fanatics need to be opposed, no matter what my father thinks. You did well, son."

That made Kirin glow. When they had tossed the last items into the second wagon and climbed aboard, he snuggled with Maia on top of the load and happily watched the small town shrink behind the departing troupe. He indulged in a little vicarious vengeance by imagining the afternoon light of the Two Suns blistering the whitewashed Temple dome.

"You've been a rascal again, like Uncle Pieter," Maia accused him with a smile.

"I confess!" he answered, kissing her. He hoped they would have a room of their own wherever the troupe stayed.

They made the next town before nightfall and found the expected inn. It had a warren of little rooms in a crooked wing that looked like it had been made by knocking three mudbrick houses together and dividing every room, sometimes twice.

"At least it's cheap," Uncle Sevan the elder sighed, handing room keys to Pieter. He jerked his chin at Kirin and turned to distract Grandfather's attention with details.

Pieter led Kirin to the first of the rooms assigned to the Troupe. "Time for the needful, son," he whispered, urging him inside.

Kirin nodded obediently, and while Pieter guarded the hallway, he closed the door behind him and sent out his Shadow.

It poured out of his chest, black as his silk performance tights, and flowed over the floor and furnishings. Darkness rose like a tide to drown the room. Within it the tiny lives of the vermin—bedbugs, lice, and ticks—glittered like sparks in his mind. He freed that stricture he normally enforced on the Shadow, and let it kill. The sparks snuffed out. A tiny pulse of life energy passed across his heart like the faintest brush of a butterfly's wing. It dived into the darkness of his Shadow and vanished. He grimly throttled the nausea that followed. There were more rooms to go.

In each he reaped tiny lives like grain. The fleas leaped about in fruitless attempts to escape before they fell dead on the floor. Kirin's face twisted up in disgust as sparks of bedbug life force flowed through him and into the Darkness. When the rooms were finally clear of pests, he gladly forced his Shadow back into its cage under his heart. Sated with its harvest of small deaths, the Shadow went with only a token struggle. Kirin trembled a little in relief when he had it locked away again. He emerged from the final room, wondering if the day would come when he couldn't make it stop killing.

"Well done, son," Pieter told him with a clap on the shoulder. "You saved us all from a miserable night and from only-The-One-knows what illnesses."

Kirin smiled halfheartedly.

They went to join Sevan and the cousins at the inn's bath house. It wasn't fancy, a big cauldron set into a brick fireplace in one corner of the courtyard with privacy provided by a woven slat fence. It did have several worn benches, a trickling fountain of fresh water, and a set of buckets. They had to bring their own drying rags or let the summer heat do it for them.

There were pegs to hang up clean and dirty clothes. An attendant fed the fire and scooped warm water from the cauldron to fill their buckets and

PETER SARTUCCI

to pour slowly over each bather. When Kirin stripped off his trousers and exposed the manumitted slave tattoo on the pale skin of his right thigh, the servant's face twisted in disgust. He made Kirin stand there, waiting with his bucket, for a long moment before ladling out a share for him.

Sevan and Kirin passed a scrubbrush back and forth. Both still had bits of makeup in their ears and hair and the creases of their skin. It hadn't taken as much of the oily white paste to make Kirin's golden skin look like an Imp. The attendant, as brown-skinned as the rest of the DiUmbra family, openly moved his right hand in a sign against evil. Kirin pretended to ignore it; one more hurt in a long litany. But he saw Pieter stare coldly at the man until the attendant went back into the inn.

Sevan and his brother and cousins quietly gripped Kirin's arms or patted his shoulders. He bent his head without saying anything and pretended to be busy cleaning his feet.

"I'm sorry that swine insulted you," Sevan muttered.

One of the cousins added, "First that country priestess and now this small town yokel." He shook his head with the lordly contempt of a born and bred City man for rural peasants.

Kirin flinched nonetheless. He knew that his unknown sire had likely been some Gwythlo conqueror; everyone knew what had happened in the war eighteen years ago. His endless shame rose up anew.

"You may well be a child of love, you know," Pieter reminded him.

"Or rape," Kirin answered bitterly, staring after the servant to avoid meeting the eyes of his adopted family. "Mama never told me which before she died. But is either one my fault?"

Pieter took him by the shoulders and turned him around. Kirin looked up into his face; his father stood a hand taller than him, like the rest of the grown men of the family. That face filled with patient kindness as familiar words formed on his lips. "Kirin—"

"I know," Kirin interrupted, dropping his gaze down to his own feet. "'We're performing in small towns where people have never even seen the ocean, where strangers from outside Silbar are rare and folks' memories are of Gwythlo conquerors and their pale skin and pointed ears. I shouldn't let people's fear hurt me.' I know."

Pieter sighed, squeezed his shoulders with both hands and lightly cuffed him on one ear for the interruption, not even hard enough to sting.

"At least I know you're listening to me," he said. "Maybe someday you'll heed me."

They finished bathing and trooped back inside with wet hair and clean clothes.

Kirin stayed quiet during supper in the inn's common room, but his eyes roved nervously. Once townsfolk had seen the DiUmbra's performance they generally liked the family, sometimes with wild enthusiasm. But until then most viewed the troupe as a disturbingly large mob of suspicious strangers. There were three merchants and their retinues in the room, too cosmopolitan to give Kirin's skin more than a glance. But easily half those present were small town dwellers with superstitious distrust stamped bone-deep into their faces.

They stared. Kirin endured.

Sevan the Elder and his wife Carmella led the evening worship for the family in proper Silbari style before the clan sat down at a long table. Kirin sang the descant with Sevan and Maia in three-part harmony. That quieted some of the suspicion in the room, though there were still plenty of looks directed at his pale skin and pointed ears.

Maia and Sevan bracketed him at the table for a meal both filling and good; even the small-beer was passable. But Kirin noticed that Maia ate litte and drank less.

"Not hungry?" he asked her softly

"Not very."

"Shall I peel an orange for you?"

"All right."

He did, removing the peel all in one long coil for Uncle Ger's six-year-old son Berrin to play with. He set the juicy wedges before Maia in a fan. She ate a few, gave the rest to the kids.

"Just tired, I guess," she said, and leaned against him.

He put an arm around her, his skin tingling at her touch. Even after most of a season he still couldn't quite believe his good fortune. This wondrous woman had chosen to marry him despite his pale skin and evil ears.

"We have our own room. Want to go to bed early?" he whispered to her. Both suns were down. The tallow candles lighting the inn's common room smoked and gave little light. "We can just sleep if you're too tired."

She gave him a grin and said, "When have I ever been *that* tired, love?"

His blood sang in anticipation.

They managed to leave the table with only a few amused smiles from the family, found their way to their assigned cubby, and disrobed in the silvery light of Calm. A big pad covering most of the plank floor in the tiny chamber did for a bed. Kirin knelt on it and straw crunched. Maia finished hanging up her clothes and turned to him, all shiring dark curves in the night. His heart beat so hard he thought his chest might burst. She bent over to kiss him and pushed him down onto his back.

"Love me, Kirin," she said, and he did.

Hours later he awoke to find himself alone in the bed. A retching sound came from the corner with the chamber pot.

"Maia?" Fear stabbed him as he sat up and pushed off the light blanket. "Are you ill?"

"No," she answered, turning her face to him. The light of the Moon of Madness glittered on fresh teardrops.

He hastily crawled to her side. "Is it something you ate? Should I call your mother?"

"No," she said again. "There's nothing wrong with me, Kirin."

"But something is wrong, isn't it?" He tenderly enfolded her in his arms and she sagged against him. "Tell me."

"I'm pregnant."

He twitched in shock. His first happy thought, *I'm going to be a father!* gave way to the frightening, *does she want to keep our baby?* There were no pregnant acrobats, for good and painful reasons. He knew they were making the best money the family had known since before the Gwythlo Conquest. Without Maia they couldn't do their most profitable show.

He pulled her into his lap and held her close. Neither of them said anything for a long while. But through his memory ran the fortune teller's words. *I will be tested with fear and loss? Please God, not Maia!*

* * *

Early next morning Kirin and Maia found a moment when they could take both Pieter and Carmella aside privately.

"But I bought you a pregnancy protection spell!" Carmella protested. "They're supposed to be good for a year!" She looked at Kirin accusingly. "You said you'd be careful!"

"Carmella, I was careful!" He protested, then glanced around and lowered his voice as he gestured at Maia's belly. "My Shadow never broke the spell, it's still there. But last night I discovered that it's got tiny holes in it, like pinpricks. I think my, um, seed, must have pierced the spell without destroying it, or being destroyed by it. I didn't know that could even happen!"

"I didn't either," Maia admitted miserably. "I know we should have been more careful, we knew the risk, but—we didn't want to stop—well . . ."

The corners of her mother's mouth pulled up unwillingly. "Saints witness, I should have foreseen that. Looks like your talent breeds true, Kirin."

"I thought I had it under control," Kirin said wretchedly. He had tried so hard . . .

"You're both young and infatuated with each other's bodies," Pieter observed drily. He'd been a monk for nearly thirty years, but he knew the world. "That's the One God's way of making sure people have enough babies for the next generation."

Kirin gripped Maia's hand and she squeezed back while her mother rolled her eyes.

"Daughter, do you want this baby?" Carmella asked bluntly.

"Yes!"

Kirin thought Maia surprised herself with her answer. He found his own heart singing. *She wants my child!* Part of the fear that had been gnawing at him all night melted away.

Maia continued more quietly, "I always wanted children out of Kirin the moment I knew I wanted him. I just didn't expect them for a couple years yet."

She leaned against Kirin and he ached with sudden desire for her.

"Mama Carmella, we talked about children," he tried to explain. "We wanted to wait until after we'd made our fame among the troupes and brought the family money and honor."

"You've already done both," Pieter assured them. Kirin discovered that it helped, a little.

"How long since you caught?" Maia's mother asked her with a sigh. "Give me your best guess if you're not sure."

"Maybe six tendays. Or seven."

"Hmmm, you can probably keep performing for the rest of this trip anyway, possibly a little longer. Don't tell anyone else about your condition while we're on the road. Your grandfather will burst a blood vessel when he hears about this, so I don't want to tell him before we're home in Aretzo."

They all relaxed a little. If they were home when Grandpa found out, at least there'd be the rest of the family for support, and Grandmother to help rein him in. Kirin wished she wasn't so frail that they had to leave her behind with the nursing mothers and the babies and the infirm of the family. The troupe's leader was a lot easier to live with when he had Grandmother with him.

Pieter said, "I'll do my best to keep him distracted. Maia, take good care of yourself. Kirin, you keep right on taking care of her, too."

"I will, Pieter," Kirin answered fervently. He hugged Maia as tenderly as a man handling spun glass, and she hugged him back. "I will."

CHAPTER 2: TERRELL

Light.

Prince Terrell DuRillin DiGwythlo dreamed of Light.

Bathing him like the two suns. Sleeting through him like tiny spears. Light, endless Light that roared stronger than a tempest. Light that assaulted him with sheer overwhelming power until his mind was swept away. Light!

Someone shook him. He gasped and opened his eyes to darkness.

"My Lord?" Pen's anxious voice finally penetrated his ears. "You were groaning in your sleep. Are you ill?"

Terrell sat up blinking. He'd pushed most of the covers off. Sweat soaked his nightshirt despite the chilly northern night. His room in Gwythford Castle faced northeast and both moons had set. The night candle by his bedside had burnt more than half way so it must be past midnight. He released Pen's hand, which looked even darker in the candlelight than his own, and rubbed his eyes.

"It was only a dream," he told his bodyguard and best friend, who had but one day of life more than his own seventeen years. "I'm not sick. I'm all right."

"You're as sweaty as my gambeson after a four hour fight," Pen answered. "You had that Light dream again, didn't you?"

"Yes," Terrell admitted.

"You promised me you'd tell Dona Seraphina if it happened again." It wasn't quite an accusation.

"I will, Pen, but I don't think there's any need to wake her now. Morning will be soon enough."

"Will you still remember it in the morning? Maybe you'd better write it down."

Terrell sighed, but Pen had the right of it. "I will."

He climbed out of the feather bed. He peeled off his sweaty nightshirt to don the clean dry one Pen brought and lit a taper at the night candle. He settled himself at his writing desk with the taper lighting a blank sheet and took a fresh quill in hand.

"Did I say anything?" he asked Pen, uncorking his inkbottle and scribbling rapidly.

"Not aloud. I only heard groaning, as if someone had cut you. That's what woke me up." Pen gestured to the open doorway beyond which lay his own small plain room. "I feared you were under attack."

Terrell scribbled for a few minutes, blotted the page and set it aside. "There. That's all I remember." He found himself yawning. "I'm going back to bed, Pen, and you should too. I'll talk to the Dona in the morning."

"As you wish, My Lord. Sleep well." Pen went to the door of his room, paused briefly while Terrell blew out the taper and crawled back into his own bed, and then closed the door behind him.

Terrell curled up in the feather bed, still slightly damp from his earlier dreaming.

This is the third time, he thought. *Each one a little brighter, a little stronger, a little worse. If this goes on . . . what's going to happen to me?*

He fell asleep wondering.

* * *

Dona Seraphina DuVigo Abnellambra read his note through twice while Terrell forced himself not to fidget.

"Light?" Dona Seraphina muttered, her brown eyes darting to him. "Are you sure you didn't simply perceive a source of magical power? Such as the Node under this castle?"

Terrell reflexively reached for the Node with his mind. He touched the upwelling magic that laired hundreds of feet below the castle's foundations, and withdrew. "I know what the Node feels like, Dona, and my dream was very different." Terrell groped for the right words. "Much, much stronger and . . . vaster."

"Vaster," the priestess repeated. "Hmmm. Hold still while I examine you."

Terrell obeyed with the practice of years. She had been his physician since his birth. Mother had brought the Orthodox Silbari priestess north with her after the famous wedding which settled the Conquest that left Silbar subordinate to the Gwythlo Empire. He knew that she'd been here twenty-six tendays later to midwife his own birth, and all the chaos that had flowed from it. Her golden yellow aura enveloped him, penetrated his skin, and warmed him inside and out. After what seemed like a long time she withdrew it and tapped his note with one bony finger.

"Your body's mana conduits are enlarged," she reported abstractly, frowning at him. "Substantially. Have you been channeling power?"

Startled, Terrell answered, "No! You know I don't have any talent but the most common one, magesight."

Her frown turned dour. "Yesterday I would have agreed, but given your ancestry, that may be irrelevant, My Lord. Your mother has none either, and yet she learned to channel the power of Aretzo's Hill of Sight during a battle."

"And did it well enough to win a marriage treaty from Father." Terrell knew a brief flash of pride that he came from two mighty bloodlines.

"Yes." For a moment the ghost of a smirk flickered across the priestess' face. "We call that war the *Gwythlo Conquest*, but who really conquered who?"

Terrell grinned; at seventeen he had begun to understand some of the truths about men and women. A maid in the castle named Serah had made it her mission to teach him.

More seriously the priestess continued, "You appear to be developing a similar capacity."

Terrell tried to understand. "You mean I'm becoming a real mage?"

"Not in the traditional sense, I suspect. Try to tap the Node."

Terrell did, with the usual result—nothing. He had enough magic perception to sense the magic source deep beneath the sprawling castle, but it remained stubbornly indifferent to his presence. He sensed three of the staff mages tapping it at this very moment, refreshing the castle wards or powering spells, but he couldn't even call forth a flicker from it.

"Hmmm. You still show no evidence of any capacity to draw on our world's inner power, which is the fundamental marker of mage talent." The priestess drummed her fingers on the table absently. "What I suspect you are developing now is different—the capacity to utilize pre-worked spells, at least those keyed to you or your bloodlines."

"Pre-worked spells?" That sounded hopeful. Terrell sat up straighter.

"You may be more familiar with the term *artifacts*, though not all artifacts contain spells and not all pre-worked spells become artifacts. Mage Shimoor will doubtless teach you much more, but I'll usurp a bit of his prerogatives today."

She went to a large ironbound chest in a corner of her office, unlocked and opened it. After a few minute's rummaging she came back to the table with a small object. When she set it before him Terrell stared curiously at a box roughly twice as long as wide and no more than a fingerwidth thick. It featured a polished bronze upper surface above a simple carved wood body. He could see a complex spell within it.

He carefully refrained from touching the object and asked, "What is it?"

"A fixed message sender. It is used to quickly send a simple prechosen message." She plucked a bit of raw silver about the size of her little fingernail from her purse and fed its magical power into the box; the silver's native glow vanished. "It is charged. Contemplate the top and, without touching it physically, attempt to trigger the message. It will most likely feel like a narrow bar in your mind, somewhat like a door handle. Try to grasp and pull it."

Terrell gingerly opened his mind to the device, trying to push his strictly limited magic perception into it. He usually couldn't do it at all, but maybe if he tried hard . . .

For a long moment nothing happened while he strained like a man trying to move a castle by pushing it with his bare hands. Then light burst as though someone had brought a dozen lit candelabras into a dark room. His awareness dropped inside the tiny space to find light illuminating the box's twisting interior. Nothing looked solid and sparkles of magic rippled over everything. In the middle a blue bar of elemental light hung unsupported. He wrapped his mind around the wispy thing and tried to pull it. For a while it

14

stayed as unyielding as the New Keep, before abruptly giving way. Something tiny and glowing shot from the end of the box. It sped birdlike through the air to Dona Seraphina. He heard a tiny sound and it vanished.

"I did it! Was that a real message construct?" Terrell asked, excited by his success. He'd never used any magic more complicated than a mage lamp or a fire starter before.

"Yes, a very small one. Try to manipulate the power in this bit of silver."

She handed him another sliver of the precious metal and he groped for the magic within it, tried to seize and shape it. As with the Node, it didn't respond at all, though he strained harder and harder.

"Stop," Seraphina said. "You'll damage yourself. Do you understand the difference between raw silver and the Keep Node on the one hand, and the message sender on the other?"

"The sender is a spell already prepared and primed; it simply had to be launched, like an arrow from a bow. The Node, and charged silver, are both power waiting to be used, the raw stuff from which that arrow might be made." His voice fell, and he looked at her pleadingly. "Does this mean that I'll never be able to wield real magic?"

She shook her head. "Too early to say definitively, but that's increasingly likely. Mage talent usually manifests before a man's voice begins to break, and yours changed more than a year ago. I've known it to appear as late as a man's eighteenth birthday and as early as his tenth. You are half a season short of turning eighteen years old."

She let that hang in the air for a while. Terrell drooped.

"Then I'll always be only a, a mechanic, operating spells that I can't cast," he said dully. He had heard ballads of the great battle mages of the past, especially his grandfather Hywel who had founded the Empire and built this castle. He had hoped—

"Do I hear your vanity talking, boy? Your father is no mage either, yet he's Emperor of Gwythlo, Silbar, Klinto, and Fehdar, plus sixteen smaller realms. Which he rules very capably indeed, especially with your mother's aid."

"But Father has Haroun's Gift. So does Pen. No mage can stand against them."

"Immunity to magical attack only goes so far, Prince. You do not yet know what you may have, or become, but there remains more than one possibility—so don't wallow in self pity."

Dona Seraphina had a sharp eye and unsparing attitude, Terrell reflected as he straightened up. "Tell me what else is possible," he demanded.

"You referred to the use of an artifact as being merely a *mechanic*, as if that is to be despised, you vain pup." She glared, and he wondered if she would rap his knuckles with a stick the way she had when he'd been small. "Yet half of your people can't even do that much. And not one in a million can manage the Great Artifacts. I strongly suspect that you will become one of that small number. But if you approach any Great Artifact with the arrogance you showed to me, it may well kill you! Do you understand?"

This time he made sure to answer meekly. He put his hands together and bowed his head briefly. "Yes, Dona Seraphina."

She grunted, mollified. "That's better."

"But—Dona, does this mean I *can* use the big artifacts in Aretzo?" He wondered if that meant he would be chosen by Silbar's Throne to be the next King after his mother died. Not that he would actively wish for her death; he loved both his parents, but it would be enormously helpful to know in advance whether he'd someday rule from the Stone Throne.

"Possibly," the Priestess temporized. "The minor functions at least; no king has been able to use the greater ones for more than a century. I wouldn't raise your hopes too high, Your Highness. As I have pointed out, most bearers of such abilities find that they settle at a low level and never progress beyond that. You may grow to be more, but you'll need training to be effective—and to avoid killing yourself. I can't emphasize enough; the Great Artifacts are *dangerous!* Still, your abilities are growing. These special talents often take years to unfold, so we'll have to see how you develop."

"Oh." Terrell deflated again. The prospect of putting up with years of confusing dreams did not entice him. But still—"Do you think Mother and Father would let me go to Aretzo and try one of the artifacts? Not the Stone Throne itself, of course," he hastily qualified. "But there are safer items that I might try, right? The Guardian, the Vault, the Pool?"

She gave him an extremely dour look. "What part of the word *dangerous* did you not understand, Prince? Any of those might still maim you. Do you want to spend the rest of your life as a mindless idiot?"

"I don't propose to try this alone, Dona." Excitement kindled in him as he dismissed the risk. "I'll take Shimoor with me! Surely Silbar's Royal Wizard is the very best mage to guide me in exploring my new abilities. It's only prudent that I be trained, and Aretzo's the best place to train any sort of mage talent. And if I'm ever to rule Silbar, I must learn the ways of its capital sooner or later."

He forced himself to stop his spate of words. He'd made the best arguments he could think of, now let them work on her for a while. Dona Seraphina looked at him thoughtfully. Good. He forced calm on himself and sat still, doing his best to project a patience he didn't feel. The moments dragged by like hours.

Finally, Seraphina nodded slightly. "I will discuss this with your mother. We shall see what we shall see."

Terrell managed a dignified, "Thank you, Dona," and quit her office before she could change her mind. He went to his mother's chapel, empty at this time of day, and knelt before the icons of the Great Seraphs, Lady Umana and Lord Haroun. Above them towered the closest depiction Silbaris ever made of their God, a many-armed silver and jet swirl.

Please, please, oh Haroun, mightiest of Seraphs, he prayed. *Intercede for me with the One God! Let me go to Aretzo and see my ancestral home. Bestow your grace on me that I may prove capable and worthy. By the Unknowable Name I pray, let me become what I hope to be—King of Silbar.*

* ⨯ *

For Terrell the next two days dragged by more slowly than tired oxen. Mother and Father were away on the annual summer tour of the Gwythlo baronies, reaffirming the oaths that held the Empire's core together. The first sign of their return came when Terrell and Pen came back from a ride in the Keep's oak forest to find the stables noisy with returned soldiers. Servants led dozens of clattering horses out to pasture, dogs dashed about yelping and every stable hand rushed to and fro dealing with the hundreds of returning beasts.

"The Silbari Brigade is back!" Terrell told Pen excitedly. "The Caniff Dragoons too! Mother and Father must be home." He and Pen dismounted in the side court that served the Forest Gate and a groom took their horses. "Viller, have you seen my parents yet?"

Viller bowed and said softly, "No, Your Highness, but Crown Prince Osrick is here." As he led their horses away he made a motion toward the open doors behind him.

Terrell's half brother came out of the stables. He had three of his Gwythlo cronies at his back and a Klinto mage behind them. Despite not having yet reached the age of thirty-four, the Crown Prince's yellow hair had begun to thin and retreat. He walked stiff-legged, both fists clenched and his normally pale face more flushed than sunburnt. He kicked aside a crotch-sniffing dog and glared at his younger half sibling.

Pen quietly stepped up to Terrell's shield side and loosened his sword in its sheath.

"Welcome home, Osrick," Terrell greeted cautiously. "How did the Fealty trip go? Did you get a chance for some good hunting?"

The Crown Prince growled, "Not while Father kept me on a short leash, and your bitch of a mother reminded everyone down to the lowest squire about my damn oath!"

"But oaths are how we hold the empire together, brother." Terrell tried to deflect the anger of his fourteen-years-older half sibling. "They bind and strengthen us all."

"Strengthen! Forty days of humiliation," Osrick spat. "She rubbed my nose in my sin every chance she got. Subtle and sly, yes, I'll grant the bitch that! The whispers were everywhere; *fratricide* in one hall and *kinslayer* in another. I wish now that I'd killed both of you in your cradles!"

"Not too late," remarked one of the nobles. He fingered the grip of his own sword and stared unpleasantly at Terrell and Pen.

Terrell sensed that Pen had gone tense, ready to draw in an instant. But there were four swords and the mage facing the two of them, very bad odds. Terrell's heart sank towards his boots. He'd never seen Osrick this filled with rage. He eyed the friends and the mage, all mature men with more than a decade of war experience. This didn't feel like a planned assassination, more like Osrick impetuously seizing an opportunity. The tumult in the stables would hide the clash of swords. Four blades against two—

Terrell swallowed, centered himself. He would have to let Osrick draw first. Could he kill his half brother, even in self defense? Become a fratricide himself? His guts were hollow, but he wasn't willing to die. He rose on the balls of his feet, ready to dodge and draw.

Osrick's sword hand moved—

"Pardon me, my lords, but it is indeed too late," said a new voice. "Far too late."

A wave of relief swept through Terrell as Pyrull walked out of the stable. The Master Swordsman wore Irreneetha at his hip, as always. The magic sword let out a subliminal hum of power. The Crown Prince's mage blanched at the sudden sound, backed away, turned and fled.

All eyes followed Pyrull as he leisurely walked around Osrick's party to Terrell's right hand. There he stopped, faced the Crown Prince, and smiled pleasantly. His own right hand, browner than Terrell's, as brown as Pen's, rested on his sword's hilt, and now a low shivering growl emanated from the blade. Three brown-skinned men faced four pale ones.

"Your father gave me strict orders not to kill you, Your Highness." Pyrull still spoke Gwythlo with a Silbari accent, which made his words to Osrick more menacing. "But he said nothing about your friends. It would be a shame to spoil this lovely day with three needless deaths and yourself wounded, don't you think?"

Osrick's pale northern skin flushed red to the points of his ears. His face twisted into a caricature of rage. For a moment he raised his fists as though about to leap on Pyrull and pummel him.

The face of the angel in Pyrull's sword manifested in the air between them.

Osrick shied back, cursed, and stormed off into the stables. His cronies hastened after him.

The angel shimmered and disappeared, and Pyrull's sword fell silent. Pen let out his breath in a gust and released the hilt of his own sword. It clicked against the silver-chased mouth of his scabbard as it dropped back in.

Terrell had to swallow to be sure his voice would come out steady. "Thank you, Magister Pyrull, for that intervention. I would hate to be forced to kill my brother."

"A shame he doesn't feel the same, Your Highness," Pyrull answered. His seamed brown face split in a relaxed smile as white as his hair. "But do not take your own success for granted. Osrick is quite good with a blade and has much more experience than you, my Prince. I am pleased that you were wise enough not to force the fight."

"I don't hate him, Magister," Terrell answered honestly, grieved inside. "I've tried to love him like a brother should, but he won't let me."

Pen touched Terrell's shoulder lightly.

Pyrull coughed. "Which does you credit, Your Highness. Unfortunately, it only takes one to hate. Now, may I be so bold as to suggest you and Baron Penghar should go change and ready yourselves to wait on your lord father and lady mother in two candlemarks? They've had a grueling journey, but they'll want to see you when they've rested a little. The Silbari brigade won the draw for first turn at cleanup, and your friends among them will want to spend a little time with both of you."

Terrell agreed, though the delay pained him. Still, it meant Dona Seraphina would see his mother before he could. She might advance his hope of visiting Aretzo.

Gwythford Castle's huge baths, built by his father in imitation of proper Silbari baths, had a steam room, cold plunge pool, warm pool, bathing room, and ample changing rooms. The cheerful bedlam of returning Silbari soldiers filled it, getting their first chance to wash in days. They welcomed their young lords and for a little while Terrell and Pen got to share again the camaraderie of men with round ears and dark skin like theirs. Men who shared their isolation here among the pale point-eared folk of the cold North. Terrell nearly managed to forget the recent encounter with Osrick.

When he and Pen, freshly washed and turned out in clean clothes, presented themselves at the door of his parent's suite, completely new worries elbowed their way into his mind.

"The Empress will see you now, Your Highness," said one of the ladies in waiting, the daughter of a Silbari noble house who had come north to serve his mother for the customary year. "Baron Penghar, Magister Pyrull wants a word with you."

Terrell thanked her and let her lead Pen aside while he moved alone through the warren of the Imperial Suite. He could hear Dona Seraphina's voice raised somewhere ahead.

"—fool I am for sending a barely trained healer with you! I should have gone myself—"

"Stop it, Seraphina." Those were his mother's cool tones overriding the priestess. "I'd have made the same choice. You'd merely have argued longer than she did."

The door opened, and he saw his mother sitting in a chair in front of the windows of the castle solar. The Two Suns shone through the many glass panes. Terrell had to squint to see details. She wore Silbar's deceptively simple silver crown as she usually did. The thumb-sized amethyst in the front of it glittered.

He crossed the room in a few strides, knelt at his mother's feet, kissed her extended hand. The skin was papery and shrunken on her fingers. He looked up into her face and gasped.

Though he knew she wasn't yet forty years old, she looked fifty. Wrinkles creased her formerly smooth face.

"Mother! What happened to you?" Looking around with growing suspicion, he found that his sire wasn't in the room. "Where's Father?"

"Sit next to me, my dear son," she told him, her voice still strong but now with a faint quaver. "There is something that I must tell you."

19

* * *

"Father's dying?" Terrell said incredulously a little while later. "How can that be? He's always been so strong!"

"No longer," Dona Seraphina interrupted, a sign of the depth of her upset. "There's a cancer eating at him, and we—I!—can't cure it. I thought that I and the rest of the healers had successfully beaten it back before the Fealty trip. I thought he'd have several years more, but I was wrong. It surged back and now it's spread to his organs. He wouldn't last another year, probably not even half a season, except that your mother—"

"I've made my decision," she interrupted the priestess sharply. More quietly she said to Terrell, "You know that your father and I married to settle a war."

He nodded numbly, taking refuge in recitation. "The Conquest, it's called in Silbar. After my Gwythlo grandfather Hywel, the first Emperor, set out to conquer Silbar, your father and he killed each other in the Battle of Black Pass. The Empire and Silbar both lost their rulers in the same hour."

His mother sniffed. "The bards exaggerate. Your grandfathers probably never got within a hundred yards of each other in that chaotic slaughter. The crucial part happened days later and hundreds of miles away."

"I remember the tale, Mother. Father led the fleet that assaulted Aretzo, while you commanded the city's defenses. Once word reached him that he'd become Emperor, he proposed marriage to you and ended the war."

"It was much more complex than that," his mother said wryly, "But that's the most important part. He proposed to me, my romantic Gwythlo enemy, on bended knee in my own Palace. How could I refuse him? Never think, my son, that your father and I had a loveless marriage of state."

Terrell gestured helplessly. "Well obviously not! Anyone who saw you two together could tell. I always knew. Osrick did too—oh." Years of thoughtless observations fell into place. "That's *why* he hates you."

His mother nodded sadly at the expression on his face. "Yes. He has never forgiven me for winning his father's love. Even at age fourteen, it made him madly jealous, I suppose because the first flush of his own manhood had come on him. It's why he tried to kill you as a baby."

"And did kill my twin brother." Terrell knew again that old ache, the loss of someone he couldn't even remember, now forever absent. *I wasn't meant to be alone.* But that was unfair to Pen, who'd been raised with him like a real brother.

He glanced across the room at the small shrine in one corner where his mother kept a candle always burning. A tiny lock of fine black hair sealed in crystal dangled on a gold chain from the lacquered frame of the icon.

So little we have left of you, Ryghar, Terrell thought. *A wisp of baby hair and Mother's memories.*

He found himself tugging gently at his own hair—pure yellow, the same as Osrick's and Father's, or rather the same as Father's hair had been before it went gray. *We were not identical, but we were twins. Damn the legends! I should have grown up with you too, Ryghar, you and me and Pen. Sometimes I dream of it—*

With an effort he pushed that thought aside. He knew better than to confide *those* dreams to Dona Seraphina, or to anyone else, even Pen. Might-have-been dreams were a trap, the Writ warned of it in a dozen places. Everyone got only the life The One gave them. Wishing for anything else was a deceit of the Pale Seraphs, a trick of the Temptress.

Only the service I make of the life I've been given will matter when I set my soul in the Grey Judge's scales. What I have lost and will yet lose on the way . . . must serve to make me stronger. There is no other path for a Prince of Silbar.

Seraphina had been pacing; now she stopped and faced his mother. "Is it love to kill yourself while your son still needs you?"

Terrell turned to his mother in shock. She smiled mirthlessly.

"I am not killing myself, Terrell. I have shared my lifeforce with your father, bound us together. I can buy him many more tendays of life this way, and thus buy time for you."

"Me?" His voice cracked humiliatingly but he ignored it.

His mother's eyes met his own and he saw there an intensity that she usually kept hidden.

"Seraphina tells me you want to go to Aretzo. Do so with my blessing. Years ago, your father decreed that Silbar would be yours to rule upon his death, yours and your line. He required Osrick to consent, and to bind himself to support you in exchange for only two duties; that you acknowledge your half brother as your Emperor, and you pay him tribute. It is part of Osrick's oath as Crown Prince, and I used this fealty trip to remind every noble of what he has sworn to. They'll all be watching him, judging him, for if he can't keep an oath to his brother, how can they trust him to keep his oaths to them? He's trapped, and he knows it."

"And furious about it." Terrell twisted his lips wryly. "He wanted to kill me after he got back. Now I understand why." *He must have realized Father is dying, too.*

His mother tensed, and her gaze narrowed. "I sent Pyrull to protect you!"

"He did. Osrick was angry but he walked away."

She relaxed. "Good. I thought he would. He is your father's son. He'll come to his senses eventually. Especially once that white cow of his stops popping out daughters and gives him a son or two to dote on. At least she's fertile, Seraphs witness."

His mother tossed her head and sniffed. Terrell almost smiled. There had long been no love lost between her and the Crown Princess. But sunlight caught the wrinkles spreading in her face and grief wrenched at him anew.

"Mother. If I go to Aretzo, will I ever see you and Father again?"

She became cold and remote, like a stone carving rather than someone he loved. He could see how much it cost her, and it almost broke his heart.

PETER SARTUCCI

"No," she said. "You won't, and that's as it must be. You are my only living child, Terrell, the last of the DuRillin-DiSilbar line. I count on you to refound that line, to restore Silbar to glory once more. You've had the best teachers and have still more of them waiting for you in Aretzo. The palace staff will serve you gladly, as will most of the aristocracy; your claim also legitimizes them. You'll have to win over the mages and the merchants and the commons, and—" Her eyes darted to Seraphina and back to him, "—the Temple Hierarchy, but you'll start with the legitimacy of my dynasty. Use it to build your own, so that when my crown returns to the Stone Throne—" Her voice caught, and she stopped speaking.

When she died, he knew she meant. Silbar's Crown would depart the body of a dead King or Queen and appear on the Stone Throne atop the Hill of Sight in Aretzo. Legends said it had done so a hundred and twenty-three times so far, ever since the first king made The Pact With God two millennia ago. Mother had made sure he knew the stories.

"I will have to stand for it as tradition demands, one of The Twenty Candidates," he nodded.

"First among them!" his mother interrupted fiercely. "You are the most direct heir in the entire Royal House. You have precedence by birthright and none can doubt it. They must let you try first!"

"Have no fear of that," Seraphina sniffed. "The tradition is firmly established, no one will question his right to be there. Not openly, at least." She rolled her eyes, leaving unsaid the caveats of Silbar's long grim history. Terrell knew that the makeup of the Twenty changed, sometimes often, as men fell aside due to age, illness, accident—or murder.

"I pray I am judged worthy," he agreed, ignoring the rest. "But that means—I have to think about this. There's so much! And to leave you and Father here—" His own voice faded as his thoughts faltered, not knowing what to do with the anticipation of grief.

"You must prepare," his mother said firmly, while Seraphina jerked her chin in harsh agreement.

Terrell swallowed the rising lump in his throat, forced himself to set aside the pain. They weren't going to die today, or for many tendays yet. He would be mad to grieve before the need arrived. "How long do I have?" he asked, knowing there were two questions in the words.

His mother chose to answer only the surface one. "You have three days before your father will send you off to Silbar with pomp and ceremony. Then four tendays to get there, and as much more as I can give you to establish yourself. You must be in unassailable control of Silbar when Osrick mounts the Imperial throne. You are my son. You can do this."

"I can do this." He nodded, excitement kindling in him. It would be the biggest challenge of his life, but he had been preparing for it for nearly eighteen years. "Mother, I need to see Father."

* * *

Terrell's sire lay napping lightly in the big bed that his parents had shared all the years of his life. Curtains across the room's great window shadowed his face. A maid pulled them aside and Terrell beheld the craggy canyons grown in his father's forehead. He looked shrunken, as though his skin no longer fit. The yellow of his hair had been fading for so long Terrell could scarcely remember when there hadn't been some gray; now most of it had gone translucent white. Mother sat on the edge of the bed and clasped one of Father's hands, wrinkled and spotted, and by that Terrell saw how much flesh had withered off the Emperor's frame. The blue eyes opened, and the same lively intelligence looked at him again.

"I'm not dead yet, boy," his father said gruffly. "So don't look at me like that. Makes me want to swat your backside, and that'd be undignified for at least one of us."

A smile bloomed on Terrell's face, surprising him. "May it please my Father; I would not want to force him to be undignified—unless nobody else could see."

The Emperor of twenty realms smiled back, pleased. "Let's skip the flowery language; takes too much breath. I promised your mother you'd have Silbar. But Osrick will still need its money. Tell me, son; can Silbar's treasury afford a tribute of a half-million pounds of silver annually?"

"That sum would be impossible to sustain," Terrell answered thoughtfully. "The silver mines produce more than twice that, but most of it has to go to support mages and spells already propping up vital functions, like bridges and harbors and the fleet. Without them, both artifice and trade would suffer, and the realm would shrivel, until it couldn't collect enough in tolls to provide any tribute at all. A healthy Silbar is necessary to support a healthy Empire, and the reverse is equally true."

"Good. You listened when I talked. Very good." The old man on the bed sighed. "Wish your brother had done as much. Maybe you can be smart enough for both of you."

"Father, I—" Terrell said as the bedroom door opened and Osrick barged in, a pair of guards not-quite impeding him. A green-clad woman followed at his heels.

"Father!" Osrick bellowed. "I—!"

"Have the discipline of a drunken plowboy!" The Emperor cut him off savagely, sitting up in the bed. His wife tucked a pillow behind him and sat next to him, one hand resting lightly on his arm. "And half the wits, since your aunt goaded you into barging in like one! Did you take even a moment to wonder why the Chief Druid in our realm might want you to provoke my anger?"

Osrick stopped in confusion, glanced aside at his green-clad aunt. "I—no, Father. I didn't think. Until now."

"Better late than never," the Emperor snorted. "You've been used, Imperial Crown Prince Osrick. Remember what it feels like." His gaze shifted to the woman in green. "Klairveen, you may have grown slightly cleverer while I've been away. I give you permission to speak, and it had better be good."

Klairveen, the Chief Druid of Gwythlo, gracefully bowed, using it to also shift a step away from Osrick and closer to the Emperor. "Your Imperial-Majesty-my-brother, please forgive my impetuous invasion of your quarters. I simply feared for your life."

"Oh, very good Klair; play upon love and fear at the same time. Note well, my sons, the artistry with which your aunt laid that one on us. You'll both find there are others better at it than she, and unfortunately, most of them will have even less true feeling behind the words, damn all their eyes. But drop the honorifics, sister, and talk plainly in front of your nephews."

The mask of concern on Klair's face slipped, settled into a chilly stare that flicked across Terrell's mother and himself like a lash. The Chief Druid of Gwythlo wasn't short on charisma when she wanted to use it, but she wasn't wasting any on them. She said, "Very well, Brion; I heard you were dying. I'm not entirely bereft of filial tenderness, hard though you make it for me to show it. The rumors made you sound at death's door. I worried that I'd not get the chance for one last try at your Edict—and a chance to say goodbye, you heartbreaking idiot."

"Put in an honest order of priority." Brion nodded. "You *are* learning. But my Edict stands. Followers of any faith from a kingdom within the Empire may worship in any other land of the Empire, no exceptions, no taxing or persecuting or massacring them. And you can drop the noise about *last try*; we both know you won't give up that fight even when I'm burnt on my pyre. Osrick, that'll be your problem then, but remember! She has a list, and once she's got the top thing on it she'll be every bit as relentless for the next, and then the next. You can't shut her up by giving in to her, only by waiting for one of her Quarter rituals and enjoying the three precious days of quiet."

"While I placate the land wights for your neglect," Klair said bitterly. "Care you nothing for the gods of your people?"

"Which people, Klair? I rule twenty realms, nineteen of which believe I already favor Gwythlo in too many ways."

"Your home," she answered forcefully. "These valleys and hills and forests and rivers! This land that birthed you, nursed you, taught you, raised you high! If its people, your true people, don't deserve some favor for that, then your heart is a stone."

The Emperor's stern face softened at those words. Terrell thought about riding in the cool forests, swimming in the slow rivers, and guessed dimly at the draw her appeal must offer to his father. And to Osrick, whose face looked more like Father's in this moment than it ever had before.

"None of us are stone, Aunt Klair," Terrell said into the silence. "I feel it too, the call of the North land that you're trying to enlarge in the hearts of my father and brother. It'll always have a place in my heart too."

"But not a dominant one," Chief Druid Klairveen answered him coldly. "Your skin tells the truth. Silbar will always have a greater claim on you, Prince Terrell DuRillin." After a pause she grudgingly added his third name, "DiGwythlo."

"Yes," he acknowledged. "And that's why I must go there, become its ruler if the One God wills it so." He shifted his attention to Osrick. "But the northern blood will still be there in my veins too, brother, you know that has to be so. It's a tie on which you can rely. While I live I'll always be part of the same truth that you belong to, even while I am part of my own. Let me be the bridge you need between them."

Osrick stared at Terrell, suspicion warring with hope in his face. Their father shot a warning glare at his sister that silenced her next words a-borning, and glanced between his sons, expectant, waiting. At last the Crown Prince nodded.

"You'll willingly acknowledge me Emperor? Pay me tribute?" he demanded.

"Two hundred thousand pounds of raw silver each year," Terrell pledged. "That's as much as Silbar can yield without damaging its ability to deliver the same the next year, and the next, into all the long years of the future. Accept a limited return now, Osrick, and it will still pay you when we're both old and gray. Demand more, sooner, and Silbar collapses like a gutted cow, leaving only hide and bones. Bones that you'll have to garrison, while they yield nothing and drain your other lands."

Osrick's face darkened. "Are you threatening me, little brother?"

"No, and I never will. You'll always be bigger and stronger than me, big brother. I'm offering a pledge of wealth to my future Emperor." Terrell met his gaze, not with a challenge but with a promise. "But only what I can actually deliver. Would you prefer I tell you lies instead, only to fail and leave you with diminished coffers? I'm sure there are plenty of others who would do so."

Osrick's face turned bitter for a moment. "Too true." His gaze cleared, and Terrell saw the decision made. "I accept." He turned to Father, made a small bow. "If my Emperor wills it."

"Nice of you to include me in this conversation," the Emperor said, but his smile robbed the words of anger. "Consent given, and well done, my son." He glanced at Terrell. "Both of my sons. Remember this moment when others try to make you forget it. You'll always be stronger together than apart."

Terrell nodded jerkily, relief flooding through him. Osrick inclined his head, neither agreeing nor disagreeing. He stared at Terrell for a long moment and then made a formal farewell. Only after the door closed behind him did Terrell slowly let out the breath he'd been holding.

"You got your way again, Brion," Aunt Klair sniped. "I wonder how long it will last?"

"You can report on that to me in hell," Father answered genially. "Since we're both probably bound there."

"Not if I can help it," Terrell's mother said fiercely, squeezing her husband's shoulder. Terrell's heart hurt as he watched another wrinkle appear in her face.

Father patted her hand as he leaned back against the pillows. His face sagged in exhaustion. "I hope you are right, my love; I hope you're right." He

25

let Dona Seraphina extend her Healing aura over him as he added, "Next time do it the polite way, Klair. Send word ahead first and knock when you arrive."

Aunt Klair's nostrils flared as if she resisted comment by sheer self-discipline. She too bowed and excused herself, with an unreadable side glance at Terrell.

"Thank you, Father," Terrell told his sire.

"No need," Emperor Brion mumbled sleepily. "Get ready to travel, son; you've got a lot of work ahead of you."

Terrell hesitated, went to the bed and kissed his father on his withered cheek. The old man smiled as his eyes drifted closed. Terrell left the room with his heart both heavy and light.

* * *

Outside the Royal Suite one of the Brigade guards bowed to him and said, "My Lord, Magister Pyrull requests your attendance on himself and Baron DiLione in your mother's chapel."

Terrell resisted the temptation to ask why. Pyrull was notoriously close mouthed, so the guardsman probably didn't know. Terrell simply said, "Take me there."

The chapel was only a quarter turn around the New Keep and on the same level; they arrived quickly. Terrell found the Master Swordsman quietly conferring with one of Dona Seraphina's healers near the door. Up at the altar, Pan knelt in prayer.

"What is this about, Magister?" Terrell asked Pyrull quietly, not wanting to break the hushed stillness of the room.

The old Silbari teacher bowed to him gravely. The slanting light that fought its way through the thick stained glass windows bathed him in purple and gold. It only accented the whiteness of his hair and the deep wrinkles of his face. "You Highness, the time approaches for Irreneetha to choose a new bearer. I wish to nominate your servant for the honor."

For a moment Terrell's mind refused to make sense of the words. He couldn't mean—

Pen rose from his prayers, bowed to the altar, and came up to Terrell. His face glowed.

"What—" Terrell stopped himself, swallowed as he gathered his thoughts. "What does this mean, Pyrull? What will happen?"

"If she accepts him," Pyrull set a hand on Pen's shoulder and an invisible bond seemed to manifest between the two men. "Then he will become her bearer; her protection will extend over him; her strengths will endow him." He looked at Penghar. "All that makes me the Master Swordsman will pass to you; my skills, my strength, and my loyalty."

"Loyalty?" Terrell asked, his heart constricting at the word. "Loyalty to whom?"

"To Her," Pyrull answered, and this time Terrell could hear the capital letter.

"Pen," Terrell struggled the force the words out through a suddenly tight throat. "You swore your fealty to me. What if—what if she takes you away?"

"I have just prayed to The One that she will not," his best friend answered, fearlessly meeting his gaze. "But She is an angel, My Lord."

And commanded a higher loyalty than any mere human could claim, Terrell knew. "Then, I could lose you." He wanted to grab Pen and drag him away from this terrifying choice.

"Terrell." Pen looked at him steadily. "I never expected this, but it is the greatest opportunity I could ever dream of. Please, My Lord."

Terrell's back prickled. "Pyrull, what happens if she doesn't accept him?"

"He can die." The Master Swordsman gestured to the waiting Healer. "Hopefully the Dona can prevent that."

Terrell squeezed his eyes shut and drew a trembling breath. *I could lose him no matter what I choose. Oh God Above, please. Do what is right for him.* "You have my permission."

Pen's solemn face split in a boyish grin and he bowed deeply. Pyrull led him to the altar and bid him kneel again, this time facing sideways.

"Bare your chest," he told Pen. "And spread your arms."

Terrell watched in terrified fascination as Pen did so, and Pyrull drew his sword. The blade glowed with an ethereal light that should have been too bright to look upon, but somehow did not hurt. Pen's eyes closed briefly as his lips moved in a prayer, then his gaze locked on Pyrull's eyes and he nodded.

The Master Swordsman raised the slender blade, her point so sharp it simply faded into the air with no clear edge. Pen took a deep breath and held it, as steady as his gaze.

Pyrull drove Her point into Pen's heart.

For an instant both men turned incandescent. Terrell squinted, wordlessly praying. *Please, Father Seraph Haroun, intercede with The One for him!*

Then Pyrull drew the sword back and the radiance around him flowed into the sword. He sagged to his knees and for a moment both men knelt, heads bowed, the blade flaming between them. Terrell stared at Pen's chest, dreading to see the arterial spurt of blood that such a fatal strike should produce.

Then Pen reached forward and gently took the sword from Pyrull's hand. Terrell's heart soared.

"It's done," the old swordsman gasped. "She is yours and you are hers, boy. Remember this when your own time comes, and do likewise."

"I promise, Magister," Pen answered, and used his free hand to help Pyrull to his feet. Terrell breathed deeply and rushed to help support Pyrull as his fear receded, but only a little way. *He lived. She accepted him. But will she take him away from me?*

"I can stand," the old man insisted heavily, and did so, though he wiped his face with trembling hands. "Dona, your aid please?"

The priestess tended to him. Terrell turned to Pen.

27

PETER SARTUCCI

Pen's shirt was still pulled open, and a wet line gleamed on the brown skin over his heart. *No, not wet,* Terrell realized. *Silvery. It's a scar.* "How do you feel, Pen?" He desperately wanted to ask, *will you stay with me?* But he did not dare.

His best friend grinned at him again, an exhilarated grin like none Terrell had ever seen on his dear familiar face. "She says I'll be taking her where she wants to go."

"Go?" A cold fear seized Terrell's heart. "Is she going to take you away from me, Pen?" He knew the bearer of a soulsword had little choice when the weapon set its mind to something. Dona Seraphina had told him that the souls of divine beings, even the lesser ones that consented to dwell in anything as mundane as a length of ensorcelled steel, tended to overawe an ordinary human mind without particularly trying, and Pyrull had confirmed it. The prospect of travelling to Silbar alone held far less attraction than the adventure he'd imagined with his best friend.

"No," Pen answered, and Terrell found immense relief in the word. "She wants me to guard you with her help!"

Terrell stared at him. "What?"

"She says you're going to need us both, Terrell," Pen added seriously, staring at him expectantly. "I'm to guard you all the way to Silbar, and beyond, if necessary for the rest of your life."

"But does that mean . . . what *does* that mean?" Terrell's thoughts were even more confused now. For a moment he floundered, trying to find words. "Is she saying that I'm going to be King?"

"I don't know," Pen answered. "But you're going to become something, *My Lord.*"

Terrell discovered that it had become hard to swallow.

CHAPTER 3: CHISAAD

Acting Royal Wizard Chisaad DuVaya DiGallio?" The Silbari Palace functionary sought Chisaad's attention in a perfectly correct and subservient way.

Long practice at controlling his anger prevented any hint from showing. More than eighteen years at this thankless task and Chisaad still bore the stigma *Acting*. He carefully paused his repair of the Palace's southeast ward spell at a safe point and let his assisting mages assume temporary control of it before he spoke.

"What is it, Fantillin?" The man's concern might or might not be worth interrupting a delicate task. The palace staff had their own opinions about relative importance and the Royal Wizard of all Silbar did not have any control over their hereditary positions, unfortunately.

"Imperial Governor Ap Marn is on his way back from Sulmona," Fantillin reported. "His mage sent a message that they are two hours out from the north gate.

"Also Mage Blue is here from the Council of Colors and insists that he must see you as soon as possible.

"And a message construct marked for your attention arrived from the Imperial Seat in Gwythford Castle shortly after you began work on the ward. I put it in your office."

Chisaad nodded. "I see. Tell Blue what I'm doing and have him wait in the Fig Court. I'll read the message as soon as I finish here and join him after. Should I assume you've already alerted the rest of the Palace Staff to prepare for the Governor's return?"

"You should, Your Excellency." Fantillin didn't change expression but managed to radiate a smug satisfaction soured by his usual badly hidden contempt for any office holder not of the Royal Blood.

Chisaad mentally added that to the extensive list of grudges he held against the efficient may-the-Tormentor-damn-him functionary. "Good. Make sure somebody tells his wife."

"Already done, your Excellency. I will oversee the preparations for his arrival."

"Thank you for telling me." Chisaad made sure he put the proper amount of politeness into his words.

Fantillin bowed his head and left with that leisurely walk that the Palace servants affected. It didn't look like running but carried him out of sight in moments.

Chisaad turned back to the ward spell. The two mages and three priestesses participating in the complex job pretended they hadn't been listening. The recording scribe pretended to be invisible. Chisaad finished extracting the small demon caught in the damaged place. The creature of smoke and shadow writhed and snapped. Chisaad successfully dodged but the demon's pseudo teeth seized on the aura of one of the mages assisting him and tore a chunk out of it. The mage stifled a cry of pain but doggedly upheld his part of the joint casting. Chisaad silently approved of the man's discipline even as he and the third mage pinned the hellspawned creature between webs of magical force. The senior priestess captured the demon in an ensorcelled flask and sealed it in with a blessing reinforced by her assistants. The inky black thing pulsated inside the glass, disturbingly like a living heart.

Chisaad completed the repair, closed the spell, reactivated the ward and checked it. The blue glow meshed perfectly with the other quadrant wards. The two Mages standing seconds to him in the delicate task voiced their agreement and wrapped their own imprimaturs over it. No mage, not even Chisaad, could change any of the Palace's labyrinth of spells without two others to observe and verify his work, and a trio of Priestesses to confirm it. The three Donas that the Hierarch had assigned to the duty solemnly attested to the repair and sealing of the southeast ward. The two junior ones carefully carried off the captured demon to be used as evidence in the trial of the fool who had summoned it.

While the scribe recorded it all in quadruplicate and the assistant mage repaired his demon-bitten aura, the third mage idly asked the senior priestess about the underlying cause of the damage. "Did the Inquestors find that madman, Dona?"

"Early this morning," she reported. "He led them a hard chase through the Sump, but there wasn't any doubt when they caught him. He still had blood from his latest sacrifice under his fingernails, the monster." She sniffed vengefully. "This will be a simple case and a quick conviction. And then a thorough purification."

Chisaad did not let his mental snort at the euphemism sound out. *Purification* in this case meant being burned alive while bound to the nine foot tall iron stake set in the plaza in front of the Mother Temple.

"A shame he didn't get caught sooner," the third mage silkily insinuated. "That poor washerwoman might have been saved."

"The Inquisitors have to be thorough," she snapped at him. "And blood sorcerers are very good at covering their tracks. As it is he nearly got away before they pinned him down. Capturing him after only three victims is very quick work!"

"I could wish his demon familiar hadn't escaped," the silky-voiced mage remarked, surveying the repaired ward and his colleague's aura repair work. "It did some expensive damage."

"*I'm* simply glad the nightmarish thing attacked the Palace and not some innocent asleep in his tenement," the senior priestess answered. "A nuisance repair is preferable to a funeral—or two, or ten if the demon had been one of the really destructive ones."

"In any case, the problem is settled now," Chisaad intervened. "The perpetrator will burn, and his summoning will be banished. I am sure the Queen will formally commend all who brought this tragic affair to such a rapid conclusion."

At that point the scribe passed out copies of the attestations for the Temple, the Royal Wizard's Office, and the Mage Guild, and Chisaad finally managed to return to his office.

The message construct perched on a wooden stand in his anteroom. The creation stood nearly a foot tall, a glowing, ever-changing shape reminiscent of feathered wings, though it was really made of intricately folded light and air. This one flashed white and blue in his personal pattern. He carried it into his private office, made very sure that his own wards were solid and nobody could spy upon him, keyed the sequence and sat down to read. When he finished he carefully extinguished the construct, then destroyed it so thoroughly that even he wouldn't have been able to reconstruct a word of it. He had to still the trembling of his hands before he could complete the task.

Can it be possible? Is this my opportunity? I'd almost given up hope . . .
For a moment the yearning shook him to his core.
The Crown in contention once more . . . it could be mine!

He looked at himself in a mirror and grimaced. Seraphs witness, he couldn't let Mage Blue see him like this, face flushed and one eye twitching in the old nervous tic that he had worked so hard to overcome these eighteen years. He didn't dare try to cover up his agitation magically, since any member of the Council of Colors would certainly notice, so he'd have to get himself under control by sheer self-discipline.

Which he did, starting with his breathing. Ten long minutes later he finally dared meet his visitor.

The Fig Court was small, and the giant namesake tree put most of it into shadow at this time of day. Blue sat on a bench under the spreading limbs and idly nibbled one of the ripe fruits. He cast the stem aside and stood when Chisaad entered the walled space, gave him the nod of equals. They both made the shaking-hands-with-himself gesture that mages used to avoid entangling their personal spells while greeting another mage. Chisaad bid Blue sit again, glad that he'd had the foresight to meet the Councilmember here. The Acting Royal Wizard took a facing bench set where the deep shade would help conceal any lingering dishevelment.

"I see that you've already heard," Blue said shrewdly.

"That Emperor Brion is dying, and his Queen-Empress has merged her lifeforce with his to give him another season of life?" Chisaad twitched one hand in a spare gesture while thinking, *Shyrill must be mad with love for the brute.* "I learned of it today. When did you?"

"Barely an hour past." The Council mage spread his hands in an ebullient gesture. "Marvelous how swift the new message constructs have become, eh? Word carried all the way from Gwythford Castle in less than three days!"

Chisaad made an agreeable noise and inclined his head. "But you're not here to crow about how fast your informant's messages fly. I invite you to save time and get to your point, Mage Blue."

"All right." Blue planted his palms on his knees, leaned forward. "You know as well as I how draining that sort of life sharing effort is on anybody, and Queen Shyrill has a limited Healing talent with which to work. She can't possibly keep him alive for more than a season or two, and then death for both. There'll be a choosing and a new Silbari King before winter ends. A new King means a chance to renegotiate the three-way compact governing use of the Aretzo Node. The sixteen thousand Mages in this city have had to scrape along with a bare pittance of power while the Temple Hierarchy appropriates three-fifths of the Node for itself. I can tell you with absolute certainty that the Council of Colors will not accept a subordinate role any longer. We intend to petition the new King, whoever he ends up being, for equal access."

"Admirably succinct and to the point," Chisaad nodded. "And you want me to endorse and support your petition, of course."

"You're a Mage, Chisaad, and one of the best of our age. Your golems alone are an unparalleled master work! When Shimoor finally dies or resigns—and he should have resigned ten years ago—you'll be Royal Wizard in full and none of this *Acting* nonsense. If you weren't locked into this fool limbo by promises made almost two decades ago, you'd have been on the Council by now."

"I took an oath to King Tollir, Blue. I don't propose to break it even for a seat on the Council of Colors." *It will take something more attractive than the prospect of sitting around the Rainbow Table with you and the other squabbling relics,* Chisaad thought. *Something far, far more tempting . . . and I think I've found it.*

"I'm certainly not asking you to break your oath." Blue waved his hands in a calming gesture and sat back on the bench. "But please, Royal Wizard, consider my plea. We mages could do so much more for the Kingdom if we weren't kept half-starved by the Hierarchy."

"A large point in your favor. But remember what the Priestesses *do* with all that power."

"Far less than they could!" Blue scowled. "I'm aware how much power they funnel into healing the sick and injured—and how inefficient they are about it. They can afford to be wasteful, they have a guaranteed supply. Having to put a little thought into their spellcasting, developing more *elegance,*" he mouthed the syllables lovingly, "Would help everybody, not least themselves."

"I'm not arguing, Blue. I'm not blind either. To missed opportunities, or to costs. But you're proposing to pick the biggest fight there could be this side of the Empire. If you want me to join your side in it, I'll expect to see a great deal more leadership from the Council than it's shown in decades.

Leadership and followership too. I don't care to step to the head of a campaign only to have it desert behind me. Can you deliver those followers?"

"Yes."

Blue radiated quiet confidence now, Chisaad noted. No bluster at all. The Acting Royal Wizard decided to set the cat among the pigeons, since word would get out soon enough. "In that case, get ready, because you don't have as long to wait as you might think. Today the Emperor will send young Prince Terrell to take over the governorship of Silbar."

Blue blinked, clearly caught by surprise, but he had an agile mind and followed the implications at once. "The Emperor's making good on his promise at last. Before Osrick takes the Imperial throne. Setting up the halfbreed to try for his mother's Crown before his jealous brother can interfere." Blue hesitated, lowered his voice. "Do you think this northern Prince actually has a chance?"

"How would I know?" Chisaad affected a testy demeanor. "Halfblood or not, he's still indisputably the Queen's son, and thus has a clear right to try for it. If the Crown chooses him, that settles the question, doesn't it?"

"And if it rejects him?" Blue speculated. "If it burns him to ash, what then? Will a new minted Emperor Osrick accept another one of the Twenty as his vassal king over Silbar?"

Chisaad shrugged as if the subject bored him. "I'd imagine so. So long as we keep shipping future Emperor Osrick his silver and sulfur and training his mages, and providing him a legion of bureaucrats to administer his territories, why would he care who sits on the Stone Throne? He has more important problems much closer to home."

"Yes," Blue nodded, obviously visualizing it. "If the One God chooses to set a half breed King over us, we'll have to bow to him, but he will need our help to actually rule. And if we get a full blooded Silbari man of our own on the throne again, why *he'll* need our help too."

The Acting Royal Wizard sent the Council of Colors mage away with a smile on his face. Chisaad wended his way through the sprawling palace to the north side and the Hill Door. Guards gossiped about the Governor's return.

"Acting Royal Wizard," the senior man said with a deferential nod. "Are you going out to watch for the Governor?"

That excuse would do nicely. "Yes," he answered simply, and the man noted it in his log book.

The curse of a literate people, Chisaad reflected sourly, was that they tended to write everything down. In triplicate.

They let him through without further comment—he'd been the Royal Wizard for most of their lives—but he knew they would watch him from their posts. Outside the door a little plaza faced the towering cone of the Hill of Sight. For a moment he gazed up the Five Hundred Steps, tempted to ascend and once again be in the presence of the thing he most yearned for. The Stone Throne at its top looked like a mere speck from here, yet he remembered every detail of it as clearly as he knew his own hands.

But he had no excuse for that. Traffic on the road would look like ants from up there and climbing the Hill without obvious need would be severely out of character for him. Instead he followed the east path that curved around the Hill, until he came to a little marble pergola perched atop the wall that encircled the giant cone. Thirty feet below it the city's cemetery stretched in an even larger arc around the Hill. The pergola faced east over the mausoleums of the nobles to the broad stony swath of the Kings Road. Chisaad took refuge in the shade and deliberately put his back to the Hill. His magesight sensed it anyway, like a banked fire warming his back right through the polished wall and the colorful mosaics.

Queen Shyrill is dying decades before her time, he thought. He knew he should feel sorrow; she was his half-sister, though nobody living knew it save him. But excitement filled him instead.

There will be a new king. I'm still young enough to be a credible candidate, except for the slight problem of my unacknowledged and illegitimate birth. A bastard can't inherit in Silbar, but does the Crown itself care whether a candidate's parents were married? Legends say it chooses the best man for the kingship, nothing less.

"Do I have a chance?" He whispered to himself. He knew the official answer would be *no.* The Temple Hierarchy invested enormous effort in trying to prevent royal bastards and ensure the unquestioned bloodlines of the Royal House. They would never let a surprise bastard join the Twenty. If they knew his real parentage he wouldn't even be allowed to keep his present post.

"Unless . . . I *create* a chance for myself?"

The audacity of the idea shook him. He knew a wise man would spurn the temptation. A wise man would be content with the post he already held.

I could be King; he finally formed the dangerous phrase in the privacy of his mind. It coiled there, glittering brighter than gold and seductive as any succubus. *I could be King!*

Trumpets jarred him out of his introspection. He glanced at the cemetery gate and the thronged road beyond it. He saw commotion out there, so he called up a distance-viewing spell and looked through the cemetery's grillwork gate at the crowd on the Kings' Road.

What he saw made him blink.

CHAPTER 4: KIRIN

K irin's heart rose as the DiUmbra Troupe's rented wagons neared Aretzo. Almost home! The trip had been the longest he'd ever done, more than five hundred miles across Lower Silbar, but they had surely made a lot of money. He had even seen Grandfather smile now and then, when the old man thought nobody could see.

Kirin rode with Maia, Sevan, and Pieter on top of the second wagon's load as the family approached North Gate. Pieter lay on his back a little apart from the younger three, straw hat pulled over his face and occasional snores wafting out. The others were too eager for home to even think of napping.

Maia had picked flowers from the roadside when they stopped for lunch. For the last ten miles she had been plucking off the withering petals and making them dance with her levitation talent. It was her only magical ability; she didn't even have magesight. She couldn't lift more than ten pounds, but everyone admired how well she had trained her little talent.

Kirin quivered inside, remembering how they danced together on stage as she sent white silk scarves floating about her. How he would weave his Shadow among them, careful not to break her spells. Audiences swooned.

He smiled in happy memory. Other than a few unpleasant people, the trip had been wonderful.

Her hand stole into his. "I've had enough of travelling," she told him. "I'm glad to be home."

The way that she always guessed his thoughts warmed him. He kissed her silently.

A wind blew off the sea as they approached Aretzo's walls. Kirin wrinkled his nose as the odors of the city met them. Wood smoke, raw sewage, horse manure, fish; strongest of all were the reeking slaughterhouses that lined the downhill side of the King's Road.

"They've grown so big," he said. "I didn't think Aretzo folk ate red meat often enough to need all this."

"It's become more popular since the Gwythlos conquered us," Sevan answered as he too gazed on the gory spectacle. "And the Navy buys a lot of salted beef."

"The stench is horrible," Maia said, wrinkling her nose.

"Even to our city-raised noses," Kirin joked as they both looked away.

Across the road from the slaughterhouses sprawled Aretzo's enormous cemetery behind its guardian wall. From the top of the loaded wagon Kirin could look right over at the elaborate tombs of the nobility. Those fretted mausoleums shrank the farther one went from the gate, fading towards the crowded plots of ordinary folk and eventually, around the curve of the towering Hill of Sight, into the Poor Field. Kirin made the sign of reverence for his mother, buried there in a grave marked with a stone so plain it didn't even have her name, only a number and her date of death.

Maia snuggled against him. Her own family's graves were crammed into their caste's part of the huge cemetery, near the Poor Field but not in it. "Do you remember her?" She asked him, knowing why he made the sign.

"Some. I was only seven when she died. She didn't talk much. Most of the time while I grew up she walked in a dream, not there with me." His forehead creased as he strained to remember. "I guess something had hurt her mind. Or somebody. She had only started to wake up from it when she died."

Maia looked pensive. "I wish I had been able to meet her, to get to know her." She lowered her voice and whispered in his ear: "She would be a grandmother to our child."

"Your own mother will be grandmother enough," he whispered back. Carmella had chattered at breakfast about seeing her first granddaughter again the instant they got home.

Kirin glanced at his brother-in-law and tried not to grin. From the gleam in Sevan's eye as he gazed at the approaching city, and the envious looks he had thrown at Kirin and Maia throughout the trip, he missed his own wife badly. Carlai had stayed home nursing their firstborn instead of risking the trip with a baby.

Kirin looked up at the huge cone of the Hill of Sight where it loomed over Aretzo. From this side the Palace and the Five Hundred Steps were not visible, only the smooth grassy slope. It rose sharply behind the thirty-foot retaining wall along the back edge of the cemetery. A decorative little stone pergola perched on the wall and looked over the noble tombs toward the road. The Stone Throne on the hill's peak could barely be seen from the wagon, but he couldn't miss the latent glow of the sleeping magic that wrapped the whole cone.

"What does it look like?" Sevan asked. He knew that Kirin's magesight let him see more than anyone else in the troupe.

Kirin suspected that Sevan's own talent was no stronger than Maia's. He'd never seen Sevan do more than move enough air to sway curtains or blow out a candle from across the room. It wasn't anything they talked about much.

For a moment a familiar pang ran through Kirin's heart. He didn't have a single real mage talent, just the ability to see magic and to move his hungry Shadow. Or restrain it rather; it moved with a mind of its own that did not always heed him.

He groped for words and told Sevan, "It looks like a blue and purple bonfire a thousand feet tall, if you can imagine such a thing."

"A thousand? Uncle Pieter said the Hill's only four hundred feet tall." Sevan looked intrigued, while his eyes squinted as if he wondered whether Kirin teased him.

Kirin shrugged. "All right, I don't know how big it is, I'm just guessing. The spells run down into the world farther than I can see." He waved a hand at the immense construct, and at that moment his Shadow shifted away from it inside him. That surprised him; his Shadow usually wanted to reach toward magic. If he let it, the cursed creature would try to drink down any spell he touched or even got too near. But it shied away from the Hill.

He puzzled over that for a moment before deciding that it had probably been cowed by the sheer power of the giant artifact brooding over the city. It heartened him to think that there might be something his burden feared. "It's the King's business anyway."

"Or will be," Sevan nodded sagely. "When we have a King again."

"The One God grant it," Pieter said, pushing his hat back and looking around.

Kirin turned to look behind them at the sound of hoof beats. "What's that?"

A horseman trotted toward the city on the long strip of greensward flanking the eastern edge of the King's Road. "Make way!" the rider shouted. "The Governor comes! Make way!"

"Uh-oh," Kirin said. "Do you think we can get inside before he gets here?"

Aretzo's North Gate lay straight ahead. The towering triple-peaked roof loomed over a fanged bastion thrust forward out of the city wall. Two immense gates pierced it, served by two huge drawbridges over the dry moat that fronted the wall. It loomed barely three hundred yards ahead of the troupe's lead horses, frustratingly close.

"No," Pieter answered crisply. Grandfather had already begun to guide the lead wagon onto the narrow western verge. They had less than ten feet of churned-up dirt between the paved King's Road and the cemetery wall. "Kirin, Sevan, get ready to help with the horses."

They bounced through ruts and over rocks as the wagons left the pavement. The wall left barely enough room to get the heavy drays out of the traffic way. The first wagon managed to pull into the broader area at the cemetery entrance. While Uncle Ger guided the second wagon as close to the wall as the horses would go, Kirin looked over the left side.

"Left wheels are still on the road," he reported.

Pieter leaped down, followed by Kirin and Sevan. They grabbed the horse's bridles and did their best to urge the beasts forward a few more steps. The left front wheel eased off the road; the rear wheel didn't.

"Good enough?" Kirin asked nervously. The rising sound of steel-shod hooves came up the road behind them. Cadoc Ap Marn, Silbar's Imperial Governor, wasn't famous for being even tempered.

"Maybe." Pieter went forward to see if he could move the lead wagon to give the second more room.

Most of the family had climbed down and gathered in the pocket of space between the wagons and the recessed cemetery gates. Uncle Ger joined

Sevan and Kirin at the bridles of the horses, gentling them with soft words and his touch of beast-magic. His eldest son did the same for the lead wagon. Kirin admired their talents; beast-magic looked so *useful.* Carmella and the other women had gathered the children between the lead wagon and the wall. Maia stayed atop the rear wagon and shouted down to the family through the growing racket.

"It's a whole cavalry troop!"

The lead horses swept past in a glitter of finery. Governor Cadoc Ap Marn rode haughty in front between a banner bearer and a herald. His pale northern face had been burnt red by a decade under the southern suns. His pointed ears were even more sunburned where they poked out of his flowing yellow hair. At a gesture from him, trumpets rang and the whole mass of horses dropped from a trot to a slow walk, preparing to enter the confined gate.

The DiUmbra family all bowed as the Governor passed. Even though he gave them less attention than the dung on the road, it was the safe thing to do.

The Gwythlo soldiers following their lord rode four abreast. Kirin guessed they must be the troops usually posted to the Grey Fort inside Aretzo's North Gate. More weathered than the Governor, the Imperial troops were all big powerful men who spent enough time outdoors to get sun browned, but still were obviously not Silbaris. They looked and sounded eager to get back to their barracks after long days in the hostile desert. Kirin heard jests and abuse traded freely in their language, of which he'd picked up enough to follow. He tensed as a few soldiers cursed the troupe's rental wagon for forcing the outer rank to squeeze past. The cursing got more frequent as the long line began to back up from the gate.

One soldier did more than curse.

Maia shrieked as a trooper stood in his stirrups and dragged her off the wagon.

"Look boys!" He shouted in Gwythlo. "I've found some fun to welcome us back!"

"Maia!" Kirin rushed forward. "Put my wife down!"

The soldier in front of the one who'd grabbed Maia lashed out with a boot. The kick to his chest knocked Kirin staggering. He bounced off Uncle Ger to fall against the cemetery gate. His head banged iron and the world swayed.

"Easy, darkie." Kirin heard the man's laugh through his dizziness. "You'll get her back when we're done."

Maia struggled in the grip of the leering Gwythlo soldier. She screamed abuse at the man as his free hand roved and pinched.

Kirin's Shadow bolted out from beneath his heart in one clean lunge. It flew at the Imperial troopers on wings wider than any wagon.

The one who'd kicked him swore and drew a sword. The one holding Maia tried to draw and lost his grip on her. She slid off his horse and landed on the edge of the road dangerously near the beast's stamping hooves. Sevan grabbed her and pulled her back among the family.

"Plethy's Tits!" swore the soldier who'd kicked him. The other managed to get his sword out and they both stabbed at Kirin's Shadow. It loomed over them like an avenging hawk, a churning opaque darkness that blotted out the suns. The tips of the blades passed through the black cloud and it closed instantly behind the steel. The horses, trapped amid the press of their fellows, began to stamp and neigh. Both men's faces paled as the nightmare grew black teeth and gaped at them. It strained against Kirin's no-kill stricture and breathed out cold death.

With Maia free, Kirin realized the danger in what he'd done. He forced his Shadow to break off the attack and flee into the cemetery, praying they would think it came from there. Once among the tombs he made it drop to the ground, sink below the dirt, and travel back to him unseen. He stayed flat while he drew it up through the cobblestones, through his back and safely inside his chest again.

The grabby soldier gasped, "What in the sodding hells was that?"

"Bung me if I know!" answered the kicker.

Both of their swords wavered around, hunting a target. The ranks beyond them were milling in confusion, the whole column disrupted.

"Make way!" screeched a harsh female voice. "Let me at these darkies!"

A slim gray hunting beast glided out of the chaos of men and horses. Some breed of dog or wolf, it stood as tall as most ponies. Claws clicked on paving stones and hungry eyes glared at Kirin on the ground. The beast stopped between the two cavalrymen, standing nearly as tall as their horses, and then crouched. A small pale woman in black and green riding leathers slid off its back—a Gwythlo Druid. Kirin stared and forgot to get up.

She couldn't be even as tall as him, but Power radiated from her like heat from an oven. Silver glinted on her wrists, throat, and belt. She moved much like her mount, teeth bared as if she too wanted to tear out throats. Her beast snarled at the huddled DiUmbras.

Kirin scrambled to his feet. The other men of the family were pushing the women and children behind the wagons, but Maia rushed to his side. He hugged her with one arm even as he raised the other to shade his eyes. The Druid's green aura flamed in his magesight.

"Where is it?" She stalked towards him. "One of you serves Darkness. Evil is here!"

Kirin nerved himself to act. His worst fear made real, here, and by a conqueror no less. He should push Maia away so the Druid wouldn't burn her too, he should run, he should—

Before he could do anything at all, there came a click and a long metal groan as the cemetery gates opened behind him.

"The only evil here is what you bring with you, Druid Boerga," said a new voice, and the cemetery's resident priestess strode out. Maia and Kirin hastily made way for her. "Your men woke one of the vengeful dead."

The new arrival wore formal yellow robes with Orthodox embroidery. Five stars glinted on her wimple. She had her silver-headed shepherds crook in her hands and two acolytes at her back. Kirin guessed she had been conducting a funeral ceremony at a noble tomb. Her own aura glowed ghostly yellow around her as she looked down her long nose at the Druid.

"Necromancer!" Boerga insulted her with a snarl while her beast whined. "My men did nothing! You must have raised that spirit yourself!"

"Honored Wisewomen," Pieter intervened, bowing so that his shaven head and silver hair rings gleamed in the sun. "That soldier offered dishonor to my niece." He pointed, and the grabby soldier shifted uneasily in his saddle, lowered his sword. "His actions awoke the spirit. It did not harm your soldiers, noble Druid Boerga, and it returned to the earth when he released her."

Boerga stared at the soldier. He avoided her eyes by sheathing his sword. Kirin fought down the temptation to smile.

The five-starred priestess gave Boerga a sardonic look. "Hear the monk. If you cannot control your men, Silbar's dead will do it for you."

The Druid glared at the Priestess. She spat, and the gobbet gleamed on the dirt between them. "That for your defeated dead!" Boerga turned her gaze on the DiUmbra troupe and snarled, "You Silbaris failed to clear the road. Let this remind you to be swifter next time!"

Her beast lunged and sank its fangs into the throat of the nearest horse. It screamed, tried to rear, and collapsed as blood gushed. The beast whirled and ripped the throat out of the adjacent horse too, and this time worried at it until it tore a mouthful of flesh free. The other two horses, trapped in the harness behind the dead ones, reared and neighed while Uncle Ger and his sons struggled to control them.

Boerga spoke a commanding word in her language. Her beast slunk to her side, licking blood off its face, and crouched. She remounted, stared haughtily at the family, and left with a swirl of gray fur. The soldiers sneered at the troupe, reformed their marching order and rode into the city.

Pieter bowed again, this time to the priestess. "We thank you for rescuing us from her attentions."

She favored him with a wry smile. "If I in fact did, Monk. Boerga never forgets a slight. The loss of your horses is regrettable. That your niece is free of dishonor—" Her gaze lingered on Kirin and Maia as they clung to each other, and on the small gold rings on their wedding fingers. "Is fortunate for you and her." She looked at Kirin. "I believe I have seen you praying at a grave in the Poor Field, have I not?" The five stars above her forehead glittered.

Kirin nodded, bowed hastily, and said, "Yes, Dona Quintissima. My mother is buried there." His heart still raced, but she seemed friendly.

Her gaze turned approving. "That speaks well of you. Go with my blessings, children."

To his amazement this priestess he'd never met before raised her free hand and moved it in the gesture of blessing. He barely reacted in time to prevent his Shadow from reaching for the holy magic. Golden sparkles billowed from her hand, settled over him and Maia and the whole DiUmbra Troupe. They glowed softly for a moment and winked out. She said, "Fare well," and returned to her funeral service. The gates clanged shut behind her.

Grandfather looked like he wanted to explode. He hissed between his teeth, unable to curse in this place or after such a blessing. Instead he said to Pieter, "Replacing two draft horses will cost us a fifth of this trip's profit!"

"But none of our family needs to be *replaced*," Pieter answered as he met his father's gaze. "Much less our best acrobats."

After a tense moment the troupe's leader let out a sigh. The whole family relaxed as he said, "Clean up the mess. Ask the knackers what they'll give for the carcasses. I'll send your brother back with two of the other horses so you can bring the second wagon along when you're done."

Pieter nodded obediently and the family all turned to the work. Sevan, Pieter, Ger and Kirin managed to unharness the dead horses and wrestle them free, then cleaned the harness. Men from the butcher yards came and dragged away the carcasses. Uncle Ger shook his head over the pittance that they paid.

"The rental master will be furious," he muttered. "We'll have to pay for replacements and pay a penalty, too."

"Too late to help that," Pieter answered. "Thank the One it wasn't worse."

"Aye." Ger sighed and glanced at Kirin but said nothing.

Kirin dragged the washed harness on top of the wagon to spread it in the sun to dry. His eye caught a swirl of copper skin and gray robes on two Duermu men herding goats toward the Bazaar. He remembered the words of the fortune teller back in that little town whose name he had already forgotten.

She said I would be tested with fear and loss. That Druid sure scared me, and we lost two horses. She also said Powers would help me, and that priestess came out of the cemetery and did. Did I just survive that 'test' or is there going to be another? What am I caught in?

The warm sunshine gave him no answer.

An hour later Sevan the elder returned with two horses and they were moving again. He had a grim silence about him that nobody dared break. Maia and Kirin nestled together atop the load next to Pieter, subdued.

"Father," Kirin asked him, troubled. "Should I not have sent my Shadow at that soldier?" Maia's grip on his arm tightened.

"I wouldn't say that, son," he answered seriously. "There were no good choices. You made perhaps the least bad choice available."

Kirin relaxed as their wagon creaked past the hulking Gray Fort and past the entrance to the Red Street. The two bracketed the road inside Northgate. They were halfway through the Bazaar and about to turn into Sulfur Street for home when Kirin noticed a change.

"Hey!" He pointed to the Bazaar space where the DiUmbra Troupe usually performed. "The Suliemons are using our space!"

Sevan the Elder nodded. "See how they've changed the name on the sign?"

"I don't like the look of that," Pieter muttered. "What happened while we've been gone, Sevan?"

"The Suliemons have stolen our Bazaar lease," Sevan the Elder said flatly. "We've lost our performance space."

Everybody gasped. Kirin stared at the Bazaar receding behind them. *How do we earn our living without a place to perform?*

CHAPTER 5: CHISAAD

C hisaad found himself torn between delight and annoyance.

His eyes could see a group of travelers, one of them at the center of the Shadow's movement. A halfbreed youth, the wizard's eyes could see him plainly through the cemetery gate. But Chisaad's most subtle spell had slid right past the boy as if he wasn't there.

He can manipulate a Shadow and can render himself invisible to magic, the Royal Wizard thought. *How has no one ever noticed him before?*

He cursed himself for an oblivious fool. Most people only saw what they expected, or could easily explain, and everybody knew stage performers practiced illusions.

Even me, he admitted to himself in the privacy of his own mind. *If I hadn't been looking at exactly the right moment to see, I wouldn't have believed it either. But I did see, and now I know.*

For a moment he thought to race back into the Palace, through its labyrinth to the internal door to the Gray Fort, and from there to North Gate, to see if he could intercept the youth. But the Royal Wizard running through corridors would attract far too much attention. And even if he reached North Gate in time, what then? He couldn't very well accost one traveler amid the horde on the King's Road to demand an explanation. Far too many people would overhear. He quivered in frustration.

Stop, he told himself. *One step at a time. Those people look like stage performers so start there. Find out about them—about* him. *Quietly, secretly. Let no one know what you suspect; let nobody discover your interest. If control of a Shadow is truly possible, it might be harnessed to penetrate the most protected of places—*

He cut the thought off and began to pace inside the pergola. *Don't build a mountain of hope on a molehill of knowledge. First find out who really summoned the Shadow; don't assume it was the halfbreed. Learn how it was controlled, and what it really is. It could still prove to be a mere entertainer's trick, useless for anything significant.*

He stopped pacing and stared at the empty road where the travelers had been.

But if it is not; if what I suspect is true! His hopes soared. *He could be the perfect tool.*

He returned to the Palace.

The Governor's arrival already had servants rushing about, though the man had barely had enough time to dismount in the Grey Fort. Chisaad positioned himself near the connecting door between Fort and Palace, and soon enough the sunburned face of Lord Cadoc Ap Marn appeared, followed by his traveling gaggle of sycophants.

It didn't take Chisaad any time at all to deduce that the Imperial Governor had returned in a foul mood. The man barked at his Gwythlo aides and cuffed the Silbari servants as they changed him out of his road-soiled riding leathers and boots into a comfortable robe and sandals. When he saw Chisaad he growled, "Wizard! Walk with me."

"Of course, My Lord Governor," Chisaad murmured, and stepped in front of a hapless military aide at the Governor's left hand. The youth gave way and Chisaad matched Ap Marn's pace.

Ap Marn strode to his office, threw himself into his waiting chair, and gestured at Chisaad.

"Sit. I've come from Sulmona. Sulfur production is down by a tenth since last year!"

Chisaad sat. Serving as Ap Marn's sounding board had proved useful before. He considered the problem. It didn't bode well for the Imperial purse. Silver and sulfur were the two main engines of magic for any Mage who didn't have a Node close enough to draw upon, which meant most of the Empire. Silbar produced generous amounts of both, the silver from mines in the Bright Mountains north and west of Aretzo, the sulfur from pits on the edge of Sulmona in the eastern deserts. A part of Ap Marn's duty included making sure that a tenth of the annual sulfur production flowed to the Imperial treasury.

"A drop that large will doubtless receive unfavorable Imperial attention," Chisaad said diplomatically. *Shrieks of outrage, more likely. Blue and his Council won't be happy, either.*

"That incompetent idiot Gwynned spends all his time drinking and wenching instead of managing the mines," Ap Marn ranted on. "I bet half the loss is due to his slack management!"

"And the other half, My Lord Governor?" Chisaad asked respectfully, since Ap Marn wasn't about to admit how much he personally skimmed off. The man's gambling debts were whispered about from the Palace to the Old City slums.

"Not enough workers," the Governor fumed. "Gwynned whines that the supply of slaves from Klinto has dried up and he demands that I make up the difference with condemned criminals." He glowered.

"You've already done that, my Lord," Chisaad said, thinking how unpopular those sentences had been with the city's poor. "There has been another objection to the practice filed by the Temple while you were away. The Hierarch likened it to the slavery that is proscribed by Silbar's Holy Writ."

Ap Marn scowled. He didn't give a damn about Silbar's religion, but he'd been made painfully aware that the Hierarchy could make his life uncomfortable.

"Those bitches," he muttered. "There ought to be some way to get back at them."

As unproductive lines of thought went, Chisaad reflected, that was a big one. He coughed slightly and changed the subject.

"My Lord Governor, has anyone yet informed you that Prince Terrell is about to be dispatched to Silbar?"

Ap Marn needed a moment to add one and one and get two. "What? Why? He's not even reached his age of majority yet."

"I am informed that the Emperor's health is declining," Chisaad answered tactfully. "Apparently he has decided to deliver on his pledge to the Queen-Empress. That her son would have Silbar as his own."

"But that wasn't supposed to happen until the brat reached twenty-one! More than three years from now!"

"The Emperor," Chisaad said delicately, "changed his mind."

And caught you by surprise, I see, he thought, carefully hiding his amusement. *You thought you'd have plenty of time to collect bribes and steal as much as you could.* He tried to sound apologetic as he added, "Apparently His Highness will arrive in four tendays, his father's grant in hand, to replace you."

Ap Marn's face underwent an interesting change of colors and expressions. The man wasn't very practiced at hiding his thoughts, a trait Chisaad had found common among Gwythlos. If the about-to-be-displaced noble could manage some control, he might be useful in the plan beginning to form in Chisaad's mind.

The Lord Governor wasn't quite stupid enough to protest aloud. He did grind his teeth, glare, and clench his fists. The sound of the bigger man's popping knuckles both entertained and intimidated Chisaad. At last Ap Marn said, "How many others know?"

"By now I would expect a number in the high dozens or low hundreds," Chisaad estimated. "By nightfall it will probably include everyone of significance in Aretzo. Gwythford Castle leaks information like a sieve, my Lord Governor, possibly with the Emperor's full knowledge, and message constructs have become quite swift."

"The yellow bitches probably know by now."

"I would be astonished if they didn't. Dona Seraphina's husband is a skilled mage and a message construct is well within his capabilities. I would not be surprised if the Hierarch knew before any other soul in Aretzo."

Ap Marn gritted his teeth again. Then he took a deep breath, blew it out, and growled. "So. Prince Terrell is on his way, you say? Did your informant tell you what route he's following?"

"No, though I expect there will be further enlightenment delivered by message constructs in the days to come. He's bringing the Silbari Brigade and a small army of attendants. His procession is bound to be well watched and duly hosted by every noble along the way. At least, every noble who wants to curry favor."

"And I'd be wise to do likewise." Ap Marn looked at Chisaad through half-closed eyes. "Tell me, *Acting* Royal Wizard, what does this change of Governors imply for your position?"

Chisaad made an intentionally nervous gesture. "I gave my oath to King Tollir, and through him to Queen Shyrill for the duration of her absence, or if she chose, to be ended at her pleasure—or displeasure. As she has been absent these eighteen years, I have remained. But that chain cannot be stretched to a third link. Once Prince Terrell assumes command here, he is free to appoint a Royal Wizard of his own and presumably will do so. There is no shortage of possible candidates."

Chisaad strove to inject the right note of worry into that last line. *Give him an opening, set the hook.*

"I see," Ap Marn said after a pause. "Well. I'm going to be very busy for the next few ten days."

"As will I, my Lord Governor. I'm afraid I may need to meet with you more frequently than we have in the past. To plan."

Ap Marn squinted at him, calculating. Chisaad stared back, calculating. They both smiled. Chisaad rose and bowed himself out.

This will not be easy, he thought as he left the Palace and made his way back to his home. *He is unbalanced and suspicious, fearful of everybody. But with care and planning, and a little good fortune, I may be able to manipulate him into a useful treason.*

Now to find those performers!

He returned to his tower in the Clerks Quarter south of the palace. He owned an old house that had once lain outside the walls of the then-smaller city, and consequently featured a fortified tower rising from one side. His mother had left it to him, a part of her legacy from her mother's family. Her much older husband had been an undistinguished mage more interested in fashioning small artifacts than in founding a dynasty. He had refitted the tower as his magic-working sanctum, and later bequeathed it to the surprise son his wife had delivered in his old age.

Did Father ever guess that I wasn't his son? Chisaad wondered as he passed through the house wards, which dutifully recognized him and opened the bespelled front door. *He never breathed a word, but I suspect he knew.* He stepped out of his overshoes in the foyer and the waiting golem collected them for cleaning. The streets of the Clerks Quarter were only marginally cleaner than those of the Old City despite being nearly a thousand years younger. The golem, an artifact of wood, wire, and fierce-burning silver, moved with grace as it carefully washed and brushed the overshoes.

The movements are almost human, but I need to tune it a little better, he decided. *I could put an illusion of humanity on it, but it's a little too jerky to be persuasive, yet.* He checked the older cleaning golem he had made for practice. It wasn't even shaped like a human, a six-legged thing that looked more like a mantis. Its virtue was that it could reach from floor to ceiling and reliably clean corners, dust shelves, and refill lamps. *Not much better than human servants, and more expensive considering the cost of silver, but at least they don't spill my secrets.*

He went to his tower, ascended the front stairs to the middle-level office and up through three more stories of storage and specialty rooms to his favorite workroom on the top floor. *I should practice climbing these stairs,* he thought, *to get ready for the Hill. Prince Terrell will want to visit the Stone Throne, probably more than once, and I need to keep up with him. I'll start walking up these front stairs and down the back ones three times a day.*

The top floor work room had tall bookshelves crowded to one side of an open workspace, now dominated by a large table. On it laid the half-assembled corpus of his newest golem.

"Better articulation," he whispered to himself, fingering the arm joints. For amusement he cast a quick simulacrum of Ap Marn's face onto the featureless ovoid of the golem's head. "Yes, you'd suit as a mechanical slave, Governor. But later."

He let the spell die and went to the big bay window that dominated the room. It looked east over the city and most of Aretzo could be seen from here. He had a device of lenses and tubes that enabled him to extend his vision all the way to the harbor seawall. He began to examine the Bazaar through it.

Those performers must be somewhere. It shouldn't be impossible to find them. And when I do, I must learn how they control a living Shadow, because I am convinced that was not a stage trick.

Their secret must become mine.

CHAPTER 6: TERRELL

T he night before Terrell's departure the dream of Light came back. This time he woke before Pen reached his side.

Terrell gasped and sat up. For a moment he saw everything in the room outlined in radiance. Then only the guttering night candle lit the darkness.

Pen's worried face loomed over him. "My Lord? Did it happen again?"

"Yes." He fought down a shudder. "So strong . . . I feel like something's prying my soul open with levers, or perhaps knives." He half snorted, half laughed. "A version of what Irreneetha did to you, perhaps, but without the scar."

"Something prying at your soul?" Pen asked, his gaze sharp. "Or . . . Someone? Are you being magically attacked?"

"I don't think so." Terrell wiped his sweating face on his nightshirt. "Any mage strong enough to get at me like this would leave a signature in the castle wards that even I could see. And . . ." he checked rapidly, finding it easier than ever before. "There's no sign of any disturbance. For that matter, if it came from a mage outside the castle, our wards should have blocked it. At the very least it would have rung an alarm bell."

They both listened, but the castle's warning bells were silent.

Terrell nodded. "If any mage powerful enough to overcome the wards without raising an alarm attacked us, why would he spend that kind of effort on me, but not damage me? No, I don't think this is a magical attack."

They were both silent for a moment, thinking of the other alternative.

"Hostile efforts by the Pale Seraphs would not, I think, be accompanied by a dream of Light," Terrell said tentatively. He had tried to pay careful attention to Dona Seraphina's lectures about the Holy Writ, but there was so much of it. And there were horses to ride and weapons to learn and strategies to understand if he ever hoped to be an effective ruler of millions of people.

"If the Good Seraphs are, umm, changing you, it must be for a good purpose." Pen spoke with more confidence than Terrell felt.

"Let's hope the Temple Hierarchy agrees with you," Terrell answered soberly. "I'm going to have to win them over if I'm ever to rule Silbar. They're sure to ask me about my dreams."

"Dona Seraphina wasn't worried about your dreams," Pen offered.

"True." Terrell brightened. "I'll ask her about this one in the morning. Before we leave."

"Very good, My Lord." Pen bowed in transparent relief and left the room.

Terrell lay back down in his bed. He stared at the frescoed ceiling, invisible in the darkness.

If this really is the Good Seraphs at work on me, he thought, *I should not resist. Pen didn't resist Irreneetha. I must do at least as much.*

He folded his hands in prayer and tried to formulate a petition to the Defender. *Oh Seraph Haroun, mightiest face of the One God, hear me! I submit my soul to Thy holy justice, and my will to Thine. Let Heaven's Plan be fulfilled in me as Thy chooseth, for Thine is the right and the glory, forever and ever, world without end.*

He composed his mind for sleep again, and when the dream returned he embraced it. Pain came with it, but now he viewed it like the discomfort of stretching a long-unused muscle. Soon even that receeded and the Light settled in him, filled him like oil filling a lamp. He slept dreamlessly after that.

* * *

Dona Seraphina gasped. "Your Highness! What have you done? How—Why—"

"I had another dream, Dona." Terrell followed her gaze back to his own chest and went crosseyed trying to look at himself. "What are you seeing, Dona?"

"Light," she answered curtly as her shocked expression gave way to a puzzled one. "Filling you like water fills a glass vial."

Terrell tried to turn his magesight on himself, with the usual result—disjointed confusion. He shut his eyes and tried to sense his internal flows as Shimoor had taught. Power moved through him now, flowing like blood in a vein. His mind could barely touch it, like sensing the castle's node. The sensation thrilled him.

"Tell me about your dream, boy," Seraphina demanded. "Everything you remember."

Terrell tried to, only to find the memory already fading as if it didn't quite fit into his mind. After he stammered several disjointed sentences the priestess raised a hand to stop him.

"Never mind, early visions are often said to be unclear and rapidly lost. Wait for the next one, assuming there is a next one, and write it down. It may take you a few tries to learn how. I wish we had someone experienced in dream interpretation to guide you." She brooded for a moment, staring at his chest with her aura extended to probe him.

"Visions, Dona Seraphina?" He finally prompted her. "What kind of visions am I having?" He wasn't sure he wanted to know the answer. The prophets described in the Holy Writ rarely had happy lives, or long ones. The mere thought made him fight off a shiver. Becoming a battle mage attracted him far more than becoming a prophet.

"Seraphs bless me if I know," she answered bluntly. "But you're being filled with divine light and having odd dreams. I don't have to be the Seeress of God's Mountain to know that something extremely unusual is going on. Be very sure you pay close attention to the next dream, your Highness, and tell me about it immediately afterwards. Wake me up if you need to."

She fixed him with that gimlet stare that always made him feel like a beast about to be butchered. His discomfort rose until he had no choice but to end it by saying, "Yes, Dona."

But two hour later he forgot vision, discomfort and all as he entered the castle hall for his formal leave-taking. Father and Mother sat on their thrones, robed and crowned in splendor, he in the heavy gold Imperial Crown that Grandfather had ordered fused from the crowns of Gwythlo and Klinto. As always, Mother wore only the simple silver circlet of Silbar, two palm-sized circles standing up from the front to clasp a polished amethyst between their overlapping rings. Something moved slowly within the gem, altering the way light struck through it.

Osrick sat at Father's right, two steps down the dais on a smaller throne, decked in the Crown Prince's regalia and his face a mask. Aunt Klair-veen stood a step lower beside him, splendid in her green and gold regalia as Chief Druid. Magister Pyrull stood two steps lower at Mother's left, Dona Seraphina a step down beside him in her most elaborate embroidered robes.

Pen walked two paces behind and to Terrell's left with Irreneetha a sheathed fire at his side. The few in court who hadn't heard yet gasped and whispered. Without the soulsword, Pyrull looked . . . diminished. His hair was pure white now, and thin.

He really is dying, Terrell thought, dismayed. *The court will be walking ghosts when I leave.*

The sight hurt; he looked around instead. Hundreds of nobles, court officials, and retainers crowded the big room.

All of them in clusters by nation, he noticed. *Decades under the Imperial Crown, and each is still fiercely separate, suspicious of all the others, and ready to break free if they see an opportunity. Father, is this all we've been able to build?* It made him sad.

The Court Herald summoned Terrell and Pen. They walked the length of the room at a measured pace. More murmurs ran around the room as those with magesight noticed Terrell's difference. Before he could kneel, his father bid him to approach. Terrell left Pen standing behind him and mounted the marble steps. His eyes drank in every detail of his parents, knowing this would be his last sight of them.

Father looked weary, his face graven with lines. Some hadn't been there three days ago. With a start, Terrell discovered that he could see right through his sire's hair to the thin skin beneath. Its paleness made his father's head look unpleasantly like a skull. The crown seemed to weigh him down, which it never had before.

This is what 'dying' really means. The thought ran through Terrell like the shock from a too-close lightning bolt. He couldn't help glancing at his mother's hand resting lightly on father's left arm. Her lifeforce flowed into him with a muted glow. *Will it ever be my lot to find such love? Perhaps, if the One is kind. But would I want that . . . shared death, to be my legacy?*

He had no answer.

They spoke the formal words so that the watching nobles and functionaries would hear and know. Words of binding, words of commitment. All the while, Terrell tried to engrave every beloved line of his father's face in his own memory, every wrinkle, and every proud angle. Only when Osrick joined them to repeat his oath did Terrell see that his sire did the same with his own face. Osrick's eyes darted from one to the other and narrowed.

Then it was done.

The rest of the formalities were a blur. A candlemark later Terrell found himself in the Keep's outer courtyard. The Silbari Brigade formed up behind him and a train of companions and baggage. Dona Seraphina and her husband shared a chair litter suspended between four big horses. Royal Wizard Shimoor had a smaller two-horse version to himself. Everybody else rode normally. Even the young court women and junior priestesses accompanying them had all dressed in divided riding skirts. The pack train ran longer than the entourage itself.

Osrick strode up before Terrell climbed on his horse.

"Brother," Terrell said, opening his arms for a hoped-for embrace. He was almost surprised when Osrick accepted, bending a little to hug him.

"I am trusting you, little brother," Osrick hissed in his ear. "I want a sign that you'll justify that trust."

"I will keep our oath to the letter, you know that," Terrell protested softly.

"I don't doubt it, since *the letter* favors you." The words were bitter and Osrick's voice rang with pain. "So I want one thing more. Don't call yourself king. You can *be* a king, if that blasted rock-chair doesn't kill you, but never call yourself one. By that I'll know."

"I am willing to agree," Terrell answered, grieved. "But what others call me I can't control."

"I don't care about others. I care about you. *Don't call yourself king.*"

"Agreed. Goodbye, Osrick."

"I'll be watching, Terrell. Goodbye."

They tightened their grips on each other, almost wrestling. Abruptly Osrick released him and strode away. He did not look back.

"My Lord?" Pen asked uncertainly from his horse's back.

Terrell's eyes were stinging. He shook his head, mounted and turned the horse toward the gate. "Let's go, Pen."

CHAPTER 7: KIRIN

T he Suliemons!" The leader of the DiUmbra troupe roared. "How did those bastard spawns of Salim steal our place in the Bazaar?"

The two older uncles who had stayed behind to manage the Troupe's reduced presence in the Bazaar both hung their heads in shame. "They showed up five days after you left, with a written order for us to get out," one explained.

"And you just meekly gave up our livelihood?"

Kirin flinched at the rage in grandfather's voice and looked around. The family had gathered together in their practice room in the Sulfur Serpent Inn's Attic, the high-ceilinged chamber that filled the fifth floor of the cavernous building. The leader of the troupe stalked back and forth across the plank floor, his fists waving in frustration. His sons and nephews rolled their eyes but said nothing. Kirin listened and worried.

"The Suliemons had City Watchmen with them," Grandmother answered practically. "They bribed the Governor. He gave them a royal grant for the space. I went to the Treasury and read the copy in the archives."

"He can't do that!" Grandfather's roar petered out.

"Of course he can. He's acting in place of the Queen." Grandmother gave her husband an exasperated look. "Do you seriously imagine *we* can persuade her to undo it?"

Everybody looked at each other. Sevan and his wife Carlai with their baby, Kirin and Maia, her younger brother Attir, her mother and father Sevan the Elder and Carmella, Uncle Ger and his wife and their three sons and young daughter, six cousins and their wives and children, and Grandmother and Grandpa DiUmbra. And Pieter, who cleared his throat.

"Father. Our Queen is more than two thousand miles away in Gwythlo," he said. "That's not an impossible distance, but even if one of us went there, without influence at court we have little chance of ever getting in to see her."

Sevan the Elder gave a heavy sigh. "Everybody says the Imperial Court at Gwythford is corrupt. We'd have to bribe someone to sponsor our plea for a hearing. The rumors in the Guildhall say those bribes run more than we make in three years! It's pointless for people like us to even try."

"Can't we take over the Suliemon's old space?" Uncle Ger asked.

Grandfather snorted. "Only if we want to starve slowly. We've twice their numbers to feed, and that's always been a bad location for business."

"Besides," Uncle Sevan added practically. "They already sold it to someone else even lower on the ladder of status than they were. Mother checked."

Grandmother continued in her *be reasonable* voice. "Which means we only have one choice. We have to find a patron who controls another performance space and persuade him to let us use it."

Sevan the Eder nodded his head dourly at his mother's words. "That's going to be tough. The old aristocrats are pretty humbled these days. Not many of them have any unrented space or are spending any extra coin. They're squeezing every copper to maintain appearances."

Ger nodded too. "The new merchants and mages have wealth, but we don't know any of them."

"Then we'll get to know them," Grandfather growled. "Everybody start looking for a way. We have enough money from our trip that we can eat for the summer without earning our usual income. But if we don't find a reasonably good performance space by the fall equinox we are in big trouble. We have to pay our lease on the Serpent then, and right now, thanks to paying for dead horses…" He paused and darted an angry look at Kirin and Pieter. "…we don't have enough saved to do that and still eat."

"We can take on small work. Embroidery and washing for the women, maybe stevedore work for the men," Grandma said thoughtfully. "That will help some."

"It'll slow the drain," Grandpa admitted grudgingly. "But we've got to stay in practice too, we can't afford to look and be any less than perfect for a new patron. That doesn't leave us much time for anything else."

Grandma conceded the point with a resigned nod.

Kirin looked around at the familiar room with its high ceiling and plank floors. The trapeze and the net dominated it. *This is my home, the place I belong.*

Maia squeezed his arm.

"We'll be all right," he told her sturdily. "We'll find something."

* * *

The next day the whole family cleaned their living quarters and the practice room under Grandmother's stern gaze. The men hauled in endless buckets of water up from the Inn's courtyard fountain on wooden yokes. Kirin's calves and thighs burned from the effort.

"It's a good way to strengthen our leg muscles for the act," Pieter claimed. Kirin and Sevan, keeping pace up the stairs behind him with their own yokes, rolled their eyes and grinned at each other. The younger men just panted.

When all the water barrels were refilled, and Maia and the other women had scrubbed the floors and walls, Kirin helped Sevan, Attir, and three cousins empty all the chamber pots into the courtyard sewer. The young men washed them thoroughly while the older men mopped the wet floors.

"Makes me look forward to trapeze practice," Kirin muttered.

"That's why Papa and Uncle Pieter make us do it," Sevan muttered back.

The dirty work done, Kirin spent hours of hard practice on the trapeze. The balance beam, tightrope, and dance floor were also crowded with the active members of the troupe. He and Sevan practiced somersaults and spins, building the timing and trust between flyer and catcher that made their complex act look effortless.

"What kind of patron do you think we'll get?" Kirin wondered aloud to Sevan during a break. "A merchant?"

Sevan shrugged. "Maybe a wealthy mage. Or one of the Gwythlo lords."

Kirin frowned. "Grandfather would hate being beholden to one of them. So would Pieter."

"Beggars can't be choosers," Sevan answered darkly as they returned to practice.

Finally Pieter decreed, "That's enough for today. Time for baths."

Kirin obediently hooked the flyer's bar of the trapeze onto its resting place, then leaped off the platform and turned a last somersault before landing on his back in the net. He flipped onto his feet and bowed to Maia with a flourish as she stepped off the polished dance floor.

She stuck her tongue out at him. "My husband, the showoff."

"Well of course!" He grinned engagingly. "Got to practice hard so I can keep up with you!" He took her in his arms and kissed her while her younger brother Attir and two of the barely-teen-aged cousins sneered and mocked.

She kissed him back, made a face at the mockers, and kissed him again.

"Get your clean clothes and sponges," Carmella reminded everyone. "Anyone who forgets has to do extra chores."

"Yes, Mother." "Yes, Aunt." "Yes, Carmella."

Kirin and Maia soon joined the rest of the family as they trooped down three flights of stairs together and out into Sulfur Street. Kirin carried Grandmother's basket as well as his own sack of clean clothes, since she walked with a stick these days. Sevan the Elder and Grandfather had left much earlier to get clean before they went to the Guildhall.

"I hope we get a new performance space soon," Uncle Ger's wife said.

Ger shrugged. "Nobody in the family has had to do this in living memory, Silla. Who knows how long it'll take? Or where we'll end up?"

The family matched Grandmother's slow pace as they strolled up Sulfur Street towards what was formally known as *King Trannel's Baths* according to the carving over the entry hall. Kirin hadn't ever heard anyone call it that; everybody referred to the enormous building as the Warrior Baths after the cyclopean bas-relief carved on the Sulfur Street side. The younger children ran in circles around their elders.

Kirin held Maia's hand as they walked side by side, with Sevan and Carlai doing the same beside them. Neighbors greeted them, some of those bound to or from the same place as the family. At the entrance hall to the Baths, Kirin handed Grandmother her basket and the men and women parted company into separate areas for each sex. Sturdy little Berrin, Uncle Ger's youngest son and newly turned six, was finally of age to bathe with the men, and proudly took his father's hand today instead of his mother's.

"How do you suppose Grandfather will find us a patron?" Kirin asked Pieter as the DiUmbra men filed into the green-and-white-tiled changing room. "Is there a place to go to find them?"

Pieter shook his head, speaking as they stripped. "I don't know, but he and my brother are talking to the Gleemen's Guildmasters about it now."

Kirin frowned as they handed their clothes to bored old attendants who gave them back wooden tags on leather thongs. "Do rich people call the guild to find troupes to sponsor?" He tied the thong around his neck so he could reclaim his garments afterwards.

"Rarely." Pieter sighed and hefted the crock of soap he'd brought along for the family's use. "We'll need divine grace to find one."

"Oh." Kirin helped Berrin tie on his own tag so he wouldn't lose it, while Uncle Ger corralled his other sons. Pieter led them to the big eight-lobed fountain and claimed a section for their use, then passed around the soap. Kirin and Sevan helped the fathers in the group make sure the younger ones lathered up properly before rinsing.

I'll be doing this with my own son someday, Kirin thought happily. *Maybe in just a few years!*

He enjoyed the thought while he took turns with the other grown men pouring water over each other and the younger ones. They scooped it from the fountain in battered wooden buckets provided for the purpose, until everyone's hair shone clean and sleek.

"You acrobats never have trouble with lice," complained a carpenter whose shop lay across Sulfur Street from the Inn. He combed his own scalp in obvious frustration.

"Virtuous living," Pieter replied, "And good soap. That cheap stuff you use is too weak." He offered the man a dab from the family's crock. The neighbor accepted a fingerful of the soft herb-scented soap to work into his brown Silbari hair.

Sevan quietly moved to stand between the carpenter and Kirin; he and Kirin exchanged glances but said nothing. Every adult in the family knew who kept their quarters free from pests, and how he did it, but also knew better than to talk of it openly. The familiar surge of resentment for his combined curse and blessing, his Shadow, surged in Kirin. Followed immediately by gratitude for his brothers and father and cousins.

This is my *family*, he thought. *Mine. I won't let them down.*

They finished washing and pulled on halfhose for swimming, which conveniently covered Kirin's slave tattoo, and herded the children into the main room. It held three connected pools shaped a bit like a huge letter 'C' wrapping around a stone shrine to the male half of the heavenly pantheon. A thrice-life-size marble statue of a powerful man, mature in years and wisdom but strong in body, represented Haroun the Father Seraph, standing naked with his sword over one shoulder and his left hand grasping the neck of Salim, the Tormenting Seraph. The marble had been carefully chosen, Father Haroun stood brown as any Silbari while Salim knelt in pale gray-white. Other members of Haroun's retinue gathered around, proud in victory and carved from the same brown marble; the lesser Seraphs were only twice life size.

Kirin and his family made prayers to the shrine before entering the water.

The northern foot of the 'C' made a shallow side pool where the small children teemed; Uncle Ger took their youngest there to gossip and splash. The big pool ran deeper and longer, where the older boys and grown men swam. Kirin and Sevan dived in and joined the many swimming in an elongated circle, up the outside and back along the inside of the pool. A towering statue of Seraph Sath dominated the smaller pool. His charge was men who love men and he presided over the waters with the stern visage of a military commander. Legend claimed that a famous general had been the model. The Sath worshippers had a separate entrance and bathing facilities at the back of the building but shared the main room.

Stern monks of a militant order maintained decorum in the big room. The Sathists private section featured in lively gossip and sometimes acid (and very frank) mockery among the married men and their sons. But the One God had made men thus, so people accepted, however grudging, when some youth answered the call of Sath and attended the other pool.

Skin color, of course, was different. The only pale skin in sight belonged to Kirin and the statue of defeated Salim.

Kirin and Sevan raced each other around the big pool twenty times, then stopped for a rest at the starting side. Kirin hauled himself out of the pool and sat on the rim, looked around at the denizens of the baths. Skinny laborers, brawny longshoremen, substantial craftsmen, big-bellied clerks, and mages who got more exercise with pens and silver ingots than with their legs, he knew most of them by name and they knew him. The Warrior Baths were free, endowed by a wise king of the past, and everybody who lived near Sulfur Street used them. Kirin turned to Sevan as an idea popped into his mind.

"Do you think we might find a patron here?"

Sevan leaned on his elbows on the edge of the pool and snorted denial. "On Sulfur Street? Maybe there's a well-to-do ship chandler or two, or a minor merchant trader, but none of them can afford what we need. No, Papa and Grandfather have got to find somebody with real money, and that means a house in Cliffside or the Promontory, or near the Mother Temple. You're not going to find anybody with that kind of money bathing here!"

"Oh. Right." Kirin's hope deflated. He looked over the plebian crowd with new eyes. "We can't go knocking on doors in Cliffside."

Sevan laughed. "True! We'd get thrown out on our asses by the Watch."

"So where do we find a patron?"

Sevan shook his head, exasperated. "I wish I knew, and I wish you'd stop fretting about it. Come on, let's do twenty more circles and then take care of the little ones while Ger and the others get some swim time."

Kirin dropped back into the pool and joined him. He always been more of a fish in the water than Sevan and made it a point to dive under his brother's steady crawl and swap sides when the crowded conditions permitted.

Afterwards they played with the little boys, teaching them to swim, until the half-hour bell rang. The family gathered together again, herded the children back to the changing room, reclaimed their clothing and dressed once more, this time in the carefully packed clean clothes. Kirin enjoyed the luxurious sensation of being really, truly clean for the first time in days. The men waited bare moments in the entry hall before the women came out to join them, to the usual amiable quarrel over who kept whom waiting.

Maia took his hand again, whispered in his ear, "Let's go to the Bazaar." Aloud she told Pieter and Ger, "Mama wants me to get some things for her and grandmother; may I take Kirin along?"

Pieter agreed readily and Ger had no objection, so the two of them handed their clothes bags to Attir and turned the other way as the family headed for home. They walked a few blocks up cobbled Sulfur Street and passed through Oldgate into the swirling sights, sounds, and scents of Aretzo's Bazaar.

A reed pipe fluted counterpoint as a snake charmer called his cobra out of its basket. A fruit seller hawked pomegranates, mangos, limes, and lemons.

Kirin breathed deeply of the aromas. Three generations of a family sold skewers of lamb broiled over pine coals while their neighbor offered clay mugs of mint tea kept simmering endlessly in a gleaming samovar. A Herdae spice merchant, swathed in a robe that left only his eyes and fingertips exposed to hide his extensive tattoos from offended Silbari eyes, hawked vanilla, cumin, pepper, coriander, and mustard. Smoky lamps inside dim tents competed with the offerings of sharp incense and sweet balms. A harness shop exhaled leather and steel, to which its neighbor contributed a hint of purging fish oil. Horses showed their paces in a corral reeking of their inevitable manure. Chains of frangipani blossoms were sold by enterprising urchins to the buyers studying the animals. Mounds of Island coconuts and barrels of northern chestnuts lent their exotic proximity to prosaic piles of Silbari almonds, cashews, and pistachios. Half the world could be found in Aretzo's Bazaar.

And plenty of strangers. Kirin automatically walked behind Maia in guard position, one hand hovering near his belt knife. With foreign goods came foreign men. Few would dare offer insult to a woman in the Bazaar, but it was known to happen. This way Silbaris who did not know him, who would have looked askance at a pale-skinned man for holding a Silbari woman's hand, could ignore him as a hired protector. Mercenary guard had long been one of the few positions freely open to halfblood men in Aretzo.

Kirin and Maia found their way to the apothecary that Carmella trusted. Maia haggled furiously and finally made several small purchases, counted out the copper coins her mother had entrusted to her, and frowned at the small pile remaining. As they left she confided, "I'd hoped to save enough to buy us each a beef skewer, but this won't do it."

"That's fine, love," Kirin assure her. "Maybe we can get some roast pork instead."

Maia shuddered and touched her stomach. "Don't say that, the thought makes me queasy. I think I could stand some chicken."

They found a stall and bought two flatbreads folded around slivers of chicken, fennel, and collard greens with a healthy dollop of spicy sauce. A shaded nook almost hidden between tents offered a place to sit and nibble. It had a stone block only big enough for one. Since they were mostly hidden, Kirin sat on it and held Maia on his lap, which despite his hard muscularity was softer for her than the stone. He enjoyed the warm armful of healthy woman nestled against him, nuzzled her clean hair and thought about the night.

She finished her meal and rested quietly against him, breathing softly into his close-trimmed married-man's beard. For a long timeless moment, he simply held her, there amid the teeming bazaar, and ached with happiness.

"Kirin," she finally whispered. "I talked with Mama about . . . about our baby."

His arms tightened a little as worry stabbed his heart, but he made himself relax. "Is everything—is he—or she . . ." He swallowed. He knew there were things that could go wrong when a woman grew a baby, terrible things that men barely whispered about, horrors that even a powerful priestess couldn't prevent. "Are *you* all right?"

She kissed him on one ear. "Yes. I'm fine. But I won't be able to dance when my belly swells, which means we can't perform Malik and Mercia. The troupe will have to do our less popular acts, which means less money. That would be hard enough if we still had our traditional space. Without it . . . the family's in serious trouble. If Grandfather's right, we could lose our home before midwinter."

Kirin understood the words she did not say. *This is a terrible time for me to be pregnant. But I don't have to stay that way.*

Unwillingly his eyes stole to a little alleyway between two hard-faced guards leaning on red stone pillars. Everybody knew that Madame Ymera, the witch who ruled the Red Street, maintained a tent there where women went when they didn't wish to be pregnant. The Orthodox frowned on the practice and discouraged it, but even the Hierarch would think twice about directly attacking a witch—and reputed vampire—as powerful as Ymera. The Purists claimed that terrible things happened to the unborn souls, while the Dissenters disputed that as they did so much else. The red pillars and the little tent remained. Kirin swallowed hard and clung to Maia.

"Don't you want—I mean, do you want . . ." His throat closed on the words.

Her arms went around his neck and she buried her face in his hair. "I want you! I want our child. I hate even thinking about—about not having our baby. But what if we lose our home? I'm scared of having to give birth in a stable or, The One forbid, in an alley." She shuddered.

"We'll still have our family," he found himself saying, and only then understood how very much he wanted to be made a father by her. "You won't be alone. Your mother, your sister-in-law, all the aunts will be there for you. I'll be there. You'll never be alone, I swear it."

They held each other wordlessly.

PETER SARTUCCI

A funeral passed by, the bier carried by eight grunting men and draped in sheer flamingo-hued gauze; the color of resurrection. Censers and a chanting Priestess preceded it, mourners followed, including a professional quartet with their hair down and garments torn. They wailed artistically, but their voices grated on Kirin's ears.

I want life! he thought.

A pair of Duermu women walked by leading a string of donkeys.

Tested with fear and loss, he remembered. *Someone powerful will help me. Please God, let it be a Patron.*

Maia sighed and kissed him on the forehead. "Let's get away from this place, love. Let's go home."

He helped her up and looked her in the face. "I will do anything you need me to do, to keep you and our baby safe. Anything at all."

"I know," she answered, and slipped her free arm around his waist to hug him. They resumed their pose of woman and guard, and silently walked home.

CHAPTER 8: TERRELL

As the miles unrolled under unhurried hooves, Terrell's sadness faded away, replaced by fascination. Within days they were beyond the Gwythford fields and woods that he'd explored as a boy, and before the first tenday they'd gone beyond the larger web of forests and villages that he'd explored as a youth. The broad valleys and low wrinkled hills of Gwythlo grew narrower and steeper.

Looking at a map fifteen days after their departure, Terrell asked General DiCervi, commander of the Silbari Brigade, "So, tomorrow we leave Gwythlo?"

"Yes, Your Highness." DiCervi bent over the map table, pointed. "Here's the Severing River. We'll cross it tomorrow morning, leaving Gwythlo for Autria, one of your father's other realms. The day after that we'll arrive in Autria's capital and you'll pay a state visit to their king."

"Who'll probably fall all over himself greeting you," Pen commented. "Folks at Court say he's scared that the Emperor will depose him if he sneezes wrong."

DiCervi flashed a smile before he resumed his usual stern expression. "After that it's a four day journey up this big tributary, Battle River, to Autria's border with Solvigi, which your grandfather also conquered on his way to taking Silbar. It is ruled directly by your father through a viceroy at the Warburg, below the Storm Pass. You'll be in strange country there. The folk of that valley are mostly wild herdsmen and hunters who speak a very foreign tongue, except for the Gwythlo military settlement around the Warburg. The Storm Pass will take us into northeastern Silbar itself. From there we travel down the Storm River." He poked the edge of the map. "To the River Amm, and down that to Aretzo." DiCervi's city accent grew strong as named the home that he'd rarely seen in the last eighteen years.

"But first the Severing River, Autria, the Warburg, and many mountains," Terrell murmured. "Before we reach Silbar. I wonder what we'll find?"

"As it happens, I've been scrying our route, Highness," announced dour Shimoor, the Royal Wizard of Silbar. He stumped into the tent leaning on a cane, dressed in gray while his cloud-white hair escaped under the edges of a hooded cape. A flicker of heat leaked from it, Shimoor had a spell going to warm his old bones in the morning chill. Despite his obvious frailty—*even more than Father's*, Terrell thought with a pang—the old wizard practically glowed with power.

"What did you find?" Terrell asked eagerly. The trip so far had been uneventful, or in other words, boring.

"One moment, Highness." The old wizard sank heavily onto a stool and grunted in relief. A servant offered him a hot tea fragrant with willow bark and wild strawberry leaf. Shimoor flicked a hand over it to adjust the temperature to what he liked, then drank half of it, visibly enjoying the way they all waited on his next words. Finally he added, "I suspect trouble ahead."

"Are there bandits?" DiCervi asked practically.

"A pack of wolves?" Terrell speculated.

"Or bears?" Pen suggested.

"None of those," Shimoor answered. "That's the problem. The forest around and ahead of us should be thick with bear and wolf and their prey. I'm seeing almost none. The land wights are silent and both the local mages and the Druids have all withdrawn from our path, though their connections to the local Nodes are as strong as ever, possibly more so. As for bandits, not a whisker. If I were a trusting wizard, I'd say our path has been made easy and clear."

"But you're not a trusting wizard, are you?" DiCervi asked with a smile.

"It smells of coordination." Shimoor scowled ferociously. "I suspect somebody is planning to surprise us."

"Where?" Pen asked, putting a hand on Irreneetha's pommel. "When?"

"Unclear. But somewhere ahead, that much is certain." Shimoor's ferocious scowl settled into a merely foreboding one and he gulped more tea.

"What kind of surprise?" Terrell asked. "And who's behind it? Do you think it is Osrick's doing, or one of the resentful barons, or—"

"Or perhaps your Aunt," Dona Seraphina interjected, joining them in the tent. "The magic of the land is her purview. If her Druids are in command of the local Nodes through the land wights, they can deny the power to us if they choose."

"But we're leaving Gwythlo tomorrow." Terrell looked at the map again. "Ah. After we cross the river. Where will we camp tonight, General?"

"I had planned to position us on this plateau right above the river plain, your Highness," DiCervi answered thoughtfully, tapping the map. "We want to cross in the morning, when the water is lower after a chilly night slows the melting mountain snows. But the plateau is open to attack from all sides, so perhaps it would be wiser to camp in this curve." He tapped the map again. "That would give us water on three sides, and we can make our crossing as soon as the sun is up."

"Unless the river is the route of attack," Pen pointed out. "There is plenty of wood in this country for boats or rafts."

"Or we might be attacked by something that swims," interjected Dona Seraphina. "I would not underestimate Klairveen."

They all looked at each other for a moment.

I didn't think she would dare try anything so direct, Terrell thought, feeling faintly sick. Sword work didn't frighten him, he knew he was strong and well-trained and had excellent weapons, horses, and armor. But magic treachery wasn't something he could fight personally.

Shimoor's tired face quirked a half-smile at him that seemed to say, *I'm still here for you, My Lord.* An overwhelming gratitude for the old wizard's decades of support and teaching seized Terrell. *The measure of a King is not in his own prowess, but in that of his people,* he recalled Shimoor saying in one of his lessons.

"No good answers," Terrell said. "Let's plan for the river campsite, but keep our people away from the banks, and patrol them. Camp as tight as we can and put up every ward we can. Shimoor?"

"Agreed, Your Highness." He nodded. "I have a few tricks under my cloak. But we planned this trip expecting to tap the local Nodes along our way, and now we must assume they may be denied to us. We don't have enough charged silver with us to replace all that missing power. If we spend too much of what we brought there on the edge of Gwythlo, and then get caught by other trouble somewhere ahead, we could have a more difficult time getting through later."

"A point," Terrell acknowledged. He thought for a moment, feeling the growing Light inside him. It circulated through his body like moving blood; he fancied he could pour it like a sluice, if he only knew how. Dona Seraphina squinted at him with the beginnings of concern in her face, while Shimoor simply squinted. "But we have to do something. We'll choose caution now."

"Very good, Your Highness," DiCervi said. "It shall be done."

* * *

"That's a big river," Pen said, shading his eyes from the setting suns to look across its width. They were standing on a bank a few feet above the waters.

"Yes." Terrell looked back at the flat meadow behind them where the brigade busily set up camp. DiCervi had ordered a hollow square formation with the royal party and the camp followers inside it. It looked like the married men were almost done getting their wives and children settled.

His gaze lingered on the travelling brothel that serviced the unmarried men. It had already been pitched on the opposite side of the royal pavilion from the family tents. He knew that red striped camp-within-a-camp was a feature provided to every major Silbari army unit by Madam Ymera, the witch who ruled Aretzo's Red Street. Dona Seraphina's husband Merritin had told him with a chuckle that the Temple Hierarchy frowned upon the brothels but had long ago grown resigned to their necessity. A banner in front of the biggest tent proclaimed, 'Lust will not keep—something must be done about it.'

Those red striped tents seemed uncommonly interesting today. He remembered some delightful explorations with Serah, a castle maid who Dona Seraphina had provided with a pregnancy protection spell. He wondered if he could ask for one of Ymera's women to be brought to him, and regretfully decided that the servants weren't likely to accommodate him without more trouble than he was willing to endure. Though his loins had begun to fret him more and more since he'd left Serah behind in Gwythford.

They were unaccompanied at the moment, so Terrell lowered his voice. "Pen, do you remember that talk about lust that Merritin had with us last year?"

Pen frowned. "A little. It all seems so distant now." He made a vague gesture that ended with his hand resting on Irreneetha's pommel. "Since She chose me I haven't been bothered by any of that." He shrugged and went back to studying the river as if they'd been talking about the weather.

Terrell knew a moment of sorrow. *Of course. Pyrull as much as told me. Irreneetha fills Pen's heart. He'll never have any other love than her. He can't.* It pained him; a difference had been driven between him and his best friend, one that went to the core of their beings and would never go away.

"Why do you ask?" Pen said absently, still looking at the river. "Are you missing your maid?"

"Serah," Terrell corrected; he needed to think of her as a person and not a thing. Then he admitted, "Some. Merritin said the palace staff in Silbar will provide me with, um, concubines. I'm just wondering, is all." He tried not to squirm.

"There's plenty of cold water in that river," Pen pointed at it as he glanced sidelong at Terrell. "I could dunk you in. That ought to mute your lust for a while."

"I might dive in on my own," Terrell answered ruefully. "It's been four days since I had a bath, or anyone else either."

"This wouldn't be the best place for swimming. Look down below us and to the left, in that big pool under the leaning willow tree. What do you see?"

Terrell squinted at a confusing mass of shadows where the pool lay hard against the steep riverbank. One of them moved and turned into a fish. A fish longer than he was tall. More than *twice* as long as he was tall. A gar, a predatory fish with a long snout, jaws to match, and teeth as big as his hand.

"Angels and Demons!" Terrell blurted, feeling slightly ashamed of the blasphemy.

Abruptly the enormous gar darted out into the river to seize a silver and green striped fish a quarter its size. The prey put up a fight, but the powerful jaws of its adversary soon broke its back. The gar retired to the pool to commence the grisly job of devouring its catch.

The teeth, Terrell decided, were larger than his hand. He found himself inadvertently stepping back farther from the bank. His imagination pictured what might happen if it lunged at him with those jaws snapping.

"Probably better not to go swimming," Pen suggested. "Unless Shimoor is willing to cast a spell that will drive it away. It and its cousins."

"My Lords, the Royal Wizard has requested that I restrict everybody to staying a hundred feet back from the bank," General DiCervi said as he approached them. "This would be easier to enforce if both of you were behind that line yourselves."

"Certainly, General." Terrell consented. "What are we doing for water?"

"There's a good spring inside the camp, and Dona Seraphina has cast a purifying spell on it."

"Very good, General."

The camp was more crowded than usual but still as orderly. Militarily precise rows of tents had been pitched behind the brass standards of the Brigade's various units. Even the family tents were pitched in rigid rows, though the children swarming among them blurred the lines. Two platoons of soldiers drove stakes cut from willow branches into the soft soil in a long curve roughly parallel to the riverside. Two mages strung cord between them. Several small boys were receiving a lecture from a sergeant about staying on the right side of the cord, together with a pantomimed 'snap' of giant jaws closing on a careless boy. The wideeyed youngsters drank in the man's words.

Terrell hoped they heeded well, as the gar wasn't likely to leave enough for a funeral.

He found Shimoor preparing a set of poles with silver insets. "Are those our temporary ward anchors?"

"Yes," the wizard grunted as he completed a spell on one of the poles. "I'm amplifying their effectiveness. Bloody exhausting work, Your Highness." He mopped his brow with a trembling hand before tackling the next. As Terrell watched, appalled, the lines in his teacher's aged face grew deeper.

"You shouldn't be spending yourself like this!" he remonstrated. "Let the other mages handle it."

"No choice," Shimoor growled. "I'm delegating everything I can to them, but I'm better at ward casting." He gestured to his two assistant spell casters working on the assembly of another ward marker; Dona Seraphina's husband Merritin helped them. "I do not like the currents I feel in the local mana flow. As I feared, somebody—almost certainly a coven of Druids—is manipulating it away from us. I'm drawing what I can from the nearest node, but I must fight for every scrap, and it's not enough to feed normal nighttime wards big enough for this camp. That's why I'm going to try for a distributed protection."

Terrell struggled to remember the finer points of ward construction. "That would make them work like a soap bubble, right? If pierced anywhere, the whole thing bursts?"

"Which is why I'm adding reinforcement spells, so that it *won't* burst if it gets pierced. We'll see if it works. If not—I hope Baron Penghar's sword arm is ready."

In answer, Pen drew Irreneetha and held her point uppermost. The steel blade glowed even to the unaided eye, a lavender shine shot through with tiny red flashes. "She knows something is happening out there," Pen said. "And it's not friendly. She's ready."

* * *

Night fell, but sleep would not come. Terrell lay awake on his cot, staring at the tent fabric over his head and listening to the sounds of the camp. A fretful child cried softly while a woman's tired voice soothed it. The men were on watch-and-watch, with the on-duty ranks formed up two-deep along the landward side of the camp and one-deep on the other three sides. The off-duty men had been given strict orders to get some sleep during their rest. He wondered how many of them really were sleeping.

"Pen?" he finally whispered.

"Terrell?" Pen's voice came back immediately.

"We're of no use lying here awake. Let's get up and be ready to fight."

"I was about to suggest that myself, My Lord."

They dressed in undergarments and helped each other into their gambesons and armor. The night air had been cool, even though they were more than five hundred miles south of Gwythford now. Terrell shivered a little and told himself the cold river caused his chill. Their rustling about woke their servants. The yawning men lit tapers and helped, after which the armoring went much smoother. Terrell and Pen exited the tent into a night that boasted only a pale crescent of Madness to light the darkness.

Terrell left his visor up as he and Pen saddled and mounted their big destriers, not the lighter rounceys they'd been riding most of yesterday. The two of them set out on a circuit between the lines.

Shimoor's wards were emplaced in a giant octagon around the square camp. Terrell squinted at the assemblage. The cords stringing them together glowed to his magesight like lines of blue-white fire. He examined the rings of protection that glowed around each individual ward pole as he rode past. The rings were wider than his arms could reach and perfectly rigid, floating in the air roughly waist high with the glimmer of a spherical dome above and below each. When he looked up, he could see a far larger dome that extended over the whole camp.

Pen had been using Irreneetha's abilities to see the same. He commented quietly, "It's like a castle made of light."

"Mmm," Terrell answered. Light. His insides were suffused with it. When he looked at his hands the Light leaked through every joint of his gauntlets.

Pen glanced at him several times, repeatedly touching Irreneetha's hilt, until finally he said, "Terrell? Did you know that you're glowing right through your armor?"

There didn't seem to be anything else to say but, "Yes."

They made two full circuits of the camp, riding inside the wards but outside the waiting ranks of men. DiCervi nodded a curt greeting when they passed him sitting atop his horse in the middle of the landward side. The mage standing night duty with the commander gaped at Terrell. Then, as they approached the middle of the opposite side—

"Do you hear a sound from the river?" Terrell asked Pen.

The giant gar leaped out of the water.

It landed on the bank twenty feet from the river's edge and flipped itself end-over-end towards them. Terrell's horse had been trained for war, but not for this. The destrier reared and dumped him out of his saddle. He barely managed to free his feet from the stirrups as the panicked horse bolted. He hit the turf back-first and saw stars. Those cleared in time to see the mighty fish land with its gaping jaws right on the ward line. Teeth that looked bigger than his head snapped shut on the cord - and cut it.

The spell discharged a titanic bolt of power into the gar's head. Bits of flesh, bone, and teeth exploded outward to batter Terrell. A gobbet smacked him on the lips and left a bloody taste behind. He sat up and spit.

The wards were pierced. A horde of creatures poured up the riverbank out of the water. Behind him the line of soldiers had been knocked off their feet by the explosion. A few began to cry warning.

The ends of the broken cord lay sparkling on either side of the wreckage of the fish. He scrambled on hands and knees towards the nearer, snatched it up, and staggered to his feet. Shaking legs carried him to the carcass where the tension in the ensorceled cord brought him up short. His gauntlet grew warm where it grasped the raw end. He stretched his arms and squatted, trying desperately to reach the other end where it spit sparks onto the turf. It stayed out of his reach.

"Here," Pen said, running up to snatch it off the grass in his own gauntleted hands and press it into Terrell's. "I'll guard, you fix!"

Pen stepped right over him and onto the fish carcass. Irreneetha shone in his hands like a spike of starlight as he called to the men behind them. "Beware! Attackers from the river!"

Terrell scrambled to his feet, tried to bring the severed ends together. They would not quite meet no matter how much he strained. The spell fractured around him, fading, he had to do something, but it was getting so bright—

The glow wasn't outside, but inside.

Light surged out from his heart and into his fingertips. It twined with the frayed ends of the ward and knit to both. A river of Light flowed out of him and into the spells that gave the wards their shape.

The cord glowed bright enough to reveal the whole riverbank. Creatures came boiling towards the camp. Crawling, leaping, shambling— hundreds of nightmare pastiches of beast and fish and beaked bird. The soldiers uttered shocked cries at the sight. Sergeants bellowed as they reformed the defensive line. Terrell stood up and tried to join the severed cords again, but couldn't. The fish had bitten part of it off.

Pen swung Irreneetha and lopped off a reaching limb from a bastard mix of crayfish and badger, then took its head on the return stroke. Another beast tried to strike at Terrell but the sword got in front of it; red ruin fell back.

Terrell jerked his head to make his visor close. With it down he'd be encased in armor from scalp to toe, and nearly invulnerable. But the swiveling metal facescreen barely wiggled. *It jammed open when I was thrown. I can't let go of the cord. I can't protect my face!*

To his left and right creatures seared themselves on the wards and reared back, screeching their pain. Snarls broke out as those behind pushed forward and the front line fought desperately to get away from the deadly cord. A tall swaying thing fell directly onto the ward. Instead of replicating the success of the fish, it was simply sliced in two. The severed halves flopped madly. A toothed beak snapped twice before a spearman pinned it down to die.

Terrell heard shouted orders, stamping feet and the ring of steel behind him. Somebody ordered the men to march forward to the edge of the ward, which was a risky maneuver with so much magic chaos. He couldn't spare the attention to look, for something low and leggy tried to dart under the ward close enough to brush his leg. It exploded and added more gore to his armor. This time Terrell managed to turn his own head aside enough to shield his face. When another monster leaped over the ward and turned into a torch impaled on the advancing spears, the mass of creatures paused.

Fanged heads swung towards Terrell and beady eyes glared. Irreneetha swung, seeming to grow longer in Pen's hands as she whistled through the air. But there was only one of her and there were dozens of them.

They've found the weak point, Terrell thought, shuddering. *It's me. I've got to do something to keep them back or they'll eat my face.*

The light pouring out of him to sustain the wards grew brighter. It almost had substance thick enough to touch. Earlier he had thought of it like blood moving in his veins; now it seemed thicker, more like dough being spun to make flatbread.

Spun . . . I can manipulate artifacts, and these wards are functionally the same as an artifact.

He groped for the light with his mind. Glowing cords came to his mental *hands* and he wound them into a ring. Small at first, he grew it fast and set it to spinning around himself and Pen. It crossed the ward spell effortlessly, the two magics intersecting without a ripple. He twisted the ring and it became a sphere centered on him. The advancing soldiers halted in confusion mere steps away, then surged to either side to attack the monsters.

The creatures boiled about the front of his spell-shield, clawed and bit at the light. They were sliced through or beheaded or exploded or simply maimed by their own actions. Gore splashed both himself and Pen and he had to spit to clear his mouth. Body fragments battered him as frenzied monsters threw themselves at the spinning barrier, some leaping up to dive down onto the glowing dome. One tried to burrow under and up but exploded as soon as it broke through the sod. He nearly fell over as a bone fragment slashed his face and his right knee went numb.

The soldiers thrust weapons past the glowing wards, stabbed and chopped at the milling creatures. Blood smoked on metal as the ward spells heated the blades. Some men hadn't donned their gauntlets first; they roared in pain even as they kept swinging.

The mass of beastly attackers broke. Monsters fled, limped, crawled to the riverbank and threw themselves in. Archers fired arrows and crossbow bolts after them, some caught fire as they flew through the supercharged wards. Soon the riverbank lay clear of living creatures all the way to the water's edge.

Terrell staggered. The spinning sphere around him and Pen faded, flickered, went out. Pen climbed down off the fish, now partly roasted, and caught Terrell as he sagged.

"Your Highness?" DiCervi's voice seemed to come from far away. "I think you can let go now, Your Highness." So very far away. Pen's voice now:

66

"Please let go of the wards." Terrell's hands didn't want to move. "Please, Terrell! Let go?"

He finally managed to open his fingers and saw the frayed ends drift toward the ground. Two mages caught them and spliced in a replacement, transferred the dying ward to the new cord and revived it.

Pen's strong arms lifted him as blackness closed in.

* * *

Terrell awoke to sunlight shining on the tent canvas. He tried to rise and immediately groaned.

"You had me worried," Pen said, sitting up on his own cot. "How do you feel?"

"Like every bit of me has been used as a target for weapons practice. By the whole brigade." He moved experimentally, touched his face. A wound throbbed perilously close to his right eye. He winced at the thought of being blinded, continued, "But I don't think anything's actually broken."

"Dona Seraphina worked on you already and she agrees," Pen reported, smiling. "Lots of bruises and strains and that cut on your face, she said, but nothing that won't heal."

"You were hit by as many exploding creature-parts as me," Terrell said to him. "Probably more. But you don't look like you even got bruised."

"Oh, there were plenty of bruises!" Pen chuckled and casually added, "But they all healed by noon today. It's Irreneetha's doing. Pyrull said she can heal me of most injuries if they don't kill me outright."

I will not envy him that, Terrell told himself. *Or at least, not too much.* Aloud: "Noon? I thought we were going to cross the river in the morning."

"We're staying for another day while you recover enough to ride. The King of Autria can wait."

"I can't complain about that. But right now, I need the latrine." Terrell struggled to his feet and leaned on Pen as he made his way to the slit trenches. When he finished he managed to hobble back to his tent under his own power. Dozens of troopers rushed to form a line and salute him; camp followers bowed. He managed to return their obeisances with a wave and a smile.

"What's all this about?" He asked Pen quietly.

"You saved the camp," Pen answered simply. "Hundreds of them saw it. Their wives and children and friends and favored whores were all on the line, and you saved them."

"You did, too!"

"No, I protected you, as is my privilege and sacred duty. But I couldn't have taken the broken ward spell in my hands and fixed it like you did. If those creatures had gotten in among the tents, dozens of our folk would have died. Maybe hundreds. Maybe us too."

"Ah." The memory flowed back, and Terrell had to lean on Pen again.

Dona Seraphina waited in his tent. She checked him over rapidly while he stood still and endured it.

"Your Light is much diminished," she reported. "Evidently it can substitute for power in a standing ward, with no immediate ill effect upon you. Though I am concerned about potential long term damage, so far it appears to have merely enlarged your body's own mana conduits."

Her healing aura washed over him, and the battered feeling faded to a dull ache. He almost fainted from the relief. But his stomach growled. "Food?" he asked hopefully.

"Plenty of that." She sat him at the folding map table and a servant put a covered dish before him. From it came a delectable aroma.

"Fish steak," Seraphina said with a twinkle in her eye. "Everyone in camp had some for breakfast, but the cooks saved you a choice bit."

Terrell cut a piece and lifted it on his knife blade. Delicious.

"Eating well is the best revenge," Pen assured him, grinning.

CHAPTER 9: KIRIN

A few days later Grandfather and Sevan the Elder returned from the Guildhall empty-handed again, with a seething rage in the old man's face that neither of them offered to explain. Grandfather pushed everyone mercilessly through practice that afternoon. Kirin endured it, driving himself with a relentless focus. Maybe if he could do a perfect double somersault the old man would stop raging at them all. He fell into the net twice from missed grabs while the troupe's leader showered him and everyone else with abuse. Doggedly Kirin began to climb the ladder for another try.

"Enough!" Pieter said. "No more flying today. Kirin, Attir, stand down."

Kirin hesitated on the second rung. Grandfather began to roar at Pieter, but he merely said, "The catcher decides when the flyer is ready to fly, and nobody else. You taught me that rule, Father. I am the senior catcher and I say these flyers are done."

Sevan the Younger, the Troupe's junior catcher, hastily backed him up with vigorous head-nodding.

Kirin looked at himself and Attir. They were both trembling from the strain. Kirin feared Attir would make a dangerous mistake from simple exhaustion.

"Father, please!" Sevan the Elder whispered something urgent into Grandfather's ear. The old man growled several more times before his sons persuaded him to give the family a break. The two men went with their father and Uncle Ger to the troupe's office in the Attic's corner for a conference.

I've got to do something, Kirin thought as he wiped himself down in the changing room. Attir had stuck his head in the water barrel and sat on a bench dripping, too tired to even wash. *I've got to find us a patron. I know who to ask. I can't keep putting it off, or one of us will get hurt.*

Kirin went to the tiny room he shared with Maia, put on a clean tunic and laced a pair of buskins on his feet. He had buckled on his belt knife and coin pouch when Maia came in.

"Where are you going?" she asked, her eyes narrowing as he put his last two silver dohba and a handful of coppers into the sadly-thin pouch. "What are you going to do?"

He hugged her and whispered in her ear, "To visit Mother Gee."

Maia's eyes widened. "Uncle Pieter won't approve," she warned. "He says she's a spy for Madam Ymera!"

Kirin grimaced at the name. Rumor about the undying witch called *Queen of the Red Street* named her the most dangerous power in Aretzo. The Kings had kept her safely bridled in her little enclave for two centuries by binding her with oaths. The Orthodox Hierarchy frowned upon her, the Purists railed against her and all her works, and the Dissenters, despite pointing out that she had kept the Law and her Oaths for two centuries, were no happier to have a suspected vampire dwelling in the City.

"I know, and he's probably right, but Mother Gee wouldn't do anything to hurt me." *Anything worse than she already did.* "Will you cover for me?"

"Yes. I'll tell him you went to a temple to pray for a patron." She kissed him. "So make sure you do, on your way back, because I don't want to be a liar. And don't take too long."

"I will, and I'll hurry," he promised, and quietly snuck out of the Inn.

He avoided the open path to Mother Gee's door. A dozen gossips would mark his arrival and departure if he went that way, and Pieter would know within a day. Instead he took the back stair out the Inn's north end, cut through four alleys and a squalid little courtyard, and entered the back of a big stable through a loose board in the rear wall of the hayloft. He had to squirm to get through; he'd grown since the last time he tried this path. For a moment he thought he'd have to use one of the four other ways instead, but he made it into the dark hay-smelling loft without scraping off any skin. He made a left and a right and another left through the labyrinth of rafters over the stables below. One of the heavy planks groaned under his greater weight, but no stable hands were near enough to notice, and the horses didn't care.

He finally found the hidden hatch, raised it and crawled into the narrow wooden tunnel beyond. He barely fit and had to wiggle along like a worm with his coin purse and belt knife both pressed uncomfortably into his groin. He'd almost reached the far end when a sliding panel opened above his head.

"Stop right there," barked a gruff voice. "Who are you and what do you want?" A blade pressed against his neck.

"Mother Gee!" His voice squeaked humiliatingly. "It's Kirin!"

"Kirin? Idiot boy, I almost cut your throat. You sounded like some fool trying to burgle me. Crawl out of there right now."

Kirin wiggled the rest of the way through the tunnel, shedding some skin on the frame of the exit door; it had been made for little boys.

"You're no boy anymore." Mother Gee surveyed him, bending her neck to look up.

Kirin was surprised at how short she was; a wizened woman barely as tall as his breastbone. She had put down the knife and now she held a mage lamp up to get a better look at him. It lit the wrinkles in her face too, her gray hair, her bent neck. He saw with a start that she'd grown old and stooped. Had she really once been a famous courtesan on the Red Street?

"Mother Gee, I wanted to visit you without Pieter knowing," he tried to explain.

"He still blames me for you getting enslaved," she growled. "Doesn't he?" He saw hurt in her eyes now and something he wasn't used to seeing there; shame. "Maybe he should."

"No!" Kirin answered forcefully as he caught her free hand. It seemed tiny and fragile in his callused paw, diminished like the rest of her. "Nobody's to blame but the Governor. He's the bastard who ordered all of us orphan boys rounded up and sold, not you."

"There were hints about his plans. I should have kept you here that day."

"It's not your fault that I got caught."

"I should have bought you off the slave block," she told him, looking down at his hands. "I had the money—"

"Gerlach would have outbid you," Kirin interrupted. "He recognized me, never mind why, and whatever you bid, he'd have raised until you couldn't match it."

Gee's hand closed into a fist, she grabbed one of his thumbs the way she had when he'd been one of her child spies and she wanted him to hold still. She stared at his face with searching eyes, and harshly said, "I figured out later what kind of monster he really was. Pieter told me you were covered in blood when he found you in the street afterwards. It was the last thing he said to me before he stormed out of here swearing never to speak to me again. Tell me the truth, boy. Did Gerlach rape you?"

The ugly memory rose unbidden and he flinched from it. "I got away. Do you really want to know more?"

"Want?" She barked a laugh like a rusty saw. "No. I *need* to know, boy. Always been my curse, needing to know. After Pieter DiUmbra took you in, I dug out every detail I could find about Gerlach's doings, the blood-magic sacrifices and all the rest of it."

You don't *know all of it, Mother Gee,* he thought. *Nobody knows but me.*

"Took me more than a season to get it," she continued, staring at him closely. "The Watch and that Temple Inquisitor did a thorough job combing the ruins of his house. By the way, did you set that fire?"

"Sort of." Kirin scowled. "It was an accident. We were fighting, and an oil lamp got knocked down." *The smell of Gerlach's burning flesh . . .*

"Fighting? You weren't even eight years old, were you?"

"That's about right."

"How'd you fight a grown man three times your size?"

"I had help." Kirin's Shadow stirred within him and an uglier memory rose behind it. He instantly pressed them both down. *No! Nobody must ever know!*

"Care to expand on that?"

"I wasn't the only prisoner in his basement," he said, lying with the truth. "Mother Gee, it's been almost ten years. He's dead and I'm alive and I plan to stay that way. I've put what happened behind me, and I don't want to remember." *I really don't want to remember!* he thought, added aloud, "Please?"

PETER SARTUCCI

"All right, boy." She released his thumb, hung the mage lamp on a bracket, and settled herself in a padded chair. "Sit, sit. Let me look at you without straining my neck. I heard about your marriage."

Kirin brightened as he sat. "To Maia! Still I can hardly believe she married me. She's wonderful, Mother Gee, I love her so much. When we dance together on the stage it's like she lifts me beyond myself." A sadder memory intruded, and he added, "I wanted to invite you to the wedding, but Pieter wouldn't let me. I'm sorry."

"No need. I don't get out much anyway. Never did care for crowds, even at a celebration." She studied him for a moment, her eyes as sharp and bright as ever. "You're looking good, boy. Acrobat work agrees with you; marriage agrees with you. I'm glad you found a better way than some of my boys do."

"I'm not the only one who's done well. I saw Raff when we performed in Dalmatzo. He's married and got two kids now, working for the Leather Merchant's Guild. He had nice clothes and a silver ring with a blue stone. He's happy."

"Glad to hear it. He and you have company. The twins apprenticed to a chandler down at the docks, and Brase went to sea with a trader. He's on his third voyage now, this time as a bosun." She smiled fondly. "He found me four orphan boys from the Sump, they've trained up nicely. I've got them working the Bazaar today, running errands and keeping their ears open. They already brought me some juicy tidbits that the Herdae paid well for."

Kirin chuckled. He'd served her the same way when he'd been young, running messages and spying out information for her clients. Knowledge had always been a coin as good as gold in Aretzo, and she'd managed to turn long strings of casual observations into more than a few gold coins over the years. "What's Tricky doing?" he asked. "I haven't seen him in two years. Have you heard anything?"

Her smile disappeared. "By now, he probably wants to die. He turned to thieving when he left me, early last year. Always had too much anger, too much cockiness in him. Got caught three days after your troupe left town on your big trip; it was his second time."

Kirin winced. "Second time thieving—that's a flogging, isn't it?" The whip would leave marks for the rest of Tricky's life, but at least it wouldn't kill him.

"No, flogging's for the first offense, second is usually branding. Ap Marn said a man who didn't learn from the flogging wasn't likely to learn from a branding either, so he sent him to Sulmona."

Cold ran up Kirin spine. The sulfur mines were a death sentence for any man less than very strong. His old friend had always been small and skinny; he wouldn't last six months under the man-killing labor there. A helpless rage filled him. "Salim take that bastard Gwythlo! Governor, hah! He's just a jumped-up thief. He sold our place in the Bazaar to the Suliemons."

"I heard." She nodded. "Half the tents in the Bazaar have had to pay bribes to keep their spots, and the other half are expecting to, as soon as he gets around to them. He's not squeezing just there, either. Word is that City Watch commissions cost a hundred pounds of raw silver now."

"Damn him! The Watch will be gouging the rest of us even harder to pay it," Kirin growled. He took a deep breath and with a wrench of shame he forced the memory of his friend, who he could not help, away. "My family's in trouble, Mother. We've got to have a new place to perform, and soon. That means a patron. Only where do we find one? Even Grandfather doesn't know anyone with that kind of money."

"Hmmmm," she rumbled with her eyes half closed. "Ought to be a few. Try looking among the new merchant houses, especially the cloth-factors—and the shippers! Tell Pieter's brother Sevan that Reshghar Bovea Millago and his wife Arriga expect their firstborn soon and are planning an extravagant child welcoming party. They'll likely want entertainment. That new ballroom they've built onto their mansion in Cliffside can hold hundreds and has a high ceiling. Ask Pernod Iola DiBellun, the victualler, about making a joint offer to Millago. If your Magister plays it right, DiBellun will jump at the chance to partner with the DiUmbras on a bid for Millago's entertainment."

"Perfect!" Kirin said happily. "Now we need to get DiBellun to talk to us." He knew the victualler had a higher social rank than mere acrobats, but the man would certainly be easier to approach than the owner of Aretzo's largest shipping house.

"I can help you there too," Mother Gee smirked. "He's married to the cousin of Dona Abbithana, Priestess Zella's new assistant priestess. She can give you a letter of introduction to him."

Kirin fished out his two silver coins and set them in her open hand, knowing that the payment meant she wouldn't tell anyone else. "Thank you, Mother!"

Her sharp eyes had noted the slenderness of his coin pouch. "I could use an extra pair of eyes and ears, boy. If you've got time on your hands, I've paying work that needs doing."

"Sorry, Mother," He shook his head. "Pieter would be angry, and Grandfather would throw a fit. I can't. But thank you for the offer."

She waved a hand negligently. "Keep it in mind. And don't be such a stranger, boy; come visit me again sometime. Only don't wait nine years, hear?"

Kirin smiled. "I promise, Mother." He kissed her on one withered cheek and left the room by a different route than he'd used to arrive.

* * *

Kirin paused at the entrance to the narrow side street that led to the Temple of Heavenly Peace, Priestess Zella's sanctuary. It lay on the wrong side of the Serpentine, the twisty street that wound along the high tide line where Aretzo fell into the half-drowned neighborhood between the docks and the Old City. He vaguely knew that centuries ago this area had once been the heart of the city, before the sea rose and turned streets to canals. For the past few centuries everybody called this tide-wracked area the Sump. Many of the sewers in the Old City drained into it. The stench hung heavy on this windless day while the rising tide backed up the canals.

He picked his way along the excuse of a street, indifferently paved and barely above the water, which lead to the old Temple's entrance. Sagging tenements rose on either side. Most of them were crammed with people. A few with bad foundations were in various stages of collapse; those had more furtive denizens. Half the voices he heard were speaking something other than Silbari.

He looked around warily; the Sump had long been the roughest neighborhood in Aretzo. There were cheap doss-houses serving sailors and roustabouts who worked on the ships and piers that lay beyond the Temple. Pieter said that Law was no more than an infrequent visitor to the Sump. Travelling through to worship with the family had always been safe enough, since even the drunkest fool wouldn't challenge a dozen very fit men armed with belt knives. But he was alone, now.

Ahead of him a seedy tavern spilled vomit and drunks into the narrow street. And fights. Garbled voices shouted as a free-for-all of wildly swinging men poured out to block Kirin's path. A pale-skinned sailor wearing a red cap blundered into him. The sailor cursed him in Klinto and threw a roundhouse punch at his head.

Kirin ducked the blow, pivoted on one foot to lash out with the other. The heel of his buskin sank into the drunk's gut and the man folded like a cut tree. A woman shrieked, more excited than frightened, and another fool tried to slug him. Kirin dodged that one and let the man blunder into the side of a building. Bricks intercepted a flailing fist with an unsympathetic crack. The drunk froze for a moment in shock, began to swear, absorbed now in his own pain.

Kirin fended off two more drunks trying to grapple each other. He dodged a punch from a cursing Xir nearly two feet taller than himself. The man's skin gleamed black as night and he bore elaborate ritual scars on both sides of his shirtless chest. The marks ran over his shoulders and up his neck to end in dramatic curls on his cheeks. Kirin shuddered to see them; Silbar's Holy Writ forbade voluntary body disfigurement.

The big sailor saw the revulsion in his face. "Shibret!" he spit the word at Kirin, weaving closer for another try. The people of Xir had a tradition of pale-skinned Imps like Silbar did, but with nastier habits.

Kirin's Shadow awoke with his own anger and uncoiled under his heart. The Xir sailor had reach to match his height. When he threw another punch Kirin barely dodged it.

The sailor spewed another insult referencing Kirin's mother and an improbable coupling with a demon and a dog. Kirin's Shadow rose into his eyes and he blocked and ducked until he found an opening and kicked the Xir in the groin.

The man groaned. He tried to draw his belt knife before he folded up but failed.

Kirin dodged him and ran. The street jinked around an old building. He leaned against a blind wall for a moment to master himself, and his Shadow.

It surged and tried to reach beyond his skin.

No! he thought at it sharply. *Down, monster!*

He ruthlessly forced it inward. It wouldn't go back under his heart, not while that same heart pounded like a drum, but after a few breaths it stopped trying to reach outside his skin. He accepted that as victory enough, pushed off the wall and began walking again. This time he kept glancing behind as well as maintaining a wary eye on the buildings and people around and ahead of him.

The street finally opened to a tiny plaza fronting the junction of two canals that bordered the sacred building. Kids played at the edge of the stagnant waters, oblivious to the stench. An arching stone bridge more substantial than the street itself leapt the channel. The other end landed next to a tilted pillar, all that remained of the courtyard entrance of the Temple of Heavenly Peace. Kirin strode over the bridge and paused to look around.

Someone long ago had tried to save the venerable building from the rising waters by filling in the lower level and raising the courtyard up to the new sea level. The replacement pavement had settled badly, tilted and cracked, with mud filling the low places so that he had to watch where he stepped. The temple's waterlogged foundations had given way and the dome and entire back half of the structure had collapsed decades ago, leaving a partly-roofed ruin with a single leaning minaret. The grand entry nave had become the sanctuary and Zella lived in a tiny set of rooms that had once housed offices.

I have to keep my Shadow under my tightest control here. He tried to drive it back into its cage under his heart, but the fight had strengthened it and it pushed back. He breathed deeply, did some of the Still Exercises that pitted muscle against muscle without arms or legs moving; Pieter had always been fond of those as an aid to prayer. Today they worked poorly. Try as he might Kirin still couldn't completely suppress the monster inside him. The best he could do was a sort of half measure, the Shadow concentrated inside his chest and hips and quivering like a shaken pudding.

He seriously considered leaving and coming back some other time. Dona Zella understood his Shadow better than any other priestess. She knew he wasn't an Imp and would welcome him even if Darkness leaked out of his every pore. Her assistant might be more easily frightened. He had a humiliating vision of a young priestess fleeing from him like some loathsome thing found in a sewer.

Please, Holy Haroun, he prayed. *Don't let me scare the new Priestess away. Please grant that she listens to me and helps my family. In the Name of the One I beg you.*

He took a deep breath and entered. The holy precincts lay beyond an archway warded now by nothing more than a bead curtain. He let the strings drop behind him and looked around. Glassless clerestory windows let light in and swallows came and went. More light poured through another arch that had once led to the circular sanctuary of the original building, now a jumbled mass of broken stone ringed by stubs of wall. A family of ferrets chased rats through the ruins while a redheaded vulture perched on a broken column and watched with scavenger patience.

A crude altar had been built this side of the open arch. On stormy days Kirin remembered rain blowing in during services to wet priestess and congregation. He found nobody in the bare room, but he heard voices coming from the living quarters. He crossed the spalled marble floor and knocked on Zella's door.

It opened to reveal a woman taller and wider than he was. Her yellow robes were stained and faded, her hair screwed back into a businesslike bun, and she wore no wimple. Richer sinecures and benefices supported their priestesses in better style. Zella's impoverished congregation barely kept her fed and clothed. Despite this she greeted Kirin with a cheerful welcome and ushered him into her combination sitting room, kitchen, and office.

A young woman in newer yellow robes wore a starched white wimple with two embroidered silver stars. The novice priestess stared at his face nervously and got up from her seat at the ramshackle table that was the largest thing in the room. "Perhaps I should go," she ventured.

"Stay, Abbie," Zella ordered. "This is Kirin DiUmbra, one of the acrobats who live in the Sulfur Serpent Inn. Kirin, this is Dona Abbithana D'Ivor Vidlet, my new assistant priestess, who arrived a few days after your troupe went on tour. You caught us finishing my sermon for this coming Holy Day."

"Dona Abbithana." Kirin put his palms together and bowed over his hands. "I'm honored to meet you. I confess that you are the reason I came here today."

Dona Abbithana had the golden aura of a healer, more prominent that Zella's own. At his words the young woman looked even more nervous. She mumbled a vague greeting while her eyes stared at his face.

No, he thought; *at my skin and ears.* He stiffened, remembering the Xir's epithets, and the old pain and anger rose once more. He blurted out, "My sire was a Gwythlo, Dona, not Salim the Tormentor. I'm not an Imp! I'm just a man."

Her face flushed mahogany-colored.

Kirin almost bit his tongue as he jeered at himself. *Idiot! Getting off to a bad start with someone you want to ask for a favor!* "I'm sorry, Dona, I've been rude. I shouldn't have been—I mean, I apologize for presuming."

From the look on her face, he'd presumed correctly.

Dona Zella chuckled. "Please forgive her, Kirin, she's from a small town in the hills west of Anagni and has never been to a big city before. She asked for an assignment that would let her minister to the 'poorest of the poor', so she's been sent to my parish. Somebody in the Hierarchy has a low sense of humor. Come, sit, and tell both of us what brings you here today?"

There were several stools around the rickety table. Kirin sat on the one that looked sturdiest. Dona Abbithana perched the full length of the table away from him. Dona Zella took her accustomed chair and looked at him expectantly.

"My family needs help, Dona Zella, Dona Abbithana." He quickly sketched in the details, ending with "I've been told Dona Abbithana's cousin is married to a man that might work with the DiUmbra Troupe to get patronage for both him and us. I'm hoping," he gave the younger priestess his best beseeching look, "That you'll be willing to introduce us to him."

"Hmmmm, I detect Gee's fine hand in your arrival," Dona Zella said, smiling as Kirin sheepishly nodded. "Pernod Iola DiBellun is his name; Abbie's cousin Millia married him a few years ago. An honest man, he could use some patronage."

The younger priestess shifted uncomfortably on her stool. "I don't know what to say, Dona Zella. I don't feel right asking my cousin's husband to do a favor for someone I don't even know."

"I'm not asking for anything more than an introduction," Kirin explained urgently. "And not for myself, for the Magister of our troupe, my grandfather Grigor Sule DiUmbra. He would put together a shared offer with your cousin's husband. I won't even be there."

He thought she found that somewhat more palatable, but she said nothing. He held his breath, desperately praying she'd accept. His Shadow churned uneasily inside him.

Dona Zella cleared her throat suggestively. "Two families might accomplish more by working together than either can apart."

Abbithana's face showed her thoughts; that her superior unfairly supported this disturbing stranger over her sister-priestess' plain preference to stay out of it. She grudgingly nodded. "I suppose I could introduce Magister DiUmbra to Magister DiBellun."

"Thank you, Dona Abbithana, thank you from the bottom of my heart," Kirin told her fervently. He hadn't known how worried he was until she agreed, and he found himself dizzy with relief. If this contact worked, if the family found a patron, if, if, if . . .

"Are you ill, Goodman DiUmbra?" asked Dona Abbie with wary concern. "You're swaying." Her golden aura reached out to envelop him as she tried a Diagnose spell.

His Shadow blocked it.

Abbithana's mouth fell open in shock.

"Sorry, Dona," Kirin muttered, hastily driving his Shadow back under his heart; this time it went. "You surprised me, I wasn't ready."

"You're a Mage!" she said incredulously. "Only a very powerful mage should be able to block my Diagnose spell."

"No! No, Dona, I'm not," Kirin hastily tried to explain. "It's just that sometimes I'm, ah, sort of blank to magic."

Zella chuckled. "Kirin's like a man with Haroun's Gift, Abbie; he has a selective immunity to magic. Except that his Talent is more erratic than the Gift. See if you can Diagnose him now."

Kirin tried to look virtuously submissive. The young priestess sent forth her aura again and this time he held his Shadow bound tight and let her spell penetrate his skin. Her Talent was considerably stronger than Zella's and he had to suppress a shiver as it brushed his heart. If she chose, she could stop its beating as easily as healing a scratch.

"This is very strange," Dona Abbie complained. "There is a place under your heart that I cannot touch. What is that? I've never known anything like it." Her aura prodded his insides.

Kirin twitched and lost control of his Shadow. It expanded, and he fought to keep it confined inside his skin, frightened of what she might think or do. Dona Abbithana might be young and wear only two stars, but that didn't make her harmless. She could take back her agreement to make the introduction.

"Look!" The young priestess whined to Dona Zella. "My aura is being swept right out of him! Even Haroun's Gift doesn't do that. How can that happen?" She glowered suspiciously at Kirin.

"It's because you're frightening him." Dona Zella reached out and patted Kirin's hand reassuringly. "Let me guess the next words out of your mouth, Abbie. You're wondering if he's a demon in disguise, or maybe possessed by one, right?"

Dona Abbithana's lips firmed and her eyes peered at Kirin with renewed suspicion, which did nothing to calm his nerves. "I am starting to wonder."

"Kirin, show her your shadow," Dona Zella commanded. "Do one of those wonderful juggling tricks."

Kirin winced. "Dona Zella, are you sure?"

"I am. Give her a demonstration." She grinned like an imp herself and added, "Do it."

He bit back the vulgarity that came to his lips at her mischievous choice of words and bowed his head. Sometimes her humor resembled the canal stench, obnoxious and hard to bear. He took a deep, trembling breath and poured forth Shadow into his hands. He molded it into a ball, and made another, and another. He began to juggle the three inky balls of Shadow. Dona Zella tossed him a clay cup with no handle and he added that to the routine, then a candle stub—unlit, fortunately, he didn't think he was up to juggling fire right now. He set the five going faster and faster. At last he snatched the cup out of the moving stream and used it to catch the three balls of Shadow, one two three, and lastly caught the candle stub. His Shadow flowed through the clay and back into him through his fingers. When he turned the cup upside down only the candle stub fell out. He passed the cup to Dona Abbithana to witness its emptiness.

The young priestess looked at it like a scorpion. She poked it with a spoon, then a finger, and when nothing snapped at her she finally picked it up and looked inside. She looked at him accusingly.

"That wasn't some clever trick—that was real living Shadow! You have a Shadow inside you! You *are* possessed!" Her aura turned bright gold and pulsated.

Kirin looked beseechingly at Dona Zella, who shook an admonishing finger at the young priestess. "Don't be hasty. What's the first rule of demonic possession?"

"That any demon can be banished," she hissed angrily at Kirin, her aura strengthening as she visibly rehearsed a spell.

"Proven thousands of times," Dona Zella agreed. "A truism of our craft, known to apply for twenty centuries without exception. But Kirin's shadow cannot be."

Abbithana looked at her in frank disbelief at this contradiction. "How do you know?"

"I've tried. By myself and in concert with my late superior in this parish, Dona Tinea." Zella arched an eyebrow at Abbithana. "Who, even in her dotage, was far more powerful than you are now, my dear. As am I, in this respect at least, though I admit your capacity for Diagnosis is better than mine. Whatever Kirin's odd little talent may be, it's certainly no demon. Will you take my word for it, or do you have to prove yourself at the expense of this unfortunate young man?"

Kirin guessed what was coming and steeled himself. Last time it had *hurt*—

Dona Abbithana's spell hit fast and hard. He only had time to gasp before the world went red and every nerve in his body caught fire. His Shadow surged to his skin, writhing in shared agony, and then it curled under his heart into an impenetrable ball. He choked, fell off the stool and curled up on the floor, not feeling the hard stone in a universe of pain.

"Enough!" Zella told her colleague forcefully as she knelt by his side. Kirin sensed her aura sweeping through him, soothing, calming. Abbithana's aura followed, probing and searching.

"It's still there," the younger priestess said fearfully. "How can it still be there?"

"I told you it's not demonic possession," Zella growled. "Help me pick him up."

Kirin's head swam as they lifted him back onto the stool. Zella held his shoulders until the dizziness ceased and he could sit by himself. Abbithana hovered over him, baffled and hunting for an answer.

"He's not physically injured," she muttered. "But his symptoms are real."

The fire in Kirin's nerves began to fade. He locked his jaws against the profanity that he badly wanted to hurl at the young priestess. He needed her help, and worse still, her ultimate superiors could order him burned at the stake if *they* decided he was demon possessed. He had to convince her that he was harmless if he wanted to win that introduction, and maybe even to live.

Zella had less reticence. "Satisfied that I'm not an inept relic?" she asked her assistant tartly. "Or do you need to hurt him again?"

"But, banishment should be a healing experience," Abbithana protested plaintively.

"Does he show any sign of being healed by what you did to him? Any sign at all?"

"No," she admitted uneasily, shifting her aura through him and wincing as it touched his inflamed nerves. "He's suffered wrenching pain, but the Shadow hasn't budged at all."

"Because it isn't a demon possessing him," Zell told her patiently. "It's a natural part of him. You tried to rip his talent out of his body. Fortunately for both of you, it's far too well rooted for that to work."

"I don't understand!" Abbithana wrung her hands. "This isn't how banishment is supposed to work!"

"Put less faith in your book learning and more effort into actually seeing the flesh-and-blood people you're supposed to be serving," Zella advised. To Kirin: "Can you sit up without support now?"

At his nod she released him. He held onto the edge of the table with one hand and looked up at the young priestess. She stared down at him, her face a roil of emotions. Revulsion, curiosity, fascination, even a dash of guilt.

"Dona," he begged. "I only want to take care of my wife and my family. We're expecting our first child this year! I have a talent to move shadows, but my tricks please people and harm nobody. I wouldn't ever hurt somebody with it." *At least, not unless it was him or me.* "I just want to live."

Kirin stopped his babbling with an effort and stared at her fearfully. Had he said too much? Too little? The fading pain left room for his fear to grow. She'd probably refuse the introduction now; would she go further? Turn him over to the Inquisitors?

After a moment she sat down on the stool next to him. Her stare now held more fascination than revulsion. He dared to hope that his muddled appeal had gotten through to her heart. She must have one somewhere under those yellow robes.

"I never met a halfblood before today," she said. "I never even saw a Gwythlo or any other foreigner before I came to Aretzo. You look very strange to me."

She probably meant ugly and scary, he suspected. Her confidence in her Healer's powers blazed; she believed she could stop his heart with a touch if he attacked her, which certainly would have been true for most men. She didn't see him as one of most men in other ways though, if that meant most Silbari men. But he thought she could see *him*, now, instead of a cypher. *It's a start.*

"I am what I am, I didn't choose it," he told her. "I can't help being different any more than you can help being a healer. Would you want to stop being one?"

She snorted at that idea. "Of course not. It's the most noble of talents. I prayed I would grow into it all through my childhood." She raised her head in pride that her prayers had been answered.

You think you're far superior to me; he thought but carefully did not say. He swallowed his own pride. "I can move my shadow. It's my only magical talent. I have some magesight too, but I can't make any of the elements bend to my will like many folks can. I can't even put out a candle from across the room, like my brother-in-law Sevan, or to float bits of cloth on the air, like my wife Maia. But together, she and I can dance and weave our talents together into something beautiful. People pay to see us, we're the stars of our family's show, the DiUmbra Troupe. Only our performance space has been stolen, and I came here hoping you would help me find a new one. Please, Dona Abbithana. Help my family."

She pursed her lips, shot a glance at her superior. Dona Zella smiled encouragingly. The younger priestess let out her breath in a huff.

"I didn't intend to hurt you," she told him. "I've banished a demon before, a small one that had seized a brain-damaged boy in our village. I thought you had a larger one hiding in you, more dangerous. But," her mouth twisted sourly, "I now see my error and regret it. And yes, I will introduce your family to my cousin's husband." She sat back with an air of *and that's as far as I'll go* and a stiff glance at Dona Zella, who merely smiled.

"Thank you, Dona Abbithana, thank you!" Kirin bowed deeply, palms together, and gave her the double nods that were the most formal way to acknowledge her rank. He promised to send Uncle Sevan and Grandfather to her before next Holy Day, thanked Dona Zella too, and left in a hurry. He paused only long enough to dump most of the contents of his purse into the alms box and send up a brief prayer of thanksgiving.

He followed a different route home—he didn't care to pass that bunch of drunken sailors and the giant Xir again—with a lighter heart.

We'll find a patron, he told himself. *A rich one who'll give us lots of work. I know we will.*

81

CHAPTER 10: TERRELL

T wo forty, two forty-one, two forty-two!" Terrell gasped as he topped the stairs of the Warburg's tallest tower. "Whew!"

"Two hundred and forty-two steps," Pen panted. "That's twice the height of the New Keep at Gwythford Castle."

"Still less than half of the Hill of Sight in Aretzo, though." Terrell leaned on the flat parapet; putting merlons and crenellations atop this tower would have been pointless. He fought for breath. "Five hundred steps there!"

"But it's got more landings, right?" Pen asked, leaning beside him.

"I think so." He looked down a dizzying distance into this sprawling fortress that guarded the northeastern approach to Silbar. The Warburg bulked nearly as large as Gwythford Castle, two battalions of men held it for the Empire. Despite that, there had been room to squeeze his entire entourage inside, though it meant a lot of doubling up on the beds and pitching tents in courtyards.

He gazed over the valley ruled from this castle. The node that supported the fortress wasn't well-situated for military dominance of the terrain, so this tall lookout had been built to enable command of the surrounding countryside. Its height let him see into the blue distance of other valleys surrounding it north, east and south. To the west a white-topped wall of dark forest and darker rock hid Silbar behind it; the Black Mountains.

"Look at that, Pen. Those peaks are amazing! Tall enough to still have snow on them even this far into summer."

"The military dispatches said the route is open and the Storm Pass road is dry all the way over to Silbar," Pen answered. "But you never know with mountains. The experienced troops say it can snow on the pass any day of the year."

"Imagine that," breathed Terrell in wonder. "Snow in midsummer! What a thing to see."

"Let's hope not," General DiCervi grated as he caught up with them, gasping for air. "The baggage train and . . . the camp followers are . . . going to have a hard enough . . . time, your Highness."

"Ah. I should have thought of that, General." Terrell turned to look down into the shadowed courtyard below, where most of the Brigade's married men's wives and children had been billeted. "Can we do something to make this ascent easier on them?"

"I already have a tenth of the force, on a rotating basis, assigned to help push, pull, or drag them along, your Highness. More than that would weaken your protection too much. There are werecreatures and worse in these mountains and I refuse to take risks with your safety."

Terrell thought about that. Then he nodded briskly. "I understand, General. I've decided to change the order of march. I'll be riding in the middle of the camp followers tomorrow. I suspect the rest of my entourage will choose to do the same. Please see to the arrangements."

Terrell felt secretly gratified when DiCervi's face went slack with surprise for an instant. A moment later the commander of the Silbari Brigade smiled.

"As you will, Your Highness." He saluted respectfully.

"Now, what about the route we'll be taking?" Terrell asked, shading his eyes to look west. The suns were sinking behind two white-tipped peaks thrust high above the tower.

DiCervi pointed to them. "Tomorrow we'll ascend to the left of that double mountain and camp at the head of the valley behind it. Next day we'll cross the pass behind it. Beyond the pass there is another meadow in a high valley, one with ample grass and a lake as well as two good springs. The Warburg's scouts report plenty of wood available thanks to an avalanche last winter. It's also sheltered from the north by a ridge and opens to the south and west so that the sun will linger."

Terrell nodded. "Which may be important if our men end up strung out on the road down the far side. We'd have more hours of light than they do down here in this narrow valley." He glanced down again; torches were already lit in the buildings below them.

"Exactly, Highness."

"Very good, General. Thank you for indulging my curiosity."

"No trouble, your Highness." DiCervi looked at the stairs and firmed his jaw. "No trouble at all."

* * *

"I think we're in trouble," Pen said, looking up at the heavy clouds. They had begun to form out of nowhere shortly after the lead elements of the entourage topped the pass. The royal party and the camp followers plodded toward a vast gulf of air where the mountain tipped down again. Darker clouds approached from the far side. A rising wind promised to carry them straight to the little hillock where Terrell and Pen's horses stood.

Terrell looked back over the strung-out line of march. The horse litter carrying Dona Seraphina struggled over the stony track. The swaying had got so bad that her husband Merritin had chosen to walk for a while. He leaned on one of the strong young swordsmen of the Brigade and gasped for breath. Terrell could see Dona Seraphina grimly enduring the jouncing of the litter while she cast spells on herself against motion sickness. He hoped both would be all right.

Shimoor's smaller horse litter had an easier time of it, in part because he'd cast a gimbal spell on the suspended litter itself. It seemed to float along between the two beasts as if they towed it rather than carried it. Terrell could feel several small Nodes under these mountains. Nothing that could support a fortress, but enough that the Royal Wizard could afford the extravagance while also maintaining an elongated protection spell over the whole entourage. Shimoor lay still in his litter, his concentration so deep that he looked asleep.

"Not trouble quite yet," Terrell answered judiciously. "But soon. A quarter of the Brigade is strung out behind us on this narrow route, and another quarter in our van. Those have instructions to prepare camp in that meadow as soon as they get there, which I suspect will be only shortly before the storm. I hope my entourage will be close to the bottom, but we'll still have wives and children on the mountainside."

"If anybody stumbles off this path in a snowstorm, they're dead," Pen warned. "We could lose dozens of our people if the winds are bad and the snow is thick."

"Agreed. We need a way to keep them together." He looked across the nearest riders, picked out the youngest of the mages and called the man over.

"Do we still have those eight ward poles that Shimoor prepared by the Severing River?" he asked.

The mage averred that they were with other paraphernalia on one of the packhorses.

"Find them, bring them to me. We're going to turn them into lanterns."

The mage caught on at once and set to work. When they were assembled Terrell touched each ward pole. It took him a long struggling moment before he found a way to divert the Light inside him into a stream that he could pour into the silver plaques. The second pole lit easier, the last easiest of all. In less than a quarter of an hour he had them all glowing brighter than the brightest flame.

"Lash each of these to a packhorse so that it stands high," he ordered. "We want as many of our people to see them as possible."

They completed the task as clouds closed overhead. Terrell rode beside Shimoor and made sure the old wizard stayed properly blanketed against the deepening chill. The other side of the valley below disappeared in the deepening dusk, then the valley itself and finally most of the mountain down which the Silbari party snaked in a long vulnerable line. But the eight glowing wards cut through the murk. Their light seemed to gain brightness even as the temperature fell. Snowflakes began to drift down and people pulled on extra clothes. The Suns faded into faint glows in the cloudy western sky.

Shimoor began to twitch and mutter; twice he groaned. Terrell got off his horse to walk next to the old wizard. Attendants had lashed the horse litter's curtains shut on the downhill side to block the wind, so he walked on the uphill side, which also helped to shield him from the cold blast. He strained his ears and heard Shimoor mumble something about nodes. He thought he heard the word *bears* and another word, *Ilvar,* but could sort out nothing clear. He considered waking the old wizard, but that would risk breaking their protection spell. He didn't know what dangers it might already be shielding them from.

Mother told me the Ilvar Clan is mostly air-mages who hold the territory on the Silbari side of the pass, he remembered. *Is Shimoor trying to warn me about them? Is there treachery awaiting us?*

"Pen," he called to his friend, riding ahead of the wizard's litter. "Pass word to the General. Shimoor is trying to warn us about something. We may have enemies ahead."

Pen nodded and rode off.

If there is treachery, what do I do about it? Terrell wondered. He knew that the Brigade was strongest when camped, or operating on an open field, but horribly vulnerable when stretched out like this.

Terrell noticed a rising turbulence in the clouds approaching from the northwest. *A change in the weather? Probably for the worse.* He considered getting back on his horse, decided to stay by Shimoor's side to see if the wizard could offer any clearer warning. The road cut into the mountainside here, the surface paved with close-fitting slabs of stone and the outer dropoff walled by a line of large close-set rocks. Patches of stunted trees grew on the slope above. The wind began to swirl falling snow into little vortexes that made moving shapes in the dusk.

Moving shapes—

Something huge and bear-shaped reared up on the mountainside above him. A ghostly black pelt glistened amid the snowflakes. Jaws opened, and black fangs gleamed.

The protection spell over the Silbaris glowed blue as lightning. It took the shape of a long slinky tube enclosing the line of people and beasts. The horses carrying Shimoor's litter stopped and stood still, forcing those behind to stop too. Fearful human faces looked up as glaring ursine ones dusted with snowflakes looked down in eerie silence. A whole line of inky black bear shapes menaced the humans from upslope.

Terrell drew his sword. "These are not natural bears!"

Soldiers pelted toward him and drew their own weapons as they lined up next to him. A scent of ashes and death rode the wind.

One man said, "If they get through the spell, they can drop right down on us!"

"We can't let them through," Terrell answered. "We've absolutely got to keep this one away from Shimoor. If it kills him the whole protection spell will go down."

The closest bear stood up on hind legs thick as trees. The mountainside rose so steeply that its hind feet were even with his face. Black claws dug into the dirt only a foot beyond the protection spell. The creature raised paws armed with night-colored daggers and slashed at the upper curve of the spell. Sparks sprayed from the glowing tube and fur smoked. The spell dimpled and stayed that way.

"Hamstring it!" Terrell shouted.

PETER SARTUCCI

He lunged up the slope, toes digging for purchase and the men at his side. He stabbed straight through the sparking blue glow and sank his sword-point into the right leg, instantly followed by two others. Shock jolted all the way up to his shoulder as his point sliced deep and grounded against bone. But no blood spurted when he jerked the blade free.

The men on either side of him snarled their fear. *It doesn't bleed!*

The creature made a weird high shrieking sound that hurt like nails being driven into Terrell's ears. But the sound gladdened his heart, for at least they seemed to have hurt it. He hacked furiously at the night-black fur.

"Chop it down like a tree!" he yelled.

The creature slashed with both sets of claws, a fast one-two strike that left deep gouges in the protection spell. Falling snow swirled and the wind rose.

If it tears through with me in front of it—"Cut it again! Keep cutting all of them, until they fall!"

He chopped at the leg in a frenzy, sent bits of black fur and flesh flying. If he could cut fast enough, he might survive.

Something whooshed overhead and struck the bear in the face.

The huge creature roared as it fell backwards to writhe against the mountainside. It bellowed madly as a second sparkling attack struck its belly. Shuddering sheets of red fire crackled across the fur, and the creature dissolved into black mist that sank into the ground.

"Prince Terrell?" said a voice behind and above him.

Terrell spun around, barely kept his footing, and stared.

The storm had opened as if a wedge of clear air had been driven into it. To the left and right the clouds were rolling back. A brightly patterned carpet floated in the air only a dozen feet away, level with his chest and undulating slowly. A man in heavy robes with a fur-trimmed hood sat cross-legged on it. He pushed that back with a mittened hand to reveal his face. Wrinkled brown skin, brown hair and beard shot through with gray, the features were Silbari.

"I hope I don't sound ungrateful for your help, but who are you?" Terrell demanded, lowering his sword.

The man bowed deeply, sat back up and smiled. It deepened the creases in his worn face but also made him look younger. "I am the Wizard Inin of the Ilvar clan, your Highness. My colleague Shimoor summoned me and my folk to aid you and yours. I am sorry that we were not here sooner."

"Your timing looks fine to me." Terrell glanced left and right. He saw more men on carpets driving back the storm, at least a dozen in all. Shimoor's protection spell had faded back to its normal near-transparency. Soldiers were getting horses back under control and straightening up the line of march. "You saved us from terrible damage."

"My duty, Your Highness. I swore my oath to one of your grandfathers. But please pardon us while we complete the task. We'll meet you in the meadow by the lake." He bowed again, and the carpet sped away to join the other air wizards battling the storm.

Terrell mounted on his horse as Pen came charging back with Irre-neetha in his right hand. Terrell raised his own hand to forestall questions.

"He said his name is Inin of the Ilvar Clan and he'll meet us by the lake. Let's get everybody safely there before it gets totally dark. And find me the Brigade's mapsman as soon as possible; I need to know more about these wizards. A clan of fliers that could fight my grandfather to a draw is bound to be important."

"Ah." Pen looked thoughtfully at the swarm of carpets driving back the storm. "Very good, My Lord."

* × *

"The Shadows of Storm Pass rarely take on flesh these days, so we have grown less attentive than we should, Your Highness," Wizard Inin apologized two hours later. He had grounded his carpet on a log before Terrell's tent and reshaped it as a seat. Campfires crackled nearby, venison roasting and stew cooking in large pots. Parts of that were gifts from the Wizard and his companions, all of whom appeared to be highly-accomplished air mages at the least. They'd beaten back the storm, created this pocket of clear air within it, and ferried in extra food from their own redoubt somewhere to the northwest. Terrell held court from another log facing the wizard, with his own entourage gathered around him.

"Shadows?" Terrell asked. "Those were lesser demonic manifestations, right?"

"Of a sort. Unlike regular demons, Shadows are usually a manifestation of the land, sometimes quite dangerous, but because they are rooted in the terrain they occupy, they have a sharply circumscribed reach. Those Shadows lurk only along this road."

"I'd been told Storm Pass is haunted, but none of the tales had anything like I saw today."

"That was an extraordinary manifestation." Inin made an expressive gesture with his hands halfway between a shrug and an appeal to heaven. "To my knowledge they have never attacked any group even half as large as your entourage, your Highness. I suspect they were goaded, though at the moment I have no idea how. Magic of the flesh and spirit my clan has through our wives, but even they have little command over manifestations of the land." The wizard's eyes travelled to Dona Seraphina sitting at Terrell's left hand and he inclined his head slightly.

"I banished one of them," the priestess reported. She sat on another log, wrapped in blankets and visibly trying not to look over her shoulder at the tents behind her. Her exhausted husband had been put to bed by two of her underpriestesses and one of the Healers tended him. Merritin had sensed Shimoor's spell weakening and recklessly poured his own personal power in to help support it. Terrell suspected only iron duty kept her here, away from her husband's side. "But there had to have been at least twenty more. I am

87

confident that it is as you have guessed; those Shadows were recently manipulated by women's magic." Her gaze shifted to Terrell and she added, "Druidic, I expect."

Klairveen, Terrell thought but carefully did not say aloud. *Her last try before I pass beyond her reach. I hope.*

The wizard nodded deferentially to her and said, "These Shadows have fed on the local creatures for centuries, Your Highness, as well as any unfortunate human they could trap. They are more than half alive now when they take material form, and thus quite dangerous."

"But they can be cut, and they know pain." Terrell nodded grimly. He remembered the shock of his sword meeting bone, and the lack of blood. When he had examined the blade later it had been dry and unstained.

"The price of equipping themselves with claws and strength, your Highness." Inin's smile turned cold for a moment. "It makes them easier to drive off, so long as one can prove one is decisively stronger."

"My mother once told me about the Ilvar clan. She said her father charged your folk with keeping Storm Pass barred to the Empire during the Conquest."

"My father led that struggle." Pride glowed in the Wizard's face. "I served as his right hand in those days. Your Imperial Grandfather's wizards were skilled, but we knew the winds and the rocks of Storm Pass better than they did. That struggle lasted long and began before they built the Warburg, but we won. They never did invade over Storm Pass."

"And today I understand why." Terrell nodded and unfolded the map that DiCervi had provided. "Wizard Inin, you have my grateful thanks. When I take up my rule in Aretzo, I will confirm the oath between your clan and my House. I only ask that you continue your good work here at Storm Pass and, when you can spare men for it, such additional patrols in east Silbar as you can manage. The Brigade's staff tell me that there are small nodes farther south in these mountains, not presently granted by the Crown to anyone. If I enlarge your granted fief to include these two. . ." He tapped the map. "Would you be able to expand your watchfulness to the valleys north of Arbatax?"

"We have enough men, your Highness." Inin grinned. "My sons and nephews are a very promising group, and twice as numerous as their elders. We would be honored to be assigned such a task." The Wizard added some detailed suggestions to which DiCervi nodded his own approval, and Terrell readily agreed. Shortly the wizard took his leave.

"Well done, Highness," the general told him. "I've been worried about that gap in Silbar's protection for years but saw no way to persuade your father to deal with it."

"Because it is not in Gwythlo's interest that Silbar be better protected from Gwythlo armies," Terrell answered. "But the moment I crossed that pass I ceased to be responsible for Gwythlo's concerns and became responsible for Silbar's. This will only be the first of many changes I will make, General. We'll discuss these issues later, for tonight I think everybody needs sleep."

DiCervi's smile broadened and he bowed and left for his own tent.

Terrell detained Dona Seraphina a moment longer. "Do you think she'll try again?"

"Inside Silbar?" The priestess shook her head. "That will be far harder to hide, and easier to block; the Hierarchy has skilled priestesses in every village. No, she's made her last throw, your Highness. Directly, at least. Now she'll have to work through other means. Exercise other influences."

Such as my brother, Terrell thought. He touched the scar on his face left by the river battle. "We'll have to deal with those as they come."

CHAPTER 11: KIRIN

Gather round, DiUmbras!" Grandfather called from the head of the stairs. Kirin alighted from his trapeze onto the high platform as Grandmother and Carmella and the rest of the family members that weren't currently practicing in the attic crowded up behind Grandfather. The troupe's leader waved a parchment in the air to beckon everybody to him. Kirin somersaulted into the net and scrambled out to join the rest.

"We have a contract!" Grandfather DiUmbra crowed. "A performance in three tendays!"

"Wonderful!" Carmella exclaimed as a dozen other voices chattered. "Where is it?"

Kirin strained to hear while he prayed for success. He had told Uncle Sevan what he'd done. Maia's father had pitched Mother Gee's suggestion to Grandfather, carefully keeping her name—and Kirin's—silent.

"At the Millago family's mansion in Cliffside!"

Yes! Kirin thought happily.

Grandfather looked around. "Where's Maia?"

"Here," she answered.

Kirin looked over his shoulder to see her walking towards the family from the women's changing room. Her steps were unsteady and her face looked gray. *Has she been throwing up again?* He rushed to her.

The troupe's leader frowned as he watched her approach. "Maia. Are you sick?"

She shook her head and almost lost her balance. Kirin leaped to catch her as she stumbled. She grabbed his hand, righted herself, and defiantly declared, "I'm fine, Grandfather."

Kirin tried to divert the old man's attention by saying to her, "Grandfather gave us wonderful news! We have a new job performing for a rich shipping magnate!"

It worked, sort of, as Grandfather turned the frown on him. When Kirin and Maia rejoined the group, the old man said, "How did you know that our client is a rich shipping magnate?"

Kirin fumbled. "Umm. I must have heard his name before, Magister, 'cause it's familiar."

Grandfather stared from him to Maia and back again. Pieter put a hand on Kirin's shoulder, silently comforting. Carmella had gone to Maia's other side to lend her own support. The rest of the family went quiet; several of the cousins stared nervously, sensing something wrong.

Kirin remembered that day Pieter had brought him home, battered and scratched from Gerlach's abuse, and told the family he had adopted a son. The same doubt that the old man's eyes had held then, looked at him now.

Sevan moved to join Pieter at Kirin's shoulder. Grandfather's frown deepened.

"Maia." The old man dropped her name into the stillness like a pebble into a pond. "Are you pregnant?"

Maia's hands covered her belly protectively. She raised her chin and said, "Yes, Grandfather, I am."

Kirin put an arm around her and braced himself.

"You promised me you wouldn't." Grandfather's voice had gone very soft, but his gaze had become as fixed as a wolf staring at a rabbit. "The family was counting on you, Maia."

"I . . . I know, Grandfather," Maia answered in a tiny voice.

Her grip tightened on Kirin's hand. He saw how her eyes fell, no longer able to meet her grandfather's gaze. His own heart felt squeezed in a giant's fist. He wanted to shout defiance.

But he could only tremble.

Sevan made a noise in the back of his throat as if struggling to talk, but nothing came out.

"I'm very disappointed in you, Maia." The old man's reproachful gaze widened to Kirin as well. "Very disappointed in both of you. You know the family's need. We counted on you to be the stars, to bring home the money that supports your kin, as we did when you were children. Instead you two put your own selfish desires ahead of the rest of us."

Maia clutched Kirin's hand so tight that her blunt fingernails dug into his skin. He forced words out through a tight throat.

"It's my fault, grandfather, not hers. My Shadow broke her protection spell and I didn't notice. Don't blame her, blame me!"

"I do blame you, you pale imp," Grandfather growled. "You and your sly lust wormed your way into her heart and her belly like a scheming snake! Are you happy with what you've done? Stolen her chance at greatness, pinned her down with the weight of your unholy seed? What viper have you planted in her womb?"

"No, no—" *I'm not a demon, I'm not!* Kirin's Shadow churned under his heart and he fought a losing battle to hold it inside. *Seraph Haroun, help me!*

"That's enough, Father!" Pieter snapped. "This is my son!"

Grandfather glared at him. "You brought this treacherous cuckoo's egg into our family, this Shadow-carrying sneakthief—"

"This star flyer and loyal worker," Pieter recklessly interrupted. "Who has carried his share and more, seen to your comfort, made our lives better!"

Grandfather's face showed his shock; nobody in the family ever interrupted him like that. Before he could speak Carmella took up the refrain. "How long has it been since we were plagued by lice or bedbugs? You know how much it used to cost to have a Priestess drive the vermin out of our quarters. Kirin spares you that! Has he ever shirked carrying even one bucket of water? Failed to clean your chamber pot when his turn came? Taken a single copper more than his due?"

"Tricks of the Pale Seraphs!" Grandfather sneered. "Now is he revealed! All he gives he will take away again—including your daughter!"

"A baby takes less than a year, Father," Maia's own father interjected quietly, stepping next to his wife. "This time next year Maia can be back performing. The family will survive a year without her in the act."

Grandfather looked at his eldest son like a betrayer. "You *approve* of this—this unnatural spawn of Salim befouling your daughter with his foul pale seed despite all promises—"

"Enough, Father." Sevan the Elder's voice remained quiet, but his gaze had grown iron hard. "Kirin is not the man who murdered your mother. Stop punishing him for something that happened before his birth."

Kirin sat stunned. He had never known Maia's great-grandmother, and only now understood why the family said so little about her. *Pieter must have known when he adopted me.*

Grandfather had rocked back in pain and outrage. "I told you never to speak of that!"

"I have been silent long enough; perhaps too long," his eldest son answered. "Father, let the past go and greet the future. I expected and welcomed children from Maia and Kirin from the moment she told me she wished to marry him. I admit that I had hoped they would wait a few more years, but what's done is done. I will celebrate the arrival of another grandchild with joy and love—as should you. For my brother's adopted son is now my son too and has been since he married my daughter. It is past time that you treat him so."

A strange feeling ran through Kirin's heart as his father-in-law spoke. His Shadow quieted itself and sank back inside. Pieter and Sevan the Younger both squeezed his shoulders and smiled.

Grandfather stared from Sevan the Elder to Pieter and back, tried to reassert his dominance. "You two league against your own father!"

"Oh, stop arguing with your boys, Grigor!" Grandmother said, tugging on his elbow. "We have a thousand things to do to get ready for the new performance. Did you and Sevan measure the space? Can we set up our trapeze there or will we need to use tightrope only?"

"Are there lamps that will be in the way?" pragmatic Carmella asked him. "How well lit is this new hall?"

"If Maia can't perform, we can't meet our contract," Grandfather growled. "In thirty days, how big will she be? The whole soaring scene will have to be scrapped. The play gutted! Our new client will be disappointed, and you know where that will leave us!"

"His ceiling's too low for the soaring scene and I already told him so," Sevan the Elder answered his mother. "We'll substitute a dance. He already knows we must rewrite the play to fit his hall, so he's prepared for changes. We can still do all the important parts."

Grandfather glared at Maia and Kirin. "The DiUmbra reputation is riding on this show. If Maia can't perform, we'll be begging on the streets."

"I can do it, Grandfather," Maia said steadily.

"We'll make it work, Magister," Kirin promised recklessly, clutching her hand.

The old man stared at the two of them coldly, and said, "You had better."

CHAPTER 12: CHISAAD

C hisaad growled and pushed his scrying contraption aside. He had risen at dawn specifically to check the early bazaar performers on the chance that his target did not have a lease to perform in the afternoons.

"Nothing!" He snarled as he glowered down at the sprawling open-air market.

In the past tenday he had examined every one of the dozen-plus performance spaces in Aretzo's pulsating heart. Literally hours of watching, and not one of them had a halfbreed actor or acrobat or bard or even juggler. He had found nobody remotely similar to the one he'd seen outside the cemetery gates. Nor did any of the performers quite look like the other members of that troupe that he'd glimpsed.

For a moment he paused, considering. The others had been an obvious family based on similarity of features. Could the halfbreed have been merely a fellow traveler, not part of the troupe at all? But the young woman had rushed to his side and embraced him like a mate, and the other men had gathered close as if ready to defend him.

No, he decided. *They were all one family. He must be a bastard got upon one of their women by some soldier during the Conquest. He looked to be about the right age.*

For a moment he knew a degree of sympathy for the mysterious youth. Both of them bastards in a nation and a people that held little tolerance for their kind. But he drove the thought out.

Sympathy is a seductive delusion. It must have been created as a subtle trick of the Pale Seraphs.

Chisaad turned away from his fruitless scrying. His latest golem lay on his worktable, a shining perfection of shaped wood, leather and wire ready for activation. This time he had built the body from individual pieces shaped to closely mimic the human bones that they represented and positioned the wires that animated those bones as if they were metal muscles. It had been far more work this way, but he hoped it would solve the articulation problem. To test it, he intended to also test his newest magical construct.

He lifted a palm-sized device of gems and silver and carefully positioned it on top of his head, gently working the spider-like legs through his hair until all eight were in contact with his skin. He cast the small activating spell and sensed the latent magic come alive. He looked at the golem on the table and gave it his first command.

Sit up.

The golem's head and shoulders rose smoothly from the table, the arms pushed it upright, and in seconds it sat facing him. He allowed himself to enjoy a moment of exhilaration before continuing.

Stand.

It did so, moving as natural as could be.

Walk.

It broke into a swinging gait that brought it straight at him. Chisaad hastily dodged while thinking *Stop!* The golem came to a halt mere inches before crashing into a bookshelf.

Turn around.

One elbow swept a row of books off a shelf as it turned in place. Chisaad sighed. It needed more work.

Back to the table.

It turned again, placing its back towards the table. Chisaad growled. Definitely needed more work.

He had to give it several more exacting commands before he got it once more lying on the table. Only then did he dare reach up and detach the command spider, before locking the device away in his vault. *I'll have to be very careful that nobody else sees this.*

He returned to contemplating the city outside his tower, feeling ironically pleased. The golem needed more work and so did his plans, but both were achievable.

If that troupe wasn't one of the ones that performed regularly in the bazaar, they must either perform elsewhere or survive as clients of a wealthy patron. He had only to ask around for such, and someone would know. He would have to do more socializing to create the necessary opportunities.

He went to his desk and sorted through the most recent pile of invitations. The office of the Acting Royal Wizard received dozens of invitations as a matter of course, most of which he politely refused, but kept general track of who invited him to what. He remembered one that had arrived this week and sorted through the pile until he found the heavy vellum envelope with a white wax seal. He opened it and read aloud.

"Reshghar Bovea Millago and his wife Arriga Viga Millago invite you to the presentation of their firstborn child. Entertainment by the DiUmbra Acrobatic Troupe."

He extracted the reply card and stared at it. *Could they be the ones I saw?* He uncorked his ink bottle and swiftly wrote an acceptance. He drew on his link to the Aretzo Node and summoned a crow, while thinking about the event. If the youth he sought turned out to be there, he would need a catspaw to help trap the boy.

Reshghar's wife was one of Lady Ymera's pupils on the Red Street, and disdains to conceal the fact. Reshghar must have been utterly besotted to marry a woman like that. He sniffed. *It is certain that Arriga will invite her old teacher. Lady Ymera is more perceptive than most, but she has her own expectations and blind spots. I can take advantage of those.*

The summoned bird arrived and perched passively on his windowsill. He tied the acceptance to its leg and sent it winging across the city to the Millago mansion.

There is no guarantee that the one I seek will be there. But if he is . . .

Finding this half breed acrobat would merely be the first step. Once he did, he would have to lure the youth into his service. Chisaad studied his waiting golem. A human would be far harder to control than this lump of material and magic. For a moment he doubted his own capacity to fulfil his plans. But the prize still glittered there in his mind. The Kingship. The power of the Hill of Sight.

"I *must* control him," he said aloud in the privacy of his tower. "Or someone else will, and that I cannot risk. If he will not serve me, he must not serve anyone."

Even if that requires his death.

CHAPTER 13: TERRELL

Cerrai is a small duchy, Your Highness," Madoc Swansea, Duke of Cerrai, said to Terrell as they reined in their horses on a hilltop. The two suns beat down on them. Terrell enjoyed the heat on his dark skin, while Madoc wore a broad-brimmed hat to shield his fair face.

The duke waved a hand at a serrated bare ridge peeking up out of the mosaic of forest and vineyard a double dozen miles to the west, then swept the hand east. "From Salim's Backbone to the River Amm, perhaps thirty miles, and from the Collusi River that you crossed this morning to my southern border at the north end of Purification Lake, barely twenty. Ordinarily it would merely be a barony, if a large one, Your Highness. Because of our family kinship your father granted me the larger title."

"So I've been told. You and my father share much, cousin," Terrell nodded, thereby giving Madoc permission to drop the formality of honorifics. He had been spending a half day with each duke and ruling baron along the route of the Kings Road, taking their measure and letting them take his. So far, he had managed to see and be seen by all of them while still making steady progress toward Aretzo. "But small land area certainly doesn't mean poor, especially when it's some of the best land in Silbar."

Terrell shaded his eyes to gaze appreciatively over neat green rows of staked grapevines curling around the hillsides, silver-gray olive groves, oak and pine trees shadowing red cattle in pastures on the higher slopes, and rich grain fields in the black-soiled bottomlands.

"True, cousin," Duke Cerrai admitted proudly while tacitly accepting the permission. "And we do have an abundance of one thing."

"Good wines!" Terrell said enthusiastically. "I've had Cerrai vintages at my father's court in Gwythford. Marvelous!"

"Yes, they even travel well," Madoc grinned. "When your father offered me my choice of rewards after the Conquest, I knew which I wanted. Of course, it helped that my heart had already been captured by my lady of Cerrai."

His duchess, brown-skinned Lady Meera DiCerrai-Swansea, smiled from the back of her own horse. "The captivity is mutual. And convenient for both your lineages, Your Highness, since I am both the heir of Cerrai and your mother's closest living female relative."

"Mother told me." Terrell nodded. "Your son Alain is my second cousin, and therefore he'll be one of the Twenty in a few years."

The duke and duchess exchanged glances.

PETER SARTUCCI

"It is good that you've paid attention to the lineages, and their implications," Madoc said. "You'll find that, since the Conquest, some in Aretzo can think of little else."

"The dispossessed." Terrell frowned. "The nobles who lost their lands to my father."

Madoc jerked his head in a sharp nod. "Yes. Some still cannot accept their losses."

"Fools," his lady said dispassionately. "They spend all their time scheming and maneuvering for scraps while living off dreams and shriveled fortunes. They build nothing for their children while steeping them in bitterness. What a waste."

"Too true," the duke sighed. "But that's a danger largely confined to the capital these days. It's been a dozen years since the last attempt to raise a rebellion. A bigger problem for you, cousin, may be the few Gwythlo lords in Silbar who still don't understand their winnings, or accept the price of keeping them." He bowed his head to Terrell to suggest that price.

Terrell frowned. "They'll bow to the Gwythlo Emperor, but not to a Silbari ruler?"

"Not necessarily. Some will offer the outward forms of obedience while defying you in their hearts. A few may carry that defiance farther, especially if you appear weak."

Terrell let his mouth quirk into a smile. "I shall endeavor to never, ever, appear weak."

"That would be wise," said Madoc. His wife reached out and took her husband's left hand in her right, squeezed it briefly. They smiled at each other.

Terrell covertly studied the two of them. Both wore bloused trousers above riding boots and midlength tunics with practical sleeves. They wore none of the elaborate embroidery and dagging typically seen on other Silbari nobles' clothing. They looked like they belonged together, despite Madoc's sun-reddened skin and the pointed ears that he currently hid under his hat.

"I have been told," Terrell said casually. "That you've become a follower of The One God and raised your children the same."

"I've gone native." Madoc grinned. "Cerrai is my home now, my life and my future. I am a Silbari, as my sons and daughters will be after me. They'll serve a Silbari king, as will I."

He made this profession so calmly that a knot of worry inside Terrell's heart melted away. *This is a man that I can rely upon.* "Thank you, cousin. One small point; to keep my brother happy I have agreed to title myself 'Prince' only, unless and until he consents to more. Though of course I cannot control what others may call me."

Madoc's grin stretched for a moment before he schooled his face. "An elegant concession. If you win the Amethyst Crown I will be content to title you as you wish."

Left unsaid was what it would take to close that final step on the path to the Stone Throne. *One thing at a time,* Terrell told himself. "I wonder who else will follow your example?"

98

"Let's discuss that after dinner." The duke gestured at his castle across the little valley behind them. "Will you accept Cerrai's hospitality tonight, cousin?"

"Gladly."

* * *

Later, as his most discreet servant prepared him for bed in the suite that Duke and Duchess Cerrai had provided, Terrell asked, "What do you think of them, Pen?"

Pen absently touched Irreneetha's hilt, paused as if to marshal his thoughts, and said, "Exactly what you need."

Intrigued, Terrell made a beckoning gesture while his valet unlaced the complex ribbons of one of his tunic sleeves. "Explain."

"First, neither of them gave me that slimy feeling I got from the dukes of Fiori and Anagni. Those two made me want a bath."

"I felt the same when I met them!" Terrell chuckled. "Second?"

"Everything your cousin does and says comes across as honest, even when it's diplomatic, like the way he talked to those hill barons on our ride. I doubt he's told you everything on his mind, but I trust everything he did say. Third, when he speaks, the local nobles listen; he has a powerful fund of credit with them, like a good leader should. If he sticks with you, they will too, and that gives you the southern half of Upper Silbar except Anagni, who they surround. And while Fiori is stronger than any two of them, it's not stronger than all of them. If Madoc can hold his neighbors together, they can check any threat that might rise against you in Upper Silbar."

"Yes, Madoc seems to have covered his flanks very thoroughly," Terrell nodded, stepping out of his trousers as his valet took them. "A man who plans, that he is. He's fortified this castle in the modern style, too, but doesn't rely on it to control his duchy for him. That system of mandatory training and service for his landholders' sons is clever, as is mixing them with the sons of his peasants and craftsmen. He's encouraging the best to rise and making it plain that those who want to keep authority, or gain it, are expected to prove their worth first."

The novelty of this idea still enthralled him. *I must find a way to implement Madoc's ideas across all of Silbar.*

"There's more than clever management going on inside his head, my Lord," Pen said earnestly. "His devotion to the One God seems sincere and deep, and the way he looks at his wife and touches her hand even in public tells me there's love between them still. He really is turning himself into a Silbari; his children will be more so. That's a good thing for your dynasty's future. You could do a lot worse than have a man like that ruling the strongest fortress north of Purification Lake and south of Fiori."

"Yes, I could," Terrell murmured, pleased, as he pulled on a nightshirt. "Thank you, Pen."

"You are entirely welcome, My Lord." Pen bowed himself out with the valet.

Before Terrell could blow out the candle and climb into the big bed, the door opened again, and a slighter figure slipped inside. She wore a simple wraparound shift and had bare feet. Terrell paused, unsurprised. This had happened in four previous castles and he had become pleasantly accustomed to it.

"And you are here for?" he inquired teasingly. The woman—clearly a woman under that thin cloth—kept her eyes demurely lowered but a happy smile played around her mouth, as if she couldn't quite believe her luck.

"For your pleasure, Your Highness." She bowed without taking her eyes off the lower half of his body. "My lady chose me, and my lord sent me." She darted a daring glance at his face, licked her lips, and peeled off her shift with one smooth motion.

Her brown skin gleamed in the candlelight and Terrell's magesight showed him the familiar glow of a pregnancy protection spell in her belly, one that he now recognized as Dona Seraphina's work. The woman brazenly gazed at his crotch, grinning. "If it be your will, Your Highness."

Her perfume reached him, something musky and every bit as arousing as her smooth curves. Terrell discovered once again that, seen through the eyes of lust, all women are beautiful. "It is. Come here and tell me your name."

* * *

Two days later Terrell leaned on the upper wall of the Tonatia, the fortress guarding the pass between Upper Silbar and Lower Silbar. "Dona Seraphina. Is this really the Scarp that God made to stop Azerin and Zablock's civil war?"

"It is, Your Highness." She gave him an inquiring look.

"I'm surprised; I expected something sharper." He pointed east along the jagged ridge atop which the fort stood. "The bards always say it was 'cut like a knife', but this . . ."

"Is what three hundred years of rain and wind do to torn earth and stone." The priestess pointed at the vast waters of Purification Lake spreading north from the ridge that cut the great valley in two. "Legends call the battle bloodier than any war Silbar has fought before or since. The twin brothers raised two great armies, each with nearly a million men, and clashed on the far side of the old river channel from here. The battlefield is underwater now, but three hundred years ago this spot we stand on was a flat plain like the one that holds the lake."

"Think of that!" Terrell exclaimed, staring along the cliffs of the rearing scarp. Erosion had chewed deeply into the north face but now he could see how it had once been sheer; the south side sloped gently. "Is there a way to look down on the lake from the ridge above the battlefield?"

The priestess sighed and rolled her eyes at the fort's commander, DiVetzi. Despite owning more than thrice Terrell's years, that worthy grinned and said, "Certainly, Your Highness. Follow me."

It took Terrell, Pen, Commander DiVetzi, and a squad of troops two hours to ride along a narrow road that grew steadily more winding, weaving in and out of great wedges and spikes of rock and bridging narrow chasms. Terrell's wonder grew with every stride of his horse. The tallest slabs towered a hundred feet above the muddy waters that laved their feet. The road followed the high ground, so they had broad views. He and Pen exchanged awed glances.

"God raised all this in a day?" Terrell asked.

"So all the accounts say," Commander DiVetzi assured him. "This road was only carved out about two centuries ago, but it follows a path said to have been made after the battle, before the waters rose. Traditionally every commander of the fort is led to the overlook and told the story." Eagerly he added, "I shall be honored to share it with you, Your Highness."

Terrell decided that DiVetzi had a bit of frustrated bard in his character. "Please do, Commander. Lead on."

The paved road ended at a round plaza next to a small watchtower built atop a sheer spur thrust out into the lake. Terrell and Pen followed the commander up echoing stairs to an east-facing parapet at the top. To their left spread the quiet lake, to their right a roaring chasm gulped down the waters as they fought their way through the huge barrier of the Scarp. The whole ridge had gradually canted downward as they rode east. Now they stood barely forty feet above the lake's foaming exit. The commander pointed over the flat water.

"Azerin held the field, which now lies underwater," he declaimed happily. "Zablock and his army had approached up the east bank, coming from Belluno." He jerked a thumb over his shoulder to indicate the half-ruined city to the southeast. Terrell could barely see it through the canyon, a distant gray blur many miles away across a fissured plain. "The battle began at dawn and had already raged for half a day before the two brothers at last met face to face and sword to sword."

"That's when God sought to stop their madness," Pen commented.

"And cleaved their armies apart by raising the Scarp," Commander DiVetzi agreed. "The legends say Azerin had struck the first blow but Zablock was only wounded, and still on his feet. Then God raised the Scarp beneath Zablock and threw him to the ground. When he regained his feet, he found himself atop the rim of the great new cliff, torn away from taking his brother's blood. He rejected God's grace and gave himself to rage, leaped off the height and fell upon Azerin. Both died broken upon the still-trembling rocks." DiVetzi sighed in appreciation of the splendid tragedy.

"Perhaps it's not a completely bad thing that Osrick killed your twin brother," Pen muttered darkly, his voice pitched for his lord's ears alone.

Terrell twitched as a chill ran down his spine. *At least we cannot end up as deadly enemies.* He pushed away the shameful thought and pointed east across the lake. "What is behind that gap next to the long red cliff? Another valley?"

"Yes, Your Highness." The commander made a lofty gesture. "The Red Wall separates Silbariki Vale from the Valley of Amm. The Vale holds the ruins of the city of Silbariki, the capital of the Flower Dynasty. When God raised the Scarp the land tilted, so that in flood season Purification Lake spills into Silbariki Vale and fills it. The old city is drowned now, along with most of its surroundings."

Terrell frowned. "It's been three hundred years. Why haven't we reclaimed that land and resettled—oh." He paused. "Hellmouth."

DiVetzi nodded and pointed northeast toward a trickle of smoke rising from beyond the horizon. "Exactly, Your Highness. The volcano is more than a hundred miles from here, but all of the River Amm between it and here is poisoned by the foul springs that pour from Hellmouth's base. The only source of irrigation water on the east bank is the river itself, and using that water makes the land sick and the people sicker."

"So that's why the east bank has never been resettled," Terrell mused. "The twin scourges of the Hellmouth Volcano and the rise of the Scarp left people no clean water."

"Yes, Your Highness. Besides, all the irrigation canals on the east side were broken and the land twisted so that they cannot simply be reconnected. They would have to be reengineered and built completely new. Also, in wet years the dry canyons flood and turn Silbariki's valley into a deeper lake that overflows back into Purification Lake. Marshes have spread over the whole eastern shore." Commander DiVetzi shook his head. "A hundred miles of the east bank is a tortured wilderness now, plagued by terrible beasts twisted by magic gone bad." Another happy sigh.

"I see." Terrell wondered if the man wrote melodramas as a hobby. "Does anyone ever go there now?"

The commander shrugged dismissively. "Occasional hunting parties go by boat, seeking the hides of giant caimans from the marshes, or in flood times one can boat right over the marshes to dry land to hunt lions and antelope. The nearer, lesser ruins were picked over long ago, the greater ones are haunted or under water." He glanced to either side to make sure his men were not close and lowered his voice to murmur theatrically, "It is said that Silbariki Vale is plagued by the ghosts of the twin brothers, still doomed to fight each other for all time as punishment for their fratricide. Some nights the dead rise again to battle back and forth across the broken lands, and woe to anyone caught in their clash."

Pen had drawn Irreneetha and held her out over the lake. Pale purple flames flickered around her point. Terrell gave his friend an inquiring look.

"There's something in that valley that she doesn't like," Pen reported, frowning. "I can't tell anything more."

Terrell stared at the distant gap, more than twenty miles away across the lake. The curve of the World put the bottom of the gap below the horizon and made it look like the lake extended between the ridges. This soon after the spring floods, he reflected, it might do so. The huge gleaming sheet of water sent shards of reflected light back at him until he had to look away.

He shrugged. "It's not an immediate problem. Let's get back, I want to reach Orantio before sundown."

They remounted and turned their horses west. Terrell spared the distant Red Wall and its gap one final glance before he left the lake behind.

Someday perhaps I'll visit that place. Something useful might be done with it.

* * *

Ten days later the royal party neared the crossroads where Pilgrimage Road came up from the fords on the River Amm and arrowed west into the Sacred Vale. The Vale made a hollow in the side of the Bright Mountains as if God had scooped it out. Terrell gazed west at the enormous bulk of God's Footstool looming over the head of the side valley. The peak speared so high that it eclipsed the setting suns and cast its vast shadow over the plain. Sunlight glinted off the snowfields covering the upper half.

"It looks more like a dream than a real mountain," Terrell heard Pen remark as they reined in their horses atop a small hillock.

"Perhaps it is," Terrell answered. "A dream that Silbaris dream together. Or perhaps The One dreams us. Who can know?"

He dismounted and knelt at a small shrine atop the hill, where he reverently touched his forehead, heart, navel and groin in respect before he prayed the quick prayer that he'd adopted as his own. *By Your grace, Father Seraph Haroun, and that of The One, let me prove worthy.*

Pen made his own silent prayers while his eyes constantly roved around the stone-fenced sheep pasture that covered this rise in the floor of Silbar's great central valley. The soldiers who had taken up positions around it waited until their lords left the hill before they gathered once more around Terrell. They rode back to the King's Road in time to find the royal entourage turning aside into a large pasture only a little distance north of the crossing. The Wizard's tent had been set up already and a knot of folk gathered around it, their voices low.

"What's wrong?" Terrell demanded, dismounting.

"Your Highness," a manservant said. "Dona Seraphina requests your presence in the Royal Wizard's tent as soon as possible."

"Is he ill?" Terrell's breath came quicker.

"She said she would explain when you arrived, Your Highness." The man looked uncomfortable.

Terrell crossed the camp at a dead run and barged through the door flaps of Shimoor's tent. Dona Seraphina had her aura extended over the recumbent Wizard, who appeared to be dozing on his comfortable cot.

"He has had a mild stroke," Seraphina reported quietly. "I've put him to sleep and I am repairing the superficial harm, but it is at best a patchwork. I cannot repair the deepest damage."

"Should we hurry him to the healing shrine at Lonigo?" Terrell asked, matching her hushed voice. "Better yet, the Mother Temple's hospital in Aretzo?

Seraphina shook her head. "Such haste would only impose greater stress on his already weakened health, Your Highness. Better we maintain this leisured pace and I continue doing what I can for him. There is no true recovery from this type of injury."

"No true . . ." He stopped and gazed at his longtime teacher. Shimoor had become so frail and withered. Terrell though he might pick up the elderly wizard with one hand.

Father. Mother. Pyrull. Now Shimoor. They're all leaving me—being taken from me—one by one. Sorrow left a physical pain in his chest as deep as a knife wound. *You taught me so much. Engineering, magic, politics, mathematics, history. What would I be without you?*

"Do the best you can for him," Terrell finally told the priestess.

"Of course, Your Highness." She continued casting minute spells around the elderly wizard's brain.

Terrell left the tent to find Pen and DiCervi waiting outside, with dozens more clustered in a respectful ring beyond them. Evening had fallen. The tents were pitched, and the bustle of normal camp life went on around this island of quiet. He must have been hovering over Shimoor for a full candlemark.

"General DiCervi. Cancel tomorrow's plans," Terrell ordered heavily. "We make for Aretzo by the most direct route. I'll visit the Sacred Vale later."

"What about Guglione, Your Highness? Your cousin Duke Darnaud?"

"Klairveen's youngest son." Terrell scowled. "There's a side trip that I don't mind discarding. Send word to him that—"

A commotion stirred the waiting crowd, people separated, and a red-headed man barged through.

"Darnaud," Terrell said without enthusiasm.

"Cousin Terrell! Well met!" The beefy redhead greeted Terrell with a cheery roar and strode forward to embrace him.

Pen tensed, nearly drew Irreneetha before Terrell waved him down.

Terrell broke the hug as soon as he decently could. Darnaud had never adopted the Silbari habit of personal cleanliness and he stank like an unwashed gambeson. "What a surprise to see you here, Your Grace of Guglione. Are you making a pilgrimage to the Mountain?"

"Haw!" The sunburned Gwythlo lord bellowed. "Good joke, Terrell, you always had a sly sense of humor. But by the Ice Hell, no! I came to visit you, of course. Brought you some of Madoc's best wine, now that you're a man we should get drunk together." Darnaud beckoned peremptorily to a pair of servants in his livery; each lugged saddle bags that bulged.

Terrell suppressed a sigh and pushed a smile onto his face. *He is my cousin, and ruler of a city on Silbar's second-most-important trade route. I should take this chance to ask him about his fief.* He led Darnaud to the royal pavilion a few steps away.

Four hours later grooms carried the snoring Duke of Guglione off to sleep in another tent. Pen helped Terrell walk the several steps to his own bed.

"Was that worthwhile?" Pen quietly asked.

"Ask me later," Terrell groaned. "Right now, bring me a bucket."

When he'd finished and washed his mouth out with cooled tea, and his face with a damp towel, Terrell sighed and beckoned for his valet to prepare him for sleep. "May the One be my witness, Pen, I've never enjoyed good wine less than I did tonight."

"The company did leave something to be desired. His Grace," Pen loaded the word with enough irony to sink a barge, "is surprisingly coarse for a man who is supposed to be a noble."

"Yes, by the third tale of his sexual conquests I did my best not to listen." Terrell didn't try to hide the contempt in his voice as he struggled to marshal his half-drunk wits; talking to Pen helped. "I did pick out a few useful bits. He doesn't pay much attention to the running of his fief, leaves most of it to his mayordomo. Who apparently is both competent and has more sense than his lord, since he found ways to talk Darnaud out of looting the trade caravans with extreme taxes."

"The work of running the place is probably helped by the amount of time Darnaud spends out hunting," Pen nodded. "But he can be poetic when he wants to be."

Terrell shrugged out of his embroidered sleeves and let his valet take the shirt off him. "Pity nothing but hunting seems to bring it out. His descriptions of the broken lands northeast of Belluno were vivid and fascinating and that long stalk following a wounded lion through the hills gave me chills. He doesn't lack for bravery, does he?"

"True, my lord, though only of the physical kind." Pen scowled and touched Irreneetha's pommel lightly. "Moral courage, on the other hand . . ."

"Yes." Terrell sighed as he stepped out of his pantaloons. "Cruel, capricious, and venal only begin to describe him. God help his people when they come before him for judgement. I'm going to have to rein him in sharply after I take up the governorship." Terrell paused, considering options through wine-heavy wits. "Tell General DiCervi to have one of his men start investigating Darnaud's forces. I'll have to make sure I can overawe him with my own if he resists me."

"Very good, My Lord." Pen bowed himself out.

Dona Seraphina entered as he left. She immediately wrapped Terrell in her Diagnosis aura and frowned. "You're not going to enjoy the morning, Your Highness."

"I know." He held his arms out to the side and let his valet wash him, trying not to sway. He badly wanted his bed right now but knew that he'd better blunt the hangover before it began. "Do what you can, Dona."

She smiled grimly as she began to cast. "You won't enjoy this very much either. Please hold as still as you can."

* * *

"Shimoor is still asleep," General DiCervi reported to Terrell the next morning. The suns were above the eastern horizon and God's Footstool glowed like a spike of ice and silver.

Terrell tried to blink the cobwebs out of his eyes. His servants had dressed him and sat him at this camp table under an awning so that he could eat while enjoying the cool breeze. It didn't help. Breakfast tasted like dust and the fickle breeze brought a waft from the camp latrines that made his stomach churn. "Wish I was," he mumbled as he flogged his wits awake. "Now tell me why you haven't wakened him."

"Dona Seraphina refuses to allow it." The General didn't quite grumble. "We need him to cast a new protection spell for today's travel."

"Let him sleep," Terrell ordered, knuckling sand out of his eyes. Pen studiously avoided comment, which only made Terrell feel worse. *Damn the drink! Wine really is Desrey's Milk, just like the old saying,* he thought ruefully. "His assistants will take on the burden of our protection spells for a few days."

DiCervi did grumble now. "That will leave us significantly more vulnerable than we have been, Your Highness. We could stay here until we can summon a replacement mage from Aretzo. Acting Royal Wizard Chisaad would be able to get here in two days if you summon him by message construct."

Terrell shook his head, then regretted it as the hangover headache punished him. "The risk is not great, General. We are in the most populated and civilized part of Silbar, where we can readily call for help if necessary, and get it from several different dukes and barons who will all be eager to outshine their neighbors in my eyes. Shimoor is to be moved to his horse litter and given an opportunity for rest while we continue as we have been."

"As you will, my lord." DiCervi coughed, waved a hand in the general direction of the tent where Darnaud snored like a carpenter's saw. "What shall we do with His Grace the Duke of Guglione?" His oblique gaze implied that while strangulation probably wasn't appropriate, the General might be willing to try it.

Terrell firmly shoved that temptation aside and scowled, rubbed his head as he considered. He discarded his next thought—to tie Darnaud across a mule and send him home still snoring—and the one after that—to tie him upright in the saddle on his horse and see how long it took for him to wake on his own. Two of Darnaud's men were standing at the edge of the royal part of the camp, helmets in hand and heads bowed, with a look of resigned patience. They were probably used to this. "Fetch Dona Seraphina to tend the—to His Grace. She can wake him enough to ride his own horse." Terrell beckoned Darnaud's men toward him and pointed to the tent. They both bowed and hurried toward their sleeping lord; one had a wineskin ready in hand.

"As you will, Your Highness." The general bowed, his face impassive.

Pen handed Terrell a beaker of strong tea; he grimaced and drank it all, pushed the remains of his breakfast aside with a shudder, and stood to allow his valet to finish the final lacings on today's garb. By the time Terrell was ready to ride, Darnaud had come stumbling out of the tent, pursued by an exasperated Dona Seraphina and assisted by the two Guglione troopers, who were trying to help their lord walk without being too obvious.

"Get away from me, you darkie witch!" Darnaud howled at the priestess. "Don't touch me! Gods, my head hurts."

"Your Grace!" Seraphina barked angrily. "You need the rest of my healing spell if you are to avoid—"

"No! Devils take you, you black hag!" He pushed one of his men between himself and the priestess to keep her from wrapping him in her aura, then gazed around blearily, missing Terrell completely. "Somebody get this bitch away from me, and bring me wine, damn all your lazy asses!"

The prepared trooper pressed the wineskin into his lord's hands and Darnaud swigged mightily, gasped, choked, drank again until wine spilled down the front of his slept-in clothes. "Ah! That's more like it. Where's my damn cousin?"

"Behind you," Pen said succinctly.

Darnaud whirled around, staggered and nearly fell. The prepared trooper caught him under his left arm and helped keep him on his feet. The man's quickness and bland expression said he'd done this before.

"Terrell!" Darnaud exclaimed with patently false cheer. "Cousin! Let's ride over to my city today, I'll show you my hounds!"

"No, thank you, My Lord of Guglione." Terrell pantomimed ritual sorrow, which apparently went right over Darnaud's throbbing head. *Right, there's no point to being subtle with you, is there?* Aloud he said, "I am eager to take up my rule of Silbar and there are still many miles to go. Thank you for a—" He had to force the word out, "—congenial evening, cousin, but I must inspect my troops and prepare to be off within the hour."

A groom had brought up horses. Terrell and Pen swung into their saddles while Darnaud blinked at them owlishly and hunted for words. Terrell gave Darnaud a last nod and a "Fare you well, Your Grace," then urged his horse away before his cousin found any.

Behind them servants began striking the royal pavilion. Darnaud's men brought him his horse, helped him onto it, and led him away. Terrell pretended not to notice the backward looks the hungover Duke cast at him before he disappeared into the crush of busy men preparing to move the sprawling camp.

"Hard to believe he and Madoc are both your cousins," Pen mused as his horse walked beside Terrell's.

Terrell rubbed his forehead and sighed. "I know. Their mothers are Father's sisters, after all. Let's circle through the west side of the camp and hope he's out of sight by the time we get to the east side. We're on good roads, I want to be at least half way to Dalmatzo by evening. I think we can make Aretzo in four days."

I'll have to start dealing with problems like Darnaud, he brooded. *I wonder how many others there are like him? Or worse?*

CHAPTER 14: KIRIN AND TERRELL

K irin! Sevan! He's coming tomorrow!" Maia's voice rang across the Attic. Kirin looked up from the rope he'd been splicing. Ordinarily they'd have replaced a frayed rope, but with money so tight Grandfather had decreed that they would make do with patches. If he had to risk himself on a patched rope he wanted to be sure of it.

Sevan looked up from testing the ropes that held the net and beat him to the question. "Who?"

"Prince Terrell of course! The Queen's son!" Maia would have danced in excitement if she weren't carrying a basket of wet laundry. Instead she pirouetted and the basket sprayed fine droplets over Kirin.

He laughed and fended her off, glad to see her so much happier this tenday. Her morning sickness had finally passed and she glowed with health. She spun around again and splashed him anew, so he put down the rope, lunged to his feet, took the basket out of her hands and set it down, and kissed her. Her younger brother Attir and one of the cousins made mocking noises, which he ignored. When he and Maia both came up for air he asked her, "How do you know?"

"Mother and the rest of us women were doing laundry at the fountain when Bertillin came by with the news." She grabbed Kirin and swung him around in a circle. "Prince Terrell will be here tomorrow morning, in a big parade! There'll be mages and priestesses and soldiers and everything, it's so exciting! Oh Kirin, Father already gave us free time tomorrow. We have to use it to go see him."

"Where's this parade going to be?" he asked cautiously. "It's bound to be crowded." His hand slipped down to touch her belly, beginning to stretch with their growing child.

She rubbed herself saucily against him and said, "Bertillin told us they're going to circle the Bazaar and stop at the Mother Temple before they go up the Processional through the Middle Court to the palace. Do you suppose Fresci would let us sit on his roof? We could see everything from there!"

"Fresci will want money—" Kirin began.

"He'd better not want it from us," Maia interrupted indignantly. "After all the DiUmbras did for him!"

"He fed us a lot of bread rolls all those years," Kirin pointed out. "Sometimes even with butter or hummus, and once with sugar."

"And he got ten times as much business thanks to our praising his wares, and don't think he doesn't know it." She adopted a formidable frown. "I'll explain it to him if necessary."

"Have mercy on the poor man!" Kirin laughed, and Sevan joined him. "Very well, love, we'll ask him. If he says yes, you're right, we'll have a perfect perch to watch the Prince's show."

"Yes!" She kissed him again, reclaimed the basket, and began levitating individual pieces of clothing onto lines strung in front of the dormers. "Sevan, I'm certain Carlai will want to come too."

"I agree." Her brother nodded and finished testing ropes. "I'll go talk to her about it."

"We should get up early to make sure of our spot." Maia rambled off into planning while juggling wet floating clothes.

Kirin smiled happily and went back to splicing rope. It did sound like fun. He resolved to bring eight of the copper coins he'd been hoarding so they could buy some sweet rolls from Fresci. That ought to make the baker feel kindlier about having his roof invaded.

* * *

"Be careful on the ladder," Kirin cautioned Maia.

She chuckled at him. "I'm not made of glass, love, and I'm only carrying a basket. Carlai's got a baby to manage."

"Yes, but our baby . . ."

"Is fine. I am so glad that throwing-up time is behind me. I've never felt better!"

"Good." Kirin braced the ladder by leaning against it with one arm on either side of Maia. "The Millago show is only six days away."

"I'll be so ready for it even Grandfather will be impressed."

She scampered up the ladder to the bakery roof. Carlai grinned at him and followed her more slowly, handing her baby to Sevan at the top while she clambered over the parapet. Kirin followed last.

The bakery stood only two stories tall, unusually low for a building facing the bazaar. It had been built of yellow stone topped by a red-tiled roof. Kirin picked his way up the long gentle slope, circled a pair of smoking chimneys, and joined the others at the front of the building. Sevan had brought an old rug to cushion the hard tiles. Kirin settled himself on it between the eastern corner and Maia, leaned his elbows on the knee-high façade wall and peered at the street below.

The bazaar looked like a sea of tent roofs when seen from this angle, crisscrossed by alleys and passages and dotted with larger openings where paths intersected. The ring road that circled it and separated it from the Old City ran broad enough for twenty men to march abreast. Three- and four-story buildings lined this side, many of their roofs filling up with spectators like the DiUmbras. Another family had followed Kirin up the ladder and planted themselves next to Sevan, with polite greetings and open excitement. Kirin looked away from the strangers, not wanting to have the happy morning spoiled by an awkward silence when they saw his too-pale face.

During the night a mist had blown into the city off the Sundering Sea. The rising suns were only now burning it off. The lacy minarets and huge golden dome of the Mother Temple on the south side of the vast opening began to shine in the strengthening light. Kirin leaned over the wall and craned his neck to look east. The ring road joined the great Processional that sliced through the city straight as an arrow from the Middle Court Gate to the towers of the Admiralty palace perched at the very eastern end of Aretzo. Though the taller building next door blocked his view of the Admiralty itself, he could see the turquoise sea glittering to the southeast beyond the sprawling Cliffside neighborhood.

"Going to be a perfect day," Carlai opined, following his gaze.

"And the Suliemons are taking advantage of it," Sevan grumbled, pointing at the stage that had once hosted the DiUmbra troupe. Their rivals were setting up a net and unrolling ropes.

"I refuse to let them make me sad today," Maia declared. "Look, there are people decorating the way, and the pavement's been newly swept. Look at all the flowers!"

Men and women were tying garlands to every upright object within ten feet of the route. Kirin had to admit that the blossoms were beautiful, gathered in bunches and woven with spells to keep them fresh. The street had not only been swept during the night, it had been washed too.

"The Bazaar hasn't looked this good in, well, ever, that I remember," Kirin said.

Sevan, from his two years older advantage, solemnly agreed.

The four of them nibbled rolls baked with honey, nuts, and cinnamon, and devoured oranges while they waited. A couple dozen more people joined them on the roof. The suns rose higher but a persistent high haze and a steady breeze off the sea kept the air comfortable. Sevan shed his hood to enjoy it. Kirin hesitated; he didn't know the folks sitting behind them. If he removed his own head covering they would see his pointed ears. He decided to keep his hood on.

Maia leaned over and kissed him.

"I love every part of you," she whispered.

Kirin kissed her back, passionately grateful for her. As he did, a rattle of drums throbbed across the Bazaar.

"All right you lovebirds," Sevan said with a chuckle while Carlai grinned at them. "Pay attention. The show's starting!"

* * *

"All is ready, Your Highness," General DiCervi reported.

"Then let's not keep my people waiting any longer. Send the signal," Terrell ordered.

Trumpets blew, and the long mass of men and horses began to move towards the city. Terrell gazed at the slaughterhouses with their newly bathed workers lined up to cheer, the sprawling cemetery, and the cone of the Hill of Sight. Pale marble flashed at the peak.

My city, my people, he thought, and prayed. *Blessed Seraphs Haroun and Umana, intercede for me with the One God, that I may be worthy of the task before me.*

The white spires and multicolored domes of the city's temples and the blocky granite towers of the Gray Fort loomed above the tan stone of the forty-foot-high walls. The enormous gate swallowed his army. He glanced up at the murder holes and quadruple portcullises in the tunnel roof.

"It's an impressively strong defense," Pen remarked over the echo of hooves on cobblestones.

"Yes, and that's good. I hope we never have to put it to the test," Terrell answered quietly.

Inside the walls a broad road separated the hulking fort from a jumble of houses. Directly opposite the fort's main entrance a street pierced the neighborhood at right angles to the main road. Fretted stonework arched over the flagstone roadway and the broad sidewalks flanking it. Dozens of women thronged the side street under the arch, all dressed in bright colors with their hair elaborately braided, curled, and adorned. Many wore scarlet ribbons, the symbol of the Pale Seraph Desrey, commonly known as the Temptress.

"That's the Red Street, isn't it?" He asked DiCervi. "Lady Ymera's domain?"

"Aye, Your Highness." The General nodded toward the center of the prostitutes' throng. "She's sitting on that platform under the arch."

Terrell tried not to stare too openly. He saw a surprisingly small woman, considering her reputation. Ymera's dress of cream silk covered her from neck to toes to conceal the fabled body beneath it. The fabric glittered, shot through with gold threads; rumor called her the wealthiest woman in the City. Skin a rich brown, hair glossy as a chestnut, she looked like any of a hundred Silbari noblewomen. But if the whispers about her were true, how could she be here in the open light of day?

The Children of Night cannot abide sunlight, he remembered Dona Seraphina teaching.

Then he saw the glisten of spells wrapping her. The glow wasn't greatly different from that around Skimoor and the handful of other great mages he had met. As his horse came near her, she stood up on her little dais and bowed deeply from her waist, the correct obeisance of a vassal noble to the king. For a moment that took him aback. Could she be mocking him? But no, he remembered that the Red Street literally constituted a domain, a gift to her from one of his ancestors. She technically held the rank of baroness and thus could claim to be Pen's peer in the nobility. The elegance of her movements, the overwhelming poise and grace of her! He'd never seen any woman her equal.

He answered her bow with a deep nod of his own, dazzled.

She straightened and her eyes met his. As if some invisible force had struck him, the shocking power of her aura flared a deep color he could not name. Not an attack, he knew that instantly. She was simply so *much* what she was, and that, he now knew, was more complex than he had yet imagined. Complex, ancient, vibrant as the dawn, and yet unimaginably weary. It quelled him in a way nothing else could have.

Warily he inclined his head through his confusion and rode on by.

"How old is she really?" he asked Dona Seraphina quietly.

"At least two centuries," the priestess sniffed, ostentatiously looking away from the Red Street. "Possibly as much as four. That voluptuous image you see is glamour, your Highness. Heaven only knows what Ymera's true appearance may be. You have been told how she survives, how she *feeds*. She's surely a vampire—do not trust her."

He wondered how many Kings and Queens of Silbar she had outlived. Would she outlive him too? In this moment he didn't doubt it and for the first time he saw himself as a small and insignificant speck in the vast flow of time. How could he stand up to that?

His own confidence awoke and shook off the beginnings of a despair he hadn't even recognized. *No. She has served my line: mine! We do not serve her, and never have.* He reminded himself that she had sworn an oath to his mother, grandfather, and greatgrandfathers back nine generations. The same oath each time, he'd been told the words of it. She would swear it to him, if he wore the Crown. And if he had a son that the Crown judged worthy, she would swear it to that son in turn, her immortality bound in service to the pageant of the Kings of Silbar.

I may be a doomed mayfly next to her, he thought as his back straightened. *But my grandfather conquered half this continent, and my father rules it. I will rule Silbar, all of it, even her.*

* * *

Interesting young man, Ymera thought as the Prince vanished around the corner of the next building. *There's potential there, and an impressive capacity for magic of some kind. Can that really be divine light filling him? Surely it must be some lesser magic, possibly one of the Temple's tricks. I wonder if the Crown will choose him? He appears competent and intelligent. He'll need to be, if he becomes King.*

She left her dais, escorted by her maids, and returned to her house. The special spells she had woven today to shield her from the deadly suns were strong, but brittle. It wouldn't do to test them for too long or too much.

She wondered how soon she should offer him her personal oath of obedience. Not until after the Queen died and the Crown chose a king, of course, but if he was chosen, perhaps immediately after. *I suspect this one responds well to loyalty when it is offered freely.*

Plenty of time to think about it. Queen Shyrill should last for this season at least. And when she goes, I will be ready.

* * *

Terrell's path had been cleared through the edge of the sprawling bazaar. A trail of flowers wound around the vast space in the heart of Aretzo, meandering towards the soaring golden dome of the Mother Temple. Cheering people lined the route, tens of thousands of people. A quarter of the City must be here crowding the stoic soldiers who held their spears sideways to fence the crowd out of his path. A bakery wafted the scent of fresh bread into the air; he glanced appreciatively toward it. There were people crowding the second-floor windows, and more leaning over the roof parapet to wave and cheer.

* * *

Kirin pointed out the banner bearer who led the parade with the royal colors on a pole twice his own height. A brilliant purple field sported two overlapping silver circles. Behind the banner bearer came two leather-lunged heralds crying out the Prince's name and lineage in melodic unison. The Queen's son himself rode a little way behind them.

"He really does have yellow hair." Carlai chattered. "That's so strange! But his skin's a normal color and his ears are round. Look how he holds himself, like a real king."

"Yep." Kirin gazed at the approaching Prince, impressed by what his magesight revealed.

He glows like a sun! How is he doing that? It doesn't look like ordinary magic power and he's not covered in silver, but he looks like a lantern shaped like a man.

His Shadow reached towards the Prince. Kirin blocked it, pinned it under his heart despite its resistance. But the Shadow's move differed from every other time he'd been near major magic and had to control it. The darkness didn't fight him; it simply reached like a beggar, in supplication.

It's not so much hungry as—yearning?
What in the Nine Hells is going on?

* * *

Terrell smiled and waved back at the people as his eyes swept the crowd. Brown skins, round ears, straight brown hair. Silbaris tended to all look alike to him after so many years in the north. His blond mane must be exotic to them. His eyes swept across the people on the bakery's roof, most had their hoods thrown back to enjoy the balmy morning but one man on the end stayed covered—

* * *

Kirin jerked. For a moment he had found himself riding a horse while thousands of people cheered him. He had looked up at a row of familiar faces—and found himself back in his own body again. Whipsawed by two sudden transitions in twice as many seconds, he fell backwards.

Maia saved him from slamming his head against the tile roof. "Love! What's wrong?"

"I don't know," he croaked, his throat unexpectedly tight. "Dizzy."

It happened when I met his eyes, he thought. *What did he do to me?*

* * *

Terrell wobbled on his horse, only trained reflexes kept him in the saddle. For a dizzying moment he had been staring down at himself riding amidst cheering mobs. *What happened? Did someone attack me?* But it hadn't seemed hostile; in fact, it left a lingering trace of bewilderment that matched his own.

"My Lord?" Pen said quietly, guiding his own horse closer. "For a moment I thought you were about to fall out of your saddle."

"I had the strangest sensation," Terrell answered softly. "Be alert, this may be a prelude to an attack." He fixed a smile back on his face and resumed waving at the crowds as Pen drew Irreneetha and held her point uppermost. But the sword's light stayed a calm white with no hint of danger in it. Terrell saw how Pen relaxed. If anything threatened, it wasn't imminent—or the sword couldn't detect it.

I looked at the crowd. He strained to remember the details. *Somebody did something to me, only not deliberately. Whoever I sensed, I could tell he was at least as surprised as me. Did some mage let a spell get away from him? Only I've never heard of a spell that lets you look down on yourself from above. What did he do to me? How did it get through our protection spells? Is there going to be a lasting effect?*

* * *

"Are you all right, Kirin?" Sevan asked, distracted from the pageantry below.

"Yes." He buried the strange sensations deep and tried to put on a happy face, but inside his guts still churned. *What if he comes looking for me? I've got to get away from here.*

Maia squeezed his hand, plainly doubting his affirmation, but said nothing.

"You missed the priestesses and officers," Sevan went on.

"Looks like the fancy part's over anyway," Kirin affected an uninterested tone. "Just soldiers there now. Can we go back to the Attic? Grandfather's bound to be annoyed with us for going out even though we have permission. Maybe if we're back a little early he'll cool down."

"Not by much," Sevan predicted. "Carlai?"

The baby chose that moment to give out a mewling cry. Carlai patted her back and said "She's a few minutes away from screaming again, we'd probably best go before that. I'd rather not have her thrashing while I carry her down that ladder."

They packed up and picked their way through the others on the roof. The row behind them eagerly moved in to claim the empty space. When they were back on the ground Kirin glanced down the alley at the long line of troops which continued to wrap around the Bazaar. None were looking towards him, Haroun be praised. All the way home, Kirin resisted the temptation to look behind them again. He feared he might see a blond-haired Silbari man on a horse, staring at him.

* * *

Who was he?

The question didn't occur to Terrell until he reached the broad Processional that formed the far side of Arezzo's Bazaar. The presence had been male, though he could not have said how he knew. Terrell decided it was much too late to send someone back to search; the man could have been a visitor paying for a place on the roof of that bakery, or one of its workers, or even a member of the family that ran it. If that mage had been even half as confused as him, and it seemed likely, he had probably fled by now.

Odd. I'm quite sure he had no ill intent. That's not reasonable. Why am I not more worried? He examined the sensation uneasily, but the confidence remained like a burning night candle nestled in his heart. *Somehow, I can tell that he wasn't an enemy. I don't know how I know that, but I do.*

He contemplated the feeling and his disquiet grew in the face of its very certainty. *Is this some demonic deceit? I must ask Shimoor and Seraphina about it. Later.*

His heralds and banner bearers had turned onto the Processional. He glanced left toward the towers of the Admiralty looming above the harbor, and right toward the imposing gates of the Middle Court and the halls of Treasury and Justice that did much of the Kingdom's work. He'd never seen such a long straight street in his life. A little ahead and to the right the Mother Temple's golden dome arched above alabaster and chalcedony walls. A veritable horde of priestesses gathered on the marble steps, where a huge choir of them sang a holy psalm to greet him. The Hierarch waited on a temporary platform built to the very edge of the Processional.

Somebody had given thought to their meeting. She sat on a small throne and the platform's height put her head exactly level with his own face here on horseback. As he drew close the elderly woman, with poise almost as great as Lady Ymera's, gave him a gracious nod without a bow, which signified the equivalence of their respective ranks.

The right to rule and command men's bodies is reserved to me, he thought. *But Mother said never to underestimate the strength of a claim on their hearts, for that is ultimately where we all live. The heart. If I'm to rule Silbar instead of merely reign over it, I need the Hierarch's willing support.*

Terrell reined his horse into the arranged stop and nodded back from the saddle, touched his head, heart, navel and groin in piety, and began the campaign to win that.

But all the time the memory of that mindtouch lurked in the back of his mind.

* * *

Grandfather had indeed decided to be angry that they'd gone out, even with permission, but as Kirin had predicted, their early return mollified him. The old man contented himself with a few words of scolding before he allowed Sevan and Kirin to get on with trapeze practice.

Yet after three hours of disciplined swinging and flying, Kirin's heart remained unsettled. The second time that he missed Sevan's hands and landed in the net, Pieter called a break.

"You're not concentrating enough, son. Did you get too much sun at the parade?"

"I don't think I could have," he answered evasively. "There were clouds this morning and I kept my hood up. I just feel a little off. Maybe it's the stuffy air in here."

"Mmmm, go out on the back porch and take a breather," his adoptive father ordered. "Attir needs more training time on the trap. We'll work him while you get a breath, then you practice on the tightrope."

Kirin obeyed, but even the porch, four stories above the alley connecting the Inn's courtyard to the Serpentine, seemed stifling in the hot still air. He grabbed the gutter over his head and pulled himself onto the Sulfur Serpent's roof, where he scrambled up the ladder-like ridges planted in the slates until he reached the building's ridgeline. There he sat looking over the city.

The harbor and its thicket of masts and sails didn't draw him today. Instead he found his gaze hunting westward. The Old City sloped up toward the gulf of air that marked the bazaar. To the right of it loomed the blocky towers of the Grey Fort. Beyond both, the upper spires of the palace bristled across the slope of the conical Hill.

Even as he watched, a banner rose up a pole atop the highest tower. He saw the spell that made it artfully wave despite the still air. A purple field with silver circles.

The Prince is there, Kirin thought. *He's taken command of the city, and the country. What will it be like, to be ruled by this foreigner?*

He snorted at himself and turned away to climb back down.

I sure hope he's better than that swine of a Governor. Only . . . I wish I knew what he did to me.

I didn't like it.

Please, oh Father Seraph Haroun, Defender of the Faithful, keep him away from us. Away from me.

CHAPTER 15: CHISAAD AND TERRELL

Chisaad resisted the temptation to curl his lip as now-ex-governor Ap Marn postured before the Prince. The man had no sense of dignity and he laid his flattery on so thick that even this callow youth couldn't miss it. Prince Terrell's eyes wandered over the assembled Palace staff as he barely pretended to listen to the posturing of the man he'd come to replace. Chisaad had a position on the ex-Governor's left, with Fantillin between. Today the wizard didn't begrudge the majordomo the proximity, as it saved him from any duty to calm the fool Gwythlo. To Ap Marn's right, his military attachés were enduring their lord's speech.

Chisaad let his own eyes wander. The Prince had his bodyguard at his right hand, Baron Sir Penghar DuVerhys DiLione. Word had already come to Chisaad that DiLione now bore the famous soulsword Irreneetha. Chisaad's last sight of it had been when Magister Pyrull boarded ship for Gwythlo with the Queen and her new husband. Fortunately, he knew the blade's reach and how to avoid its attentions, though that wouldn't be easy. The angel within would have difficulty penetrating his spells, since her metal form and even more importantly, the mind of her bearer, limited what she could do in the world of matter. He would still have to discipline his thoughts every time he came nearer to the blade than this.

And now Pyrull lies dying in the cold north, he thought. *As will the Queen, and soon too. How much time do I have to maneuver?*

The Prince had a six-starred priestess at his left, the famous healer Dona Seraphina, but Chisaad had little interest in her. *All the Donas are essentially fingers of the Hierarch's hands, and I know what she wants.* His gaze moved on until it found a withered face, some old man in plain gray robes leaning on a staff. Recognition hammered him.

God Above! It's Shimoor!

The round smiling face Chisaad once knew so well had gone thin and gaunt. White wisps of hair strayed out from under his hood across a liver-spotted forehead. The eyes, once so warm and vibrant, were dim lamps in sunken pits where life and power both ebbed like the tide. The Royal Wizard's hands were thin knobby sticks where they clung to his prop.

My Teacher! Are you fallen so low? Chisaad's chest hurt to see him like this. For a long moment he could only stare in anguish, his public persona forgotten as memories stormed through his mind. He remembered those early years and the joy of learning under his beloved teacher's wise tutelage. Stretching and disciplining his newgrown talent to make it the finely crafted instrument of his will that it had become today. Without Shimoor he knew he would merely have become some journeyman mage, forever stuck toiling in a greater mage's service.

You taught me so much, gave me a path to my golden opportunity. Without you . . .

Shimoor's gaze intersected his own and a tremulous smile lit the old man's face.

He remembers me! Chisaad was torn between wanting to caper like a child and needing to weep.

Abruptly he noticed that the Prince's gaze had flickered back and forth between both mages. *No! He saw my feelings!* With effort Chisaad brought his face back under control.

The years have flown too fast. I am no longer a callow apprentice. And I play now for stakes that I once could have barely imagined. I must not lose sight of my goal.

Yet his heart ached within his chest.

* × *

That may be significant, Terrell thought. *The Acting Royal Wizard was upset to see his old teacher. I think—no, I'm sure—that Shimoor's condition profoundly moved, even grieved, him.* He considered that and found in it a dash of melancholy satisfaction. *This Chisaad will regret Shimoor's passing, perhaps as much as I. Is he a man with more love in his heart than ambition? I must find out. If so, I'll keep him on.*

Finally the transfer ceremony finished. Ap Marn, belatedly realizing that he had done more damage to his stature than good with his ill-conceived oration, ended it, and allowed majordomo Fantillin to take over. Terrell concealed his relief and thanked the outgoing Governor politely, steeled himself to make the offer courtesy demanded and prudence required.

"If you are willing, My Lord Ap Marn, I ask you to delay your departure by a few months and stay on to assist me in learning about my realm." *I need to wring out of you every scrap of knowledge I can get.*

The old Governor put on a good show of bowing to royal will, but underneath Terrell could tell the man had practically swooned with relief.

That's unexpected. Is he simply relieved that he won't lose his status quite yet? He doesn't feel lazy to me, there's ambition inside that head, so I don't think this is relief over not having to move his household. Does he hope to accomplish something here still, and is glad that I won't put a premature end to his plans? I need to find out what he's been doing.

"We'll discuss matters of the realm in your office at the ninth bell tomorrow morning, My Lord Ap Marn," Terrell told him, and noted how caution instantly tempered the man's relief. *Yes, I need to know more about him.*

The palace majordomo urged Terrell away and he turned his attention to the vast home of his ancestors.

Now to be mine, he reflected. *If I can keep it.*

* * *

Chisaad approached Shimoor as the crowd dispersed, some to follow the Prince and most back to their interrupted tasks. He bowed more deeply than politeness required, did the shaking-hands-with-himself courtesy—he certainly wouldn't presume to mesh spells with his old master uninvited!—and found himself at a loss for words.

"Shocked to see me so decayed, my dearest pupil?" the old man asked him in a quavery voice. His sunken eyes were bright and searching, his fire banked but not yet out.

Chisaad could sense the frailty of the body behind the old wizard's spells. Shimoor looked like a blown glass bubble with a candle inside, bright but terrifyingly fragile. The Acting Royal Wizard hesitated while his throat tightened again, and finally choked out, "Yes, Teacher."

Don't be a fool, he scolded himself immediately. He forced his mind back to the old habits of discipline and duty.

Shimoor's eyes were still sharp enough to catch the effort that took. The old man smiled. "Ah, Chisaad, it warms my heart to see you. Come, let's go to my—now yours!—office. On the way you can tell me about affairs here in the city."

Chisaad matched pace with him as Shimoor glided over the marble floor. It startled him to realize that his old mentor had a levitation spell supporting him. The old wizard had good control, but Chisaad caught a faint tremble in the movement.

He can't walk, the younger wizard realized. *He's tapping the Node to power a levitation spell and relied on it to get through the ceremony. He's even closer to death than he seems.*

Chisaad found it unnerving to walk beside such a display of power and frailty. He suppressed the feeling. *This is my chance to convince him that I'm worthy to be his successor. He'll expect me to do no less. To avoid awakening his suspicions I must present exactly what he expects.*

"Mage Blue and his Council of Colors seek to reopen the allocation of the Aretzo Node," he began. "He's offered a potent argument, but the Hierarchy will certainly counter—"

* * *

"This is the approach to the Royal Apartments, Your Highness."

Fantillin gestured gracefully at a marble ramp that led west from the big anteroom of the Hill Door. Terrell wondered if the man ever did anything clumsily, and if so, whether he scripted that as thoroughly as the rest of his actions.

"Does Ap Marn live there?" he asked Fantillin.

"No, Your Highness, he dwells in the Diplomatic Court adjacent to the Gray Fort." The majordomo's smile glinted with barely-hidden triumph. "Your mother left instructions that the Apartments be maintained against the day of her return, or that of her heir. She never saw fit to amend those instructions, so no one else has dwelt here for eighteen years."

Which probably infuriated Ap Marn, Terrell reflected. *But I don't think that has much bearing on his suspicious degree of relief. Unless he's nursing an old resentment? More to the point, I hope Osrick doesn't take umbrage. He said I could be a king, as long as I didn't call myself one. And be a king is exactly what I'm going to do.*

"All is in readiness for you," the majordomo continued as he led Terrell's party up the ramp and into an arched passageway. "Only the initiated servants of the Palace, the Royal Family, and those persons designated by the King, may pass through the bridge guardian."

"Guardian?" Terrell looked down the passageway using his magesight. This corridor looked no different from the rest of the palace; marble floor, vaulted ceiling pierced by translucent panels that lit the frescoed walls. A little way ahead the walls opened to let in even more light; the spells that wrapped the building strengthened there. He followed the majordomo and discovered that the passageway made an enclosed bridge from one part of the sprawling palace to another, physically separate, building. He walked out into it, Fantillin at his elbow, and looked curiously to either side.

The side of the Hill had been cut away to make a moat at least fifty feet wide. It ran three stories deep beneath the bridge, the sides sheer and the bottom fanged by fourfoot spikes of stone. The moat curved away in both directions to enclose a building perched on a huge pier of rock, itself a mere bump on the lower slopes of the Hill of Sight.

It's a smaller palace inside the big one.

Outside the righthand windows the peak of the Hill loomed to the north, its bottom slopes held back by a retaining wall of titanic granite blocks. The whole cone blazed purple-white in Terrell's magesight, many times brighter than the node under Gwythford Castle.

What must it be like to grow up next to such power?

He looked in the less-disturbing direction. The outer wall of the moat sank lower as it rounded the south side of the Royal Apartments, its top supporting another wing of the sprawling Palace. The inside curve of the moat remained thirty feet high and had been made so smooth below the Apartments that it reflected sunlight. A water-filled channel hugged the foot of that gleaming wall and shaded into marshland between the stone spikes. Black cormorants dived into the moat for fish and squabbled over choice catches. An osprey swooped among them like a thunderbolt, seized a fish out of the water, and flew up to the roof to eat it.

"Impressive," he told Fantillin. He looked ahead to the midpoint of the enclosed bridge. There the walls and roof stopped to leave a gap. The space stretched a dozen feet wide, wallless and roofless. In the center of the gap a fancifully-carved ring of stone sprang from the right side of the floor, circled overhead in an arch wider and taller than the hallway, and returned to the floor on the left side. It had been decorated with dozens of faces of creatures. All their eyes were made of gems, and they gazed across the corridor at their mirror images on the opposite side of the ring, some of those inset into the floor. The Two Suns made the eyes glitter. Terrell's magesight revealed animating spells that ran through the ring and under the floor.

"Observe," Fantillin said as he gestured to a waiting attendant on the ring's far side. The woman opened a small box. A butterfly emerged and immediately flew straight toward Fantillin. When it passed through the ring—

The jeweled eyes lit like lamps. They bathed the corridor in brilliant color as they instantly wove a web made of beams of light. It covered the opening and caught the butterfly, suspending it in midair between one wingbeat and the next.

Terrell glanced to either side of the bridge. That glow must be visible to any guards for hundreds of feet around. Sure enough, he spied two guardsmen on a tower overlooking the moat and bridge, both diligently watching the royal party.

"The Ring Guardian also stops inanimate objects," Fantillin said. A second attendant stepped forward on the far side, raised a bow and shot an arrow into the ring. Terrell forbade himself to flinch; the archer had aimed well over their heads. The arrow stopped halfway through the glowing web and hung suspended.

Pen looked ready to jump up and pluck it the rest of the way through. Terrell put a hand on his sleeve to stop him and quickly asked the majordomo, "How do I control this spell?"

"I have set it to respond to the next member of the Royal House to touch the web." Fantillin gestured Terrell forward. "From within it you can direct the Guardian to accept an individual by simply taking their hand and drawing them through while you remain in the web. Thenceforth it will recognize that person, and the web will not be activated when they pass."

Terrell put his right hand into the web of light. He could feel the heavy stream of it, as thick as wind or water and quivering like a living thing. He stepped into it and the stream flowed around him, lines of light bending to wrap him in a warm embrace. It bathed him right through his clothes, a disconcertingly intimate touch. He closed his hands around one stream. It constricted to rush across his palms at a speedier rate. The multiple colors all merged to become pure white.

Fantillin smiled. "You are your mother's son, Your Highness. The Guardian recognizes your kinship."

"This is one of the Lesser Artifacts," Terrell breathed in wonder.

"Correct, Your Highness." Fantillin coughed discreetly. "Though not so 'lesser'. In addition to capturing intruders, it notifies the Inner Servants and the Palace Guard. Right now, bells are ringing in my office and that of your Guard Captain, though he knows to ignore them for now."

Terrell nodded. "How do I release the butterfly?"

"You can cup it in your hands and pass it back to its keeper. The arrow may simply be grasped and handed back."

Terrell did both. The spells stretched to cover him as he moved. Pushing his hands straight away from the Guardian's glowing plane carried the butterfly and his hands out of the light. The woman servant deftly took the fluttering creature from him without touching the web and carried it off. The archer gravely accepted the return of his arrow the same way, bowed and left.

Terrell turned back to Pen, who waited with quivering intensity. His friend and bodyguard eagerly seized his offered hand and stepped inside the web with Terrell, keeping his other hand on Irreneetha's hilt. Terrell sensed as well as saw the web draw back from the soulsword. *It recognizes her, of course. When Pyrull bore her he lived here with my grandfather and then my mother.* Pen craned his neck to look around the inside of the web, grinned a *you did it!* grin at Terrell, and stepped on through to the far side. One by one Terrell pulled the rest of his party through, Dona Seraphina, her husband Merritin, and Fantillin last of all.

"What about my personal servants?" He asked the majordomo, not wanting to be parted from their familiarity in all this strangeness.

"They are being reinitiated to the servant's tunnel as we speak," Fantillin explained. "They were all chosen from among the Inner Servants by your mother and went north with her. You have been enfolded in the care of the Royal Household from birth, Your Highness. We are delighted to finally welcome you home."

Terrell limited his relief to a single nod and the word, "Good."

The glowing web had faded away as soon as everyone passed through. Pen tested it by stepping back across without effect, then he examined the outer surface of the stone ring. "This thing is slick as grease on the outside," he told Terrell. "I thought an assassin might be able to cling to the outer side, avoiding the faces, and swing around it to a window instead of going through it. But there's nothing to hang on to." He nodded approvingly.

Fantillin coughed discreetly. "The guardian's power also covers the windows in the remainder of the bridge."

Terrell smiled. "My ancestors had many generations to make their home secure."

They made their way through a branching corridor lined with apartments for the royal healers, valets, and others. A stunningly beautiful courtyard garden held banks of flowers around ancient willow trees that trailed their branches over a pool big enough for swimming.

Terrell gazed around, enthralled but also slightly dismayed. *'Enfolded,' Fantillin said. I will have to take care that doesn't become 'caged.' This palace-within-a-palace is uncomfortably like a beautiful prison.*

At last they reached the double doors opening into the royal suite. Mirror-image embossed reliefs of a dragon graced each golden panel, tails coiled but front quarters reared up to strike. The two dragons' eyes were rubies and emeralds, and they tracked him as he approached. He paused with one hand on each panel. The magic here tasted different.

"These are alive," he said wonderingly.

"Indeed." Fantillin looked pleased. "They are lesser spirits, summoned by a great Priestess among your ancestors and invited to dwell within the metal home prepared by her son, one of the greatest mages of his day. Only a member of the Royal House can persuade them." He fell silent, watching expectantly.

This is a test, and he's not going to tell me what to do.

He half closed his eyes and concentrated on the strange sensations emanating from the golden panels. Like Irreneetha, and yet not; he'd never received any sensation from Pen's sword other than a cool distance, an almost palpable I-am-not-for-you message. These were . . . inviting.

There are personalities *here. I think I could talk to them.* He struggled to open his mind to the spirits in the metal. They were disturbingly vast, more alien than an ocean, and yet he had a sense of intimate presence like two tiny voices perched inside his ears. They spoke in a strange language and for long moments he grappled with it, comprehension hovering out of reach.

His Light surged inside him, flowed through his hands into the golden carvings. The dragons glowed, their eyes blazed. An affirmation like a mighty choir singing homage rang through him. Followed by a stepping-back sensation as the doors opened silently of their own accord.

Fantillin's face split in the first unguarded smile Terrell had seen from the man. "Very good, Your Highness! Welcome home."

In the beautiful sitting room beyond the dragon doors, three even-more-beautiful women rose from couches and bowed. Terrell gazed at them in confusion. "Are these the Inner Servants you mentioned?"

Fantillin beamed. "No, Your Highness. They are your concubines."

Terrell's jaw dropped as he stared. "I didn't know you would be so beautiful," he said to the three, receiving smiles in reward. "What are your names?"

"Rose," declared the one on the left, who wore a brilliant pink gown and had rose blossoms in the knotted crown of her piled hair.

"Wren," sang the next, clothed in saffron silk and sable with an avalanche of brown curls across her shoulders.

"Mist," whispered the third, clad in shimmering white, her chestnut hair a sweeping fall caught by a single golden comb studded with emeralds and rubies.

"I meant your full names," Terrell explained. "Who are your families?"

"You are not permitted to know that," Dona Seraphina interrupted. "The Hierarchy judges it unwise for the King to develop a close affection for any concubine. Your love must be saved for the wife that you will someday marry. Therefore, the three names, Rose, Wren, and Mist."

Terrell stared at her. "What? But that's . . . Dona, are you telling me that this is the Hierarch's policy?"

"No, it is that of the Hierarchy. All of us." She stared into his eyes without flinching. "We have argued this through and through, Terrell, all the seventh-ranks of the Hierarchy assembled in conclave, and we are of one mind. The realm is too fragile to survive a repeat of the Bastard Wars. You must not sire any children out of wedlock. The survival of Silbar in the years ahead will depend upon clear and unarguable bloodlines. It has been Seen."

Terrell's objections foundered on that final word. "Seen? By the Seeress of the Mountain?"

"No, thanks be to Umana and Haroun! If it had been *her* vision, there would be no escape. No, this came from a lesser seer, and is a possible future, not an inescapable one. The Hierarchy cannot and will not disregard the danger." She finished fiercely. "You must not sire any bastards!"

"Dona—" he protested, then stopped with an effort and held his tongue. *This is not the time or place to argue.*

But he looked at the three and his desire awoke. *This . . . may be a problem.*

CHAPTER 16: CHISAAD AND TERRELL

Be calm, Chisaad told himself sternly. Do not give your ambition away through carelessness.

He waited in the anteroom before the Hill Door and wrestled with his own impatience. Another delay in his meticulous search for that performer.

No. This meeting with the Prince is a crucial step I must take toward my goal, not a distraction. I must know if the Stone Throne will accept him as a member of the Royal House, as it did me. If it rejects him, which it may well, one problem is solved, and I can concentrate on the rest of the Twenty.

A bustle down the corridor announced the Prince's arrival. Baron Penghar and his sword were with the youth. Chisaad disciplined his thoughts and bowed low.

* * *

Terrell found himself wishing Irreneetha hadn't chosen Pen. The three concubines had roiled his thoughts as much as his loins, possibly more, and he badly wanted to talk to his old friend about it. But Pen was no longer someone with whom he could share those feelings.

They're all so beautiful, and I can bed any of them any time I wish. His desire stirred at the thought of the coming night. *But I can't learn their real names?* Uneasiness countered his ardor. *I'm going to have to sort this out. But not right now.*

"Acting Royal Wizard Chisaad," he greeted the waiting man. "Shimoor has spoken about you favorably. I take it you will be my guide to the Hill of Sight?"

Chisaad affirmed that and gestured to the Hill Door. The waiting guards opened both huge bronze leaves.

It's more of a gate, Terrell thought as he strode through, passing more guards outside the door. He found himself on a little stone plaza pinched between the Palace and the grassy mass of the Hill. To left and right the plaza narrowed into paved paths that curved around the vast cone and out of sight. Straight ahead a flight of stairs climbed arrow-straight up the slope, the marble treads wide enough for six men to ascend side by side. His eyes followed them up to the distant flash of white at the top. A thrill ran down his spine at this glimpse of the Stone Throne. *The most powerful artifact in Silbar.*

"The Five Hundred Steps," Chisaad stated, and Terrell could hear the reverential capitals in the man's voice. "I see that you are impatient to ascend, Your Highness, so I ask only that you wait for me on the ninth landing, before you reach the top. There are important explanations that you must hear before you approach the Stone Throne."

Terrell nodded eagerly and launched himself up the steps, Pen at his back. *I climbed the Warburg in one go. I can handle this.*

Their legs strengthened by years of war training, he and Pen breezed through the first landing and charged on up the second flight. By the time they had put a hundred steps behind them, Terrell's eagerness had barely begun to ebb. The second landing gave a broad view of acres of Palace roof. The towers of the Gray Fort and the sentries on them were below him now. Terrell barely glanced at the watchers and charged on, putting the third and fourth flights behind him before he paused on the fourth landing. His lungs weren't working quite as hard as they had on the Warburg's stair. *The air is thicker here.* But his legs had remembered the difference between climbing and riding or fighting. Pen had kept up with him, but they were both breathing strongly now.

"Next flight," he told Pen, and they charged up another fifty steps to the fifth landing.

"Two hundred and fifty steps," Pen panted, standing with his legs braced a little apart and his head back to suck in air while he studied the remaining route. "Half way. What did we climb on the Warburg?"

"Two hundred forty-two," Terrell panted back, glancing over the city. The Palace spread its maze below, the royal quarters looming as a blocky island on its north edge.

"Perhaps we should wait for the wizard, My Lord?"

"On the ninth landing." Terrell attacked the stairs again.

The cone of the hill grew narrower, but the stairs stayed the same width. The landings too remained the same size, each big enough for half a dozen sedan chairs. Terrell toiled up the eighth and ninth flight by sheer stubbornness, his calves burning and lungs heaving. He wavered on the ninth landing before deciding that leaning on the balustrade would not be undignified. Besides, the view amazed him. He sucked in air while he stared.

The Palace lay like an intricate toy below, the Gray Fort a blockier one next to it, and the government buildings of the Middle Court seemed only a handspan farther away. Beyond them the city unrolled like a bejeweled map. Terrell mentally labeled what he saw from his memory of the parchment map that he had studied every night since crossing the Storm Pass.

Pen had paid attention to parts of it; he pointed across the Palace to the city's hulking South Gate, which birthed the coastal road that ran to Rovigo and the other cities of the south coast and eventually to distant Cape Woe.

"Is that the Clerk's Quarter there between your government buildings and the gate? I remember Pyrull told me most of your judges, their clerks, and the Treasury workers live there." He frowned. "They don't seem to be guarded by much; anybody could walk from the Bazaar right into that neighborhood."

"The city's not like Gwythford Castle, with every wing walled off from every other one and guards between each," Terrell answered. "People live more mixed together here. I think Wizard Chisaad lives among the clerks, and two of the judges I'll inherit from grandfather live in the Cliffside neighborhood." He pointed to the more orderly spread of houses lying to the east of the South Gate, on a plateau where the southern edge of the city fell into the sea.

"I thought that must be full of priestesses." Pen waved at the rows of houses spotted with palm and fig trees. The tidy Cliffside neighborhood arced behind the golden dome of the Mother Temple and the ordered religious buildings that nestled close to it.

"And merchants and mages and people who work for merchants and mages and for the Temple and Collegium and Hospital and the rest of the Hierarch's domain," Terrell nodded. Half of Aretzo lay on that broad promontory thrust into the sea, sheer on the south and gently sloped on the north and northeast.

"What's that palace out there on the east end?" Pen demanded. "Is that one of yours?"

"In a sense. That's the Admiralty Palace, from whence my ship commanders operate Silbar's Navy. I think the Navy Yard is mostly hidden behind it, in the corner of the harbor that we can't see." Terrell paused to admire the walls and towers of the long breakwater enclosing the placid harbor. Even for a boy who had grown up in Gwythford Castle, Aretzo's harbor fortifications were awe-inspiring.

The granite wall atop the harbor's breakwater stood a good thirty feet above the high tide line and stretched north and west again for more than a mile, forming a vast arc pierced by three openings through which ships came and went. His magesight showed him the busy sorceries of the Harbor Wizards as they guided ships in and out; even from up here the wealth of magic in use could nearly blind him. He dropped his magesight and relied on his mundane eyes, which might be more easily fooled but were less uncomfortable.

Pen frowned. "What is that ungodly mess between the harbor and the Bazaar? It's bigger than any of the cities we passed through on our way here, all by itself! Compared to the neatness of Cliffside, it looks like *those* streets were laid out by a demented cow trying to find her pasture. Even Fiori made more sense than that."

"That's the Old City; the original part of Aretzo." Terrell studied the untidy clutter of roofs, domes, spires, towers, tenements, and other buildings rolling up the slope from the half-sunken Sump to Oldgate. The Red Street lay tucked between the Old City and the Gray Fort. But something pricked at his mind, he couldn't quite bring it into focus.

Terrell called up his magesight again and narrowed his eyes, trying to look beneath the tumultuous surface spells of the tens of thousands of mages and priestesses. More spellcasting went on in Aretzo than he'd seen in every other place on this trip put together. Abruptly he succeeded, and immediately gasped. "Pen. Do you see that magic?"

"See which magic, My Lord?" Pen shook his head in perplexity, leaning his weight on one booted foot propped on the balustrade as he clutched Irreneetha's hilt and stared. "The whole city's rife with it, I can barely separate one piece from another."

"There's an enormous glowing oval underlying the city, it's bigger than the city itself. It runs out under the harbor too, and north under the slaughterhouses and marshes." He squinted, looked directly down at the grassy slope under his dangling feet. "The Hill also has one under it, though not nearly as big. They almost touch. No, they do touch, under the Palace."

"What you are seeing," Chisaac panted as he toiled up the ninth flight of steps, "Is the Hill Node and the Aretzo Node. The latter underlies the City and is one of the largest Nodes in the known world, Your Highness, as you no doubt have been told. The Hill of Sight enables you to view both at the same time and still tell them apart."

Terrell's busy mind abruptly assembled scraps of rote knowledge into a whole. "This is the key to my line's rule over Silbar, isn't it? Control of the Hill Node gives control of the city's Node too."

"More precisely, Your Highness, it gives powerful influence, not absolute control." The wizard tried a smile on his face that fit badly, discarded it in favor of several quick gasps for breath, and continued. "Bear the distinction in mind. Though the Hill is significantly smaller, its controlling spells have been devised by your ancestors to be operated by one man, from one place." He waved a hand at the remaining flight of stairs and looked at the stone treads with visible disfavor. "The Aretzo Node is not so simple. It lacks the sort of geographic focus that the cone of the Hill provides and is much too wide to be controlled from any single point. Any user of magic can tap into it, and if all were allowed to do so without limit they would soon overdraw it, and local spellcasting would be hobbled. Therefore the Kings working through the Hill Node have imposed limits on how much draw they allow from any given mage or priestess."

"The Aretzo Compact." Terrell nodded. "Shimoor told me how it works, though he didn't go into the why part much." Guiltily he thought, *or my attention wandered to riding horses that day, and I didn't listen.* He looked at the slope below his feet and frowned. "I don't understand how you can call the Hill Node small, it's at least twice the size of the one under Gwythford Castle."

"Certainly the Hill Node is only small compared to its neighbor," the Wizard agreed. "Though tightly circumscribed—it is no wider than the Hill itself—it is very deep. Definitely the deepest Node in Silbar, possibly the deepest in the known world. And the deeper into our world a Node extends—"

"The more power may be drawn from it." Terrell interrupted, feeling his skin prickle as awe swept through him. *Deepest in the known world!* He pushed himself back to his feet. The Stone Throne waited close ahead and he could feel the power of the Hill narrowing to a point under it. "What do I need to do?"

"First, Your Highness, caution." The wizard waved an admonishing finger at him, so much like Shimoor that Terrell blinked. "This much concentrated power can easily kill, and not only you, but potentially everyone on the hill as well. I would greatly prefer you refrained from doing anything rash that killed *me*, Your Highness, and I rather expect Baron DiLione feels similarly."

Pen gave Terrell a dry look and touched Irreneetha's hilt again. "I don't know what she can protect me from, My Lord, and what she can't."

Terrell had no trouble filling in the unsaid *so let's please not find out today* codicil. "Understood. Caution," he acknowledged as he curbed his impatience. "Next?"

"There is no harm in simply sitting on the Stone Throne, Your Highness, so long as you do not attempt to draw upon its power," the wizard lectured. "Only the wearer of the Amethyst Crown may do that safely. To others it will either not respond, or it may kill them." The wizard paused, regarding him narrowly before he continued. "But supposedly any member of the royal bloodline can use the lesser spells that have been linked to the Throne, notably including the various sight spells."

Terrell nodded again. "Mother did that during the Conquest. You helped her, didn't you?"

Chisaad's face went even blanker than it had been. "Indeed, Your Highness. It is well established that your Silbari blood is attuned to the Hill. The question is whether your Gwythlo blood will interfere enough to deny you that access."

Anxiety stabbed Terrell. "What happens if it does?"

"That depends. Most likely is simple rejection; the Throne will not respond to you. However, in extreme cases, Your Highness, the results are tragic." Chisaad shook his head dourly. "The last recorded instance occurred a little over a hundred and fifty years ago when King Chighar's son Xigren, by his Xir second wife, attempted to use the Long Sight spell."

"What happened to him?"

Chisaad gestured to the grassy slopes on either side. "He's fertilizing flowers, Your Highness. The chronicles say his ashes were quite fine and a strong breeze spread them over the Hill before anyone could gather them for a proper ceremony. His father grieved so hard that he died two months later."

"Has any halfblood ever succeeded?" Terrell asked slowly.

"In using the sight spells of the Throne? A few." The Wizard rattled off some names from history. "Been chosen King? Never in two thousand years."

The wizard let Terrell think about that.

I really can die here. Terrell turned that over in his mind; it intimidated him in a way that the Shadow-bears on Storm Pass had not. He knew how to swing a sword, but this struggle atop the Hill wouldn't involve blades. *Is that why the palace staff insisted on introducing me to the concubines first? To show me life can be sweet, but I mustn't be rash?*

Point taken.

Chisaad glanced at Pen, returned his gaze to Terrell and continued in a more positive vein. "Shimoor has conveyed to me your magical education so far. Every eager young candidate for the Twenty wants to try the Sight spells. I imagine you are no different. But approach it slowly, with your shields down and your mind open. Allow the Throne time to recognize you and determine your bloodline. It will change color when it has done so and then fade back to white when it has settled your ancestry to its satisfaction. Only after the Throne completes the color change and returns to white will it permit you to operate the lesser spells. If I may remind you again, Your Highness—"

"Caution." Terrell nodded. The prospect of being burned to ash had more than a little quelling effect on his curiosity, but not enough to stop him. "What color will it turn when I'm accepted?"

"That varies. If it stays white and does not change, you have been rejected. Any of the colors of the rainbow signify a degree of acceptance, purple being strongest and red the most conditional. Black is bad, a final warning. Very final, as Prince Xigren discovered."

"Right." The slow radiance of the Node beneath his feet renewed his eagerness. "If that's all, let's go."

"That is all, Your Highness." Chisaad made an open-hand gesture toward the final flight of stairs and bowed his head.

Terrell took the last stair at a measured pace; his calves had had enough rest to protest at renewed movement. The platform came into view as he topped the final steps. He paused to stare at it.

It's bigger than I thought it would be . . . and smaller too.

He had expected the Stone Throne to be in the center dominating the flat space, but it sat to the northwest side facing inward. The throne's small size surprised him, and the way it perched on a tiny dais that raised it only one step above the pavement. White marble traceries made the blocky chair seem draped in snowy linen. He moved towards it, noticing the patterned pavement under his feet and the ring of squat bollards around the outer edge. The light of the Two Suns flowed over him like honey poured from heaven. His scalp prickled, and the air seemed thick with ghosts.

Hundreds of my ancestors have walked here before me. Perhaps they left some bits of themselves behind? Or is this how the Throne examines me?

Shimoor had taught him how to raise and maintain elementary shields around his mind, as everyone with any magical sensitivity was taught. Now Terrell firmly pushed those barriers lower with each step. *If you can hear me, creation-of-my-ancestors, here I am.* When he reached the Stone Throne, he lightly touched the nearest arm. Despite the Suns the marble slid cool and slick under his hand, as if it had been carved yesterday instead of millennia ago.

Weather and time do not harm it.

The white marble began to sparkle, then ripple with pale colors that strengthened from red through orange to sun-yellow and green and finally blue, shot through with veins of turquoise. The prickling sensation in Terrell's scalp grew stronger. A cowardly voice inside him insisted this was madness, he should flee. He ignored it, held onto the arm while the rippling peaked and faded back to white. Then he stepped up onto the dais, turned and sat.

Instantly he plummeted into the same sensation he had known when he learned to operate the little message sender back in Gwythford Castle, so many tendays ago. Only here the Stone Throne seemed to rise around him, to cup him in a giant embrace of layered spells. Instead of a single shining bar crossing his vision there were dozens of them in a wide array of colors and shapes. They shifted constantly, each one moving nearer as he focused his attention on it and leaping away as his gaze shifted. The circular plaza could still be dimly seen beyond the ghostly swirl. Pen hovered a few yards away, an anxious blur beyond the bewildering veil of spells.

The wizard circled Pen at a distance to take up a position at Terrell's right hand. His voice seemed distant as he said, "It activated for you in blue, Your Highness. That's a very positive sign."

"That my Silbari blood is ascendant?" Terrell asked. Relief washed over him "Which of these are the Sight spells?"

"They should appear to you as a set of green bars. If you want the long-sight spell, which can reach across the city and beyond, use the crossed pair. Grasp them with your mind and point them where you wish to look. There will likely be some disorientation at first."

Crossed green bars. Where are the crossed green bars?

There were a hundred swirling geometric shapes here, in all the colors of a rainbow and a few he had never seen before. A set of red circles tempted him; they looked important and powerful.

And they might kill me if I misuse them. Better not touch.

He finally found the right shape, reached with his mind as if it were a third hand, and after a struggle, managed to grasp the center of the cross. Much to his relief, all the other spells faded away and the green cross hovered before him, faintly pulsating. The top of the hill, the city beyond, and Pen and Chisaad all looked sharp as cut glass.

He also discovered a strange sense of presence, noticeable now that the distracting cloud of spells had muted. It gave him a sensation oddly like seeing himself in a mirror. He shook off the feeling and focused on the task at hand.

Where do I want to look? Let's try the harbor.

Terrell pulled the crossed bars to the left and the view swung dizzily, like being thrown from a horse. He fought down the desire to vomit, thanking the Seraphs that breakfast had been hours ago, and strove to look at the distant towers of the Navy Gate. It took a few tries, but he found he could focus on individual stones in the towers, peer through the glass windows in the top and see the harbor wizards at work managing ship traffic. He tried leaning in closer, found himself looking into some junior wizard's ear. It needed a thorough washing. He pulled back, searched left and right, gradually growing comfortable with the moving point of view.

This must be how a bird sees the world. I wonder if I could find an individual? Such as that mage who touched my mind during my procession? I wish I had some idea what he looked like. I must make time to discuss him with Shimoor.

He tried to look at the Bazaar and quickly gave up that notion. The swirling crowds were far too numerous.

The city is too big. No one man could look at everybody, even using this amazing device.

He sighed, and his mind reluctantly let go of the Sight spell. The green bars faded into the background and the bewildering array returned. Only now that brooding sensation grew sharper, more watchful. As if a face not his own looked at him out of a mirror.

"Chisaad, that's amazing. Can any member of the Twenty use the Throne this way?"

"Theoretically, though the less gifted find it wearying. Had it activated for you in red you would be exhausted now. In practice, most of the older candidates do not try until there is a choosing. It is fairly rare for there to be a candidate as young as you are now, Your Highness."

The wizard indicated the twenty cylindrical stone bollards that ringed the platform, each shaped vaguely like a stool and a little more than knee high. The sides that faced the throne had chiseled numbers in an archaic script. "Speaking of that, please note the seats for the Twenty Candidates. As the only son of our reigning Queen you will have number one, with the right to attempt to claim the Amethyst Crown first." He cleared his throat and gestured to the nearest bollard.

Terrell reluctantly stepped down from the Throne. The spells immediately furled themselves and it became only a gleaming marble chair again. He went to the bollard and dutifully seated himself there. No spells rose to serve him; it was simply a shaped rock.

"You've been told the names of the current members of the Twenty," Chisaad lectured. "Tradition demands—"

Terrell listened with half his attention to the details, while the rest of his mind followed his gaze back to the Throne. That brooding sense of a face in a mirror remained.

It's more than a fabulously powerful tool. When Chisaad referred to it as something that would examine me, he wasn't using a metaphor. There's a presence there.

CORRECT.

The word rang in Terrell's mind and he completely lost track of Chisaad's words. For a moment he sat frozen, listening for that bell-like voice again.

Is someone there?

IN A SENSE. GREETINGS, TERRELL DuRILLIN DiGWYTHLO.

The voice seemed to be coming from the Throne. Terrell stared at it. *What are you? An Angel?*

NO. I AM JUDGEMENT.

Are you judging me now? He fought down a surge of panic, he hadn't prepared for *this*.

NO. THAT WILL COME WHEN THE CROWN RETURNS, IF YOU PRESENT YOURSELF BEFORE ME.

Relief, then curiosity as Terrell asked, *What happens then?*

I CHOOSE THE NEXT KING.

Daringly, he asked, *Will it be me?*

YOU SHALL SEE.

The voice ended on a note of finality that discouraged more questions. Terrell blinked, thinking furiously. *That's the Throne—no, it's something that lives in the Throne. Something not human, something cold and analytical. Spell construct? Spirit? Whatever it may be, it's not done weighing me.*

And I must appeal to it, somehow, if I want to be King.

* * *

"What are you thinking?" Pen asked him quietly as they slowly descended the Hill.

"That this is a more complicated challenge than I understood," Terrell answered. "Mother never said very much about using the Stone Throne. I suppose that's because she did so little of it before Father took her away to Gwythlo. It's the key to actually being King, and I knew that, but there's knowing and there's really *knowing*." He resisted the temptation to glance back over his shoulder at the peak of the Hill, still aware of that brooding presence. "I don't only need the Hierarchy's support to rule, or the loyalty of nobility and commons to get things done. I need that, that *thing's* consent too. Else, no matter what else I accomplish, I won't be King."

"Well, of course," Pen said, sounding faintly surprised. "But you can do it."

I must, Terrell thought. *Or somebody else will.* He squared his shoulders. "Yes, Pen. I can do this. I will."

* * *

Chisaad turned the Prince and his bodyguard back over to Fantillin's eager fawning with a relief that he couldn't let anyone see. A servant told him that Shimoor had gone to his Palace quarters to rest, so Chisaad shut himself in his office to let down his guard for a few precious moments. He stared out a window at the cone of the Hill towering above the city and allowed himself to think the thoughts that he hadn't dared think while Sir Penghar and his damnable sword hovered so near.

It talked to him, I'm certain of that. He brought it up to blue. Blue! I only managed green. The halfbreed pup is acceptable to the Throne. He can use its power. It might even . . .

134

He swallowed hard, hating the thought with a sudden acid jealousy.

It might even choose him to be King.

He turned his back on the window, sat at his desk and leaned his forehead on his fists.

No. It must not. IT MUST NOT! I cannot let this Gwythlo bastard become King of Silbar. I won't. As the One is my Witness, I will not let that happen.

He sat up, straightened his robes while he thought. He would need to gather resources, most importantly a means to pry this pup away from his cocoon of protections without any of those protectors realizing that their charge had been spirited away.

I need the right tool. I need that acrobat, and more help besides.

Ap Marn's quiet voice followed a hard rap on his office door. Chisaad admitted the man and found him accompanied by another, a man wearing a concealing robe and hood who moved with a fitful energy. The wizard bowed them in, shut the door, made sure his spells would prevent anyone from overhearing them, and turned a questioning look on the ex-governor.

The other man threw back the hood and shrugged out of the Silbari robe as if wearing it disgusted him. He had bright red hair and a perpetual sunburn to match it—Duke Darnaud, the younger son of Gwythlo's Chief Druid Klairveen.

Ap Marn's face looked strained. Darnaud looked sulky.

When the workman needs them, the tools will come to hand, Chisaad remembered the old quote. *And here they are; one ex-governor and one disaffected noble.*

"Governor Ap Marn and Duke Darnaud of Guglione." Chisaad ushered the two into chairs before drawing one up for himself. "How may I help you?"

"The question is, how may we three help each other?" Ap Marn answered. His steady gaze held the Wizard's for a long moment.

Chisaad deliberately relaxed. "Indeed." He glanced at Duke Darnaud. "Your Grace, the gossip already says your mother attempted to slaughter the Prince before he left Gwythlo, and again on Storm Pass. Then he snubbed you on his procession through the valley. Are you perhaps feeling less than secure in your duchy?"

Darnaud growled, jerked his head in a hard nod. "Ap Marn says you feel likewise."

"Indeed." Now Chisaad let a small smile rise to his face. "I believe the Governor has phrased the question most exactly. How may we help each other, my lords?"

CHAPTER 17: TERRELL, CHISAAD, AND UMERA

"Shimoor's allotted span is ending, Your Highness," Dona Seraphina reported sadly.

Terrell closed his eyes for a moment, feeling the upwelling grief. He stopped his servants in the midst of clothing him for Millago's party. "How soon?"

"He will not see midnight."

"Take these off," he told his valets with a gesture at the fancy clothes. "Bring me something plain and comfortable. Fantillin, tell Ap Marn to convey my apologies to the Millago family, but I will not be attending their child welcoming tonight."

"Your Highness!" gasped Fantillin. "That is one of the most important social occasions of the year! It's your first chance to impress the leading—"

"I understand that," Terrell interrupted firmly. "And I don't underrate the importance of the social dance of influence. But loyalty to those who have served me must come first. Take my message to Ap Marn, and make sure Chisaad knows too."

To Seraphina, "I'll sit with Shimoor."

"Very good, Your Highness." She bowed to him more deeply than usual.

Fantillin bowed stiffly and departed to deliver the messages.

* * *

Melancholy dogged Chisaad as his carriage rattled over the cobblestones on the way to the Millago mansion.

I should be with Shimoor, he thought, and knew a moment of profound sorrow. He tried to force it away by telling himself wisdom required his presence here. *This excessive grief threatens my good sense. There's a risk that I might reveal too much in front of the Prince if I did stay with them. And this opportunity to find that halfbreed is too important. I must keep my mind on my goal.*

Yet his heart still ached.

His carriage delivered him to the mansion and he swept through the entry in appropriate style to his office. It took only moments to verify that Ap

Marn had already arrived and informed the Millagos' majordomo why the Prince would not be attending. Chisaad knew a moment of amusement at the way Reshghar Bovea Millago's face lit up when the house herald announced the arrival of Silbar's Acting Royal Wizard. Somehow the first adjective didn't bite quite so hard tonight. *Tomorrow I may finally gain the title in full, but would that serve my ambitions as well as not having it? While I dangle in this uncertain state like him, Ap Marn is inclined to trust me.*

Chisaad descended the seven steps to the floor of the grand ballroom at an unhurried pace, casually flicking his gaze over the vast room. He had arrived neither early nor late, in accordance with his usual preference. He inclined his head to his hosts and spoke the customary greetings, repeated the Prince's apologies to be sure. Millago and his wife bowed low and gushed their thanks for his presence, and their condolences for the soon-to-be-loss of his mentor. Chisaad made sure he added the right touch of melancholy to his acceptance, before he admired the new baby and generally did exactly what everyone expected of him. After the obligatory banal exchanges, he managed to extricate himself smoothly from their company and began a circumambulation of the crowd, muttering polite nothings as appropriate.

All the while his eyes searched for his target.

The south end of the ballroom had been marked off with velvet-wrapped ropes. Curved rows of chairs faced a raised stage where two workmen tightened a brace for a long tightrope above the platform. Ladders and other ropes were already anchored into stout wooden braces around and behind it. Drapery and paper screens covered the frescoed walls. It all looked stark and simple compared to the few other productions he had seen, which surprised him.

Ahhh, I see. It's meant to concentrate our attention on the performers.

Chisaad recognized the two testing the ropes as part of the family he'd seen outside the cemetery gate. *I was right, it is this DiUmbra clan that's sheltering him.*

He moved on into the swirl of guests, greeting Ap Marn and a dozen others. Distantly he heard the bells of the Mother Temple ringing the hour. The play would not start for some time yet; he curbed his impatience.

I hope Ymera arrives soon. I must manipulate her into my debt.

* * *

"Dear Arriga," Ymera murmured to herself as she tucked the invitation into her sleeve. "You've done your old teacher proud. It will be lovely to see you again." She adjusted her protection spells and nodded to her servants to open the front doors of her House.

The Two Suns had already impaled themselves on the peaks of the Bright Mountains, which bled their deadly light away. Ymera paused on the front steps to enjoy a brief defiance of those ancient enemies. Not too much, not too long, or she'd have to rebuild her shield spells again; but a few moments could be afforded. Their last light showed off her new dress magnificently, the fine white silk decked with the same scarlet ribbons that were the mark of a prostitute in Silbar. As ruler of the Red Street, she would flaunt her pariah status and challenge anyone to look down on her tonight.

Several early customers, older men mostly, paused in astonishment. One missed a step and had to be saved from a fall by one of her more alert manservants. Ymera mentally marked that man for bonus pay. All eyes turned to her for a lovely long moment, a tasty precursor of the greater effect she hoped to inspire at the celebration.

She descended the steps lightly as two maids carried the train of her dress. That was redundant, since she had woven an extra spell into the exquisite fabric to repel soil and dust. But it added to her status to display her servants this way.

She wondered who else might be present tonight. Arriga's husband Reshghar Bovea Millago had awesome wealth but lacked any noble lineage. He had grown rich on the trade in silver and sulfur and other ingredients of sorcery, and richer still on the export of its products throughout the Gwythlo Empire. Rumor claimed that he owned an interest in every eighth ship that left Aretzo's docks, and Gee's spying had confirmed it for her. A party thrown by him would be one of the chief social events of the year, one which even the bluest of Silbari blue-bloods could scarcely avoid attending, lest their peers regale them with un-toppable anecdotes.

Tonight's guest list could be entertaining.

She settled herself inside her carriage with her maids on the facing seat. The vehicle rolled out of her Street into the Bazaar's swarming mass of tents and booths.

Sounds assaulted her, unmanaged and careless out here beyond the harmonious artistry of her carefully controlled Street. She drew it all in, the snatches of music, tears, laughter, haggling, and occasional screeching imprecations too, as Aretzo's thousands milled and shopped in the cool of evening.

I haven't gone out often in the last decade or two, she mused. *Perhaps that's unwise.*

Outside her carriage the pullulating masses of the city ebbed and flowed. She saw a well-dressed Silbari woman furtively moving down an alley between two red pillars toward that very special booth Ymera maintained. An Orthodox priestess glanced at the furtive woman and glared helplessly at Ymera's carriage. Ymera did not allow her flash of triumph to show on her face.

The women of this city support me in more ways than one. Willingly. And as much as the priestesses want to stop them, every Dona in the Hierarchy knows they cannot.

When she'd been younger, such petty triumphs had given her a heady rush of another kind of power. She'd learned better, only grateful to have survived the learning. Silbar's millions might be mayflies dancing desperately on the rushing wind of time, but they could walk unheeding under the Two Suns.

Her driver maneuvered her coach to join a long line of other coaches filing past the big plaza before the Mother Temple and its Orthodox Collegium. Priestesses robed in yellow and white walked the Sacred Precinct, acolytes and postulants trailing in orderly rows. Ymera could smell the power that filled the domed sanctuary with a clear light. She cast a little unglamour over her coach while they passed. It wouldn't do to provoke the Hierarchy too much; there were thousands of priestesses in this city and only one of her. She was stronger than any of them, even the Hierarch herself, but Ymera knew she would never be stronger than all of them.

The cost of prudence was low, after all, and the return could be critically high.

Her carriage soon discharged her on the doorstep of the mansion recently rebuilt by Arriga and her upstart husband. Her maids arrayed her dress for a proper entrance to the arched marble of the great ballroom, where leaded glass windows, ornate new mirrors as big as her coach, and tiered chandeliers glittered as if the stars had been brought down for this spectacle. She paused in brief admiration, also to allow the herald time to announce her and the assembled multitude to notice her. That didn't take long; her name and dress guaranteed it.

A shocked murmur ran around the room almost instantly as her fluttering scarlet ribbons were seen. Though not, she judged, quite as shocked as she had expected.

Can I be losing my sensibility? Ymera thought, feeling the beginnings of alarm. *Have I spent too much time away from the dance of style?*

Ah. No. The student has learned well, and nearly outdone her teacher!

She controlled her budding smile and swept down the few steps and across the lavish room. Arriga and her husband waited on a dais to greet each arrival. Only when she had curtsied and stood face to face with her hostess did she let the humor blossom to full freedom.

"Darling Arriga, you look lovely tonight."

The flushed young woman in the cream-colored silk bedecked with the dozen—yes, those were scarlet—ribbons, curtsied back in matronly dignity, then spoiled it slightly by seizing the hands of her former mistress and beaming like a child. She did manage to maintain a reasonable semblance of a cultured voice.

"My Lady Ymera, thank you ever so much for attending! And what a perfect dress!" Arriga gestured at the thousand scarlet ribbons bedecking Ymera's own dress, with as much poise and polish as if welcoming the most notorious madam in all Silbar constituted an everyday occurance and not a daring thing to do.

Nice to see my training hasn't slipped! Ymera chuckled inside. They exchanged ritual greetings followed by introduction of the husband, who still looked as doting as he had a year ago. And why not? Their firstborn son lay in a cradle tended by a self-effacing nurse and appeared robust as any newborn and more so than many.

Ymera carefully did not approach the child, but only nodded and smiled from a distance. She sensed a subliminal lessening of tension from the father at this obvious restraint—and even from Arriga. The nurse's hand made a small gesture of aversion behind the crib, her eyes wide.

Sadness pierced Ymera, instantly suppressed. *They know how I must feed to live.* She tasted again the bitter dregs at the bottom of the cup of her life. *Yet they want to trust me. That is my reward for two centuries of restraint; that they truly want to trust me. I will not begrudge the effort that it costs them.*

She bowed herself away into the swirl of the crowd, drifting through it as wavelessly as possible in a dress with a train longer than she stood tall. Her maids warded the fabric from careless feet as she warmly acknowledged all who acknowledged her. Which included nearly all, to her gratification, though some were more frightened than friendly.

Speak truth, she scolded herself. Most *here are more frightened than friendly. A pity the Prince is absent; I would be pleased to see how he handles this assemblage. But there will be other opportunities.*

The city's wealthiest corn factor murmured polite words over her hand, his nervous eyes darting to her face and away again. He had received his young-man's instruction in the ways of pillowing two decades ago at her own House, she remembered, as his attendant wife must suspect. Ymera responded with distant correctness and they both relaxed fractionally.

Nervous children, she thought tolerantly. *Fearful that I might spank them from irritation. Ah well. If I must choose between being feared and being loved, I know which one is more dependable.* She tasted again the familiar chill that thought left behind; it stopped her motion for an instant. *You came here to impress the crowd, and to listen. Walk and do both.*

She forced herself into motion again and studied the crowd as she strolled. The rising merchant class dominated it, shipmasters and factors and Magisters of a hundred workshops. Also well-leavened with dispossessed aristocrats who were not too proud to rebuild their devastated fortunes through trade, the only avenue left open by their conquerors. A few of the new Gwythlo lords were present too, their pale northern faces often burned ruddy.

Only mad dogs and Gwythlos go about uncovered under Silbar's noonday sun! She greeted several of the newer Lords, noting which ones had already patronized her Street.

Wailor Reesford, the dissolute Count of the Harbor, featured on that list. She remembered him as a proud northern conqueror striding down from his war-battered ship onto the docks of defeated Silbar at his Emperor's right hand. The new ruler of the city had casually gifted his ship captain with the richest port in the known world on his way to receive Queen Shyrill's surrender. Wailor the pale-skinned young lion had gazed about, feet planted on the teak wharf, awestruck at his good fortune.

Now his paunchy face swayed over her hand, sagging like over-risen bread dough. He had the pointed ears of his Gwythlo ancestry, his pale skin discolored by liver spots and his blond mane gone stringy gray. Already armored in a fine miasma of wine fumes. Conquered by his own indulgence.

She kept pity and contempt off her face as she answered him politely.

His impatient eldest son pawed the floor like a stud horse at his side, unhappily bridled by etiquette and parental authority. On Wailor Junior the ears and skin only accented a natural devilment, the more handsome for his hard muscularity. He reminded her of popular religious paintings of the Imps of the Tormentor, though those usually featured black hair instead of blond. She amused herself imagining hooves inside his northern-style boots, and a barbed tail coiled uncomfortably inside his pants.

He'd been punishing the wine already, the oversized goblet in his hand mostly empty. His young eyes took fire as the boy-man gazed on her in thoughtless adolescent lust.

In your dreams, child. I've no interest in being a vessel for you to pleasure yourself. She gave him her most ancient smile and left him blinking, taken aback by an almost-glimpse of the fanged skull beneath her perfect skin. *Remember what I am, and what you are.*

And then the swirl of people parted, and she found herself facing the yellow and white robes of the leader of the Purist sect. That role, titled the 'sixth rank' or Hectissima, belonged to a harridan named Hellas D'Illbinth D'Isernia, tonight accompanied by her granddaughter Keldra D'Illbinth D'Ilar, harridan-in-training. Who had come clad in an astonishing confection of silver and white threads not woven, but magically felted into a spectacular hourglass shape that branched and trailed a full three yards behind the girl in a double train. It practically glowed with all the magic pumped in to sustain its flaunting artistry.

I know how you've been spending the collection plate. Ymera bowed low, in a courtesy so respectful that it neared insulting. *Last tenday you denounced me from your pulpit and called for my execution, for the fifth year in a row. Time for a little retribution, delivered my way.*

"Hellas." Ymera softly addressed her enemy with a familiarity sure to annoy and then switched to a more obsequious tone as she pitched her voice louder. "Dona Hectissima, what a magnificent dress you've clothed Dona Keldra in tonight. I confess astonished envy."

Keldra looked torn between apprehension and gratitude. It couldn't be easy to be the focus of the harridan's hopes. Her rich brown skin showed off the silver threads to perfect effect as they shifted endlessly, a movement probably intended to create a winking glitter but which Ymera privately thought looked like crawling worms.

More thoughts of death? Or am I simply wishing destruction to the harridan's seed? My struggle is with her grandmother, so let's not be uncharitable to the girl. There's no need to perpetuate this feud another generation.

Hellas' eyes went to the scarlet ribbons on Ymera's dress and her gaze narrowed. "I see you are still flaunting your sordid profession in the faces of decent folk." She omitted any acknowledgement of Ymera's rank, not even nodding her head.

Ymera made a small tutting sound and smiled indulgently in a way calculated to goad the Purist priestess beyond bearing. It worked.

"If The One grants my plea," Hellas spat back, "I'll hear you confess your unholy nature to the crowd at an Extreme Inquisition. And burn!"

"My goodness, how choleric of you, Dona Hellas." Ymera's smile grew wider. "Do be more careful or that unhealthy temper of yours may aggravate your heart problem. It would be a tragedy for you to send yourself to an early grave."

Hellas' face flushed even redder but this time she realized she was being baited. Her eyes bulged as she strained to control her tongue.

Ymera bowed again and swept away, smiling.

"A most expertly cruel exchange," a familiar voice observed neutrally.

Ymera turned to find Chisaad standing by. The Acting Royal Wizard wore a typically bland expression, a blank detachment that he'd been cultivating so long that she wondered if his facial muscles could still smile, or frown. Considering the ticklish duty that he'd inherited when his mentor and superior had been hauled off to Gwythford Castle by Emperor Brion, she could not fault him for such self-protection. *And now Shimoor is dying . . .*

"She chose this conflict," Ymera answered. "And chooses it again each year. I would be perfectly willing to avoid her entirely, but if she remains determined to thrust her arrogance and anger upon me, then I will continue to resist."

"Mmm. Yes, I saw a copy of her latest denunciation of you. Stridency tends to become self-defeating. As does spite."

He left that observation hanging. Her lips curved up in an appreciative smile.

"Why Chisaad, I do believe I've been scolded. And by the Royal Wizard, no less!" She put on a mock downcast expression.

"Scolding is a rather strong word for such a commonplace observation, almost a platitude." He made a small self-deprecating gesture, as spare and economical as the rest of his public persona. His facial muscles betrayed no hint of movement.

"And you would never stoop to anything so abrasive, so basely aggressive, as scolding, would you?" She grinned at him with mischievous amusement.

"I might entertain the possibility with you," he conceded thoughtfully. "From the point of view of the Crown, you are a valued force for stability in these troubled times. The desire of some to overthrow even a small part of what little stability the nation possesses is cause for worry among those who make policy."

Probably meaning former Imperial Governor Madoc Ap Marn, Chisaad's direct superior. Word had already spread that the new Prince had kept him on for a few months to ease the transition. She doubted that Chisaad referred to the Prince, since the youth hadn't been here for long. She glanced over Chisaad's shoulder and found Ap Marn standing a little distance back and turned half away, but he watched her from the corners of his eyes. Nervously.

"And therefore, those of us who must carry that policy out," Chisaad added, not quite acknowledging his immediate superior's presence in this little charade, as if that would prevent her from knowing on whose behalf he spoke.

"Nicely two-edged," Ymera remarked admiringly. "Will you be rebuking her in like tactful fashion tonight?"

"If suitable opportunity presents itself or can be arranged." He inclined his head politely and added, "I hope you will enjoy your evening, Lady Ymera," before he drifted on.

Tactfully rebuking the harridan will be a difficult project, Ymera thought with amusement; Hellas D'Illbinth possessed all the subtlety of a bronze club. Ymera carefully bowed her head in Ap Marn's direction, enough to acknowledge receipt of the message, and smiled to see the fractional relaxation of the man's rigid posture.

He's a snake. But he still has fangs. As do I, oh soon-to-be-ex Governor of Silbar. Do not forget that.

* × *

Chisaad did not allow his satisfaction at the exchange to show. *She now knows I have sympathy for her side of that stupid rivalry and will want to cement it into outright favoritism.*

He would have to be extremely careful. She was easily the most perceptive magic user in the city thanks to her unique nature. No other woman, and certainly no man, could command flesh, spirit, and elemental magics to the extent she could. The Aretzo Node Compact reserved one part in five hundred of the Node for her own use, a luxury as great as his own, and she had fewer duties to support with it. So she could meddle more than most, if she chose.

But with care, he could turn that perception to his own ends.

* * *

Ymera glanced up at the sound of silver chimes. Servants tapped xylophones to draw the assembly toward their hosts, who preened atop a dais accompanied by the baby and nursemaid. The crowd positioned itself before them and Ymera's maids folded her train inward so that others might crowd closer, though few did. Hellas' maids did the opposite with Keldra's train, claiming extra space for their charge.

The leading priestess of the Dissenting sect took the forward space on the stage. Ymera suppressed a savage smile. Of course Arriga's upstart merchant husband would be a Dissenter, neither Orthodox nor Purist. That would surely stick in the harridan's craw.

Don't gloat, she scolded herself. *Simply enjoy what serendipity the evening throws your way and remember this too shall pass away.*

Arriga and her man looked happy enough to burst but carried off their roles faultlessly. Ymera happily noted how Hellas stood wooden and stern, trying to mix approval of the ceremony with her obvious disapproval of the Dissenting priestess conducting it, and managed only to look sour.

Endearing yourself to absolutely nobody in this room, Ymera laughed inside as she joined the audience in polite applause for the presentation of the baby boy and the plucking of a few infant hairs from his scalp. Those were immediately sanctified and sealed away to be delivered to the Records Hall at the Mother Temple. The priestess followed that with the reading of the little boy's three names and the anointing. Last came a brief closing prayer to which Ymera carefully bowed her own head as deeply as any. *A nice spare ceremony, not long enough to bore anyone except Wailor's whelp.* Most of the Gwythlo lords had learned to accommodate Silbar's religion. A few had even converted to it, much to the chagrin of the Druids that the conquerors had brought with them. Ymera had already noted that none of those were here tonight.

They know that they are losing their struggle with the Temple Hierarchy, she thought dispassionately. She had no stake in that fight and had been careful to stay apart from it.

Nursemaids bore the baby away to sleep, none too soon as a long wail accompanied them out the door. Arriga and her husband accepted congratulations. Ymera kept her own brief but did exchange mutual hugs.

My student has reached a pinnacle of social achievement, Ymera thought as she gracefully moved away to let someone else approach. *May there be many more for her.* Unbidden, a melancholy thought interposed itself like a cloud: *before age claims her too, as it has all the ones I trained before.*

She moved well aside and kept her face carefully smiling, but inside her mind the ashen years counted themselves. How many girls had passed through her hands, been placed into good marriages, found lives of fulfillment, and turned their backs on the Street where they started? Forgotten the ageless teacher that propelled them outward and upward? Even the few that did not forget still grew older and eventually died. Their daughters usually preferred not to remember their mothers' questionable beginnings.

No. I will not indulge in melancholy, not here, not now.

Servants respectfully herded the multitude to the evening's entertainment. They led her to a place on the left of the assemblage but in the front row. The stage thrust out into the audience enough to bend the rows of seats into long arcs. Arriga and her husband had seats in the right wing of the front arc, Ymera in the corresponding position on the left wing.

Another nice gesture. Arriga is signaling to the whole city that she'll neither disavow nor forget me. Ymera hoped it would be true.

Wailor and his whelp were positioned on her left, Mage Blue beyond him. That seating must rankle Blue, though of course the leader of the Council of Colors gave no sign. Wailor promptly spoiled the careful ordering by swapping seats with his son. While his elders exchanged low comments, the youth peeled off his long Gwythlo surcoat, tossed it over his seat, plunked himself down and fidgeted next to her. Ymera noticed him swig from a wine cup and cast another lustful glance over her and beyond, to settle on Keldra like a hunting wolf. Ymera rolled her eyes and pointedly looked away from the boy-man.

Chisaad and Governor Ap Marn sat to her right between herself and Dona Keldra, with the harridan immediately after, followed by Mage Yellow and assorted other leading lights of Aretzo's Council of Colors filling out the ends of this arc. Wailor Junior had practically drooled as he stared at Keldra's dress, or rather, at the newly-ripe body displayed so effectively within it. Ap Marn managed more circumspection, but no less focus.

Ymera suppressed a grin. *I should arrange for Wailor's pup to be properly trained by one of my women so that he at least becomes a competent bed partner. His future wife will thank me. Ap Marn, I suspect, lacks any willingness to learn, and Chisaad has never seemed to care.*

Keldra's maids had arranged her split train in a sweeping double arc that cupped her feet and curled artfully on the floor in front of her. The mass reached almost to the edge of the stage. Keldra herself posed on the edge of her chair, bosom thrust forward and alternately concealed and revealed by her fan in a move that would have been clever if it weren't so obvious. Ap Marn's gaze grew every bit as transparent.

Hoping for a last fling before the Prince sends you home? Ymera thought. Ap Marn had a wife and a mistress and a roving eye—and a coldly practical expediency little colored by any sense of gratitude. *This should be interesting. Is Hellas hypocritical enough to dangle her granddaughter in front of the outgoing Gwythlo Governor for a fleeting advantage? Her sect claims that Gwythlos don't even have souls. And soon he'll be gone back to the North.*

From the angry look the harridan shot at Ap Marn, her answer would be a resounding *No!* accompanied by a high degree of frustration.

Aha. If the Prince had been here, that seat would be held by him. That's why Hellas attended this event in the first place. She expected to dangle her granddaughter in front of the potential new ruler of Silbar! Who, despite his halfblood, is indisputably the leading member of the Twenty and a prime candidate for the Crown before this year is out. Instead she must tolerate a pale-skinned lecher who can offer her nothing. I detect Arriga's hand in this seating. Ymera suppressed another laugh. *Thank you, my pupil, for providing me with such entertainment.*

* * *

It pleased Chisaad to find Ymera on his left, Ap Marn on his right and an unobstructed view of the stage before him.

The word in the crowd is that the DiUmbra Troupe does indeed have a halfbreed star performer. But how to woo him to my service without being obvious to the rest of the magic users gathered here? I must look for opportunity.

Chisaad glanced at his outgoing superior. Dona Keldra and her astonishing dress had him totally engrossed. *Good.* Chisaad dropped both from his thoughts and quietly adjusted the precast scrying spell he had devised for this occasion. He concentrated on the stage and prepared to present the façade that he wanted Ymera to see.

* * *

Ymera overheard Ap Marn exchange a few words with Keldra as Arriga's household herald stepped up on the stage. The herald bowed to the audience with a flourish calculated to bring attention to his words.

"Lords and Ladies, Donas, Magisters, and Good Gentles all, pray attend as the DiUmbra Aerialist Troupe brings you that most beloved of Silbari tales, the Dance of Malik and Mercia!"

Ymera perked up at this choice both traditional and inspired. The DiUmbras had a good reputation. She recalled seeing works of theirs several times over the generations, though none in the last decade. *I really must get out more.* They might do interesting things with the old tale.

Chisaad's profile caught her attention.

He's fascinated, she thought, bemused. *I didn't know Chisaad liked acrobatic plays.*

* * *

Kirin tried not to fidget. The troupe had waited for hours in a stuffy little courtyard squeezed between the ballroom and the kitchens. Setup had been simple since Millago's carpenters were skilled and they didn't argue with the exacting demands of Grandfather and Sevan the Elder. Pieter and Sevan had carefully tested the tightrope and the other ropes before the audience began to arrive. Now they waited.

"At least we've got a place to sit," Carmella said to break the boredom.

Maia nodded silently where she sat on a bench against the wall. Her belly had begun to swell with their growing child, not too much yet but enough that the women of the troupe had devised a new costume for her to conceal it.

Kirin was glad they had had to cut the soaring scene and all of Maia's trapeze work; it would have been dangerous for her now. He leaned beside her with their hands touching on the smooth wood of the old bench. His face glistened with fresh makeup and he tried to rest quietly to avoid smearing it before the white paste set. He could feel his wife's withdrawn quiet. He turned his head to look at her, softly spoke with his voice pitched for her ears alone.

"It's going to be fine, love."

A smile flickered across her face and she nodded.

Within the hall, musicians began to play.

"Places, everybody," Grandfather called. "Time to start."

* * *

Drumbeats drew Ymera's attention to the stage. A tightrope had been set up, ten feet off the stage and running across the center. Two muscular male dancers in black tights strode out on it, edgy, aggressive, meeting in the middle as if in combat, then between them unrolled a billowing sheet of black fabric to symbolize Hell. They hung it from another rope and leapt down to shake the cloth, reminding all present of the strife and violence of the Pale Realm. Others tumbled across the stage, miming pain and fear as they passed back and forth.

An acrobat vaulted up onto the wire from behind, probably lofted by his fellows. He posed momentarily above the fray, perfectly balanced and wearing black tights and black vest both savagely slashed with red dagging. His exposed skin had been blackened until he looked darker than a Xir from the Lesser Continent. The traditional fanged black helm masked his face and he bore a black sword and whip in his hands. Salim, the Tormenting Seraph, Lord of the Nine Hells, leaped down among his victims and drove them from the stage. When it he had emptied it of all save him, he strode to the front and raised his weapons high in exultation. But behind him white and yellow banners waved from side to side above the quaking black backdrop, reminding him and the audience that Hell still lay prostrate beneath Heaven, and would stay so until the end of time.

The Tormentor raged back and forth, tossed high by black-clad acrobats as he struck uselessly at the air above. He came back to the stage, weapons drooping in frustration, to sing of his envy and hate for the Good Seraphs, his wish to humble them. His voice turned cunning and he sang of his plan to waylay one of their angels, to break her and make her his own. And for that plan he summoned his chosen instrument, the Imp Malik.

The dancer who played the Imp leaped onto the high wire, cartwheeled across it and dived down to roll across the stage. He landed at his master's feet amidst gasps from the audience. Her first sight of him made Ymera clap her hands together with delight at such a delicious and daring choice.

White paint coated the youth's face, but his bared arms and chest revealed his real coloration. Golden brown skin under hair black as night with, yes, pointed ears showing amid the tied-back curls. Almost certainly a Gwythlo halfbreed on some Silbari woman of the Sump, or at least the Old City. Roughly eighteen years of age, too, bound to have been sired within days of Emperor Brion's first step on the docks. She guessed that his mother must have been kin to the DiUmbras to gain him entry into the Troupe. From his poise and physique, he hadn't wasted the opportunity. Now would he be up to the challenge of the story?

* * *

Chisaad's had carefully adjusted his personal spells so that he could use his scry spell passively and undetected. It let him give full attention to the play's star.

The halfbreed youth wore only black slippers, black tights, and black ribbons on his arms. His lighter skin gleamed as he knelt before his master,

147

bowing lower, lower, until the Imp lay prostrate at Salim's feet with arms and legs outstretched in submission. The Tormentor sang his intentions; the beautiful angel Mercia, to be lured into his domain and broken forevermore. The imp recoiled into a crouch, protested his inadequacy to the task and his terror of the Light. He dropped to his knees and begged to be assigned some lesser task that would be within his capacities. The Tormentor laughed and placed one foot on his chest, pushed him back and pinned him down supine to emphasize his hopeless enslavement to this most demonic of masters. Salim commanded him to undertake the task anyway. The Tormentor sang of the tortures that would befall the unhappy imp if he failed, for there was nowhere on or under the World that Salim could not reach one of his own.

Salim the Tormentor leaped back atop the wire with the aid of two more black-clad acrobats, sang of the triumph he would soon have, and exited to a drum crescendo.

A reed flute played softly as the unhappy Malik crawled to the front of the stage. The imp dragged himself to his feet all cowed and miserable, and bemoaned this fate that saddled him with an impossible task. For how could a flawed and ugly imp hope to lure the perfect beauty of an angel into Hell? The reed flute sank into silence and the imp went to his knees at the edge of the stage, despairing.

The youth is a complete blank, Chisaad thought. *Bereft of mage talent, like so many others. Or is he?*

* * *

Beautifully done, Ymera thought, and knew from the stillness that the crowd agreed. *Now can they deliver on this opening promise?*

Pipes wailed as a new character took the stage, skin covered with white makeup and clad in flowing red cloth subtly patterned with black. A plunging neckline reached below her waist and her skirts were slit all the way up the side. Desrey the Temptress positively slunk across the boards, oozing passion and singing of deception, the ancient bone-white seductress out for ruin and destruction of any she could misguide. She stalked the despondent imp, holding a long veil of grey gauze, every movement flaunting her body and her cruelty.

Ymera shivered. She understood the temptation of that path all too well. Perhaps Chisaad had been right to chastise her. Though she couldn't forbear noticing that Desrey's costume cleverly enhanced assets of the actress that were past their prime.

Golden-skinned Malik raised his black curls, looked at Desrey with a woebegone expression as she wrapped her grey veil about his chest and pinned his arms to his side. Aggressively she hauled him close, still on his knees, and sang to him of all the ways a human woman might be led astray. Were not the angels only a little more resistant?

Slowly his body moved from despair to eagerness, and gradually she loosened the imprisoning veil, releasing him entirely when he jumped to his feet and cried out his hope of success. He cartwheeled around her, sprang to the high wire and danced down it, caroling his surety of capturing Mercia. In his eagerness and ambition he dived off the wire and disappeared.

The Temptress laughed, mocked the foolish overconfidence of the imp, and predicted the coming disaster. She exited gloating, and the first act ended.

Ymera blinked. That had been surprisingly good. It pleased her to find that she enjoyed this show. The young man playing Malik fascinated her. Such energy!

The black-clad pair drew up the black curtain and two others in white hose replaced it with a shimmering blue banner. They tumbled off the opposite sides and immediately came back with long green sheets that they ran across the stage and let settle to the floor. Two small girls in yellow pirouetted through, emplacing pots of real flowers, probably provided by Millago's gardeners. They were followed by other dancing women with more pots; some of the blooms stood over a yard tall. The stage became a garden where white-clad Mercia danced with other angels, all save her robed in colors as varied as summer blossoms. One by one the other angels drifted offstage, leaving Mercia dancing alone. The angel, perceiving her aloneness, slowed in her dance and spoke to a tall flower. Red petals poured up from it, formed a whirling column in the air, and danced with her.

Superb levitation skill, Ymera thought. *She shapes their movement to suggest the dance partner that she doesn't have. Beautifully done! I remember hearing that the DiUmbras have developed a reputation for clever illusions. I should attend more of their performances.*

A movement at the edge of the stage, a ripple in the shadows, and the white face of the imp appeared. Malik spied upon the angel, clothed in a shifting darkness that moved with him as he crept about.

Ingenious trick with the imitation shadows. And that youth, ah! He moves superbly! I'll wager that half the women in this room already want to bed him. She chuckled silently. Then the corner of her eye caught Chisaad.

The Acting Royal Wizard stared, completely absorbed. But not at the beautiful angel—at the muscular imp.

I didn't know he inclined toward Sathist ways, she thought, amused. *He's never married; perhaps that should have been a clue.* She gave herself over to enjoying the show.

The old tale followed its predictable course. Malik tried to dance with Mercia and won pain and rejection for his efforts. The angel excoriated him for his nature and drove the imp to his knees with the lash of her tongue. She danced to the edge of the stage, prepared to depart—and took that long fateful glance back at the contrite Malik, still kneeling, but yearning towards her with one hand outstretched. For a long instant they locked gazes, then the angel fled.

The hook is set, Ymera chuckled inwardly. *But who is caught by whom?*

Malik sought help from other Imps and finally approached the Temptress for the ensorcelled gem that would weaken the angel's resolve.

Trickery, scheming, it all unfolded in beautiful choreography and understated stage effects that brilliantly enhanced the old story.

But it's the young halfbreed and the girl who carry this production, Ymera decided. *They're both magnificent, the rest are merely very good. And the spare elegance of it! No spectacular sets or splashy illusions, only subtlety. Those simple tricks they do with white kerchiefs and fake shadows are excellent. But she's tiring, there's a strain there that's barely showing now, but getting worse. I wonder?*

She called up a subtle spell to adjust her vision and saw it. *She's pregnant. From the exquisite care he's taking with her, he knows it, too, and he's straining to cover for her eroding agility. I wonder if he's the father? What a piquancy that lends to their performances! The lust of the imp shading over into the tenderness of the husband. Brilliant!*

The moment of transformation came. Malik the imp, now hopelessly in love with the angel Mercia, broke faith with his Master and freed her from the very trap he'd set before Salim arrived to claim her. The Tormentor's terrible rage ended in cruel vengeance upon Malik. The despondent imp, limbs broken, was chained into Hell's depths under the savagery of his fellows, never to know movement or freedom again. The audience groaned in pity.

Then a general indrawn breath as Mercia dared what no other angel would chance; the journey into Hell to rescue Malik.

They have captured us, Ymera knew in the back of her mind. *Not a human soul in this audience could look away now.* She glanced aside at the Acting Royal Wizard's profile and smiled to herself. *And Chisaad's gaze tells me he'd like to get to know that youth very, very well. Mercia, you have competition!*

Clever use of ropes and beams portrayed the long journey downward, Mercia dodging other imps and demons and all manner of nightmarish denizens as she dared the depths. Until at last she found the chained, broken Imp. And even in his misery, Malik bid her flee and save herself, for how could an imp who could no longer walk hope to escape Hell?

Yes, I can see why Chisaad is fascinated by that young man, Ymera thought, and admitted uneasily, *as am I.* That disconcerted her enough to break her entranced state. *Why? Is it his maleness? I've seen thousands of handsome young stud-humans before and bedded more than a few. Yes, he's intriguing, but at the end of the night there's nothing new there.* She brushed the distracting thought aside and concentrated on the play.

* * *

It's not a stage trick. Chisaad decided. *He really does command an actual Shadow. Ten other Mages and Priestesses are watching, and Ymera too, yet none of them see it!*

For a moment he marveled, then smiled. *We are so accustomed to seeing what we expect, and every Silbari knows that stage performers practice illusion. If anyone were so rude as to send a detection spell at the Shadow, they would receive nothing, and so assume they dealt with an illusion and look no deeper. What complacent fools we are!*

He put the feeling aside to examine later. Right now, he had a shining opportunity, if he could find a means to bring this unique youth under his control.

Ymera has noticed my attention. Now I must walk my own tightrope between being too subtle and not subtle enough.

* * *

Maia's Mercia freed him from his bonds. Kirin collapsed to the stage while miming broken limbs. Then Mercia put forth her power to Heal the broken imp, raised him to his feet, and they sang the Love Duet.

Kirin sensed her strain, trying to keep up her part of the Duet. The even more demanding Escape scene loomed. *How can I help her through it?*

They began the difficult Escape, climbing tilting pieces of stage and angled ladders. Once Maia nearly missed a step and Kirin managed to stabilize her without being too obvious. He caught and carried her across the Bridge of Fire, set her down on the far side and felt the brief gratitude in her touch. *So far, so good. We can do this.*

Before Malik could step off the tightrope that did duty for the Bridge, Sevan burst onto the stage as the demon Fear, right on cue. He and Kirin mock fought back and forth on the tightrope as Kirin made his Shadow flicker around them both.

Meanwhile Mercia drew back the oversized bolts on the Door Out, with much pantomiming of strain.

She's not faking that. Her cramps have come back.

But he had shifted his attention away from his own moves for a moment too long. His foot came down on empty air. He flailed his arms like a windmill as he toppled.

* * *

Ymera saw the youth lose his footing and fall. A drop that awkward, from that height, could break bones. This couldn't be part of the script. A collective gasp came from the audience as the more quick-witted shared her realization. With the practice of centuries of instant decision-making, she hurled a feather spell to cushion his impact.

Her spell hit the youth an instant before he landed—and it vanished.

* * *

Kirin barely knew the spell had hit him. His Shadow swallowed it completely. He caught an angled ladder with one hand, managed to push off it enough to not land on it ribs-first. That saved him from broken bones but converted his fall into a roll, one so fast that he rolled right off the stage. He landed on something soft and magical that tangled his limbs.

His Shadow, its appetite whetted, gulped down that spell too.

A cloud of silver puffed into the air. Nearly blinded, Kirin gaped up from the floor. A naked woman clutched at fistfuls of silky thread in a vain effort to cover herself.

Next to her sat a Purist Priestess wearing six stars.

* * *

For an instant the whole audience held their breaths as Keldra's dress flew apart. She leaped to her feet and shrieked loudly enough to rivet all attention on her. Someone sniggered, someone else chuckled, and the crowd dissolved in choked barks of laughter.

Chisaad ignored the junior priestess' humiliation and her grandmother's outraged scream. He kept his gaze on the halfbreed. The youth scrambled back onto the stage with silver threads scattering in his wake. His face bore a terrified expression as he fled back to the girl and the young man playing Fear, who had both come down to the stage. The two of them seized him protectively and hurried him away. All three gave backward glances at the crowd.

They know! Chisaad thought triumphantly. *They've been concealing him in plain sight.*

Chisaad turned his gaze to Ymera. Thanks to his preset scrying spells he had seen her attempt to cushion the halfbreed's fall. *Did she see what happened to her feather spell? Does she understand what he must be?*

By the puzzled look on her face, the answer was mixed. *She knows her spell didn't work correctly but doesn't realize why. I must lead her to the answer that best serves me.*

Dona Hellas had been sputtering, now she found her voice. "You did this!" The senior priestess of the Purist sect shouted. She leveled an accusing finger at the ruler of the Red Street.

Ymera drew herself up haughtily. "I did not. You think I'd stoop so low as to humiliate your granddaughter merely to bait you? Arrogant conceit!"

"I saw you throw a spell!"

"In an effort to save the actor from a misstep, that the show not be interrupted. You are simply not that important to me, Dona Hellas. Consider instead those to whom Keldra's shame could actually matter."

Ap Marn had his surcoat half off, obviously intending to offer it to Dona Keldra. When the harridan spoke, he hesitated. The possibilities in Ymera's words visibly flashed across his face, and those of a hundred other attendees. There were any number of people in this audience who might wish to see the leading family of the Purist sect humiliated. But to do so in a neutral place like the home of the wealthiest merchant in the city, implied a willingness to upset the social order guaranteed to offend Aretzo's leaders. It would take a foolhardy man to dare that, unless he wasn't planning to be around much longer anyway. Ap Marn's jaw set in angry reaction.

Wailor Junior eeled past Ymera, Chisaad, and Ap Marn to drape his own surcoat around Keldra's shaking shoulders. She clutched it close and gave the blond Gwythlo youth a look both wary and grateful.

Hellas glared at the young Gwythlo, more implike in his pale skin and pointed ears than the Governor or even the actor. Her hostile gaze shifted from Ymera to the two Gwythlos and back as if she couldn't decide which she despised most.

Chisaad had remained seated. Now he rose, faced the crowd, and spoke.

"My Lords and Ladies, Mages and Priestesses, good Gentles all, I saw what happened. Lady Ymera did indeed save the young performer from his misstep, a generous act on her part that likely averted a serious injury for him and prevented the premature end of the performance. Unluckily, her spell arrived a fraction of a moment too late and it interacted badly with the troupe's own illusions. Those of you who deal in magic know how unpredictable it can be when two spells collide. Three is even less predictable, particularly when one of them is new and comparatively untried." He made a small gesture at the threads still floating in the air. "Good Dona Keldra has suffered the effects of an unfortunate mischance, not an act of malice."

The crowd muttered like a convocation of doves, many cooing their satisfaction at this explanation. Hellas visibly sensed the tide of public opinion pressuring her to accept this facesaving solution. She struggled against it for a moment before surrendering without grace.

"I suppose it must be as you say—*Acting* Royal Wizard."

Ap Marn's clenched jaw relaxed. He favored Chisaad with an approving look, and young Wailor with a resentful one.

At that moment a servant came running with what had to be one of Arriga Millago's own dressing gowns. The hostess led Keldra away to a private place to change, Wailor Junior trailed after, and the herald bid everyone to return to their sets and prepare for the resumption of the performance.

Chisaad called up a spell to privately project his voice to Ymera's ears and whispered, "We must talk."

She glanced at him out of the corner of her eye and gave him an infinitesimal nod.

* * *

"God Above, boy, could you have bungled that scene worse?" Grandfather thundered.

Kirin hung his head, still shaken. The nightmare of the bursting dress came back and he trembled. "Yes Magister, I mean no, I mean—" *My fault, my fault!*

"And you two, rushing him offstage like that!" Grandfather rounded on Sevan and Maia. "What were you thinking?"

"Grandfather, that's a Purist priestess out there!" Sevan blurted out.

The old man snorted. "And two Orthodox and a Dissenter, and most of a dozen mages! So what, my fool grandson?"

153

"She's wearing six stars! She could burn Kirin!"

Grandfather opened his mouth to say something, but visibly changed his mind as Maia glared at him. Carmella winced and rubbed her forehead, smearing the Temptress' makeup.

Pieter interrupted. "No, here in Aretzo she would have to get the Hierarchy's permission first. Which is unlikely to be granted since the Hierarch and her Circle are Orthodox. You panicked, all three of you, and made a bad situation worse."

"Yes, Father, I did," Kirin admitted humbly, flooded with shame. "I'm sorry." The eyes of the family cut like flensing knives. *I failed them all.*

"The show has to go on," Grandfather growled. "All three of you get yourselves ready to pick up where you left off. Stage the fight on the boards if you're not calm enough to do it on the wire. Maia, you look like cracked glass. Can you finish the scene?"

"Yes, grandfather," she said, raising her head high.

"And the play?"

"I have to, don't I?" She stared back at him, but everyone saw the frailty behind the brave words.

"You do." His glare included all three of them in that you. "To your places, everybody. We resume on my word."

* * *

Chisaad watched carefully as the play continued. The cast members were plainly shaken, struggling to renew the intensity of their earlier scenes. The woman had abandoned her levitation tricks and the halfbreed barely showed any of his Shadow, and that only in ambiguous hints.

This audience is distracted, Chisaad thought. *No longer emotionally invested. The actors feel it. Millago looks unhappy, even angry. The Purists will blame him for this. He knows this mess will damage his reputation and his business and I can guess who will suffer for it. That might give me the opening I need.*

The play limped to its conclusion. The audience offered halfhearted applause that soon ceased. The acrobats vanished behind their curtain and were not seen again. The wealthy and powerful resumed their dance of influence while servitors set out an elaborate dinner. Chisaad found a moment to speak to Ymera alone. He activated his private speaking spell, but she cast a circle of privacy about them both and spoke first.

"Your explanation placated the harridan and put me in your debt." Her words whispered into his ears. "You'll want something for that." Her gaze had gone very cold now, a thin mask of human womanhood that barely concealed the monster behind it.

"A small thing," he assured her, allowing a little of his very real nervousness to show. He arguably ranked as the most powerful mage in the city, but knew himself not even close to her equal.

"That I avoid the bitch and her grandpup?" An ugly hiss lurked behind the words.

"I think you'll choose to do that on your own," he answered. "I want . . . something else." He swallowed as if the words were hard to speak and found that they were. *So much at risk.*

Ymera eyed him for a long moment, probably scrying him in half a dozen ways. "What?"

"The halfbreed." He let his gaze drop, brought it back to her face and stared defiantly. "I want him."

"Why not seek him out yourself?" The question purred between those rouge-tinted lips. "Insufficient courting experience?"

Chisaad could feel his face heating. "True, and I don't know the Old City. Searching, finding, c-c-courting," He gulped. "In that place. I don't know how to do any of those. You do."

"Do you know that girl is pregnant, probably by him?"

"What?" For a moment the question left Chisaad whipsawed. "What—oh."

She nodded. "He may spurn your advances, especially if made clumsily."

"I—I will, ah—" He swallowed hard and looked down at his feet. *So much at stake.* "I will have to risk that, won't I?"

He looked back up in time to see a smile bloom on her face like a painted rose on a porcelain plate.

"So be it. I will let you know what I discover, and help you meet him. Persuading him is your problem."

He could only whisper, "Thank you, Lady Ymera."

She dispelled her circle and moved away into the crowd.

Chisaad heaved a sigh. Silver chimes called the attendees to dinner. He made very sure he had his customary bland expression back in place before he answered.

* * *

The gates of the Millago mansion shut behind the DiUmbra troupe. The cold clang stuck a dagger in Kirin's heart.

His family plodded home through the clean streets of Cliffside, across the Processional and the Bazaar to the stinking cobbles of Sulfur Street. Nobody said anything until they had carried everything back into the Attic and Uncle Ger had returned the horses and wagon.

"How bad is it?" Pieter finally asked his father when the family crowded around their dining table. They had gathered to eat a scrounged-together meal in place of the one they had not been fed by Millago. Kirin huddled with Maia and Sevan at the far end. The bits of cried fish, withered olives, and stale flatbread tasted like wood on his tongue.

Grandfather brought out the little pouch Millago's mayordomo had thrust at them before they left. He upended it on the plank table. Five one-dohba coins clattered on the wood. They lay there, dull gray depleted silver stripped of its power before being minted. Everybody stared at the pitiful pile.

"We spent three on the wagon rental and four more on makeup and supplies," Grandfather said dully. "A net loss of two. The damage to our reputation? I can't even guess."

One of the candles lighting the room guttered and went out. Twilight faded into night outside the windows. Maia clutched Kirin's hand.

I'm under Salim's curse, he thought. *My Shadow has ruined my family.*

* * *

Shimoor's gaunt face stirred on the pillow. Terrell held one withered hand in his own, feeling the birdlike bones under crepe skin and listening to the Wizard's shallow breathing.

"Old teacher," Terrell whispered, remembering. Lessons in perception, learning to use his magesight to see the flow of power in the world. Lessons in politics, seeing and understanding the dance of influence every being exerted upon every other. Engineering, numbers, so many truths revealed, so much understanding gained.

Shimoor stirred, opened his eyes. "Terrell," his breath gusted in a bare whisper.

"I'm here."

"Chisaad." A sad sigh carried the name.

Terrell nodded. "He served you and Mother faithfully all these years. I won't forget him."

". . . beware . . ."

"Beware?" Terrell repeated, startled and confused. "Of what?"

The aged wizard seemed about to say something more, but his eyelids fell shut. A twitch ran through his body. His chest sank down and did not rise again.

"He's gone," Dona Seraphina reported, and began the Litany for the Dead. Terrell joined her in the words, trying to find solace, while tears dripped down his face. Pen gripped his shoulder and wept with him.

CHAPTER 18: YMERA AND KIRIN

The next day Ymera rose early and crafted a message construct to send to Gee, her spy in the Old City. It took only a few minutes to cast the spell, write a cursive message upon the charged air with one glowing finger, and fold it for sending. Gee ought to be able to assemble interesting information on a troupe as well known as the DiUmbras, but Ymera had a detailed desire in mind.

There is something odd about that boy, beyond the color of his skin, she thought as she launched the glittering construct. *Gee is skilled at discovering secrets. She'll find it.*

* * *

Kirin stepped out of busy Sulfur Street into the quiet of the little walled courtyard. A pair of ancient date palms shaded the green door that he had once known so well. Pieter hesitated inside the arched entry, stared at the copper nailheads that made an intricate swirling pattern on the painted wood.

"Do you know what that pattern means?" Pieter asked Kirin abruptly.

Kirin looked at it, really seeing it for the first time. "That this is Mother Gee's place?"

"More," Pieter growled. "The curls along the bottom are Bhinnish script. They say 'under Ymera's protection.'"

"Oh." Kirin looked at the door, looked back at his father. "You never told me that before."

"Nine years," his adoptive father sighed. "When I found you in the street outside Gerlach's burning house, looking so lost that it broke my heart, I was furious with Gee. With myself. We should have saved you from ever being enslaved or bought you off the auction block."

"You didn't have any money, and Mother Gee couldn't have outbid Gerlach." Kirin searched for the right words. "After I got away from him, I remember sitting in that Temple garden with you. You . . . you let me sit without touching me, until I could stop remembering what he did to me, and simply lean against you. Until I could stand to be touched again. You saved me, Father."

"I was too slow." Pieter answered bitterly. "Almost too late."

"But you weren't." Kirin flexed his arms, raised his head proudly. "Look at me, Father. I'm grown now, thanks to you. Maia and I are going to make you a grandfather soon. I turned out pretty good, didn't I?"

Pieter smiled at last. "That you did." His smile fled again as his gaze returned to the door. "But it sticks in my throat to take money from her, especially when we don't know what she wants, who she wants it for, or why."

Kirin's own gaze fell a little. "Father. It's my fault that Millago didn't pay us."

His father sighed. "Partly true, son. You made the mistake on the tightrope, but Sevan and Maia both panicked with you. If any of you had kept your heads and continued straight on, or even paused to give my father time to call intermission, it would have been much easier to salvage the situation. Instead you lost yourselves in fear and couldn't find your way back into your roles. All three of you. Remember that for the future, son, but don't let the memory crush you. You will make mistakes in this life, because you are human." Pieter deliberately tweaked him on one pointed ear, and repeated, "Human. Face your mistakes, redeem them if you can but at least learn from them, and continue living."

Shame eased its grip on Kirin's heart. He pushed the memory of the fiasco aside and nodded. "Do you think there's any way we could convince Millago to give us a second chance?"

Pieter shook his head. "I doubt it, son. After the embarrassment of Dona Keldra's dress, the Purists would see him employing us as a poke in their eyes. Why would a rich man risk that? I doubt he'll pick a fight that he doesn't need."

"Then other merchants might think the same." Kirin scowled. "It'll be even harder to find a patron now."

"It might be easier, too." Pieter gave him a wry smile. "The Purists aren't widely loved in Aretzo, and the Orthodox and Dissenters might be privately glad to give us business now. Trouble with the harshest—and smallest—faction could turn out to be good for us. Or at least, not bad."

That thought eased Kirin's heart and offered the first hope he'd known today. "Really?"

"We'll see. It could take hard work and time to find another patron, but I'm not worried."

Kirin accepted Pieter's words and looked at the green door again. "Ten dohba is still a good offer for a little talking."

"Suspiciously good." Pieter glowered at the painted wood.

Kirin sighed. "Father . . . you said it could take some time to find another patron, and we need the money . . . please?"

"All right, son. Let's see what she wants."

They ascended the stairs inside the green door and knocked on the plainer door at the top.

"Come in," said Mother Gee's voice.

Kirin opened the door and glanced around rapidly. The little room remained unchanged from nine years ago. Over there stood the same low bench where he and the rest of her boys had gathered to report what they'd seen and heard, over here the table with the bubbling samovar of tea with which she plied her customers. Swathed in a loose robe of faded rose and violet stripes, she occupied a comfortable chair behind the table. He thought her face had gained more wrinkles in the last few tendays.

"Mother Gee!" he greeted her with as much cheer as he could muster. "You sent for us, here we are."

She greeted him and Pieter with their names and waved them to two chairs facing her table. A cat sat on a shelf behind her, purring contentedly. Mother Gee had a pile of coins in front of her: ten silver dohba.

Kirin found the offered chair had a rag-stuffed cushion. She offered tea from mugs freshly poured and waiting under a heat spell. She took such obvious pains to welcome them that it surprised him.

Pieter sat next to him and gave the coins a sour look. "We're here. What do you want?"

"I heard about the accident at Millago's house," Gee said. "I want to know everything about what happened." She pushed the pile of coins across the table into Pieter's hands.

That surprised Kirin even more. He'd seen her buy words from people before, but she never gave them the coins until fully satisfied.

Pieter's nostrils flared, and he gave her an unfriendly look. "If this is some disguised attempt at charity—"

"It's not. I'm not a Temple almshouse. I'm a businesswoman." She gave Pieter a swift glance that Kirin couldn't read and turned to him. "Tell me how the events looked through your eyes, Kirin." Her face remained stiff.

He remembered the way she had seemed to him when she first took him in, harsh and demanding. He'd soon learned she had a kindness underneath that she rarely showed to anyone but her boys. That had won his loyalty all those years ago. He answered her willingly now.

"It began well," he said. "But near the end, I made a bad mistake."

* * *

Ymera had been pleased by the promptness of Gee's message. She had activated the difficult spell that she had cast upon one of her cats before arranging for the beast to be in Gee's office today. It let her look through the cat's eyes and hear with its ears. She had settled herself comfortably when the young halfbreed arrived, ready to watch and listen.

Then events veered into strangeness. Gee had addressed two people, but only one had entered. Ymera recognized him as the older acrobat who had played the Tormentor. She saw him take a seat—and the empty chair next to him moved as well. Gee offered a mug of tea to the empty chair and the mug vanished!

Ymera found herself mesmerized. Clearly Gee carried on a conversation, prompting a third person to address points she wished, asking questions. But Ymera saw nobody there.

Wrong, she told herself. *The young halfbreed must be there, for she addressed him familiarly. But I cannot see or hear him. My spy spell is completely missing the youth.*

She marveled for a moment at the unprecedented lapse. In a flash of shocked realization, she understood.

He is invisible to my spells. By all the Angels and Demons, probably to any spells.

It took her only another heartbeat to reach the next conclusion. *That means he can walk through any guard spell and not set it off. Or he could destroy it, the way he destroyed the spell on Dona Keldra's dress and destroyed my feather-fall spell.*

She didn't know whether to laugh or weep at her own blindness. She had seen him do it and hadn't even recognized the truth before her eyes.

And I'll wager the rest of the crowd didn't either.

The advantages that such an extraordinary ability could confer were frightening to contemplate. It sent cold prickles down her back, activating the fear-reactions of her kind that made her hands curl into claws and her white lips peel back from teeth bared in a fanged snarl. No trap or spell-lock could keep that boy out if he wanted to pass through.

Probably not even mine. That must be why Chisaad is interested in the boy. This isn't romance, this is recruitment. *Chisaad must have come to that party already knowing about this halfbreed. I thought it odd that he showed such interest in acrobatics. But this boy is the reason for his interest in this troupe. And he doesn't want me to realize that.*

She frowned, wondering if this could be part of some last-minute maneuver of Ap Marn's to cling to the governorship and his lucrative graft.

No. That venal fool hasn't the necessary imagination. But Chisaad does. Would he tell Ap Marn? Unlikely. Chisaad's oath is to the Silbari throne, not the Governor. He would hug this knowledge close to his heart rather than share it with any Gwythlo. He might be playing some deep game of his own. But most likely he told Shimoor while trying to understand the boy's power. Chisaad trusts few, but Shimoor heads that list.

Would Shimoor tell anyone? Of course! His loyalty to the Crown is legendary. He would certainly tell Prince Terrell.

She examined her reasoning carefully. It remained possible that Chisaad acted on his own, but at least as possible for the Prince to be behind this. Indeed, this was exactly the sort of clumsy foray into subterfuge that a young ruler might try, not realizing that someone with Ymera's experience would investigate the boy first.

Wait. Shimoor or Chisaad would have warned him. If the Prince knows that I'll realize what his wizard has found, he may be testing me! Testing to see how circumspect I am, perhaps? Will I do his concealed bidding and never mention it?

That had the ring of truth. She elevated one fine eyebrow for a moment, impressed with the pup. *Yes, if my suspicions are correct, this young Terrell may be subtle enough to take and wear the Crown. Chisaad might still be acting on his own, but it's hard to see what he gains from that. Clearer is what the Prince gains.*

But should she help him, or not? A weapon like this boy could be used against her as well. That should frighten any sane magic-user. She looked at her clawed hands, touched the savage rictus of her face. Her servants had instructions not to disturb her, but if anyone chanced to barge in with an 'important message' she would probably shock the poor fool to death. She took a long breath and willed herself back into the delicate, brown, un-threatening shape she had worn for so long.

Would she be wiser to simply arrange the boy's death? He was obviously a mortal, and they died of so many things.

The temptation made her shiver, and that reminded her why she had resisted similar temptations in the past.

No. I would not truly be safer; there is no safety for my kind! I would merely risk the Prince's anger if he suspects. I am already vulnerable to the King in half a dozen ways, with the power of the Stone Throne not the least of them. That is why I have offered my oath to a parade of Silbari rulers. To bind them to me, for my safety. That balance is not changed simply because the Prince may acquire a new weapon.

She speculated. If she helped him acquire this boy, she might be able to add a new and different thread to that tapestry binding the possible future King to her. The boy-Prince's decision to stay with dying Shimoor signaled that he knew the meanings of the words gratitude and obligation. That could be very valuable to her someday.

I'll do it. But first I want to learn all that I can about this amazing young acrobat.

She returned her full attention to the cat.

* * *

"We had their hearts in our hands, Mother Gee. Maia danced the Descent beautifully, I could see the crowd's faces and she had them all praying for her. When she freed me—freed Malik, I mean—we sang the Love Duet so perfect, I think some of them stopped breathing. But then we moved into the Escape, and that's where things went wrong."

Her eyes were intense, but she tore her attention away from him long enough to dart a glance at Pieter before returning that commanding gaze to Kirin. "Tell me everything that you saw. Everything that you experienced."

Kirin paused. He had never told her about his Shadow. For the first time in years, he wondered if she knew about it, and wondered if she meant that she wanted to know more. But why not ask him directly? She'd never been hesitant before. Before he could decide the limits of his willingness to tell her, Pieter intervened.

"Why are you asking my son these questions, Gee?" He leaned forward to squint at her. "Who wants to know?"

"Not everything I do is for a client," she answered, bland as skimmed milk. "Sometimes I want to know for my own understanding."

Pieter snorted disbelief. "Don't treat me like a child. You offered us money!"

She bobbed her head in an oddly nervous gesture and glanced rapidly from Pieter to Kirin and back. "There will be complicated consequences descending from that evening at Millago's mansion, Pieter. Many powerful people were there. Some are likely to grow curious once they have had time to think about it a little more. That curiosity will beget questions, and attention. Attention that doesn't much care about the people that it fastens on, but only cares about how they can be used. Your family could suffer from that kind of attention. Or could benefit, if I direct any inquiries into . . . safer channels." She gave him a long steady stare.

Kirin glanced at Pieter in time to see his father's face go grim. "No," Pieter whispered. "You wouldn't sell us out—sell him! Not after Gerlach!"

"Never!" She spat the word fiercely and stared at Pieter again with a pleading expression. "But you have very little room for maneuver. I can help you there."

Kirin looked away. His chest hurt at the mere thought of such betrayal. *Mother Gee wouldn't sell me . . . would she? But why? What could make her do that?*

His gaze caught the cat sitting on a shelf and watching them all with unnatural intensity. A complex spell wrapped it, focused into whirling circles around the ears and the eyes.

A spell on its eyes and ears . . . a watching and listening spell? Why would Mother Gee have such a thing?

He knew she had no powerful magic. Her talents ran to small things like the heat-spell on the mugs. But she had more than enough magesight to have noticed this. The cat sat there in plain sight, she could reach out and touch it. She must be allowing it. Who would have put a spell on a cat?

Then he knew. Anger boiled up from his heart, his Shadow rising with it. He called some of it into his hands, rolled an ebony ball and threw it at the cat. The creature didn't seem to notice it coming, it only sat there until his Shadow struck the spell and ate it. The cat yowled as if bee-stung, leaped off the shelf and disappeared.

* * *

The abrupt death of her spell shocked Ymera. She half-rose from her seat, settled again. *Did the boy do that?*

She tested the spell; simply gone. Even if the cat had died, the break shouldn't have been that sharp. And a dispelling would have left traces that she had too much experience to miss.

Yes. He had to have done it. Gee and the one she named Pieter were still arguing. How? Does this mean the boy has magesight? I think he must have. Yet he showed no trace of mage-abilities at the party.

If he destroyed my spell because he guessed he was being spied upon, he'll demand Gee reveal the watcher. What will Gee say?

The information-seller's stiffness during the session troubled Ymera, as did that argument with the older man. Gee had too much skill to make such elementary mistakes.

She didn't want me to learn all there is to know about the boy. She's protecting him. He must have been one of her boys once, there's no more likely explanation. Given her tension and her vehemence with that Pieter, she'll tell him the truth.

That disturbed her on more than one level.

I am surprised that Gee has developed such a strong attachment to him, strong enough to compromise her loyalty to me. There must be something deeper there.

Ymera set that thought aside for later. Right now, there remained the issue of the boy, especially his unilateral destruction of her spell without consulting Gee or his older companion. That indicated a certain amount of recklessness. What would he do next?

What any other rash youth would do. He'll come here.

She smiled and began to prepare.

* * *

The echo of the spell's power rippled through Kirin and vanished, leaving behind only a faint scent of lilac and fear. The idea of being spied upon by the Witch-Queen scared him down to his toes even as it fueled his anger.

Pieter tensed with alarm at the cat's screech, demanded, "What did you do?"

"Broke a spy-spell," Kirin answered as he turned to accuse Gee. "Madam Ymera sent that cat, didn't she?" Before the old woman could answer, he plaintively added, "Why, Mother?"

Gee let out her breath in a whoosh and seemed to shrink. "Yes, she was listening. She sent me word that she wanted to know about you and sent the cat to watch. I owe her too much to refuse, and it would have made her suspicious enough to do something more dangerous. I called you here and gambled that I could make you cautious without giving myself away to her. Probably a fool's dream; she has centuries of experience smelling out lies." She eyed Kirin, visibly wondering. "When you were with me you had to touch a spell to break it, but today you never left your chair. What was that dark thing you threw?"

"My Sha—" Kirin began but Pieter hushed him.

"Enough, son." He turned to Gee. "Why does she want to know about Kirin?"

"Exactly what I told you. Because he made such a big mess at Mil-lago's party." She gave Pieter a hard glance before adding to Kirin, "I've had two inquiries already about you, and three reports from different sources. How else did you think I knew enough to question you?"

"Big mess . . ." Kirin remembered that moment when the dress flew apart and the crowd of mages and priestesses gasped. "Some of *them* are asking about me? Oh dung. Dung, dung, *dung!*"

Her face had gone dour. "Yes. You've come to the attention of the powerful, boy. That's never good. I'll steer them as best I can, but my in-fluence is small. You need a powerful protector of your own, and you need him soon."

She paused, looked Kirin straight in the eyes with an intensity that set his simmering anger back. "Or her."

Pieter sucked in his breath. "You can't mean you want Kirin to serve Ymera?"

"I do." She kept her eyes on Kirin's. "You haven't much time, boy. I can stall the ones asking questions for a day, maybe two, but not longer. You could do a lot worse for a protector than Ymera."

He stared back. The Witch-Queen, interested in him . . . as his protector? Or for some darker purpose? A flash of erotic fantasy crossed his mind, followed by shame that made him clench his fists. *No! Maia, forgive me for even thinking that!*

Pieter interrupted. "Gee, don't give us this noise about a *protector.* What does she want from Kirin?"

Mother Gee made a palms-to-the-heavens gesture. "I don't know what she wants. She may not know herself. She may simply be curious. Or she may have intentions far beyond anything I can guess. Trying to outguess her is a fool's game. But I'll have to send her a message about him, and I can't wait very long to send it, or she'll get suspicious." She glanced aside at Kirin. "More suspicious."

"Father—" he said, but Pieter made a quick gesture to silence him. Kirin bit back his annoyance as Pieter rose from the table and motioned for him to do the same.

"Gee, we're leaving. I made a mistake ever agreeing to come back here. As for your money—" he threw the ten silver coins down on her table so hard that they bounced. "Keep it!"

"Pieter!" She caught a rolling coin with one hand even as she stretched the other out in supplication. As he turned away she cried, "Wait!"

Pieter ignored her and stormed out of the room. Kirin followed, hesitated at the door, looked back at her.

"Kirin, please think!" She implored him. "Ymera's not going to leave you alone because you broke her spy spell. She'll send more of them, and if she gets curious enough she'll come looking for you herself. Damnation, boy! She's the most powerful witch in Silbar. You've got to treat her respectfully!"

"Respect?" he answered slowly. "When has anyone powerful ever offered me any respect, Mother?"

"You don't ask a lioness for respect. You either stay out of her way or you give her what she wants." Gee's voice had gone quiet now and her gaze didn't waver. "That's how little folk like us survive. I want you to live, boy. Please!"

Conflicting feelings warred in his head. He had always trusted her, but could he trust her now? Ten years ago he had learned to call her Mother; but today she had been ready to pass his secrets to the Witch-Queen without warning him. Some of his secrets, anyway, and with only an indirect warning. His heart hurt as much as his head.

"I'll think about it." He turned away and followed Pieter.

CHAPTER 19: KIRIN AND YMERA

Kirin woke to the sound of Temple bells ringing the tenth hour. He quietly slipped out of bed. He should have been spent and sleeping like Maia after their evening's lovemaking. Instead his mind twitched restlessly around old memories of horror. He gritted his teeth and forced them away as he padded on bare feet to the room's one window. Slivers of moonlight lanced between the thin curtains. He peeked through the gap between them, eyeing the inn's courtyard and the jumbled roofs beyond. On the west side of the city lay the Palace, the Gray Fort, and the Red Street. The familiar vista from this fourth-floor window had always been a comfort. It told him that he had a place rooted in the centuries-old traditions of the DiUmbra family.

Tonight, it seemed as frail and threadbare as the curtain itself. Who knew what the Witch-Queen could do?

She might be watching me right now.

Conscious of his nudity, he went to the wall-pegs that held his clothes and pulled on hose and a shirt. Cautiously he went back to the window. He peered with his magesight at the courtyard and the walls and roofs of the surrounding buildings. Nothing seemed out of the ordinary. If any creature out there in the night carried a spell, it stayed far enough away that he couldn't see it from this window.

Madame Ymera. He brooded over her name. *She kills unborn babies so she can live! She's a monster. I can't have anything to do with that. Haroun be my witness, I can't!*

Then a mosquito bit him in the sensitive spot behind one ear. Instantly he slew it with his Shadow. The tiny life flickered through him and into the Darkness.

The brutality of his unthinking habit stopped him cold. *I kill too. I do it every time I clear the vermin out of our rooms.* He remembered what he'd tried so hard to forget for nine long years; the taste of Gerlach's life as his Shadow drank it. The horrible forbidden richness of it, damnation in that terrified swallow. The heat of his anger drained away and he shivered.

Maybe I'm a monster too. Maybe . . . maybe I'm like her.

He tried to fling the horrible thought away. It circled back to him like a black fly, persistently biting. *Please, Father-Seraph Haroun, not that! I don't want to be a monster. Please, please, please, I beg of you, anything but that.*

A shooting star arced across the night sky. A promise, or a condemnation? He could think of only one way to find out.

He tenderly kissed Maia on her sleeping forehead and let himself out of their room.

Less than an hour later he picked his way through the revelers on the Red Street. The Silbari Brigade was back in town, uneasily sharing the Gray Fort with the now-outnumbered Gwythlo troops that would escort Governor Ap Marn home in half a season. Men from both forces strolled the flagstones whose color originally gave the Red Street its name. Freshly-washed soldiers still emerged from the baths at the entrance facing the Gray Fort. Ymera had long let it be known that she expected her women's customers to arrive clean and with money in their pockets. Kirin gave way to a swaggering pair of soldiers headed for a whorehouse. He stepped aside and ducked his head even as sullen anger burned in his heart.

She spied on me. I'll show her. I'll spy on her!

Festive lanterns with red-and-orange panes hung from ropes overhead and pushcarts sold food and trinkets. Bawdy laughter and singing echoed from the cheaper houses crowded full of soldiers waiting their turns. Perfumes and music wafted from every house; some of the ornate buildings crowded the very edge of the pavement and towered four stories high. Others were set back amidst gardens where naked couples cavorted shamelessly.

Kirin blushed and averted his eyes. He must be hideously conspicuous in his battered buskins, worn hose, and stained shirt. He hadn't even brought his coin-purse, and his belt knife looked puny compared to the swords worn by the bodyguards escorting lordly patrons. A wealthy young merchant scion passed by, peacock-proud in silks and gems, and spared him a disdainful glance before turning to enter a brothel so exclusive that it had gilt-framed glass windows lit by expensive mage lamps within. The women who welcomed the merchant were dressed even more richly. Two of the man's guardsmen settled themselves to wait with several others on benches outside; another went on to a nearby house where handsome young men clad only in loincloths lounged on open windowsills.

Kirin belatedly remembered that he had no idea which house Madame Ymera laired in. He stopped in the shadow behind a corner of a brightly-lit four-story building that looked like it catered to officers and upper-level civil servants. Grunts and soft cries of ecstasy floated down from open windows overhead.

This is her domain, he reminded himself. *The spells here will all be her own.*

His magesight showed him only a baffling blur of spells on the street. He'd never seen so many spells at once, even on the audience at Millago's house. He closed his eyes and called up his Shadow. It flowed outward from that secret place under his heart until it filled him to the skin. His magesight strengthened and an orderly web of spells revealed itself under the confusion. Wards on the buildings, wards on the street itself, they were all connected by strands of control that gathered together like bundles of invisible strings.

His Shadow greedily reached for the power in the stone wall at his back. He had to rein the dark creature in lest it break something she would notice. Ethereal cables of spells floated overhead, leading down the Street. He followed them.

They led to a House merely three stories tall and converged on the cupola that adorned its slate roof. If not for those skeins of spells, he might have entirely overlooked the place. Not particularly large, it sat back only a couple dozen feet behind a modest front garden that could not be called grand. But a flight of tiled steps led up to a broad front door of elaborately-carved wood, all the windows were glass, the music refined, and subtle perfumes wafted from open windows. The guards that waited in the garden were the most finely-equipped that he'd ever seen. And attentive, too; at least three of them watched him with thoughtful eyes as he gaped at the place.

He hastily turned away and hurried past her house, and the next one too. There he found an alley, obviously meant to serve the kitchens and support areas hidden behind the grand frontages. He ducked into it and discovered it had been blocked a few feet in by a spell stretching wall to wall. Intruders weren't just unwelcome here, but actively barred.

He hesitated, turned back toward the Street. There might be a better way.

A Duermu man carrying a sack strode by the mouth of the alley, paying him no mind. The smell of sweet incense lingered in his wake.

The fortuneteller said I'd suffer fear and loss, Kirin thought. *I thought the Gwythlos at the cemetery were what she meant, but if Millago's house wasn't both, then I'm a monkey. She said Powers would help me, and that priestess did. I'm only steps away from Ymera's back door.* He turned back to the alley.

He took a deep breath, wrapped his Shadow over his skin and stepped through. As the spell rippled over him he sensed a repulsion woven into it that smelled like dung and vomit.

Another spell lurked beyond it, this one woven of fear and pain; it left the taste of blood on his lips.

The third spell stank of steel and death.

He staggered through them, his Shadow churning in frustration as he refused to let it eat the magic. On the far side he leaned against a blank brick wall and panted while he struggled with his Shadow. He had rarely been so near to so much magic before and it drove his burden ravenous with hunger. The Shadow boiled against his will until he feared it would throw off his control and gorge itself. Ymera could hardly fail to notice if it ate dozens of her spells. For an agonizingly long moment he wrestled with it in the darkness of his mind, until, reluctantly, it submitted.

Relief filled him. He still had control over his Shadow and the ward spells hadn't even noticed him.

But passers-by might. The alley ran arrow-straight and contained nothing big enough to hide behind. He let his tamed Shadow flow out a little farther, merging himself into the lesser shadows around him. The blank brick walls ran well over a hundred feet back before they made a sharp turn. When he got to the corner he retained the wit to listen carefully rather than stick his head around the angle.

Two male voices gossiped desultorily; they had to be guards standing not very far away.

Kirin backed up a few steps, examined the brick wall. It didn't have enough space between bricks to squeeze his fingers in and climb like a ladder. But it stood only ten feet tall.

He crouched, leaped, caught the top and pulled himself up and over to find a paved path on the far side. The soft leather soles of his buskins barely made a sound as he landed. This narrow passage seemed to lead around the house next to Ymera's own. He hurried to the back corner, found a kitchen yard with a compost midden and an ash-pit. A solid wooden gate barred access to the back alley. Thankfully the two gossiping guards were on the far side of that. A detached kitchen and bakery on the yard's far side stood silent and separate from the house proper. Of course; a whorehouse wouldn't need bread until noon at least, so the oven would merely be kept warm with a banked fire at this hour of the night. He glided quick as he could down the alley between them, sure-footed in the dark. It ended at a blank wall of smooth close-set stone separating this house from his goal.

Atop that wall, something slithered and glowed.

He gaped up at it for a moment. It looked like a snake with a beaked head surrounded by a bushy mane of long feathers. The top of the wall had been made flat and broad enough for the thing to coil along with a writhing motion that made his stomach twitch. The head turned this way and that; it had four eyes and they swept across him like a hawk searching for prey. But the baleful gaze moved on, and he knew it hadn't—couldn't—see him.

It might have other senses. He watched in fascination as it slithered on towards the front of the property, moving fast. Perhaps he could climb the wall behind it quietly enough to avoid drawing the creature's attention.

Before his courage could falter he rushed forward, leaped and caught the top. Magic tingled through his palms and he struggled against both his Shadow's hunger and the slick stonework. He managed to drag himself up on top, looked down into a landscaped bower centered on a small round pool bracketed by two stone benches. Trumpet-flower vines climbed a set of trellised arches and the nearest stood right in front of him. He heaved himself over the wall, grabbed the trellis and descended it like a ladder. Laths creaked and leaves rustled, but he made it to the ground without a cry being raised. The patrolling guardian kept on slithering away down the wall, oblivious to him as he basked for a moment in his personal triumph. He'd gotten through all her guardians without getting caught

"I am impressed. Five spells on that wall and you didn't alert any of them."

Startled, he spun around to face the house. A side door had opened to reveal a woman and he didn't know how he could have missed her, she glowed so brightly with power that she should have been visible right through the wood.

"You—" Before he could speak armed men poured out of the shrubbery. Four spears were leveled at him and a man advanced between each shaft with a drawn sword.

CHAPTER 2c: KIRIN AND YMERA

Kirin almost drowned the garden in Shadow before he realized the men were too close for him to escape that way. They need only lunge blindly forward and at least one blade had to find him.

They had stopped with the four spear points pressing his shirt against his skin. The two blades in front prodded his belly; those behind threatened to skewer his kidneys. The swordsmen were worse. The one behind him had already relieved him of his belt knife while the men to his left and right touched the tips of their blades to his throat. The man in front had knelt as he advanced and now the point of his sword hovered at Kirin's crotch.

His guts trembled. His balls tried to crawl up inside him. He stayed very still and fought to hold his Shadow inside as well. If it escaped, those sharp points would surely stab.

The woman descended two steps from the house, advanced to the bench on the far side of the pool and stared at him over the head of the kneeling swordsman. Layers of spells made a shifting veil draping her head to toe, but her face shone through them all like alabaster. There were sharp, pointed fangs behind those pale lips and he couldn't help staring at them. People whispered about her but seeing still shocked him.

* * *

He's staring at me, at my face—no, my mouth, Ymera noticed. *Ahhh. He can see through my superficial spells.* She smiled at him and noted how his attention sharpened. *An aspect to his power that I'd not considered. He does more than simply devour or evade magic.*

"Ordinarily I'd be quite cross with a lad who invaded my garden un-invited," she told him. "But it happens that I desired to speak with you, so you've saved me the bother of sending an invitation. I'll consider that adequate compensation for your failure to use my front door."

His body's tension ebbed a trifle at her words and he no longer looked quite so ready to fight or flee. His eyes followed her as she settled on a bench and contemplated him across the little pool. *I am his world at this moment. Now how can I persuade him to reveal what I want to know?*

"Please pardon me for not asking you to sit down quite yet," she added drily. "You do still have a strong air of violence about you, young Kirin DiUmbra. Perhaps that's to be expected, given how poorly many Silbaris treat those who look—different." She made a graceful gesture at him, turned the same hand on herself.

Confusion flickered across his face, then his eyes widened.

That's right, boy, she thought. *You have eyes and a brain. Use them.*

* * *

Kirin's thoughts raced. *She's telling me something. She's disguised to look like a beautiful Silbari woman, but underneath she really looks like a monster. I don't have any disguise spells. I always look like a halfbreed. Underneath*—He squeezed his eyes shut and trembled. *Is she telling me that I'm a monster too? Please, Father Haroun, not that. I don't want to be like her. If I have to kill babies to live—I'd rather be dead!*

Her next words brought his thoughts back to the garden.

"You have gone to significant trouble to gain an opportunity to talk to me. If you give me your soul's word to offer no harm to me or mine, I am willing to grant you privacy for that talk. Can you make that pledge honestly?"

He'd expected her to threaten him, and the lack of it threw him even more off balance. This hadn't turned into the outraged confrontation he'd expected. A chance to talk; she was so old, she must know so much. What if she knew what he really was? Would she tell him? Could he trust her if she did?

"As the One God is my witness, Lady Ymera," he croaked. "I don't want to hurt anybody. Not you, or any of yours. Just, please, Lady, *please . . .* tell me."

She stared at him inscrutably for a moment before she said something in a language he didn't know. The eight men surrounding him drew back their blades, retreated and left the garden. He almost fainted in relief. She pointed to the bench opposite hers. He stumbled to it and dropped onto the hard stone. She made a swift gesture and cast a spell that encircled them both only an arm's length away, arching over their heads as if they we inside a giant soap bubble.

"Now we have privacy," she told him.

He nodded gratitude, not quite trusting his voice to speak. His earlier anger had evaporated like dew in the morning sunlight.

"Welcome to my House, Kirin DiUmbra. I thank you for not damaging any of my guardian spells. Am I correct to assume you could have destroyed them had you wished to do so?"

That heartened him. He raised his chin a little defiantly. "Yes. I could."

Her hand caught his attention and he drew a sharp breath and stared. The delicate little fingers were a veil over something with claws. Fangs in her mouth, claws on her hands.

"Ah. You see more than most, don't you?" She didn't sound surprised. "As do I. Which makes you quite disturbing to contemplate, young man." She stared fixedly at his chest. "Quite disturbing."

Hearing those words from her lips heartened him more. Kirin let his gaze wander over her. His eyes told him he looked at a diminutive Silbari woman with beautiful brown skin, round ears, and flowing chestnut hair, as petite and unthreatening as some pampered merchant princess who had never set foot outside her father's house. His magesight showed the layers of gauzy spells wrapping her, ablaze with all the colors of power.

His Shadow showed him her claws, fangs, lithe strength, and pallor whiter than any Gwythlo.

"What are you?" he blurted out.

Her lips parted in toothy amusement. "Exactly what you think I am, I suspect."

"You don't even look human!"

"Perhaps I'm not, now." She twitched her hands in a dismissive gesture. "I was born like anyone else, longer ago than you can probably imagine, but as I grew I changed. I've learned that most who are born like me don't survive that change. I was uncommonly fortunate. I learned caution early and found a way to be tolerated amidst ordinary people. Thus, I lived, and became what I am now."

A gesture of her hands took in their surroundings, her power and wealth and position, all the things that he didn't have. Resentfully he demanded, "Do you drink babies' blood to live?"

"What a repulsive thought." Her perfect lips shaped a moue of distaste, disturbing when his vision also showed her fangs. "No. I choose to feed much more cleanly than that. There, I've now told you more than any other living being knows about me, though many suspect. My turn. What are *you*?"

"I'm a DiUmbra, an acrobat." He hesitated, and she gave him a sardonic expression that pushed him to put words to the obvious. "I'm a half breed. My mother was Silbari but my father must have been a Gwythlo. I don't remember him; he might have been a merchant that she fell in love with. Or," he swallowed against the humiliation. "A soldier who raped her. She died when I was small and Pieter DiUmbra took me in. Adopted me."

"That's who you are," she said delicately. "Not *what* you are. What are you, mysterious Kirin DiUmbra?"

Her words reminded him of that Duermu fortune teller who had insisted on reading his fortune, many tendays ago and far away. "I don't know," he whispered. "I hoped . . ."

"That I could tell you?"

His throat almost closed on the words and he had to force them out. "Yes. Lady Ymera. Please. I need to know."

She tilted her head, half closed her eyes and gazed at him. Her eyes roved up and down him in a way that would have been lascivious if it weren't so cold. He had to resist the urge to cover his crotch with his hands.

When her spells followed her gaze, he grappled his Shadow and fought it to a standstill, forcing vulnerability on himself. Her magic felt like and unlike a priestess' Diagnosis spell, delicate and yet harsh at the same time. After long moments of that torture she said, "Your aura doesn't taste of demon—and don't ask me how I know, it's not a memory that I am eager to dwell on. You lack the specialized features of someone like me, and you are old enough that you would have developed them by now if you were ever going to do so. Your mage-gift is difficult to see, you are as opaque as one of the utterly untalented. I suspect you have nothing more than magesight, correct?"

He nodded jerkily, not trusting himself to speak. *Not a demon, not a vampire, that's good, very good!*

"Yet a Shadow nests in you. You let me see it at Millago's and I simply thought it a clever illusion. A sign that I've grown too complacent, alas. Now that I realize what it is, I am astonished. I have seen living Shadows before, and always they were rooted to a place. A Shadow rooted in a person is unprecedented."

Unprecedented. It took him a moment to parse out the big word and when he did his hopes sagged. *Not a demon, not a vampire, but maybe still a monster.*

She still studied him. "Do you command that living Shadow?"

"Yes," he whispered. "Most of the time. Sometimes it fights me."

"Do you always win those fights?"

"So far."

She stared at his face unblinking for a long moment, nodded. "Your Shadow ate my feather-fall spell, and the spell holding Dona Keldra's dress together?"

"Yes."

"If you loosed it at me, would it eat my personal spells as well?"

He twitched at her bluntness, forced himself to answer. "I think so. Yes."

"Which could mean my death." She sounded very matter-of-fact about it, but he caught the tension in her voice and saw the way her claws flexed. "As I said, quite disturbing to contemplate."

Hastily he assured her, "I already said I don't want to kill you and I meant it! I don't want to kill anybody! I keep it leashed, I only kill fleas and ticks and vermin like that."

"You know something of restraint. I wonder if . . . yes, let's find out." She made a gathering gesture at the fountain-pool with one hand and held up a shining globe of air as big as his head. "You kill fleas? Here are a few water-fleas. Kill them and show me what you do with their life-force."

He hesitated. Slaying on command always nauseated him. But his instinctive refusal to kill without need stuck in his throat.

"Let me sweeten my request. Show me how you kill fleas, and I'll show you where the souls of the dead go." She tossed the spell toward him like a ball.

Reflex made him catch it and the fragile spell broke in his hands. Three water-fleas clung to his fingers, tiny sparks of life. They weren't doing him any harm, but she had asked him to kill.

They were just fleas.

He nerved himself, focused his Shadow, and slew all three of them. The tiny sparks of life flowed through him and into Darkness.

The way her eyebrows twitched hinted at how much she'd been impressed. "That," she declared evenly, "Is not something I've ever seen before."

Kirin's hopes fell. *She hasn't seen anybody like me. She doesn't know what I am.* "You said you would show me where the souls of the dead go."

"That I can and will do, if you truly want to know."

Kirin closed his eyes as his thoughts raced. *I killed Gerlach while he tortured me, but where did his soul go? What really happened? Am I a soul-eating monster?* He didn't trust himself to speak, only nodded more violently than he'd intended.

She made a gesture of agreement and added, "I warn you, you may not enjoy the experience, and I will hold you to your word. Come."

Her privacy spell winked out as she rose to her feet and beckoned him to follow. She led him into the house through the side door, which led to a hallway and stairs that wound upward two levels. He heard grunting and moaning from the rooms they passed and blushed furiously. It was one thing to hear his kin making love in the family home; listening to strangers somehow felt more shameful. The top level had separate spell-wards and he wrapped himself in his Shadow to walk through them without a ripple.

She glanced at him. "You slip through my defenses as if they weren't there. Even a swordsman with Haroun's Gift wouldn't be able to avoid my warning spells. Have you any idea how terrifying your mobile Shadow is to a mage?"

"No, Lady." He turned the idea over as she led him into a room and through it to a steep narrow stair. He barely noticed the luxurious bed and elaborate lady's dressing table. He found comfort in the thought that he wasn't the only one afraid of his Shadow.

The cupola room shook him out of his abstraction. Hundreds of spells converged upon it from the Street outside. He gazed in awe at the twining skeins of them embedded in the walls, and breathed relief that they didn't extend into the room itself. He doubted his ability to avoid wrecking some of them in the confined space, barely a dozen feet on a side. Then he saw the silver bowl brimming with sparks.

"That—those are—what *are* those?" Kirin demanded, not wanting to believe what his magesight told him.

"What you think they are, I expect," she told him soberly. "The lives of the unborn, or rather, the never-will-be-born, since all of them are now severed beyond hope of reattachment to the flesh that nurtured them. Does that disturb you?"

"Yes!" he answered fervently, backing away from the bowl until his rump pressed against the wall. His Shadow surged restlessly in his mind's grip and one corner of a windowsill jabbed him in the buttock.

She scooped up a double handful of sparks and looked at him over it. "You are about to see what I have rarely allowed another living being to see. It is necessary in order to show you what you want to know. I will not be surprised if you are repulsed by my actions; but listen to my words."

PETER SARTUCCI

He stared in horrified fascination as she raised hands to her lips and spoke to the tiny sparks.

"For me to live, you must die. I do not ask your pardon."

Then she drank them all down, her long white throat moving in delicate gulps. The light of those tiny sparks merged with her own and her power brightened.

His first thought gasped, *She really does kill to live!* Followed by: *But she's so neat about it.* And by, *is that what I do to fleas? Eat their lives?* His empty stomach roiled in queasy affirmation and he had to stop his Shadow from eating a spell in the wall behind him.

Then she exhaled, and he saw the fine mist of gray souls. Saw the tenderness with which she bound them together. The sharp honesty of it slapped him like a cold wind off the mountains. *Monster, but . . . not* only *a monster.*

He panted several breaths, fighting queasiness and his Shadow together, until his garbled thoughts settled and left one thought uppermost. *Maybe I don't have to* be *a monster even if I* am *one.*

He tried to exhale the memory of Gerlach and knew bitter disappointment when nothing happened.

She looked at him thoughtfully while the swarm of souls hovered before her. "Now you have seen me feed. Does it illuminate your own ability?"

"Yes. No. Maybe." He struggled through his confusion to shape a question. "After I killed the fleas, did I glow like you do?"

"No. You remained quite opaque. You still are; one might easily mistake you for an ordinary blank human with no talent. Whatever you did with those tiny life-forces is not evident. Tell me, what sensations did you know when you slew them?"

"Like all the other times I've killed vermin," he answered slowly. "Like I'm a tunnel and their lives move through me and away. Only my Shadow lives in that tunnel and it *takes* from them as they pass. Like a robber in an alley. And when they've passed on, they leave behind a taste." He resisted the temptation to spit in the clean little room and swallowed instead. "I've never liked it."

"I can imagine that a diet of fleas does not appeal to one's palette." Her lips shaped that delicate moue again. "Ticks too?"

"And bedbugs," he added morosely. "I hate them worst of all. Well, I guess they're not the worst. Once I killed a pigeon by accident and it took a whole bowl of spicy lentils to get rid of the taste. Worse than if I'd eaten the cursed thing raw."

He remembered the taste of Gerlach's life. No spices could drown that out.

"You perceive these lives as moving through you and into that Shadow of yours." She watched him thoughtfully over the swirling cloud of gray souls. "You don't gain any of their power for your own use?"

"Nooooo." He hesitated, thinking of Gerlach. "No. It goes into my Shadow, and it's gone."

176

"Do you dream about them afterward?"

"Not . . . the fleas. Or the ticks and bedbugs." He made himself ask. "Do you?"

"Yes. The more life-experience a soul has, the stronger the dreams." She contemplated the cloud of gray souls. "And the opposite as well. I suspect the normal fate of my kind is to go mad from the dreams, at least for those who feed on adult lives. The memories must be overwhelming. But the unborn do not have memories, so the dreams they induce are shallow things. My particular, very narrow role in human society seems to have saved me from that fate."

"You get life and power without danger?" Acid envy touched him.

"You mean, other than the not-inconsiderable danger that your Hierarchy might burn me in the public square?"

Kirin flinched. *They might do that to me too!* For a moment the old fear stirred in his heart, but her words in the garden came back to him. *She said I'm not a demon, and she must know.* He found a strange sort of relief in being told by a monster that he wasn't a demon and believing her.

She still watched him in that thoughtful way; now she gave him a tiny nod. "There is also a responsibility, which I will show you."

She folded back the wooden louvers covering the north window. He noticed that they were mounted on clever bronze hinges; he moved two steps closer to see what she did. That also got his hungry Shadow away from its persistent straining for the spell-filled walls. She reached over her head with one clawed fingertip to touch the top of the window frame. When she drew her finger downward in a smooth slashing line, the air split open.

Beyond the windowsill an unbelievable vastness gaped ahead and down. His Shadow abruptly reversed its reaching for the spell-wrapped walls and lunged for the hole she'd torn. He stopped it inside his chest but had to take two steps toward the opening before he caught his balance again. The windowsill, weirdly bent and stretched, lay close enough that he could see over it.

He had never known vertigo in his life, but he knew it now. His heart beat faster as he stared into the vastness below. His lungs heaved as if some mage had taken away half the air. Streams of gray wraiths advanced from all sides, some from right under the room, to pour over slick cliffs red as blood. They plunged into a vast dim crimson well that went down, down, and yet still down for an impossible distance.

"What *is* it?" he gasped.

"A portal looking into the Well of the World." She answered him matter-of-factly.

He found in her voice an anchor for his reeling senses. "And those gray things?"

"Wraiths. Severed souls of dead people, hastening towards judgement like your Silbari Holy Writ claims. Down there lies Hell."

"And the door into Heaven." He added that by rote; if the priestesses were right, he looked on the place toward which his life's journey had always been bound. It terrified and fascinated and he couldn't look away from it, until she shepherded her fog of tiny souls through the opening. He tore his gaze from the Well to watch the gray mist pour down into the rushing flood. The surging dead absorbed the unborn lives with barely a ripple.

"What happens to them?" He found that he deeply wanted to know, like an awakened itch inside his chest that he couldn't scratch. His Shadow still surged and strained to reach for the portal, pushing him right to its edge.

"Careful! Flesh cannot safely pass through, and the portal might sever your soul from your body. You could find your answer in a very personal and permanent way." She twitched her shoulders in an elegant gesture. "Indeed, I expect that the only way to truly know would be to follow the dead into Hell, which I decline to do today, thank you very much. But if the Writ is accurate, they go to judgement, after which some will pass on to Heaven and some will not."

"You mean babies might have to stay in Hell?" That thought shook his unthinking faith in the certainties of his world. *Will I? Am I damned to spend the rest of eternity in the Pit like the priestesses say she will?*

"Or perhaps be sent back to life, reborn into new bodies for a second chance." An acid tone crept into her voice. "I have listened to learned theologians of the Writ expound on this subject and I don't believe that they know any more than I do."

"But why? How can—" Words failed him, and he struggled in an internal storm of confusion. *Did Gerlach's soul go down there?* Aloud, he demanded, "Do all souls go into Hell?"

Her lips twitched. "You are asking me? How would I know? I only see these few that pass while I have opened the skin of the world. I cannot maintain this portal for long."

Already the sides had begun to shrink inward. She began to sweep her hand upward from the windowsill, reversing the motion that had opened this window into the abyss.

Kirin seized the edge with his bare hands and tried to hold it open. "Wait! I need to know!"

The portal distorted, one side shrinking in while he tugged the other wider. Black wisps of Shadow wrapped his hands as if it too sought to stop this entrance to Hell from closing. The little room shuddered. Dust puffed from the walls.

"Stop!"

Her command was so strong that he let go of the edge. The portal snapped shut with an audible smack like giant lips, but now a faint gray line ran across the window, a wound in the Skin of the World. He clenched his hands into frustrated fists. Beyond the window frame lay only the roof of her house and the dark night. Inside his chest his Shadow shrank into a hard, sulky ball.

She had recoiled from him. "You are both the bravest and most foolish youth I've ever met, Kirin DiUmbra. I am astonished that you still have your fingers, or for that matter, your life. That portal cuts like a knife."

He looked at his hands, hard and callused from trapeze-work. They looked no different than usual. The edge of the portal had been as slippery as a live fish and twice as cold. Not like a knife at all. But she knew far more of these things than he did. Had he had a narrow escape from death? A shudder ran up his spine. Cascading souls . . .

"I need to know," he said, and the words seemed pale and limp compared to his burning desire. The good manners that Carmella and Grandmother had drilled into him reasserted themselves, and he added contritely, "I'm sorry if I broke your spell, Lady."

She half-lidded her eyes and he saw her veil of spells rearrange itself and settle back. "Damaged, but not broken. It will require repair before I use it again. You badly need training in the use of your abilities, young man, else you may leave more wreckage in your wake than you can imagine."

He remembered Mother Gee's words. She thought he needed a protector, but he saw now that she had the wrong solution to his problem. *I don't need protection. I need knowledge.* "Lady Ymera. Will you teach me?"

She shook her head. "I dare not. When the magic users of this city truly understand what you are, there will be a collective outcry of horror. I live on sufferance as it is. I will not risk being the target of such fear and outrage. You need a powerful mentor, and it cannot be me."

His head bowed at her rejection, but before he could say anything she spoke again.

"I will send you to the Royal Wizard."

* * *

From her cupola Ymera watched him leave. Her guard captain punctiliously returned the boy's knife at her front gate, with a flourish of courtesy that Kirin seemed to appreciate. The boy stood a little taller as he walked away into her street.

Men and their weapons. Her lips twisted in a wry grimace.

The guard-captain's formality told her something important. She had hired and promoted him because he'd proven to be a perceptive man not easily fooled by deceits, magical or otherwise. *He senses very real danger in the boy and chooses to fend it off with formality and courtesy. Wary of that which he does not understand, and suspects could be mightier than himself. Hopefully young Kirin DiUmbra will not carry any resentment of me or mine away with him tonight.*

She hugged her arms across her chest for a moment, trembling with the release of tension. *I took a monstrous risk. I knew it, but even I didn't understand how great a risk. Should I have tried to kill him while he opened himself to me? And what would I have done if I failed? Probably he would have killed me, perhaps without even meaning to do so.* She shuddered at the thought, feeling death brush her like a moth's wing. *Sometimes the only path to safety is to take a great risk.* She turned back to her tattered gate spell and began repairs.

PETER SARTUCCI

He put his hands beneath the Skin of the World and drew them back whole. He nearly tore my gate open while doing so. What manner of nightmare is he?

* * *

"The Royal Wizard?" Grandfather repeated, staring bug-eyed at Kirin.

Kirin shifted on his stool uncomfortably. The leaders of the family were gathered with him and Maia in the DiUmbra's tiny dining room. Most of them were looking at him like he'd grown two heads.

Sevan's stare turned envious. "You sneak into the Witch-Queen's own garden, and instead of frying your ass, she asks Magister Chisaad to teach you? Kirin, that's like falling in a dung-heap and coming up with a gold brick."

Pieter looked worried. "They are two of the most powerful people in the City. Mixing with folk on that level is dangerous for people like us. I wish you hadn't gone there, son."

Maia, who had been clutching Kirin's arm ever since he got home, nodded her head vigorously. For a moment Kirin felt abashed at the way he'd snuck out without telling her. His mind still struggled to think through the night's events.

Sevan the Elder looked thoughtful. "What's done is done, Pieter. I'm worried too; but think of the possibilities. We've known for years that Kirin has an unusual talent. After the recent unfortunate events," he cleared his throat and Kirin cringed as Grandfather's stare sharpened into a glare. "It's obvious he needs training in how to control it. There could hardly be a better trainer in the whole city than the Royal Wizard."

Pieter's frown sank into a general unhappy look and he didn't disagree.

"This family badly needs a patron," Grandmother pointed out. "We need a connection to somebody rich and powerful if we're going to keep eating. Kirin needs training to use his magic safely. If the Royal Wizard consents to take him on, that gets us two-thirds of the way to where this family needs to be. Where else is Kirin going to learn what he needs to learn?"

Grandfather's gaze changed to a calculating one and he nodded decisively. "Yes. This really might be the gold brick in the dung heap. But only if the wizard takes him on for free. We can't possibly pay for apprentice-level training. We'll have to hope Kirin can interest the wizard enough to make him a charity case. Can you do that, boy?"

Kirin gulped. Grandfather looking at him with hope was a new thing. He rallied. "I'll find a way, Grandfather."

Pieter sighed and capitulated. "My prayers go with you, son. But be careful."

Relieved, Kirin smiled as he patted Maia's hand. "I will, father. I will."

* * *

The Wizard's tower loomed fortress-like over the surrounding houses. From the sumptuous front courtyard Kirin saw crows perched on its slate roof. More of the scavenger birds wheeled and soared like inkblots splashed across the morning sky.

Their flights were as agitated as his stomach. Two hours past dawn, he stood here freshly bathed wearing his best tunic and hose. He stared at the Wizard's front door.

I'm stalling. He forced himself to walk across the geometric patterns of the courtyard to the imposing entry. He pushed his Shadow into its cage under his heart before he gingerly lifted the ensorcelled doorknocker. When he slammed the knob down on its brass inset, the sound echoed through the house and sank into his bones.

The door opened. A tall grave-faced man wreathed in spells stared down at him. Kirin gulped and tried to stand straighter as he recognized the Royal Wizard from that disastrous night at Millago's house.

"Kirin Sule DiUmbra," Wizard Chisaad said to him in a smooth voice. "Welcome to my house."

CHAPTER 21: TERRELL

Ninth petition," the Clerk of the Queen's Court announced with rigid formality. His voice was only slightly leavened by the anxiety in the glance he gave Terrell, who as Governor substituted for his absent mother. The clerk knew poison when he read it on a scroll. "An appeal originally submitted by Sir Gellir DuRicci DiSolera, formerly Duke of Lonigo, now amended and consolidated to include appeals from three other former nobles or their heirs."

Terrell resisted the temptation to roll his eyes as the clerk read a list of names. Each man stood forward when identified; a former duke and three former barons or baronial heirs, all dispossessed by the conquering Gwythlo Empire. In the waiting audience four Gwythlo nobles pressed against the edge of the petitioner's dais. Terrell recognized the current Duke of Lonigo, Rhet Cadigan, among them. The clerk continued reading.

"The undersigned come before the court of Her Majesty seeking redress of wrongs—"

"I've read the petition," Terrell interrupted. "Twice. Skip to the requested action."

The clerk hastily unrolled the heavy parchment to the end and read, "That they be restored to possession of their proper rights, titles, benefices, privileges, and duties, by the order of Her Majesty and the grace of the One God."

Terrell rubbed his brow for a moment and sighed. "Sir DiSolera, step forth."

The senior petitioner proved to be a florid, gray-haired man with a proud bearing and expensive clothing stretched over a belly that didn't look like he'd ever missed any meals. His haughty face creased into a permanent scowl. He bowed with an antique flourish and murmured "Your Highness," before he stared at Terrell with dark eyes lit by a demanding hope.

Terrell regarded him without favor, aware that the man was his third cousin and thus close enough to be one of the Twenty candidates. "Sir DiSolera. You and your fellow petitioners would have me, by simple fiat, undo the consequences of the Gwythlo Conquest and return you to the seats from which you were deposed by my father. Or in the cases of Sir DiNivir and Goodman DiBrollino, to grant them baronies of which they are the closest heirs of the previous Baron. Correct?"

DiSolera, DiVaragga and DiBrollino had the mother-wit to simply nod their heads respectfully and affirm his words. DiNivir expounded on his written argument. Terrell cut him off with a polite, "A simple 'yes' will do, my lord."

DiNivir choked off his voluble flow and managed the one word. In the audience the four Gwythlo nobles glared at the petitioners but waited for their turns.

"You four cite your hereditary rights and your family's suffering and shame as reasons that I should support your request, but you provide no other arguments. I give you opportunity to amend your petition. For example, do you, Sir DiSolera, claim that Lonigo is badly governed by the present Duke?" Terrell opened his right hand in the direction of Cadigan, who stared haughtily at DiSolera.

DiSolera glanced at the Gwythlo with a sneer that made his ample jowls quiver. "I do, Your Highness. He has broken traditions stretching back centuries, dispossessed loyal knights who followed my family for generations and given their fiefs to his own creatures, allowed rampant disrespect for proper social order, and worst of all, permitted foul northern Druids to establish a fane within the city walls!"

DiSolera offered more, but Terrell soon extracted the salient point. It seemed that the one manor the former Duke still retained turned out to be inadequate to support him in the style to which he had once been accustomed. When DiSolera took a breath before launching additional embroidery on this theme, Terrell stopped him.

"In keeping with tradition, His Grace the present Duke of Lonigo shall now have an opportunity to speak." Terrell gestured the man forward and Cadigan practically leaped onto the respondent's dais.

"Your Highness, officers of the court, and Sir DiSolera." In Cadigan's mouth the last name dripped contempt. "The petitioner's words do but affirm that I have served the crown, and the Empire of which it is a part, more than well! I established my own military control of the duchy, permitted trade to flourish by eliminating monopolies and fees that fattened his favored parasites instead of enabling commerce, and granted the same freedom of worship that has long been allowed in Aretzo. Sir DiSolera has surely noticed that foreign traders have been permitted to establish their own houses of faith here in this city since Your Highness' four-times-great grandfather's day."

DiSolera glared back and prepared to launch a blistering response when Terrell stopped him again, this time with a raised hand, and gestured to his Treasurer. The official read off a prepared list of annual tax payments from Lonigo to the crown that stretched back to before the Conquest. DiSolera's expression grew noticeably more choleric while the numbers grew smaller as the dates stretched farther back in time. Cadigan let a modest smile grow on his face.

"Whatever other results may have come from the present rule," the Treasurer noted, "His Grace's contributions to the realm's coffers are a third higher than those in the years before the Conquest. The Lord Justicar also reports that Lonigo's dungeons are less than half as full as they were under the previous regime."

Terrell gestured invitingly to the clerical priestess waiting by the Treasurer's side. She stated in a clear voice, "The Lonigo Temple's almshouse reports that the city's people are better fed and more prosperous than they were twenty years ago. Their contributions to the Faith have also grown, enough that the Lonigo Autarch has commissioned a new bell tower to replace the unsound one that presently graces, or threatens, her Temple." She turned a sharp smile on Duke Cadigan. "While the Hierarchy does not of course approve of the license granted to that alien faith, attendance at Temple does not seem to have suffered from the presence of a Druidical fane in the city. Indeed, the contrast of those unsavory practices may have helped strengthen the people's loyalty to the true faith."

Terrell thought Cadigan did not seem disturbed by this observation. *There might be truth in the rumor that his wife has been secretly attending Silbari religious services.*

"But cousin!" DiSolera appealed. "He turned my knights out of their lands! Forty of them have been forced to enlist in the army as simple foot-soldiers, unable to afford horses any more. Without land to support followers, they cannot even bring a single man-at-arms to your service!" Belatedly it occurred to him that presuming on their kinship might not be a good idea, and added, "Your Highness."

Terrell, aware that much of the Silbari brigade had been built out of such dispossessed men, decided to ignore the presumption. He turned an enquiring look on Cadigan.

"I had to be sure that the landed knights of the duchy would serve me and not him," Cadigan acknowledged. "Ten of his fifty knights gave me their oaths, the rest I replaced with a mix of ambitious Silbari men and second sons from my brother's Gwythlo estates. More than half of those men married kin of the dispossessed knights, adopted Silbari ways, and have raised their children to be as Silbari as Your Highness might wish."

DiSolera glanced at Terrell's yellow hair and away, recognizing the double-edged blade in Cadigan's comment. A half-blood Prince wasn't likely to consider it a bad thing in knights or nobles. "Such dispossession remains a shocking betrayal of generations of loyal service, Your Highness. What man anywhere in Silbar can feel safe in his lands and titles, knowing they can be so readily torn away from him despite his loyalty?"

"They were loyal to you, not to me," Cadigan pointed out. "I had to assure the loyalty of the Duchy's people for myself."

Terrell glanced at the petitioner and remarked, "My lord DiSolera, you ask me to do to Duke Cadigan and his knights what he did to yours, and without the justification of a freshly-lost war. That would add a new injustice to an old one and lay a new wound over an eighteen-year-old scar that seems to have largely healed."

DiSolera glowered, his wounded pride a long way from healing. "Is the age of an injustice a license to allow it, Your Highness?"

Terrell chose not to address that point yet and turned his gaze on the other three. "Have any of you anything to strengthen your claims? What about you, DiNivir?"

The thin noble cleared his throat and launched into a lengthy recitation of grievances, most of them wounds to his personal vanity and finances. Terrell let him run long enough that even DiSolera looked bored before he cut the man off. "Enough, my lord. I offered you the opportunity to present evidence, or even claims, that your uncle's former barony is badly managed. You have presented nothing of the sort. I grant you one last chance."

DiNivir looked at the smiling Gwythlo baron who had displaced him, looked at the Royal Treasurer standing ready with papers in hand, looked at the priestess, then shut his mouth and shook his head.

Terrell turned to the last two petitioners and opened a hand suggestively. "Sir DiVaragga? Goodman DiBrollino? Have either of you anything of substance to add?"

DiVaragga frowned thunderously but shook his head, unhappy and aware that he had already lost.

DiBrollino smiled wryly and said, "I could cite my successes in trade over the last decade, Your Highness, and my demonstrable contributions to civic repair in the funding I provided for the new roof on Aretzo's South Gate. But I suspect that you would take those as indications that I am better suited to remain where I am than to add a muddy barony on the shores of Purification Lake to my holdings."

Baron Rhys of Bontemna looked insulted at this description of his barony, a third of which lay under the lake during flood season. Terrell interjected before Rhys could protest.

"I see. If it is a title that you covet, Goodman DiBrollino, I might be willing at some point in the future to consider other alternatives. Alternatives that do not dispossess someone who has been faithfully performing their duties to the crown, for which loyalty and service I am duly grateful."

Baron Rhys settled down at this praise and reassurance. The other three Gwythlo lords also looked mollified; DiVarraga looked calculating and DiSolera simply looked furious.

"Your Highness is most kind," DiBrollino said. "But that is a matter for the future. Today I withdraw my name from this petition." He bowed and stepped off the petitioner's dais, disassociating himself from the other three. DiSolera and DiNivir gave him angry looks.

Terrell looked sternly at the three remaining petitioners. "I conclude that your requested outcome is not desirable for the realm. Such an act would embolden a dozen other claimants and sow discord the length and breadth of Silbar. That I will not permit. The Conquest cannot be undone, by my word or by that of any man. While I rule, whether as Crown-chosen or as Governor on behalf of my mother the Queen, my eyes will remain fixed on Silbar's future, and not chained to its past."

"Do justice and kinship mean nothing to you, Your Highness?" DiSolera snapped.

"Duty means more, my lord." Terrell held the older man's gaze until it dropped. More softly he added, "I note that all of you have other paths open before you, such as investing in trade as DiBrollino has, or partnering in the new mage workshops that have produced much wealth over the last decade. DiNivir, I understand that your younger son is actively managing several such investments and has forged a profitable alliance with a significant merchant house."

DiNivir's face reddened to the color of mahogany. "You need not rub my face in the actions of my offspring, Your Highness." The man's nostrils flared but he choked off further words and simply glared at the four smiling Gwythlo lords on the other dais.

Aha, Terrell thought. *He sees his son's marriage to a merchant heiress as shameful, even though it rescued the DiNivir family from destitution. Dinner with his in-laws must be a tense affair. I'd better try to guide the son's ambitions away from the father's brooding.*

"The choice is yours, my lords," Terrell told the three. "This matter is dismissed without action. I will not entertain any such petitions again unless they come with allegations of substance, such as a gross dereliction of duty or an outright violation of Silbari Law. You may all depart."

Terrell carefully ignored the grumbling at the door as all eight men crowded through.

"Nicely handled," Pen said quietly. "Any more of these hot coals tossed into your lap today?"

"That's the last, thank the One!" Terrell sighed. "But those fires aren't quenched, merely dampened. I'm sure DiSolera, at least, will find a new way to cause mischief, and eventually I must face him atop the Hill of Sight during the Choosing."

He stood and stretched. "Now for a sadder duty. We have a funeral to attend."

* * *

Hours later the soft breeze atop the Hill of Sight stirred Terrell's yellow curls. He breathed deeply of its scents as he topped the final tread of the Five Hundred Steps. Flowers on the grassy slopes, smoke and manure from the city below, and the salty odors of the sea beyond. The funerary urn seemed far heavier than its size warranted.

It's the weight on my heart that I feel. Shimoor, Shimoor, I already miss you dreadfully.

Pen had offered to carry it, and accepted Terrell's refusal without comment.

Dona Seraphina alighted from her carry-chair. The tasseled ends of her black and pink stole fluttered in the wind as she joined Terrell, Pen, and the Royal Wizard. Terrell looked around the gleaming marble space atop the Hill.

"Is there a traditional place?"

"Downwind?" suggested Pen helpfully. Dona Seraphina gave him a dry look.

Wizard Chisaad cleared his throat after a quick gasp for breath and said, "Baron Penghar is correct, Your Highness. It is traditional to distribute ashes off the north side, which on most mornings is downwind. It is also the side visible from the cemetery, where many of your people have gathered to watch."

"Thank you." Terrell carried the urn to the opening between the first and second bollards, set it on the seat that would be his on Choosing Day, and pried off the cap. He hefted the urn again and stepped to the edge of the platform beside Seraphina. Chisaad adjusted a voice-amplification spell and nodded to her. She began the traditional ceremony for dispersing ashes. Her voice carried all the way down the Hill to ring across the crowd gathered in the cemetery.

Terrell tried and failed to prevent his mind from wandering. The Hierarch had conducted Shimoor's actual funeral in the Mother Temple three hours ago, after which Chisaad and the entire Council of Colors had overseen the magical cremation of the former Royal Wizard's cast-aside and preparation of his ashes for this dispersal. The urn was still warm in Terrell's hands even though they had cast chilling spells on the carefully-ground ashes before loading them into it. Terrell hoped no bit of bone or scrap of tooth had escaped their grinding spells to bounce embarrassingly down the Hill. He looked toward the waiting people and waited his own turn.

The Hill fell away below him in a long smooth slope starred with black-and-pink blossoms. *Black and pink,* he thought. *The colors of death and rebirth.*

Dona Seraphina finished the standard oration and a murmur of anticipation went through the waiting crowd as she turned to him. Terrell cleared his throat and nodded slightly to Chisaad, who switched the amplification spell to him. Terrell's lips and throat tingled slightly as the spell settled and he began to speak.

He commenced with a recitation of Shimoor's humble beginnings in the Old City, spoke briefly of his rise through the ranks of the Mage Guild, lingered over his long service to the Silbari Throne, and delved into his own training and teaching at the old mage's hands. By the time he reached his final lines emotion tightened his voice.

"May you go to your promised rebirth, Shimoor," He prayed aloud. "As sure as the suns rise in majesty every morning, the Door to Heaven will open for you."

He tilted the urn forward and a fine shower of gray ash flowed out. The breeze took it, spread it into a long plume that flowed a hundred feet down the hillside before it settled into the grass and flowers. He poured until the urn was empty, shook it to send the last fleck downwind with his prayers. Below, the thousands gathered in the vast cemetery and along the roadside, on the towers and parapets of the Gray Fort, and in the windows of the Red Street, watched in silence as the ash plume slowly settled and vanished. A long sigh floated up from the multitude, followed by the murmur of prayers. Shimoor had never forgotten his roots among the folk of Aretzo, who counted him as one of their own.

And now he has the final and supreme honor of having his ashes spread on the Hill of Sight with the Kings and Queens of old, Terrell thought.

That cannot help but please the common people. Even after death, my teacher, you still help me. May Father Haroun and Mother Umana carry your soul to the One.

Chisaad shifted the amplification spell back to Seraphina, who gave the closing prayer and benediction, and it was done. Seraphina boarded her carry chair and headed back to the Palace while Chisaad carefully folded up the spell. Terrell consented to let a servant carry the empty urn. He paused at the top of the Five Hundred Steps to gaze over the Palace and the city. Chisaad stopped beside him and Pen waited behind them both while, at a slight gesture from Terrell, the servants went on ahead to escort Seraphina.

"I am minded to appoint you Royal Wizard in full," Terrell said to the mage. "Would that please you?"

Chisaad hesitated, even quieter today than usual. "Once I would have loved few things more," he slowly answered, his eyes squinting against the sun's light. "That form of acceptance and status used to loom large to me, in my younger days. Yet I have functioned for more than eighteen years with the title *Acting*, and now I find it to be a light burden. One that I can readily bear for a little longer, if it please you, Your Highness."

"It is no dishonor to Shimoor for me to speedily promote his pupil to fill his title," Terrell pointed out. "And I need a Royal Wizard."

"You already have one, who has borne the burden for many years," Chisaad answered. "And you face a momentous choice before the summer is over, as Shimoor warned you after I warned him. Mage Blue and the Council of Colors are readying their petition to reallocate the Aretzo Node between mages and priestesses. He will submit it within the next few tendays. I am told that the Council has secured more than twelve thousand signatures of Aretzo mages, including every Magister-level mage in the city who does not serve the Hierarchy."

Terrell twisted his lips in acknowledgement. "Yes, the gossip is everywhere. I'm certain the Hierarch is preparing a counter-petition." *Haroun help me. I need her support, but I need the Mage Council's support too. This is going to be much more challenging than a handful of whiney dispossessed aristocrats!*

"Therein lays the problem, Your Highness," Chisaad said apologetically. "I will be supporting the Council, indeed leading its effort, as she surely must expect. To promote me immediately before such a struggle is joined will be seen as declaring favor for the Mages before you have judged their petition." With delicate understatement he added, "The Hierarchy will not be pleased by that."

"But there isn't any doubt that you deserve the title!" Terrell protested. "Every mage I have consulted agrees on that, including the few who've been at odds with you in the past. The priestesses too. Dona Seraphina is very favorably impressed by your record of working with the Hierarch's appointees to the Palace."

Chisaad made a gesture of polite disagreement. "What I do or do not deserve is not the issue here, Your Highness. The issue is avoiding a breach with the Hierarch early in your reign."

Terrell snorted. "I could do that simply by siding with her and rejecting Blue's petition."

"Which I doubt you will do, because he has powerful arguments on his side," Chisaad replied calmly. "The priestesses are unquestionably less efficient in their use of the Node than are the mages. Every priestess in this city has a personal allocation of power that is more than half again as much as the share granted to each mage. Some of the Hierarchy exceed their limits repeatedly, which would lead to sanction and even punishment if they were mages. Instead they are barely even chastised. This wastefulness means that less work may be done by the mages, which produces less wealth, which limits the Crown's revenue from trade and taxation. That is why I have chosen to support the Council on this matter."

He didn't mention how helpful the extra revenue would be towards the tribute I have to start paying to Osrick, Terrell thought. *Tactful.*

"I see your point." He sighed regretfully. "Better a victory of substance, with as few ruffled feathers as possible, than one merely of symbolism."

"Exactly, Your Highness." Chisaad smiled wistfully. "I can hear Shimoor's teachings in your words."

For a moment they stood there, each mulling over bittersweet memories. *What would Shimoor suggest if he were here?* Terrell wondered. *He'd say don't deceive yourself, strategy must always triumph over tactics. I play for the long term, as Chisaad knows I must, and so he signals that he, too, is prepared to wait. Ahh, Shimoor, this will be much harder without you, but at least I have the loyalty of your best pupil.*

Pen shifted uncomfortably as Irreneetha hummed a lamenting descant to the murmur of the departing crowd below, then settled back to his watchful waiting.

Terrell shook off his sorrow and spoke briskly. "Very well. We'll leave you in your comfortable limbo for a season longer, until Blue's petition is settled. I shall revisit the issue after the Hierarch's feathers are smooth again."

"I can wait," Chisaad said blandly. "I have ample work to occupy my days."

CHAPTER 22: CHISAAD

C hisaad breathed a quiet sigh of relief when the prickly watchful sensation emanating from Sir Penghar's soulsword passed down a side corridor and beyond range. He shut himself into his office where, for a while, he could relax the fierce discipline over his thoughts required to deceive her.

I must separate him and his damnable sword from the Prince if this is to work, he thought. *But how to do it?*

A soft knock on the door announced Ap Marn, who slipped inside and shut the door quickly. Without a word Chisaad led him into the inner office, secured the privacy spells, and sank into a chair. His knees were aching from climbing the Hill for the third time in six days.

"We have got to do something about that damned bodyguard," the ex-governor snarled. He slammed a fist into his opposite palm. "His cursed sword puts my back up."

"Yes." Chisaad stroked his close-trimmed beard, thinking. "The latest message from Gwythford Castle indicates that our queen won't last another forty days. You need to provide the Prince with a sufficiently strong incentive that he'll willingly send his most trusted servant away on a task that will occupy him for at least four or five tendays."

"What are you talking about?" Ap Marn scowled at him.

"We both know why he's keeping you here by his side." Chisaad stared boldly into the other man's eyes. "He's collecting evidence of your peculation to use against you. When he's satisfied that he's got enough, he'll try and convict you and strip you of every asset he can. Your ill-gotten wealth would go a long way toward that tribute he'll eventually have to pay Osrick."

Ap Marn flushed an angry red but didn't deny the truth. "I can't leave. He's made sure the Gwythlo garrison officers all know he has been given direct command over them by the Emperor. Not a one of the sodding sons-of-bitches will take a risk for me. And between the Harbor Wizards and the Navy he's got the sea-routes in his pocket."

"If you do nothing, he'll snare you in webs of evidence at his leisure and ship you off to Osrick in chains," Chisaad agreed. "I suggest, My Lord, that we need to start taking some risks. You need to enable that Treasurer of his to find enough evidence that he can trace part of the stolen sulfur to your tools in Sulmona."

Ap Marn went pale. "What good would that do?"

"The sulfur pits don't draw as much attention as the silver mines, but they still represent a sizable part of the Crown's revenue," Chisaad pointed out. "Prince Terrell must plan to sort them out sooner or later but for the immediate future he dares not leave the city, not with the Mage Guild about to pick a fight with the Hierarchy. If he feels pressured to deal with them sooner—"

"He'll send DiLione." Ap Marn nodded. "But even after we sideline him and his sword, there's still all the bureaucracy and guards loyal to him and his bitch of a mother. It makes me sick the way that whoreson Fantillin fawns over him! And there's this damned Palace too, with all its spells." He looked at the walls without favor and lowered his voice. "The Gods only know what tricks he can make it do for him."

"I can deal with those." Chisaad gave him a chilly smile. "If you get Di-Lione out of here for long enough, I've been working on some special tools to handle the magic side of our problems. But timing is crucial. DiLione must be in Sulmona before the Queen dies, and must not return until after the Choosing."

Ap Marn studied him for a moment. "And what happens when the Queen dies? Is this Silbari ritual really so damned important?"

"Yes," Chisaad answered, with a profound understatement that he knew the foreigner would not understand. "Handled right, you'll be Governor in fact if not in name, because we'll have a weak King that we can manipulate. Give new Emperor Osrick a few years to establish his control over the Empire before you remind him how you kept the silver flowing and Silbar stayed peaceful. He won't care how you got your money. And by then I'll have raised the Mage Guild to primacy over the Hierarchy, and thereby have won my heart's desire too."

Ap Marn shrugged. "I'll take your word for it. If we don't pull this off, I'm dead anyway." He glanced at Chisaad's face through half-lidded eyes. "And you after me."

Chisaad smiled. "It appears that we understand each other. Good."

He managed to get Ap Marn gone swiftly, afterwards leaned against the inside of his inner sanctum's door, thinking.

He's not the best of tools, but he is competent. This will take a bit of finesse and some courage on his part. It will be a good test for what must come after . . .

CHAPTER 23: KIRIN AND CHISAAD

You've been spending more and more time with that wizard in the last few tendays," Maia told Kirin, shifting her swollen belly uncomfortably while she trimmed Pieter's hair and beard. She looked more than twenty-four tendays pregnant. "It worries me."

"Worries? Love, there's really nothing to be worried about," Kirin assured her as he took his good hose off the drying line and pulled them on. "I know I said I was a little suspicious of him at first, and sure he's not the kind of man I can invite home for beer and fish stew. But he's been honorable and straight with me on everything."

Pieter looked thoughtful. "You told me about those tests he set for you. It's pretty clear you don't have any spellcasting abilities at all."

Kirin winced as he pulled his tunic on over his head, remembering how badly that had gone. His Shadow had eaten every bite of power in the sulfur he'd tried to use to make beginner-level castings. It had also gulped down the spells powering two of the small artifacts that Chisaad had tested him on. Worse yet, when Kirin got too close to the wizard's cleaning golem, his Shadow had devoured the spell animating the ugly thing's longest arm.

That had been so embarrassing that the memory still made him cringe. For a moment Kirin had thought his new teacher would explode in outrage. The Wizard had flushed red as a beet and his eyes opened so wide Kirin had been able to see whites all the way around.

Chisaad had slowly exhaled a long breath and said, "We both must bear this in mind, Kirin. Your ability, undisciplined, can be severely damaging to property and thus, potentially, to people. You have a duty to develop unfailing control over it."

Kirin knew his error had to have cost the Royal Wizard a pile of charged silver, or whatever powered the weird thing. He still knew a pang of shame every time he saw the cleaning golem, or the more human-shaped one that washed the Wizard's dishes and clothes.

"That's sure the truth, Father," he agreed morosely with Pieter.

"But you can drain or destroy spells cast by others," Pieter continued. "You said he is teaching you how to be more skilled at that?"

Kirin nodded as he laced his tunic closed. "The last ten days he had me pick one spell from a bunch and take only that one out."

"How do you do that?" Maia asked, touching up the edge on the hair-shears with a whetstone. "Do you sit at a table and poke at spells with your fingers?"

"He had me do it that way at first, but I got really bored. I couldn't stand sitting still for hours, and by now I'd be getting flabby from not moving enough." Kirin grinned. "Instead he's been finding ways to make it more fun."

Outside a temple bell began to ring the hour. He hastily straightened his tunic. "Got to go, love." He kissed her goodbye and ran out of the family's quarters in happy anticipation.

* * *

Two hours later Kirin eeled through layered spells in a controlled lunge and dodged between three zigzagged pillars flaming with even more spells. His heart pounded with the excitement of a bold trapeze move. Some of these spells carried stinging sparks or disgusting odors if he set them off.

I'm doing this! he silently exulted. His Shadow surged and struggled inside his chest as he denied it one tasty spell after another.

He glided under a bar hanging from threads without jostling the glass fishermen's floats balanced atop it, crab-crawled through a narrow tunnel with mere finger widths of clearance on either side. White and red itching spells rippled over him without effect. At the tunnel's far end he leaped high, grabbed the first of five rings embedded in the ceiling and swung to the next without touching the floor. Each ring anchored a different spell; none reacted to his passage. After the last he dropped onto a beam barely half as wide as his own feet while evading the clatter-alert spells that rippled up and down it. He swiftly strode down its flexing length without losing his balance or triggering any magic. He leaped to another beam and at its end vaulted over a packing case. He landed in the middle of a circle of blue flames where he finally loosed his Shadow. The magic flames went out instantly.

"Very impressive," Chisaad acknowledged from where he stood in an out-of-the way corner of the room. "Twenty-three separate spell-traps and you didn't trigger any of them. All while moving faster than I'd have believed possible in such cramped spaces."

Kirin grinned with the triumph coursing through him and punched his fists in the air. "Yes! I promised you I'd do everything right if you let me be physical too, didn't I, Magister Chisaad?"

"And you kept that promise," Chisaad nodded while shutting down the complex assembly of spells. "We've determined that your invisibility to magic runs the full range from tiny movement-detectors to full-scale guardian spells, and even hair-trigger-dangerous projectile traps."

Brimming with confidence, Kirin boasted. "You should let me try a real trap, Magister. Something with an arrow or a spear, instead of these padded sticks."

"Are those words from your reason, or do I hear your stones talking?" Chisaad inquired warningly. "Pride is one thing, recklessness quite another. How would I explain it to your family if you got your liver impaled?"

Kirin thought about what Pieter or Maia would have to say about that and deflated a little. "I guess that would be a problem." To himself he thought, *I wouldn't get speared. I can sneak through anything!*

"And speaking of 'a problem,' I do hope you are being circumspect in what you tell your family about the tests we run here," the wizard cautioned. "Remember that I have been giving you opportunities that are not generally made available to less than journeyman mages, when you are not even an apprentice yet. I would be severely criticized for that if word got around. The Council might even bar me from teaching any student, much less you."

Kirin gaped at him, shocked. "But you're the Royal Wizard!"

"Acting Royal Wizard," Chisaad corrected. "Still subject to Council discipline as any other mage. The Prince can dismiss me at a whim and may yet do so."

Kirin bridled at the injustice. "But you've served his family for years! Doesn't he have any sense of honor?"

"When it is convenient for him," Chisaad muttered wryly. The wizard looked Kirin in the eye as he added, "Remember that blood counts for less of a man's character than most people think, and upbringing for more. Despite your pale skin, Kirin DiUmbra, you are Silbari through and through. Prince Terrell was raised in the north among barbarians. A superficial polish of training and education can hide but not obliterate that unhappy truth. He will never really be a Silbari the way we are; at most he can but imitate one. Underneath—"

The wizard stopped and shook his head. "I shouldn't have said that. It could endanger you."

"I've been careful, Magister," Kirin promised, feeling flattered by the confidence. "I don't gossip about my training with anybody, not neighbors, not even the rest of my family. Only my wife and my father know what you're teaching me."

"We must hope that is good enough." Chisaad looked at him solemnly. "You have a new and wonderful talent, Kirin DiUmbra. The rags of old spells littering this city are a frequent nuisance to any mage casting new ones. You can cure that problem. I think I can train you to use this ability effectively and safely. Bear in mind that we are both exploring new ground in this effort and therefore we must expect demanding challenges at some point."

Yes! Kirin exulted inside. *I'm going to be important and powerful soon!*

"But word of you has spread from the unfortunate events at Millago's party," Chisaad continued, watching him closely. "The gossip is mostly wrong and for that we should both be grateful. Nobody beyond Ymera has any accurate idea of your abilities yet, therefore they underrate your capacity. If certain ruthless individuals among this city's mages or priestesses should come to a correct understanding before you have the training to establish yourself securely, I fear for what may happen to you, or to those you love."

"Those I—" Kirin gulped, shocked, as his agile thoughts leaped ahead. "You mean, someone might threaten my family to control me?" Visions of strange men waving knives at pregnant Maia, or at Sevan and Carlai and their little girl, crowded his mind. *No!*

"Yes," sighed the wizard, wearing a sad expression. "That is why you must be very, very careful of your words. Tell nobody what we say or do here, until you are established as someone they dare not threaten. Only then will your loved ones be safe."

"Yes, Magister," Kirin promised from the bottom of his heart. "Thank you for warning me." *When I am* established *as he says, nobody will threaten my family! Else I'll rip their spells to pieces and, and, and I'll make them regret it!*

The wizard waved a hand. "Enough of such grim thoughts. Let us get back to practice."

"Yes, Magister." Kirin hesitated, dared. "Only . . . when will I become your apprentice?"

Chisaad raised one eyebrow as if he hadn't thought about it. "There is no reason that it cannot be tomorrow. I had intended to register you with the Council sometime in the next tenday, but now that I think about it, sooner would be wisest. At least a few of the less-scrupulous figures in Aretzo will hesitate to threaten my apprentice. The rest, alas, will not be so easily put off. But it cannot hurt and may help. Wear your best clothes tomorrow morning and we will pay a visit to the Council offices."

"Thank you, Magister," Kirin said gratefully, and in a smaller voice added, "But these are my best clothes."

"Ah. I have been remiss. Here." The wizard plucked a coin purse out of a cabinet and tossed it into Kirin's hands. "Let this be your first four tendays' salary. Buy yourself something new and clean to wear and meet me at the Rainbow Hall when the tenth bell sounds."

Kirin hefted the little pouch, stunned by the weight of it. A peek through the drawstrings showed the glint of depleted silver coins and he gulped. "I didn't know apprentice mages got paid a salary."

"They normally don't." The wizard's face creased in a fleeting smile, but his eyes were intent. "Ordinary recompense is room and board and a few coins for journeymen, and apprentices are expected to pay. But it is important that you accelerate your training as fast as you possibly can, Kirin. You need to progress to at least journeyman-equivalent this very summer, if you are to keep your family safe. The work will be hard and will require that you spend many afternoons with me, which will take you away from your troupe and prevent you from contributing to their income. Thus, thirty silver dohbas every four tendays should adequately recompense them for the loss."

"Thirty!" Kirin gulped again. That was almost as much profit as the whole Troupe's normal tenday take performing at their old spot in the Bazaar. Half the amount that Millago had promised for his party. He would have to spend one, maybe one and a half on new clothes, but—"Thank you, Magister. I'll work hard every day and learn everything, I promise you!"

"I have confidence in you, Kirin." The wizard nodded to him soberly. "Now. Let us see if you can pass through a highly dynamic spell without disrupting it. I am going to make that brass plate there float back and forth across the room in an irregular pattern. Try to move through the supporting spell multiple times and see if—"

* * *

Hours later Kirin walked home through twilight gloom with the pouch carefully concealed inside his tunic. Chisaad watched him go from the topmost room of his tower. The boy quickly disappeared into the torchlit Bazaar.

I believe I have found what moves him, Chisaad thought. *Now I must pull those strings delicately to shape his thoughts and especially his fears, yet not alert that father of his, who is clearly far more sophisticated than the boy.*

He turned back to the table where his new golem lay, still under construction. The ovoid head sat detached on a cradle. For amusement he cast a simulacrum of the Prince's face upon it. It looked quite life-like sitting there.

I shall have you ready soon. The Queen steadily fades in Gwythford Castle. Before she dies I must move. So, which tool will motivate the boy properly? His wife? Or his father? Either would probably work, but which can be threatened most effectively?

His gaze fell on a clear glass vial of prepared sulfur, fresh from the mines of Sulmona, and he knew the answer.

A pounding on his front door distracted him. He descended the tower and answered it to find Duke Darnaud, swathed in a dark blue cape that didn't do enough to conceal him.

"I thought the brat would never leave," the Gwytho lord grumbled after the door closed behind him. He handed his cape to the insect-like cleaning golem after it wiped his shoes. "You told me never to let him see me near you, but I didn't expect to have to cool my heels in an alley!"

"An unfortunate necessity," Chisaad soothed. "Were you successful in placing the link in Silbariki?"

"Yes." The Gwythlo smirked and produced the other half of the enchanted link that Chisaad had provided. "I think you'll laugh at the place we chose. I'm eager to try this, can we do it now? Ap Marn's men have been told to expect the two of us at any time."

"Certainly, Your Grace. Follow me; the decagram can be ready in half a candlemark. While it charges, I'd like to discuss with you an idea I had tonight. Would you be willing to acquire a servant that you'd dispose of—permanently?"

Duke Darnaud chuckled. "Tell me more."

CHAPTER 24: KIRIN

H e kept you later than usual." Maia set a late dinner in front of Kirin and sat next to him.

"We had a lot to talk about after practice," Kirin reported before filling his mouth full of polenta, leeks and fish.

"What did he want to talk to you about, son?" Pieter asked; the three of them were alone in the family's little dining room while everyone else put kids to bed, except Grandfather and Sevan the Elder who were at the Gleemen's Guild hunting for work.

"Me. He wants me to become his apprentice tomorrow, and he's going to pay me a journeyman's salary!" Kirin proudly slapped the jingling pouch on the table. "I'm supposed to buy new clothes out of this and meet him at the mage guild hall to get registered!"

Pieter picked it up and spilled it on the table; thirty silver dohbas glinted. "This is far more than you need for clothes. Is this an advance on that salary for the coming year?"

Maia stared at the coins. "We'll have to be careful to make it last."

"It's my pay for the next four tendays," Kirin answered smugly. "I'll get thirty more at the start of every fourth tenday."

Pieter's attention sharpened, and a troubled look came into his eyes. "Why so much?"

"He said I'm going to have to work really hard and get better control over my Shadow. I won't have enough time to contribute to the family the way I did, so this is to make up for that while I'm training." Kirin stuffed more food in his mouth to cover his hesitation. He didn't want to talk about the Wizard's darker concerns in front of Maia.

But she frowned at him after exchanging glances with Pieter, scooted her stool closer to him and laid a hand on his thigh. "Husband-mine, what else? I can tell there's something more."

Kirin dodged her gaze to look at Pieter, hoping for intervention. That resulted in a stern look and a finger crooked in the 'out with it' gesture. He swallowed, sighed, and said to her, "He told me the same thing Mother Gee told Father and me, Maia. Powerful people have heard about me and some of them are dangerous. That's why he wants me to spend so much time training. He wants me to be ready to prove I'm powerful too, and as soon as possible, before somebody tries something." He left the something undefined and hoped Maia wouldn't notice.

Her frown darkened. "Don't try to hide things from me, Kirin, I can tell when you do. He's worried that somebody will threaten me to make you do what they want."

Kirin curled one hand over hers in a quick squeeze, met her eyes and let his own worry show. "Yeah."

Her other hand crept across her belly protectively and they both looked at Pieter.

He nodded his head slowly. "I'm glad the wizard sees the problem."

"That pouch will really help the family," Maia pointed out, rallying to put the moment of fear behind her. "After Kirin buys clothes, the rest of it will feed us all for a good ten or twenty days."

Pieter reluctantly assented. "I don't like this situation very much, but I can't think of a better way to handle it. Wizard Chisaad is probably strong enough that nobody will dare try anything with his apprentice, or the rest of us. But since we can't be sure, you had best do as he says. And we'll all have to be extra careful from now on. Maia; don't go anywhere without at least two of us with you every time."

She looked down at her swollen belly and wryly said, "Simple enough, Uncle Pieter. I won't leave the Serpent until after the baby comes. My feet will thank me for it and the stairs are already difficult."

Pieter nodded approval. "Kirin, I'll change our practice schedule so that you do all your sessions in the mornings, before you scamper off to the Wizard's tower for the afternoons. But tomorrow, first thing I'll take you to buy new clothes and get bathed, so you make a good impression on the Mage Guild."

"I can do that." Kirin relaxed in relief. He hadn't been completely certain that Pieter would consent. *This will work. We'll be fine.*

* * *

Kirin wandered in dim alleys of haunted sleep. He dimly knew that he fled an unnamable danger with Maia, the two of them alone and afraid. They hurried along hand in hand while she tried to support her swollen belly with her other hand and wept in silent fear. Faceless men with knives lurked around every corner. He moaned and thrashed, trying to drive them away, only to have them slip past like dancers and close on her despite all he could do. Their faces all looked like Gerlach, but the blood-mage's Fehdaran features conflated with something horrible not of their world. Terror shook him as knives glinted red in the night.

"Mrrph? Kirin?" Maia yawned, waking him; they'd been sleeping like spoons with her belly resting on a special pillow that her mother had sewed. She leaned back against him, craned her neck to peer over her shoulder at him where he nestled against her back. "What's wrong, love?"

He held her for a moment while indescribable relief flooded him. Only then did he discover that he had been shuddering. "Bad dream," he managed to whisper into her neck. He pressed his front against her back and buried his face in her hair.

She reached back over her hip to stroke his thigh, and saucily wiggled her buttocks against him. That got the usual reaction and she chuckled. "Let's do something to banish those bad dreams," she suggested. "Help me turn a little."

They fell asleep together a while later, and he slept dreamlessly until dawn.

But the next night the dream returned, Gerlach in all his horrifying foulness. And the next. And the next.

Please, oh Blessed Seraph Haroun, he prayed each night. *Intercede with the One for me. Don't let this be the madness that Ymera warned me of. Banish Gerlach from my mind, lock him away.*

He tried to build a wall between the dread memory and his own mind. He didn't quite succeed, but the dreams faded enough to let him sleep, most nights.

* * *

Days later Kirin hurried through the Bazaar toward the Old City's evening-dark streets. Torches were being lit and customers thronged in the evening cool. His arms and legs ached in unaccustomed places from the Wizard's latest tests, but the glow of triumph buoyed him up despite his recent nightmares. Today he had selectively killed three spells while leaving six others untouched. Then he had absorbed the residual fragments of two other broken spells without disturbing their replacements. All while moving through narrow places and over obstacles. He grinned to himself as he rounded a harness-repairer's tent and almost ran into his younger brother-in-law.

"Kirin!" Attir hailed him excitedly. "We got a job!"

Sevan and Uncle Ger and Ger's eldest son were with him, and Pieter and Grandfather and Uncle Sevan right behind them. All but Grandfather were wearing tights and clearly ready to perform.

"What is it? An exhibition piece?" He guessed, added, "For some Gwythlo lord and his friends?" since none of the family's women were with them.

"Yes, for Duke Darnaud of Gugione," Pieter explained. "Not much challenge, but good pay and exposure to potential patrons." He clapped Kirin on the shoulder approvingly. "You look happy and tired. Your teacher put you through your paces today, I'll bet." Keeping things ambiguous for the listening ears around them in the crowded Bazaar, he added, "Your control better today?"

"You bet!" Kirin almost spilled the details, caught the warning in Pieter's look, and contented himself with saying, "A perfect three-in-a-row!"

Pieter nodded understanding and hugged him while Sevan and Attir pounded Kirin on the back. "Excellent. I'm very proud of you, son."

The others congratulated him too, even Grandfather unbending enough to say something positive. Which the old man immediately followed with a harrumph and a pointed reference to the setting suns. Kirin gave them the traditional acrobat's well-wish of "Touch the sky!" as they hurried off to their appointment.

As he watched them disappear he thought wistfully, *I wish I was going with them.* But he'd been at the Wizard's tower most of the day with no chance to rehearse whatever exhibition Grandfather and Uncle Sevan had devised, and he knew better than to try any acrobatic maneuver without practicing it first. Besides, with most of the adult men gone the women and children would be almost alone. He turned his face back toward the Old City and hurried.

He halted in annoyance at the sight of the sulfur caravan's huge wains groaning through the narrow passage of Oldgate. The line looked to have recently arrived, so it would be the better part of an hour before the gate cleared enough for foot traffic. He could cut around east through the warren of alleys in the Old City and try to get ahead of the caravan. If he was very lucky he'd be able to cross Sulfur Street before the wagons reached the Serpentine and cut him off, but he knew from previous tries that game rarely worked. He also briefly considered trying to swarm over and across one of the moving wagons. His tired muscles and Pieter's warnings about stupid risks put that thought to rest.

Instead he stepped into the alley next to Fresci's bakery and went to the laundry located behind it. The laundress provided a urine bucket for passers-by to relieve themselves and supply her with the valuable basis for cleaning fluids after it had fermented. He used the bucket while trying to concentrate on the fading scent of the day's baking rather than the appalling stench of the fermenting vats. When he finished he laced his hose up and headed back toward Oldgate through the silent alley.

Before he got there a stranger in a long robe stopped him. Kirin's Shadow immediately filled him to the skin and he used his magesight on the man. He saw layers of complex spells, including one on the surface that shifted the stranger's real features to look quite different.

He's wearing a disguise spell. But I remember seeing his real face at Mil-lago's house. He's Mage Yellow from the Council. Kirin recalled Chisaad's warning about unprincipled mages as his scalp prickled and his heart quickened.

The man had pushed back his hood and displayed a friendly smile as he said, "Say, aren't you Kirin, the star acrobat of the DiUmbra family? I've seen your troupe perform." He waved a hand in the direction of the space now occupied by the Suliemons.

"Yup." Kirin looked Mage Yellow over. Fancy slippers were protected from the muck of the Old City's streets by spells. The man wore quality clothes similarly guarded, with an extra spell laid on to make shoes and clothes look coarser and poorer. Half a dozen more spells wrapped him; to Kirin's magesight the man positively glowed. He might as well have brought a herald to declare the presence of money and power.

A season ago such a combination would have frightened Kirin. Even a few tendays ago he'd have been nervous and deferential. Now ten nights of bad dreams and more days of building confidence joined to spark a different response. *I'm powerful too, and in a way that'll surprise the hell out of you.*

He boldly said, "You're a mage disguised as a young scribe. Pretty good disguise too, you even have fake ink stains. But your real hands are clean, and you don't have pimples and you aren't young. I'd say from the wrinkles on your face and the gray in your hair that you must be nearly fifty." He couldn't resist smirking.

The Mage's smile changed into something colder and more calculating. "Very well, boy, you can see through my disguise spell. Impressive, since I see that you have no spells of your own. I do wonder how a youth with no visible mage talent manages such a trick." Even as he spoke he brazenly launched a probing spell.

Kirin let his Shadow gulp it down whole, snapped back, "Why in the nine hells would I tell you?" He poked the mage's disguise spell with a finger and ate that too.

The mage gasped and stepped back, his eyes wide and his hands raised. A violet glow of power gathered in his palms.

"Don't try it," Kirin growled. "If you had any respect for me and my talents, you'd have come to me honestly and not like a sneak-thief. My teacher warned me about mages like you."

"Chisaad?" The mage barked a laugh as he took another step back. He gave Kirin a bitter sneer, hands lower but still holding spells that glittered like blades. "That's rich. He's a bigger schemer than Blue, bigger than the whole Council! He's survived eighteen years as Royal Wizard, boy, and that takes more lies and dealings than a peasant like you can imagine."

Kirin propped his fists against his hips and sneered back. "'Grimy arse,' said the kettle to the pot.' You're no better, Mage Yellow. Yeah, I recognize you from Millago's party. I've heard plenty about you, and not just from Magister Chisaad."

Mage Yellow visibly throttled his own words, lowered his hands, took a deep breath, and went on in a softer voice. "Look, we got off to a bad start here, and I'm sorry for that. But whatever a bunch of jealous backstabbers say about me, you should think about maybe relying on more than one teacher." His eyes widened in eager anticipation and in a wheedling tone he added, "You know, I can be very helpful to a novice like you."

"Dung to that. I already know you can't be trusted." Kirin pressed closer, poked another spell with a finger and ate that too. "Stay away from me and mine or I'll make you sorrier than *you* can imagine."

Yellow yelped and scrambled back several more steps. "How are you doing that? Have you got a demon familiar?"

Kirin's spine chilled at the implied threat. His mind skipped to an image of himself tied to the Temple's iron stake while flames seared his flesh and boiled his blood. He glared. "Watch your tongue, mage, or I'll cut it out. If I start hearing evil slanders about me, I'll know where to look. Get this through your head right now; I can hurt you a lot worse than you can hurt me."

He leaped across the distance between them, let his Shadow gulp down the spells the mage hurled, and raked Yellow with claws of inky darkness. The rest of the mage's spells shattered and the man went reeling back against a wall. Kirin's Shadow lapped up the fragments and left the mage naked of spells. Yellow sagged and gasped, his hands raised in helpless protest and his eyes wide as a dried fish.

Kirin stood over him with his fists balled, trembling with anger so strong he could barely stop himself from pummeling the man. "Now get out of here and leave me alone. If I hear anything about this, if you cause me any trouble, you'll get worse." He pointed to the alley entrance. "Go!"

Yellow bolted with a strangled gasp and vanished into the Bazaar.

Kirin leaned against the wall to give in to a fit of shaking. More visions of being burned in front of the Mother Temple swam through his mind and made his guts churn, each one worse than the last. "Bastard!" he whispered, gulped and fought down his fears. *I'm not a demon! Lady Ymera said so. The Royal Wizard himself thinks I have a new talent never seen before. Not a demon!*

He didn't know how long he leaned there, caught in his own private terror. Eventually he noticed that the distant rumble of the sulfur caravan had faded. He pushed off the wall, straightened his tunic and tried to saunter casually back to Oldgate. He couldn't help looking around every corner for the thrice-cursed mage. A pair of Temple Inquisitors in black and yellow robes passed by. He hid in an alley and shuddered in fear until they were gone. *I'm not a demon!* His mind conjured threats everywhere.

By the time he made it to the Sulfur Serpent his neck threatened to cramp from trying to watch everywhere. He climbed the main stairs and took off his buskins on the top landing as usual, then racked them inside the door to the family's private floor of the Inn while jauntily calling, "Hey everybody, I'm home!"

A muffled groan answered him.

"Maia?" Terror boiled through him. Had Mage Yellow gotten here first and taken vengeance? "Maia!" He ran to their room. "Maia!"

"Stop yelling," Aunt Silla told him in a brusque tone as she blocked the door. "You'll wake the kids and we barely got them to sleep."

Kirin's heart skipped a beat when he saw that her hands were full of soiled, bloody cloth. He danced in frustration as he tried to get around her. "What's happened? Is she hurt?"

"No more than usual," Silla tossed the bloody cloths into a laundry basket sitting outside the door. "For a woman who's just had a baby. Come back in a candlemark and you can help name him."

She shut the door firmly in his face.

For a long moment Kirin stood there staring at the wood panel. Finally, his thoughts managed to focus on one word.

"Him?"

* * *

Carlai collected Kirin and took him to the family's little dining room, made him sit and eat something while she nursed her own baby and chattered.

"Sevan and the others are at that private party, I suppose it'll be another couple of bells before they return. I hope this Duke Darnaud likes them and has them back again, Grandfather said the man paid the whole fee up front! It's only an exhibition, not a real performance, but it gets us seen by his guests and who knows? One of them might want to be our patron. I'm so glad Grandfather didn't make a fuss about working for a Gwythlo lord. I told Sevan we'd better get used to it, they've got most of the money now, and besides, the old man never complained when there were Gwythlos in our crowds in the Bazaar. Some of them threw good money."

Kirin mechanically ate what she had put in front of him while her words washed through him. His thoughts roiled around the enchanting word. *Him. I have a son. I'm a father!* The amazing thought went around and round through his mind. He was no different, and yet utterly transformed. *I'm a father!*

Finally, half of eternity later, Aunt Silla fetched him to see his wife.

Maia lay on their bed looking utterly exhausted and yet triumphant. Carmella tucked a little wrapped bundle against her breast. He heard a tiny cry before the baby latched on and began to suckle.

"What will you name him?" Dona Abbithana, acting as midwife priestess, asked as she packed her bag. She still tended to look warily at him but a season of ministering to the DiUmbras had softened her suspicions.

Kirin looked at Maia. "Do we still want to name him after Grandfather?"

Maia nodded. "It's a good name, and it might soften his heart towards you."

Kirin turned to the priestess and said formally, "Our son is named Grigor Sule DiUmbra."

Dona Abbie wrote it down, tucked her tablet in her bag and congratulated him in a low voice, and quit the room. Kirin barely heard her and did not see her amused smile. All he could see, as he knelt on their bed-pad next to Maia, was the incredible beauty who had married him, and the wonderful, terrifying, marvelous, astonishing new life she had brought forth.

Kirin curled up, still clothed, on the bed next to her as the rest of the women vacated the room. He tenderly kissed her and whispered, "Hello beautiful. Looks like you lost some weight."

"Traded it for something better," she told him with a tired smirk.

He took her free hand in one of his and kissed it too, then lay next to her and watched their son enjoy his first meal.

* * *

He woke up hours later to voices in the hallway. Maia had set baby Grigor between them while she slept. Kirin got up and went out to see about the noise.

"—course not! It has to be a terrible mistake," Sevan-the-younger protested.

"Terrible doesn't begin to describe this!" His father snapped. "The Watch dragged him away in *chains*!"

"That wasn't a mistake," Grandfather growled. "We were set-up, used to cover up a murder and take the blame for it. Probably the reason we were hired in the first place."

Grandmother began to keen softly in grief. Grandfather put his arms around her as he glared at the ceiling and declared, "I should never have trusted a Gwythlo lord."

"What's happened?" Kirin demanded as he stared from face to face. "Tell me!"

Sevan-the-younger, Attir, Gir, and Gir's oldest son stood around hanging their heads in grief as other family members came out of their rooms into the hallway. Sevan the Elder looked at Kirin and his craggy features softened. "I'm sorry to have to say it, son. Pieter's been arrested. A man was found dead at Duke Darnaud's party, with Pieter's belt knife stuck in his back."

CHAPTER 25: CHISAAD

T he next day Chisaad went early to his office in the Palace. He refreshed all his ward spells to be certain nobody could spy on him and placed the glyph on his office door that warned the Palace staff that he was occupied with delicate casting and should not be disturbed. Then he rolled back his office carpet, took out the little rug he had concealed in his robes and spread it on the marble floor.

It had taken him days to embed a very specific and complex spell into the fibers. He had invented it and tied it to another spell set with even greater labor into the floor of the topmost room of his tower. The two had to operate in perfect harmony for the first step of today's plan to work. Delicately he adjusted the casting until the decagram embedded in the rug's weave flashed twice and settled. He rolled the carpet back over it and made sure the spell remained aligned even in concealment.

He checked the palace's ward spells; not a ripple. He allowed himself a smile. Linking a spell inside the Palace to one outside it without triggering any of the various wards was an impressive achievement, but today he intended to dare much more. He began the work by stepping into the decagram and, with a whispered word, teleported to his tower.

He experienced no dizziness or vertigo from the movement; he was simply in one place, then in another, travelling without moving. The roots of his hair and all his finger-and-toenails prickled with exhilaration and he drew a great lungful of air in sheer delight.

Two miracles accomplished. Now for the third and most important.

On his worktable lay his new golem, clothed in one of his spare robes and wearing a simulacrum of his features. He used a mirror to compare his face to the imitation, for even a small error could draw the eyes of observers and raise questions. He picked up the silver-and-jet spider he had crafted, set it onto his own head and covered it with a fez. It settled securely while he placed a similar fez atop the golem's scalp and pinned that in place. When he had the spider prepared, he linked his mind through it to the elaborate construct inside the golem's head.

The golem's stiff face flexed, became alive. It blinked and stood up, smoothly counterfeiting his natural movements right down to the small hesitation in his left leg where he'd overstressed it from climbing the Hill so often.

Chisaad silently ordered the golem into the decagram. It obeyed as casually as if the command had originated within its false skull. He teleported them both back to the Palace, settled himself comfortably in his chair, closed his eyes, and shifted his mind's attention entirely to seeing through the golem's crystal eyes.

It disturbed him to look upon his real body leaning back as if asleep, so he turned the golem's attention away. He made the creature walk to and open the door to his outer office. He carefully closed it behind itself while sealing the protective spells and walked the golem out into the Palace.

He had practiced this sort of movement enough that his mind quickly fell into an unthinking rhythm with the artificial body. He passed several servants and gave them preoccupied nods in return for their bows. None gave any indication of having noticed that the spell-wrapped thing before them was not the Acting Royal Wizard.

First test passed. Now to try it on a mage. It should work, since I couldn't tell the difference.

He visited the office where his subordinate wizards worked. He entered as if he owned the place—*before this year ends I shall!*—and barked orders to the two mages to report on the latest repair to the Gray Fort's spells. They did and faithfully explained their meticulous analyses of the break, all leading to the same conclusion. The Gwythlo battlemages and the Silbari battlemages had been showing off and the Gwythlo's druid, Boerga, had egged them on until they made a mess, which would require costly repair. They would schedule it for the next few days, and recommended that the battlemages be forced to supply most of the power from their personal allotments. As for the Druid— they were both transparently glad she was some higher-up's responsibility.

When Chisaad grunted approval they both relaxed as if they had passed one of his frequent tests. He found the golem's face smiling as he walked back out and quickly forced it back into a concealing blandness. Perhaps the golem responded to his mind a little too readily?

No, it responds as it must if I am to deceive anyone who knows me well. Now to test it on a few more.

The Temple bells rang the eighth hour. Fantillin normally conferred with the Commander of the Palace Guard and his captains at this time. Chisaad had long made it a point to drop irregularly. He sent the golem strolling that way while trying to minimize the small but aggravating limp it had developed in its left leg.

He found the Commander with Fantillin, greeted both with the shaking-hands-with-himself gesture. He had barely taken a seat when the Prince's personal Healer, Dona Seraphina, entered. For a moment Chisaad almost fled. He hadn't intended to risk the presence of any powerful priestess until he had a chance to refine the golem's spells based on today's test. But walking out now would draw unwelcome attention. She greeted him normally, clearly not perceiving his deception, so he relaxed and listened.

The Palace Guard's three captains stood spear-straight and stared at their Commander as one of their number delivered an abbreviated report on the results of the battlemage's mess in the Gray Fort. Chisaad added his staff's verification and noted, "The Druid Boerga clearly instigated the conflict, my lord."

"In other words, we need to get the Gwythlo troops out of the Gray Fort and on their way home," the Commander acknowledged heavily. "Especially their damn Druid. I will talk to the Prince about it."

The Commander, his captains, and Fantillin departed. Chisaad moved to do the same when his left leg twinged and made him limp again. He had to pause and barely kept his balance.

"Hold still, Wizard," Dona Seraphina ordered. "Let me fix that." Before he could stop her, she sent her aura into his hip.

This time he froze in petrified fear. She could sink his hopes and cost him his position simply by telling the Prince! Then her healing aura penetrated his real body where he reclined in his office chair, a tenth of a mile away.

"Will you please relax your protection spells a bit, Wizard? You mages always make it so difficult for us to heal you," she grumbled. "There, that should help your leg for a while. If it still bothers you in two days, come see me."

He managed a half-strangled thank you and got out of there, hurrying back to his office and sealing the door behind him.

Only when he had the golem safely standing on the hidden decagram did he relax his control and open the eyes of his real body. He stretched and gave vent to a happy sigh.

It worked. Even the priestesses can't tell my golem from the real me. I can replace the Prince, and no one will be able to tell, save possibly Sir Di-Lione and his damnable sword. I shall have to wait until he leaves before I try anything else.

He got home to find even better news. Darnaud's efforts had succeeded and Kirin's father had been arrested for murder.

Now to make sure the man is condemned, and Kirin blames the Prince.

CHAPTER 26: TERRELL AND KIRIN

Third fall," the referee declared. "Baron Penghar wins, two out of three."

"I should be on to your tricks by now," Terrell chuckled.

"Second time I've used that one on you." Pen nodded as he helped him up off the wrestling mat. They were both stripped to loincloths and dripping sweat after more than a dozen rounds of wrestling, several with the Palace Guard trainers and the last six with each other.

Terrell heard the implied 'so you should have been ready for it' in Pen's voice and nodded ruefully. There were advantages to knowing each other for as long as they had. *If being scolded in a way that nobody else can hear counts as an advantage!* Aloud he said only, "Let's wash up."

The suns were still more than three hours short of noon. Their light already baked this walled courtyard of pale yellow stone and white marble pilasters. Pen passed Terrell a bucket of water from the corner fountain before dunking his own head under the flow and splashing like a big brown tiger. Terrell slowly poured cool water over his own head, enjoying the feel of it sluicing sweat and dust away, scooped up more and did it again. Servants brought big sponges for the two of them to use, followed by towels to dry themselves off, and fresh clothes. Terrell idly watched spilled water evaporate off the sunbaked flagstones as his valet dressed him. "Have you thought about my offer, Pen? Are you willing to become my Hand?"

His bodyguard's face creased in thought while his own batman helped him into a loose silk shirt that would not interfere with drawing his sword. "I'm honored by your trust, Terrell, and I can't say it isn't tempting to be offered that kind of power and responsibility. But I'm supposed to be by your side to protect you. Serving as your Hand will take me away from you, sometimes for days at a time."

"Nobody's tried to kill me yet," Terrell pointed out, holding out one arm so the sleeve could be laced up. "Even that Druid I banished yesterday, Boerga. And I do have a brigade and a half of soldiers in the Gray Fort, plus more than two hundred men in the Palace Guard. Dear as you are to me and much as I will miss your company every time I send you on a mission, I suspect that four of them at a time will be adequate substitutes for you and Irreneetha. Especially if I take a mage along as well whenever I step outside the Palace."

"Take two," Pen advised. "I'll worry every time I'm away from your side. But I do understand the importance of having someone you trust to be your eyes and ears elsewhere in the kingdom. Yes, if something comes up where you need me to go out and act for you, I'll do it."

"Thank you." He clapped Pen lightly on the shoulder, letting the touch speak to the depth of his gratitude. A temple bell rang the ninth hour. "Let's get going. I promised to look in on the Law Courts today."

Pen buckled on his sword belt and drew Irreneetha's point from the rock where he'd placed her while they wrestled. "You may want a bath after that, too." He clicked the soulsword into her sheath.

* * *

The Law Court was high-ceilinged, completely made of marble, and brightly lit by fancy chandeliers and high windows of real glass. Kirin had never seen a more intimidating place. The family, except for Grandfather, Uncle Ger, and Sevan the Elder, were required to stand behind a marble railing that separated the back half from the main part of the room. Pieter's case would be the third of ten. The family members of other men already jammed the observers' space so the DiUmbras had to stand at the back. Kirin peered between the heads of the crowd and did his best to catch glimpses. Not for the first time, he wished he were taller.

The Judge, a stern-looking gray-haired Silbari man of corpulent girth, sat enthroned behind a tall desk while various people sat quietly or stood and talked in the open space below him. One case finished as the family filed in. The cold-eyed Judge asked the accused, "Have you anything else to say before I pronounce sentence?"

"The bastard deserved it," growled the pugnacious young man who rattled his chains. "He tried to rape my sister!"

"And he desisted when you intervened. Had you challenged him openly, he accepted, and you wounded or killed him during a duel, you would not now be sitting where you are," the judge answered ominously. "It has been proven in open court to my satisfaction that you instead chose to sneak into his house at night and stab him in his sleep. You offered nothing of substance to dispute that proof. Such an act is not protecting your sister's honor, it is cold-blooded murder, as well as violation of the sanctity of a home. For these crimes I sentence you to servitude in the sulfur mines for ten years from this day, or as long as you shall live, whichever comes first."

The Judge rapped a brass gong and the sound reverberated through the room. Bailiffs hauled the protesting man away while the sister and mother of the condemned wept. Kirin shivered. Law had always been to him a mysterious and terrifying force that wise denizens of the Old City kept at a distance. Now Pieter was caught in it.

A door opened behind the Judge and Prince Terrell came through, closely followed by his bodyguard. The Judge gave him a deferential gesture and whispered something. The Prince shook his head and said, loud enough to be heard across the room, "I'll simply observe, Riccon." He took a seat beside the Judge. The crowd murmured.

Kirin stared between the people in front of him. He could barely see the Prince through the crowd. *Will he intervene to save Pieter? Please, Father Haroun, let it be so!* But he uneasily remembered the Wizard's words.

He will never really be a Silbari the way we are . . .

"The Law versus Pieter Ille DiUmbra," intoned a clerk. Guards brought Pieter into the room still wearing yesterday's clothes, and still in chains. Kirin balled his fists and squeezed his Shadow down under his heart, praying. *Please, Father Haroun. Please.*

What followed bewildered his inexperienced mind. Witnesses were called, testimony given about an argument between Pieter and the man later found dead, who had been one of Duke Darnaud's recently-hired Gwythlo retainers.

Grandfather spoke, and Uncle Sevan, pointing out that the dead man had started the argument, which Pieter affirmed. They protested that Pieter had never been a violent man and reminded everybody that there was no witness to the actual murder. Pieter had not been wearing his belt knife during the exhibition, anyone could have stolen it out of the room where the acrobats had left their personal items while performing. Pieter had only discovered it missing afterwards. When he went looking for it he found his knife stuck in the dead man. Uncle Ger testified to his cousin's honesty.

Kirin's hopes soared. Surely the Judge must see that his father couldn't have done this.

The steward of Duke Darnaud's townhouse reported that Pieter had been found by another retainer leaning over the fresh-killed body. Both steward and retainer swore to that, while admitting that they hadn't seen the actual killing. The discovering one stoutly declared that there'd been nobody else in the house close enough to the bleeding body to have done the deed. One of the Duke's other retainers, a lawyer, reminded the Judge that Pieter had fought against Gwythlos during the Conquest, and been tortured by them. He insinuated that such a painful memory led Pieter to harbor secret resentment against all Gwythlos, one expressed by this killing.

Kirin scowled at this slander. He looked to the Prince between the blocking heads of the other onlookers. Surely, he must see how wrong that was? But the glimpses he got of the Prince's face revealed nothing.

Grandfather and Sevan conferred, tried to call Kirin up as a witness to show how untrue the insinuation had to be. Duke Darnaud's lawyer objected. The Judge limited the DiUmbras to only the witnesses who had been there at Duke Darnaud's house. Kirin slumped in worry.

The Duke made an aggrieved speech while he pointed an angry finger at Pieter. "I welcomed this man into my home, paid him—in advance!—to entertain my guests. I did not expect him to murder one of my men in a fit of rage. Now I have been deprived of my man's services. I only ask for justice to be done."

The dead man's widow, a Gwyzhlo like her husband, cried for vengeance against the slayer of the father of her children, and wept. The Judge looked moved by her words.

Kirin clenched his hands together and bit a knuckle. But Pieter couldn't have been the murderer!

Grandfather made an impassioned plea for his son's freedom, repeating all his arguments in one long rush. Duke Darnaud's lawyer countered with a learned spiel that lost Kirin in moments, talking about circumstances and extrapolation and other big words. But it seemed to affect the Judge, who nodded slightly three times.

Kirin began to fear.

Everybody stopped talking and waited. The Judge tapped his gong once and turned to confer with the Prince.

* * *

"What's your assessment?" Terrell quietly asked Judge Riccon.

The judge made a small open-hand gesture. "It's all circumstantial, but collectively quite damming. The acrobat had means and opportunity, and seems to have had motive, though that's the weakest leg of this stool. Murder—and a knife in the back is clearly murder—in a fit of anger must be dealt with firmly, lest it spread. The lower classes are appallingly violent as it is. I'm minded to convict."

Terrell frowned. Something about the case didn't feel right. *Is it simply that Darnaud is involved, and I don't trust him as far as I could throw him?* But he found it hard to see how this could be a scheme, and even a Duke had to deal with ugly surprises. "Those circumstances disturb me. I'll reserve my right to review the case personally."

"Of course, Your Highness." Riccon hesitated, bowed his head slightly and turned back to the court.

* * *

Kirin could barely see the Judge and the Prince talking, there were too many heads in the way. If it had been less crowded he would have tried to push his way through to the railing, but several men had already given him unfriendly looks and he'd heard a muttered 'half breed' only a moment ago. He struggled to stand still as dread rose in his heart.

The Judge tapped his gong again and Kirin's attention fixed on him.

Judge Riccon cleared his throat and declared, "Pieter Ille DiUmbra, it has been proven to my satisfaction that you had motive, opportunity, and means to commit this murder. The lack of corroborating witness to the deed itself is troubling, but the circumstances are so damming that I come down on the side of the accusers. I hold you guilty—"

The rest of his words were lost as Kirin's heart thudded in his chest and a great roaring filled his ears. His Shadow churned inside him and he barely held it in check. *No! Oh no no no!*

Aunt Silla tugged on his arm and pulled him out of the room. In the hallway she hugged him, crying unashamedly. "Oh Kirin, this is so awful! How could they? Two years in the sulfur mines! Even Pieter, strong as he is, might not survive that. We must pray that the Prince commutes this horrible sentence."

Kirin's mind seized on her last words. *The Prince can free Pieter. Please, please, please oh Father-Seraph Haroun, let it be so!*

* * *

"That acrobat case bothers me," Terrell confided to Pen as they walked back through the Palace labyrinth.

"How so?" Pen asked curiously. "The Judge's reasoning seemed as sound as it could be, since there isn't a handy witness to the actual murder. Somebody certainly did it."

"Is that what Irreneetha thinks?"

Pen shook his head. "She's not a Truthteller or a Seer. She doesn't peek inside people's heads unless they push their intentions on her by thinking about directly hurting you or me. And if they are close enough for her to sense their thoughts, because her reach isn't very long. That's why I take her out of her sheath when she's not in contact with me. Ordinarily she senses the world through me, but she can perceive some things directly if she's exposed to the air. I received no sensations from her while we were in that room."

"Perhaps it's Darnaud's involvement that troubles me." Terrell scowled.

"Hmm. Well, I can tell that Darnaud doesn't much like you and is afraid of what you might do to him, but so were the Dukes of Fiori and Anagni and a dozen lesser lords we met on the way here. DiSolera wanted to strangle you with his bare hands when you ruled against him, but he's calmed down." Pen shrugged. "When everybody's scheming about *something*, it's hard to sort out the ones who'll go too far, until they have."

Terrell grunted. "That's unfortunately much too true."

* * *

Kirin fumbled through the pathetically small hoard of treasures that he and Maia kept under their bed. He found the creased bit of parchment and took it out as Maia came into their bedroom with a lit tallow dip in one hand and baby Grigor on her hip. Kirin told her. "I'm going to go to the Mother Temple and make sacrifice for Pieter's release."

"Good." Maia set the tallow-dip down, reached past him and plucked out the gold-threaded hair ribbon that her parents had given her when she became a woman. "Take this with you and sacrifice it for me. I love Uncle Pieter too."

Kirin took it reverently and folded it inside the parchment, carefully tucked both inside his belt pouch. "I love you," he told her before kissing her thoroughly.

"I know." She kissed him back, her belly no longer interfering but with the baby perched on one hip. "Hurry back and be careful out there in the night streets."

"Always."

He did hurry, up Sulfur Street to the Bazaar, across it and across the wide Processional into the Sacred Precinct. The last service had ended, and the Priestesses, acolytes, attendants and others had dispersed to rest or other duties. He scurried up the thirty-two broad marble steps to the Mother Temple's wide portico, slipped through the middle door and into the holy building. The yawning scribe on night-duty barely glanced up as Kirin bowed to him and went inside.

The cavernous interior of the Mother Temple's dome arched overhead. Alabaster walls and chalcedony pillars ringed the circular travertine floor, frescoes receded into dim heights. Eight giant statues of the Seraphs upheld the dome, Mother Umana with her ewer, Father Haroun with his twenty-foot sword grounded in the temple floor, and others of the heavenly pantheon. The huge room lay still and quiet with only the sacrificial fire and one large night candle burning.

Kirin had no problem with the dimness; he'd always been able to see in the dark. He prostrated himself once at the entrance and twice more as he approached the altar and its four-foot-wide bronze dish holding the ever-burning fire. He made the proper ceremonial gestures and prayers as he set his treasure on the edge; his original slave-manumission certificate that Pieter had bought for him after Gerlach's death. He wrapped it in Maia's hair-ribbon and used the waiting bronze tongs to drop them both into the blue heart of the fire. There among the ashes and cinders of other sacrifices, the parchment and ribbon caught at once and burned fiercely. A gray tendril of smoke spiraled up. His eyes followed its ascent toward the ocular, the round opening at the top of the dome. Outside stars twinkled in the night sky.

Father Haroun and Mother Umana, he prayed. *It's me, Kirin. I beg you to help save Pieter from the sulfur mines. He's not a murderer, he's being blamed for someone else's evil. Please, Seraphs, please intercede with The One on his behalf. Soften the heart of Prince Terrell, persuade him to pardon Pieter and set him free of this terrible punishment. In the name of That Which Cannot Be Named, I beg this.*

The smoke dissipated as he waited tensely. The room wrapped him in stillness, its thick walls deadened the night-sounds of the city outside. Stars shone down through the ocular and twinkled silently.

A white owl flew through the hole in the dome, circled the room thrice, and flew back out. Its wingbeats were strong, purposeful, and silent, a feathered ghost in the night. Kirin remembered the story of Uboe, Mother Umana's owl who had led the Hero Gordin through the desert. Was that the Seraph's answer?

But what does it mean?

He waited while the night candle burned down a full notch, but no other answer came. Eventually he went home.

CHAPTER 27: TERRELL AND CHISAAD

H ow much did you say?" Terrell demanded incredulously, leaning forward over his desk to stare at the ledger. The number remained obstinately unchanged. "I see it, but I'm having trouble believing it." Behind him Pen stirred, then quieted; even he had been shocked.

"One million, two hundred and fifty-eight thousand, five hundred and twenty pounds of sulfur," Lord Treasurer Snowdon repeated, curling his blond moustache with pale ink-stained fingers. "That's my conservative estimate of the total amount missing from the royal inventory over the last fourteen years."

Osrick will have someone's head on a pike for this, Terrell thought, appalled. *If his rage doesn't go even further.* A little head-chopping seemed more than appropriate right now, but he throttled his own anger. *Recovering as much of the money as possible is more important.*

"The thefts appear to have begun two to three years before my lord Ap Marn was appointed Governor," Snowdon explained. "The sheer brazen nerve of the thieves apparently carried them through his term." The new Treasurer glanced sideways at the former Governor.

Ap Marn sent back a smoldering look at his fellow Gwythlo before he ground out, "I began to suspect early this year, when my own reeve noticed the same discrepancy that I brought to Lord Snowdon's attention. This time the drop in sulfur production from the Sulmona mines was sharper than ever before."

"But it must have been dropping for years!" Terrell stared very hard at Ap Marn. "Yet you didn't notice until now?"

The ex-Governor's face flushed brick-red and his jaw tightened. "I had a dozen years' records of steady production until now; why would anybody have looked further?"

"It's true, Your Highness;" Snowdon coughed apologetically. "The official production reports really have held comparatively steady over that time, with occasional small dips and rises that add up to a very slow overall decline of perhaps one part in a hundred. Apparently the Sulmona mines' production has in fact climbed substantially, but all the increase has been stolen."

"Until this year, when they got greedy and stole even more, whoever they are," Ap Marn growled. "Your Highness, Gwynned took over as the mine

Intendant fourteen years ago, right before the stealing began. I went to investigate personally only a few tendays before your arrival and he put on a very convincing show of being short of labor. I realize now how he must have been deceiving me. He has to be involved in these thefts right up to his eyeballs."

"Lord Gwynned, or someone he trusts." Terrell's gaze focused on Snowdon. "How confident are you in these figures?"

"I'm very confident that matters are even worse than this ledger indicates, Your Highness." Snowdon explained his investigation and reasoning. "I strongly suspect, based on reported levels of sulfur usage in various parts of the Empire, that the real production is a fifth higher than my numbers. And all of that is being stolen."

Terrell added it up and silently cursed. *Over three million pounds stolen. That's a quarter of the Kingdom's total revenue last year!* He took a deep breath, then another as he fought for equanimity. "Fourteen years. I suppose we must assume most of that is beyond hope of recapture. What can be done now?"

"Immediately seize the Sulmona mines, Your Highness," Snowdon replied. "Imprison Gwynned and everyone who works for the Intendant's Office, right down to the pit supervisors. Have the Hierarch's Truthtellers question them all to find the start of the lies and unravel the web from there until you find the thief. It might be Gwynned, it might be someone in his entourage, but it has to be someone who can consistently falsify the reports, so it can't be someone outside the immediate operation."

"That investigation would take three or four tendays," Terrell immediately pointed out. "Simply to get there would take half a tenday! I can't spend that much time in Sulmona. I have far too much to do here."

"Your Highness must send someone trustworthy who can spend the time," Ap Marn suggested. "It would help if that appointee had unimpeachable authority and your unquestioned trust." He looked over Terrell's shoulder.

Terrell turned and followed the ex-Governor's gaze to Pen, who looked torn. "Pen?"

"My Lord." Pen bowed his head quickly, scratched his chin while his brow furrowed. "I'm no reeve. I won't know if the numbers are lies."

"I have a whole staff of reeves, including the three who put together this compilation for me," Snowdon observed. "I can easily send two of those with you. They can do the actual searching, as long as they have someone unshakable supporting them."

Pen said, "I'll need some troops."

"Take a full company from the Silbari Brigade," Terrell told him. "I'll ask the Hierarch for a couple of her Truthtellers to go with you and remind her that unraveling this theft-scheme will put both of us in a good light with my brother the soon-to-be-Emperor."

The last four words sent a pang through his heart. The latest report on Father's health brought nothing good, and Mother the same. It would not be long.

Pen nodded assent. "How soon should I leave?"

"That will depend upon the Hierarch, so I'll send her a message immediately." Terrell rang a bell for his secretary and the old man appeared with pen and paper. "While we're about it, your badge should be ready."

He summoned two other servants and gave orders, then dictated a letter to the Hierarch. "Fill in the flourishes and put it on the finest paper, have it delivered with all ceremony as soon as you can get it written. That ought to please her." The secretary bowed and hurried out as one of the other servants came back with a gleaming wooden box.

"Perfect." Terrell opened the box and drew out a silver badge mounted on a square of heavy cloth. The backing had been dyed the same royal purple as his family banner flying above the Palace. The badge had the shape of a right hand, held palm forward with the fingers together and pointing up. It gleamed with a magically-enhanced shine.

"I declare you, Baron Sir Penghar DuVerhys DiLione, to be my Hand in all matters touching on the Kings' Law and Silbar," Terrell intoned formally as he fastened the badge to Pen's tunic with a long silver pin. "With the right of the Three Justices, High, Middle, and Low, and the authority to speak for me when I am not present."

Pen's lips twitched up into a grin. "That'll do for the 'unshakable authority' part. I'll ask General DiCervi to pick the troops for me." The grin faded as he added, "When I find the guilty ones, what do you want me to do with them?"

"Haul them back here in chains," Terrell growled, his own smile vanishing. "Osrick will want them made into an example to discourage any other clever thieves—and so do I."

Ap Marn didn't quite succeed in suppressing his twitch. Terrell noticed; he and Snowdon exchanged glances.

Yes, my former Governor, Terrell thought. *Eventually I'll get around to you too. After you've finished throwing all your collaborators to my wolves.*

Chisaad arrived at that moment with three secretaries, each laden with scrolls. He glanced from Terrell to Ap Marn to Snowdon and said, "I apologize if I am interrupting something, Your Highness, but Mage Blue's formal petition is here. You had indicated you would wish to see it immediately." He pointed to the huge scroll carried by the first secretary; it glowed with spell-affirmations and eight dangling wax seals the colors of the rainbow. "The Hierarch's counter petition has also arrived." He indicated the slightly smaller scroll in the second secretary's arms; that one had a single golden seal dangling from it and looked even heavier. The third secretary, in the livery of the Law Court, produced a fan of additional parchments at Chisaad's gesture. "And Judge Riccon has sent over orders for your affirmation; perhaps you'd like to get those out of the way first?"

Terrell sighed, dismissed Ap Marn and Snowdon, and beckoned the secretaries forward. Four soldiers appeared on their heels, brought by the second messenger. "Yes. Pen, I'll have General DiCervi's men here replace you while you prepare. I dare hope the Hierarch's Truthtellers will arrive soon, so you had best go pack. It appears I will be spending the rest of the day reading."

He quickly glanced over the Law Court orders while Pen left. Terrell signed most of them but stopped at the acrobat's case. He stared at the sentence.

Two years in the sulfur mines? Riccon thinks he's being lenient, but something isn't right here. Now that I think about it, I realize Darnaud wasn't actually upset by the murder of his man, he was pleased. *But trying to hide it. I don't want to undermine Riccon by changing his sentence, but mercy is my prerogative and no judge can resent that. If I pardon this acrobat, Darnaud may be annoyed enough to let something slip. I'll have my redheaded cousin watched.*

He wrote in his own judgement below Riccon's, commuting the man's sentence to a single night in jail. He handed them to the Law Court secretary before picking up the bigger scroll. "Chisaad, return in the morning and I should have my preliminary questions ready."

"As you wish, Your Highness." Chisaad bowed himself out with the secretaries.

Terrell opened the Council scroll and, alone in his office but for four bodyguards and a dozen guardian spells, began to read.

* * *

Chisaad followed the Law Court secretary around four bends in the Palace labyrinth. When the hallway held only the two of them, the wizard struck. A prepared spell, a quick swap, and the secretary continued on his way. Unaware that he'd lost a minute of his consciousness and now carried a different document than the one that had been entrusted to his care.

The wizard hurried on home after that, the purloined pardon hidden in his robes. Once safe in his personal sanctum, he thoroughly destroyed it. Then he sent a message construct to Darnaud and settled back to wait.

All depends now on whether I've read Kirin correctly, he thought, forbidding his fingers to drum nervously on the table. He glanced at his prepared golem and the waiting decagram. *I roll Ifni's dice, and on the outcome hangs my life. Or his. Or both.*

CHAPTER 28: KIRIN AND TERRELL

Ten years!" Grandmother recoiled in shock at Grandfather's report. Most of the DiUmbras were packed into their little dining room in the Sulfur Serpent Inn to hear the news. "Oh, my son, my son!"

"Nobody survives ten years in the sulfur mines," Uncle Ger said in a hushed voice.

"My poor brother," Sevan the Elder lamented as he and Carmella hugged each other and wept.

"But why would the Prince do this?" Kirin asked, horrified.

"The Duke probably asked him to. The bastard!" Sevan cursed.

"Those Gwythlos are all bastards!" Grandfather railed. "They stick together! We can't trust any of them."

"Oh, Uncle Pieter!" wailed Carlai, hugging her husband and her baby, who began to cry.

"Can we get him free somehow?" demanded Attir, staring wildly around.

Sevan's eyes settled on Kirin. "Can you?"

Kirin's stomach clenched as tight as his fists. How could his talent for breaking spells be used against a guarded caravan of men in chains? He didn't even know how to use a sword, other than the pretend wooden ones the family used in the show. A real soldier would laugh at his swordsmanship—one had once, when he performed in the Bazaar.

"I . . . I don't know," he answered, ashamed of the tremble in his voice.

Grandfather looked at him with contempt and turned away.

Baby Grigor wailed and Maia jiggled him, offered him her breast. She stared at Kirin and in a quiet voice said, "What are you going to do?"

"Get help," he said thickly, and ran out of the Sulfur Serpent Inn.

* * *

Kirin didn't remember running up Sulfur Street to Oldgate. He found himself at the edge of the Bazaar's ring-road. A mass of people blocked the way, none of them moving. Impatient, he scrambled up on the pedestal of one of the massive sculptures that flanked Oldgate, a bas-relief of an ancient battle. From this unsteady perch he grabbed the marble wrist of a dying soldier, leaned out and peered over the heads of the crowd.

Gwythlo troops marched along the ring road toward the Processional that led to the harbor. The crowd murmured in protest, but the soldiers carried shields and unsheathed blades. In their midst walked men wearing chains, linked together into a long coffle.

One of them was Pieter.

He still wore the clothes he'd worn to the ill-fated exhibition at Duke Darnaud's town house, now wrinkled and stained. Kirin saw with shock that Pieter's scalp lock had been cut off and his silver hair-rings taken. Despite that, his father held his head high.

"Father!" Kirin shouted, his eyes burning and throat hoarse. "Father!"

Pieter's head turned. His eyes met Kirin's and his step faltered. One of the guards prodded him and Pieter had to turn back. He tried once more to look over his shoulder at Kirin, but the moving line carried him out of sight. The mass of prisoners and soldiers continued toward the barge that would take them upriver to Amm Crossing and the hard road to Sulmona.

"Father," whispered Kirin, tears on his face as he clung to the cold stone.

The crowd dispersed and left him alone in the emptied street, save for an old Duermu man leaning on a bent stick as he hobbled toward the Bazaar.

Tested with fear and loss, he thought numbly. *This is the third time. Someone powerful will help me, and I think I know who.*

* * *

"I am sorry for your loss." The wizard shook his head sadly. "I had hoped the Prince would be different."

"You warned me, Magister," Kirin choked, smearing the back of one hand across the tears that still leaked from his eyes. "He's a Gwythlo. A murdering bastard like Ap Marn!"

"Yes." Chisaad stared at him with a penetrating look. "Tell me, Kirin; if you could change him . . . would you?"

"What?" Confused, Kirin gaped at the wizard. "Me? Change the Prince?"

"Exactly." The wizard's gaze grew more intense. "If you could change the Prince to no longer be cold and callous, but instead to become someone better—would you?"

"But I don't have any magic like that." He wrinkled his forehead. "Even a priestess can't do that, or they'd change the blood-sorcerers instead of burning them. Dona Zella said so."

"Yet people do change," Chisaad said. "Your family accepts you as Silbari despite your ears and skin. Your neighbors do too, don't they?"

"Well, most of them," Kirin admitted, mystified. "But they've known me for years."

"If the Prince had spent the last few tendays with your family, wouldn't he have known that your father could not be a murderer?"

"He'd have to!" Kirin scowled as he struggled to parse the new thought. "If he ate with us, practiced with me and Sevan, met Grandmother and Aunt Carmella and Uncle Sevan—though Grandfather might not be so friendly . . .." He worried that one over for a moment. "But Grandmother would make him behave for the Prince. Especially if that could get Pieter released!" He brightened at the thought.

"If the Prince spent time with your family, you and they could teach him what a Silbari should be," the wizard pressed his point. "He's not stupid or cruel by nature, he's simply ignorant, and has been taught the wrong things. He never has a chance to meet people like you when he's caged inside that Palace."

"If he really knew us," Kirin said, then balled his hands into fists in frustration. "But this is crazy, he'd never agree to live with a bunch of acrobats."

"Nor would the Palace Staff help him to do so," Chisaad agreed. "Not if they, or he, have a choice. It could only happen if somebody powerful overrode them to *make* it happen." He paused for a moment before he quietly said, "Or two somebodies. Two powerful magical somebodies, with very different talents."

Kirin stared at him. "You think that *we*—that you and me, can make this happen?"

"If we did." The wizard held up a finger in warning. "If you brought home Prince Terrell, with his voice and appearance magically disguised as an ordinary man, would your family accept him into their home and teach him how to be Silbari?"

As Kirin hesitated, the wizard added, "It could be the only way to set your father free."

Somebody powerful will help me, the fortune teller said. "They'll do it," Kirin declared, convincing himself. "I know they will. But how can I get the Prince to agree?"

"He must not be offered a choice. It must be arranged and done in secret, so that he simply awakes in a new place with new people."

"But he'd only run back to the Palace." Kirin protested.

"Not if a spell confined him to the top floors of your inn." The wizard leaned forward and stared at Kirin eye to eye. "Not if you and your family share with him your lives, show him what it means to be an acrobat, teach him about your father."

Kirin thought hard about that one. "That would mean that I couldn't hate him." He'd been hating the Prince a great deal for the last hour. *Dona Zella said hate leaves no room for love, we must pick only one.* He agonized over that, but in the contest between hating the Prince and loving his father, there could be only one winner. He raised his head, stared at Chisaad's face. "Yes. What do I need to do?"

The wizard smiled. "Let me show you." He led the way up the main stairs of the tower to the topmost room.

Kirin, who had never been above the ground floor before, stared around in amazement. There were tall shelves with strange apparatus crowded in among more books than he had ever seen. A decagram graven on the floor glowed with energies. A table held a carving so life-like that he had to look twice to be sure it wasn't a sleeping man. He froze, scared to damage something, and fought his hungry Shadow to a standstill.

The wizard touched the recumbent form. "Here is the means to compel the Prince to listen to you and your family." He activated a spell on the carved shape and it took on the appearance of flesh. Prince Terrell's flesh.

Only then did Kirin recognize it as another golem like the wizard's other servants. *No, not like them. Much, much better!* It sat up and swung its legs off the table, pivoted smoothly and sat there staring vacantly into the air. It didn't seem aware of them. The resemblance to the Prince astonished Kirin. *Does he really have blond hair in his crotch like that? I guess he must since his head is blond.*

Chisaad's intention became clear. "You want to switch this golem for the Prince!"

"Exactly." The wizard smiled a thin smile.

Kirin marveled. He knew magic could do amazing things, but this seemed like a dream. A dream that he badly needed right now. "Won't people notice?"

"By itself, yes. However, I have another spell that will give it the Prince's voice, ways of moving and speaking, even his knowledge. It will not last for more than a season, so you must befriend and persuade the real man in that time. Do you think you can do that?"

"Yes." Kirin jerked his head in a decisive nod. "I have to." *The Duermu seer promised me powerful help, and here it is. Besides, Maia and Grandmother could charm even a snake, with that much time.*

"Let us begin."

* * *

"I still don't feel right leaving you here without me," Pen muttered under his breath to Terrell as they strode out of the Diplomatic Gate. This part of the Palace opened into Messenger Street, the broad thoroughfare that separated the Gray Fort from the Treasury. Late afternoon sunlight threw shadows over the street.

Terrell answered, "I'll still have five companies of the Silbari brigade here with me. We must break up this sulfur plot before the principals can escape. I cannot leave Aretzo now, not with the Mages and the Hierarchy in contention. I'll miss you dreadfully, Pen, but it has to be this way."

Pen nodded in wordless concession and looked at the waiting entourage prepared for him. The Truthteller priestesses reclined in a two-person horse litter like the one that had carried Dona Seraphina and her husband to Silbar; their husbands rode horses to either side. The two young reeves had mounted their own horses and waited eagerly for this adventure to begin. The company of soldiers flanking them were all cavalry and dragoons, mounted, phlegmatic, and ready.

"I wish we had that Ilvar clan here," Pen said. "They could fly me to Sulmona in a couple days. Wouldn't that surprise Lord Gwynned?"

Terrell chuckled. "There aren't any wizards in Aretzo talented enough to sustain a levitation spell like the Ilvars. Chisaad said even he couldn't manage one for long enough to reach Sulmona. And how would we get your soldiers there? Sorry, Pen, you'll have to ride."

"I'll be as quick as I can," Pen said, looking pensive. "I do hope I can get back here before . . ." He left the thought unsaid.

Terrell's own face saddened. "The latest dispatch says Father couldn't rise from his bed the day before yesterday. He won't last a great deal longer. But I'll delay the Choosing ceremony until you return, no matter what."

"Thank you." Pen's face lightened a little at that.

They embraced each other fiercely before the Prince of Silbar's best friend mounted his horse and rode out Messenger Street toward Northgate. Terrell stared after him until the last of the train of soldiers and pack horses had followed. Then he sighed and turned back through the Diplomatic Gate. The day aged and he had work to do.

* * *

"He looks like a normal man," Kirin whispered to Chisaad, as they gazed down on the parting from the upper works of the Diplomatic Gate. "Except for the hair."

The wizard had gotten him into the Palace through the Clerk's Gate. The guards there had been introduced to Chisaad's new apprentice and had made appropriate notations in their registers with friendly solemnity. A twisting path through the labyrinth had brought them here in time to watch the departure.

"He is a normal man," Chisaad murmured back. "Unfortunately raised and badly taught by Northern barbarians, but little older than you, I expect. If he had only been raised here, imagine how different he would be."

Kirin nodded. *I've got to teach him about us common folk*, he thought. *He'll be a better king that way.* He squared his shoulders and followed the wizard as Chisaad showed him around the Palace. Tonight, Kirin knew he would have to find his way through it while avoiding human guards. Best to memorize where they were usually found. For the rest, he would have to trust to his Shadow.

* * *

Prince Terrell yawned, pushed the Mage Guild's scroll away from him and let the end roll up. A Temple bell rang the tenth hour; most of the city and the Palace were already asleep. "That's enough for today. We'll finish in the morning." He sent his secretaries to bed and vacated his office.

PETER SARTUCCI

The Palace corridors were echoingly empty. He could feel the watching spells more keenly than usual as he made his way through the labyrinth with his bodyguards.

I miss Pen already. Simply his rock-steady presence there at my elbow, always reliable, always comforting.

At the bridge into the Royal Apartments the soldiers perforce stopped at the Guardian, saluted, and left him as soon as he had stepped through. His two personal servants and his valet hovered on the far side, alerted by the Palace's web of spells. Dona Seraphina stood in front of them and looked as immovable as a tree.

"Past time for me to check you over, Your Highness," she said in a voice that implied *you disobedient puppy!*

He sighed, stood still and let her aura sweep through him. It was quicker than arguing.

She squinted as she worked. "The Light inside you grows steadily stronger."

"It declines each time I use the Stone Throne," he disagreed.

"Only temporarily, and by smaller amounts each time," she countered. "It is enlarging and eroding your mana-conduits, which worries me. Such damage can take a long time to heal. Perhaps you should find a way to drain off more of this Light regularly."

"Climbing the Hill every few days has certainly strengthened my legs. Perhaps using the Throne will strengthen my mana-conduits too."

She made a noncommittal sound and withdrew her aura, bowed to him and stepped aside.

His servants followed him into his suite. "Bring me food," he ordered. "And have, hmm, Wren attend me tonight."

An hour later, replete in two different ways, Terrell kissed Wren before she left his bed. "I wish they would let me know your real name," he told her drowsily.

She smiled and stroked his chest. "This is the way it must be. Someday, after you are married, perhaps we will meet again, and you will know me and be glad. For now, My Lord, sleep." She left him and firmly closed the door to the concubines' suite behind her. He wondered if she and her sister concubines would stay up exchanging gossip about him, or simply go to sleep.

He stretched in the silken sheets; the windows were open to let in such breezes as the warm summer night offered, though heavily shielded by spells. They faced north across the moat at the western flank of the Hill of Sight. He deliberately did not call on his magesight, preferring that the blazing power of the cone not disrupt his sleep.

Pen's door stood ajar and his room dark and palpably empty. Pen usually closed it while Terrell enjoyed his concubines, then opened it again to bid him good night after they left. But not tonight; by now Pen must be camped along the Kings Road or more likely staying at an inn somewhere many miles north of the city.

Terrell sighed and composed himself for sleep.

* * *

Kirin rubbed his eyes. They'd grown weary from staring at a huge map of the Palace on the inner wall of the Royal Wizard's office. It had markers for every spell in the enormous building and he had to stay a yard away from it at all times to calm his Shadow.

"Have you memorized it yet?" the wizard demanded irritably. They had been cooped up in his office for hours, skipping supper and working well into the night as Kirin strove to figure out a way into the Prince's bedroom.

"Yes, Magister," Kirin answered, controlling his impatience. This wasn't too different from the tension before a performance, except tonight he hoped to go completely unseen. He checked the two brass cylinders he had tucked inside his vest, containing special concoctions prepared by the wizard that had no magic to attract his Shadow's attention. "When can I start?"

As he spoke a spell-marker changed color on the map of the Royal Apartments. "His servants have left for bed, all except for the one tasked to stay awake if the Prince calls for anything," Chisaad announced with satisfaction. "Be very sure that you take that one out first, and quietly! If you wake the Prince and he has time to call for help—"

"I know, Magister," Kirin interrupted, rolling his eyes slightly. They had been over this half a dozen times already. *You'd think he's got stage fright.*

The wizard flicked him an irritated glance before his features smoothed into blandness. "Remember to exit through the Diplomatic Gate. It is busy throughout the night and the guards will think nothing of one more late departure."

"Yes, Magister. Can I start now?"

"Go."

CHAPTER 29: KIRIN AND TERRELL

The obvious way to get there went over the roof, Kirin had decided. All the interior corridors were guarded. According to Chisaad there would be more guards the closer one got to the Royal Apartments. Unfortunately, the many buildings making up the Palace were not all the same height, or even close, so getting from one roof to the next would make noise and draw attention. The guards were aware that some mages could fly, so they kept watch over the palace from towers as well as inside. Kirin checked two different routes before reluctantly concluding that he'd have to get closer to the Royal Apartments before going aloft.

He worked his way through the labyrinth, remembering turns and corridors from the map in Chisaad's office. Parts of his route passed through broad airy two-and-three story hallways with upper floor balconies under barrel-vaulted ceilings. Oil lamps were few and far between, so most denizens who had cause to move around inside the Palace at night used candles or mage lamps to find their way. Shadows were the rule and light the exception.

Shadows were his friends. He wrapped himself in his own as he prowled.

The vast roofed corridors were only a little bigger than the Serpent's Attic, but their colorful frescoes and carved marble pillars, arches, and doorways were strange to his night-sighted eyes. He stayed under the second-floor balconies as much as possible and hugged the walls. Several times individual servants passed him on nocturnal missions. Twice clusters of young men returned from the Red Street reeking of wine, perfume, and sex. Once he nearly walked right up to a youth in servant's garb crouched behind a pedestal that supported a massive urn. Kirin waited impatiently several steps behind him until a maid with a candle came down the hall, slipped behind the urn, and the two indulged in a passionate kiss. They finally took themselves off down a side corridor and he glided on, his bare feet silent. He had tucked his new buskins and the two brass vials into a sack tied across his back. It made him look like a hunchback, but bare feet were best on unfamiliar surfaces and he counted on not being seen at all.

Malicious fate nearly undid him.

The closer he got to the Royal Apartments, the more vigilant—and frequent—the guards became. Soon a broad hallway crossed the one he followed. Twisted columns upheld the intersecting vaults of the ceilings, one pair per corner, perched on wide pedestals ornamented with statues and more of the huge urns. Glass skylights soaked all four corridors in stripes of moonlight and shadow. He looked both ways and listened carefully before gliding across in one of the shadowed bands. Unfriendly moonlight lit the floor to either side.

He made it only halfway when two guards walked out of a side corridor. He dashed across the rest bent almost double and prayed neither of them saw him.

"Dung!" one man choked.

Kirin flattened himself against one of the corner pillars as the guard's partner asked, "What?"

"Something moved!" The first voice said, amid the sound of a sword hissing out of its scabbard. "Like a shadow of something big! Right there!"

Another sound of drawing swords and two pairs of footsteps advanced together.

Kirin silently cursed and stared around wildly. Too much hallway stretched between him and the next hiding place, he'd never make it there in time. The second-floor balcony didn't continue on this side and the marble walls were too slick to climb. But one of the big urns loomed over him, four feet tall and standing on a waist-high pedestal. He grabbed the rim and hauled himself up and in.

The two guards rounded the corner slowly, swords at the ready and covering each other. They poked sharp metal into all the shadows, did the same on the other side of the hallway, and finally stood together in the middle.

"There's nothin' here," the second said reasonably. "You sure you saw somethin'?"

"I thought so." Kirin could hear the scowl in the first voice.

Second Voice sheathed his sword with a loud click, suggested, "Maybe a bat flew overhead, threw a shadow through the winders."

First Voice sighed and sheathed his own sword. "I need a smoke. You got any?"

"Sure. Gimme your pipe, you get us a light."

There were footsteps, shuffling noises, and the click of a wall lantern's brass case opening and closing. Puffing sounds as someone got a pipe drawing. "Quick! Before it burns my fingers," First Voice implored.

Kirin sweated inside the tall urn and breathed as shallowly as he could. He had to crouch low to keep his head hidden below the rim. A moment later a "Yeow!" echoed through the hallway, then a curse as the burned guard flung the hot ember away, followed by—

A flaming splinter dropped on Kirin's head.

His thick curly hair caught the splinter and held it away from his scalp. He almost gave himself away when he shook his head so hard the splinter flew back out of the jar. Luckily the flame had gone out and neither guard noticed the dark ember drift to the floor.

First Voice and Second Voice traded gossip, bellyached about their commander, and swapped boasts about recent prowess on the Red Street.

Kirin resisted the need to sneeze and tried to hold off cramps by doing some of the Still Exercises. Just when he thought the two would never leave, their voices came closer.

"Time we git moovin'" Second voice said from right outside the urn. "Gimme your pipe and I'll empty it with mine."

A moment later the bowls of two pipes appeared above the rim of the jar, rapped sharply, and dumped hot ashes on Kirin. He held himself rigid as the ashes slid down the inside of the jar. They burned hair off his arm and singed one thigh right through his tights. He forced himself to wait and listen until the guards rounded the next corner.

Then he leaped out of the jar, somersaulted to the floor and slapped embers off himself. Assured that he wasn't on fire, he continued down the corridor while mentally swearing all the way. The burns were minor, he'd had worse from ropes a dozen times, but it galled him to have to stay still and take it.

A side corridor, an inconspicuous stair, a service door guarded by spells that didn't notice him, and he gained the roof near the bridge to the Royal Apartments. Bats soared through the night air pursuing pale moths. A narrow band of shadow thrown by the east-bound Moon of Madness let him crawl unseen to the start of the bridge over the moat. Kirin looked south. Close at hand a tower reared near the moat's edge, he could see two guards vigilantly watching. Farther to the southwest another tower had been set only a little way back from the moat, also boasting two guards. He thought he could avoid the eyes of the farther tower by staying on the north side of the pitched roof over the bridge. But the near tower looked right down onto it, those guards could hardly miss him.

Unless he gave them something else to look at while he crossed the bare top of the bridge. He had made his Shadow dance with Maia's white kerchiefs. It could just as well dance by itself.

He rolled onto his back on the hard roof, poured Shadow into his hands, and began to mold it. His first attempt came out awful, his second merely laughable, but the third one worked, and by the sixth his shadow-bats looked good enough for night-time work. He sent the four best bats soaring like their fleshy fellows while he remade the first pair, made two more, and soon he had eight Shadow bats circling the nearer tower.

The guards exclaimed and jabbered, taking them for real creatures. Kirin took his courage in his hands, drew his Shadow over himself, and crawled out onto the bridge roof.

He didn't dare move fast; sudden motion could catch the guards' eyes even with his Shadow-bats' distraction. Slow and steady crawling brought him to the gap in the roof between the two halves of the bridge where the glowing Guardian waited.

If there hadn't been men in the towers he would have chanced a running start and a leap right over the thing to the next roof. Instead he stuck his head down below the rim of the roof, made sure the bridge was empty, and flipped himself down to the floor. Getting back up and out would be a challenge, but the roof jutted only a dozen feet above the floor and the broad window sills would provide a useful step up. He remembered to draw his shadow bats down into the moat and under the bridge, then back up to him through the stone. They tried to snack on the spells, but he managed to stop them.

He stared at the big stone ring of the Guardian. Its many faces were all silent and unlit, but the glow of latent magic rippled over the surface. Chisaad had told him about it, though the Royal Apartments were not part of his wizardly duties; some mage named Fantillin managed this artifact.

It's just a bunch of spells. It can't see me, Kirin assured himself as he wrapped Shadow tightly around his skin.

He took a deep breath and walked straight through the carved stone ring.

Nothing happened.

He exhaled happily and skipped the rest of the way across the bridge.

The corridors of the Royal Apartments were dim, the courtyard pool a burnished mirror in the moonlight. Midnight had passed into memory and Kirin had heard the second bell ring some time ago. Two small magelamps burned in the main hallway. He avoided both and made his way to the double doors into the King's Suite. The brass dragons embossed on their panels glittered in the dimness. Spells writhed over them so that their eyes seemed to track him as he approached.

They can't see me either. He reached out with both hands to push one of the doors open, expecting it to be so heavy that it would be a strain to move. But as his palms touched the cool brass, the dragon eyes lit.

He froze as two vast presences crowded into his mind.

WHO COMES? They asked in voices louder than trumpets. *NAME YOURSELF.*

I'm Kirin! He cried, the darkness of his mind now shattered with light. Two incandescent beings pinned him between their pitiless gazes and held him fast.

For an excruciatingly long moment they scrutinized him while he despaired. He'd failed, the guards would come, and they'd take him to prison, or to the iron stake in front of the Temple. Pieter would die in the sulfur mines. Death and shame, shame and death, nothing else lay before him.

YOU MAY PASS.

Their gaze released him, and he nearly fell over as the two big doors silently opened inward. He stumbled into the room beyond and dropped to his knees on a soft rug.

They saw me! Did they call the guards?

He trembled, sicker with fear than he'd been even after Millago's, even at the news of Pieter's sentence. Long minutes passed while he waited for doom, but except for the doors silently closing again, nothing happened. Surely guards would respond faster than this?

The dragons not only let me go, they let me in here. Why? Do they know why I'm here?

No answer came.

Whatever they wanted from me, they're letting me continue. Maybe the angels approve of what I'm going to do for the Prince? Maybe they want him to learn from my family.

Encouraged, he looked around.

Chisaad had only been able to describe the Prince's personal apartment in general terms, since he had never been here himself. Kirin discovered that he had stumbled right into the middle of a big sitting room. Slanting moonlight lit the long dim room through three large skylights. A small mage lamp burned on an elaborate inlaid table next to one of the many long soft couches. A sleeping youth in servant's garb had begun to stir.

Kirin grabbed one of the wizard's brass cylinders out of his pack, took a deep breath to hold, and twisted off the top. A drug-soaked cloth fell into his hand and he clapped it over the sleepy face as the boy's eyelids began to flutter. The youth twitched, sighed, and sank into a deeper slumber. Kirin frantically stuffed the cloth back in the cylinder and slapped the lid on before he ran out of breath. The hand that had touched the cloth stung like a sunburn. He backpedaled away from the couch, sucked in lungfuls of clean air, and looked around.

There were four doors, unevenly spaced, in the long wall opposite the dragon-doors. Which one lead to the Prince's room?

He combined rumors with what the wizard had told him. The prince had concubines, and his bodyguard slept here too. But Sir Penghar DuVerhys DiLione had gone to Sulmona, and the concubines slept in a separate room according to rumor.

Kirin wondered at that. It seemed an unnatural way for a man and a woman to sleep.

The four doors waited. They had handles but no latches. The left one and the second-from-left one were widely separated from each other and from the other pair, which were closer together. The bodyguard would probably have a smaller room than the Prince or his concubines. Kirin took a deep breath and tried the second-from-the-right door. Moving very gently and slowly, with his Shadow extended to block all sight of the moonlit room behind him, he pushed the heavy panel open one finger width at a time.

Empty. A neatly made bed lay undisturbed. From the personal possessions on shelves and the garments incompletely returned to a wardrobe, he guessed this must be Sir DiLione's room. Another door in the side wall stood slightly ajar. From beyond it came a faint snoring. He tiptoed to it and cautiously peered through.

The bedroom beyond had ten times the space of the room he and Maia shared. The bed by itself was bigger than their whole room. A man lay on it, yellow curls disarrayed around his sleeping face. He glowed with an inner light.

The Prince.

Kirin slipped through the door. He drew the other cylinder from his pack as he padded across the plush rugs and tile floor. When he reached the bedside, he stood a moment staring down at the sleeping man. Prince Terrell's face shone. He didn't look cruel or harsh. Kirin clutched the drug-cylinder and hesitated.

He's . . . young. Like me. But all that Light spilling out of him! How does he stand it?

His Shadow reached for the man on the bed and touched him delicately, worshipfully. The Prince's glow diminished, and only then did Kirin realize that his Shadow had drunk some of that upwelling Light.

Like a vampire.

Hastily he seized his personal monster with his mind, tried to forbid it from touching the Prince. It churned unhappily around him like a storm of black clouds but stopped drinking the Light. Kirin decided that he could hope for no better.

I've got to do what I came for. The angels let me in, they must approve. I can teach him how to be a real Silbari. I've got to do it to free Pieter.

He pushed through his uneasiness, took a deep breath as he twisted off the cylinder's lid, bent over the Prince and pressed the drugged rag over his mouth and nose.

An instant before it touched, Prince Terrell's eyes opened.

* × *

Terrell gasped in shock and got a deep breath of something heavy and strange. His hands had instinctively grabbed at the muscular arm pressing something against his face. His eyes followed that arm to a face wrapped in darkness, out of which two black eyes stared . . .

. . . and with a dizzying jerk he found himself looking down at his own face half-covered by a cloth clamped in a golden-brown hand that was not his own.

Sleep overcame him and he knew no more.

* * *

Kirin almost passed out on the bed beside the Prince. He managed to stagger away, and his head cleared enough that he remembered to stuff the drugged cloth back into the cylinder and seal it again. He tried to put it back into his pack, dropped it instead. Thankfully the metal tube landed on a plush rug and not on the echoing tile. He fell on his face when he bent over for the brass tube. He managed to catch himself on his hands and knees, again grateful for the rug, and had to crawl to it. On the third try he finally got the tube put away secure.

He lay there trembling in a pool of moonlight.

It happened again. What did he do to me?

He covered his face with his hands and remembered one of Pieter's sayings. *Once is just the thing itself, and twice might be coincidence; but if it happens a third time—*

Kirin's mind groped for an answer. There had been such a wave of surprise both times that he couldn't believe the mind-swap had been deliberate. Could it be a special talent of the Prince? There hadn't been any gossip about any such thing, but maybe he had kept it a secret.

Remembering the shock in the other mind, he thought it upset Prince Terrell as much as it upset him.

Holy Haroun protect me, what if it happens while I'm teaching him trapeze work? He imagined the confusion, a missed catch, an embarrassing and dangerous fall into the net. *It happened both times when I looked at his eyes.*

I better not ever look him in the eyes again.

And with that he remembered that he lay on the floor of the Prince's bedroom while Chisaad waited outside.

Kirin got to his feet, still unsteady, and made his way to the room's middle window. All three were open to admit cool night air. Layers of spells screened them, woven so thick that they wouldn't allow a gnat through. He knelt and rested both hands on the low sill, hesitated for a moment remembering the dragon-doors, then took command of his Shadow. He leaned forward and stuck his head and shoulders through the screen.

The spells parted around him; his Shadow didn't even try to eat the magic, which surprised him. He found himself looking at the southwest side of the Hill of Sight. Using magesight through his Shadow revealed the vast core of spells woven into it, a multi-sided column of blazing purple fire that saturated the Hill and ran deep into the World. He hurriedly closed his magesight and blinked to rid himself of the after-images. When he could see normally again he stared at the north flank of the Hill where only ordinary protection spells flowed and coiled. Chisaad had said he would conceal himself on that slope in the shade of the western pergola, under an illusion spell.

Kirin found him. The wizard crouched on a carpet that floated above the wall-less pergola's floor. Without the illusion spell he looked as obvious as the proverbial priestess in a whorehouse. But only someone immune to magic could see him. Kirin stretched his arms apart, shaped his Shadow into an open-ended tube, and pushed back the window spells to the very edges of the frame.

The wizard saw. His carpet lifted and flew arrow-straight at the window. Kirin strained to push every bit of his Shadow out from the inside of the tube. Chisaad neatly threaded the gap and landed his carpet silently on the floor of the Prince's bedchamber. Kirin let his Shadow collapse back into him, still without trying to snack on the spells, and sagged back onto a rug.

The wizard tossed spells at all three doors to bar anyone from entering, then hurriedly flipped back one of the plush rugs. He took out a rolled cloth and spread it on the floor, aligned it minutely until spells on it activated to make a glowing blue decagram. He shot a hard look at Kirin as he said, "Be sure you stay well back, there's no time to fix this if you damage it."

Kirin nodded, not trusting his voice yet. Between the drug and the mind-swap, the floor seemed like a fine place to be right now.

Then Chisaad rolled up his flying carpet and stepped on the decagram, spoke a word—and vanished.

Kirin stared. Chisaad had told him the decagram carried a teleporttation spell, but he had had only a foggy notion what that meant. Moments later the wizard returned with his golem, still looking eerily like the Prince. The golem peeled back the sheet and effortlessly scooped up the drugged Prince, carried him to the decagram, and the two of them and Chisaad disappeared again. Several very long minutes passed before the wizard returned with the golem and without the prince, and now the golem moved with a fluid and natural ease that it hadn't had before, and glowed with the same Light the Prince had shown. Chisaad gestured to the bed impatiently and the naked golem climbed in and drew the sheet over itself while Kirin stared.

On the surface it looks exactly like the prince, right down to his Light. It even moves like a real man. Only when I look under the spells can I see the golem. Wow.

Chisaad gave a relieved sigh and relaxed, looked at Kirin. "Why are you still sitting on the floor?" He whispered. "Are you injured?"

"No." Kirin scrambled to his feet. "The drug made me dizzy."

The wizard shook his head. "You should have followed my instructtions more exactly. Give me the canisters."

Kirin turned them over. "I'm sorry, Magister."

Chisaad tucked the drugged canisters in his robes, then looked at Kirin's face intently. "We're almost done. Are you able to make it back out of here? Can you find your way to the Diplomatic Gate?"

Kirin bridled a little at that; he had made it in here, hadn't he? But he contented himself with simply saying, "Yes, Magister."

"Good." The wizard did something to the decagram and then scooped up the cloth that had carried it. The glowing pattern remained on the floor, muted but still visible to Kirin's eyes. Chisaad rolled the rug back over it, which hid the glow not at all, then carefully dispelled his locking spells from the three doors. Without another word or even glance at Kirin he stepped onto the decagram, said the triggering word, and vanished. A moment later the decagram's glow also winked out.

Astonished, Kirin lifted the edge of the rug and peeked under. The ten-pointed diagram had gone as if it had never been. He dropped the rug and looked around.

He was alone in the Prince's bedchamber, save for a sleeping golem.

He sighed and set about the task of sneaking back out of the Royal Apartments.

CHAPTER 30: KIRIN AND TERRELL

The third bell had rung before he made it through all the long hallways to the Diplomatic Gate. Fate had been kind this time. He had made it back onto the roof without being noticed—he had worried that his shadow-bats wouldn't be enough this time—and no guards had been in the long corridors while he passed through.

The Dragon Doors had opened to let him leave as if he had every right to do so. He tried to convince himself that was good, but it still unnerved him.

The route from Chisaad's office to the Diplomatic Gate went easier, as guards expected people to be about in this part of the palace even after midnight. Dozens of Palace officials and servants actually lived along those corridors. The Gate guards were sleepy and incurious, what attention they had left at this hour focused on anyone entering. He gave them his name and status and they looked him up in one of their books, where his name had already appeared since this morning.

"Wizard's got you working late on your first day, eh?" One guard said.

"Lot to do," Kirin grumbled, shifting the empty pack on his back. "Hope I can get something to eat before I have to come back. Some sleep'd be nice too."

The guard chuckled and waved him through.

Kirin didn't relax until he reached the end of Messenger Street. Traffic had ended for the night, he saw nobody but a trio of men repairing a wagon's wheel. He hesitated at the corner, looking east into the Bazaar. Even at this hour someone would be awake and selling food and drink, and hunger gnawed at him.

A knife almost got him.

Kirin twisted aside at the last instant. The blade grazed his ribs with a deadly promise. The man wielding it had been working at the wagon wheel a moment before. The attacker stabbed again, barely missing as Kirin kept dodging.

What in the Nine Hells? Kirin thought through his shock. *Why is he attacking me?* Then, as the other two came after him, *Oh dung!*

A cowled and caped man stood up in the wagon bed and growled, "Gut him, you fools!"

Kirin had heard that voice in the Hall of Justice. *It's Duke Darnaud!*

The three tried to surround Kirin, which would have been death for an ordinary man. Instead he drowned the street in Shadow.

He dodged the first blinded-man's stab in the darkness, kicked a knife out of a second one's hand and then kicked the cursing thug in the crotch for good measure. Kirin danced out of the way of the third flailing attacker before the disoriented fool ran into the first man.

Then he turned, ran out of his billowing Shadow, and found himself face-to-face with a growling wolf-beast as big as a pony. It carried the druid he'd met outside the cemetery gates a season ago, whom the priestess had named Boerga.

"I knew you were evil's servant!" Boerga cackled in Gwythlo. She kneed her beast in the ribs. "Kill!"

He hurled Shadow in their faces as the beast lunged for him, then dodged and drew his knife. The snapping jaws closed on air half a foot from his elbow. The Druid swung a wickedly-curved sword in a vicious arc that missed him completely. He stabbed the beast, his knife sank in and grated along bone. The big creature jerked away, and Kirin barely held onto his blade.

Boerga snarled commands as her steed tried to double back at him, almost unseating her. In the confusion in the Shadow's darkness, beast and rider staggered for footing. The Shadow drank the power from her silver jewelry while her sword hunted Kirin. She shrieked something frustrated that he didn't catch as he fled into the maze of the Bazaar.

He drew his Shadow back inside him as he dodged between stalls and leaped over obstacles hidden in shadows. He paused behind one tent, wiped his belt knife clean on a washrag left to dry on one of the ropes, and then ran on. Behind him he could hear a growing uproar as the beast crashed into a stall and wrecked it. Rudely-awakened merchants howled, the druid cursed, and the beast whined in pain. He hoped the wound he'd dealt it was enough to stop it from chasing him.

Long minutes later he slipped across the Processional while a cloud covered the moons. Shortly he crossed the South Road with a quick look north towards the plaza in front of the Middle Court, where the North and South roads met. He couldn't see the mouth of Messenger Street from there, or the tangled mess he'd left behind in the Bazaar, which meant Duke Darnaud and Boerga couldn't see him. The clean streets of the Clerk's Quarter accepted him as he slowed to a walk and got his breath back.

Understanding finally hit him.

Duke Darnaud and Boerga; they knew I would be there. They were waiting for me.

He stopped between one pace and the next, in the shadow of a fig tree leaning over a courtyard wall. Only one person had known he would be leaving the Palace by the Diplomatic Gate and Messenger Street. His stomach churned and he tasted acid at the back of his throat; the world suddenly seemed made of knives. He shrank into the tree's shadow, into his own Shadow, then looked across the cobbles and up. The top of Chisaad's tower loomed over the neighborhood. Mage-lit windows glared at the pale moons.

Oh no. Please no. Magister wouldn't betray me like that.

But even Mother Gee had betrayed him to Ymera. He remembered Mage Yellow's bitter words.

"He's survived eighteen years as Royal Wizard, and that takes more lies and dealings than a peasant like you can imagine."

Kirin crouched against the wall while his thoughts raced.

I did what he wanted. I kidnapped the Prince out of his own Palace. Magister replaced him with a golem. What if . . . what if that was the whole point?

Kirin wrapped his arms across his chest in an agony of doubt. *Holy Haroun help me! What do I do now?*

The top of the wizard's tower blinked and drew Kirin's attention back to it. A moment later he saw someone moving between a mage lamp and the windows. Two someones, throwing shadows on the glass.

He said he would put spells on the Prince to disguise his face and voice, so I could bring him home with me, and then a spell to keep him inside. But what if he isn't doing that at all?

Kirin shivered. *I have to know what's really happening.*

He stood up, wrapped his Shadow close about him, and glided toward the tower.

A carriage waited at the curb in front of the wizard's residence. The yawning coachman wore the Governor's livery. Kirin felt sick; if this scheme included Ap Marn it must be even more twisted than he'd thought. In the courtyard three bodyguards lounged on the front step, gossiping and waiting. There would be no getting in unobserved by the front door.

Kirin slunk around the block to the alley behind the house. Tower and house both blazed with spells that had been strengthened since yesterday. A barred gate denied entry to the delivery tunnel leading into the back courtyard and he couldn't possibly squeeze over or under its heavy timbers. The tower had a rear postern door opening into the alley, also firmly shut; he remembered that Chisaad kept it barred on the inside. The rectangular tower had no windows on the outer side at all for the first two floors, only a small window in the back stairwell above the postern door.

It stood slightly open.

He measured the distance with his acrobat's eye. About twenty feet up to the window, too high to jump, but the massive door frame below offered a path.

This could be a trap.

He stopped, stared at the glass panes. Nine of them, arranged three by three in a wooden frame. There should be a latch on the inside and the gap could pass a hand to release it.

Magister might have told the Duke where I'd be. If he did, then he tried to get me killed. Maybe this open window is a trick.

Kirin hesitated. Another thought followed.

If I don't find out what he's really doing, I'll have nothing to tell my family except that I helped kidnap the Prince and then Duke Darnaud tried to kill me. Maia and Sevan would believe me when I say the wizard betrayed me; would anyone else?

I have to know more.

He gulped, steadied himself, and began to climb the door-frame.

The spells didn't notice him, but their glow distracted him, he had to strain to ignore it. Slow centuries had worn away the mortar, in some places the gap between the cut granite blocks ate as much as three finger-widths deep and half that wide. He found enough purchase to make it to the windowsill and slip into the back stairwell. Voices drifted down from above, indistinct. He began to ascend, his soft buskins making no sound on the stone treads.

He found a tiny landing and a door at each floor. The door into the tower's top floor had been shut but not barred. He tried to remember the big room, pictured the decagram in his mind, the table where the golem had rested, a lot of book shelves, but no back door. Some of the bookshelves had been pushed back to make room for the decagram and left standing in untidy disarray; this door might be behind them. Gently, slowly, he pressed the wood panel open, bit by bit. He prayed it wouldn't creak.

The voices became clear. The room was brightly lit but the door got none of it. He had guessed right, two large bookshelves had been shoved in front of it, only an arm's-length away. One had spilled books and scrolls to leave a gap at waist height that he could look through. He slipped through the door, knelt and stared.

The prince lay naked on the table with his wrists and ankles bound, still unconscious. The wizard did something to his head while talking to former-Governor Ap Marn.

"There, the anchor is ready. The final step is to link the spells on my golem with the spells on his mind, so the golem knows everything he knows."

Chisaad whispered something and made a gesture. The Prince twitched, groaned, rolled his head back and forth, and awoke. Kirin stared in horrified fascination at the glittery spider nestled amid bloody hair on the top of Prince Terrell's head.

* * *

Terrell awoke from bad dreams to find himself muttering incoherently. His head pounded with the worst headache he'd ever known and he wasn't in his own bed. He turned his head side to side as he took in the surroundings. A strange room with two familiar faces leaning over him: Ap Marn and Chisaad.

"Wh- what happened?" he asked through the headache. "Where am I?" Then, belatedly discovering his bindings, he demanded, "What's happening?"

Ap Marn chuckled. "You replaced me, so I replaced you, young fool. Enjoying the sensation, My Lord?" An ugly bite freighted the words and an uglier glare filled the Gwythlo Lord's eyes. "I hope not, because it's about to get much worse, and that *worse* will last for as long as your bitch of a mother lives. After that we won't need you alive anymore."

Terrell flicked his gaze to Chisaad. "Conspiracy, Chisaad? Why?"

"Because I need you alive until the Choosing, Your Highness. Don't bother asking more, you wouldn't understand. Meanwhile we're sending you to a place we've prepared for you. I'm afraid you'll find the accommodations rather rough, but you'll have an excellent view of our ancestors' folly."

"Accommodations?" Terrell pressed, desperate for information. "Ancestor's folly? You mean the Scarp? Or Purification Lake?"

"Oh, very good, Terrell, excellent deductions from very little evidence. Shimoor would be proud of you." Chisaad smiled. "But still a few miles off. You expressed a wish to see ruined Silbariki, so I've arranged it. I'm afraid you can't be allowed to wander around—it's half-underwater anyway—but you'll be able to see the most impressive part from your prison."

Terrell tried to surreptitiously test the knots while the wizard spoke, but Ap Marn caught him at it and laughed. "Don't bother, boy, I still know how to tie a good knot." The ex-Governor looked at Chisaad. "Do we really need him awake for this?"

Yes! Terrell thought; the next few minutes might hold essential clues he would need to escape.

"No," said the wizard calmly, twisting the lid off a canister.

Dung! Terrell turned his head aside as Chisaad slapped a familiar-smelling rag across his face. He tried to jackknife himself off the table with his legs but Ap Marn held him; he tried to hold his breath, but the fumes worked their way with him anyway. His last sight was of a pair of familiar black eyes staring at him through a shelf half filled with books. For an instant he saw himself struggling against his captors' grips. Then the drug took him, and his consciousness spiraled down into darkness.

* * *

Kirin bowed his head, nauseated as much by the brief renewal of the mind-link as by the conspirators' words. *Three times, it happened three times!* The Prince's tightly-controlled terror shook his soul. He fought the urge to vomit despite the emptiness of his stomach.

When he looked up again, Ap Marn had brought one of his men into the room to lift the sleeping Prince. The big Gwythlo carried him to the decagram under Ap Marn's direction, the wizard joined them there. With a swift flash of power, they were gone.

Kirin fumbled his way back into the stairwell, barely retaining the presence of mind to shut the door behind him. He nearly fell as he descended the stairs, caught himself and breathed deeply, then made it back to the little window. He had to dash tears out of his eyes before he looked out to make sure nobody waited below. It took several breaths to calm himself enough to descend the wall. He lost his grip only at the end. He dropped the final few feet to the pavement and caught his balance with long practice.

Then he ran blindly through the streets of the city with his Shadow drawn around him like a fraying cloak, his mind churning as badly as his gut.

This is my fault! What do I do?

CHAPTER 31: MAIA AND KIRIN

You will all remain quiet or your children will die."

Maia heard the Gwythlo woman's imperious declaration and believed her instantly. The weathered woman and the silent cowled man at her elbow had growled at the DiUmbra family as soldiers poured into their quarters and rousted everybody out of bed. Those pale-skinned men waved unsheathed swords to herd the family into the corridor. Maia clutched baby Grigor tightly and he mewled a protest.

The woman's eyes fixed on her like a beast sighting prey. "You. Are you his woman? Is that child of his seed? Tell me!"

Maia cringed, then forced herself to raise her chin. "I'm Maia Sule Di-Umbra. My son is Grigor Sule DiUmbra. My husband is Kirin Sule DiUmbra. What do you want?"

"Him," the woman said unpleasantly. "The rest of you are means to that end. You," she pointed to Grandfather and the other men of the family; most of them wore loincloths or nothing in the hot summer night. "Take your women into your rooms. Lie on the floors with the doors open. Do not show yourselves at the windows, do not cry out, do not speak at all. Your children will be held in there," she pointed to the family dining room. "If you are silent, if you are still, if you *obey*," she stressed the last word, "they will be released unharmed. You have my word on that, and my promise of vengeance if you disobey me."

She glared at them all and Maia could practically feel the magic crackling in her, and the rage. The combination terrified her. This Gwythlo had to be stronger than any priestess Maia had ever met. The swordsmen held their blades point-up and ready. Grandfather, tense with outrage, opened his mouth, but Grandmother grabbed his arm and squeezed it. He shut his jaws with a snap and stalked with her into their room. The rest of the family did likewise with many backward glances. The Gwythlo woman allowed Carlai and Sevan to keep their baby with them, but separated Ger and Silla from their five children. The Gwythlos swept Attir in with the smaller kids, who clung to him and his two eldest cousins for reassurance. Attir's mouth firmed as he gathered them to him and led them into the dining room, head held high.

"Not you." The blonde woman turned back to Maia. "You and your whelp stay near me."

Maia looked beseechingly at Sevan as he shepherded his wife and child into their bedroom. He looked torn as he hesitated in the door, hands opening and closing helplessly and as stark naked as Carlai. But the pale cowled man raised his sword and gestured with it. Sevan dropped his gaze and followed his wife.

"Now." The woman said coldly, staring at Maia with hard blue eyes. "You will take me to your room."

Maia bowed her head and did as directed while her mind raced. She settled herself on the bed pad and gave baby Grigor her breast while the woman hung a lantern from a clothes-peg and arranged it so that it lit the bed and window but left the door-end of the room in shadow. The woman stood and stared at her and the baby like a reptile. Maia found it impossible to hide her fear.

"Half-bloods are abominations," the Druid suddenly announced. "Mingling pure Gwythlo blood with you darkies ? It's like mating with hyenas!" She spit as if she couldn't get the taste of the words out of her mouth fast enough. Abruptly the woman knelt on the end of the bed. "Hold still," she hissed as Maia tried to shrink away. Then the Gwythlo laid one rough hand on the baby's head. Maia could feel the magic flowing around them both.

"Ahhhh." The woman drew back her hand as if she had touched something foul. "You lay with him and begat that willingly, didn't you?"

"He's my husband!" Maia objected. "I love him!"

The woman shook a finger at her. "Answer only the questions I ask, slut. You enjoyed rutting with that tainted blood, didn't you?"

Maia raised her chin in defiance. "My husband pillowed me with kindness and consideration every time. Could anything be more joyous this side of heaven?"

The woman slapped her. "Demon-lover."

Maia tasted blood where her teeth cut the inside of her cheek, and wisely kept silence. But in her heart the fear that had taken root the moment these pale strangers awoke her, now blossomed. *This one wants my husband dead and our son with him.*

The cowled man slipped into the room and nodded to the woman. Maia looked down at baby Grigor to avoid both their gazes while she listened.

"You have your outside men hidden well?" the woman demanded of the Gwythlo man in that language. "They must not frighten him away."

"Am I a babe?" the man answered in the same tongue, his voice a surly whisper. "Look to your own task. Are you sure he will come here?"

"Yes," the woman answered in a low voice. "The land-wights tell me this is the seat of his heart; he will not willingly stay away from it for long. If we must wait for dawn, we will. Be sure all the other rooms are dark. We must draw him in thoroughly. If we do not get him inside these walls he will escape again."

The big Gwythlo grunted angrily. "Do not forget who gives the orders, Druid." But he left the room.

Maia suppressed a shiver. *Whatever that man may want, she wants Grigor and Kirin to die. What can I do? He may be home any moment!*

Baby Grigor refused the nipple and began to hiccup. Maya put him against her shoulder, deliberately holding him in a position which made him cry.

The Druid scowled at her. "Quiet that noise."

"It's too hot and stuffy," Maia explained. "I wish we had a breeze."

The Druid hesitated, visibly calculating, then nodded decisively. "Display yourself at the window," she directed.

She means to dangle us like bait, Maia thought, fighting her fear while her thoughts raced. She knew what happened to both bait and fish in the end. But the window offered her opportunity, too.

Maia stood in front of it, shifting Grigor down against her stomach where he would be more comfortable. He burped loudly and stopped crying, began to drowse. Her eyes grew accustomed to the night outside. The clouds had cleared, and both moons lit the Inn's courtyard. She stared at the empty space while desperately hunting for the flicker of shadow that would mean her Kirin had arrived. Half praying he would not be there, half fearing he would.

* * *

Kirin slipped through the back alleys in his moving blot of Shadow. He hadn't seen any sign of Duke Darnaud and his Druid since escaping the fight. He hoped that meant they had given up on killing him.

Hah, he sneered at himself bitterly. *I know too much now. I've got to get Maia and Grigor and escape the city. Or maybe go tell Mother Gee and let her tell Ymera? But Ymera sent me to Chisaad; she might be in on his plan. I wish Pieter was here. Who can I trust? What am I going to do?*

He vaulted over a garden wall into the Inn's courtyard and headed for the exterior stair at the building's north end. Then his eyes caught sight of Maia standing in the window of their bedroom holding Grigor, and he changed course to pass below her.

She made no sign that she saw him, though she was used to his Shadow and knew the difference between it and normal moon shadows. Then, before he could whistle to her, she did something that froze his voice in his throat.

She dropped the baby out the window.

His heart skipped a beat before he realized that she still held Grigor with her levitation talent. The baby slowly floated down through the night air like a leaf. A wail burst forth as Grigor wobbled above the paved yard and drifted farther from the Inn. Maia had to be straining her small talent to hold him at such a distance.

Kirin raced to get beneath his descending son. Why—

A man's voice shouted, a woman snarled. Maia's straining body leaned against the window frame. With shocking suddenness Kirin saw a length of steel blade burst from her belly as someone skewered her from behind. Her levitation failed; baby Grigor wailed as he plunged.

Kirin caught him.

Then Maia tipped forward and fell four stories from the window. She landed with a thud like a sack of flour hitting the pavement and drops of her blood splashed him. Kirin's heart went numb. Duke Darnaud roared from the window above and brandished a bloody sword.

Eight men appeared out of the Inn's west wing and moved across the courtyard in a line toward Kirin, waving their swords like a moving hedge of steel. Two more came out of the alley to the Serpentine and blocked it.

Rage and shock warred in his heart as he clutched his crying son close. He wanted to run toward Maia but knew it was useless. Instead he charged the nearest of the two men. His Shadow ravened forth faster than a panther's leap. It seized the swordsman's throat and drank his life in one gulp. The man's sword fell from limp fingers and bounced on the pavement as he collapsed, dead before he hit the cobbles.

The forbidden rush of blood-power almost knocked Kirin off his feet. Like Gerlach ten years ago, only now Kirin knew what he tasted. A life— memories of sweet apples, savage frozen winters glittering in wan northern sunlight, a welcoming yellow-haired girl in a hayloft, first taste of wine and oranges and strong Silbari curry, pride in a sharp sword and the blood shed by it, a glorious lord to follow—and ashen bone-pale death.

Grief howled through him, acid regret splashed across his own pain and loss in a twisted skein of sorrow so overwhelming he could barely walk. But Maia's killers were coming for him with bared steel.

He staggered past the body and dodged the dead man's partner, who charged into the Shadow slashing left and right. The attacker slipped on the dropped sword and sprawled on the cobbles while Kirin ran into the alley. The other eight closed behind him. More men pounded down the open north stairway of the Inn towards him, but before they reached the ground he had already made it to the Serpentine. He cut left away from the Inn and ran. His Shadow filled the Serpentine behind him and blocked the pursuing swordsmen.

He ran through the stinking alleys of the Sump, clutching his infant son and weeping into the uncaring night.

CHAPTER 32: DARNAUD

You should have let me kill them all," Darnaud grumbled in his native tongue. He stamped his feet in fury on the night-dewed cobblestones outside the Sulfur Serpent Inn. He dared not defy Boerga, but he wanted to. A few of his men still held the acrobats' floor while the rest fruitlessly swept the surrounding streets and alleys for the youth, Kirin.

"I gave my word," she answered fiercely. "Even to darkies, it was my honor pledged! Bad enough that you violated it by killing the woman. Dishonorable and stupid! While she lived we had something to coerce him with, maybe even bargain his life for hers. Now we have nothing, and if you'd killed his whole family we'd have less than nothing, and a mess that the City Watch would have to heed."

"It wasn't me who let the bitch slip her baby away and warn him at the same time," Darnaud sneered, smarting under both the lash of her tongue and the infuriating knowledge that she was right. "Be sure Ap Marn will take note of that! He'll—"

"This bickering is pointless," she cut him off. "The night isn't over yet, we still have a chance to find him. We need to guess where he will run and go there."

Darnaud scowled, but she had a point. He fought down his temper and thought hard. "The wizard only told me a little about him. Of his friends and allies I know nothing. If he runs toward power, well, he already knows we have the civil rule in our hands, now that the Prince will no longer overrule us. He can't know how many mages Chisaad has won over, so he'll probably stay away from the Council. The damn Witch-Queen could be a problem if he runs there."

"Nay," Boerga disagreed. "She sent him to the wizard in the first place, he'll not likely trust her either. There's only one power in Aretzo he dares trust, one that has shown him favor before, curse their yellow robes. We need to know which Temple he'll likely seek for sanctuary. If it's the main one then we are ruined, but a lesser one could still be assailed with the men you have."

Darnaud snorted; the woman dreamed. "How many men do you want me to lose tonight? Those bitches can kill with a touch!"

"As can I, my lord." She bared her teeth in not-a-smile. "As can I."

The reminder chilled his anger. Grudgingly he said, "Give me some time with one of these peasants and—"

"Nay, my lord, your blood is still too hot." She matched his scowl, then tossed her head. "I will find out where these peasants worship. Meanwhile you gather up your men."

Darnaud grunted unhappy assent and went to make it so.

CHAPTER 33: KIRIN

K irin stopped before the bridge to the Temple of Heavenly Peace. He leaned his forehead against a cracked stone wall and retched again.

I'm a murderer, he thought for the twentieth time. He spit, but the taste of the life he had drained still lingered on his tongue. The Gwythlo fighter's angers and fears, loves and delights, they all flickered across his mind with horrifying intimacy. *I killed him like Gerlach.* He desperately wanted to vomit, as if that would void his memory too, but his heaving stomach had nothing.

Baby Grigor stirred unhappily against his ribs. Kirin had tucked him inside his shirt for shelter and to have both hands free. Now he cradled his son through the fabric with one arm while he snuck through the night-vacant streets of the Sump. He hesitated at the sight of someone ascending the arch of the Temple's bridge.

Calm slipped free of the clouds as the robed figure got to the top. Kirin recognized Dona Abbithana. She walked slowly, head down as if grieved or exhausted, and cradled a wrapped bundle in her arms. She passed over the top of the arch and disappeared into the ruined temple's courtyard.

He looked along the crossing streets and canal; nothing moved save for a few scurrying rats. An owl seized a bat overhead and the tiny flyer died with an agonized squeak. Kirin nerved himself and then darted over the bridge, across the muddy courtyard, and through the string curtain into the sanctuary.

Dona Abbithana uttered her own squeak of surprise and he saw her aura brighten as she called upon the City Node for more power. Then baby Grigor uttered a little cry. The young priestess relaxed at this evidence of innocent intent. "Who goes there?" she demanded, peering at him as she hesitated outside the rooms she shared with Dona Zella.

"Kirin Sule DiUmbra," he answered quietly, fearful even here of giving himself away. "And my son Grigor. Please, Dona Abbithana, I need to talk to Dona Zella." Grigor cried louder.

Kirin saw the priestess' white teeth flash in the dimness. "You are fortunate, since I must wake her anyway. Come."

Inside the office-kitchen he took Grigor out of his shirt while she woke her superior. Only then did Kirin discover that he had been bleeding on the baby. The assassin's knife had come closer than he thought. Dona Abbie exclaimed over the mess, took Grigor from him and changed the child into a fresh diaper while cooing to him. Yawning Dona Zella came out during the changing and discovered Kirin's wound. She immediately sent her aura into him while Dona Abbie sat on a stool and rocked the baby. Kirin endured her questions while she knit his skin closed and swabbed off the blood. Fortunately, nearly all of it had been absorbed by the diaper. She set that to soak in a bucket and then unwrapped the bundle that Dona Abbie had brought.

"What tragedy is this?" she exclaimed, revealing a dead baby.

"Merria's firstborn," Dona Abbie reported sadly. "He never breathed, and nothing I could do would call him to life. It was a hard birth. I doubt she will be able to have another child." She stroked baby Grigor's back gently.

Zella sighed and rewrapped the tiny corpse, set it reverently aside, and for a moment Kirin saw every one of her fifty-six years graven on her face. "I'll arrange for a funeral in the morning." She turned back to Kirin and said, "Right now, you tell me what brought you here, bloody and carrying your infant son."

Kirin gulped and steadied his nerves. In a voice roughened by tears, he began to speak. Half a candlemark later he had poured out his story with all its pain, grief, and regret, save for one thing; the method by which he had killed the Duke's soldier. *Maia, Maia, I've lost you and stained my soul forever.* The tears flowed freely by the time he finished.

"Oh, my dear, dear boy," Zella shook her head sadly. "You placed your life in the hands of a powerful man. Did you not see the implications of any Mage controlling the Prince? Chisaad is leading the Mage Guild in a struggle with the Hierarchy over access to the Aretzo Node. Now they can simply re-apportion the Node as they will. They've probably already begun. The Hierarchy will be weakened, and the Guild strengthened. Worse still, the entire succession to the Throne could be thrown into a hideous bloodbath as bad as anything from the Red Years. You said Ap Marn told the Prince that they only needed him alive until the Queen dies?"

"Yes; then they're going to kill him." Kirin's stomach clenched; he remembered Prince Terrell's fear and bravery from that last brief touch of minds. *He's not a cruel man, I know it now; so why did he condemn Pieter? Chisaad and Darnaud must have persuaded him to do it just so they could convince me to kidnap him.* He had only a murky guess at the depth of the plans that had ensnared him, but the sheer cold-hearted abuse of it humiliated him. *They used me. They used me and when they were done with me they meant to kill me. And they nearly did.* He touched his healed scratch through the hole in his shirt. *I went to the wrong powerful person.*

"They probably have supporters among the Twenty to dare so greatly." Dona Zella stared at him thoughtfully. "Were they so careless as to have named any?"

"No." Kirin shook his head wretchedly. "The Gwythlos must be in it too, but until tonight I had no idea that Chisaad was dealing with anybody." He almost gagged on the words, "I really thought he meant to help me." *So wrong, so wrong!*

"Why were you willing to trust the wizard in this?"

Kirin hesitated, turning the question over in his mind. He couldn't bring himself to confess his experience with the Duermu fortune teller, so he temporized. "I guess, because I wanted it to be true. Wanted to believe that . . . the prince would free Pieter if only he really knew us." *Why did I believe that? Why do I still believe it?*

"Well, kidnapping him might not have been the best way to plead your cause."

"I see that now, but it sounded so right when he explained it," he agonized. "Dona Zella, Maia's dead. What if Duke Darnaud has killed my whole family?" *Fear and loss—please God, no!*

She didn't try to hide her own worry at that thought, for which he was oddly grateful, but she did offer him solace. "Consider that possibility in light of their conspiracy. They have committed a monstrous crime, but only you know it and can testify to any details. They dare not attract too much attention before they capture you, or before they achieve whatever goal is served by excluding the prince from the succession. A slaughter of your whole family, or even part of it, would be sure to attract lots of attention. There would be questions among the Hierarchy and recriminations against the Watch, possibly petitions from the people of the Old City to the Governor. I pray that they don't want that level of unrest and scrutiny. The immediate question is, what are you going to do next?"

"I can tell the Hierarch." But his mind stumbled over his own part in the crime. *Tell her that I kidnapped the Prince by using a living Shadow that I carry under my heart? Tell her that I killed a man with it? That'll get me burned!* He had heard it said that the blood-sorcerers and demon-possessed hoped for suffocation in the smoke before the flames reached their flesh.

He looked at Zella's face and for the first time in a decade of knowing her, it occurred to him to ask. "Umm, Dona Zella, have you ever told the Hierarch, or any of her people, about me?"

"Not yet." She didn't look away, but she didn't quite meet his eyes either.

Dona Abbithana sucked in a breath and stopped rocking baby Grigor. "Dona Zella! You told me you informed the Hierarch of everything you knew about him!"

Dona Zella shook her head. "No, Abbie, I told you that I've written a letter. I didn't tell you that I've sent it, because I haven't, at least not yet. Maybe not ever."

"You misled me! Why?"

"Did you ever wonder why I choose to dwell here in the poorest and most degraded part of Aretzo?" Zella raised one eyebrow at her assistant. "My sister is the Autarch of Belluno, a broken, half-abandoned and poverty-stricken city, but a city. I certainly have the seniority and influence to swing a more prestigious seat than this. Why do I stay?"

"I thought you love serving the poorest of the poor," the idealistic young priestess answered slowly.

"Which is quite true. But I've got more than one reason." She sighed. "I despise the decadence and luxury of the upper Hierarchy. They've allowed themselves to become corrupted by worldly temptations. Kirin would represent an even more terrible temptation for them, as much as he does for the Mage Guild. The temptation of using him to take power over others in a way that can't be fought by any normal means. I wish I had understood how far-reaching his strange talent is." Aside to him she added, "I confess I never imagined you could walk through the Palace's spells, my dear boy!"

"I didn't either," he mumbled, shamed.

Returning her attention to Dona Abbie, Zella said, "But my limited imaginings were bad enough. I won't subject him—or the leaders of my faith—to that terrible temptation if I can find any other way."

Dona Abbie stared at her in consternation. "What are you going to do?"

"I don't know yet." She looked Kirin in the eye. "What do you want to do, Kirin?"

He dropped his gaze to his hands, unable to meet her eyes while his thoughts whirled. *I can't trust any mage. If Dona Zella is right, I can't really trust any high-ranked priestess either.' Who can I go to? Who has enough power to help me, that I can trust? I think the Duermu fortune teller meant me to go to somebody other than Chisaad, but who?*

Everybody knew that real power in Aretzo rested on a tripod. *The Temple Hierarchy and the Mage Council, who both need the City Node. And the King—right now the Prince—who controls it.* While Ymera was certainly strong by herself, she was small next to those three.

He remembered the three times his mind had touched that of Prince Terrell. They had been brief, but the longer he thought about the sensation, uncomfortable as it had been, the more he remembered from the man's own mind.

I know he's sad because his brother hates him. I know he loves his mother and father—though how anyone can love the Emperor I don't understand. He cares about his friends, and cares about the Kingdom too. He wants to do the right things. But he doesn't always know what those are. I think . . . I think Chisaad, whether he knew it or not, got it right. If Prince Terrell knew my family, if he knew my father, he would never have listened to Duke Darnaud. Maybe God meant me to find a way to beg his help instead of going to Chisaad. He trembled, remembering the Prince's face as the drug did its work.

But I made a terrible mistake and kidnapped him. Chisaad only has him because of me. Kirin gulped at that thought. *Prince Terrell might condemn me to death for that alone. If he did . . . I would deserve it.*

His stomach got queasy from even thinking about it. Between being murdered by the Mages, burned by the Temple, or executed by the Prince, what was there to choose?

He can free my father. That's what matters. It's not whether I live or die; it's whether I can save Pieter from the sulfur mines. The Prince can do that with a word. Kirin swallowed a lump in his throat. *If he wants me to die as the price of Father's freedom, then I will pay that price. At least then, I might get to see Maia again.*

Then his eye caught an old fresco on the back wall, partly crumbled away. The piece remaining showed a Duermu playing a pipe in the Bazaar.

It's a sign. Zella has power. The Prince has more.

Aloud he said, "I need the Prince. He's my only chance to not be a tool in the mages' hands, or the Hierarch's. I dreamed of being powerful, but I'm not really. I'm one man, alone. So is he, but he can command other men and they'll listen to him even though—" He gulped again. "Even though he's a halfbreed too. He's still Prince, and Governor. If I get him back in his palace, maybe he'll put both the mages and the priestesses in their place. Nobody else can." He added, "Only, how can I get him back?"

Dona Zella smiled at him. "I'm confident that anyone who can kidnap a prince right out of his own palace is surely able to get him out of a half-drowned ruin."

"But I don't even know where this Silbariki place is."

"That's easy. I do. I've even seen it from a distance."

He couldn't have been more astonished if she'd grown an extra head. Coarse, humorous Dona Zella who had ministered to the poor of the Sump since before the Conquest? "You? How?"

"My dear boy, I've never made any secret of the fact that I wasn't born in Aretzo, though I've spent most of my life here. I just told you I'm from Belluno, where my eldest sister is Autarch of the Temple." She pointed at the old painting on the wall. "Do you know where Belluno is?"

"Um." He tried to remember the DiUmbra Troup's performance trip across Lower Silbar. "Somewhere north?"

She looked at him reprovingly. "It's the first city south of the Scarp. From the highest cliffs north of Belluno you can see the ruins of Silbariki in the distance, beyond the lakes."

She rummaged through a chest while talking. "I suppose I don't talk about it much; this is home to me now. Let's see, I know I have that somewhere—aha!" She pulled out a leather tube. "Here, look, my father gave me this many years ago." She opened the tube and took out a scroll that she spread on the table in front of him. "This is a map of Lower Silbar, from the scarp to the sea."

Kirin stared at it in fascination. He had seen maps before, but not often. Grandfather had rented one for their exhibition trip. That had been the most detailed map he'd ever seen, and this one rivaled it. The vellum had been seared with a hot needle to make lines and words. He made out Aretzo and the sea on one edge and the River Amm threading up the middle to the Scarp and Purification Lake. Cities and roads decorated it like beads on strings. Dona Zella put her finger on a blot near the upper right corner.

"This is Belluno." She tapped a dot on the map, then moved her finger several finger widths to the northeast. "Silbariki lies here, partly drowned by this smaller lake in the south end of its valley. We always called that Ibis Lake for the birds that flock there, you can see clouds of them overhead. It is past midsummer, so the waters should be down enough for you to get to the ruins. You'll have to be careful of wild animals, lions and hyenas on the plains and crocodiles in the reed-marshes, though it's rare that any of them attack a man. Carry water with you whenever you find some, the lake water is not good to drink." She rummaged in the chest again, found a leather water-bag and thrust it into his hands.

He gulped. The DiUmbra family's trip had taught him something about Silbar's true size. He would have to—"Dona, what'll I do about Grigor?"

Dona Abbie had resumed rocking him. "He'll need to nurse in the morning. I know a woman who lost her own baby tonight, she can care for him."

She did not say *until you get back*, Kirin noticed, but he accepted it as a given. "Thank you, Dona Abbie, and please thank her." The offer relieved him so much that for a moment he knew shame. But the task awaited. "Dona Zella, can you help me get out of Aretzo without anybody else seeing me? I'm going to go rescue the Prince."

She smiled then, her approval better than a warm fire in winter. "Certainly."

* * *

"There, now your skin looks more Silbari," Kirin heard Zella say many minutes later, after painting his face and hands with brown dye. He had kissed his son goodbye and Dona Abbie had carried baby Grigor off into the night. "Are you ready?"

He fumbled for the waterproof bag. "I think I've got everything." He squeezed it again, trying to force the last bit of air out before he plugged the vent with a wax-coated cork.

"No, boy; are *you* ready?" She held his eyes with her calm steady gaze. "Ready to do whatever it will take to undo the damage you've done?"

He paused, swallowed the first words that came to his mind, and centered himself before he nodded. *It's the only way. Even if I die in the trying.* "Yes, Dona Zella. I'll find the Prince, free him and get him back here. After that—"

She held up a finger to cut him off. "Will come whatever comes. Keep your thoughts on your task and leave the rest to the Seraphs, Kirin." She patted his cheek, blessed him, and said, "Now follow me."

Zella led him out the back of her quarters to a path around the ruins of the old sanctuary. Mud squelched underfoot as he followed her. It ended at a little stone-walled basin overhung with mangrove trees. Cracked stairs lead down into the water and a rowboat bobbed at the end of a tether, tugged by the ebbing tide toward an opening barely visible through the low-hanging branches.

"I'll row," she told him. "You don't know the way. Watch out for anybody out there on the water with us, I don't want to run into another boat."

They both got in and Kirin held the branches aside while she rowed them out into the canal. Most of the buildings were dark, save for one drinking house lit by oil lanterns and raucous with drunken singing; dawn wasn't far away but the waterside taverns never closed. Kirin drew his Shadow over the boat like a shield while Zella grunted at the oars. They slid past the noise and out between two long wharves lined with sleeping ships. A faint lightening of the eastern sky warned of dawn's approach.

Few lights shone in the harbor where anchored ships slumbered. The New Trade Gate had closed for the night and the only moving ship rode the falling tide out through the Old Trade Gate. Zella turned her rowboat toward the high seawall closing off the north end of the basin. Soon they bumped gently against the wet stone.

"Let me see, Kirin," she grunted quietly, and he drew his Shadow back inside him. Moonlight bathed the wall and the slick fronds of seaweed exposed by the tide. "Find the drain-gate."

Only a few feet away his night-sighted eyes picked out the top of an arch where it poked above the water. "There it is, Dona." He helped pull them along the wall until the prow of the rowboat butted the keystone. The ebb tide pushed at them as it tried to cram a quarter of the Harbor's water through an opening only twelve feet wide and half-blocked with crisscrossed granite slabs. The steady flow pressed the rowboat against the stones.

Zella shipped the oars. "Right. The passage is twenty feet long. The smuggler's opening is near the bottom on the right side. Be careful that the bag doesn't snag on anything, or your clothes either. I don't want you to drown down there in the dark and wet."

"It won't be dark to me, Dona," he told her as he tied the double lashing over his shoulders and around his waist to snug the pack against his back. Wearing this soft leather shell made him feel like a turtle.

He rolled over one side of the boat while Zella balanced it by leaning the opposite way, then he held to the gunwale while she leaned back and looked down at him. Her hand brushed his wet hair aside to touch his forehead.

"Come back to us, boy," she whispered to him.

"I will," he promised. "Thanks for everything."

Then he took several deep breaths, exhaled most of the air, and dived.

CHAPTER 34: ZELLA

Zella rowed the dinghy back to her temple. The harbor remained empty of moving vessels, the one taking the night tide had gone and the rest slept at their anchors and docks. Years of practice helped her find her way through the night-dark canals of the Sump without Kirin to play lookout. The waning tide made it harder work than rowing him out to the seawall had been. But she managed, and gratefully grounded the little rowboat's prow against her rickety dock. She rubbed her aching back, wishing she had a decade or two fewer years, then plodded back to her half-ruined Temple. A light flickered behind the window. Abbie must be back and would certainly have a hundred questions.

Zella sighed. As she opened the back door she noticed a black shape moving on the grounds. She paused on the doorstep and demanded, "Who's there?"

A soldier, and then two more, appeared out of the night. The trio held drawn steel and their faces and hands were pale; Gwythlos. Their eyes were wide in the night and the tips of their swords trembled. Zella recognized frightened men on the verge of doing something violent simply because they were afraid. She held very still and scolded herself for failing to expect this. *Everyone in the Sulfur Serpent knows where the DiUmbras worship! Of course Kirin's enemies would find out.* She pushed down her fear and locked it away, controlled her breathing.

Then a harsh Gwythlo-accented female voice spoke from inside her rooms.

"Come in and sit down, Priestess. We will speak."

Zella startled and peered inside to find Abbie sitting at the far end of their rickety table. A single candle flickered in front of her worried face. Behind her loomed a large pale-skinned man in a cowled cloak, holding a naked sword in gauntleted fists, and five more men behind him. Beside him stood a woman with a glowing green aura twice the size of Zella's own; a Gwythlo Druid.

So much power in her! She must be Boerga, the Gwythlo military chaplain.

At the look in Boerga's eyes, Zella's breathing quickened despite her best control. She read hatred there like none she'd ever seen before. Her knees went weak. *Mother Umana, lend me your strength! And Seraph Shali, your tongue, for surely I need clever words now!*

The men behind Zella closed in, threatening to prod her with the tips of their blades. She stepped inside, went to her own chair and set her hands on the back. Haughtily she demanded, "Who are you, to invade my temple with armed men at your call?"

"Sit," Boerga ordered.

"I prefer to stand," Zella answered curtly, meeting the other woman's eyes unflinchingly. The man growled and the swordsmen behind her stirred, but Zella stayed where she stood. "What do you want?"

"Where did you take the acrobat?" Boerga snapped, glowering. "We know he came here, leaving tracks in the mud of your courtyard. But he did not pass out that way, and is not here now, so where did you take him?"

"Kirin? To the harbor, of course."

"Where is he now?" The Gwythlo woman's fingers twitched and her aura throbbed.

"Well beyond Aretzo." Zella shrugged, added carelessly, "How fast does a ship sail? The wind is to the southeast and fresh. I suppose it might be as much as ten miles out by now. Perhaps he's looking back at the city right this moment as we disappear behind him."

Abbie sat still as this not-quite-a-lie fell from her superior's lips. Boerga snarled something in her own language and the man growled wordlessly back. Then the Druid stared at Zella again, teeth bared in an expression nothing like a smile.

"And his spawn?"

"Spawn?" Zella stared at her. "What do fish have to do with—oh."

"His cursed child!" hissed Boerga, raising a fist. "It must nurse, he would have to leave it with a woman. Where is the little darkie abomination? Tell me!"

At that moment Abbie pointed to the pathetic wrapped corpse on the sideboard, and said in a patently false voice, "Right there. If you had asked me earlier, I could have told you then and saved you time."

Zella's heart sank. If Abbie had kept quiet and pretended ignorance, there had been a chance that the younger priestess might have lived through this. Zella mentally composed herself as she tightened her hands on her chair's back. *Father Haroun, aid us now!*

Boerga strode to the sideboard, peeled back the wrapping, then whirled back to glare at Abbie with a thunderous scowl. "This is not his! But you know where it is, don't you?" The Druid's aura thickened, and she raised her hands threateningly toward Abbie, for the moment disregarding the older priestess.

Zella spun in place and flung her chair at the three men behind her. Without waiting to see whether she hit any of them, she dropped to the floor with a pained grunt and rolled under the table.

The men shouted, drawing the Druid's attention back to where Zella had been standing. She scrambled under the table and out the far side, tearing her skirts as she lunged for Boerga's ankles. If she could touch the woman skin-to-skin first, maybe she could still give Abbie a chance.

She barely made it. Boerga hurled lightning at her back. Unbearable pain lashed Zella as her spine shattered. But her hand closed on the point where the woman's riding breeches met her boots. Fingernails dug into the gap, into the skin, and with her last breath Zella willed the command she had never used before.

Die.

The Druid shrieked and jerked free of her grip before collapsing. Zella strained to reach her again to finish the job, but couldn't. Abbie's cry cut off mid-syllable with the wet sound of metal slicing flesh. Then Zella's mind spiraled down into darkness and she knew no more in that life.

CHAPTER 35: KIRIN

Even in fall Aretzo's harbor wasn't cold, and Kirin's Shadow gave him night sight as he dived. But he couldn't see far through the murky water. The leather pack tried to bob upward, he had to fight it for every foot of depth. He found his way downward as much by pulling himself along as by swimming. The granite slabs that denied this passage to invaders left one-foot-square holes for the tide, which rushed through strongly. It kept rubbing him against the crusted barnacles and slick seaweeds.

When he found the smugglers' passage he almost turned back from the two-foot-by-two-foot square. Only the flow of water into it assured him that it came out somewhere.

He had no time to waste, his lungs already craved air so much that his chest hurt. He maneuvered himself into the hole headfirst.

The pack immediately snagged against the ceiling. He rolled over and used his hands and knees to crawl through the long stone tube upside-down, while the pack and his straining lungs pressed him against the ceiling.

The far end seemed bright as day when he burst out of the stone gullet. Air had never tasted so sweet. He swam to the beach below the fish-ponds, hid from sight between two rocks to disrobe and wring water out of his clothes, then dressed and looked around.

Aretzo lay behind him. North, the vast open valley of the River Amm gaped between the Bright Mountains and the Ash Needles. The peak of God's Footstool caught the approaching dawn and kindled like a beacon. He had memorized Dona Zella's map; many miles north lay ruined Silbariki.

Zella had loaned him a worn brown robe from her alms-box. He took it out of his waterproof pack and pulled it on. It only fell to his knees but covered his arms to the wrist. With his dyed skin, black hair tied back, and the robe's hood up to hide his ears, he hoped he could pass for a normal Silbari.

Half a mile north of the city the shore road met a cluster of stubby piers, hovels, and warehouses called Fishtown. A double pair of warehouse doors were propped open and a wagon parked in front of them in the pre-dawn dimness. A man and a little boy lead four big dray horses up to it. The man tied off the lead ropes to the wagon and then visibly startled when he saw Kirin looming out of the fading night. The boy moved closer to the man. Their own hoods were pushed back to reveal the brown skin and straight brown hair of typical Silbaris. The man—probably the boy's father, Kirin thought with an ache in his heart—wore his robe belted above heavy boots.

Both belt and boots showed wear, but his neatly-patched robe had been cleaned recently.

"I need a ride north," Kirin told the wagon master. "I can pay."

"Hmm." A dubious look followed. "How far do you want to go?"

"To Belluno."

The man shook his head. "I only go as far as Isernia."

Belluno lay only a few miles farther north. Kirin thanked the Seraphs for this good fortune. "Close enough."

"Show me your money," the wagon master demanded. When Kirin produced the two silver dohbas that were most of what he had in his pouch, the man shook his head and said, "That'll only get you to Amm Ford."

Kirin licked his lips and choked back the plea that tried to force its way from his mouth. It wouldn't do to show desperation when bargaining. "I can work for the rest of it."

The wagon master looked him over again, eyes flicking over the thickness of Kirin's arms where he filled out the too-small robe, and the muscles of his calves beneath the robe's hem. He nodded slowly and pointed to a barrel inside the warehouse. "Show me. Get that up the ramp into my wagon."

Kirin went to it, rocked it slightly. Damp, heavy, probably full of pickled fish by the smell. There had been an acrobatic trick the troupe did with empty barrels, but this wasn't the place to show off tricks, not if he wanted to escape Aretzo unnoticed. He rocked the barrel onto its side, rolled it up a pair of planks the man had pulled out of the wagon, and levered it upright again into a corner of the bed, all with barely a thump.

"You'll do," the man decided. "You load here, unload there, and haul water and feed for the horses. We'll share our food with you and you can sleep under the wagon at night until we get to Isernia. Fair trade?"

Kirin handed over his two coins and they shook hands on it. The man smelled of old sweat and road dust, like a million other working men, and had a strong grip. If he noticed anything odd about Kirin's skin or garb, he said nothing.

The wagon could hold twenty-four barrels standing upright. Kirin packed them in, sweating and straining and racing the moment when Chisaad or Ap Marn or Duke Darnaud thought to look for him outside the city. In half a candlemark the barrels were done. Then he lashed two layers of bulky sacks of sea-sponges above the barrel-tops. Last, he helped the wagon master's son Ammin raise a stained white canvas awning on wooden ribs mounted over the load. When they were done Kirin had made sure he still had enough room to crawl inside between sacks and be hidden from view.

The wagon master had his horses fully harnessed, four big sturdy yellow beasts with white manes. He inspected the load and the knots and gave Kirin an approving thumbs-up sign. "What's your name?"

"Veglic," Kirin answered, borrowing the name from a pot-boy who worked in the Sulfur Serpent's kitchen.

The man flicked a glance over him at the lack of second and third names but made no comment. "I'm Varrin Culpatha Chiaver. Hop in, Veglic."

PETER SARTUCCI

The wagon pulled out of the little dock complex north of the slaughterhouses as red Fathersun peeked over the horizon and began to lead white Mothersun into the sky. The pale wraith of the Moon of Calm hadn't quite set behind the Bright Mountains to the west. The wagon rattled up the dirt side road from Fishtown, across the strip of greensward maintained for messenger-horses, and onto the Kings Road. There the heavy oak wheels began to thunder on the stone pavement, a sound soon lost among the dozens of other wagons that joined them.

Kirin peeked out from under the tented awning, anxiously watching for pursuit. His anxiety didn't fade as the wagon plodded north. Cavalry could move fast, and message constructs flew faster still.

"You hungry, Veglic?" asked Chiaver's son Ammin. Kirin nodded his head as his stomach, reminded that he hadn't eaten since early yesterday, growled.

Ammin grinned and offered him a handful of dried figs from a sack. "We've got lots," he boasted. "Our landlord has a tree at home and he lets us keep half of what we pick."

Kirin made an impressed noise at this privilege and thanked him, then nibbled on the dense, sweet fruit. It stilled his belly's hunger but did nothing for the ache in his heart.

Maia, Maia, his heart cried. He fought back tears, with limited success.

"You look so sad," Ammin observed with a child's innocence.

Chiaver glanced at Kirin, startled. "Is something wrong, Veglic?"

"My wife died yesterday." Stating it so baldly made his throat tighten and the tears broke through. "Please, I need some time," he choked out.

Chiaver's face softened. "Why don't you crawl in back and take a nap."

Kirin did and curled up on sacks of sea-sponges. He pulled the robe's hood over his face and, hidden from view and masked by the noises of the road, wept for Maia, until at last sleep took him.

CHAPTER 36: CHISAAD

You *what?!*" Chisaad, the Acting Royal Wizard, bellowed at the top of his lungs, surprising even himself. In a slightly calmer voice he continued, "How could you let him get away?"

Duke Darnaud drew himself up, put a hand on the pommel of his sword, and glowered. "You forget yourself, darkie mage!"

Chisaad bit back a retort as Ap Marn stepped in. The former Imperial Governor peremptorily demanded, "Explain, Your Grace. You were supposed to kill one man and you had twenty at your disposal, plus Boerga and her wolf. What happened?"

Darnaud looked sulky. "It was his bitch's fault. She warned your damned tool by tossing her baby to him, right out a fourth-floor window."

At this Chisaad's anger exploded again. "Window? You tried to trap him in his home, amidst that huge family of his?"

"Wizard!" snapped Ap Marn. "Hold your tongue while I handle this." To Darnaud, the former Governor icily said, "You were supposed to kill him in the street outside the Diplomatic Gate. We even arranged for the Watch to be absent and the garrison to be looking the other way. Why didn't you do it there?"

The Duke glowered at Chisaad once more, then turned to his fellow Gwythlo and superior, and told of the botched attack. "So we went to the place Boerga said he would go, that big inn, and laid a trap for him there. This time I had my men line up shoulder to shoulder with their swords out, so that they could still get him when he tried that shadow trick, which he did. But he killed one of my men and escaped." The Duke made the Gwythlo sign against evil and his face grew paler. "There wasn't a mark on the body! What kind of demon kills like that?"

Icy fingers of fear ran up and down Chisaad's spine at the thought of Kirin at large somewhere in the city. He could be anywhere, could be seeking help right now—

Then Darnaud's last words penetrated Chisaad's mind and he relaxed. "That's the answer. Report your man's death as a murder by the demon-familiar of a suspected blood mage. That will dispose the Temple Hierarchy against him. Even if he talks about kidnapping the Prince, it won't matter. The Hierarchy will never trust the word of a blood-mage. Meanwhile, My Lord Governor can alert the City Watch to search for him."

Ap Marn nodded, following the logic. "But if he has already run to the Hierarchy, the yellow bitches will have heard his story first. They'll be suspicious of a counter-story."

"He hasn't," Darnaud interjected. "He's left the city."

"What?" Ap Marn snapped. "Explain."

"He got help from a couple of the Temple bitches down by the docks, we caught one rowing back after she took him out to a ship in the harbor. She said it had already left with him by the time she got back to shore."

"Then he probably told his story to her, and she's likely in the Hierarch's office right now repeating it," Chisaad groaned.

Darnaud grinned in a way that reminded Chisaad unpleasantly of a shark he'd once seen hauled out of the harbor.

"She won't be repeating anything, even if they raise her," the Duke boasted. "Boerga took care of that after we killed them. Bitches must have known something 'cause they attacked us. Stupid."

"You killed two Priestesses?" Chisaad demanded, torn between being appalled and envious.

Darnaud sneered. "I said so, didn't I? Boerga made it look like a demon attack."

"Very clever of her," Ap Marn said. "But that won't fool them forever, and we can't count on him to stay away for long. Where is the ship bound?"

Darnaud admitted his ignorance.

Chisaad made an impatient gesture. "Any ship leaving on the night tide is aiming for the open sea, so it can't have been a coastal trader. That means they plan to cover a distance, and he can't get back here without switching to another ship at the end, then sailing all the way back, which takes many tendays. Four is more than we need, half that might do. The Queen is dying, and we control her brat. Once the Choosing is done, nothing that went before will matter."

"As long as we also control the new King," Ap Marn pointed out, gazing at him through narrowed eyes.

Chisaad sensed the suspicion in that gaze and immediately moved to neutralize it. "That is what we should be working on right now, My Lord. We need to manipulate the roster of the Twenty Candidates so that the most capable are sidelined or killed. While also neutralizing Baron Penghar and searching for Kirin. Killing him is still essential, and the sooner the better."

Darnaud snorted, turned to Ap Marn. "That's more to my liking. Tell me who to kill first and I'll handle it."

"Thank you, Your Grace." Ap Marn frowned, obviously resisting the temptation to remind Darnaud about the night's failure. "Penghar can wait a while, before that we must make very sure Kirin has left the City and send an assassin after him if he's sailed to another port. But first, we need you to report your man's death as a demon-slaying and connect it to the deaths of those two priestesses. Come, let's arrange that now. Wizard, I'll meet with you after this detail is taken care of, and we'll discuss the Twenty—and this unexpected talent for dealing death that your apprentice has shown."

260

Chisaad nodded unhappily and saw the two Gwythlos out of his tower. He checked the door after them, locked and barred it, and then double-checked every other window and door. Spells were not enough against Kirin's talents, as he was all too aware, but there were sophisticated tricks that he had been thinking about ever since he met the youth. The best involved a spell resting lightly on the house wards, a spell that every few moments simply sent a soft chime to his ears to tell him that the wards were still functioning. He would get used to it and cease hearing its monotonous reminder after a while, until it stopped. It took him most of an hour to construct and install, but he felt better afterwards. Since Kirin had never been shown how to counter this, chances were good that he'd break it if he tried to enter the house or Tower, and alert Chisaad.

Did he really flee the City? It makes the most sense. He's young and cocky, but under that shell he's a scared boy. But if he's still here, if he runs to Ymera instead, what steps do I take against her, or to win her to my side? She sent him to me once, but I better not count on that happening again. For that matter, what if Darnaud is wrong and Kirin didn't *leave the city?*

He hoped Ap Marn and that fool Darnaud took care of the false trail quickly.

If it is a false trail. For all I know, Kirin really does have a demon within him.

He shivered and returned to work.

CHAPTER 37: TERRELL

Prince Terrell DuRillin DiGwythlo awoke on a hard floor.

For a while his drug-addled mind knew only the chilly surface under his back. Gradually the fog cleared from his wits.

Drugged. Somebody drugged me. Chisaad? Yes, but before him somebody else. I saw myself, twice . . . like that time with that mage in the Bazaar.

Discordant images tumbled through his thoughts. His bedroom in the Palace. Somebody standing over him, somebody with the blackest eyes Terrell had ever seen. He remembered breathing something bitter-smelling and remembered passing out. *It had to be that same mage swapping his mind with mine.*

Memory finally crystallized. *He held a drugged rag over my face, right, I remember now. I fought, but he was as strong as a warrior, much stronger than any mage I ever met. Then I woke up somewhere else. Inside the Palace? But that room looked shabby and stark, I'd swear it didn't have a shred of decoration in it. Not the Palace. So Chisaad took me somewhere. How did he get me out of the Palace without the spells and the guards stopping him?*

Wait, I remember Ap Marn there. The traitor! They had me on a big table. There were bookshelves and a glowing diagram on the floor, a decagram. Wizard things. Maybe Chisaad's home? Ap Marn with Chisaad and somebody else.

That mage! I saw his black eyes looking at me through a gap in a bookshelf. Why peek at me that way? One of Chisaad's servants could surely have stared openly. Unless he wasn't supposed to be there? That makes no sense.

Terrell let his aching mind rest for a while and simply looked around. He lay flat in the middle of a huge round space as big as the Mother Temple in Aretzo, manacled to the floor with his arms and legs splayed out. Being naked added to the discomfort and made it even more degrading. The tiles under his back and buttocks chilled him. High overhead the room's ceiling curved into a dome, with a circular opening or ocular directly overhead. Outside he could see cloudless blue sky. He slowly turned his throbbing head to look around.

Glassless windows ringed the base of the dome and provided light. It had been a generously proportioned and beautiful room, with marble walls, travertine and tile floors and an elaborate coffered ceiling decorated with vine-like traceries. Spalled places revealed where carvings had been removed. That vandalism and long neglect left the walls cracked and bulged. Fragments fallen from the inside of the dome littered the floor. He could see no trace of furniture, nothing but bits of windblown debris in the corners. Open doorways to his left and right led into other spaces that he could barely see. If he'd awoke the next morning then those would be east and west, and a third opening lead north. His magesight revealed that all three were barred by fresh spells, as were the windows and overhead ocular.

This is a Silbari Temple. Or the ruin of one.

He inhaled deeply. A muddy stench pervaded the air, flavored with stagnant water, rotting weeds, and nastier odors that hovered below his ability to identify them.

He said he was sending me to the ruined city. Silbariki. That decagram had to be some kind of teleporter, a huge one. Big enough to send a man?

Terrell had heard of recent experiments to use such devices for sending messages much faster than a message construct. If that one had been used to send him here, then Chisaad had come up with a new variant. Such a sending must take great power or great subtlety, probably both. He wondered if any other wizard had noticed such a large draw on the Aretzo Node.

Then Terrell cursed himself for a fool. Chisaad's duties included tracking such things; if he chose not to make note of it no one would question him.

Yet. But his subordinates will know he did something. Has he enlisted them in his treason, or is he simply pressuring them to keep quiet? Surely that will only work for a while. People like to talk, and mages are as gossipy as anyone else. If he uses such powerful magics often, eventually one of the Council will notice too, or the Hierarchy.

But that reed was too slender to bear the weight of his hopes. Eventually might be a long time. *Nobody's going to rescue me. I must find a way out on my own.* He had to admit that his chances of doing that did not look good.

His headache remained, throat sore and mouth dry, and stomach getting hungry. He tested his bonds by tensing his muscles. The manacles were fastened to spikes driven into the floor and allowed only a few finger widths of movement. Perhaps by tugging them back and forth he might loosen one enough to get an arm free.

Then footsteps approached.

Terrell raised his head, endured the resulting ache, and saw one of Ap Marn's Gwythlo military aides stride through the eastern door. A silver badge flashed at his neck, probably the passkey that let him through the ward spell. His memory fumbled for the man's name—Dylan Fenman.

Fenman stopped a yard from Terrell's side, surveyed him critically. The aide's pasty complexion stood out in the gloom. "You're awake sooner than the wizard thought you'd be. I'm surprised a darkie like you recovered this fast. Maybe your Gwythlo blood is stronger than it looks."

Terrell made sure his voice stayed calm before he replied. "Fenman. How did he enlist you for this treason?"

The man chuckled. "It's not treason for me. I'm only obeying my sworn lord, Ap Marn. Your bad favor with the land-wights looks sure to put him back on top. I'd be a fool not to prosper on the side."

"I see." Terrell kept his voice flat only with effort. He wanted to rage at the traitor, but that wouldn't set him free. "So, you let yourself be bought."

"Oh yes. With two thousand pounds of silver," Fenman boasted. "Enough to get me a full officer's commission, buy a little farm, and pay for my wedding too." He grinned broadly. "Thanks for being so valuable, darkie princeling."

Terrell clenched his jaws against further words.

Fenman looked faintly disappointed as he knelt by Terrell's side and held out a cup. "Water. I advise you to drink it, since you'll get no more until evening." He dribbled the fluid slowly into Terrell's mouth.

Tepid and alkaline, but water. Terrell swallowed, managed not to choke on it. Fenman kept staring at his face. *No, he's staring at the top of my head.* For the first time Terrell became aware of something there. He swallowed the last dribble and tried shaking his head.

Agony turned the world red.

Fenman grinned and waved an admonishing finger at him. "Unh-uh, darkie. Shake the spider too much and you'll regret it. The wizard said to make sure you know this; it's already read your mind. You can't sabotage his plans by destroying it, but you can kill yourself prematurely by trying. That silver spike runs right through the top of your skull. Shake it free and your brains leak out too. I bet that'll hurt! So be a smart princeling. Lie here quietly and you get a couple extra tendays to live."

Fenman got up and left. Terrell waited until the pain in his head had subsided and he could no longer hear the man's footsteps. Then he very gently moved his head from side to side, this time sensing the small weight clinging there.

Spider, he called it. It's already read my mind? What good will that do? Sooner or later I'll be missed; it must have already happened. The Palace servants will have raised a cry, alerted the Temple, sent word to Pen. Dona Seraphina must already be questioning everybody and searching for me. Even if Chisaad's pretending to join that search, suspicion must eventually fall on him. He's keeping me alive for some purpose, but if his device has read my mind, why bother? They'd be wiser to kill me.

Fenman didn't seem worried about that at all. In fact, he seemed to be anticipating some denouement that pleased him. Did he have actual knowledge, or only a hope?

This doesn't make sense. I'll have to get him to talk to me more.

He gave up wondering for now; without information it was pointless. Instead he began probing the spider with his magical sensitivity. It stayed infuriatingly opaque. He could not find a single way into it or any way to affect its operation, even when, frustrated beyond bearing, he gave up on subtlety and tried to overwhelm it with Light. The thing simply sat there atop his head, busily doing Seraphs-Knew-What to his mind.

Chisaad knew about my special ability, he talked with Shimoor and me about it twice. He must have figured out a way to shield his creation against my tampering. The thought depressed Terrell. He had extended his trust to the Wizard simply because the man had been Shimoor's star pupil. *Everything I confided to him, he can use against me.*

He tried testing the stakes that held him. For a timeless time, he alternately tensed and relaxed his arms and legs, trying to work the iron spikes free. The beams of sunlight through the windows and the ocular moved across the floor and onto the opposite wall. Occasional bird-cries filtered in from outside the windows. He grew hungrier. His bladder filled and for a long time he held it until the discomfort grew too great to stand. Then he endured the shame of pissing himself. And the stink. At least urine dried quickly. He continued to work the stakes until his muscles were trembling with exhaustion, his wrists were chafed, and his eyes stung from dried sweat. The metal showed no sign of loosening.

Maybe I can keep at it tonight. But if—no, when, I free myself, how do I get out of here?

He had spent time listening during his rest periods. There were occasional noises through the eastern door that Fenman had used, distant echoes of something heavy being moved. For an hour or more he heard the monotonous sound of an axe chopping wood or perhaps somebody working at a pell with a sword. Once he thought he heard the smash of a ceramic dish dropped on a floor and a faint stream of curses following it. That last didn't sound like Fenman's voice, so his captors must have left more than one guard with him.

He examined his manacles as best he could, moving his head slowly to prevent a repeat of the pain. They had been made of spell-shaped iron molded to his wrists and showed neither seam nor lock. They gleamed like something new-made, so Chisaad had to have set this up quite recently.

He said they need me alive until the Choosing. That must mean he's supporting another one of the Twenty, but which one? He's stayed well clear of all of them while I've been there. This may be a sudden change in allegiance, or part of a deeper-laid plan.

He went back to tensing and relaxing, over and over until his muscles burned. Hours crept by, the suns passed almost overhead. The shaft of light shining down through the ocular moved away from him, and still he lay there alone.

The sunlight had climbed more than halfway up the opposite wall when Fenman finally returned with a bucket of water. He ladled three cups of it into Terrell and between them fed him a few bites of dried beef. It wasn't enough to satisfy Terrell's stomach but it took the edge off his hunger.

"Can't have you dying too soon," the Gwythlo aide said with indecent cheerfulness.

"Why not?" Terrell asked. "I don't understand why I'm still alive, if this thing on my head has truly read my mind."

Fenman laughed. "Don't ask me to explain it, I'm no mage. My Lord says keep you alive until the wizard doesn't need you anymore. Good enough for me."

Then he poured the rest of the bucket over Terrell from crotch to face. "Have a bath, darkie. The less I have to smell you, the better. See you in the morning."

While his jailer walked away, whistling, Terrell counted footsteps. It took Fenman twenty-five steps to cross the sixty feet or so of floor between his staked-out position and the east doorway, then another hundred before the man set his bucket down with a clatter. That made it less than three hundred feet from his prison room to the room that he guessed Fenman stayed in. He heard voices again, indistinct, and then nothing.

The sunbeam slanting through the ocular slowly climbed the inside of the dome and pinched out. The light through the windows followed. Stars appeared in the darkening sky above. For a while candlelight flickered and sounds from his guards' quarters echoed down the corridor, then the candle went out and silence ruled.

The wet stone beneath him grew no chillier and the air remained warm and humid. In winter this room probably grew cold enough to kill him overnight. But Silbar in autumn still baked under the Two Suns, and winter was still tendays away. The stone walls and dome metered residual warmth back at him. Hunger gnawed but not enough to cause more than annoyance yet.

All day long, in between bouts of straining at his bonds, he had been stretching his magic sensitivity as far as he could reach. This ruined temple lay rife with rags of old spells attenuated by time to mere wisps. Newer spells tasted familiar, probably Chisaad's magic, but they were few. He sensed one somewhere beyond the door like that diagram in Chisaad's chamber and guessed it must be the near end of the Wizard's teleportal link. The spells on the openings of his prison were plain, and he caught a tantalizing whisper of several more down the hallway toward whatever room his guards were living in. Far beneath the floor he could sense a node under the ruins, about the size of the one under Gwythford Castle. It didn't respond to his mind and its magic seemed sick somehow, or else something terribly warped fed on it. A few moments of exploring it left him as befouled as if he groped barehanded through the sludge of a sewer.

He pulled his sensitivity back inside his skin and the slimy sensation faded. The Light within him remained a gentle pressure, a soothing familiarity that washed him clean again. But he couldn't use it without a magical device or focus in which to pour it, and the only ones within his range were his prison spells.

Could he overload those ward spells by pouring more power into them? He divined their shape and construction with his mind, a painfully slow process, until he knew enough. Pour in power here, push it there, and the ward spells would probably collapse. He briefly considered trying it, if only to have something to do. But that wouldn't free him of his bonds, and those unfortunately were simple iron merely shaped by magic, not magical devices themselves. Without the ability to cast an actual spell, he couldn't affect them.

I can be a vandal, but I can't set myself free.

More hours passed. He'd never been alone like this before. Mysterious creaks came from the building around him, and the monotonous whisper of wind against stone. The silence intimidated him more than a threat would have. He wanted to call out for someone, anyone, so he wouldn't be alone in the dark.

No. Fenman will mock me, and I'll be even weaker in his eyes than I am now. I've got to stay strong.

He tried to sleep. The moons spilled their radiance through the windows and limned the old temple walls with bars of light and shadow. Eventually sheer nervous exhaustion carried him off to a restless sleep far from any comfortable oblivion. For in that night there were dreams that he couldn't remember, and one rude awakening that he wished he could forget.

He woke as something pawed through his mind like a robber looting a home, carelessly tossing aside anything that did not catch its fancy. His very thoughts were bruised in its wake.

What's happening? Is this thing on my head reading my mind again?

The sensation didn't last long. Before it ended he sensed a distant echo.

Chisaad! I can hear him through the spider. He's giving orders to someone—or maybe something? Something that isn't me.

The sensation faded, and he found himself alone with a throbbing headache. One thread of hope gleamed in his mind.

Does he know that I can hear him? If not, how can I use that?

CHAPTER 38: KIRIN

K irin soon learned that wagon master Chiaver had meant it when he promised plenty of work. They stopped for the night in a tiny roadside caravanserai, barely more than a pounded-dirt plaza shaded by ancient trees and wedged next to the road. The owner dispensed hay and grain from a mud-brick barn in exchange for copper coins. *Veglic* hauled buckets of water for the horses from a spring-filled cistern behind the barn while Chiaver unharnessed them and rubbed their yellow hides until they were glossy. Then Kirin hauled feed to the beasts, and more water, and shoveled the team's fresh dung onto the owner's compost pile in exchange for a couple coppers off the nightly camping fee.

When he finished the work, the wagon master bought the three of them a rude meal from the caravanserai owner's wife. The steaming flatbread wrapped around boiled lentils, butter and greens tasted like ambrosia. They ate by moonlight, squatting on stone blocks under a grapevine trellis leaning against the barn, amid the scents of horse manure and the huge jasmine vines wreathing half the building.

Chiaver exchanged gossip with the half-dozen other wagon masters that populated the caravanserai. They clearly all knew each other, and their curious eyes stabbed at Kirin. He'd mumbled out a story during the day, a mix of lies and truth that he repeated for them now. A young widower bound north to bring word of his wife's death to her family in Belluno. He stole Zella's connections to fabricate that and hoped she would forgive him. His obvious grief kept their questions at bay and he retired to the wagon as soon after evening prayers as decently possible. There he gave vent to some completely honest weeping.

Maia, Maia, he cried inside his head, curled into a ball among the sacks of sponges. He silently cursed the darkness inside him and cursed the power that had brought this disaster down upon his family, even while praying desperately that Sevan and Carlai and the others were still alive. His only consolation was the confidence that Grigor at least was being cared for. The waggoneers' gossip had included nothing about happenings in Aretzo. Whatever Chisaad and his allies might be doing had not come to the attention of these folk.

Chiaver roused him before dawn, whispering blearily, "Veglic. Wake up and get yourself ready. Breakfast in a bit."

Kirin stumbled to the outhouse next to the barn, then through morning ablutions at the cistern with his employer and the other men. The place had nowhere to bathe so he could get away with merely rinsing his dyed face and hands and did not have to reveal his too-pale body. Zella had told him the dye would withstand water but not strong soap. The caravanserai wife fed them yesterday's leftover flatbread wrapped around warm scrambled eggs and diced greens, all washed down with steaming mint tea.

Kirin discovered that his muffled sobbing during the night had validated his story in the minds of the listeners. The waggoneers' reserve had cracked, several gave him kind words and even blessings, which he accepted with what grace he could manage. After he watered the horses and shoveled dung again and while Chiaver and Ammin re-harnessed the beasts to the wagon, the caravanserai-wife slipped him a trio of oranges. Surprised, he tried to thank her, but she merely patted his arm and returned to her endless work.

The icy peak of God's Footstool gleamed in the early morning sunlight as the wagon's wheels hit the pavement again.

Chiaver and Ammin let him curl up among the sponges and rest in silence. The two of them sang low rumbling songs, about travel on the roads and tales of Seraphs and Kings. The wagon passed through laden orchards of pomegranates and oranges where birds chattered and hawks swooped, then through miles of irrigated fields. The rank scents of manure and growing things filled the humid air. They stopped at a spring under the cover of a grove of spreading trees while a brief afternoon thunderstorm rolled through. It soon sailed on north into the Valley, billowing clouds lit by the Suns like a fleet under full sail. The air smelled clean and sharp.

Ammin brought out the sack of figs again and Kirin shared the three oranges given to him. Chiaver looked surprised, then pleased.

"Thank you, Veglic," the big man said in his gruff voice, with a warm smile.

Kirin's heart warmed as well. They all nibbled on sweet succulence while the stolid horses plodded onward. Afterwards the boy played delightedly with the single long peel Kirin had stripped from his own orange. Kirin watched him wistfully. Would he be able to play with Grigor like this someday?

Not if Chisaad wins. I've got to rescue the Prince, no matter what.

Evening brought another caravanserai much like the last. Kirin understood the rhythm of wagon-life now and threw himself into his tasks before Chiaver said a word. Work, food, sleep, more work, and another day's travel. The miles crept by as they plodded towards the harsh wilderness of the distant Scarp, and the reckoning that Kirin both prayed for and dreaded.

Will the Prince free Pieter? Will he have me killed for kidnapping him? The worries chased themselves through his mind without answer.

Four days bled together, during which Chiaver and Ammin asked him few questions and he volunteered little, but the three of them grew comfortable in each other's presence. They sang Orthodox hymns together and Kirin let his voice soar on the descants even while his heart ached for Maia.

At night he dreamed of her, and sometimes wept anew. Other dreams were unhappy in a different way, featuring bonds on his wrists and ankles, the pain of forced immobility, hunger and thirst, and the ache of loneliness. Were the Seraphs sending him revelations of what the prince suffered? *My fault*, he thought, shamed anew before he finally drifted into an exhausted sleep without dreams.

Then one morning they turned off the King's Road and rattled down Pilgrimage Road toward Amm Crossing. Kirin perked up despite the humid heat. His family's trip had not come this way.

"We're headed for Guglione next, Veglic, after we cross the river," Chiaver explained.

Kirin shivered inside when he remembered that Duke Darnaud ruled Guglione. His Shadow stirred uneasily inside him after days of quiet withdrawal. He immediately suppressed it, afraid of what these people would think.

But the wagon master continued blithely, "That's where we turn north toward Isernia and home. More than halfway there now, though you'll have another day's walk to get to Belluno. Maybe you can find a wagon making the trip."

Kirin nodded and muttered thanks, grateful inside that he wouldn't have to do that in Guglione. The farther he could stay from Duke Darnaud, the better.

An hour after lunch the road passed through a four-arched triumphal gate commemorating a long-dead King's victory. The wagon wheels clattered as they entered a walled-in granite ramp lined by double rows of lotus palms and espaliered bougainvillea vines. It led east for more than two miles in a long straight descent to the river's edge, the walls broken periodically by gates to hidden places behind.

"Quite a sight, eh, Veglic?" Chiaver asked him proudly. "Nothing like it in the world."

Kirin gawked and nodded silent agreement.

Two giant statues flanked the river-end of the ramp, each more than thirty feet tall and standing on oversized plinths higher than his head. The figures faced the river but as the wagon came closer he could see that both were female, clad in floor-length gowns, with bare upraised arms holding silver globes balanced atop their heads. Skeins of spell-fire trailed from each globe to connect to the far side of the broad water. A low rumbling came from the river, growing louder as they approached.

Two officious clerks and a muscled guard stopped the wagon. The guard wore a Temple badge, half-armor and helmet and a sword, and had a horn on a strap slung over one shoulder. The clerks wore yellow robes with a prominent black symbol, two vertical lines and a longer horizontal one between, the mark of the special Temple order that ran the Crossing. The shorter clerk carried a paint-pot in one hand and a pointed paintbrush in the other.

"Four dohba," the taller clerk demanded in a bored voice while the shorter one began painting something on the wagon's left side.

Chiaver paid without objection while Kirin leaned over the sacks of sponges, curious to see what the painter did. The yellow paint glowed in his magesight and the man's rapidly-moving brush shaped it into symbols on the wagon's side. Symbols that faded and went out. A brief flicker of power drained through Kirin into the Darkness. For a moment he didn't know what had happened.

The painter stopped and stared at his work in consternation.

"Are you done?" the money-collector asked, a note of annoyance in his voice.

"The anchor-spell broke," the smaller man complained.

"Well, paint it again." Impatience this time. The bored guard glanced at them and rested a hand on his sword's pommel.

The painter repeated his strokes as Kirin moved back into the wagon, hiding his chagrin and gripping his Shadow tightly in his mind. It pushed back restlessly, awakened by the proximity of so much magic in the Crossing. He lay down between sacks where the officials could not see him.

"It worked this time," the painter announced with audible relief. The money-collector muttered something caustic under his breath, then told Chiaver to move along. The wagon master flicked his reins and they plodded a couple hundred yards ahead to join a stopped line of other wagons.

"Now we wait," he announced to Kirin. "Looks like it won't be too long, must be more than thirty wagons already. They send us across forty at a time."

Kirin climbed onto the end of the driver's seat and shaded his eyes to see the waterside. "Are we allowed to go down to the water while we wait?"

"Papa, can I go there too? If Veglic comes with me?" Ammin asked eagerly.

Chiaver smiled indulgently. "Yes, both of you, but come right back when the first gong sounds."

Kirin and Ammin both scrambled over the wagon's right side and dropped to the pavement. Ammin took one of Kirin's hands and they walked toward the riverbank. Kirin counted thirty-two wagons in line ahead of them, mostly freight wagons like their own. But two carried pilgrims returning to their homes in eastern Silbar or points farther east. An enclosed coach occupied by an Annubhinish merchant and his family filled out the line, with mounted guards before and behind it. Veiled women and girls leaned out the windows and made remarks to each other in their language. Kirin knew enough of the Bhinnish tongue to realize that one woman contrasted his shortness with the thickness of his muscular arms and legs and made extrapolation to other body parts. Embarrassed, he flushed beneath his brown skin-dye, clutched Ammin's hand harder and hurried past. Gales of laughter followed his departure.

He and the boy joined a crowd of other youths and men on the river's shore. The statues were set back a dozen yards from the ramp, and the riverbank between them and the ramp had been filled by flat plazas with stone balustrades. Men and boys crowded the south plaza, plus a sprinkling of women.

"The next king ought to put in a bridge," one young man declared loudly. "Then we could stay dry."

An older man snorted. "River is all that kept the damned Gwythlo army out during the Conquest. Mages can shut down the spell, can't do that with a bridge!"

Others chimed in about cost and convenience; it sounded like an old argument. Kirin lifted Ammin onto his shoulders so that the boy could see over the crowd, then gazed around himself, amazed.

"First time here, lad?" asked the old man who had argued with the opinionated younger one. He smiled kindly as Kirin flushed and nodded. "You're in for a treat. We wade the whole width of the river on the back of Crossing Ridge, with spells to keep the current from sweeping us away." He gestured grandly at the river.

The ramp ran straight into the Amm. Muddy water swirled around double rows of granite bollards the size and shape of men that marked the outside edges of its path every ten yards. They were worn with age; Kirin vaguely knew the Crossing had been built centuries ago. He had also known that the Amm was a wide river but hadn't known how wide. Here it looked to be two miles and more to the far bank, with the cones of the Ash Mountains fading into the skies to the southeast. The spells followed the lines of bollards, diminishing in the distance to a double line of dots. Several hundred yards out a row of wagons plodded towards this shore, with spells and water swirling around them. He couldn't hear a sound from them thanks to the bellowing roar downstream.

South of the bollards, the river broke into chaos. From the bank Kirin could see how it fell off the ragged edge of a long ledge that bore the crossing. Tapering fingers of still water ran out into the churning maelstrom before they too succumbed. Ragged black rocks reared from the white water, each skirted with glistening foam. The whole massive river dropped into a brawling battle between earth and water that raged for a thousand feet downstream and extended all the way across. The deep rumble shook his bones and a cool mist blew in his face. It smelled of a clean wetness quite different from the briny life-heavy sea. For a while Kirin simply stared, soaking in the cool and the noise.

Then the other wagon train arrived at the shore. The horses waded through the final shallows with much splashing and punctuated the background roar with the clatter of iron-shod hooves. The beasts' legs were wet to their bellies and they smelled of their exertions. A string of pilgrimage wagons carried chanters reciting a hymn of gratitude for safe arrival. Some of the smaller, shorter wagons spilled water that had leaked into their beds. A merchant cursed in four languages as colored water draining out of his too-low wagon betrayed an expensive leak. Wagon after wagon thundered ashore.

Ammin shouted to Kirin, "They'll call us to go pretty soon. Let's go see the mages before we go back to Father." Kirin reluctantly turned away and carried the boy over toward the south statue.

The river side of each plinth jutted forward a good ten feet from the statue it carried, supporting an awning and three wooden chairs. The middle seat had been shaped like a lounge. A mage reclined there, with another on his left and a priestess on his right, all in the same Temple livery as the clerks. Between the mage's seat and the water-end of the plinth stood an iron rod knobbed with five silver bulbs bigger than Kirin's fist. Spells ran from it up to the silver globes held by the mighty statues, and more spells connected the mage to the bulbous control rod. The power sheeted around each plinth, welling up from a small node deep below. Kirin kept a wary distance as his Shadow stirred inside his chest, fretted by all this power.

"Let's get closer!" Ammin urged, wiggling as he enjoyed this ride on his new steed.

Kirin balked. "This is close enough." A loud gong rang from the north statue. "Time for us to go back anyway."

He lifted Ammin off his shoulders, preparing to set him down. The boy resisted, stiffening and protesting with the eternal childhood lament, "But not yet!" Kirin had to heave the spindly child over his head to get him free. Then Ammin relaxed, and, off balance, Kirin set him down faster than he'd intended. Ammin's belt caught on Kirin's hood and pulled it sideways off his head before he could stop it.

A man right behind them drew in his breath sharply. "Imp!" he accused, pointing at Kirin's exposed ears. "Spawn of Salim!"

"No!" Kirin denied, snatching his hood back up as a prickle ran up his spine. He shivered. *Not here, Father Haroun, I beg you! Not now!*

"Half breed," another man said with contempt, and turned his back on him. Several others in the crowd turned to look at him with doubtful expressions on their faces.

Kirin grabbed Ammin's hand and hustled them both away. The boy had a bewildered look on his face and had to scamper to keep up as Kirin practically ran back to the wagon. There he tossed the boy up to his father and scrambled up and inside as fast as he could.

"No need for that much haste," Chiaver laughed. "We start slow and don't move faster than a walk all the way across. Settle yourselves."

A second gong pealed out, two strikes this time, and the lead wagon lurched into motion. One by one all the rest followed it. Most of the crowd had returned to their own wagons. The plazas were nearly empty by the time Chiaver's wagon reached the water. The big yellow horses waded right in with the calmness of experience. Water rose around them as Kirin stared from side to side. The heavy wheels threw up rooster-tails of spray and waves lapped the bottom of the wagon. The river surrounded the moving train and its immense power pressed on their fragile wood and flesh.

The spells closed in as well.

The ethereal webs spun out from the silver globes delicately wrapped the wagon and horses. Kirin stared, dismayed by the shifting rainbow of power holding the wagon against the strengthening current. The magic crawled over wood and cloth like the shimmering threads of Dona D'Illbinth's dress.

Oh no! It reaches inside *the wagons too! Seraphs help me!*

Kirin retreated among the sacks of sponges to hide from the relentless magic. It did no good. The webs crawled over the awning, between the sacks, reaching closer and closer. His Shadow groped for the magic and he fought it back. One shining tendril of the shimmering web touched him. His Shadow bit off part of the spell before he could prevent it.

The wagon shivered in the current. Ripples spread up and down the row of other wagons as the entire web twitched at this sudden maiming. The downstream rapids roared. Chiaver gripped his reins harder and darted frowning glances up and down the line. The horses tossed their heads uneasily, tried to stop, but he urged them forward.

Behind them Kirin saw the silver globes flicker. He could see the entire web stretch and start to deform. The mages on the plinths were casting furiously, trying to patch the damage before it spread.

Kirin screamed silently at the monster inside him. *You'll kill us all!* His mind grappled it with renewed terror. *Father Haroun, lend me your strength!* The wounded spell leaked power into him to feed his darkness. He could only match it with his willpower.

The whole row of wagons trembled, and several horses neighed. Shocked voices were raised in fear in the other wagons. The pilgrims in the wagons ahead began to pray loudly. Chiaver muttered under his breath and squeezed the reins. He glanced back over his shoulder into the wagon and his eyes widened as they met Kirin's.

Kirin curled into a ball, trying to fold his Shadow inside. He shut his eyes and battled it with all his concentration. Slowly he squeezed it inward.

Then the spells crawled across his skin as the mages strengthened their web. Over his eyes, through his hair, in his ears, up his nose, and down his throat—

He nearly lost control then and the whole web shuddered. The horses squealed, and the wagon jerked. Somehow, he held the Shadow back and locked it down, refused its raging hunger and held it fast.

The web stabilized. The wagon master urged his beasts onward, tension in his voice as thick as the rapids' spray. Past the river's midpoint, past the canyon of the deepest channel where the water fell right off the road-edge between two bollards. Past the three-quarter mark, the east bank growing closer with every step.

Kirin stayed curled into a ball until the sound of hooves on pavement told him they'd arrived. The spells fell behind as they clattered up the eastern ramp. Only then did he dare relax his fierce internal grip on his personal monster. He sat up and blinked in the suns' light.

Chiaver reined the wagon to a stop and turned in his seat to stare at Kirin. "What did you do?" he demanded in a voice that shook. "What *are* you?"

Ammin, staring with eyes wide as saucers, whispered, "A man at the shore called him an Imp."

Belatedly Kirin noticed that his hood had fallen back and his ears were exposed. He snatched it back up. "I'm not an Imp, just a man! My father was a Gwythlo, that's why I have pointed ears. That's all!"

"I saw that dark spell you cast," Chiaver answered angrily. "You almost killed us! Get out of my wagon!" He reached under the driving seat for Kirin's knapsack and threw it at him. "Go!"

Kirin scrambled over the tailgate and cropped to the pavement, driven as much by the fear in the wagon master's voice as by the lash of the man's anger. Other wagons were rumbling past them. He ducked between two and ran to the verge of the ramp. An especially large pair of lotus palms and an untrimmed bougainvillea created a shady nook next to the stone-lined ditch that watered them all. He stopped to fill his water bag from the chuckling canal and take stock. Chiaver's wagon had disappeared up the road.

Kirin looked around the huge stone ramp, twin to the one on the west bank and full of busy strangers. Had any of them connected the near-destruction of the crossing spell with him? He wanted to hide in the nook until nightfall. But Pieter wouldn't get freed if he didn't free the Prince.

Kirin shouldered his pack, made very sure his ears were covered, and began walking.

The ramp ended with a pair of head gates that gushed water into the flanking irrigation ditches. He crossed a bridge over a large canal and the pavement ceased, replaced by a pounded clay surface whose shoulders were sandy dirt splashed with bits of grass and weeds. Plenty of manure coated the road and two industrious farmers shoveled it into a goat-cart while their harnessed goats nibbled weeds. A big campground opened on his right beyond the curb. He avoided that and headed up the road, drawing a bit of cloth across his face to keep out the dust.

An hour of sweaty walking brought him to a crossing where a battered road ran south toward huge clay pits along a broad sandy wash stippled with acacia and cedar trees. Smoke trickled up into the brassy sky from the ovens that made Guglione's famous amphorae. Another road ran west up the valley of the wadi into sere desert. The last turned north and curved under the frowning walls of the big battlemented city itself. His goal lay past it.

Other men walked north from the clay pits, many pulling small handcarts piled high with fresh amphorae. He stepped into an empty place between two of the carts and tried to be inconspicuous. There were hours yet before sunset.

The closer he got to Guglione, the less he liked it. A dry channel liberally scattered with sharpened stakes moated the city and the walls held dozens of gibbets, every one dangling a corpse. Some had been nibbled by carrion birds till they were more bone than flesh. A fresh one had been stripped naked to display the marks of a whipping that nearly flayed the man. Crows quarreled over his eyes. Nauseated, Kirin looked away.

Most of the men plodded straight ahead onto an iron-bound drawbridge that served the city's open gate. A side road paralleled the moat; Kirin turned onto it to circle the place. Surly guards watched him, their hands on their swords, and for a moment he feared they would seize him and drag him inside the brooding maw. But they let him go without comment. He didn't breathe a sigh of relief until he got far enough around the curving city wall to be hidden from their gaze. Another road branched off paralleling a canal that watered the city; he gladly followed it away into farmland. The pavement soon leaped the canal on a sturdy stone bridge and bent north again at a stone obelisk with an arrow and the name Isernia carved on it. Heartened to know the right direction, he picked up his pace.

The road cut through irrigated fields where green growing scents tried to wipe away the memory of rotting flesh. The arrow-straight road boasted little traffic. He thought he could see Chiaver's wagon a few miles ahead and slowly leaving him behind.

His heart hurt. The man and his son had been kind to him when they thought him a Silbari like themselves.

Until Chiaver saw my ears, and my Shadow. Bitterness welled in Kirin like a black tide and for a moment he wanted nothing more than to be home in Aretzo with Maia and Pieter and all his family. But Maia was dead, and his father would be, if he didn't rescue the Prince. He dashed tears from his stinging eyes and kept walking under the hot afternoon suns.

CHAPTER 39: TERRELL

awn woke Terrell. Fenman brought him water in the morning and water and a morsel of food in the evening. By then his stomach was growling so badly that he wolfed it down gratefully. He had spent all day alternating between straining at his bonds and stretching his magical sensitivity, and accomplished nothing with either.

But five separate times during the day, the spider on his head had let him hear Chisaad speaking.

He's ordering someone around, but he's being very precise in his wording, and very cold. As if whoever he talked to wasn't even human? I wonder what that's about.

The aches bred by his forced position on the floor made sleep harder that night. The Moon of Calm sent a sliver of its light through the dome's ocular to creep across the wall.

Sound caught his attention, a peculiar rasping that echoed softly. Something scraping against stone? He thought it sounded like fingernails on slate, or maybe claws. It came a third time, louder now, and definitely from the east entrance.

He turned his head to look, careful not to shake the spider atop his head. For a moment he thought he saw a dog moving in the darkness beyond the door, then he remembered the monumental scale of the ruined building and his breath quickened. Whatever moved there was as big as a pony.

Then it came into the moonlight. He gasped.

A twisted asymmetric nightmare of a beast stared back at him. A forked tongue licked at the ward spell, then withdrew behind double rows of fangs longer than his fingers. Seven legs upheld the lumpy body, four on one side and three on the other, and a long scaly tail swept back and forth behind. It raised itself up, lifting the front pair of limbs entirely off the floor as it sniffed the ward spell.

No, he realized with sick certainty. *It smells me.*

More scales glittered on the belly. The raised limbs pawed at the ward spell, which glowed blue and repelled them. It tried again, leaning its weight into the spell. The ward glowed brighter, trying to push it back, then slowly dimpled as the beast lifted two more legs off the floor and leaned with more of its weight.

It's trying to get at me. He shuddered at the thought of those savage teeth. *It might almost be a mercy if it goes for my throat first.*

The ward began to bow inward as the monster pressed harder.

Terrell's mind grasped for the thin edge of the guardian magic. It wasn't terribly different from using a message sender or the Stone Throne itself. When he had it, he called forth his Light. It flooded into the spell, strengthened and stiffened it until the monster had to retreat. The creature uttered a low throaty growl that scraped Terrell's nerves.

Its stench reached his nose and he gagged.

What is it? The body looks a little like a bloated crocodile, save for the extra legs. But that head! It's as bad as anything Aunt Klairveen conjured to send against me in the river battle. Is this what has corrupted the node? Or has the corrupted node made this beast?

For a while the scaly nightmare plodded back and forth, lashing its tail in slow waves of cold frustration while it stared at him. There were two eyes on one side of the horrific head and one on the other. Branching growths like soft antlers waved from the top of its skull. Moonlight bleached its color, but the hide looked leprous. Dark patches blotched the pale scales.

Terrell nearly gagged from the stench, but he kept feeding the ward spell. Finally the creature turned away and vanished into the darkness. He heard a faint slithering sound as it moved, then a distant thump and splash. The ward spell faded to its normal transparency.

Sleep eluded him the rest of the night. When Fenman appeared the next morning, Terrell warned him about his night visitor. The Gwythlo laughed at him.

"There're plenty of those things prowling around this place. You can spear them if you're quick, though the meat's no good. Guess that'd be no consolation to you if it had gotten through the wards, hah!"

He didn't seem much worried by the possibility. When he left, whistling, Terrell came as close as he'd ever come to cursing someone individually.

No, he sighed after a struggle. *If I'm ever to be King I must rise above that sort of temptation. The King's curses have weight; I won't be worthy to wear the crown if I waste them on personal vengeance.*

Restraint offered little comfort.

Terrell concentrated on the metal spider atop his head, listening to every quiet sound within it. He discovered that he could hear other voices than Chisaad's. One sounded like Fantillin, another like Dona Seraphina. Both baffled him.

They don't sound like they're talking to Chisaad. I'd swear Dona Seraphina said my name! What is going on?

He continued to listen, and by the time his jailer returned with his third evening of water and food, he understood. Sheer loneliness led him to blurt it out.

"Someone is masquerading as me," he declared to his captor. "Using this spider-device to raid my memories so he knows what to say and do."

Fenman chuckled. "You're mostly right, darkie. Now drink up."

Terrell had to swallow his questions with the water, and then chew up the dried bit of beef as best he could. Fenman doused him with the remaining water again and left, whistling once more. Terrell gritted his teeth and endured the chill while the water drained away through cracks in the floor. He resigned himself to another long night.

Sometime well after midnight he awoke to find Madness shining through the dome's western windows. The little moon bathed him in its ill-omened light. Then movement warned him that the beast had returned.

This time it immediately reared up and clawed at the eastern ward spell. Again, Terrell strengthened the ward until the monster gave up trying. Instead it squatted on its haunches and stared at him unnervingly, blinking now and then. Terrell wanted to turn his face away but didn't dare. Once his gaze had locked on the beast's, he suspected that he had better convince it he wasn't prey, though only The One God knew what really went on inside that horror of a head. The staring contest continued until Terrell's control grew ragged. He wanted to scream at the thing but did not dare. Abruptly the creature turned its head away and slithered back to the water. Terrell found his heart racing and lungs panting as if he'd run a mile in full armor.

Father Haroun, hear me! he pleaded. *Give me the strength to face that evil thing. I beg you to intercede with The One for me. Send me a way to escape this prison.*

He prayed a lot as the night dragged on. Moonlight crawled across the floor and wall to eventually expire against the inside of the dome. He finally fell asleep only to wake to another dreary dawn.

The fourth day offered no change.

And the fifth.

And the sixth and seventh, each so much alike that he feared for his sanity from laying there in his own filth and pain. Every night the monster tested the wards, stared at him for a while, and then left, as if it found purpose in depriving him of another hour's sleep.

But the morning of the eighth day was different.

CHAPTER 40: KIRIN

The city of Isernia made a walled oval spiky with towers. It squatted across Kirin's route like a giant hedgehog. He circled it at a distance through farm roads and canal paths, wary lest the wagoneer Chiaver had alerted the local priestesses against him. Rich farm country sprawled around him, well-irrigated and at the height of harvest season. Everybody wanted workers and some weren't picky about their appearance.

Hungry, he paused at an outlying farm to trade work for food, and spent a whole afternoon climbing date palms to cut free their ripe burdens. Then for half a candlemark after nightfall he picked itchy bits of dry palm-frond out of his clothes. He finally fell into exhausted sleep in a hayloft above two plow-mules. In the morning the farmer paid him with breakfast and a double handful of hard-baked traveler's biscuit plus a small sack of shelled almonds, both of which Kirin crammed into his pack. He bowed to the man in gratitude, but the farmer waved him away—and made the sign against evil.

He'll hire an imp, Kirin thought sadly. *Even feed and pay him, but nothing more. I guess I should be glad he didn't try to cheat me.* His heart ached anew. He pulled the hood over his head as he returned to the road.

Several miles north of the city he crossed a decaying bridge over the last working canal. Beyond sprawled the wrecked lands that had been torn by the rise of the Scarp.

The road immediately fell out of repair, patched only by windblown dust and sheep dung. People still used it, for there were clear trails winding along the route, even marks of wagon wheels, but plainly no one maintained it. The land heaved up in wrinkles and gullies that broke up the old irrigation ditches and repeatedly cracked the road. Most buildings were little more than heaps of rubble, trees long since decayed to stumps or simply depressions where the roots had been gnawed away by ants. He found a lonely living date palm standing in a hollow next to the collapsed remains of a shrine. There he applied his new skill to help himself to a meager harvest. This prickly experience feeding himself in bare countryside without inns or farms warned him that he'd better collect any food he found. The travel biscuits would not last long.

His restless feet ate the miles. Broken irrigation ditches slashed weed-grown fields dotted by collapsed homesteads overgrown with thistles. Near sunset two young toughs with bad teeth and stained knives tried to jump him from a ruin leaning over the road's verge. He threw Darkness in their faces and fled as one cursed and the other prayed. Neither pursued him.

The experience both heartened and frightened him. *I'm powerful, but if they'd had bows, I'd have been dead before I knew they were there.* He moved more cautiously after that, noticing the furtive movements of rabbits and jackals in the weeds. The distant blowing of rams-horns as shepherd talked to shepherd brought him no comfort, for they might be passing word of him as easily as the two outlaws. The local law would be thin protection for a half breed.

Nightfall brought him no place to rest. The broken road crested another rise and he saw Belluno off to the northeast. The decayed city formed a dark block against the writhen soil. Its few whole towers were lit by only moonlight and a handful of torches. Rising Calm and setting Madness vied to light his way. The road followed a dry canal toward the dim city.

Kirin stopped at a broken bridge, rested on a fragment of balustrade, and thought. His Shadow gave him vision even when the moons hid behind clouds. This coolness was much better than the day's heat. And robbers would be easier to avoid in the dark. He resolved to travel by night from now on, and as he plodded he let his Shadow ooze out to completely hide him.

Hours later, Calm neared the western horizon as he approached a blocky ruined temple standing near the track. A long day and night of effort had left him and his water bottle dry. A green wetness rode the breeze from the broken building, barely detectable beneath the heavy overlay of sheep. He drew his Shadow close until it coated him like paint and picked his way through rubble. A woven thorn-fence blocked the gaping entry and more such screens plugged every window. He circled the ruin as a black man-shape ghosting past bits of fallen stone and broken tile.

In back two arthritic cypress trees bracketed a spring. A jackal raised his wet muzzle in sudden consternation, blinked wide eyes and fled. A fan of luxuriant rushes trailed from an overflowing pool like a bedraggled skirt. Kirin found the ruin's back door blocked like the front, but scented the ashes of a recent fire within. Sure enough, the shepherd's snores rode the wind. He probably caught up on much-needed sleep while his flock slept safe behind stone and thorns.

Kirin filled his water bag, drank deeply, filled it again, and continued around the old temple. The dome had fallen in and the point of the single minaret's spire had snapped off, but the small room at the top of the main shaft looked intact. He had to climb cracked walls and then wiggle through the minaret's lowest unblocked window, afraid he would wake a sleeping sheep in the big room below. Inside he ascended a spiral of dusty stairs past nests filled with sleeping swallows. At the top the prayer-caller's airy chamber welcomed him. Dried mud obscured the tile floor; starlight shone down through the hollow stump of the spire. He leaned on one of the eight waist-high windowsills to gaze across the ruined land.

Much nearer now, the ragged top of the Scarp cut across the north. The few taller peaks in the ridge were separated by sharp canyons, one clearly broader than the others. The wrecked road he followed lead straight toward it. East, the barren hills wrinkled up like a carelessly-dropped blanket. West, the great central valley of Silbar opened to the stars, fenced by the high spine of the Bright Mountains eighty miles away. Their feet lay hidden below the curve of the World, but their white heads shone in the fading moonlight. The peak of God's Footstool loomed above the rest, impossibly tall and pale in the night. Soon dawn would touch that point with fire and the shepherd would wake.

Kirin wrapped himself in his one thin blanket and curled up on the hard floor, his pack for a pillow and memory for comfort in the chill. At home he lived with the endless background of spells and workings drawing on the city Node, a traffic operating too deep below the city for his Shadow to touch, but close enough to feel. He still hadn't grown used to its absence even after six days and nights. But the toll of unfamiliar exertion left him tired enough to sleep through dawn and noon both, to awake as the Two Suns kissed the Bright Mountains.

A cautious look over the windowsill showed the rubble-strewn temple floor empty of sheep, though the thorn barrier had been carefully closed. Some surreptitious scanning showed sheep flecking a field a mile or two to the west. Satisfied, he packed and descended, ate a few dates and drank at the spring, added his contribution to the shepherd's privy, and resumed his walk with a lighter heart.

This wasteland isn't so hard, he told himself confidently.

* * *

A day later, as he struggled down the brutal north face of the Scarp, he took the thought back. He'd begun this descent after nightfall and now dawn already bathed him in a new day's heat.

The old road had disappeared completely a few miles from the edge, dissolved into wandering animal trails. He had picked one that seemed to run more-or-less straight toward a low part of the ragged edge, lost it in a maze of gullies, found it again, and followed it into this canyon. The walls grew higher as the floor descended in a tight series of water-carved steps, each larger than the last. He had slid more than his own height down the previous drop. Now he could see the broken ground below, tantalizingly close, but still better than three times his height below the little ledge on which he stood. He leaned out as far as he dared but could not see what lay below his perch.

I can't get back up. He stared back the way he had come. *There's nothing to hold onto. I have to go down.*

But what if there were sharp rocks? What if he broke an ankle or even his leg? He would die of thirst in this wilderness. He shuddered for a moment, then swallowed his fear. *There's no choice.*

He lay on his belly and swung his legs out over the emptiness. Jack-knifing in the middle let him put the toes of his buskins against the rock and test for a foothold. He found one, eased his weight onto it, and then gripped the crumbling rim as he did a one-legged squat with his face and belly pressed into the stone and his other leg feeling for the next foothold. For a frightening moment his toes found nothing, then caught on a bit of protruding stone. He eased down onto it, fingers barely clinging to the ledge overhead, and put all his weight on it.

The rock snapped off. His weight hung on his fingertips. His hands held, and he breathed a sigh of relief. Then the ledge above his head broke off.

He slid feet first down the face of the cliff, crumbling sandstone banging his knees and ribs and scraping his chin and fingers bloody, until his feet slammed against another ledge with a shock that made his teeth rattle. There he clung to the cliff with fingernails and willpower. After his heart calmed he dared look down to see how much farther he had to go.

A foot below his heels, a dimpled fan of sand and gravel spread out.

He stepped down onto it and leaned back against the rock for a moment to get his breath. The detritus under his buskins merged with a corrugated plain sloping gently down towards a marsh some hundred-odd yards away. The broken road he had been following emerged from the detritus-fan and dived into the marsh, parting the reeds for a hundred yards before they overwhelmed it. Beyond he could see more mud flats emerging from Purification Lake as it shrank in the summer heat. Clouds of flies buzzed, birds flitted, and a lizard peered at him from atop a waist-high rock, then flicked away. The rising sun-warmed stench of the mud flats warred with the burgeoning life-smell of the marsh and the harsh scent of warming rock.

He pushed off the wall, climbed atop the lizard's rock and looked about. West, the land and the Scarp both descended until the lake lapped at the cliff itself. East, the valley floor sloped gradually up towards the wrinkled desert hills. Those were banded and streaked with pastel ochre, gray, and brown. The marshes didn't reach the hills, so he hoped he could pass between them.

He jumped down off the rock and headed east along the feet of the cliffs.

Two hours later, the suns finally high enough to no longer be in his eyes, he found a canyon opening in the face of the Scarp. A lightly-trodden but unmistakable horse trail issued out of its dry depth. He could see it switch-backing up the canyon wall toward the top.

I could have walked *down here? I should have looked farther. Salim take me for a fool!*

The horse trail branched into more trails headed north, northwest to the lake, and east into the hills. A rude rock shelter and a rough corral had been built outside the mouth of the canyon, neither looking recently used. He puzzled for a while over the sigil carved on a rock in the shelter wall, it looked familiar, but he couldn't remember why. He shrugged and followed his nose behind the shelter. There a small spring filled a stone basin ringed by lush grasses and fading flowers. He refilled his water bag, ate a bit, and curled up to sleep in the most shaded corner of the shelter until night. Memories of Maia tormented his sleep.

Only after he woke at sunset did he remember where he had seen the carved sigil. Duke Darnaud's men had worn it at Pieter's trial. This must be his hunting camp.

Kirin stared about in fear, then remembered that the canyon would have echoed the iron-shod steps of any approaching horses. He quickly gathered his gear, covered himself in a cloud of Shadow, and strode purposefully onto the trail that headed north.

Many hours later he toiled his way onto a long low treeless plateau that lay above Purification Lake and below the hills. Antelope ran from him, and an owl swooped low to look at him, then veered away to the northeast. Distantly he heard a lion's roar near the lake and shivered in dread. His Shadow thickened about him.

He found a paved road in surprisingly good condition despite grass sprouting from every crevice. The moons and his night-vision lit the vast emptiness, so unpeopled and frightening that it made him crave the comfort of walls. He began to run, eating the miles with a loping stride as the road gradually curved east toward a huge gap in the hills. When he got to a junction where another road ran up arrow-straight out of the big lake, he stopped, weary and panting, next to a tumbledown shrine. A head-tall pedestal held the broken stump of a statue. After a little rest he climbed onto it to look east.

He could see the road descending into an oval basin much smaller than the great valley that held Purification Lake. A second lake filled the south part of this vale and glinted in the moonlight. He remembered that Dona Zella had called it Ibis Lake. It stretched north into the heart of the oval vale, where its steely waters met blocky black shapes.

Ruined Silbariki.

His heart thumped as he gazed on his goal. The ancient city looked bigger than Aretzo, the stumps of walls and broken towers spread for miles across Ibis Lake's northern shore. Lines of shining water extended deep into the wreckage like the flooded roads of Aretzo's Sump. They converged on a clump of ruins in the center, where a soaring dome ringed by eight broken minarets still rose above the city.

He stared at the dome's curve with his magesight and caught the flicker of spells. Somebody had warded the place. *They have to be keeping Prince Terrell there.* To be within sight of his goal restored his flagging confidence and he hunted for a way to get there.

A deep gash in the landscape ran from Ibis Lake to Purification Lake, draining smaller lake into the bigger. He saw no bridge across the artificial canyon, no trees growing out of it, only a yawning trench cutting off northern travel. North of it the imposing height of a sheer red-colored cliff rose to tower over the gap that joined the two valleys. He could barely see the distant thread of another road at the cliff's foot, arrowing toward the drowned city. It looked like the obvious approach, but that trench lay between him and it.

The first light of approaching dawn began to lighten the night. He needed a place to shelter, and soon. A smaller ruin down the road looked promising. The lion's roar had frightened him down to his bones, he wanted stone walls around him before he lay down to sleep.

The ruin had been a walled monastery. The gates were long gone, and a side road led into a partly-paved courtyard. The temple squatted in the center in a ruined splendor of carved stone. Directly in front of the broad steps leading to the building's doorless entry lay an oval pool of shivering water. A spring still poured into it from a stone spout carved like an angel's face. Two elderly orange trees and a hoary fig spread their branches above a riot of weeds and garden gone wild.

It looked like heaven.

Kirin circled to the upper edge of the pool, with the deepest water and a stone rim still whole and clear. A nightjar trilled in the fig tree. He slipped off his pack, stripped to his hose, and slid down into the pool. He gloried in the coolness and squeezed mud beneath his toes as he immersed himself completely in blessed, cool, clean water.

He managed to retain the sense not to tempt fate for long, but scrubbed himself and his clothes swiftly, refilled his water bottle from the spring, and then entered the temple.

Behind the grand façade lay a collapsed wilderness of stone and the stump of the eastern minaret. Its stair had mostly fallen but with effort he made his way up the narrow fragments of steps remaining to reach a second-level room. Bats had coated the floor with guano, but the next set of stairs was whole, so he continued to the third level. A bit of roof survived next to an arched window looking north and down onto the front courtyard. Another window on the east side faced the soon-to-rise suns. The high perimeter wall lay right below it, eroded but not broken. Nothing could get at him here unless it could climb or fly.

Satisfied, he made a nest in the sheltered corner, spread his clothes to dry, and slept.

But not for long. Less than two hours past dawn he awakened to howls that sounded like laughter. A pack of hyenas had arrived and taken over the courtyard. They woke him when they found his scent at the water's edge, raised their hunting chorus, and followed his trail.

CHAPTER 41: TERRELL

T errell's eighth day dawned with aches and boredom. Fenman perfunctorily brought him water and left again. The hours began to crawl. Then a heavy tread announced the arrival of someone new. Terrell's hopes rose as he saw the familiar form.

"Darnaud?"

Terrell choked back the temptation to say anything more as his cousin strode across the cracked floor. *He's with Fenman, which likely means Ap Marn and Chisaad own him too.*

The Duke of Guglione stopped next to Terrell and stared down at his face. He wore half armor—back-and-breastplate on his torso plus vambraces on his arms—and had sword and main-gauche at his belt. For a long moment he stood there, silently looking Terrell up and down while Fenman waited a pace behind and to his right. The aide looked nervous, even fearful. Darnaud looked gloating.

That's not good, Terrell thought. *He's trying to make me feel trapped and helpless. Which I am, but I don't have to let him know that I know it.* He stared back, studying Darnaud the same way. He noticed a recent dent in the Duke's breastplate. The man's left vambrace had also been freshly scored, and blood stained his trousers where they bloused above his boots.

"I see you've been fighting, My Lord Duke," Terrell observed in as close to a detached voice as he could muster.

"Killing darkies," Darnaud answered, and smirked. "Three of your damned 'Twenty' got my blade in their guts. Not much challenge in it, but a man has to take his fun where he can." He drew his sword.

For a moment Terrell thought he was about to be run through. *Mother Umana, accept my soul!* Then Darnaud laid the flat of the blade's tip against Terrell's inner thigh. Fenman drew a sharp breath.

"No darkie should have blond hair like yours," Darnaud remarked casually, sliding the sword toward Terrell's crotch. The sharp edge shaved off some of the fine blond hairs growing between his legs. "It's not right."

Terrell felt the blood drain from his face. He'd never thought he might have to endure death by torture. He locked his jaws against speech or screams and gave himself to prayer. *Father Haroun, lend me your courage!*

Darnaud continued, "You won't be using your manhood again, but you've had enough practice to know what you'll be missing without it. I think I'll start by cutting one of your balls off, then--"

"Your Grace!" Fenman interrupted, his face aghast. "Damage done to him will affect the golem! My Lord Ap Marn's orders are quite specific. He is not to be harmed until it is time!"

Darnaud's blade stopped with the sharp edge touching Terrell's stones, which were trying to withdraw into his body. For a long moment the cold steel paused there while Terrell stared at Darnaud and the Duke stared back. "Time. Faugh."

When he withdrew the sword Terrell almost fainted in relief. Darnaud sheathed it without taking his eyes off Terrell's. "I'll have to wait a bit then. Just as well. I need to go kill your pet darkie with the magic sword. He'll be a real challenge. I'll have to backstab him, so he can't use that damned thing against me. Maybe send three men against him first to distract him, then come up behind. I know! I'll cut off his head and bring it back here for you to see before I get to work on you." Darnaud grinned and leaned over him to add, softly, "That'll make your despair sweeter."

"Pen will kill you, you triple-damned traitor!" Too late, Terrell clamped his jaws against further words. *Idiot!* He berated himself. *You let him know he's gotten to you!*

Darnaud smiled cruelly. "Well then, maybe I'll poison him first. Then while he's dying I'll run a pike up his ass and bring him back here whole. His carcass can stand watch while I take my time with you."

He sauntered away, throwing back over his shoulder as he left the room; "Think about that while you wait for me, darkie."

Darnaud chuckled as he exited through the western ward spell, with Fenman scurrying along behind him.

Pen, Pen, be careful of this bastard. Terrell thought desperately. *Don't let him get behind you!* Would his best friend recognize the man's treachery in time? *Father-Seraph Haroun,* he prayed, *Alert Irreneetha to his evil intentions. Don't let Pen be taken by surprise.*

Terrell added many more prayers while the day waned, and the Two Suns' light made its monotonous journey up the inside of the dome. Fenman returned at the usual time to feed and water him, and even took a little extra time to clean him off before dumping the bucket over him. The aide did not talk and his eyes refused to meet Terrell's.

"Will you watch while he tortures me to death?" Terrell asked Fenman quietly.

The aide flinched, kept his gaze turned doggedly aside. "Not unless I must." Soon he finished and left, moving faster than usual.

Terrell sighed when Fenman had gone. The aide might feel guilty or even ashamed of his role in this treason. *But it's clear that he thinks he is too committed now to do anything else. I wonder. If I promised him a Royal Pardon and money in return for setting me free, would he do it?*

Probably not. He knows I can't ever trust him after this.

Then, darkly, he wondered if he could make such a promise and never intend to keep it.

Father-Seraph Haroun, save me from ever having to follow that road. If I can't trust and be trusted by people, there's only madness ahead of me.

But if he had no other route to getting his freedom back? Or to keep his life?

His head hurt from thinking about it.

He lay awake on the floor for hours while every muscle in his body ached, and tried to think about Chisaad's scheme, or anything else but the horrors Darnaud had showed him. The memory of cold steel touching his crotch burned. *Hardly had time to learn to use my manhood right, and now Darnaud—*He cut that thought off savagely. *No. I won't let him haunt my thoughts. Those, at least, are my own, and he shall not own me that way!*

Fenman said 'golem'. He must mean Chisaad has made a golem that looks like me and it's taken my place. I wouldn't have believed that possible. Anyone can see that his other golems are not people, only things. This spider must be empowering it to fool everybody, even Fantillin and Dona Seraphina. Otherwise there'd be a huge search going on for me by now, and I don't think Darnaud or Fenman could keep quiet about that; they'd boast how safe they were from being found.

I wonder if that mage who kidnapped me is responsible for this spider-spell? It doesn't feel anything like that mind-swapping he did to me, but it involves my thoughts. He might be skilled in some esoteric forms of mental magic, though I've never heard of anything like this before. Is it a good thing that I never asked Chisaad about that first mind-swap episode? Could the kidnapper have already been working for Chisaad, maybe practicing the spell that runs this metal spider? Chisaad had to have been planning this for seasons, maybe even years.

He thought about trying to break the spider, but he had no idea how sturdy the device might be. An experimental shake brought the blinding pain back again, but no sensation of the thing moving. Shaking it loose might well require more endurance than he still could claim. If Fenman spoke true, the thing had already gained enough from him to continue its masquerade indefinitely.

Yet it still rifles my mind now and then, he remembered, loathing the sensations. *It must sometimes meet people or situations that it doesn't know how to deal with, and that's when it digs into me again. If I wreck it, then maybe someone will realize Chisaad's creature is not me.*

But he still had a hole in his skull. If the spider fell out, his brains, or at least his blood, might follow.

And even if I succeed and somehow don't die, that just removes any value I still have. They'll likely kill me immediately and feed my body to those monsters in the lake.

Or remove the ward spell and simply let the night-visitor eat me.

That triggered a still-more-unpleasant chain of imaginings. Between being cut apart by Darnaud and being torn apart by the monster, he saw little to choose.

No. I am not totally helpless. I can still hear that thing that wears my face. I can hear everybody it talks to. I'm learning at least some of what they're up to, though I still don't see how Chisaad gains from any of it. I may yet be able to stymie them.

I won't despair. Not yet.

He settled down to wait for the monster's nightly return. Madness rose and sent its wan light shining through the ocular onto the old temple's exit. He strengthened the ward-spell again to protect himself, knowing that as he did he also protected Fenman and his cohort. The accumulating Light inside him made him feel fevered, but he dared not discharge more than a fraction into the ward spells lest he break them. Eventually, despite his worries, he drifted into sleep.

CHAPTER 42: KIRIN

T he hyenas' hunting cry jolted Kirin awake. He threw off his blanket and ran to the window. A pack of the beasts poured into the ruined temple and sniffed at his trail. One looked up, spied him, and raised the laughing howl again. It sounded like some damned soul wailing from the Pit.

Kirin jerked back into hiding. *Idiot! Now they know I'm up here.*

He doubted they could climb the broken stairs, but they might be able to jump high enough to get to the second floor. From there they could easily climb the stairway up to his level.

Hastily he packed, listening to the beasts scratching back and forth below. He heard a thump as one tried to leap and fell back. He might not have long before the pack swarmed up the steps into his aerie, and he had only his knife.

Could he kill the whole pack with his Shadow? They were sort of like large fleas, in a way. Very large and vicious fleas. He remembered the taste of Darnaud's soldier and shuddered. A whole pack of man-sized beasts—what would eating their lives with the Shadow do to him? Would all those memories of being a wild beast overwhelm his mind and turn him into something less than human?

Then it dawned on him that he had another choice.

I can run. Run wrapped in my Shadow. They won't be able to see me. I can run to the lake and wade out deeper than they can go; their legs are short.

Another scrabbling thump decided him. He ran to the east window and looked out. The top of the exterior wall loomed only a few feet away and a little lower. He tightened his pack so it wouldn't bounce, gauged the distance to a solid-looking part of the wall, then vaulted over the windowsill. He landed with barely a sound, ran lightly along it to where debris had collected and lowered himself down the outside. Shadow wrapped him and the rising Suns faded to gibbous disks. The land took on an eerie clarity when he used his Shadow's sight in daylight.

He fled down the road that led to Ibis Lake, three miles away.

After half a mile the hunting cry grew muddled. They had made it into the tower and discovered him gone. Too soon the cry rose again, clearer now, as the pack issued from the ruined entry and pelted after him. Either they heard or scented him, or his Shadow attracted them.

Kirin tried to increase his speed, but the cracked and uneven road forbid it. The pack slowly gained on him, while his feet ate one mile, then two. By the time the sandy shoreline loomed ahead the vanguard of the pack snapped at his heels. He spread his Shadow wider to fend them off and won a brief reprieve. Dried mud crackled under his feet. An instant later water dragged at his steps. The risk of falling forced him to slow.

One of the beasts leaped in big hops that took it in and out of the water and right at him. He slapped at it with the densest part of the Darkness, his Shadow forming fangs. The hyena dodged and found itself in deeper water, had to swim.

They can swim? He almost panicked as his hoped-for refuge turned out to be an illusion.

Kirin waded deeper to stay ahead of the swimming one. But the pack splashed in after it while howling their demented laughter. He slogged waist deep along the flooded road. Some of the hyenas gave up, but three of the biggest paddled toward him with their fangs a-gape. He had heard that once a hyena locked its jaws in its prey, only cutting its throat could make it let go. He drew his belt-knife to wave it.

I have a tooth too!

They paddled closer, snarling. One knife against three sets of fangs.

He did what he had to do.

The Shadow sank teeth of black mist into the nearest and largest of the beasts. A startled yip, a jerk, and the swimmer went limp in the water. Savagery coursed through Kirin's mind, a primal empty-belly hunger raging for the taste of fresh blood. Food for the pack, food to fill the cubs' empty bellies and feed the nursing mothers. Food!

The other two hesitated at the leader's sudden stillness and their ghoulish howls stilled. Sick with the primal hunger raging through his veins, Kirin stabbed the floating carcass and flung drops of blood in their faces. One recoiled at the taste of its own kind's blood and turned back to shore. The other swam back and forth looking for a way at him. He countered its every motion with blade and Shadow, until finally it too gave up and paddled away.

The Shadow tried to follow it. Kirin shuddered as he struggled to reel back the darkness. The Shadow fought him in tandem with the raging desire of the beast burning inside him. For a long moment the struggle balanced on a knife-edge before Kirin forced his darkness to heel. For a while he stood there panting, watching the pack shake lake-water out of their fur and pace back and forth on the shore, watching him.

He'd survived the pack, but he couldn't swim the length of the lake to reach the sunken city. He needed another way. He stared around the sunlit water and discovered he wasn't the only thing poking out of its calm surface.

Fleeing the hyenas had brought him to double line of stones that appeared on either side of him parallel to the lake shore. He felt along the submerged road with his feet, found the edges, and traced a T intersection. He could go north or south, and it looked from the stones like he would stay away from the shore and the hungry pack.

The stones were pillars thicker than his leg and almost flat on top, they projected a foot or so out of the lake. He put his knife away and then heaved himself up on one pillar. He managed to balance and then stand on it and looked around. The suns were still close enough to the eastern horizon to make it painful to gaze that way for long, and the pack prowled to his west.

North lay the ruined city miles away across the water. Between him and there the shore had been cut by the sharp trench that drained the lake. He stood barely sixty feet south of it. Ripples pointed into the cut like watery arrows. Even from here he could feel the current.

If I try to swim across that, it'll suck me in. A roar echoing out of the stone trench warned of rapids at least, maybe a waterfall.

South looked more promising. A ruined building rose from the lake, far enough from land to confound the hyenas. He climbed down from the pillar and began slogging toward it.

For a little while the pack paralleled him along the shore, but well before he reached the swamped building they gave up and loped away. That heartened him; clearly, they didn't regard his destination as something accessible to them.

The ruin turned out to be a small palace built of white-and-red stone. Lacy terra-cotta wall-screens and big windows made the ruin airy and inviting despite the water flooding it. He stumbled up the stairs of the ruined building to a gaping entry bereft of doors.

Inside the floor lay under ankle-deep water. He nearly stepped in a hole where part had collapsed into a flooded lower level. The floors were slick with drifted silt and the parts close to the windows boasted luxuriant beds of green water-weeds. He picked his way to a flooded courtyard at the back of the building.

The courtyard had possessed several raised flowerbeds, only two still jutted above the surface. An enormous fig tree grew from one and the second hosted a maze of trumpet-flower vines that had clambered over much of the ruin's roof. Their sweet scent contrasted with the stagnant odor of the water and the pungent lime from generations of birds nesting on the roof. Cooing and occasional raucous cries filled the air as ibis and ducks paddled or took wing.

Kirin's gaze narrowed in on the vine. Its several trunks were thicker than the ropes his troupe used. Moments later he had made it up the living cable and reached a dry floor.

The upper level looked as empty as the lower. A few patches of sparse grass grew in the thin drifts of sand and dust that had blown in. The only furnishings left were made of bronze and marble, and so massive that he marveled how the floor still held the weight. Then he found a closet with an intact door, the first door he'd seen. Only then did he realize that the building had been stripped of all other doors and windows. Somehow this one had been overlooked or ignored.

The bronze panel had badly corroded in its frame, impossible to open. But by tugging it he managed to drag the whole door, frame and all, out of the wall until it toppled forward with a clang that must surely be audible from shore. For a moment he feared the floor might collapse.

That exposed a closet as big as the room he had shared with Maia in the Sulfur Serpent Inn. Dust motes billowed, and he sneezed. But the tears in his eyes came from thinking of her, the lilt of her voice, her sweet touch, the bone-deep pain of missing her. For a while he sagged to the floor, huddled against a wall, and wept.

But grief couldn't hold forever. After a time, he knuckled tears from his eyes and got back to work.

The closet held several rotted wooden boxes with unidentifiable contents, a couple bronze-and-gold fan-clasps holding the shriveled stumps of ostrich feathers mounted on five-foot-long handles, and a huge clothes-chest with a rounded lid. The lid had been decorated with inlaid silver and gems that still glowed weakly with a preservation spell. The spell died when he touched it.

Clumsy fool! he scolded himself as the last dregs of power ran away through his Shadow.

Gingerly he opened the lid; it had neither lock nor latch. A baron's ransom of silk garments filled the inside with a stunning variety of colors and cuts. He held one up and recognized nobleman's clothes. He pulled garment after garment out and tossed them on the floor outside the closet, hoping something more useful might lie at the bottom, but the chest held nothing else.

He remembered then that the Prince had been naked. He doubted Chisaad had clothed him since. He chose a couple of the bigger garments in hope that they'd fit and stuffed them into his pack. The round-topped chest, longer than his height and more than a yard wide, offered a way to cross the lake. If he could detatch the lid from the ponderous bottom.

He worked at the hinges for hours before they gave way, then spent more time cutting up silk to braid a rope and jury-rigging a paddle from a fan. Some wrestling got it into the lake, where it floated well. A few more minutes to stock his craft with his pack, paddle, and rope, and he pushed off.

The last light of the two suns slipped behind the peaks as he paddled his makeshift boat through the ruined palace. Ibis were flocking back to their nests on the roof, sending shrill calls into the sky to greet the appearing stars. Old memories of childhood in the islands, in the time before he came to Aretzo, rose unbidden as his body remembered the rhythm of paddling.

The growl of rapids warned him to stay well out in the lake to avoid the current draining into the trench. Once past the danger he made for the ragged bays of the western shore. The east and south shores were one smooth crescent that felt hideously exposed. Gliding a few feet from the reeds seemed safer, close enough to hide among them if he had to but far enough out that his paddle didn't dig into the mud. The birds had mostly settled for the night, save for an owl silently gliding overhead. It circled him once, then arrowed away toward the ruined city. An omen or a warning? He wished the Seraphs would be less obscure.

A sinuous shape glided out of the reeds. Yards of serrated backbone cleaved the water. The crocodile stretched more than twice as long as his makeshift boat. He froze, staring at its bulbous eyes. As it approached, huge jaws parted to reveal many teeth.

I am going to die, a calm corner of his mind proclaimed. The rest gibbered in primal fear. He raised the heavy fan like a spear. He wasn't going to get eaten without a fight.

Then the beast closed its jaws and sank beneath the opaque water. A moment later a thrumming vibration shook his makeshift hull as its jagged back slid beneath. He almost stabbed blindly with the crescent edge of the fan but held back. It hadn't done anything to him yet, and he didn't want to break his paddle.

The ripples quieted and vanished. His arm muscles began to cramp from holding the heavy bronze fan over his head. At any moment he expected the monster to erupt from the water and go for his throat. But nothing happened.

Finally, he lowered the fan and, tentatively, began to paddle again, as quietly as he could. He didn't relax until he'd put two hundred yards between himself and that bit of marsh.

A spell gradually intruded on his awareness as he approached the city. Something old and powerful, tied to the node under the deepest foundations. It curved out of sight around the ruined city like an invisible fence. His Shadow tried to eat it as he paddled through, but he forbade it. The One God alone knew what it did, and he had no wish to attract attention.

Ruins rose from the water around him. Several times collapsed walls or patches of reeds blocked the way. Twice he had to back up and seek another route. Eventually he found a broad boulevard and followed it until its muddy pavement rose from the shallowing water.

A ruined building with a big stair walled one side of the street, complete with a line of bollards to separate traffic from steps. He tied his craft to one by looping some torn strips of silk through a broken hinge and around the bollard, and then waded up the steps to dry stone. Leaving his escape method so exposed worried him, but he had no place to hide it. He shouldered his pack, thickened his Shadow, and headed for the soaring dome and its beckoning spells.

He clung to the edges of the street, sometimes cutting through buildings or rubble when collapsed facades blocked the route. The ruins were alive with insect chirps and lizards slithering, while the night sky hosted fluttering bats. Occasional whiffs of wood smoke leavened the pervasive swamp-reek of mud and rotting plants; somewhere there were people in the ruins. The ward-spells on the temple dome drew him like a beacon.

More flooded road forced him to detour. He climbed to the elevated main floor of an imposing but roofless shell that faced the old temple. The rooms were cluttered with fallen beams, roof tiles, and smashed remnants of furniture. Finally he approached the open plaza at the city's heart. Here the lake had invaded again to make a shallow reed-spotted pool running out of sight down another boulevard. He mentally kicked himself for not finding that route. He could have paddled right to the main stairs of the temple itself. It rose from the water on the far side of the plaza, close enough to hit with a long spear-throw.

Then he noticed what moved in the plaza among the rubble and reeds. Dozens of sinuous shapes rested on mud banks or slithered around scattered stones. They had bulging heads with branching antler-like fans that twitched and waved like a peacock's tail. And teeth; lots and lots of teeth. The clawed feet were nothing compared to all those teeth. One raised its head and uttered a growl like grinding bones.

Kirin shrank behind a fragment of wall, overwhelmed by terror at his aloneness and danger. His goal lay so near, but a moat filled with monsters blocked his way and he had no idea what guards might lie beyond it. Still, somebody had come here to set things up for Chisaad, and they had to ride a horse or walk. *There's a way in, I only have to find it.*

He stiffened his nerve and explored the ruined building around him. A long corridor to the east took him past rubble-strewn rooms under the jeweled sky. Calm showed a bare crescent thinner than a nail paring, by to-morrow night she'd be gone. Madness hurtled high overhead, fickle and wan. The little moon shone through a gap in the walls. Kirin went to the hole's edge and peered through.

One of the temple's fallen minarets had toppled right across the nar-rowing plaza and the spire had smashed this hole. Farther east the plaza narrowed to a road that rose out of the water.

It took some work, but he made it to that encrusted road. Curled-up plates of dried mud as big as his foot coated the pavement. He tried to pick a way between them but hadn't got far when he stepped on one. The clay snapped with a crack that filled the night.

Kirin froze in place, listening. The ridge of rubble left by the fallen minaret blocked his view of the plaza and, he hoped, blocked any sight of him from the scaly denizens there. After a while he resumed his steps, but soon broke another. Then another. And four more before he reached the far side.

The sound of grinding bones came from the plaza. A second growl answered it, and a third.

Kirin hastily scrambled up a stair into the ruined temple. A long corri-dor under a barrel-vaulted ceiling led into the gloom. Remembering the guards who had almost caught him at the Royal Palace, he wrapped himself in a cloud of Shadow and crept along, his ears straining for a human sound. Up ahead, spells glowed in his magesight.

The first spell simply blocked the hallway at a junction. He throttled his Shadow and slipped through it readily. The second lay only a little farther and was as simple to pass, but now tracks appeared in the rubble and dust on the floor. He could smell wood smoke and stale cooking odors. Kirin listened, heard a trio of steady snores. Then something creaked, boots slapped on stone, and a pale-skinned man came out of a side-room up ahead. He wore half-armor and the leaf-bladed killing sword of a Gwythlo soldier. The guard crossed the corridor with a bored glance each way—Kirin didn't dare even breathe—entered the room across the corridor, and soon the quiet sound of splashing echoed. Moments later the guard returned, still tying his codpiece shut, and went back to the first room. This time Kirin saw the shine of a ward passkey at his collar. Sure enough, the sleeping room had a separate interior ward spell.

Kirin dithered for a moment. The sanctuary of the old temple lay straight ahead, and around it the biggest spells. He thought the Prince would be there, but maybe one of those snores in that room belonged to him.

He had to be sure.

He eased closer, until he could look into the guardroom. Four sleeping men lay on pallets on the floor, a fifth on a more elaborate pallet a little distance away; Kirin guessed he must be an officer. A banked fire glowed inside a broken ceramic stove patched into a repaired chimney. Driftwood had been hauled in and piled near. The awake guard sat on a pile and tried to get a pipe going using a splinter from the fire. None of the men in the room had dark skin like the Prince.

Kirin withdrew, gradually thickened his shadow until it blocked view of the corridor from the room, and then glided across in silent care. He stopped on the door's far side to slowly draw the Shadow back into himself. The guard puffed on his pipe unconcerned.

Kirin quickly picked his way along a path through the dust and rubble. He came to a side room with a warded doorway and slipped inside to examine a glowing decagram on the clean-swept floor. His magesight detected the umbilical tap that ran down into the World, drawing on a Node far below. This spell had to be connected to the one in Chisaad's tower.

Kirin hesitated. The spell slept now, but he remembered how the wizard had brought the one in his tower to life with a word. At any moment someone, or a whole squad, might come through. He couldn't leave it behind for the guards to spread swift word of the Prince's escape.

His Shadow flowed out and blotted up the spell like a sponge gathers water.

He slipped out without damaging the ward spell. Let the guards figure that out! He moved on to a wide-arched entry at the end of the hallway, again warded by a spell. This one he slipped through the same way and gazed up at the vast hollow of the old temple dome. On the floor beneath the ocular hole lay a naked man—glowing.

CHAPTER 43: KIRIN AND TERRELL

Terrell woke from bad dreams. Darnaud and his sword featured prominently, but the worst included Pen falling to poison. He shuddered and almost shook his head before he remembered the spider.

His arms and back ached, his wrists were chaffed bloody, and his buttocks and the backs of his shoulders were raw from rubbing against the gritty stone floor. He stared up at the ocular overhead, a too-small circle of stars in an oppressive darkness. Darnaud had probably left Aretzo by now, on his way to murder Pen.

Father Haroun, hold your hand over Pen in protection, he prayed. *Grant that Irreneetha detects Darnaud's evil and saves Pen from poisoning. And Mother Umana, lend me your strength. Help me face what I must with courage and dignity, even if it be death by torture. In the Name of That which cannot be named, I pray for this.*

He heard a sound and looked to the east entry, expecting to see the monster again. Nothing. When he looked to the west, a billowing cloud of utter darkness flowed right through the ward spell. It advanced on him across the floor.

Terrell didn't know whether to greet the monstrous billow with words or screams. Abruptly it shrank to the size and shape of a man. A short man wearing an open robe knelt at his side and whispered in a deep voice, "You're awake, good. Give me time to get these off and let's get you out of here."

Then he wrapped both hands around Terrell's wrist and began squeezing the manacle. Terrell couldn't imagine what the stranger thought that would accomplish, but before he could speak the solid iron broke into pieces. The man moved to his ankle and did the same thing, then the next ankle and finally the last wrist, each manacle taking less time than the previous. Terrell levered himself up and stifled a groan, gingerly checked his wrists and ankles while staring at his rescuer.

The man looked to be carved out of black marble, but moving. Terrell guessed him to be a few finger widths shorter than himself, narrow-waisted but broad-shouldered and powerfully built. Terrell had never seen a mage as muscular as this one; he wondered if the darkness tricked his eyes.

The stranger took a pack from his back and pulled something out of it. "Here. It's the best I could do," he whispered, and shoved silken pantaloons and shirt into Terrell's hands.

Terrell dragged the shirt on while his overstressed arms made every movement torture. He fell when he first tried to get to his feet. The stranger helped him up and steadied him with a hand on his shoulder while he pulled on the pantaloons. The solid grip reassured him even though the man remained an inky shadow.

That must be a disguise spell, Terrell guessed. *Or perhaps a concealment spell? Though I've never heard of either one working like this.* He tied the shirt closed with silken laces, then carefully explored the spider on his head. He'd been itching to touch it for days, and found it more complex than he'd guessed. Pain warned him not to prod it any harder, so he desisted.

The stranger stared at his head. "Damn. Highness, that thing--"

"Don't touch it!" Terrell warned. "There's a spike in my head holding it on. I need a priestess before I dare take it out."

The stranger nodded back, or at least seemed to; it was hard to see his features. "All right. Now let's get out of here." A hand drew him toward the east entry.

Terrell resisted. "There's a creature out there. Look!"

The beast had returned. It lifted its horror of a head, jaws parted, and once more leaned on the ward spell. This time a second creature joined it, one even uglier than the first.

The stranger flinched. "Haroun defend! Right you are, Highness. Back the other way instead."

They hadn't made it five steps when a clatter of footsteps announced the guard and three other soldiers. Fenman snapped, "How'd you get free?" Then he did an almost comical double-take as he noticed the stranger. But the young Gwythlo officer immediately shouted to his men, "Swords out! Take them both!"

The stranger grabbed Terrell's arm again and the room went black. A yank made his abused body protest and nearly pulled him off his feet as he stumbled through darkness. Moments later they passed under the northern archway into a dusty corridor where he could see again.

"That ought to slow them down," the stranger mumbled, still pulling him along. "Can you see well enough to walk, Highness?"

"Yes," Terrell answered, then promptly stubbed his bare toes on a piece of rubble and stumbled again.

The stranger prudently kept a grip on his arm with a hand as strong as any swordsman's. Could the man be a battlemage? Debris jabbed the bottom of Terrell's feet, but he pushed pain out of his mind. He missed his shoes but resolved that he'd run his feet bloody to get away from his jailers. Though he hoped he wasn't running into the arms of worse trouble by following this stranger.

He's got to be a mage, though I'm boggled if I can name the school or even the discipline. Whatever's covering him looks disturbingly like those

Shadows that attacked us at Storm Pass. Terrell used his magesight and could not detect any spells emanating from the man, not even the weird texture of the Shadow Bears, which relieved him. *If this is an illusion, it's very effective!*

They came to the end of the corridor, turned right into another and soon met a pile of rubble where the roof had come down. The stranger helped Terrell clamber over it, and on the far side they descended through a big hole to a street outside the building. Water stretched southwestward, glinting in wan moonlight reflected from the ripples thrown off by a sinuous swimming form. The stranger cursed under his breath and dragged Terrell northeast. Mud coated the pavement, soft and slippery at first, then dry and hard. Terrell ignored the occasional sharp edges and concentrated on putting distance between himself, the warped crocodiles, and his prison. His atrophied muscles were slowly awakening. Several times the stranger paused to check side roads that ran south, but all ended in more water or heaps of rubble.

"No good way through," the stranger panted. "And not enough time. We have to try for their horses, Highness, and hope we get there before they sort themselves out again."

"Then you didn't kill them?" Terrell panted back, forcing his aching legs to keep moving. He'd been wondering about that sudden Darkness.

The man flinched. "Umana save me, no!"

Terrell wondered if that meant he couldn't kill, or if he feared the consequences if he did. Perhaps this mage's art trespassed a little too close to demonic sources for comfort? Overall, Terrell decided that flinch reassured him.

The hand on his elbow urged him to greater speed, and he obliged as best he could.

Wind-drifted sand and patches of dry grass marred the road. Occasional tracks of horseshoe and boot showed that it had been recently used by men, and therefore must lead somewhere. More alarming tracks also crossed it or even followed it for a distance, some shaped like hooves bigger than dinner plates. Others looked like a giant bird's-foot twice the size of the human prints. Sharp indentations at the end of each 'toe' showed that it had claws.

Terrell and the stranger ran faster.

He estimated that two miles of ruins had flowed past while the pain in his feet steadily grew. They came to a fallen column that had strewn drum-shaped segments across the road. He deliberately stopped and parked himself on one to check his feet. The abrasions on his buttocks did not thank him for it.

The stranger jittered back and forth for a moment, then stopped.

"Have you got anything I can use to wrap my feet?" Terrell asked, picking a thorn out. The sparse vegetation growing in the road ran to stiff stems and sharp points. "If I don't protect them I'll soon leave a trail of bloodstains."

The man pulled off his pack again and rooted around in it, produced another silk robe and began slicing it up with a belt knife. It didn't take him long to wrap Terrell's abused soles in improvised slippers that gave his feet some protection. The silk cords that had held the garment closed served as shoelaces.

Terrell studied his rescuer covertly. The illusionary darkness covering him had drained away while they ran. He looked like an ordinary man now.

No, not ordinary, Terrell thought. The man had strangely colored skin, dark as an ordinary Silbari on his face and arms, but nearly as pale as a Gwythlo where his pushed-back hood and open robe revealed more. *He's dyed most of the exposed parts. And he's got pointed ears peeking out of that curly black hair. A halfbreed, like me, only more towards the Gwythlo side in his ears.* The earlier impression of hard muscularity hadn't been an illusion, under the open calf-length robe the man had the build of a warrior. *Yet he must be a mage too, to do whatever he did to free me. That's an unusual combination. I'd guess him to be a battle-mage from Lake Van; probably his mother had southern blood. But he speaks Silbari like a native-born and hasn't used a single Gwythlo word yet. Of course, he's hardly used twenty words in total. Time to change that.*

Casually, Terrell asked, "What name should I call you by?"

"Kir—" The stranger hesitated, his shoulders hunched for a moment, then he relaxed. "Kirin will do, Highness."

"Kirin," Terrell said agreeably. "Old Silbari name, isn't it? I believe it means Black Eyes?" He tried to engage Kirin's gaze, since eyes were the windows of the soul. But the man avoided looking directly at him.

The hunch returned. "Yes." The man tied off the last improvised slipper. "Let's keep moving, Highness."

"Gladly." Terrell stood up and tested his footing. "But where, or what, are we moving toward?"

Kirin scanned the road in front of them. "I hoped we'd find some sign of a place where they've been keeping their horses, but there's nothing yet. We'll have to move more carefully when we reach the city wall. They're probably stabling them there under guard."

"Good plan." It took Terrell a moment to find his stride in the clumsy foot-coverings, but they blunted the rocks and thorns very nicely. Soon he achieved a faster pace than before. Kirin kept up with him with apparent ease.

A round bastion loomed ahead on the right, its twin fallen in ruin to the left. Beyond them the rubble-strewn cityscape ended and a wall towered. Terrell's magesight showed a ward spell on the standing bastion. Kirin put a hand on his arm and led him to the shadowed side of the road.

"Time to creep," he whispered.

Terrell nodded and slowed, picking his way along in the shadows as best he could. His rescuer seemed as sure-footed in the dark as in moonlight. The intact bastion showed no light, but Terrell smelled horse manure. Kirin pressed him to stop in the blackness under a snag of wall. Terrell obligingly sat on a stone and waited while Kirin slipped ahead, his shadow-covering in place once more. In an instant he had vanished into the night. Only a slight sound of one pebble hitting another gave him away.

The moon made the night seem paradoxically darker. During his time staked to the floor Terrell had noticed how accustomed he had grown to candles and other forms of night-time illumination, and how much he missed it. His thoughts wandered to the strange tracks he'd seen on the way here. If one of those creatures found him here, weaponless and alone . . . he huddled on his stone seat and tried to be absolutely quiet.

Several subjective centuries later Kirin returned, appearing out of the night so abruptly that Terrell jumped to his aching feet.

"Nobody there," Kirin said in a low discouraged voice. "No horses either, they've left."

"Could Darnaud have taken them?" Terrell wondered aloud, new fear seizing his heart. He had assumed that Darnaud had to go back to Aretzo by the teleporter spell and ride his own horses from there to Sulmona before he could try to kill Pen, but it might be a shorter journey from here.

"Duke Darnaud's here?" Kirin blurted out in a worried voice. His posture tensed as if to fight or flee.

There's a world of fear and hatred in your voice when you say my cousin's name, Terrell thought. *Why do* you *hate him?* "Earlier today," he confirmed. "Threatened me, threatened to kill my bodyguard and Hand, Sir Penghar. Who is in Sulmona right now on a mission for me. Could Darnaud have taken the horses across country to reach there?"

"I don't know," Kirin said. "But there haven't been any horses here for three days at least. The manure is dried."

"Then he didn't take these horses." Terrell relaxed fractionally. "What do we do next?"

His rescuer didn't answer with words, but led the way to the fallen gate. Someone had long ago cleared the rubble from it, a broad dusty passage led through. But the air itself seemed to hold him back. He looked with his magesight and found an enormous spell running across the opening. It sank into the wall to left and right.

"What is that?" he whispered.

"Barrier spell, I think," Kirin answered tersely. "Wraps all the way around the city."

"Can we get through it?" He tentatively touched it, ready to snatch his hand back if it proved to be damaging. It pushed back, not strongly but unquestionably there.

"Guards did. We can too." Kirin took a grip on his sleeve.

His rescuer's dark disguise spell flowed over Terrell again, blinding him. He fought down reflexive fear. *He must be hiding us from the spell.* Then Kirin pulled him forward, not ungently but steadily, for four paces.

"That should do it," Kirin remarked, and abruptly Terrell could see again.

They were on a stone plaza outside the city wall. Terrell gazed about in awe.

The vast bowl-like basin holding the ruined city stretched north for more than a dozen miles. The floor looked smooth, probably deceptively so, since he could see a web of roads and broken canals covering the whole valley. West and north the basin's edges rose in sharp cliffs, ranks of them piled one atop another. The western set glowed faintly rusty even in Calm's wan light. That had to be the other side of the Red Wall that he had seen more than a season ago from beyond Purification Lake. Whirling little columns of wind-blown dust wandered the basin. Faintly across the miles, the roar of a lion came to his ears.

The hairs on Terrell's neck prickled. He didn't even have a belt knife. Then something about the dust storms caught his attention and he stared, nonplussed. They were growing bigger, organizing themselves into two opposing masses.

"Dung," Kirin cursed in a low voice, staring at them too. "What monsters are those?"

The dust took on shapes and Terrell understood. Awe shook him as he said, "Azerin and Zablock! Their ghosts, at least. Reenacting the battle where they killed each other."

"How do you know?" Kirin demanded in an astonished voice.

"Commander DiVetzi warned me about this." He shook his head. "Never mind. They're fighting right on top of the road to Purification Lake. I don't think we can get through those sand-storms they're raising. Not alive, anyway." He looked longingly to the southwest where the peak of God's Footstool gleamed in the moonlight. There were five hundred men garrisoning the Tonatia Fortress on the crest of the Scarp and he doubted Ap Marn had been able to corrupt many of them—the Tonatia brigade had long been one of the most loyal in Silbar's entire army. If he could get to them, he could race that force down the Kings' Road to Amm Crossing and block Darnaud from getting at Pen.

"Agreed, Highness," Kirin said. "But we can't stay here. Your prison-guards will come after us and dawn is only a few hours away. So we've got to go there instead." He pointed east, away from the ghostly combat.

The eastern edge of the valley had at least three canyons slashing through the cliffs to reveal jumbled hills beyond. The nearest and most southerly spread a vast fan of sand and rocks before it. The plaza under their feet threw off a road that ran straight toward that canyon.

"We've got to hide before dawn," Kirin explained. "Sulmona has to be somewhere beyond those hills. Maybe that road even goes there."

There's hope in his voice, thought Terrell. *Sulmona is important to him too. Why?* Aloud: "Agreed. But hiding won't do any good if our tracks lead right to our hiding place."

"Ah." Kirin looked around, then rooted in the weed-grown rubble at the foot of the fallen tower and came up with a handful of brush. A strip of silk for binding and a stick for a handle turned it into a broom. "You walk in front. I'll wipe away any tracks we leave."

Terrell nodded consent and began plodding, sticking as much as possible to bare stone. The occasional scratch of twigs against sand told him when he missed. Resolutely he drove on, ignoring aches and pains from his too-long sojourn on the temple floor. He wondered how Fenman dealt with his escape, and whether Ap Marn and Chisaad already knew about it. His judgment of Fenman's character told him the young aide would try to recapture his escaped charge before admitting the truth to his superior. *I hope. The longer he takes to call for reinforcements, the better my chances of escape.*

"I should have tried to wreck the teleporter," he mumbled to himself. Though time had been precious and escape more important, that would not matter if Chisaad recaptured him.

"Already did it," Kirin muttered back, bending to wipe away another footprint and then bouncing back upright with easy grace. "Broke their wards too. Hope the monsters keep your jailers busy. Highness."

Startled, Terrell looked back over his shoulder. Kirin had covered himself with that black illusion again, he looked like a fuzzy man-shape in the fading moonlight. For a moment, white teeth flashed in the darkness, then there were only dark eyes looking back at him for the briefest instant before Kirin bent to wipe footprints again.

But Terrell had seen. Black eyes gazing at him out of darkness. *He's the mage who kidnapped me!*

It took all his self-possession to turn his back and keep walking.

Madness had already set and Calm poised above the distant mountains, throwing the shadow of the Red Wall across the basin. Terrell plodded on toward the hills and the fragile promise of concealment. Behind him the man who had got him into this nightmare erased their tracks. Pain gnawed at him as abused muscles and tender feet protested.

My kidnapper is helping me escape. Or is he? If this is some sort of double-cross, what do I do about it?

CHAPTER 44: CHISAAD

C hisaad strode into his office and cast the spell that filled every crack around his door until neither sound nor breath could pass through. Only then did he drop his inscrutable expression in favor of a grimace. His plans were mostly working as he had hoped, but the exceptions were galling.

The golem was the brightest star in his plan's constellation. The spells had held perfectly. So far it had completely fooled Fantillin and Dona Seraphina and all the lesser servants in the Palace. Chisaad enjoyed a little glow of pride at this accomplishment. If Sir Penghar and his damnable sword could be kept away, that part of the plan should work perfectly.

The winnowing of the Twenty had gone less well. Silbaris expected a certain amount of bloodletting when the Crown was in contention, or looked like it would be soon. But Darnaud's deadly duels had resulted in most suspicion falling on the Prince—and on the Emperor. Ifni-worshiping gossips had begun to claim that Emperor Brion had ordered the deaths before his illness to raise the odds that his son would win the Kingship. Others whispered that Osrick had instigated them, preferring the Crown go to a brother he disliked rather than to a stranger he trusted even less.

That turned Chisaad's grimace to a scowl. If such a claim got back to Gwythford Castle, it might draw unwelcome attention to the Choosing. So far Osrick had stayed busy with his own maneuvering, content to accept Ap Marn's carefully slanted reports. Chisaad did not want the future Emperor's attention drawn to Aretzo prematurely.

Most of the Twenty had barricaded themselves in their Aretzo townhouses to wait for the Queen's death and the formal day of choosing. Chisaad considered that an advantage, since it handicapped their own scheming and offered fewer distractions for him. Alliances were being negotiated with furious urgency by go-betweens, and probably broken almost as often.

Good. Let them waste time on each other. Once I take the Crown for myself they'll have to fall in line no matter how much they hate it.

The religious situation worried him more. Accusing Kirin of bloodmagic, especially with Darnaud's two murdered priestesses to blame on the boy, had tied up many but not all of the Temple Inquisitors. It would be even better if they issued a warrant for Kirin's arrest and trial, so that he could be seized when his escape ship arrived in Haresalaam. While the brat would likely babble his role in Chisaad's ascension if they managed take him alive, the Temple Court ground slowly indeed. Chisaad would have the Crown securely in his grasp by the time the religious bureaucracy drew the right conclusions. By then it simply wouldn't matter, with Heaven's mandate resting in his hands.

Unfortunately, hints percolated out of the Mother Temple that tumorrow the Hierarch would exercise her prerogative to take control of the Hill of Sight for the Choosing. Not waiting for the Queen's death would be a very public hint that she suspected an unusual level of misbehavior going on.

And of course, she's right, damn her to the bottom of the Nine Hells.

That kind of interference could too easily turn into disaster. He couldn't shut the damned priestesses off from the Aretzo Node without using the Crown. If the Hierarch positioned any of them on the Hill prematurely, they'd start prying into the Royal Wizard's preparations for the Choosing. Once they figured out what his spells were really designed to do, they'd demand his death as a traitor.

I can't afford the time for this, there's too much else to do! Chisaad dropped into his chair with a sigh. His Office only had limited control over the Hill's link to the City Node, just enough to manage ordinary power allocations among the thousands of mages and priestesses. Serious changes could only be made by the King wearing the Crown, which meant he'd gone as far as he could right now. He had hidden spells readied for the moment of Choosing, spells no mage would ever have dared cast if he wasn't of the royal bloodline himself. And no Royal Wizard ever had been, before him.

I can tilt the Throne's choice to me, I know I can. I'm so close to wearing the Crown, I can feel it. He took a deep breath, let it out slowly. *Stay calm, keep your eye on your goal, and bluff your way through,* he told himself.

At least he had finally got Darnaud and his household troops dispatched to Sulmona to eliminate the threat of Sir Penghar's premature return. Ap Marn had squeezed half a company of Gwythlo regulars out of the commander in the Gray Fort to send with him. It would have to be enough. Even if they failed, merely pinning Penghar to Sulmona for the duration should be sufficient. When Chisaad became King, he could dismiss the man and appoint his own Hands.

Chisaad wished his half-sister the Queen would hurry up and die.

His door chimed; a quick check of the spy-spell revealed Ap Marn. Unscheduled meetings made Chisaad nervous, especially since the tightness around the Governor's eyes presaged bad news. He hurriedly unsealed it to invite his co-conspirator in and then prudently sealed the wards again.

"Message construct from Haresalaam," Ap Marn said cryptically. "Your apprentice never sailed on that ship."

Chisaad's heart skipped a beat. "You mean he's still here in Aretzo?" The prospect of Kirin creeping through his wards chilled his spine.

"Doubtful," Ap Marn growled, shaking his head. "I've had his family watched and your spells have consistently told us that they've no idea where he went. With the yellow bitches alert for him too, we'd have heard something before now."

"Then he did leave the city, at least," Chisaad said aloud, his thoughts racing. "Where did he go?"

"Did he know where you sent the Prince?" Ap Marn's gaze had grown narrow and hard.

"I didn't tell him," Chisaad said, then paused. "Which doesn't mean he couldn't find out. Or guess. He's quite clever and Darnaud's men have been our weakest point from the beginning. I laid subtle spells on them to keep quiet, but such things aren't fully reliable. Then there's whoever Darnaud himself may have boasted to."

Ap Marn made a disgusted sound. "I know, but you use the tools you've got."

The Governor's gaze narrowed and Chisaad made very sure his bland expression didn't slip.

"I've kept the decagram powered," Chisaad said quietly. "Can you take a candlemark for a *private conference* with me?"

Ap Marn jerked his head yes. "My aides are waiting outside your door with orders to keep us from being disturbed."

Chisaad activated the decagram on his office floor and a moment later they stood on the larger one in his tower. Only yesterday he'd used it to send and retrieve Darnaud from Silbariki, to reassure the guardsmen posted there. A quick reset and Chisaad spoke the word that would send them on a repeat of that journey.

Nothing happened.

Chisaad's throat clenched nearly shut and he shivered. *The spell is broken, and so deftly that I couldn't tell.*

Ap Marn swore profanely. "Don't," he added dangerously, "call this a coincidence."

"Kirin's work," Chisaad acknowledged, battling his shock. "Has to be."

"How soon can you repair it?" the Governor demanded urgently. "My man is there with half a dozen guards. They may have taken the little bastard but if he broke their emergency message-sender too, then they have no way to assure us."

"I can't repair it from this end alone," Chisaad admitted. "We have to get another anchor-spell planted there, then I can rebuild the linkage."

"Even with fast riders that will need three to four days." Ap Marn's fist clenched, then relaxed. "I'll see to it. You—" He visibly stopped his next words, instead said, "Get ready. Whatever's happened can't have been longer ago than yesterday, since Darnaud came back without a problem. We'll need scouts to find your brat at least, and maybe to find *them*. I'll arrange the men."

"I'll ready the spells."

Chisaad took the two of them back to his office, bowed his putative superior out, then shut the door and leaned against it trembling.

How did Kirin do this? If he's got the Prince, then he could break the spider at any moment!

Hurriedly Chisaad checked. The golem busily signed documents in the Prince's office, his link to it undamaged. It wasn't doing anything that would require it to draw on Prince Terrell's memories yet, and its own ability to imitate the man convincingly had improved every day. But later this day the *prince* would have sword practice and then a physical checkup by Dona Seraphina.

It will have to tap into Prince Terrell again for both. What if Kirin is waiting to break the link when it does? Seraphina will realize it's not the real prince! Chisaad's thoughts raced and his heart beat feverishly as he teetered on the verge of panic. Then he forced himself to draw a deep breath and calm down. *Wait. Terrell's got to realize the spider's spiked into his head. He probably won't risk uprooting it until he has a priestess ready to repair that wound. I have a little time to get ready. Then with some luck and daring I may be able to turn the tables on them.*

He wiped his sweating forehead and almost prayed for the first time in years. Then he caught himself and angrily dashed the thought away.

I am not some callow boy, to pray to gods because I feel helpless! I've learned a great deal about how Kirin's talent works and does not work. I can capture both of them. It will merely be difficult.

He opened a spell-warded cabinet in his office and took out a magical instrument shaped like two dulcimers merged at an odd angle. Even Shimoor had never known about this. He set it on his desk and awoke the dormant spells on it. The instrument gave forth a soft shivering note that throbbed in the air.

You can hide in your Shadow, Kirin, he thought harshly. *You can be invisible to every spell in the world. But you can't hide your absence.*

CHAPTER 45: KIRIN

Kirin swept away another stretch of their tracks. Dawn had revealed a canyon floor made of alternating patches of sand and gravel with occasional ledges of rock. Now the midday suns blasted down into the narrow space and heated everything their light could touch. He and the prince tried to stick to bare rock when they could. When the canyon floor didn't cooperate Kirin's back got a workout wielding his makeshift broom.

I need to find a longer stick and make a better handle for this cursed thing, he thought as he straightened up with a wince. They had passed occasional windrows of debris caught on the rocks, but none boasted sticks both long and thin enough to use. Some of the debris had been snagged higher up the canyon wall than his head. He couldn't imagine this bone-dry place with that much water running through it, but the broken fragments of old road hinted at the power in such floods.

"Wait," Prince Terrell panted. "I've got to rest." He collapsed onto a flat stone and stared up at the sky.

Kirin hesitated. *I'm afraid of his eyes. What if he does that vision-swapping thing to me again? Can he do more than that to me? But I need him to save Pieter. I'll have to be careful to never look directly at his face unless I've got my Shadow over me. I'd better think up an explanation for that, too, so he doesn't decide I'm a demon.* The rock could easily hold both of them so Kirin stretched out flat in the shade.

He passed one of the two remaining figs to the Prince and nibbled the other. He mentally kicked himself again for not stuffing his pack full at the sunken palace. The water bag at his hip also hung too lightly. Water looked like a worse problem than food.

Their route had climbed slowly but steadily as they left the dead city behind. The walls about them were steep now, stacked cliffs layered by treacherous talus slopes and slashed with side canyons. Patches of grass were rare and trees rarer, nothing but twisted little junipers on the canyon walls.

The prince turned his head to look at him. "We're going to have to find a place to hide."

Kirin avoided meeting the man's eyes as he answered. "I know, I've been looking." He forced himself to sit up. "But we also need to get as far away from the Gwythlos as we can."

His charge answered in a dry voice. "Hard to do, when we're both part Gwythlo ourselves."

Kirin scowled in the prince's general direction, feeling insulted. "I'm a Silbari, Highness. I'll never be a Salim-be-damned Gwythlo."

The prince didn't respond aloud. Instead the man levered himself up, clenched his teeth against a groan, and got back to his feet. Then he plodded up the canyon once more.

Kirin followed, dutifully sweeping away footprints. *At least I don't have to herd him.*

An hour later they found a large fragment of the old road. Prince Terrell diverted their path to follow the bare pavement instead of the sandy canyon floor. Kirin silently approved and stretched his aching back. The road gradually climbed the canyon wall until they were a dozen feet above the stream bed. A branch canyon opened, and the road turned to a stone bridge leaping over it.

The prince paused, looked over the edge and said, "Water."

Kirin joined him and gazed down at a small puddle in a hollow of the little canyon's floor. As Kirin vaulted over the masonry side of the bridge the prince cautioned, "Don't leave any tracks."

Kirin bit back a retort and instead nodded shortly. The wet hollow lay at the bottom of a steep little side-canyon gouged into stair-stepped basins, all dry save this one. He coaxed as much of the precious fluid into his water bag as he could manage, then corked it and threw the gurgling sack up to the prince. Only then did he bend down and stick his head in the hollow to drink. He stopped when he got coarse sand in his mouth, sat up and wiped his lips with the back of one hand. He noticed that the dye had begun to fade and peel off with his skin.

Prince Terrell sat with a grunt and dangled his legs over the edge of the bridge, drinking more neatly. "Thank The One for this."

Kirin frowned at the dangling feet. "Highness. You're bleeding."

Terrell glanced down, inspected one stained bundle of rags and shrugged. "Broken blister, I guess." Then, frowning, "Have I been leaving blood-stained tracks?"

"Not yet. Let me look at it," Kirin requested, using the excuse to avoid the prince's gaze again. He unwrapped the stained rags as carefully as he could and stared in dismay. "Highness, the bottom of your foot looks like raw meat. Four broken blisters, at least, and another ready to go." He took out his knife and added, "Hold still."

Prince Terrell stiffened for a moment, then did as asked. Kirin carefully lanced the blister and trimmed away the rags of skin from it and the others. He scooped up the last of the water from the rock basin to wash the oozing skin, then cut up more silk to make a bandage. After he rewrapped the foot he held it for a moment, soaking his Shadow into the cloth. If The One God was kind it might kill any vermin lurking in the water or sand. He did feel a few tiny puffs of life passing through him, barely detectable but there. He gave the other foot similar treatment, using the last of the silk and holding it for slightly longer. When he finished he glanced up to see the prince staring down at him. Kirin hastily looked away, fearful of the man's eyes, and cursed himself for a careless fool. He should have waited until his charge slept before using his Shadow.

"I saw that. What did you do?" Prince Terrell demanded in a tight voice.

Kirin's shoulders hunched, then he forced himself to stand erect while not meeting the other man's gaze. "It's my own special talent, Highness. It kills vermin and such. My wife thought it stopped evil plagues from entering wounds, too. I—we can't risk you getting sick out here."

The prince's gaze beat down at him. Kirin refused to meet it. For a long moment he stood there and endured.

At last the prince said, "I see. We'd best continue." He levered himself to his feet.

Kirin breathed a sigh of relief as he leaped up to catch the stone railing and heaved himself onto the old road again. His charge took a few testing steps, then the prince's stride lengthened and became more confident, though the bandaged feet must still have been painful.

The old road stayed above the stream channel now, occasionally eroded to a narrow shelf or torn by an outright gap. Twice Kirin helped the prince scramble across teetering slabs undermined by vanished floods. Their route wound around sharp curves and crossed frequent side canyons as the suns sank behind them. More and more they walked in shadows with direct sunlight shining only on the canyon wall. The air rapidly cooled from its pounding noonday heat, falling to comfortable and then chilly. The light on the higher hills vanished and stars began to appear. Prince Terrell walked as steadily as if his legs were made of iron, but his feet flinched when he put them down.

He's hurting, Kirin thought. *We should walk all night, but he's not going to be able to keep this up. He'll have to rest. What'll I do if those soldiers catch up to us? I've got to find a place for us to hide.*

He passed the water sack to his charge again. The prince drank a little, handed it back silently; it was already down by half.

Kirin drank even more sparingly; he hadn't lost any blood. They passed a side-canyon that exhaled chill air at them. They were miles from the humid valley by now and the canyon wound steadily upward. He heard a growl from the prince's stomach and his own echoed it.

After a while the canyon curved and a shelf appeared on the far side of the sandy bottom. Some past flood had piled it high with debris. *Thank you, Lord Haroun.*

"Highness," he said. "Look at that mess of broken trees down there. I think we could hide there for the night."

The prince stopped walking and stared into the canyon. After a moment he nodded.

Kirin helped him down the steep bank to the sandy bottom, carefully erased their footsteps as they crossed, then scouted among the jumble of smashed tree trunks. He wondered how the stream had found enough wood to make this jam. At the highest point the pile stood taller than him. There were several gaps under the larger trunks, the biggest one floored with sand and easily large enough for them.

"Are there snakes in this country?" Prince Terrell asked.

"Snakes?" Kirin stared at the pile, unsettled by the thought. "I don't know."

He didn't want to give the prince more cause to distrust him, but he would rather that than get bitten by some viper in his sleep. He put his hands on parts of the pile and poured his Shadow into it, trying to keep it within the mass and as unnoticeable as possible. Lizards yes, he detected plenty of them, and even some mice and a little garden-snake, but nothing larger. That nest of scorpions, however, had to go. He slew them without hesitation.

"I think we're safe now," he reported, drawing his Shadow back inside.

"Useful talent you have there," Prince Terrell remarked to him in a very dry voice.

Kirin deliberately ignored the remark. They crawled inside. Kirin took food out of his pack, pressed a traveler's biscuit into the prince's hands. There were only two of the twice-baked rations left.

His charge eagerly crammed the tough biscuit into his mouth and chewed avidly. Kirin wondered how much he'd been fed during his captivity. Or how little.

"Want some roasted almonds, Highness? I've got a few."

"Water first, please," the prince practically begged. Kirin passed over the water bag and saw how Terrell's hands trembled as he uncorked it and took a gulp, then made himself pause and regain control before he took a smaller second swallow. He passed the bag back immediately afterwards like a man exiling temptation.

Kirin pressed a dozen almonds into the prince's hand. Terrell carefully popped two into his mouth and chewed, eating with a dreadful concentration.

Eight days chained to a stone floor. Kirin visualized the waiting, imagined knowing his captors would have to kill him in the end, and being unable to move. It made his heart hurt. *Mother Umana, help him. No surprise that he's in pain. It's a wonder he can walk.*

The cold settled in deeper. This hidden cave had been shaded most of the day, unwarmed by the suns. A shiver ran down the prince's arms and he dropped the last almond and had to grope for it. Kirin reached over and plucked it out of the sand for him. The way the prince's hands trembled as he lifted the nut to his lips decided him.

"Highness, I've only got one blanket. We'll have to share it." Kirin hadn't shared a bed with anyone but Maia in more than a year, but he figured the prince wouldn't be much different from sleeping with Attir and the cousins in the Boys Room back home. Maybe smellier; neither he nor Prince Terrell had had a proper bath in much too long.

The prince nodded tiredly, drooping a little even as he shivered. "I understand. You've got the knife and you're in better shape than I am if it comes to a fight, so you should be on the outside."

Kirin hadn't thought of that; his respect for his charge rose a notch.

He arranged the blanket against a log at the back of their cave and ushered his charge into it, then lay down in front of him and pulled the blanket over them. They had his pack for a pillow, but the confined space didn't allow either of them to stretch out. The prince lay half-curled on his left side and spooned against Kirin's back in an uncomfortable intimacy. Warm breath brushed the back of his neck. The blanket barely fit around both of them, little chilly drafts kept sneaking under the front edge. But Kirin's back rapidly warmed up and the Prince's shivering soon stopped. They had each tucked their left hand under their heads, which meant Kirin had the prince's left elbow under his neck.

Is this going to put his arm to sleep? He wondered, visualizing Terrell waking them both up from pins-and-needles in his limb. That would be a nuisance, but they'd live. A guard finding their hiding place in the night worried him more. Before crawling inside he had carefully swept away all traces in the sand outside, then jammed his tattered broom and a few other bits across the entrance like a mass of weeds caught in the wrack. It wouldn't fool a close inspection, but it might pass a casual one. As a last defense he stuck his knife in the sand where he could readily grab it if needed.

The prince gradually relaxed against Kirin's back as they both warmed up. His breathing smoothed out and he yawned. Kirin thought he must be on the verge of sleep. So it came as a shock when his charge's voice drowsily whispered in his ear.

"I hope tomorrow you'll tell me why you set me free—and why you kidnapped me in the first place." Another yawn, then a whispered, "Good night."

Kirin went rigid. *He knows!* He was torn between wanting to bolt and fearing to move. If they didn't stay close the cold outside might kill the prince in the night. Kirin agonized over a hundred different scenarios as his charge's breathing settled into the regular rhythm of one deeply asleep. *Is he angry at me? Maybe not. Or maybe he's biding his time. Then why did he tell me? Does he want to put me off balance? That worked! I'm a fool to lie here with him at my back. But there's no choice, without me and the blanket he might die, and then Pieter would die.*

Finally, one thought made it to the top of his mind and stayed there.

He wants me to tell him why I kidnapped him. Do I tell him the truth? When he fell asleep, he still didn't know the answer.

CHAPTER 46: TERRELL AND KIRIN

Terrell dreamed. He hung by his hands from a wooden bar suspended on two ropes and swung through the air. A crowd of people stared up at him. Someone else swung nearby, upside-down with his legs hooked over another bar suspended from ropes like this. The speed and motion ought to have made Terrell dizzy. His legs pumped as he drove each swing higher. Then he let go and soared.

His stomach wanted to flip over and dump itself. His body folded through a bewildering series of contortions while land and sky traded places once, twice. Then he raised his arms over his head and his hands slapped against the other man's wrists. Their grips locked and held against a tremendous force trying to drag all four of their arms out of their sockets.

The watching people cheered.

Two more swings as he pumped his legs. The other man threw him back into the air. His mind wanted to gibber in panic, but his body knew what to do. Another bewildering contortion while the world tumbled around him, then his bar slapped against his hands. He found himself back where he had started but facing the other way. More cheers as he levered himself up onto the bar, standing and bowing to the crowd even as he swung back and forth. He finally noticed that he wore nothing but hose, and his skin had become a pale golden color.

The dream vanished as if it had been washed away. Terrell awoke in darkness, warm and curiously relaxed despite the frightening disorientation of the dream. The human presence against his chin, chest, belly, and thighs comforted him. He and Pen had gone winter hunting in the far north on young Duke Vanford's estate and stayed for the night in a rough camp before the dawn stalk—

Then belated memory awoke. Danger threatened Pen too far away for Terrell to help, while he lay wrapped in a blanket with the mage who had kidnapped him. And bewilderingly, also set him free. He had found no answer to that conundrum, so before falling asleep he had thrown the riddle back on his rescuer.

He said his name is Kirin, Terrell thought. *It means Black Eyes, and they certainly are. He conjures spells blacker than night, too. He said it should kill any sickness attacking my bloodied feet. I haven't felt any worse than I expected to feel, so perhaps it worked. I think he used the same dark spell when he examined our hiding place. Never saw anything like it. He's a very strange mage.*

If he's only a mage. Is he also demon-possessed? The idea that he might be wrapped in a blanket with a demon gave him an urge to shudder and push away, which he resisted. *If he is, I must know. He's asleep, I'll risk a little prying. Father Haroun, be my shield and guard now. For what may be seen with magery, may also see me.*

Delicately Terrell opened his mind and his magesight. The man so close in front of him was completely opaque, like one of the utterly untalented. Beyond and around them he could sense the tissue-thin wrapping of life over this harsh desert land, sense a small node somewhere ahead and the large warped one under the ruined city not many miles behind them. Much too close behind them. They desperately needed to get farther away from Silbariki and Ap Marn's soldiers. But his exhausted body rebelled at the thought and pressed for more sleep. He denied it a little longer, stretching his magesight to probe at Kirin. But he found no magic at all in or around the sleeping form pressed against him. And absolutely none of the queasy sensation leaked by demons.

I don't feel any evil emanating from him, certainly nothing like those Shadow-bears or Klairveen's creatures. But blood-mages are hard to detect, they conceal their auras very thoroughly. And I'm no mage myself, to defeat a spell like that.

He remembered Kirin's reaction to being asked if he had killed the guards. *He called on Mother-Seraph Umana and he looked frightened at the mere possibility. Frightened of killing? Or frightened of killing with his magic? Genuine fear, too, if I'm any judge. I don't think a blood-mage would have dissembled that way.*

Though he had to admit that it might also mean that the mysterious mage had in fact killed with his power and didn't want to do it again. This Kirin wouldn't be the first skilled killer who had no taste for it. The memory of Pyrull with his hand on Irreneetha's hilt came to Terrell.

I think I'd be wise not to underestimate how complex—and dangerous—this Kirin might be.

Terrell became aware of something else. The pressure that had grown inside his chest for the last few days, as his Light accumulated with no place to go and too little to spend it on, had eased. It trickled out of his chest in a steady rivulet and flowed into Kirin's back.

For a moment the sensation unnerved him, and he tried to stop it. But he didn't know how it even happened, he simply sensed the flow and concomitant release of pressure. Was this necessarily a bad thing? If it reimbursed whatever power source Kirin had drawn on to cast his own magics, it might be an important key to their survival.

The real question is, do I need him in order for me to survive? He does have the food and water and blanket.

Terrell made himself think about the situation coldly. *Right now he's deeply asleep and completely relaxed. He's very strong, but I don't think he's ever trained for war. He doesn't hold himself like a warrior. There's no instant readiness to fight in his movements or his resting poise. He's wary, but not ready to attack or be attacked, especially not now while he's sleeping. I could probably break his neck and take those things off his corpse—and decent clothes too.*

The thought briefly tempted him. The man had kidnapped him, he was confident of that. Death had always been a just reward for treason in Silbar. *But that would leave me alone in a wasteland with only the faintest idea where I'm going. I'd have to conceal my own tracks as I go.*

He listened to the night, much quieter than the ruined temple had been. There must be far less life inhabiting this dry canyon than the swampy ruins. He heard the skittering of a mouse in the deadfall and a cold breeze fluted mournfully through the sandstone walls.

No. For better or for worse, I need his help.

Inside his mind his honor gave a snort and challenged his vanity. *Be honest with yourself, Terrell DuRillin DiGwythlo. You also need his company, or this empty unpeopled land might drive you mad with loneliness. You spent eight days chained to a stone floor with only twice-daily visits from your jailer, and one very unpleasant visit from Darnaud. Your parents are dying, Chisaad is scheming to put someone else on the Stone Throne, and your life will be worthless if you don't find a way to out-think him. You're too close to madness as it is.*

Terrell contemplated a painful truth. *I do not know how to be alone. It terrifies me more than death.* Then he allowed himself to sigh.

Pen, Pen, with all my heart I wish you were here with me.

A tremor ran though Kirin's sleeping body. Terrell wondered if the mage dreamed, and if so, what he dreamed about. *Impossible to know.* He closed his useless eyes on the night and allowed his tired body to carry him back to sleep, while his abundant Light continued its steady streaming into the dark stranger.

* * *

Kirin dreamed. He knew that he dreamed, for Maia was there. Maia, laughing and whole as they completed another perfect performance of *Malik and Mercia* in the Bazaar. A crowd cheered and threw money at their feet while she glowed on his arm. Later that night, in their tiny room in the Sulfur Serpent, the glow had been for him. Grief stabbed him repeatedly, ten thousand cuts that he couldn't heal.

Then Maia's face changed into another woman, someone extraordinarily beautiful and enthusiastic, but no one he knew. Yet she called him Lord, and they made love to each other in sumptuous surroundings that were strange yet familiar. Beneath the pleasure lurked a sadness in his heart that he didn't understand.

He awoke, panting and frightened. He knew that room. It was the Prince's bedchamber.

The warm presence at his back went from comforting to threatening. Kirin barely stopped himself from throwing off the blanket and rolling away. A chilly gust hit him as the blanket's front edge lifted a little, and he shrank back under it. Cold ruled the air outside their hiding place. No moons lit the narrow canyon.

He won back control over himself before he woke the prince. The soft steady breath against the back of his neck didn't change. Kirin breathed deeply, forced calm on himself.

Why am I dreaming about him bedding his concubine? No, why am I dreaming about being *him while bedding his concubine? This is madness, when Madness isn't even in the sky!*

He became aware then of the steady flow of warmth from the prince into his own back. Not only warmth; the glowing Light within the man spilled out and into him. His Shadow nestled quietly under his heart, contentedly swallowing the flow. *It's drinking from him again, like a vampire.* The thought sent a quiver down his spine; could his Shadow be draining the Prince's life? But the man breathed normally, he certainly wasn't gasping for a final breath. Kirin got no sensation of personality with the flow, nothing like he'd received when he killed Darnaud's soldier in Aretzo. That had been a single giant gulp of life, the living whole of the man uprooted and swallowed as casually as a farmer plucking a radish for lunch.

The dead soldier's memories rose in his mind like a haunt bidden to appear. Kirin shrank from the tumbling images and struggled to submerge them before they could trigger worse ones. For a moment the memory of Gerlach hovered at the edge of his waking mind, a stalking horror about to pounce, with the dead hyena at his side.

Then the soothing flow of Light gently submerged both memories, and he could be safely himself again. Whatever mystical power he received from the Prince right now, he didn't think it included either the man's life or soul.

Mother Umana, Kirin prayed in silent anguish. *Forgive me for what I've done. I don't want to be a blood sorcerer or a vampire. I'm sorry I used my power to kill people—well, to kill the soldier anyway. Gerlach needed killing even if I did do it by ripping out his life. I beg you to pour over me your Water of Forgiveness and grant me absolution for those terrible sins. Even though it was them or me . . .*

His prayer collapsed in a welter of confusion. He couldn't wish that he'd died too, not when Grigor's tiny life had depended on him. Heartsick fear for his infant son vied with helplessness as he struggled to think of anything he could do for little Grigor. At least Dona Zella and Dona Abbie were overseeing his care.

And tomorrow the prince wanted him to explain why he had kidnapped him. Did he have any way to do that without earning the man's utter contempt? His mind cringed away from the memory of how stupid he'd been to fall for Chisaad's plan. As for admitting that to Prince Terrell—*I'd almost rather he has me hung for treason.*

Stop this or you'll go mad, he told himself. *You've got to keep your mind on your goal; rescuing Pieter. Get the Prince to Sulmona and get him to free Pieter. That's what matters.*

Nothing else. Just that.

He forced himself to stop thinking and mentally chanted a child's prayer for sleep. He never noticed when it worked.

CHAPTER 47: KIRIN

Kirin woke to a poke in the ribs and a voice in his ear.

"Wake up. You, Kirin, wake up! I can't move until you do."

A faint predawn light filtered through the opening to their hiding place. Kirin peeled the blanket back. The rush of chilly air hit him as he pushed their makeshift concealment aside and crawled out.

Rough sandstone cliffs towered over him. The canyon lay deep in gloom but a peak above the northern wall glowed redly. Dawn had already come to the rest of Silbar.

"We've got to get moving," he said blearily. "I didn't mean for us to sleep this late."

The prince crawled out after him, dragging the blanket and Kirin's pack. "Agreed. The One only knows how soon there will be searchers following us." He handed over the pack and began to fold the blanket while casually asking, "Have you decided what you're going to tell me?"

Kirin gulped. *Dung!* His mind tried to scramble for words even as his gaze shied away from the prince's eyes. "Umm, yes. Err, no. No, I mean yes!" He stopped to pull out the water sack and swallow a single gulp from it. That eased his throat and triggered something like brains to work inside his head. "My tongue takes a while to wake up, Highness. Give me a moment."

"Why?" The prince inquired in a bland voice. "Will more time change what you have to say?"

Dung dung dung! Kirin barely avoided looking at the prince's eyes as he blurted out, "No, Highness! I was stupid to believe Chisaad, but I wanted you to meet my family! If you knew us, you'd know my father couldn't be a murderer, no matter what Duke Darnaud told you." Kirin choked off the flow of words as despair rose in him. *Wait! I'm telling this all wrong!*

Prince Terrell's voice took on an *aha!* tone. "Murderer and Darnaud. I remember the last time those two items were together. Is your father that acrobat who Darnaud accused of murder?"

"Yes, Highness, but he couldn't have done it. Please, I know I did the wrong thing, but you've got to believe me," Kirin pleaded, keeping his gaze below the prince's chin. "He's innocent! Please, please, let him out of the sulfur mines."

"I didn't send him there," Terrell contradicted. "I commuted his sentence to one night in prison. He should have been home the next day."

"But I saw him marched away in the prison coffle!"

Terrell's voice turned doubtful. "Are you certain? There were quite a few condemned criminals that tenday. Might you have mistaken someone else for him?"

"You saw him in the courtroom, saw the scars on his head," Kirin answered angrily. "They cut off his hair and stole his silver order-rings, but I know my father and he knew me. He tried to talk to me, but the guards wouldn't let him."

"Ah," Terrell said bleakly. "Chisaad left my office right after the clerk of the Law Court. I suspect that my commutation never reached the judge." The prince took a slow deep breath, let it out, and clenched his fists. "He laid his plans deeply, that wizard did." Then the prince stared at Kirin closely. "On the strength of that false condemnation, he bought your treason?"

Kirin's mind whirled, sickened to find matters even worse than he'd thought. He wasn't only a fool for trusting the Wizard, but twice a fool for distrusting the Prince. "Yes," he answered mechanically. "I'm the one who kidnapped you, but only because Chisaad said—I mean, I didn't know he was going to make you his prisoner. I thought he'd help me keep you with us. With my family."

The prince's voice grew dry again. "You meant me to be your prisoner instead?"

"No! I mean, only until you knew us and understood!" Kirin stopped, miserably sure that his runaway tongue had wrecked everything and hung him beside. He dropped to his knees and put his hands together in supplication as he bowed his head before the prince. "Highness, I know I've done wrong. I'm a fool, I've committed treason, I deserve to hang. Kill me if you want, but please, please, please, free my father. That's all I ask."

He saw the prince drop the blanket, revealing Kirin's own belt knife in the royal hand. The blade gleamed wanly in the morning light. Father had always taught him to keep it clean and sharp. Would the prince execute him with his own knife?

A cut throat is supposed to be a fast death, Kirin thought hopelessly. *Maia, I'm so sorry. Mother Umana, Father Haroun, please take me to her.* He closed his eyes, raised his chin, and waited. Would it hurt? Probably, but he could face a little pain to be with Maia again. Though she was surely bound for Heaven, while he didn't see any escape from the Pit for himself.

Cold metal forced its way between his clasped palms. Startled, he opened his eyes and found his knife-hilt in his hands. He gaped at it.

"Time enough to discuss treason when we're out of here," Prince Terrell told him quietly.

Kirin raised his eyes, met Prince Terrell's blue ones looking down at him, and—

He looked down on himself kneeling, seeing a stunned expression on his own face that would have been funny if he hadn't journeyed so far into despair—

* * *

Terrell gazed up at himself, standing tall and grave after taking an enormous risk. This young fool was an admitted traitor for all that he'd been coldly manipulated into it. Possibly a blood mage too, there was still that eerie darkness he had conjured that didn't *feel* like a demonic Shadow, but certainly *looked* like one—

* * *

"I'm not a blood mage, please God I'm not!" Kirin blurted, even as the sick memory of the soldier's life ran through him and away into the Darkness. His mind shouted, *I don't want to be a vampire!* Ymera herself had assured him that he wasn't one—

* * *

Terrell's guts twisted as the horrible memory ran through his mind. The victim's life flew through him in an eyeblink, barely time for the man to know he'd been killed. But Terrell also saw the soldier's sword swinging in that moment. This was a death, yes, but no slaughter of an innocent. Could this youth be a blood mage if his victim wasn't innocent and didn't suffer? It wasn't the death that drew the demon-familiar, but the suffering of the innocent coupled with the deliberate maiming of the perpetrator's soul in pursuit of power. And here all the suffering seemed to be happening to the mage. As for being a vampire like Ymera—

* * *

Kirin writhed at the Prince's revulsion and pity, shamed beyond bearing. He pressed his knife-point against his own chest even as he prayed. *Oh God, why did you give me this power? I don't want it!*

* * *

Shame stormed through Terrell, years of being showered with contempt for his ears, his skin, the slave tattoo on his thigh, Osrick's jealousy and bitterness, Maia's murder, Pen's absence like a missing tooth, all snarled together until Terrell couldn't separate Kirin's memories from his own. But the despair—his hands flashed out to seize the kneeling acrobat's clenched fists.

* * *

For a moment they struggled over the blade, its point perilously threatening them both. Then Kirin stopped. That warm flood of Light was back, pouring through the Prince's hands into him and soothing, soothing, quieting his Shadow's insatiable hunger. He could kneel like this forever and his Shadow would want for nothing more. He gulped air, tasting the desert harshness of it, seeing every line of his own face through the Prince's eyes and knowing Terrell saw his own the same way.

What is this? Kirin asked wonderingly. *What are you doing to me?*

Me? Only stopping you from taking your own life. Terrell answered. *Is this a spell? I hear your voice, but your lips aren't moving.*

Neither are yours, Kirin protested. *I don't have any magic but magesight. I never have. Even Magister Chisaad couldn't teach me how to cast, but he figured out that I can eat spells right down to the roots, using my Shadow.*

Is that what this dark thing is? Terrell's mind brushed against the Shadow like a blind man trying to understand a statue by running his hands over it. *I thought it might be a demon, but it's nothing like the Shadow-bears at Storm Pass.*

Careful! Kirin twitched. *It killed Darnaud's soldier. It killed Gerlach.* Memories of that horrific night in the blood-mage's basement stormed through him, ending with him staggering out of the mage's burning house as the awful taste of Gerlach's twisted soul coursed across his mind. *He tried to sacrifice me to conjure a demon.*

Terrell withstood the horror. *Mother Umana save you! What an evil man. You were a child?*

Yes. The memory faded from Terrell's mind, replaced by Pieter finding him covered in blood and wandering in the street. A wash at a Temple fountain with the help of gentle hands, food and drink, and strong arms to hold him while he cried out the dregs of terror. Then being carried into the DiUmbra's home, falling asleep to the quiet words, "This boy is now my son, and will ever be."

Wonder from the prince, mixed with admiration and a dash of envy. *Then he wasn't your body's sire? I wondered if your mother came from Gwythlo.*

Old bitterness renewed. *Some raping Gwythlo soldier sired me.* Shifting images of his brown-skinned mother, her vacant stare too-rarely animated with any semblance of mind. *Pieter DiUmbra is my Father in every way that matters. Please, Highness, do what you want to me, but free him.*

I will free him, if I live. I swear that much to you. Your father and my dearest friend are both in Sulmona. We must go there, but I need your help. It's taking all my strength to walk. I need you to find the way, and find us food and water.

Kirin got to his feet, still holding the Prince's hands as the warm Light flowed into his Shadow. *I can do that.* He barely suppressed a gasp when Terrell released his hands and the flow stopped. His Shadow quivered under his heart as if it wept at the loss. Resolutely he sheathed his knife, picked up his rough broom, and waved Terrell to precede him.

They walked for hours, alternating blazing sun with cool shadow as the canyon twisted. Once they found a pile of washed-down rubbish with a stick long enough to make a decent handle and Kirin rebuilt his broom. After that his back complained less when he swept away their footprints.

But more and more they were able to stay on the old road following its shelf above the river. At times it climbed until it hung more than twenty feet above the stony floor. Once a landslide had carried it away and they had to backtrack to find a way down, then follow the hard bare canyon floor for an hour before the road descended to meet them again. Miles steadily passed beneath their aching feet as he listened for pursuit. Twice Kirin thought he heard voices echo in the canyon behind them, but never clear enough to be sure.

In all that distance they didn't once find water.

They finally stopped for a rest during the brutal afternoon heat. The pavement leaped another twisty side canyon that writhed away into the wilderness, and underneath lay blessed shade. The arch offered easily enough headroom to stand erect in the middle, but Terrell crawled aside until he could sit leaning against the cool abutment. Kirin sat beside him with the broom between them. Both of their throats hurt with thirst, mouths painfully dry and their water bottle as empty as Chisaad's promises.

Kirin winced a little at the pain in his feet, then understood it wasn't his own feet that hurt. *Do you want me to re-wrap your bandages again?* he asked silently.

The reply came back the same silent way, sparing both their throats. *No, not until we have unneeded water to wash them. I'm not losing much blood anymore and the wrappings are catching it.*

Good. Let's rest a while before we move again.

The prince gave him a wordless assent. Kirin leaned back against the huge cut stones of the bridge foundation. The bottom row tilted back enough to support him comfortably and the shaded rock cooled pleasantly. Prince Terrell's relief flowed through him, and he knew the prince also felt his. The knowing wasn't as comfortable as the feeling.

This is a remarkable talent you have, his charge commented. *This conversing without speech. Are you sure it's not a spell?*

Me? I told you I'm not doing this. It must be you.

I assure you, I've never had any such talent before today.

So maybe you're a late bloomer. Ought to be handy for a king to be able to talk to people without being overheard. Kirin paused. *Or could anybody hear us?*

A long pause followed while the prince's busy mind turned over the implications.

That's a very good question, Prince Terrell answered slowly. *The only way to find out will be to try it.*

Kirin found himself oddly flattered that the prince had taken him seriously. He turned his head aside to gaze out into the main canyon. The brightness outside the bridge's shadow made him squint.

A rock rattled.

Kirin tensed, forced himself to relax and listen. He could feel the prince doing the same, both of their ears alert for a repeat.

Gravel crunched, then footsteps slapped on flagstone. A voice, uncomfortably close, panted, "Sir, I still can't find a trace of their tracks. Since we're almost out of water, may I respectfully suggest—"

"We are not turning back," a familiar voice growled. "You heard those echoes. They are somewhere ahead of us and we are going to find them. The other men will catch up to us with extra food and water soon enough."

Kirin's mind heard Prince Terrell's exclamation. *Fenman!*

Is that your guard? he asked, grateful for the ability to speak silently. If he really was . . .

They both waited in frozen stillness, not even daring to think, as the footsteps crunched closer. There were two sets, and both men were panting hard. One of them stumbled on the bridge and a dropped shield clattered.

"Watch yourself, Cottar!" Fenman's low voice snarled.

"Sir," bleated the tracker's voice. "Begging your pardon, sir, but a moment of rest would be a fine thing, sir."

Fenman gusted a sigh. "All right."

A thump as Cottar set his shield down against the bridge balustrade above Terrell's head. Metal scraped as both men sat.

We're only hearing them through our ears, Prince Terrell said inside Kirin's head. *Not in our minds. I don't think they can hear us talk.*

Kirin hesitated for a moment, but the one called Cottar chose that moment to speak.

"Sir, if we do catch them, there are only two of us—"

Fenman cut him off sharply. "We're in half-armor with swords and shields, Cottar. Our prisoner's got no weapon and I saw nothing but a knife on his rescuer, no sword, not even a leather jerkin. We can take them. Remember that we want the Prince alive if we can capture him, but better he dies than escapes."

"But that creepy darkness the mage cast, sir!" Cottar's voice waged a losing battle against fear.

"An illusion." Fenman's voice oozed confidence. "Nothing more. It harmed none of us. If he casts it again, use your ears and get your blade into him as fast as you can."

Kirin winced inside. With all the sand and pebbles in this canyon he had no chance of moving silently.

"Yes, sir."

Kirin heard a water bottle being uncorked, a noisy gulp. Then the shield grated again, and Cottar's voice sank to a whisper. Both men went very quiet.

Damnation, Prince Terrell swore inside Kirin's head. *I think he's remembered that they didn't check under this bridge.*

Kirin suppressed three different curses. *Highness, stay low against the foundation. I'll try to baffle them enough to get my knife into them one at a time.* He began sending his Shadow out from his chest to thicken the bridge's mundane shadow. Very carefully, he got to his feet—and dislodged a pebble. It rattled down the dry wash until it hit sand.

Kirin could practically feel the two men's attention sharpen. There were no more words, only soft scrapes as they positioned themselves on either side of the span.

They're sure to come at us simultaneously, Prince Terrell warned. *They'll probably vault over the balusters to drop on each side, and hope you have your back to one.*

Kirin agreed wordlessly and thickened his Shadow to its blackest. The world took on a weird sharpness to his eyes even as Terrell closed his own to the artificial night.

The two Gwythlos landed with simultaneous grunts—and Kirin buried them both in Shadow.

They charged in anyway.

The taller man in a plumed officer's helmet must be Fenman. He had landed well, sword at the ready and shield held in tight to cover him from crotch to throat. His long, leaf-shaped blade chopped viciously. Kirin swayed aside, felt the wind on his skin, then darted in and jammed his knife under the man's chin. The point scraped across the helmet's chin-strap, losing some of its force, then sliced into the right side of Fenman's neck.

The officer gasped and tried to ram his elbow into Kirin's ribs. He connected but not with the sharp armored point, only the muscle of his upper arm. It still threw Kirin off balance. He had to grab Fenman's shoulder to stay close enough for a second stab. Fenman tried to tuck his chin to protect his bleeding neck, and by blind chance forced the knife-point down and into his windpipe. Kirin drove it through with all the strength of his arm and sliced both the windpipe and a big blood vessel. Fenman staggered, fell to his knees and spilled dark liquid on the ground. He dropped his sword, pawed at his fountaining throat, and collapsed.

Kirin whirled to see the other soldier, Cottar, land hard on his back. Terrell had swung the broom-handle blindly and caught the man behind his knees. Cottar flung his arms wide in a useless attempt to salvage balance. His helmet and shield boomed as they slammed against the rocky floor of the channel. Malicious fate did him dirty as the tip of his sword flashed a foot over Terrell's crouching head and jammed into the bridge's underside. The tremendous torque forced the blade to bend like a bow. The fine spring steel, too strong to break, flipped itself out of the man's grip.

Prince Terrell, who had been on his knees, dropped the broom and swarmed onto the supine man. Still blind in the Shadow, he grappled the stunned Cottar by touch, feeling for his weapons.

But Gwythlo soldiers were trained to be tough and quick. Despite the blow to his helmet and the pitch darkness, Cottar swung his shield back to pin Terrell against his breastplate. Terrell shoved, tried to lever himself free while still groping for the knife that had to be somewhere. But his antagonist knew where his own weapons were even when blind, and his hand got to the dagger first. He drew and raised it to plunge into the Prince's exposed side.

"No!" Kirin shouted, and sank the Shadow's fangs into Cottar's throat.

The man's life poured through him fast as lightning, slow as the most fiendish torture. Indelibly there and yet gone in an instant, replaced by a bewildered sense of loss that lingered like a wound.

Terrell freed himself from Cottar's dead embrace as the Shadow drained back into Kirin. The prince scooped up the knife fallen from nerveless fingers, found the sword too, and only then looked at Kirin, who swayed on his feet.

"He had a wife and two daughters," Kirin croaked, and collapsed into a trembling ball.

CHAPTER 48: TERRELL

Terrell sat quietly next to unconscious Kirin. He'd shifted him into a more comfortable position and put the blanket under his rescuer's head before he searched the bodies. Between them, Ap Marn's men had another two meals of travel biscuits and two water skins, both almost empty. They'd have had a thirsty trip back to Silbariki if they hadn't met their ends here.

Fenman's clothes were soaked with blood but Cottar had been close enough to Terrell's size that he could wear the soldier's boots, shirt, and pants. Stripping the corpse had been unnerving. There wasn't a fresh mark on the body that Terrell hadn't put there himself during their struggle. Now he sat next to Kirin, waiting for him to wake up, and debated with himself.

He killed Cottar with his Shadow. Killed like a priestess stopping a man's heart, only men don't have command of flesh like that. But demons might. He shivered despite the heat, staring at Kirin's sleeping face while fingering Fenman's belt knife. He had the officer's sword too. *Did a demon do that for him? Is Kirin really a blood-mage? Or demon possessed?*

And the hardest question: *Should I kill him now, while I can? He gave me one chance and I passed it up. But now . . .*

Terrell teetered on the edge of the decision, then set it aside. *I need to know more. I don't think he knows that I looked him over magically last night. I'll dare to try more. I can still hear his mind churning. I'll look deeper this time.*

He closed his eyes on the distractions of the canyon and reached inside his mind for that link that had carried their thoughts earlier. Still there. Cautiously, with more practice now, he reached toward the mind next to him.

His mind ran right into a wall; a shivering, shifting wall, but still impassable. No matter how he searched and prodded, Kirin's mind stayed totally opaque. Terrell could tell he lived and might be dreaming, but discovered nothing more. There was no push-back. Whatever guarded Kirin's sleep didn't try to retaliate for Terrell's probing. But it didn't let him in either.

I'm going to have to risk this with him awake. He clutched the knife for a moment, reliving that terrifying instant when he understood what Kirin had done. *Killed without even a touch. Cottar was at least ten feet away! Not even the highest-ranked Priestess in Silbar can do that. Aunt Klairveen couldn't do that. A mage would have to use a spell, like a lightning bolt or fire strike, to kill at a distance, and it would leave a mark. Same with an arrow or spear.* Nobody can kill from a distance like that without leaving a mark. Nobody human.

But Kirin could. Kirin had.

Kill him, or don't. But decide.

Terrell set the knife down and leaned over Kirin, took his sleeping hand. That strange connection formed again and Light flowed out of him across the contact of skin. It laved the barrier in Kirin's mind and diffused into him. Kirin twitched, mumbled, and awoke, his thoughts a chaotic jumble of images. Two girls perhaps six and eight years old. A woman old enough to be the girls' mother. Ap Marn and his banner, and a roiling mix of love and contempt.

Cottar's love for Gwythlo and contempt for Silbaris, Terrell guessed.

Yeah, Kirin replied groggily. *God forgive me! I didn't want to eat his life, but it was the only way I could stop him from killing you.*

Terrell let out his breath in a gust, nearly bowed under the weight of Kirin's grief and sorrow. *I don't think a blood mage would feel that way,* he ventured.

Kirin shuddered against the stone. *Then what am I? I don't want to be a vampire—and Ymera said I couldn't be one, I don't show any of the signs. She's got claws and fangs like a wolf, Haroun witness! She said I'm not a demon either, but I've drunk three lives now. I hate it!*

Terrell said, as gently as he could manage, *May I look inside your mind?*

Kirin stared up at him; their faces were barely a foot apart. *You're wondering if you should kill me, aren't you? I saved your life and you're thinking about killing me.* Anger flickered against the consuming guilt and shame before he continued softly, *I almost wish you would.*

I'm frightened by your talents, Terrell answered unflinchingly. *Worried about what you may become. You can kill without touching, and without leaving a mark. You must know how terrifying that is. But I owe you a debt of gratitude for taking down both Cottar and Fenman when they would have taken—possibly killed—me. Tell me, did you drink Fenman's life too?*

No. Kirin shuddered, his whole body quaking. *Haroun be thanked. Ymera said drinking adult lives leads to madness. Three men are three too many. Even the hyena was too much.* He clenched his fists and shook his head violently, then sighed. *Go ahead. Look where you want.*

Terrell's mind pressed against that wall as it vanished. Aching grief poured out of Kirin, the scent and touch of a woman Terrell had never seen but knew intimately, as he knew her name and knew that she was dead. *Maia. A baby. That man on the trapeze bar. More men like him; Kirin's family?* Then the sensations changed, became darker and more painful. *Cottar. Another soldier, one of Arnaud's men. A hyena. And that disgusting blood-mage.*

Both Terrell and Kirin flinched away from that memory. Terrell found his awareness back inside his own body, still dizzy from the storm of Kirin's memories.

I learned about blood-mages when I studied magic, Terrell told him. *The lust for power generally consumes them from the inside out, hollowing out their moral awareness until no foulness seems too low. That's what draws the demons to them, the self-destruction of their own souls. You feel to me like a man tormented, but not destroyed. Not even close. Whatever you want, it's not power.*

I want my family back. More painfully, with a surge of grief that almost overwhelmed Terrell, Kirin declared, **I want my wife back. But I can't have her, unless God grants a miracle. And who am I to get a miracle? I just want to raise my son and be a DiUmbra.**

I believe you, Kirin DiUmbra, Terrell told him silently. **I'll take a chance on you, frightening as you are. Can you get up now? We don't know how close Fenman's other men may be.**

"Yes," Kirin croaked aloud.

Terrell released his hand and stood up with the acrobat. That steady flow of Light cut off and for a moment he knew Kirin's sorrow at the loss. Then the acrobat shook himself and strapped on Cottar's sword belt before they set off again. Terrell already had Fenman's, and he had put the few other items of plunder into Kirin's pack with the silk rope and cut-up bandages. They plodded on up the canyon at the fastest pace Terrell could manage. Wearing Cottar's boots helped.

There's no point in trying to hide our trail now, Terrell told Kirin. **By not returning, Fenman sends as much of a message as if he'd sent a construct, if not as quickly. We've got to get out of this canyon and find the fastest way to Sulmona.**

I'm not arguing. Kirin stripped off the brush and handed him the broomstick. **Here, use this for a walking stick. It'll help you move faster.**

They drove themselves along at the best pace Terrell could manage. The suns sank behind them, clouds patched the sky, grew and slowly darkened. The canyon twisted monotonously, once bending back so far on itself that the dry bottom punched through the thin wall and they walked under a titanic arch. The afternoon heat peaked early and ebbed fast. They listened for the pursuit that they dreaded but heard only wind in the stones. It had grown louder and the clouds overhead were shot with lightning. The growl of thunder stalked the canyons.

Terrell squinted as the suns fell below the cloud layer and their light reflected off pale stone walls ahead. He had already finished Fenman's water bottle and the man's ration biscuit; tomorrow they'd be hungry again. He glanced at the clouds and longed for rain, though none looked to be forthcoming here. He imagined a stream of it flowing down the dry canyon. Splashing from ledge to ledge and filling the hollows of the stone. Imagined slaking his thirst and dangling his feet in its blessed coolness.

"Do you hear a sound?" Kirin asked aloud, stopping. They were at the start of a straight stretch perhaps a quarter-mile long, a bare channel of scoured stone flanked by cliffs topped with broken talus slopes on either side.

Terrell listened hard. Ahead he could faintly hear a rumbling noise, a throbbing of the air. "What is that?"

A wall of muddy water appeared around the distant bend. It grew into an unstoppable fist taller than their heads, racing toward them.

CHAPTER 49: KIRIN

T his way!" Kirin snapped.

He grabbed Terrell and dragged him into a steep little side canyon barely over a yard wide. Three steps and they hit a vertical wall as high as his chest, the lowest tread in a giant flight of water-carved steps. Terrell flung his stick as far up as he could reach and tried to climb. Kirin seized him by the waist and threw him atop the step, vaulted himself up after. Before Terrell could climb up the second step Kirin hurled him up that too. The roar of the approaching flood filled their ears. They made it up one more step before the flood reached the mouth of their side canyon.

The crest surged past like a raging army. It spun off a tongue that tried to lick the little canyon clean. Water swallowed the first step, surged up and over the second, climbed the third. Kirin desperately shoved Terrell up onto the forth step as the flood rose about his ankles, knees, waist, chest. It slammed him against the rock with bruising force. Spouting water splashed off the walls.

The wave churned against the fourth step, battered Kirin from side to side in the narrow canyon. Then the muddy water sank backwards with a terrible sucking force. Kirin's feet lost all grip on the slick rock. He slid backwards as the flood took him.

Terrell grabbed his wrist with both hands, braced his feet on either side of the narrow slot, and hung on.

The wave slammed Kirin against the rock walls again, twisted him, but couldn't tear him free of Terrell's fierce grip. Kirin gasped as his head banged against rough stone, then choked on a lungful of more water than air. His free hand scrabbled for a handhold as he hung, helpless in the wave's power. Then Terrell dragged him out of it. The water churned resentfully, spat more wavelets, and sank down. It revealed the steps one by one until finally the wave drained completely out of the side canyon. There was only muddy water dripping down the walls.

Kirin hacked and wheezed till his lungs were clear. Each dry breath was better than wine.

I prayed for water. Terrell said inside Kirin's mind. *I should have been more precise.*

Yeah. Kirin spit mud. *If you hadn't grabbed my hand . . .*

If you hadn't tossed me to safety first . . .

Kirin looked at his face and croaked, "Thank you for saving my life."

And you, mine. Terrell's eyes met his gaze frankly, blue eyes to black.

Their minds merged in shared gratitude like two handfuls of water flowing together. The sensation was so intimate that Kirin jerked back from the prince and banged his head against the canyon wall.

Are you hurt? Prince Terrell asked him, mental voice full of concern.

Kirin rubbed the back of his head and found no blood. "No, just another bump. Let's get going."

They climbed down while listening for another flood. The wet canyon walls were banded with mud farther above their heads than either could reach. They continued slogging east, away from Silbariki, and soon became as beslimed as their surroundings. Both looked longingly at the many pools left behind amid the rocks.

Still more mud than water, Terrell thought at him, poking one puddle with his stick.

Kirin hesitated a moment, that uncomfortable intimacy too fresh in his mind. But he was grateful the prince had saved his life, and he could tell that the man hadn't meant anything harmful by it. He opened his mind to the link again and agreed. *Maybe the flood caught the rest of Fenman's troops.*

We can hope. Terrell's agreement held a dash of vicious satisfaction.

Kirin thought about being chained to a floor for eight days and said nothing.

They slept that night under a long shelf of rock raised above a fragment of the old road that had escaped the waters. The mud dried on their bodies to an itchy misery that almost made them forget their thirst. Cold breezes probed the blanket as they huddled together, linked by the endless flow of Terrell's Light into Kirin's Shadow, and by the fear of being found.

The next day lacked even a morsel to break their fast. Speaking was torture for dry throats and all the mud puddles had vanished overnight. They slogged on.

Then, around an innocuous bend, mud returned to the canyon floor.

There's water ahead! Kirin thought, and they both picked up their pace.

A hundred feet farther the canyon opened into a mountain-ringed basin. Trees towered on a plateau several feet above their heads. Birds sang and a hawk patrolled the sky.

Look. Terrell pointed. A little waterfall trickled down a sandstone wall to feed the muddy channel.

They scrambled to it. The falls were wide enough for both to crowd against it, licking the raspy rock as they filled their mouths with blessed clear water. Kirin scraped up handfuls of water and tried to rinse mud off his face and clothes. Terrell, cautious of the spider still spiked into the top of his head, put his hands in the flow and gently washed his face and hair between gulps. Then he ran his fingers over the wall beneath the water. *This is artificial!*

Kirin's fingers traced the rectangular stones under the water's flow, slick with travertine and moss. *Yeah, somebody sure built it.*

Terrell looked around, pointed to a steep flight of steps that Kirin had not noticed, carved in the rock wall beside the falls. *There must be a proper stream above.** The prince darted over to the ladder-like stair and climbed. Kirin followed.

Together they topped a beveled stone dam to find a pond jammed wedge-like into the plateau. The upper end was choked with reeds but the water at their feet lay deep, clear, and inviting. Kirin dropped his pack, unbuckled the sword belt and dropped that too, then dove in buskins and all. After an instant's hesitation Terrell stripped off his own weapons but waded in more cautiously, keeping his head and the spider above water.

Bless Mother Umana for this! the prince's mind said as he opened his clothes and washed himself fastidiously. **I've never gone so long without a bath, not even in winter.**

Kirin wordlessly agreed. He didn't quite dare disrobe, not in this strange place, but he loosened his drawstrings and scrubbed himself as best he could while still clothed. Then he dived deep. Waving fronds as long as his forearm carpeted the bottom and little fish darted about. A turtle perching on a rock ate one of them and then gave him an inscrutable look. Kirin surfaced and blew, splashing for the sheer joy of it.

Tension from Terrell's mind warned him. **We're not alone.**

Kirin turned himself in the water to see what Terrell stared at. A woman stood on the shore next to one of the trees that shaded the pond. She wore a gray goatwool mantle and hood over black hair and copper-colored skin. Her forehead was graced by a single joined black eyebrow and the gray eyes under it gazed on him with a look of great satisfaction. He remembered that face in a rural theater, on the family's performance-trip more than a season ago.

The fortune teller!

You know her?

Not exactly. She told my fortune once. A chain of memories flashed through Kirin's mind and Terrell caught them. **She said I'd know loss and need guidance, and she was right about that.**

Terrell snorted silently. **Easy prediction. Those are true of everybody. What's she doing here?**

Duermus live in the desert, so this must be her home.

I'm not sure I like the look on her face. What is she so pleased about?

Father Haroun save me if I know. Kirin swam toward her, found footing on a long ridge of rock that led up out of the water to her feet. He stood up waist deep in the water a few yards away from her and made a clumsy bow while water dripped from his hair.

Before he could speak she said urgently, "You are both in danger, especially the yellow-haired prince. Come with me at once."

"Fenman's troops?" Terrell asked as he waded up the sloping dam toward their weapons.

Kirin waded towards her and asked, "Are more soldiers coming up this canyon?"

"Not Gwythlos--" she barely got out when the brush crackled, and half a dozen copper-skinned men swarmed out onto the dam. Terrell dived for the sword that he'd left on the shore. Two Duermus got there before him and seized the weapons and Kirin's pack. The rest grabbed Terrell and dragged him out of the water.

Kirin tried to lunge toward him, stepped off the ridge into deep water and floundered. By the time he got his feet under him again Terrell recognized that the odds were hopeless. He allowed two men little older than him to pin his arms behind him.

Better stay there, he warned Kirin. *No sense letting them catch you easily.*

Kirin hesitated, waist deep in the pond again. A Duermu man in a sand-colored burnoose walked up to Terrell. Curved sword and dagger hung from his broad leather belt. He stood no taller than the rest, perhaps twenty years old, and displayed the same copper skin on hands and face. His hair and beard were black, and he moved with the prowl of a leopard.

A war leader, Terrell thought. *He knows how to use those blades, I can see it in his walk. Be very careful of this one, Kirin.*

The other Duermus gave way to the leader with swift tugs of their forelocks. He scowled at the prince, then at Kirin dripping in the pond, then stared at the fortune teller with unconcealed pleasure.

"Jina." The war-leader had a deep voice and the next words from his mouth were unrecognizable. Kirin caught only the word "prizes."

He saw chagrin flash across the woman's face and she rattled something back, addressing the man as "Herrip."

Herrip grinned and replied with obvious glee. The grin faded as he turned his gaze on Kirin again and spoke in accented Silbari. "Come here, boy."

"The water's fine," Kirin drawled back, letting his hands drop down into it. "Why don't you join me instead?"

Herrip barked a laugh. "The God sent me visions of you. I Saw you swimming in the sea far away. Water is your element, not mine." He made a gesture and a man drew a long knife and held the point at Terrell's throat. "No, boy. You come here, or this yellow-haired one bleeds."

Don't do it! Terrell thought sharply. *If he has us both, he can do anything he wants!*

Kirin thought frantically for a moment, then smiled with a confidence that he didn't feel. "Did your visions include this?"

The Shadow that he'd sent through the water lunged up the dam's slope and caught Herrip around the knees. The man gasped and before he exhaled again Kirin surged the Shadow farther, till the knife-man and the two holding Terrell were also snared. His men muttered in consternation as the Shadow rose and fell in little heaves like the panting of a great beast, barely under control.

"I can kill all four of you with a thought," Kirin told them loudly, overriding the shocked voices. He forced away the memories haunting the back of his mind and shouted, "If any of you harms Terrell, I'll do it!"

Herrip's stern face melted into a weirdly happy smile. "You truly are the two that I Saw. Your deaths will bring the war that breaks Silbar and Empire, and sets us Duermus free. Against that, what do any of our lives matter?"

Kirin's gut twisted in terrified anticipation. If he drank four lives at once, would the madness that Ymera warned of overwhelm him? What if the men kept coming and he had to kill all of them? He gulped and prayed for strength. "I'm warning you!"

"Herrip, stop!" Jina shouted, her hands raised in helpless protest.

"Kill them both," Herrip calmly ordered.

CHAPTER 50: TERRELL

No," said a penetrating voice.

Terrell had been about to fling himself sideways in a bid to escape the knife. At the word he checked his motion.

An old man in a dun robe had stepped out of the bushes. The elder addressed a stream of words to the pair holding Terrell. They dropped his arms as if they were hot coals. Terrell stayed ready to bolt and carefully watched the knife man. That one sheathed his weapon and bowed to the old man. Herrip's mouth creased in a thin line and his face went blank. Terrell rubbed his wrists and tried to watch everybody at once.

Kirin's afraid that he'll go mad if he kills too many men with his Shadow. But he was willing to risk that to save me, and I could tell that he meant it. I could feel him nerving himself up like a man going into a battle. Is that only because he needs me to save his father?

The old man looked at Kirin and said in Silbari, "Strange mage, I ask you to free our men. They are guilty only of impetuous youth. They will not threaten your companion further."

Kirin hesitated.

Terrell thought at him, *I think he means his words literally, Kirin. Look at the young men's postures, the respect they're showing him in the way they stand. He has got to be some kind of authority among these people, maybe even their ruler.*

If you say so. Kirin drew his Shadow back into the pond and waited tensely. Herrip's eyes narrowed but he said nothing and did not move.

Terrell walked up to the old man, nodded his head in a formal bow and said, "I am Prince Terrell DuRillin DiGwythlo, Governor of Silbar by grace of my father Emperor Brion and my mother Queen-Empress Shyrill. Whom do I have the honor of addressing?"

The old man stared at the glittering spider on his head for a moment, and then looked at him with an annoyed expression. "Spare me your fine words, Prince. We know of you and your companion. The Elders have listened to the paths proposed by Herrip and Jina, and today we choose. You will come with me."

He pointed at Kirin, crooked a finger. "You also. Come."

Highness? Kirin thought at Terrell a little desperately. *Should we trust this old man?*

Terrell thought furiously for a moment, but there were still a dozen men here ready to obey the elder's words. *I think we must.*

Kirin waded out of the water and through the waiting men, his Shadow fitfully wreathing him like a black mist. Terrell saw several of the men flinch away and make the Sign Against Evil like a devout Silbari. Kirin took up a position at his side, turned a little away to watch Herrip. *Highness, don't let that one near you. We surely can't trust him.*

Agreed. Terrell looked at the men who had Kirin's pack and their weapons belts, then thought better of demanding their return. He turned back to the old man and said, "Where are we going?"

The old man had been staring at the spider again, frowning. He answered only, "You will see," before he turned on his heel and led them through the chest-high bushes.

Terrell discovered a winding trail, invisible from only a few feet away but plain while he walked on it. A dozen yards later they passed through an opening in a fence of woven sticks into a pasture spotted with black and white goats. The old one moved with surprising speed and Terrell had to stretch his stride to keep up.

Kirin kept pace with him as easily as before, and silently asked, *Are we heading toward bigger trouble?*

Almost certainly, Terrell replied wryly. *But also, opportunity. The old man clearly isn't friendly, but he isn't letting Herrip kill us either. If I can think of a way to appeal to him and these Elders, maybe he'll show us a direct path to Sulmona. These folk must know this country better than either of us.*

To himself he thought, I don't like the way he stared at the spider. He clearly doesn't know what it is, but doesn't like it, perhaps for that very reason. I suspect telling him will diminish the strength of any arguments I make, so I'd best keep quiet about it and act like I always wear glittering head-jewelry. He hoped that Chisaad couldn't manipulate him through it. Or see what I'm doing either; that would leave me nearly as much a prisoner as before!

He glanced back over his shoulder at Jina, who looked both happy and distressed at this outcome. Beyond her, Herrip's impassive face gave little away, but a small smile flickered across it as he caught Terrell's gaze. Terrell turned back to watch the path while a little chill stole up his spine.

Kirin, seeing the image in Terrell's mind, remarked, *Herrip doesn't look unhappy.*

Then he sees opportunity too. Terrell sighed.

Dung.

The path led them through another pasture of goats and sheep, then up over a rocky rise. The sides and top bore widely spaced incense cedar trees a yard thick and fifty feet tall. Dried fronds crackled underfoot and the trees' smoky scent mingled with animal dung and the sharpness of wild sage. Overhead wispy clouds scattered before the Two Suns' relentless glare.

Terrell looked around as they picked their way through the dry spacious forest and over a ridge of eroded rock. Five canyons came together here to make a star-shaped basin, perhaps half a mile across and ringed by towering cliffs and sculpted peaks of sandstone. *A hidden valley,* he remarked. *I don't remember my teachers ever mentioning such a place.*

I thought the Duermus were just goat herders. Kirin waved his arms to either side as they descended again with Jina behind them. *But look ahead. I didn't know they had anything like this!*

The route took them between irrigated fields watered by little stone channels. A maze of such covered the heart of the valley. They passed fruit trees dripping yellowed autumn leaves and being gleaned by women in robes the color of camels. The women wore blue mantles to shield themselves from the hot sun. Their copper-skinned arms never stopped moving even as they gossiped in musical voices. Some of the older women pointed at the two of them and made warding signs against evil. Hushed words were exchanged, and frightened glances.

Kirin flinched at that and Terrell caught the edge of a bad memory flashing through the acrobat's mind. *Damnit, Highness, they've seen people like us before, and not in a happy way.*

Terrell nodded. *At a guess, they remember my blond hair and your pointed ears on Imperial troops, probably after the Battle of Black Pass and before Mother and Father's marriage ended the war. There was plenty of fighting and looting here east of the Amm, and slave taking too. If those are the only Imperials these folk ever saw, then little wonder they fear us.*

Kirin hunched a little and his hand groped for the belt knife he didn't have. *That's not good. They're afraid of losing what little they've got, and frightened people are halfway ready to kill.*

Unfortunately true, agreed Terrell, then he added: *Seeing this fertile place makes me wonder what other secrets they have.*

And how they're going to feel about us learning them, Kirin answered.

Terrell carefully did not look back at the armed young men following them.

The old man led them into a narrow grove along a canyon floor, willow and other trees planted and coppiced to win as much lumber as possible from the miniature forest.

Ah, Terrell thought. *They grow the cedars for big logs, and these for the small uses.*

The air cooled in the dimness and the old road reappeared. It had been walled up several feet above the channel, where a trickling stream wandered between banks glistening with fresh mud. Drops of water trembled on every leaf tip.

This is bizarre. It rained here, Terrell thought wonderingly to Kirin. He reached up to wet his hand by brushing water from the leaves. *But not back there where the flood hit us!*

Kirin shrugged. *That's how rain is in Silbar. Sometimes you're under it, sometimes it passes you by—but that doesn't mean you'll be either dry or safe.*

I never thought of a rainstorm being like a passing army, Terrell answered thoughtfully.

Better, Kirin averred. *Rain brings life. Armies bring death.*

Or, Terrell answered him archly, *they stop enemy armies from bringing death to us.*

336

Kirin didn't answer the jibe, but Terrell sensed his mind working.

He's intelligent, the prince thought. *But poorly educated and saddled with the prejudices of his class. Well, I shouldn't be surprised. At least he was clever enough to find and rescue me.*

Trees vanished as the canyon tightened until the walled channel and the raised road twisted along between sheer cliffs. The pavement, now barely wide enough for the two of them to walk side by side, bent sharply with the stream. Terrell pointed up at a little stone building perched thirty feet up atop a cliff across the channel.

Archer's redoubt. From there they can easily pour arrows and spears down on this road. Anybody here shooting back has a much harder shot. And look above us—another one, with openings to drop rocks on us.

So, whatever's ahead is well protected? Kirin asked him.

Very well protected. I don't see any way to get at those redoubts from down here. There must be tunnels, or perhaps paths we can't see across the slopes above us. It would be expensive to conquer this approach, though with enough men and engineering it could be done.

Let's not be thinking about attacking people who outnumber us, please? Kirin sent back a little desperately, reminding him that they had no weapons. More men and women had joined the procession, over fifty people walked behind them now. *I don't think I can kill them all and survive.*

The two soldiers rose in Kirin's memory and Terrell winced at his pain. *I'm sorry. I didn't mean to torment you with an impossible task. I'm wondering why the old man shows us all this. Is it to impress me with their strength, as a negotiating position? While we're disarmed and surrounded.* He shook his head in frustration. *This is a painfully weak hand to play.*

The canyon abruptly pinched down until they could stretch out their arms and touch both walls at once. The road became a series of stone slabs laid above the stream, like the treads of a giant staircase. Gaps between the treads were more than wide enough to catch a careless foot. The water gurgled hollowly beneath them. The sheer walls folded back on themselves and the road climbed steeply. A quarter-mile after leaving the hidden farmland, they passed through a tall arched gate.

Terrell noted the stone slabs ready to be dropped across the passage, and the murder holes in the ceiling overhead. Several men on the parapet gazed down at him sternly. *Do they think I'm the vanguard of an attacking army? But the old man said they know about us. Probably they had watchers tracking us as we approached. They certainly know how helpless we are right now, unless Kirin uses his Shadow against them. But that would leave him carrying their memories too. How many can he carry before he goes mad?*

He thought again of the horrifyingly vivid memories Kirin had already shown him, and his gut clenched. A madman with Kirin's powers could be an unprecedented horror.

I must find some other way out of this. But the more they let us see, the less willing they'll be to let us go. Father Haroun, lend me your wisdom!

PETER SARTUCCI

On the gate's far side the canyon opened out again. It took Terrell a moment to make sense of what he saw. Elaborate doorways, ornamented windows, and monumental carvings in the sandstone walls. Tall second- and third-floor windows wider than a grown man's reach. Women and children staring down at him.

"It's a city!" he blurted aloud.

"Carved into solid rock," Kirin agreed in an awed voice.

Terrell gazed around with dawning understanding. "Aha. This must be the Stone City that was ally to Azerin during the Twins War. The stories say it was destroyed when God raised the Scarp, but evidently only the road disappeared."

Jina the fortune teller smiled at them. "Welcome to Artep, home and heart of the People—we who you Silbaris call Duermus. You know us only as minstrels and corpse carriers and shepherds." She raised her head proudly.

The old man led them into a little plaza tucked into a bay in the canyon wall, then through an arch in a high wall and up a flight of stairs. A roofless room at the top held two men and two women sitting on a curving stone bench raised on a dais. Behind them the towering canyon wall had been carved into a huge bas-relief of the many-armed swirl that signified the One God. The old man joined the waiting elders and Terrell found himself the target of five pairs of eyes.

Not one of them smiled.

Terrell shared the sensation when Kirin's stomach went queasy as the realization struck him. *Dung on a stick! Terrell, we're standing on a stage!* Kirin's left hand flicked out in a gesture at the five watchers. *And this is the toughest crowd I've ever seen!*

Do they expect us to perform somehow? hazarded Terrell, examining the elders as they conferred with the old man. Their language sounded almost familiar, yet he couldn't understand it.

I don't think my juggling tricks are going to be enough. Kirin commented ruefully as he moved a little closer to Terrell. *You got any idea what the lines of this play are supposed to be?*

Terrell frowned. The old man had said the elders were going to make a decision, but he hadn't offered them a chance to speak yet. *Not enough clues to say.*

Kirin gulped. *So we improvise? I hate that.*

You've done pretty good at it so far, Terrell pointed out, realizing as he spoke how true it was. *Found your way to Silbariki, got me out of shackles, fought off Fenman and his man, saved us both from a flood and then from being murdered by Herrip. If this is how you improvise, I want to see something you've actually planned.*

Kirin shrugged. *I had to do those. You're the only way I can save my father.*

Terrell sensed the reticence behind that declaration. *Truth—but not all of it. Then again, I'd be a fool to expect more. He's still a peasant and I'm a noble, and he knows it.*

Herrip had approached the Elders, gone down to one knee and spoke to them in a ringing voice. The words sounded like Silbari but Terrell still couldn't understand most of them. *It has to be a different dialect.* After a moment Herrip got up again, bowed, and went to stand against the left wall of the room beyond Kirin. Jina took his place, again an incomprehensible conference, then she also rose, bowed, and moved to the right wall.

Terrell glanced from her to the elders, who still spoke among themselves. How close were they to settling his fate? *Should I interrupt? But that could offend them when I can least afford it. Still, I can't passively wait here!*

"I am not your enemy," Terrell told the five elders, breaking their conversation and drawing their eyes to him again. "You fear loss of your people's freedom, and loss of this too-small oasis of comfort that you tend so carefully. I want neither. Instead I offer the same just lordship to you that I pledge to all of the realm. Slavery will remain banned in Silbar, your people shall not be carried off by Gwythlo or Klinto slavers any more, and I will punish any that try. Your lands will remain your own, and the only tribute I demand is that you defend both yourselves and the other peoples of Silbar against the enemies of us all. You are not mighty enough to stand against Silbar's millions, but you can stand with them and share their might as your own."

"Promises," remarked a male elder. "Such have been made to us before—and broken."

The woman on the end of the row had not been participating in the discussion, but watching Terrell and Kirin instead. Before he could respond, she frowned and said accusingly, "It is as Jina claims. They speak to each other mind-to-mind, as did the two who ruined us." A murmur went through the five elders and their gazes became, if anything, sharper.

Terrell's skin prickled. *If the fortune teller is the one who told them, then either she's very observant, or she knows through arcane means, or she can hear us.* "Oh wise woman of the Duermu," he dared to ask, "Who are these *two* that you mention?"

"The twin princes," the old woman answered, staring at him rather like an owl. Which Terrell remembered was also a predator.

The conversation among the others intensified and she leaned over to join it.

Who? Kirin asked, baffled.

She has to mean Azerin and Zablock, Terrell sent. *The Stone City of legend was caught in their war and it went badly for them, as it did for everybody. They must have been promised aid in recovering, aid that never came.*

But the past isn't our fault! Kirin answered indignantly. *Besides, I'm no prince!*

Two good points. I wonder. Jina, Terrell thought directly at her, *Can you hear our thoughts? Can the Elders?*

He waited a moment but neither she nor they responded, or even seemed to notice.

That's a relief, Kirin mentally muttered.

We've been careless, Terrell thought at him. *We have both been making gestures as we would when talking aloud.*

And Jina told the old woman to watch for that? Damnation, these people are too clever for a bunch of goat herders. Highness, I'm swimming out of my depth.

At that moment the conference ended and the five sat up straight on the bench. Kirin sent nervously, *I think that's your cue.*

The old man stared at Terrell. "Is it that device amidst your yellow hair that speaks thus mind to mind?"

"Not as you think." Terrell gestured to the spider, careful not to actually touch it. "This is but a wicked tool of a mage who sought to enslave me and usurp my position. I have escaped his control with the aid of my companion, and I would remove his device if I dared. But that would leave a possibly fatal hole in my head. I need a skilled Healer to help me take it off."

"Can it spy upon us?" Another elder demanded in heavily accented Silbari.

Terrell hesitated. "I do not believe so. I am using it to hear the orders he gives in my absence; if he knew I could do that, I do not think he would speak as freely as he does." He hoped they found that more reassuring than he did.

Evidently not, from the consternation on their faces. Herrip smiled.

Terrell hurriedly cleared his throat and said, "Wise ones of the Duermu, my companion and I are at a disadvantage. You appear to have been told quite a bit about us, but we do not know how complete, or accurate, it may be. May we know what Herrip and Jina have told you?"

The fortune teller received a permissive gesture from the old man and turned to plant herself in front of him. "Herrip climbed the Skyrock and claims to have had a vision of a day to come when the Duermu are free of the Silbari Crown, as he thinks we were a thousand years ago. A vision which will only happen if neither of you," her eyes flicked between Terrell and Kirin, "takes Silbar's throne. Should any of the rest of the Twenty become the next King, Emperor Osrick will crush the world in war, and he thinks we will own the ruins."

Terrell frowned at her. "Skyrock? I've heard—wait. Neither of us?"

She nodded calmly. "One of you must become King for there to be peace."

Terrell saw Kirin gape at her. "That's crazy! I'm not even noble, never mind one of the Twenty!"

Herrip laughed. "I have Seen you at the Stone Throne with the Silbari crown in your hands, Black Eyes. What does that make you? And I have Seen the days that splay forward from that moment like blood spilled on stone if someone else becomes King. The Pale Seraphs will be well fed! Then we Duermu will finally stand free once more, as the God meant us to be." He strode closer, stared hungrily into Kirin's face. "Your deaths will make us great again."

"No, you simply wish destruction on Silbar," Jina contradicted angrily, stepping between Herrip and Terrell to his carefully-hidden relief. "And thus, you betray the gift of Sight that the God has given you."

"No! I—have—Seen!" Herrip seized Kirin's hand.

Terrell saw how Kirin jerked his arm back, but his hand couldn't escape the Duermu's fierce grip. The acrobat stiffened for a moment and then sagged as if the strength had been drained from his body. Terrell caught Kirin's free arm to help him stay upright—and then sagged himself, as Herrip's vision cascaded through Kirin into his own mind.

The Stone Throne blazing as if it were a lantern made of purple and gold. Kirin holding Silbar's Crown aloft while strips of Shadow clothed him like a corpse-wrapping. Then Terrell himself holding it, purple light wreathing him too. Next someone else wearing the Crown without the purple light, a mélange of his Mother's kin melting from one to another all through the Twenty as the Throne's light faded through the spectrum toward a sullen red. Silbar's purple-clad armies fighting soldiers in Imperial red on fields heaped with dead. Aretzo in flames, Gwythlo Castle broken and smoking, ships burning and cities and countryside laid waste across the length and breadth of the Empire and beyond. Duermus picking over heaped bones before gutted homes where orange trees withered in desolation. Many of the dying trunks had pitifully small skulls nailed to them.

"Not the only path," Jina said as she grasped Terrell's other hand. "See."

Terrell's vision changed. Armies dissolved like mist, Aretzo stood whole while children played and ships sailed in and out of her harbor. Atop the Hill of Sight Kirin and Terrell faced each other across the opalescent Throne, the Crown silver and purple on the seat between them. Shadow and Light, staring at each other.

"And then what?" Herrip sneered tauntingly. "He must still be your enemy, Black Eyes, as you must be his. Only one of you can rule."

"Get away from me!" Kirin demanded, jerking his hand free.

His revulsion at the fanatic's touch echoed in Terrell's head, as did Kirin's visualization of the things he might do if he were King, and could give anything in the world to his infant son.

He is tempted, Terrell realized, and felt a little colder.

"Do you want to live?" Herrip asked forebodingly. "Sooner or later he must move against you. Do you think you will survive if he is King?" In a cunning voice he added, "If a mage has enslaved him once, it may happen again. He must be a weak reed, to be so easily taken. Let us kill him now and your own path to the Silbari throne is clear!"

"No!" Kirin shoved the Duermu away. Terrell thought he was the only one present who understood the guilt in the acrobat's voice as Kirin shouted, "You don't know me, you don't know him! This is moon-addled madness! I'm not one of the Twenty!"

Terrell resisted the temptation to agree. A tiny voice in the back of his mind clamored for attention that he didn't dare spare. "You are wrong about both us and the One God," he told Herrip, hoping the words were true. "Men are not pawns on a board. God grants us the power and right of learning and acting on our own. Visions only give us warnings, they don't turn us into puppets."

"Deny all you want," Herrip answered serenely. He turned to the gathered elders. "Before us stand the two who will doom us to more years of subjugation. Jina denies the truth of my Seeing and counsels a timid caution in the face of God-sent opportunity. What say you, Elders of the Duermu? May I kill at least the yellow-haired Prince, who may be a spy for an unseen enemy behind him?"

From the looks on their faces at least two of the Elders leaned toward exactly that. Terrell tensed, wondering if he and Kirin could possibly fight their way out of this city. Relief swamped him when the other three shook their heads. Herrip smoothly continued, "Better still is to kill them both and launch our people on the path that will exalt us once more."

"Or destroy us," Jina said. "If we take their choice away from these two, usurp their fate solely to advance ourselves, it will be the One God's ire that we draw, not Herrip's imagined bliss. His vision will die stillborn along with our people. The only freedom we will gain is that of the grave. Resist the temptation to believe that murder solves all and ushers in our heart's delight, for the blood guilt will instead curse us."

The five Elders put their heads together. Herrip and Jina each retired to their respective sides of the room, leaving Kirin and Terrell alone in the middle again.

Arrogant bunch, Terrell grumbled silently, trying to choose the right words to speak next. Having to admit to the spider's effect had surely weakened his already scant chances. He wanted to know if that *Skyrock* place was indeed—

Herrip's mad! Kirin insisted defensively. *You know I can't become King; the crown would kill me for trying. It has to be you.*

But he had such a clear vision, Terrell fretted, juggling several thoughts in his mind at once. *Why does he think you could take the crown? Is your shadow power stronger than the Stone Throne?* That idea alarmed him in a way that the mere threat of death had not.

Kirin shook his head. *I don't think it can be. My Shadow's afraid of the Throne, or at least, it leans away from it when I'm near the Hill.* Kirin's mind again touched on things he'd do if he were King; hire a nursemaid for his son, free Pieter and all the mine slaves, execute Ap Marn, give all the Bazaar spaces back to their dispossessed tenants. Terrell could tell the acrobat strained to sound certain as he sent, *This is crazy talk.*

Or maybe it's not, Terrell thought uneasily. *His vision showed the Throne glowing purple for both of us, the highest degree of approval.* Terrell chased a stray thought but could not quite catch it.

Kirin sent back incomprehension; the young acrobat had no idea how the Stone Throne operated.

Before Terrell could formulate an explanation, the Elders finished their talking. The old man they'd met at the pond pointed at both of them and said, "We have decided. Ordinarily we would kill any Silbari or Gwythlo who came into our valley uninvited as you did. But the God's plans are not to be trifled with by mortals, so we will take the great risk of freeing you both. We forbid either of you to be slain, and we require of you no oaths or promises in return."

Herrip's face went completely expressionless, but his hands clenched into fists before he relaxed into leopard-like waiting. Jina smiled. Terrell knew relief, then thought *but? I can hear a 'but' in there.*

The old man continued, "By your actions alone will we see if this decision be wisdom or folly. Know only that the curse of the People will follow you both if either of you prove false to Yellowhair's words. Meanwhile you two cannot stay here, where your mere presence will sow further division. You may choose a destination and we will order you taken to the edge of our lands nearest to it; but you must choose now." He clapped his hands three times.

Herrip bowed to the elders and stalked out. Jina came over to Terrell and beckoned him and Kirin to follow her. They left by the same stair they entered, only now the courtyard outside had been filled by tribesmen who seemed to favor Jina. Terrell noted the way Herrip and his men filed into a different cavelike dwelling with more than a few sharp glances back at him.

Kirin let out a relieved breath as his pack and their weapons were returned. "So that's it? We can just go?"

Jina's smile faded and she nodded her head. "I will guide you out."

"Can you show us the quickest route to Sulmona?" Kirin asked urgently.

"Wait," Terrell interrupted. "This Skyrock place, is it a sharp mountain with a Node inside it?" Kirin frowned at him for an instant, then listened.

"A node; that is what you Silbaris call a well of magic?" Jina answered. "Yes, the roots of Skyrock drink from the eternal springs under the Skin of the World. We Duermus have woven much magic from that well."

"That's where we need to go," Terrell told her firmly. "Also, is there a Healer that I could beg help from, to get this cursed thing off my head?" He made a gesture to the metal spider.

"Not here, and there is no time to fetch one." She glanced back at the cave where Herrip had gone. "The elders want you gone and Herrip schemes. You must follow me now."

"Ah." Terrell nodded, swallowing his disappointment and matching her pace as she began walking. "Herrip has lost a battle but not a war?"

"Yes. We must get you out of here before he chooses his next attack. He will not disobey the Elders openly, but that does not make you safe. And two at least will not mourn if you die after all."

Their way out of the hidden city lead up a narrow stair through another gate and then down a different canyon that twisted like a snake. Terrell guessed they had walked two miles down it when they paused at a dripping spring in a side alcove, all hung with green moss. While they all refilled water bags, Kirin's mind flung questions at him.

343

"Terrell, what is this Skyrock place? Why are we going there?" The acrobat asked, striding along like a tiger lashing its tail. "Shouldn't we head straight for Sulmona?"

"The legends I have heard say it's a powerful node out here somewhere in the desert," Terrell explained. "Inside a tall spire of rock." He added a silent codicil. *If I can use it, I can summon aid that will get us to Sulmona in hours instead of days, and with a lot less walking.*

Terrell felt Kirin's mind withdraw into uncertain acquiescence, and saved his breath for the walk. Jina set a fast pace, with occasional glances behind that showed just how much she feared Herrip.

Less than another mile later the twisty canyon opened into a vast basin. Terrell and Kirin shaded their eyes and squinted across the miles of sand. Out there loomed an immense pier of dark stone.

"Skyrock," Jina confirmed before either could ask. "We must move quickly, the day already fades."

She folded her mantle over her head and stepped out onto the firm sands. The men surrounded Terrell and Kirin and urged them to follow her into the wastes.

Kirin submitted with ill grace. "Damnit, we're getting farther away from Sulmona, aren't we?"

Terrell could feel the acrobat's worry for his father. *I'm sorry, but this truly may be the swiftest way to reach our goal. If that rock is the thing Shimoor once told me of, I may be able to use it to summon the Ilvar Clan's help.*

"Help would be good." Kirin answered aloud, and hurried along at the pace Jina set. He squinted at the dark rock ahead. "Do you think you could send an order to Sulmona to free my father from the mines?"

"If it has a message construct generator spell in place, I can try." Terrell found himself cheered at the thought of being able to warn Pen about Darnaud.

They both moved a little faster after that, until Jina had to restrain them to a pace she could handle. Despite the miles they had already walked, Terrell felt invigorated. *Soon I might be able to do something more than merely run away from Ap Marn's men! And there are healers in Sulmona who could repair this hole in my head.*

Later, as they followed a silent Jina along the crest of the latest dune, Terrell paused and glanced to the west in time to see the lower rim of Mothersun dip below the edge of the world.

Kirin stopped beside him, followed his gaze. "Look at our tracks."

Terrell did. The sands formed long rolling ridges, not terribly high but endless, and Jina stuck to the top of them as much as possible. Their tracks should have stretched back as far as he could see. Instead, moving grains of sand were busy filling each mark. Barely fifty paces behind the last man in their escort the dune lay featureless again.

He guessed what Kirin had not said. *We're dependent upon these people for guidance in this waste. If they won't show us a path to Sulmona that we can follow, and you can't summon help, what chance do we have of finding it on our own?*

The jumble of mountains and canyons behind them all bled together into rocky chaos, a dry fortress of mystery hiding the Duermus' home. Ahead, the sharp spire of Skyrock loomed above them.

Kirin sampled his waterbag sparingly and resumed walking.

He's avoided sharing his thoughts with me ever since we left the Elders, Terrell thought as he followed. *Should I be worried about that?*

He looked around at the sprawling sands. Distant hills rose to the north and east, none near enough to be more than bumps on the horizon.

Worried or not, there's no choice but to keep walking.

CHAPTER 51: CHISAAD

The old temple in Silbariki reappeared around Chisaad with the last light of the Two Suns in its western windows. He swallowed against a sudden pressure in his ears, made sure his cleaning golem still had the loads he'd assigned, and tossed a magelight spell onto the ceiling of the decaying room. Ap Marn's men, crowded uncomfortably close on the decagram, promptly spread out with their weapons at the ready. Two relieved-looking soldiers, one of them visibly wounded and the other the fast rider that Ap Marn had sent, rushed in and babbled relief at their arrival.

Chisaad checked the ward spells he'd so laboriously cast on the crumbling building. The ones on the personal quarters were still whole, but the vast chamber of the sanctuary had been stripped completely. Not even the nubs of the ancient magics once littering it still remained.

Kirin has been here.

"Where is Fenman?" Ap Marn demanded.

"He took Cottar east with him and sent t' other four up the north and northeast canyons, chasin' the escaped prisoner." The wounded man hung his head and shivered. "And the spooky mage what rescued him."

"We don't need him yet," Chisaad told his coconspirator as he launched prepared guard spells. He soon had the three entrances to the sanctuary warded again. Inside the vast chamber he put up another mage light, not caring if somebody outside the ruins noticed. There wasn't time to minimize risks; leaving the golem unattended like this was insanely dangerous even though he'd ordered it to go to bed early and sleep. Only recapturing the prince could be important enough to take him away from the Palace now.

He hurried to inspect the shattered manacles and found the metal dull and crumbling, all the binding magic leached from it. *Of course. They weren't forged mundanely so the metal didn't set normally. Kirin's quite strong, and the base metal went brittle without the spells. He simply crushed it.*

He shivered, discarded the fragments, and busied himself unloading and setting up the tripod that he'd brought and linking its devices into the damaged node under the ruins. It disgusted him to touch the corrupted magic but he steeled himself to finish the task.

Meanwhile Ap Marn had reorganized the shattered local command and assigned one of the men he'd brought to stay with the wounded man. He came up behind Chisaad to demand, "Tell me where he is now, Wizard."

"In moments, My Lord." Chisaad lit a graduated time candle to start the spells running. The green crystal atop the device warmed and began to rotate in its brass housing. "I've linked my new finder to the spider, each turn it will cast a wider net until it catches him." *Or at least catches the spider,* he thought uneasily. He wasn't sure what he would do if Kirin had killed the eight-legged device, or if the prince found a way to remove it from his head and leave it somewhere. But the Prince's simulacrum had still been behaving normally before they left the Palace. *The spider wasn't dead then. I've recorded hours of its connection to Terrell, so I'll still be able to sustain the golem for a little while. But not forever.*

Ap Marn watched like a wolf, his impatience rigidly held in check. Chisaad remembered again how this man had risen so far in the Imperial service. When Ap Marn's interests were threatened he could outwork twenty demons—or outwait them. Presently the former Governor said, "I see. The more circles it turns, the farther away he is. But why is it slowing down?"

"The farther it has to look, the broader the sweep of land it must cover," Chisaad explained, praying it wouldn't need many more cycles. "Therefore the longer each pass requires." *And the lower the accuracy of the finder. Ten circuits so far. They must be more than twenty miles away by now. It's been most of four days; how far can they walk in four days?* He had no idea. He monitored the marked candle, calculated distances, and tried not to worry as time melted by.

"I expect him to run to the Tonatia and raise the troops there," Ap Marn remarked. "That's nearly thirty miles from here across the big lake, but far longer by land. If he's still slogging through those marshes, will your device find him?"

"Marshes, mountains, canyons or city, it makes no difference, My Lord. If the spider is still spiked to his head, the finder will find him."

"And if it is not?"

"Then the task gets harder," Chisaad replied with a forced patience. "Which is why I brought other devices." He lifted the two-headed dulcimer from his carry-golem and set it up to play. A few strums were enough to prove that Kirin had left the ruined city. Farther would have to wait until he had an indication of direction, as he could waste the night on blind tries and simply exhaust himself.

Ap Marn eyed the devices, refrained from asking questions.

They settled down to an uneasy silent waiting. Halfway through each circuit Chisaad tried the dulcimer again, seeking the void in the world's magic that Kirin made, and not finding it. Full night had set when, on the twenty-sixth circuit, the rotating gem finally flashed from green to red and stopped. It sent out a pencil-thin beam of light to stripe the floor and mark the cylindrical wall of the old temple.

"They went east!" Chisaad caroled happily, marking the wall with a dab of paint and calculating. "Fifty-two miles from this spot and approx.-imately four degrees south of due east. Terrell must be making for Sulmona, though he can't have reached it yet." He tried the dulcimer and detected a faint anomaly. *Kirin's got to be there with him. I can find them both!*

"Impressive," nodded Ap Marn, visibly estimating distances and locations in his head as he spoke. "Darnaud may be able to intercept him after he settles Sir Penghar."

"I'll prepare a message constr—" Chisaad began, when the world flashed purple. He heard a sound like silver trumpets and a chill raised the hairs on his neck. He found himself on his hands and knees with no memory of how he'd gotten there.

Ap Marn bent over him in concern. "Wizard? Wizard! Are you ill? What is wrong?"

"We've got to get back to the palace," Chisaad muttered thickly, fighting off dizziness as he pushed himself to his feet. He couldn't afford to show weakness. "Right now!"

"Why?"

"The Queen is dead. The Stone Throne has summoned the Twenty to choose a new King."

CHAPTER 52: KIRIN AND TERRELL

A too familiar chill returned to the air as the Suns vanished; Kirin shivered. Soon after the stars came out but before the twilight faded, Jina led them to a trail that turned to a paved path at the foot of Skyrock. It wandered between outflung ridges radiating from the central spire. Kirin welcomed the relief the ridge granted from the incessant wind, and knew Terrell did the same. He resisted the temptation to touch that busy mind directly.

Herrip and Jina have got to be wrong about me. I can't sit on the Stone Throne, I'm a peasant! It'll kill me!

But Terrell's speculation that his Shadow might be mightier than the most powerful artifact in Silbar kept haunting his thoughts. *Ymera said every mage in Silbar would fear me, practically told me that I could stand against any of them. Even her. What if—*

Visions of the things he could do if he were King swam through his thoughts. Not only free Pieter, free all the slaves in the sulfur mine! Make the City Watch treat people decent, stop demanding bribes, and catch the real thieves! Give people in the Bazaar back their rightful places. And then the damn judges, replace them with fair people who understood—

He shook his head to banish the thoughts. *But I don't know how to be a king.*

He wondered if Terrell might teach him.

Right. I take the Throne that he thinks should be his, and expect him to teach me how to do the work that should be his? That's the craziest idea of all!

But he couldn't stop thinking about it as the desert wind moaned among the rocks.

* * *

Terrell stumbled along the paved path, finding rocks harder to cross in dusk than the dunes had been. Then a broad cave appeared in a ridge of Skyrock, right before the path turned to carved stairs that wandered up between rocks and into darkness. Jina's relief was palpable. Terrell peered into the cave, glad to find some place out of the wind, and suggested to Kirin, "Perhaps you should clear the place of vermin."

Kirin simply grunted assent. He glanced at the Duermus; the men gathered bits of brush from among the rocks to start a fire in the open mouth of the cave, while Jina sat on a rock wrapped in her mantle and watched him. She smiled at his look.

"I have Seen what you can do," she told him in an amused voice. "Go ahead."

Terrell watched Kirin send his Shadow into the cave, slaying scorpions and anything else dangerous. It didn't seem quite as horrifying this time. *Am I simply growing accustomed to his strange power? Yet it's unquestionably a form of death-on-command, it should be terrifying. It looks like something demonic, yet my Light does not repulse his Shadow. Indeed, it seems they share a kinship of sort, by the way they link so seamlessly.* Suspicions to which he couldn't yet give voice thronged the back of his mind.

Jina smiled serenely and said nothing. Terrell flushed with a brief anger, then grew annoyed with himself. *Of course she has her own goals and desires! What else should I expect?*

Terrell chose one of the many shallow alcoves in the cave to lay out their one blanket, while wishing he had thought to ask for another at the village. The Duermus wore heavy robes and had brought no blankets at all. They built a tiny fire, cooked something in a pot, and shared the food out equitably. Before the crescent of Madness had cleared the horizon they were done and the men had spaced themselves in a row across the mouth of the cave, with Jina in another alcove at the very back of the cave. Six of the eight Duermu men promptly went to sleep, the other two watched vigilant in the night.

Terrell shared a water bag with Kirin to wash down the meager meal, then set the sword he'd taken from Fenman's body by his head before he crawled into the blanket. Kirin did the same but put his knife close to hand before he lay down in front. Terrell rested his head on his left forearm and flipped the blanket over them both. He let Kirin press back against him as the acrobat pulled the front edge down to close in what warmth there was. Their bath in the pond had cut some of his body stink, but there was no doubt they were two young men working hard and sweating accordingly. *At least we don't smell like goats,* Terrell thought.

As soon as they were in close proximity that mysterious link between them reappeared. Terrell knew again that gentle relief as his accumulated burden of Light begin to drain into Kirin's back. Kirin stiffened, then slowly relaxed into the flow.

It's strange how comforting this is, Terrell thought at the mind of the man whose greasy black curls tickled his nose.

Kirin stiffened again. For a while his mind stayed as tightly shut as a door.

Terrell waited patiently for an opening of the other's guard, and then added encouragingly, *I suppose we get accustomed to anything eventually.*

Another long moment passed before Kirin responded. *Yeah. Still makes me feel like a monster.* He shuddered against Terrell.

350

Monster? A monster wouldn't grant me so much relief, I think. Terrell thought for a moment, tried to explain. *The Light wells up in me all the time, I can't stop it—and I don't want to. It's a gift from the One and such gifts must not be spurned. But I'm a man, not an angel, and I can only contain so much before it burns me. I can drain some off by using artifacts, especially the Stone Throne, but I've got no artifact here. If you weren't here, well, after so many days I'd be in pain from the surfeit.*

You sure I'm not hurting you? Kirin's mind fumbled for words. *It's just that—I wonder—I remember.*

He cut the thought short, but Terrell soon knew where it led; to Gerlach, and a horror of fear and pain. Kirin relived the humiliation of being used to satisfy another's lust, not simply without any care for his own joy, but with active malice, the will to harm and maim and ultimately, to kill. The sharp, sharp knife tracing Kirin's nerves and blood vessels under his skin, Gerlach's gloating words as he explained what would follow the blood-mage's embrace, the better to torment his victim for the demon summoning.

Terrell endured the horrific memory, the awful sensation—nothing erotic about it, all power and pain. Kirin shuddered and wept silently. Terrell resisted the temptation to offer comfort by touching him, recognizing barely in time how it would be perceived in the face of such a memory. So he simply waited, while two soldiers paraded through Kirin's mind next, and the hyena almost comforting in its thoughtless and brutal simplicity. The second soldier haunted Kirin with the memories of a wife and daughters that the dead man would never know again.

In time the memories receded, and Kirin lay against him quiet and exhausted. *I hate remembering them,* the acrobat thought dully. *But I can't get rid of them, especially Gerlach. He's always there, inside my head. Now that he's got those two soldiers for company, I can't stop thinking about all three of them. Is this how madness starts?*

I don't know, Terrell admitted, worried himself. *It may be happening because the two soldiers were so recent. Did Gerlach fade in the years after you—* killed seemed to be the wrong word, murdered was definitely out, Terrell settled on, *executed him?*

Some. Kirin considered, added, *Mostly. I didn't think about him much at all after I became a performer with our troupe. Especially not after I, uh, noticed Maia.*

An erotic memory of Kirin embracing his wife, a closeness between them that Terrell envied. Kirin hastily turned his thoughts aside to other matters, the small doings of his family, and memories of the acrobat that had adopted the lost boy. Pieter loomed larger than life in Kirin's mind, a heroic figure loved and adored and emulated. And maimed; a time-softened memory of seeing Pieter for the first time in the baths, the knife scars in his groin, and understanding why his adoptive father had never taken a wife even after his Order disbanded and he returned to the family.

Somebody castrated him? Terrell thought back, reflexively cupping his free hand over his own crotch.

Gwythlos. After the Battle of Black Pass. Kirin frowned. Terrell could sense him sorting memories; this must be an old one much dimmed by time. *I asked him about it a few years later, when my man-hair grew. He had torture scars on his head and chest, too, everybody at the baths respected him for that, though he never made a show of it or anything. He'd been a war monk, fighting with the Sons of the Defender order during the Conquest. He told me about defending a bastion in the Pass where they got overwhelmed and taken. Something hit him on the head. He woke up more than a day later, staked out on a rock before a Gwythlo Druid cut him. First she tried to do a magic to enslave him, but his Temple ward defeated her, so she took revenge by cutting off his balls. She did it to all the monks that lived through the battle, though some died afterward.*

Ah. Terrell winced in shame. *I'd heard rumors about that. Mother said Father wasn't pleased. He had words with Aunt Klairveen about it later. After that he announced his Edict on freedom to worship and her Druids weren't allowed to torture Silbaris, or anyone else, any more. Part of the reason, I guess, that she hates Mother and me so much.*

Kirin thought back, *Pieter didn't let it make him bitter. He told me that he'd already chosen celibacy when he joined the Sons, so losing his balls made it easier to keep his vow. He said he was grateful that she'd left him his cock, so he could still pee standing up.*

Terrell's eyebrows climbed at the blunt honesty of Kirin's thought. *I don't think I could be so . . . philosophical if such a thing happened to me.* He found his right hand cupping his groin again. I don't want to be celibate, especially not involuntarily!

Kirin evidently caught the gist of the thought, for he chuckled. *Me neither!*

They lay silently for a while, Kirin remembering his wife in melancholy.

Someday I too will have a wife, Terrell reminded himself. The closeness in Kirin's memories could make a stone envious. A night with the concubines had never been the same, and for the first time Terrell understood what his parents shared. Will that be my fate? Royal marriages are usually arranged for mutual gain, not mutual happiness, and I can tell Osrick hasn't been happy with his wife. He certainly isn't faithful to her.

Somewhere in the desert a jackal howled. Beyond the cave mouth bats flew across the faces of the moons.

The women in our lives redeem us or damn us, according to their choosing, Terrell remembered Father once saying to him after an argument with his sisters. Mother had merely smiled and linked hands with him.

Then Terrell's mind returned to the faint memory trail that had been bothering him earlier. Something about Herrip's vision.

I have a request that may make you sad, Terrell told Kirin.

The acrobat's answer was guarded. *What?*

Please remember your mother. Terrell held his breath as he waited.

For a moment Kirin hesitated, then his mind swirled with memories that peeled back in layers. A grave where masked corpsetakers carelessly shoveled dirt over a body that didn't even have a shroud, much less a coffin. A woman lying on a pile of straw, her face bruised from a terrible beating, eyes closed and breathing labored. The same woman healthy and vibrant, dancing while pale thuggish men with pointed ears leered, until the strongest among them stepped forward to claim her. The woman sitting on a woven mat under palm trees surrounded by other women as brown of skin as herself, only now her face had a vacant expression as she plaited palm fronds. A close memory of her prying nutmeats from their shells with a bone pick, face still vacant as she fed the fruits of her labor to Kirin. All the memories made her and everyone else in them seem huge, so Kirin must have been no more than six or seven years old.

Terrell remembered Herrip declaring that he'd seen Kirin swimming in his vision. *Where did you live when you were small?*

On an island in the Sundering Sea. Memories of sand and blue water under an endless arch of sky. *We called it Pearl Island, for the pearls that the men took from giant clams in the lagoon. Xir traders would come once a year to trade for them. That was our undoing, eventually, when a Klinto ship full of Gwythlo and Klinto slavers followed the traders and found us. They attacked, captured most of us and carried us off to their own island.* A memory of violence that made Terrell wince.

That dance she did, he asked. *Were those the slavers around her?*

Yeah, they were separating all the children to be sold together, the men to another buyer and the women to a third. She didn't want me to be separated from her, so she told me to hide in the jungle when no one was looking, while she danced to distract them. It worked, I hid, and the buyer left with the other kids but not me. She tried to explain it to me afterwards, but it wasn't until I grew up, years later, that I finally understood. Their chief made her his woman, but he treated her cruelly. It took us most of a year to escape, and she'd become very sick by the time we did, feverish and babbling nonsense. She died the night we finally made it to Aretzo. Old grief mingled with new.

Terrell hesitated, then delicately asked, *Did she ever tell you anything about your father?*

Surprise, then resentment, but Kirin answered, slowly thinking through the old memories. *No. He must have been a Gwythlo because of my skin and ears. The villagers called Gwythlos rapers and said one surely got me on her. The other kids tormented me over that.* Memory of pointing fingers as brown-skinned children sang a cruel song at him.

Did she ever confirm that? Terrell asked, holding his breath for the answer. His guess looked like a certainty, but he had to be sure.

Hunh? Kirin's thoughts sounded bewildered now. *No, Mother hardly ever talked at all; people called her simple. Except after the slavers took us. They hit her in the head, and when she woke up afterwards she didn't remember me at first.* More old sorrow, a pain worse than a body blow as the face he knew best gazed on him with doubt. *But she changed after that, *got more aware and clever. I hid in the woods on the slaver's island and she put food out for me. Sometimes the other slavers tried to catch me, and I had to hide for days, but she always found a way to get food to me. Even when the slavers went out after new slaves we couldn't really talk much. The slavers' own women didn't have any way off the island, and the chief always left a couple of older men behind to watch over us. Even when those got drunk we still had to be secret, because the slavers' women didn't like Mother and were mean to her when they could get away with it.** A mental picture of a bevy of angry pale-skinned women hitting the brown one he had called mother.

What did she tell you during that time?

Not much. Even in the forest we couldn't talk for long or the slavers' women might find us. Resentfully Kirin answered, **Why are you asking me all these questions?**

Terrell hesitated, then slowly said, **Because I think perhaps I may know who you are.**

Bafflement as Kirin demanded, **What in the Nine Hells are you talking about? I'm Kirin Sule DiUmbra, an acrobat with the DiUmbra Troupe!**

Terrell shook his head, feeling Kirin's black curls brush his nose. **One more question then. Was your mother native to that island?**

Perplexedly, Kirin thought, **No. They found her in the lagoon one morning tied to a mess of wreckage after a terrible storm. The villagers told me about it. She had me, only a newborn then, tied to her breast with a piece of fine cloth. The women still talked about that cloth years later though it had rotted away by then. She must have been on a ship that sank.**

And took twenty loyal lives to the bottom with it. Terrell nodded again, his own heart filling with emotion. **That's why Herrip's vision showed you holding the Crown, why Jina saw us both standing before the Stone Throne.**

Kirin wrenched his body around violently, the blanket flapping as he turned to stare directly into Terrell eyes. **What are you talking about?**

Osrick tried to kill you and your nursemaid, and everybody thought he'd succeeded because no mage could find you, even using your birth hair for a link. Terrell raised his free hand to trace the bones of Kirin's face, so close to his own. Kirin flinched yet did not pull away. **But no mage can ever find you, because you can walk through any magic ever made by man and it doesn't see you unless you want it to. Until you walked through the Dragon doors of the Royal Chambers in the Aretzo Palace, right?**

Kirin stared at him, his mind in a whirl that Terrell shared as if it were his own. **They opened for me. I thought they must approve of, ahh, of what I did.**

They let you in because the spirits that inhabit them knew you belonged there, Terrell told him, a churning mix of emotions filling his chest. **Because you are my twin brother, Ryghar DuRillin DiGwythlo.**

* * *

"That can't be true," Kirin whispered, shock roaring through him.

He pushed away from the prince, rolled out of the blanket into cold night air and staggered to his feet. "It can't be true!" Kirin cried to the uncaring night.

Jina and the men stirred in their blankets. Both sentries lay still on the sand, black blood glistening in the moonlight while a dim form got to its feet. Another rushed at him with glinting steel.

He barely dodged the blade, knew a tug as it sliced the sleeve of his robe and kissed his left arm with fire. The attacker, a man wrapped in black cloth almost invisible in the night, recovered his balance and bored in with another lunge. Kirin reached for his own knife—and it wasn't on his belt.

The second stab tore his shirt and scratched his ribs.

Kirin's attacker stumbled; Terrell had flung a rock and hit the man. Kirin kicked the attacker's knee to send him tumbling, but the second attacker rushed forward. In the corner of one eye Kirin saw two more struggling with three of the Duermus.

Catch your knife! Terrell sent, tossing it.

Kirin reached for the flying weapon's handle and missed, saving himself from slashed fingers. The knife clattered among rocks.

"Dung!" Before he could add more, the second assassin came at him with a knife in each hand while the first scrambled for his own dropped knife.

Kirin buried them both in Shadow.

The new attacker slashed wildly with both blades and again Kirin dodged. This assassin cocked his head to listen for footsteps, then lunged again almost correctly. Kirin let him get close enough to kick him in a knee, and nearly got spitted in return by the lefthand knife. He backed up and circled while the second recovered his balance and the first managed to regain his feet. Both men wobbled in pain for a moment and then stood there, knives poised and listening. Jina crawled through the Darkness along the foot of the cave wall. Four men fought two outside the cave mouth, while four others lay too still.

Where in the Nine Hells did they come from? Kirin demanded, his heart pounding.

Are they all Duermus?

Yeah. Single eyebrow, copper skin, stink like goats.

Then likely Herrip sent them, Terrell answered, drawing his own sword and discarding the sheath. *Watch out, the two out front might join this fight.*

Kirin looked over his shoulder. Terrell had got to his feet and stood with his back to the rock wall of the cave. The Shadow didn't cover him but blocked him into the alcove like a wall. The prince listened intently. Kirin tried to watch both of his attackers while also keeping an eye on the fight out front. For a moment everybody stood still, looking or listening or both.

A distant jackal howled in the cold night.

"You shall die," the first assassin said in a loud voice. "Accept your fate."

"The hell I will, you smelly bastard!" Kirin growled back, then knew himself a fool when both assassins charged the sound of his voice.

The second managed to run right out of the Shadow for a moment before Kirin hastily lapped it over him again. But the moment had been enough. The assassin redirected his run to head for Terrell.

Watch out! Kirin warned, dodging the first as the man grimly hobbled at him.

Let me see him!

Kirin managed to draw the Shadow up off the ground enough that Terrell saw the assassin's legs two steps before the man reached him. The second assassin burst from the darkness barely a foot from the tip of the prince's sword. Incredibly, the Duermu managed to twist aside and block Terrell's stroke with one knife. He nearly got the other blade into Terrell's right shoulder as he passed; the point ripped the prince's silken sleeve. Terrell ducked, dodged, and then the assassin had his own back to the rock wall and the prince staggered into the shadow blindly.

He's fast! Terrell gasped. *Stung my shoulder but I can still use my sword arm.*

He's too damn smart, Kirin growled back. *Keep your guard up! He might charge you again. Give me a moment.*

He kicked the first man again to send him sprawling, then used the moment's respite to search among the rocks. He found his knife and sheathed it, then picked up two fist-sized rocks and began carefully walking wide around his own attacker toward Terrell. *I'm going to try to lift my shadow off the ground enough that you can see your man's legs, but he can't see us.*

But before he got there the second assassin charged again, this time toward the noise of Kirin's footsteps. Kirin set himself and heaved one rock, then the other.

Both hit. The first grazed the Duermu's right hand and clanged off a knife, the second smashed the assassin's nose and broke two teeth.

"Bastard of a whoreson pig fucker!" The second assassin snarled, spitting out teeth and blood. He weaved side to side while slashing furiously all around him. "I swear by The One I will feed you your own balls!"

The first man snapped something in a pain-wracked voice, evidently making sure his slashing partner knew where he was, but this time he didn't try to rise. Kirin hoped he had broken the bastard's knee.

Kirin backpedaled while drawing his Shadow off Terrell and closer around both assassins. *As soon as you see him,* he sent, *Cut him!* Aloud, he said for the assassin's benefit, "Bite yourself, you desert goat fucker! You must have been banging every nanny in Silbar, you stink so bad! The billies too!"

The second assassin growled and shifted his attention towards the taunting voice. Kirin threw another rock, this time hitting the Duermu on the left collarbone. A bone cracked and the man dropped that arm, but didn't lower his other weapon. Kirin went on with a description of the assassin's ancestry and a catalog of even more unsavory habits, trying to hold his attention as he lifted his Shadow up off the ground.

356

The other two assassins, fighting the three surviving men of Jina's entourage, both bolted toward the sound of his voice. They charged into the Shadow without hesitation, then slowed.

Terrell crouched, peered under the floating Darkness until he could see the second assassin and gage his footing, and then darted in. The man, despite his pain and Kirin's taunts, nearly skewered the prince. Terrell backed away barely ahead of the knife, but his sword had opened the assassin's leg. Blood poured from the cut.

"Die!" shouted the second assassin as he threw himself after the prince.

Kirin rang the third assassin's head with a rock. The man stumbled but forged on doggedly, weaving a net of moving steel in front of him as he searched for his target. The fourth one took up a station at his right and wove a third knife into the matrix. Jina's men hesitated, ran around the outside of the Shadow to find and guard her. She had reached the mouth of the cave by crawling along the back wall.

Kirin drew his knife and darted up behind the second assassin. Before he could stab him, the man twisted like a snake and nearly knifed him instead.

Then Terrell sank his sword into the second assassin's lower back and twisted; the man dropped to his knees. For a moment he tried to rally, stabbing toward Kirin's legs, but his strength gave out and he collapsed face first in the dirt. Kirin stomped on the nearest knife hand to disarm him before he saw the blood gushing from the assassin's back. Terrell had opened a kidney and the second assassin bled out in moments.

Then the first assassin almost hamstrung Kirin. The tip of the knife sliced a finger-long hole in his hose and left a shallow gash across the back of his leg.

"Dung!" Kirin swore, whirled, and jammed his knife through the man's eye. The first assassin joined his partner on the cave floor.

The last two were still slashing the air and slowly forcing Terrell back, any moment now they'd break out of the Shadow. Kirin strained to raise it off the floor while sending, *Get down!* to Terrell.

The prince obediently dropped to a crouch as the Shadow rose, looked under it and found his target. The third assassin's knife flashed over his head as the prince lunged from his crouch and ran his sword straight through the man's belly. The third assassin strained to stab him, only tore his sleeve. Then the fatally wounded man fell backward as Terrell's sword ripped free and spilled his intestines. He dropped his knife and curled around his ruptured guts with a mewling sob, pain finally triumphing.

The fourth sensed his partner fall, turned toward Terrell—and Kirin jammed his knife under the assassin's right ear. The man dropped like a puppet with cut strings.

Any more of them? Terrell demanded, hastily cleaning his dripping sword on a dead assassin's garment while he crouched under the Shadow and peered about.

Kirin looked around. The three surviving Duermus had made a protective triangle around Jina where she crouched against the wall of the cave.

The Shadow billowed scant feet from them and their eyes were white rings in the night, bugged out in terror, but they didn't run.

Kirin thought the fight had probably made enough noise to scare off every wild thing nearby. Jina said something sharp to her escort and they spread out slowly, looking carefully around the outside of the cave. The rocks revealed no more assassins bearing down on them with deadly intent. Outside the cave Calm's wan crescent peered over a shoulder of Skyrock.

I think that's all, Kirin answered tentatively. *If Herrip had more than four to send against us, I think he'd have used them all at once. I hope.*

Terrell stood up as Kirin drew the Shadow back inside his chest. *They were too eager. They should have waited until we were both asleep.*

Kirin snorted bitterly as he cleaned his knife. *Maybe the bastards thought we were. Or maybe they wanted the fight. Maybe they got impatient.*

Thank The One for that. If they had waited until we were truly unconscious—

We'd be dead. Two sentries were no match for four assassins. Kirin gave in to the shudder that wanted out, gasped a few times before he could master his breathing again. He knew Terrell did likewise as the prince shared his own horror. But also, a shaky triumph. Their minds united in the same thought.

We're alive!

But four of their escorts were not, and a fifth had been badly wounded. Jina finished working on him, left him propped against a rock in more-or-less comfort and approached them. Her eyes were wide with more than the night as she pointed to the blood on their clothes. "Are you injured, young lordlings?"

The slash on Kirin's leg chose that moment to dump its hoarded pain on him and he winced as he looked at it. "Yeah, but it's only a bleeder. I just need something to patch it."

"My healing talent is small, but I may be able to close your wounds if you wish, Shadow-lord?"

"I'm not a Lor—" Kirin choked off his reflexive denial. *Or am I?* He managed to nod, and stand still while her touch slowly knit the raw edges of his skin back together. His Shadow surged and strained against his control but he bottled it inside his chest long enough for her to work. The three Duermus had built up the fire, two stood watch while one spoke with their injured companion. They all gave Kirin awed looks while Jina worked and he strained to keep his face impassive. The healing seemed odd, he had never had any other Healer work on him but Dona Zella.

When Jina finished, the prince touched the spider on his head and asked hopefully, "Do you think you could heal the hole in my head if I remove this?" He knelt and let her examine it.

Kirin saw her horror when she discovered how deeply the spider had been spiked into Terrell's skull. "Who did this to you?"

"That doesn't matter," Terrell answered patiently. "I need to know if you can heal the hole, should I take the device out."

She gently touched his head with yellow glowing fingers, then shook her own head. "I doubt it, Prince. Working with brains is delicate, I would fear to fail."

The prince sighed, thanked her and stood back up again. *It's not all bad,* he sent to Kirin. *At least I can tell when the damned impostor is giving orders in my name.*

Glad to hear that much. Kirin's eyes ran over the malevolent thing and a cold shiver touched his spine. He hurried to change the subject. *Was that the first time you ever killed a man?*

Yes. A half-smile, half-grimace flashed across Terrell's face. *Klairveen's monsters and the Shadow-bear on Storm Pass don't, I believe, count. Though I didn't exactly kill that bear, since it wasn't alive in the first place, and I had lots of help.*

Kirin tried to think up an appropriate answer; congratulations didn't seem quite right. His mind still groped for the right word when the world turned purple. He reeled and fell to his knees, then found Terrell had done the same. Silver trumpets of unearthly beauty played inside their heads, every note bearing mingled grief and joy.

What was that? he demanded of the prince, more shaken than by the assassin's attack.

Proof that you are my twin brother, Terrell answered in a mental voice full of sorrow. *That was the Stone Throne summoning the Twenty for a choosing. Our mother has died, which means our father is dead too. The crown has returned. At dawn the Hierarchy will begin two days of ceremony, and a golem wearing my face stands ready to usurp my place. Which is also your place. We must cross the miles to Aretzo to stop whatever Chisaad has planned.*

Kirin's thoughts stuttered over the terrifying events hanging before him. *You mean I have to climb the Hill of Sight too? But I've never been trained for this! What if I do it all wrong? What if it just kills me?*

That is the risk our line runs. It's the price we pay for being born to the Royal House. I grew up always knowing it. You would have too, if Osrick hadn't tried to kill you and you weren't lost to us for so long. More gently he finished, *I'm sorry the hard truth gets dumped on you all at once.*

Kirin gulped. My mother's really the Queen? Pieter, I didn't ask for any of this. I just want you back. Aloud; "You promised me you'd free my father from the mines. You promised me!"

* * *

Terrell hesitated, struggling inside. The survival of Silbar might hinge on him being there for the Choosing. But if I start my reign by betraying this promise to my twin brother, will I even deserve to become King? This could be what that thing inside the Throne is watching for, the choice that makes me fit or unfit for the crown. Which answer will it consider right?

Then he remembered Dona Seraphina's husband teaching him long ago. Merriten's words rang in his memory still.

"All your choices are cumulative, my prince. Good and bad, you cannot escape even the least of them, and they will all shape you. When you choose honor and justice and keeping faith with that which is greater than all of us, you lay up the strength you will need if you are to be King. Expediency, arrogance and cowardice, those weaken you. Choose wisely."

If I turn my back on Kirin, will I set us both on the path followed by Azerin and Zablock?

"I'll keep that promise." Terrell sheathed his cleaned sword. "But time is more precious than silver. Do you think you can see well enough in the dark to lead me up this stairway?"

"Hunh?" Kirin answered, baffled. "Yeah, I think so, but why? It'd be easier in daylight. Safer for you too."

Terrell shook out the blanket and folded it. "I need to be on top of this rock before dawn." In his mind he added, *Do you feel the node inside Skyrock?*

* * *

Kirin looked at the towering mass. *It's a focused node, like the Hill of Sight. Not as big, not nearly, but not tiny either.*

Which means it has prepared spells set into it, * Terrell explained. *That's why we've got to get up there. We're more than a hundred miles from Aretzo and the King Choosing will happen in two days. We have got to be there, or the Throne may choose another one of the Twenty instead—and Herrip's hope may come about by default.* * His mind shared remembered visions of the world at war and Aretzo burning.

Kirin swallowed a lump in his throat. How would his family survive that? What would happen to his tiny son in such chaos, without him there? *Dung. All right, let's get going.* *

But in his heart he wondered, *what do I do if you betray me?*

CHAPTER 53: TERRELL AND KIRIN

Terrell tested the crumbling step before he put his weight on it. He couldn't see it in the dark and had to feel for the stone through the thick military boots he'd taken off the dead soldier.

Stay to the left here, his brother—*my* true *brother!*—told him. Terrell sent back a silent assent and groped his way forward in Kirin's wake, his left hand on the mountainside and his mind trying to ignore the deepening gulf of air to his right.

Jina had agreed with Terrell's decision and given it her blessing. "Your paths run together from the ruined city to the Stone Throne," she told them. "I know not what you will do after that, but those paths narrow every day. Speed is your chief ally now. May the One God bless and keep you, princely brothers." Then she and her remaining men had left them at the foot of the long stair and withdrawn to the cave.

The long stair often constituted little more than chiseled niches between stretches of steep pathway. The route wound back and forth like a snake across the narrowing bulk of Skyrock, whose central mass seemed to be made of hexagonal columns of black stone welded together. At first they were in the rock's shadow and, almost blind, Terrell had to allow Kirin to lead him by the hand. The steady flow of Terrell's Light into Kirin's Shadow felt weirdly comforting on the fraught trek; Terrell tried to keep his mind on his feet. But presently the trail shifted to the southern face of the huge monolith and Calm's light lit their way. They made better time after that with Kirin walking ahead to scout the steep trail, but Terrell's awareness of the tumbled slopes dropping away beside them grew stronger.

He tried to convince himself that it was no different from crossing Storm Pass, but this trail wasn't a tenth the width of that one and had no comforting exterior wall to ward erring feet. Several times they had to step over cracks in the mountainside that dropped sheerly into darkness. One gaped more than a yard wide and he had to nerve himself up and jump, trusting Kirin to catch him if he missed.

He's so comfortable in the dark. The way demons are supposed to be. Terrell pushed the thought aside, but it didn't quite go away. *I couldn't do this without him. I'm not even sure I can do it with him. But every hour is precious and dawn is still far away. I must take the risk.*

Then the zigzagging path curved around an outthrust buttress and dived into a black crack.

"It's stairs again," Kirin reported from the darkness. "Almost a ladder. Looks like it goes to the top. Can you manage a ladder in the dark?"

Terrell steeled his will. *I must. Lead on.*

The climb wracked him with growing terror of the lengthening fall. He couldn't see his hands and feet or what they touched.

Terrell sensed Kirin doing his best to help. The acrobat swept small pebbles to the side and chucked larger rocks far out into the gulf of air, to give Terrell the cleanest footing that he could. Terrell knew his growing fear of the long fall behind them leaked through the mental bond. He struggled to keep it under control.

I'm a Prince of the Royal House. I can do this. I will.

* * *

Is that what it's like to fear falling? Kirin wondered, astonished at the sensations from the prince's mind. *Horrible! How is he ever going to climb down again?*

When at last they crawled onto the top of Skyrock, the prince simply lay panting for a while as he clung to the flat stones like a lover. Kirin, embarrassed for him even as he admired Terrell's bravery, looked around.

They were on the eastern edge of an oval space perhaps a dozen times the size of his room in the Sulfur Serpent. The top of the mass of hexagonal columns had been smoothed by some art; he could clearly see how they were welded together with barely visible seams between them. Skyrock fell away sheer on all sides and the edges were crumbly. Some of the outer columns had cracked free and even fallen; he stayed clear of those. All around stretched a vast gulf of night air.

The triangular peak of God's Footstool loomed above the western horizon, its moonlit ice gleaming in the night. To the east, beyond basins and low hills, the icy tops of the Black Mountains surged like a frozen wave. North and west the sullen fire of the Hellmouth volcano glowed below the rim of the world. South the desert sands stretched to the horizon. This must be the Sand Sea that he'd heard about, that lapped close to the western edge of Sulmona.

Beneath them the Node sank deep into the World. He could feel it without even trying, constrained by powerful spells into a column of power that made his Shadow fret in hunger. His mind kept a tight grip on his personal monster as he turned to Terrell.

"We're here. Now what?"

* * *

All the way up Terrell had fought the quivering terror gnawing at his gut. *I climbed the Warburg stair and the Hill of Sight, and both were taller than this*, he told himself sternly. The terror answered with a scream of *but I couldn't fall so far on either of them!*

The flat top of Skyrock gave him blessed relief.

At Kirin's question he forced himself to sit up and look around. The edge of the constrained node lay right under him. He could feel the structured spells wrapping around it like helical ladders, forcing the node into a tight cylinder filling less than a third of the stone spire. Kirin had knelt just outside the edge of the node and from the way he looked at it, was none too happy to be even that close. It must be a little like staring at the point of an arrow in a drawn-back bow aimed at your face.

I can do this. Terrell got to his feet and walked to the center. The confining spells forced the node's power upward, an awesome potential trembling under the smooth caps of the hexagonal columns. His Light burned in his chest in response. The Duermu magic differed from any other he'd ever dealt with, but not, he thought, impossibly so. *It must work at least somewhat like the Hill of Sight. Activation first.*

He sank his magical awareness into the node, much like using the Stone Throne. There were wards and simple trap spells, almost laughably easy to bypass. He swept them aside in his haste, searching for the action spells.

"Oops." Chagrin took him as a guardian spell rose to block him. It manifested as blue manacles that extruded from the stone floor to lock onto his ankles and hold him fast. A message construct launched itself from the node and flew west, probably toward Artep. Capture and alarm in one.

"Did you mean to do that?" Kirin asked him skeptically.

"Argh. No." Terrell tried to cajole the spell into releasing him; nothing happened. *Idiot!* he berated himself. *Of course the Duermu mages had a subtle trap waiting!*

After several more fruitless tries Terrell had to admit he was truly snared. *This is so embarrassing.*

Kirin got up, ambled over and stuck his hands into the blue bonds. The spell abruptly died and the glowing manacles disappeared. Kirin smirked and strolled back to resume his seat.

I deserved that. Terrell suppressed a sigh and searched—very carefully—for the activator. This time he found it and gingerly opened it.

A cloud of spells appeared around him, evidently crafted by generations of Duermu mages and priestesses. He knew gratitude that there were less than half as many as cluttered the top of the Hill of Sight. Then he settled in to the search for one that he could bend to his desired use. A mental push here and pull there, and—

A blazing column of light shot up into the night sky.

For a moment Terrell simply bathed in it, glorying in the sensation of disciplined power at his command. Then he modulated the column into alternating bursts of short and long beams. It took long enough that the first faint hint of dawn touched the eastern horizon before he finished. The encoded message would repeat until he stopped it. Confident at last that the node would keep pulsing light into the sky without his attention, he staggered out of it and collapsed next to Kirin. *Should I think of him as Ryghar? But that's not the name he expects to be called by. Better I stick with Kirin.*

"All right, I'm impressed," his twin brother said testily. "But what's it *doing?*"

Calling, Terrell answered smugly, leaning back flat on the stone to watch the pulsating column ascend toward Heaven.

Calling who?

The only ones who can get us to Sulmona and Aretzo on time; the Ilvar Clan.

And who in the Nine Hells are they?

A black speck appeared against the lightening eastern sky. *That was fast, they must have had a night lookout on duty. I didn't know they were willing to fly in the dark. *The flying wizards, who can get us to Sulmona in a day. We're going to rescue your father and my best friend Penghar.* He gestured toward the speck, which slowly grew bigger. *That Ilvar mage must be setting new speed records for crossing the desert.*

Terrell added, *At least, I hope we are. If we're in time.* It would be a horrifying irony to arrive late, to find Darnaud triumphant over Pen's cooling corpse. Exactly the sort of cruelty in which the Pale Seraph known as Salim the Tormentor delighted. But if Pieter were alive and Pen defeated Darnaud, perhaps Kirin would want to stay in Sulmona with his father?

If I use such excuses to prevent him from exercising his right to try for the crown, will that not be only a degree better than actively betraying him? Terrell wondered. *Did Azerin and Zablock walk this path before me? Father Seraph Haroun, shield me from Desrey's temptation! Now more than ever I must cling to the path of honor in every particular.*

Kirin stared at the distant mage. Terrell sensed his twin's hopes soar. Together they waited as the mage raced the rising suns toward their perch, and Skyrock continued to blast its summons into the sky.

* * *

More than a full candlemark later, Terrell silenced the summoning spell moments before the carpet slid to a stop on the rock. He recognized one of the younger Ilvar sons through the man's bundled robes even as the seated mage bowed from the waist.

"Your Highness." The Ilvar pulled back a scarf covering the lower half of his face as he spoke reverently. "My uncle told me the code you two agreed upon, but I little dreamed that I would have the honor of answering your summons. How may I serve you?"

"First, by flying myself and my companion to Sulmona, and second by summoning the Master of the Air and the other fast fliers of your clan to meet us there. My Royal Wizard has betrayed me, a usurper wears my face in Aretzo, and the Twenty have been summoned."

"Then do you wish me to send a message construct to Aretzo to delay the Choosing until you can arrive?"

"No." Terrell scowled to the southwest. "I can't trust any message sent to the Palace to get through, and I don't want to give away my location. I don't know who else may be collaborating with him, but the mage guild at least is likely compromised. I fear the Hierarchy may be as well. But the Stone Throne itself cannot be suborned. We must get to the Hill of Sight with all possible speed, but first, a message and then ourselves to Sulmona, where the life of my closest friend is threatened."

The young wizard face blossomed in a delighted grin. "Then wrap yourselves in your blankets and sit close behind me, My Lords, for the wind is cold when you travel as we do."

Wait a minute, Kirin protested, sending Terrell a memory of Kirin's struggle at the river crossing. *He needs to use magic to hold that thing up. What happens when the spells meet my Shadow? We'll all fall!*

Then you must restrain it, Terrell told him somberly. *You will have the help of my Light. We'll share the blanket in flight as we did in sleep.*

An echo of Kirin's answering gulp quivered in Terrell's throat. *Dung on a rope. I hope this works.*

As do I, Terrell thought back. *For I will not leave you here at the mercy of Herrip's assassins—and we must rescue your adoptive father.*

Kirin's jaw firmed and he nodded decisively. *Thank you.*

A quarter-candlemark later, with message constructs cast and sent to warn Pen and summon the Ilvar Clan, Terrell knelt close behind the mage. Kirin pressed against his left side and they wrapped their lone blanket about them. Kirin had to clutch the blanket's front edges together with both hands to keep the wind out; his teeth clenched nearly as hard. Terrell reached beneath the blanket's bottom edge to grasp the mage's belt with his right hand and slipped his left arm around Kirin's shoulders. He hugged his blood brother close to share body-heat, and to feed Light to the hungry Shadow. "We're ready, Mage."

The young Ilvar answered happily, "Then hang on, My Lords!"

The thick fabric under their knees stiffened and rose, and away they flew through risk and fear and hope, as the rising wind cut at them and the Sand Sea unfolded beneath their fragile craft.

CHAPTER 54: PIETER AND PEN

T he chains had put bloody chafemarks on Pieter during the long walk up the dusty camel trail to Sulmona. At the mine barracks the receiving guards had taken the chains and his clothes and left him nothing but sandals and a loin cloth, but they did bandage his wounds. Pieter had submitted to their rough handling with stoic grace, accepted the narrow shelf in a five-stacked bunkbed assigned to him, and soon found himself in the mine stuffing sulfur chunks into a battered wooden hod. A single jug of water to drink and then wash came with the mean supper of porridge, served in a bare courtyard with a single drain where they were all ex-pected to empty their bladders and bowels and drain their wash water. The guards issued him one thin blanket against the cold desert night, and required him to surrender it again the next morning when the meal got reprised for breakfast. The next day was the same, and now on the third day he understood they would all be the same.

He gathered his fifteenth load since dawn while the suns blistered the vast pit. He and a couple hundred other men worked on scaffolding propped against the crumbling cliff face, which gave little shade.

He noticed that some of the men had torn scraps from their loincloths and used them to shield their skin from the raw sulfur. The precious stuff ate at his hands despite his callouses.

"Why don't they issue us rags to shield our hands?" he wondered aloud.

"To shame us a little more," said a youth working against the pit wall. He moved like one of the clockwork automatons that rang the carillon bells at the Mother Temple in Aretzo, prying fresh chunks out of the ragged yellow face. He had a voice as dull as the sound of his wooden mallet hitting the bronze wedge he wielded.

Pieter thought he'd never seen a more hopeless face, even in the pris-on camps after the fall of Black Pass. But at least this one was still willing to talk; some of the prisoners did no more than grunt. As he packed more sulfur into his load he asked, "What's your name, son?"

The youth tensed and looked at him suspiciously, then glanced at Pieter's crotch. "Right, you're the ballless one," he muttered, relaxing. "I guess you aren't gonna rape my ass. I used to be called Tricky. Now they call me Skinny." He hammered at another spot.

The name fit; Pieter could count every one of the youth's ribs. By the curly brown hair in his armpits and chest he wasn't a boy any more, but his half-starved face had a waif-like air. They were laboring at the farthest end of the scaffold, wedged between the working face and several blocky pillars of non-sulfur-bearing rock that had been left behind by the mine's advance. It offered more shade than the front part, but Pieter also had to cover a longer distance to deliver his load.

An overseer snapped something sharp, then cracked his whip for emphasis. Pieter obediently raised the hod to his shoulder and joined the line of men toiling up a ramp to the waiting oxcart. Once there he dumped his load in and headed down another ramp back into the pit, an endless loop of moving men. The mine sprawled at least a mile across on the narrow side and more than twice that long, and it descended in long slopes and cliffs cut into the hillside. A hundred men on the scaffolding chewed at the working face, a hundred more carried the fruit of their labor.

Pieter found his way back to Skinny and began scooping up the heap of loose chunks that had collected at the youth's feet since the last load. Sulfur dust and tinier fragments sifted down between the boards and collected in windrows under the bottom level, where the workers would be sent to scoop it up at sunset. As long as there was daylight, they worked.

A supervisor down on the uneven mine floor leaned on a staff, rubbing his forehead above bloodshot eyes. Pieter recognized an epic hangover. A haughty official harangued him and waved irritably at the wooden braces holding up one of the pillars. The supervisor shrugged helplessly and the official stormed out. The supervisor went back to leaning on his staff and swigging from a water skin. Pieter's parched tongue already hurt and there would be no more water issued until evening; he looked away.

Thus his gaze crossed a timber brace in the same instant as a crack shot through the overstrained wood. Yellow dust puffed as three more cracks split it in rapid succession and the brace shattered. Two more braces to either side followed it instantly and the entire massive pillar of unmined rock leaned toward him.

Pieter grabbed Skinny and shoved him toward the scaffold's exit. "Run!" he shouted as thousands of tons of rock came down on his back.

* × *

"Has Lord Gwynned agreed to talk yet?" asked Sir Penghar DuVerhys DiLione.

The Truthteller shook her head regretfully. "He's quite stubborn, My Lord. I have attempted all the usual tricks to begin conversation, but he has rebuffed every one of them. I suspect that he believes he will be rescued from his predicament by some form of superior political intervention." Her eyes went to the gleaming silver hand pinned to Pen's shoulder, then she uttered a slight snort at the sheer ridiculousness of that dream. "He clearly will be a long-term interrogation project."

"He's not the only arrow in our quiver," Pen told her. "But keep trying, in case he breaks. And make sure he stays uncomfortable unless he starts talking."

She grinned at that. "Trust me, My Lord, we are already working on that. He has been denied a dozen luxuries that he once considered essential, and certain subtle discomforts have been imposed upon him. Nothing blatant, of course, but continuous. Eventually his ire should reach a boiling point and we hope to steer the resulting complaints into a productive channel for His Highness' purpose."

Pen nodded assent and left Gwynned's prison cell to make his way to the Records Room. "Any news?" he asked the two reeves busily poring over massive tomes.

"Our suspicions are confirmed, My Lord," one said, showing him a cutout page in one volume. "Somebody made a significant effort to purge these books of incriminating evidence before we arrived. Fortunately, they did not get very far, and there is more than enough remaining to document the magnitude and frequency of the thefts. Most of the entries refer to another book that we have not yet found. Your men ransacked Lord Gwynned's personal chambers to no avail, so I am told they have moved on to other possible hiding places. We'll find it if we have to tear this entire palace down brick by brick."

"Assuming, of course, that they didn't simply burn it, My Lord," added the other reeve dourly. "They may have been desperate enough."

"I thought of that and had all the furnaces, ovens, and waste bins checked already," Pen grunted. "Nothing as big as these account books has been burned lately."

"Then either they took it completely outside the palace, or it's hidden here somewhere, My Lord," grinned the first. "We'll reconstruct most of it from the others if we cannot find it."

"Good work," Pen told them and left.

His men were spread thin controlling everything. The biggest problem had not turned out to be the men overseeing the mine, most of whom were pathetically eager to betray every scrap of confidential information they'd ever learned in hope of diverting Royal ire. It had been the sheer volume of lies, half-truths, and half-remembered statistics those worthies were dumping on his other Truthteller. It would take days to sort the wheat from the chaff.

He went to the Palace mage station, where the Silbari military mage that he'd brought assured him no messages had come in since they arrived three days ago.

"Which is odd, Sir DiLione," the man commented, wrinkling his forehead. "Their logs indicate this station usually receives at least two a day."

And last night the Throne summoned the Twenty, Pen thought uneasily. *Irreneetha heard it. I expected Terrell to recall me the instant that happened. A message construct shouldn't have taken later than the fourth bell this morning to arrive. It's now well into afternoon. What's keeping him? Or . . . keeping his messages?*

Message constructs were hard to intercept, but not impossible, especially if one merely wanted to destroy them and not read them. Pen thanked the mage and headed back to the front hall, slapping his hands together moodily. *Who can I trust in this dungheap?*

"Sir DiLione?" One of the soldiers addressed him. "Another merchant has arrived and is quite irate that his shipment has been impounded. He claims he will lose thousands of Imperial marks if he cannot depart tomorrow with his sulfur. He says his name is Dylan Allsford and he demands to speak to you personally."

Pen gave his man a sardonic look. "And you told him I was the man in charge, did you?"

The soldier's gaze shifted to a point a little above and to the left of Pen's left shoulder. "Well, my lord, your status and reputation do make it easier to deal with most of them. Unfortunately this one is being very stubborn."

"Tell him I don't give a damn!" Pen shrugged irritably; why hadn't Terrell recalled him yet? Then Irreneetha made a reproving sound and he sighed. "No, don't do that. Give him my regrets for the damage to his business, offer him a chance to file a claim against the crown for any losses he suffers, and send him to wait with the others."

"Ah, Goodman Allsford claims to be the second son of a Gwythlo knight, My Lord," the soldier explained delicately. "He says he's delivering a contract to the Governor of Pitar, and has suggested that his client has the ear of Crown Prince Osrick. He's quite insistent that he won't leave unless you speak to him first. Also, his retinue and their beasts are clogging the front courtyard and blocking anyone else from getting in or out."

"So he's an arrogant third-string noble from some backwoods manor on the ass-end of nowhere, puffing up his connections." Pen pressed his lips together in annoyance. "Very well, I'll chew him out myself."

He strode down the corridors to the front door of the Sulmona Palace, which while not exactly a hovel, definitely came off poorly compared to Aretzo or any other significant city in Silbar. *Probably helps make this arrogant little frog of a merchant feel superior,* he thought. Two guards opened the double front doors with timed heel clicks to magnify his status and he strode through. For a moment he blinked in the bright sunlight and unconsciously set a hand on Irreneetha's hilt so she would shield his eyes for him.

Her warning came barely in time.

Two spearmen charged him from the shadows on either side of the front door. He drew and slashed in one motion and the first spearhead fell in the dirt. The second man slowed his charge, feinting skillfully, and Pen danced back two steps to avoid his point before he slashed it off as well. The soldier who had accompanied him out the door fell to his knees with a sword through his back. Four other men swarmed the door guards.

Dung! I've put my back to the mob!

He whirled to face the courtyard again and chopped the point off a third spear; attackers nearly surrounded him. *This is bad!* Irreneetha rang against a sword and gouged a wedge out of the inferior blade. Five other swordsmen closed in on him. *I've got to get my back against a wall or I'm dead!*

He charged a fighter, broke the man's blade and slashed his sword hand right off as he passed. But there were two more behind that one and others reached for his back.

CHAPTER 55: TERRELL AND KIRIN

T he Ilvar mage slowed his carpet as they approached the front courtyard of the Sulmona Palace. "Looks like a caravan clogging the place, Highness. Should I land in front of the door?"

Then that door opened and Terrell saw Pen come out, blinking in the bright sun. An instant later steel flashed as two dozen men in the yard all drew blades and went for Pen.

"Pen's in trouble!" he gasped, releasing his grip on both Kirin and the mage as he groped for his own sword. "Get us down there now, then fetch help!"

The carpet plummeted right onto the heads of two swordsmen, flattening them, and hovered a yard off the ground. Kirin swept the blanket off their shoulders into the face of another attacker as Terrell rolled off the other side of the carpet and drew his sword. The Ilvar mage soared away and Terrell found Kirin at his side, belt knife in hand.

"Draw your sword, not your knife!" Terrell told him. The attackers had been rocked back by the sudden arrival but were recovering fast.

"Got something better," Kirin replied, and black Shadow poured from his free hand.

"Pen!" Terrell shouted, stabbing a man blocking the way to his best friend. "Make a triangle with us!"

Pen obeyed. The attackers growled and resumed their charge. The next several moments were a berserk fury for Terrell as he stabbed and slashed, using every trick his teachers had ever drilled into him. Then the attackers' faces turned fearful and they drew back, giving him and Pen some breathing space. Between gulps of air Terrell demanded, "Are you hurt?"

"No," Pen panted, then waved his free hand behind him. "What magery is this?"

Terrell glanced back and saw a billowing mass of darkness taller than his head. He knew a moment's profound gratitude. Kirin had *made* them the wall they didn't have to guard their backs. Terrell didn't see him so he must be inside it.

"I brought a friend!" he gasped, then they were both fighting for their lives again.

* * *

Kirin eeled through his darkness, gliding between men frozen in fear or stumbling blindly while their swords wavered. He stabbed a hand and snatched the dropped sword away, slashed an arm and grabbed that sword too, trying to disable or disarm as many fighters as he could. Choked screams followed his weaving path. Two men dropped their weapons, fell to their knees and spewed Gwythlo prayers; he ignored them. Another, standing alert and listening despite the blinding Shadow, nearly stabbed him as he approached. He ducked aside, lunged, and planted his knife in that man's throat. He could feel Terrell's fury matching the fire in his own veins. Then hot blood cascaded over his knife hand and his gorge rose.

It's kill or be killed, Terrell's mind warned.

Pox and damnation! Kirin answered as he fought, and knew he killed inexpertly but too well. His Shadow devoured small magics on the attackers, thirsted for their lives too, but he denied it. *I don't want any more dying memories in my head!* His clothes collected three more slashes, one leaving a burning slice on his left arm, before he had accounted for the half-dozen men trapped in his Shadow.

A remembered voice outside the darkness snapped commands. *Duke Darnaud!*

* * *

Irreneetha glowed red as Pen swung and men fell back in fear. He had cleared more than half the space in front of them but two swordsmen still hard-pressed Terrell.

"Get behind me!" Pen told him as he charged the lefthand man. The noise of the fight would draw his own soldiers, but they were scattered through the Sulmona Palace and would need time to gather.

A bow twanged and an arrow lofted over the heads of the men in front of him. It fell between him and Terrell and the arrowhead gleamed wetly.

"Ware poison!" Pen shouted.

The next arrow came straight at him. Irreneetha shattered it midair with a beam of light. Then he heard a familiar voice roaring orders.

"Darnaud!" Pen made the shout a curse.

Six bows twanged together.

* * *

A chevron of seven men charged into the darkness packed shoulder to shoulder with spears leveled.

Kirin thought, *If I let them through they'll be on Terrell's back!*

He flung his knife and then the sword he'd taken at the men on the two ends, then dived under the lead spearpoint to bounce up into the wielder's face.

The heel of his rising hand caught the man's chin and snapped his head back hard enough to crack neck bones. Kirin caught the spear and twisted it enough to knock the next two men sideways, slashing one. They crashed against the last two and the whole chevron disrupted as men fell over each other.

But right behind them came Darnaud, clad in armor and helmet with two swords swinging. Kirin remembered barely in time that the Duke might be blind in the Shadow, but it made him no less deadly.

Kirin dodged back, tripped over a dropped spear and threw himself into a backwards somersault. Darnaud tripped on a body, windmilled both arms to get his balance back, and accidently sliced an ear off one of his men trying to regain footing. Kirin got his own feet back under him and snatched up a spear.

* * *

Darnaud paused, listening. His men wore leather boots that made a distinctive sound against the stone. When the damn shadow mage had leaped off that flying carpet there had been a glimpse of buskins. His men groveled noisily on the flagstones with pained groans, scraping weapons—and a soft whisper of supple leather on sand and stone to his right. He stabbed his right-hand sword and hit flesh.

"Got you!" he exulted, twisting the blade as he brought his left hand sword around for the finishing stroke. His victim gasped something in Gwythlo.

Then a burning fire tore into the left side of his gut below his brass chestplate. It rocked him backward to fall over another body. His head slammed against the stone hard enough to make his helmet ring and he lost one sword. The fire chewed deeper and his legs went numb when the point found his spine.

"No," said the acrobat's voice. "I've got you."

Darnaud slammed his remaining sword against the spear shaft, nearly cut the stout ash wood. The movement tore his guts further but he ignored pain as he chopped again. The shaft broke, he cut backhanded into the space beyond it. The little turd had to be close to lean his weight on it like that.

Then another spear nailed his sword arm to the dirt. The Darkness surged backward and a face looked out of it into his own.

"For Maia, you heartless bastard," Kirin said, his eyes black as hell's deepest pits. "Die."

A blade took Darnaud in the throat. He tried to raise his own sword one last time but his arm wouldn't work. A terrible roaring filled his ears as he sank through darkness into blood and nightmare. Gray wraiths seized him and dragged him over the lip of a vast hole. He fell and fell and fell.

* * *

Kirin had to yank the sword free of the Duke's throat and use it to parry another wildly slashing soldier. He managed to trip the man and then kicked him in the head hard enough to make his helmet fly off. One more spearman had gotten to his feet and stood slashing his spear in a big circle through the Darkness encompassing him. He missed Kirin but gashed two of his own compatriots when they tried to rise. Kirin timed his swing, dashed in and cut the man's throat.

He stood panting for a moment, looking around and listening. No man in his Shadow still stood save him. The cries and groans of wounded Gwythlos echoed off the courtyard walls. Where was Terrell?

Kirin found the prince kneeling scant feet outside the Shadow while the knight with the flaming sword knocked arrows out of the air. One arrow stood up straight out of the top of Terrell's skull.

Kirin's gut churned. His shadow swirled behind him as he knelt facing his twin. "Terrell?"

Terrell's eyes opened. "Arrow hit the spider. Didn't quite break it. I can still hear the golem and Chisaad. He's casting something. I feel sick; poison?" He swayed.

Kirin caught Terrell in his arms as he sagged forward. He gently rested the prince's chin on his shoulder and held him with one arm while Light torrented out of Terrell into his chest. With the other hand he explored the shattered mess of wire and gems on his brother's head. "The spell is breaking down, I don't know what it'll do to you when it goes. Should I kill it?"

"Yes," Terrell sighed, hugged him, and closed his eyes again. *Now.*

Kirin grasped arrow shaft and spider both, sent Shadow through his palm into the wreckage, and slaughtered the animating magic. A spell on the arrow died too. The spike came loose, the arrow also, and he flung bloody arrow and spider both to the pavement. He slapped his palm over the leaking wound in his brother's head. "It's out!"

Thank The One. Terrell voice sounded drowsy. *If I die—be a good king.*

Terrell's voice faded out of Kirin's mind.

"You're not going to die!" Kirin told him, struggling to his feet. Terrell had become a limp weight in his arms but still breathed. "I'll find you a Healer. Sir Penghar, we've gotta find him a Healer!"

"Looks like the Ilvar already thought of that," Pen answered, lowering Irreneetha as Silbari soldiers poured into the courtyard and ended the fight. Darnaud's bowmen and his mage surrendered rather than be slaughtered. Pen pointed at the approaching carpet where a Priestess' yellow robes fluttered.

Kirin carried Terrell to meet the healer as it landed, not even noticing that his billowing Shadow shrank and drained into his back, or that men scrambled away from him. He dropped to his knees before the priestess, holding Terrell across his lap, and begged, "Dona! Please save him!"

The middle-aged priestess opened her tight-shut eyes and pried her shaking hands from the Ilvar's belt. Without a question or word she sent her aura into the prince. "I've got him. Lay him on the carpet but hold his head up so it doesn't leak."

Kirin followed her orders, heartsick. *I didn't want this! Father Haroun help me, help him. You gave me a brother I didn't know I had, don't take him away so soon.*

Time crawled like a snail, though the Suns had barely moved, until the priestess sat back and sighed. "There, that will hold him. I'll check him again later."

Kirin had sensed Terrell's mind shift from unconsciousness to simple sleep. He rubbed one eye and said, "Thank you, Dona," as the depth of his own gratitude surprised him.

The Priestess answered briskly, "My duty. Now hold still while I fix your arm."

Kirin found her aura invading his arm before he knew it. His Shadow, sated by the warm flow of Light from Terrell, remained blessedly quiescent under his heart. Kirin looked at the top of Terrell's head while she worked. The ugly gash in the prince's brown scalp had closed to leave a small pink bald spot. The Priestess finished with his arm and went to help others, and still Kirin sat there holding Terrell's sleeping head in his lap and staring at that scar.

He only had that wound because of me. We're only here because of me. If I hadn't fallen for Chisaad's lies, Terrell would be at the head of the line tomorrow to see if the Throne will make him king.

Kirin gulped a sudden lump in his throat. *Instead, he'll wait for me to go first. Oh God Above, do I want to do that? I'm a traitor, I should be hung for kidnapping him! Instead I get to maybe take the Crown myself?*

The visions of what he might do as king returned, meting out justice and putting a stop to evil and cruelty. *I'd make some of those bastards pay, I would!* For a moment he filled with righteous indignation. Then the sobering thought followed. *I never would have discovered my kinship if I hadn't—no, wait, the flash and the sound of trumpets. I would have thought I'd gone mad without Terrell to explain, and I'd have run to Dona Zella about it. Would she have known what it meant?*

He could picture the consternation on her face if she did. *Wait, since I heard the call too, that means the Throne knows I'm one of the Twenty. It must have always known. Whoever thought they were last, number twenty, didn't get called. He'll probably tell the priestesses, and they'll look for the missing candidate. God help me! Can I even get out of this if I want to? And do I want to? Grigor could grow up to be a prince. What's best for him?*

Pen cleared his throat and broke his introspection. For the first time Kirin noticed that the knight had been standing there behind him throughout Terrell's healing.

The knight's voice came out flat and hard as he said, "If you'll release His Highness' head, stranger, I'll arrange to get him to a bed."

The young Ilvar mage smiled. "Allow me to float him, Sir Penghar, and he will have the gentlest possible ride."

Kirin touched Terrell's face once, then slid out from under him and tenderly set his head down on the carpet. The Ilvar mage bowed to Kirin and the knight as if they were equals and then his carpet rose smoothly. It floated toward the palace doors as a soldier led the way. Kirin's Shadow stirred when Terrell's light stopped feeding it; he squeezed the monster back under his heart. It had devoured the spells and stripped the cast magics from every man he'd swathed in its darkness, but stayed as hungry as ever.

"Who are you?" Penghar demanded harshly, his sword still unsheathed and glowing. The knight stood several fingerwidths taller than Terrell, which made him loom over Kirin.

Kirin didn't like the sensation. Taken aback by the challenge in Pen's voice, he snapped back. "I'm Kirin Sule DiUmbra."

The name obviously meant nothing to Pen, who immediately demanded, "And what are you?"

The knight's gaze bored into him as if he wanted to squeeze out all his secrets. It put Kirin's back up worse. "I'm the man who rescued Prince Terrell from Ap Marn and Chisaad," he answered levelly, staring right back without a bit of the deference a peasant owed a knight. But his shadow flinched away from the soulsword and he couldn't help flicking a fast glance at the uncomfortably close blade.

Sir Penghar's eyes widened, then narrowed. "Explain." He didn't lower his sword.

Kirin growled back, "What do you need to know? Chisaad and Ap Marn had him kidnapped and replaced him with a golem. It's been pretending to be him for a tenday and a half now. I went where they had chained him and freed him. In return he promised to free my father from the sulfur mines where those lying bastards put him." He scowled up at the knight. "I kept my part of the deal. Since he's out cold, will you keep Terrell's word for him?"

Pen's eyes had been growing wider with every word, until he looked like a dried fish in a market stall. "That's not an explanation! That's the most ridiculous pile of—"

"Think so?" Kirin interrupted, his temper fraying. "Here's more. I saved him from the Duermu fanatics that tried to kill both of us. I freed him from that thrice-damned slave-spider that Chisaad spiked into his head, the pieces are lying right there." He jabbed a finger at the wreckage. "And I killed Darnaud and five of his men while defending Terrell's back, and yours! Your ass would be deader than a mouse in a snake pit if not for me! Least you could do is take me to my father."

Pen's face had been darkening toward mahogany and his eyes narrowing to slits through this speech, but at the ending his gaze widened. "DiUmbra. You're that murder's son? You expect me to believe that you—"

"My father's no murderer!" Kirin stormed. "Darnaud framed him! And I expect you to be a prick, that's what I expect!"

He turned his back on a spluttering Penghar and stalked away across the courtyard, flinging back over his shoulder, "I'll find the sulfur pit without your damn help!"

He was so angry that he didn't notice how quickly everybody in the courtyard got out of his way.

An hour later, after wandering through the maze of workshops, overseers' houses, and other buildings making up the pathetically small and crooked city of Sulmona, he found his way to the lip of the mine. The sheer size of the pit daunted him for a moment, but he had enough residual anger that it carried him to the ramps and the loading gate. A nearly filled cart stood waiting while an endless line of men carried hods full of sulfur rock to it. Two guards lounged at the entrance behind a low wooden gate cut into a waist-high stone wall, obviously meant more as a boundary marker than a defense.

Kirin glared at them, letting his Shadow fill him to the skin and leak out. The guards, engaged in a game of dice, didn't look up when he spoke. "I'm looking for my father. He got here in the last tenday in a prison coffle from Aretzo."

"No visitors," the taller one grunted as he picked up the dice. "Be off with you."

The smaller looked up at that moment and met Kirin's eyes. His own went wide and he gasped as Kirin reached over the gate, grabbed the front of his tunic, and dragged him close.

"Where is my father?" he breathed into the guard's face in his lowest voice. His Shadow billowed around him.

"I dunno!" the short one squeaked. "Gurrin!"

The taller guard shot to his feet, tried to draw his sword and instead jammed it in his poorly-cared-for sheath.

"Don't try it," Kirin told him, sending Shadow through the gate to wreath both men's legs. "I don't need to touch you to kill you. Tell me where my father is!"

"'E's a mage!" the short one gurgled to his partner, clutching Kirin's hand as he was lifted onto his toes. "Don't make him mad, Gurrin!"

Taller Gurrin gulped, let go of his hilt and raised his empty hands placatingly. "Got here in the last coffle? They all went into the mine, all're working right now, 'cept the ones caught in the cave-in this morning."

Kirin's blood chilled at the last words. "Cave-in?" He let go of the short guard and vaulted over the gate, obliterating the scratched game board when he landed. "What happened?"

Gurrin lowered his hands part way and then hastily raised them again. "Pillar fell, crushed a bunch. They're in the hospice." He pointed away from the pit toward a gaggle of buildings against the inside of the wall.

Kirin's fists clenched as he demanded, "What were their names?"

Gurrin shrugged helplessly, but the smaller guard hastily said, "A young guy named Skinny, I don't tink he got hurt too bad, but the old bald guy with a lotta scars got pretty busted up. Couple others got killed dead—"

"Bald? Scars?" Kirin interrupted, his throat tight. "No. Please God, no." He ran for the buildings.

A whitewashed hut did for the hospice, with the sign of a religious order next to the one rough wooden door. He hesitated, drew his Shadow fully back inside his skin, and cautiously pushed the door open. The room inside had been whitewashed too, it held a desk with a single chair and an elderly Priestess telling her prayer beads. He bowed his head when she gave him a serene smile.

"Dona," he begged. "May I please see the men who were hurt in the cave-in today?"

She gave him a compassionate look and led him into a longer room. Six rough beds lined up against one side. Light slanted in through high windows in the opposite wall to shine on the occupants. The last two beds had blankets drawn up over the faces. The fourth bed held a skinny young man with one leg bandaged and splinted and raised on a pad; he snored like a saw cutting wood.

The third bed held Pieter.

Kirin fell on his knees next to it, reached out a trembling hand.

"I wouldn't touch him," the Dona said in a kindly voice. "His spine is crushed, seven ribs and his hipbone broken plus both of his legs, in multiple places. Internal damage, well, too much to describe. We've numbed the pain and he's sleeping."

"Will he—can he—" Kirin choked, seeing the answer in her sympathetic eyes. "Can't you?"

"Only the legs or only the hip, certainly." She sadly shook her head. "The spine too? He's paralyzed from his armpits down and the damage is extreme. No one here has that kind of skill, not even our best Healer, who's at the palace right now. He would never survive a trip to Lonigo or Aretzo. I doubt he'll survive to sundown. I am very sorry, son." She didn't seem to notice his pointed ears and pale skin as she patted his shoulder. "Stay with him if you like, he might awake. He can't feel most of the pain."

Kirin didn't notice when she left. He stared at Pieter's bruised and swollen face, at the old scars on his scalp, his shorn scalp lock, his closed eyes. The rise and fall of the blanket over Pieter's ravaged body continued, but so painfully slow. Kirin found Pieter's left hand tucked under the edge of the blanket, slid his own in to clasp it.

"Father," he croaked, tears sliding down his face as he leaned his forehead against the bedframe and wept. "Father!"

He didn't know how much time passed before he noticed his surroundings again. The bed behind him creaked. He looked up to find Penghar sitting on the end of it with his unsheathed sword resting across his knees. The soulblade gleamed calmly now, her former red glare dimmed to pale white. He squinted; did he see a face in the glow? Yes. He looked away, ashamed. *What must an angel think of me?*

"Did you see her?" Penghar asked curiously. "Many mages can't. Can you?"

Kirin shrugged desolately. "Yes."

Penghar contemplated him for a moment, almost long enough for Kirin to get angry again. Then he said "Darnaud's men talked. He came here to kill me, part of a plot against Prince Terrell. None of them really knew any more than that, but a couple told me some interesting things about you."

Kirin laughed, stopped himself before it became a laugh that would never end. "I'll bet. Did they tell you he murdered my wife?"

Penghar nodded. "Also a story about you draining the life from a man without leaving a mark on his body." The knight's eyes bored into his.

Kirin looked away. "True." He put his head against Pieter's bed again, gently squeezed the old man's still, calloused hand. He almost said, 'I could kill you where you sit', but he didn't actually know what the soulsword could do, so that might not be true. He could feel it there behind him and knew that face still stared at his unprotected back. "Is Terrell going to be all right?"

"Healer says yes. He still slept when I left him. You're mighty presumptuous to use His Highness' first name without title. Did he give you permission?"

"In a sense," Kirin sighed, irked but not enough to lift his head. "Yes." *Or our mother and father did, through conceiving me with him and giving us both birth. God please help me, I was born first; I'm the highest noble in all of Silbar right now.* The knowledge brought pain and relief mingled, and he had no inclination to share either with the arrogant lordling at his back.

"I talked with the healer," Pen continued. "She examined that evil device and the damage it did to his head. She said it had to have taken the most precise casting she's ever seen to make and attach it, and the same to remove it without hurting him. I saw you take it out, and heard Terrell give you the order. Chisaad made it?"

"Yes." Kirin left that hanging.

After a while Pen said, in a cautious tone, "You were his apprentice, weren't you?"

"Right again." Another long pause, which Kirin grimly enjoyed.

"I heard he'd taken one, but never knew, or at least connected, the names until now." Pen paused, then said deliberately, "Did you have a falling out?"

"The biggest. He lied to me, used me, and tried to kill me."

"Oh. Well, he is a traitor."

Kirin sighed a long mournful sigh. "So was I. I offered Terrell my life if he would only free my father. He refused to kill me, and said he already had commuted Pieter's sentence. But Chisaad made sure that didn't happen. Damn him. Damn him! Damn him."

Pen sat quiet for a while, possibly trying to figure out the target of that triple damnation. After a while he stirred as if about to speak.

Pieter gasped. His hand convulsively squeezed Kirin's. Kirin sat up and leaned over him in hope. "Father?"

The old acrobat's eyes had opened. "Son?" he whispered. Blood flecked his lips.

"I'm here, Father." Tears swelled in Kirin's eyes.

"Good," Pieter sighed, and for a moment his eyes closed. Then they flicked open again. "I'm dying, aren't I?"

Kirin could barely bring himself to say the words. "Healer says so."

Pieter lay silent for a moment, then smiled sadly. "At least you're here. So many things I thought I'd say to you, boy. No, that's wrong, you're not a boy any more. You're the man I raised, one I'm proud to leave after me." He panted for a while and more blood leaked from the corners of his mouth.

"Father, I'm so sorry . . ." Kirin fumbled for words.

"Don't be." Pieter's eyes drank him in. "I had a good life. You just love your wife, love your children and your family and your people. That's all you have to do." Pieter smiled again, though pain clouded his gaze. "Makes living almost easy, when you do that."

"Oh Father!" Kirin knuckled tears from his eyes, clutched Pieter's hand with both of his.

Pieter's eyelids drooped. "So tired. I love you, Kirin. You are . . . the best son . . . I could . . . ever . . . have."

Kirin stared numbly as Pieter's eyes sagged closed. Fresh blood spilled from the corner of his mouth. The red trickle pulsed, then slowed and stopped. Pieter's chest sagged down and did not rise again.

Kirin put his forehead against the bedside and wept.

It seemed a long time later when he finally stopped. He raised his head, found Penghar still patiently waiting. The knight had sheathed his sword but kept one hand on her hilt as he spoke. "I'm sorry for your loss."

Kirin managed a nod of acknowledgement. He rubbed his eyes on his dirty sleeve. *I should get up,* he thought, but the effort required seemed beyond him.

Penghar got to his own feet, said, "Terrell should wake soon according to the Dona. I suspect he's going to want both of us there. There's a plot against him and the Twenty have been called, so there isn't much time left to counter it."

He held out his hand.

My son is in Aretzo, Kirin thought. *Where Chisaad is trying to do—what?*

He took Pen's hand, let the knight heave him to his feet. Kirin lingered for a last moment, looking down at Pieter's still body. The youth in the next bed still breathed with his face turned away in sleep. The priestess came in and began a benediction for the dead. Kirin turned his back on the room and followed Sir Penghar out.

They hurried across Sulmona through the fading desert heat. The suns poised above the hills west of the city, the day nearly spent. Kirin and Pen reached the palace courtyard as Kirin's mental connection to his twin awoke.

Kirin?

Terrell! I'm glad you're alive.

You too. Where are you?

On my way into the Sulmona palace.

Did you find your father?

Yes. Grief followed the word.

For a moment their minds merged in shared sorrow. Fathers, mothers, all dead. Kirin paused on the palace doorstep. Then, with an effort of will, he followed the knight and said to his twin, *You know how this Choosing works. What do we have to do to prevent Chisaad from winning?*

We must fly to Aretzo as soon as the Master of the Air arrives. Tonight.
How did I know you were going to say that?

Terrell chuckled. *Because you're in my mind. Oh, poor Pen is going to be so confused by us.*

Kirin's back stiffened as he followed Pan down a corridor. *Don't tell him.*

You mean you haven't?

Not, not yet. I have to get used to this first. This brother-ness. He won't—he'll find it hard enough. Let's first see . . . who becomes King. Before we tell anybody.

There followed a moment of silence while Terrell's busy mind wrestled with the implications of Kirin's words.

Kirin blinked and steadied himself against a wall. All those thoughts running in tandem with his own, like two rivers joined in the same bed yet running side-by-side. One clear and quick, the other muddy and slow, and he wondered which one he was.

If that's what you want, then very well, Terrell answered slowly. *We'll do it your way, my brother Ryghar-called-Kirin.*

Thank you.

Pen opened a door where guards braced to attention and led Kirin into a room. Terrell looked up from the bed where he sat.

Kirin knelt and bowed like a peasant. He could feel Pen's happiness at the gesture as the standing knight used the half bow that was his privilege.

You are wiser than you know, Terrell sent to Kirin whimsically. Then he bid them both rise, welcomed them, and said to Pen, "Does this place have decent baths? I haven't had one in days, and I'd like to be clean when the Ilvars arrive to take us home."

Kirin saw the happy grin on Penghar's face and didn't have to guess the knight's joy at having his lord back.

For now. But the Throne awaits, he thought to himself. We're still halfbreeds; what if it just kills both of us?

CHAPTER 56: CHISAAD, TERRELL AND KIRIN

T|he spider nestled in his hair itched abominably. Worse, Chisaad had to constantly dedicate part of his mind to monitor the golem no matter what else he did. The sheer effort required wracked his nerves and shortened his sleep.

Chisaad had the Golem's illusion spell running in a loop reprising the last several hours of its connection to Terrell, before it had gone abruptly silent. But the loop eventually repeated, with minor but real consequences for the Golem's physical appearance. The resulting shortened cycles of fatigue and health could only be glossed over, not hidden. The Hierarch didn't know the prince well enough to notice, but Dona Seraphina did. At any moment Chisaad feared she would become suspicious. If she sent her aura into the golem without the active connection to Terrell, she'd surely realize that the prince's Light had deserted this body. Chisaad knew he couldn't fake that flow well enough to pass a serious inspection.

He squinted at the suns, morning-bright here on the little plaza at the foot of the Five Hundred Steps. The succession ceremony had begun. The Hierarch intoned her blessing on the gathered Twenty, though only seventeen were actually present. Two more waited in the crowd of nobles, still stunned that they had not heard the Call despite established bloodlines that should have guaranteed them a place.

They don't know about me, Chisaad thought with smug relief. *Mulghar DiMerio is still bedridden from the wound Darnaud dealt him, which is perfect. He was the most dangerously competent candidate after Terrell. And there's probably another bastard at large somewhere too, one meek enough to keep his head down. Everybody else is here.*

He fought down impatience once more. If he could get the golem climbing the Five Hundred Steps, he could keep it separated from Seraphina for a while. The procession had lined up, the 'prince' in the lead and Chisaad standing subserviently at his left to operate the voice-carrying spells and the rest of the customary magical panoply. The space where Baron Sir Penghar should have been on the right remained conspicuously empty.

I should have received word of his death by now from Darnaud, Chisaad fretted in a corner of his mind. *Did that fool bungle his opportunity? Is*

Penghar on his way back right now with Darnaud's head in a saltbox and vengeance in his heart?

Relief flooded him when the Hierarch finished her speech and she and the old Healer got into their separate sedan chairs. Chisaad silently directed the golem to graciously wait a few steps to let them get ahead, then ordered it to start climbing. It took the steps with mechanical precision, face composed in a smile that revealed nothing. The men lined up behind followed with the customary three steps between each. The older among them would find the Hill a serious challenge; tradition insisted the rest wait for them, and the sluggard's pace made him want to scream his frustration.

Even so, Chisaad thought, plodding along beside his 'Lord.' *In less than a full candlemark we'll be at the top, and moments after that I'll be King. Then nothing else will matter.*

* * *

Terrell squinted at the land beneath them. The rising suns' light had swept down from the peak of God's Footstool to illuminate the Valley floor. From a hundred feet up he could see the works of humanity in road and canal, fields and towns. It exhilarated and terrified him. The wind of their passage bit harder and the carpet twitched beneath him.

"Master of the Air, are we going to make it in time?" he asked.

"Now that we have daylight I can see our route easier, and fly faster," answered the senior Ilvar wizard happily. "We'll make it in time, Your Highness."

Terrell had been watching the King's Road unreel a hundred feet below the carpet's edge ever since they reached Amm Crossing. He knelt behind the older man as he'd done with the wizard's nephew when flying from Skyrock, clinging with one hand to the mage's belt while gripping Kirin with the other. They had warm robes now over clean clothes that Pen had extracted from Gwynned's stores, and thick kerchiefs around their faces to cut the wind, but it had still been a long chilly trip. *This method of travel has its benefits, but I suspect flying on a carpet is never going to be popular.*

Kirin had locked one arm with him and held the mage's belt with his other as Terrell fed him Light to calm his Shadow. Their minds mingled and withdrew, mingled and withdrew again as each wrestled with his own role in the event racing towards them.

We're nearly there, Terrell told him, trying to be encouraging. *That bump straight ahead is the Hill, barely ten miles away.*

Terrell. If it kills me? Kirin asked. *Will you take care of my son?*

Absolutely. I'll have him brought into the Royal House and raised as the Prince he's entitled to be. After all, he's my nephew. But it's not going to kill you. If you aren't chosen, you simply won't be able to move the crown. If it really doesn't want you, it'll warn you when you approach it. Remember to keep your shields down so you can hear it.

You told me. But I haven't got any shields. I told you I'm not really a mage at all.

Then keep your Shadow caged under your heart, that should be good enough.

Thank you. Kirin's mind withdrew again into a muddy contemplation that Terrell couldn't follow.

Terrell glanced back over his shoulder. Another carpet followed with Pen, who hadn't been happy at being assigned to seize control of the Gray Fort. But he was the only man other than Terrell himself with sufficient rank to give orders to everyone in it, Gwythlo or Silbari. He'd swallowed his objections and agreed.

I think he found it harder to see me take Kirin with me, Terrell thought sadly. Jealousy from Pen was a new thing, one Terrell hadn't known Irreneetha's bearer could feel. *Even though I told him I needed a mage on the Hill to counter anything Chisaad tries. Which I do. A mage, or Kirin.*

"Five more miles," the Ilvar chieftain said. The carpet's speed increased again. "I'll have to charge at the Hill as fast as I can fly to get us up it, Your Highness. We'll have to trade speed for height on a slope like that."

"But you managed much higher slopes in the Black Mountains," Terrell answered, puzzled.

"Their nodes are under Ilvar control, they won't resist me. The Hill of Sight most certainly will, though I hope it will recognize you and refrain from blasting us out of the air." The Master of the Air grinned. "This will be a new and exciting challenge!"

Kirin looked at Terrell and rolled his eyes.

"Four miles!" The Ilvar mage shouted joyously into the rising wind.

* * *

At every landing on the Five Hundred Steps the procession paused, an acknowledgement that the eldest candidates found the climb a serious challenge. Chisaad curbed his impatience, stuck to the Golem's side, and watched the Priestesses' carrychairs ascending ahead of him. Their bearers stopped at the ninth landing as planned to let the women off, turned and came back down to the eighth to wait.

"Welcome to the Fifth Landing," Fantillin, the Palace Majordomo, intoned as servants fanned out along the line to offer watered wine to all. "Please drink sparingly, My Lords. You resume in forty breaths."

Chisaad had the golem decline, and did the same himself. He glanced over the balustrade down the slopes of the Hill. The roofs of the Palace and the Gray Fort were packed, every Silbari soldier in the Fort waiting and staring. There hadn't even been a protest when the prince ordered Gwythlo soldiers to man the city gates today, which would simplify Ap Marn's seizure of power when the Choosing ended.

He thinks. Chisaad forbid himself to smile. *He doesn't know half of what the Hill can do with a King in control. I can send a cleansing fire through both gatehouses and rid myself of most of the Gwythlos right there. Then I'll arrest Ap Marn and send him home in chains with a list of his thefts and his stolen wealth as tribute, that ought to buy off Osrick for a while. Time enough for me to organize the mages the way they should be organized, and to make Silbar supreme and independent. The people will hail me for that!*

"It is time, My Lords," Fantillin declared as his staff withdrew from the line and the last candidate swallowed a final gulp. "Please resume."

Chisaad had the golem incline its head slightly in acknowledgement and set forth once more. The procession continued in lockstep. DiSolera and the elder DiMerio candidate and a couple of others were already panting like dogs. The younger men looked solemn, suitably awed by the ritual in which they were participating.

Chisaad smiled a grim smile and matched his creation's pace. His mind caressed the hidden spells he had planted in the Hill. Soon.

* * *

"Last mile," the Ilvar Master of the Air shouted into the roaring wind, and Kirin gulped. He pried his gaze from the blazing purple cone ahead to look down.

The outer edges of Aretzo flashed beneath the speeding carpet, the fishermens' village, the stockpens and slaughterhouses, the cemetery wall and the arcing rows of graves that wrapped half the Hill. He saw thousands of faces turning to look up at them with mouths agape. He'd never seen the cemetery so packed. The Hill approached like a giant hand about to swat them out of the sky. He clenched his teeth as they crossed the thirty-foot wall around it and plunged into the purple fire.

Then they were rising.

Kirin's stomach tried to drop through his groin. Every particle of his body got dragged down, down, like the fastest trapeze move but much stronger. The Hill's defensive spells besieged them, tried to penetrate them and slow them down.

His Shadow awoke, surged to his skin and fought back. Attacking spells ripped where they touched him, leaving a trail of flinders as the carpet soared up, up, and still up, slowing with every breath but still climbing.

Help me stand! Terrell's mind shouted as his legs fought the dragging weight.

Kirin shifted his grip to catch the prince about his hips. Terrell stood, raised his hands against the drag, and addressed the defending spells.

"Let. Us. Pass!" he ordered.

The spells obeyed.

Vertigo slammed them as the carpet leaped.

* * *

At the ninth landing the procession paused again while the eldest men panted and trembled. It wasn't unknown for a frail candidate to collapse or

385

even die before reaching the top. The Hierarch took station on the other side of the golem from Chisaad and Dona Seraphina stepped to her far side, the four of them arrayed in a line facing the final flight. The Hierarch raised her censer and chanted; the golem smiled beatifically, looking like a man too rapt to speak.

Chisaad glanced aside over the crowds below the Hill. The mass churned oddly, arms pointing at something behind the towering cone.

Then the Hierarch and the golem stepped forward simultaneously to approach the last fifty steps. Chisaad moved in lockstep with her, the long tail of candidates on their heels. He was so close to success that he could taste it.

A shout wafted up the Hill from the crowd. His pulse began to pound.

The Hill's defensive spells activated—on the back side. Streamers of magic wreathed the top. He gaped and missed a step, as did everyone else in the procession with any magesight. *What?*

Then the defending spells furled themselves exactly as if commanded.

"Excuse me," Chisaad muttered. "I must attend to the Hill." Through his spider he ordered the golem to ascend slowly, then hurried up the steps ahead of the sedate procession. The Hierarch frowned after him but did not object. She set her aged feet on the first step at the measured pace of the golem. Everyone else, bound by tradition, followed.

* * *

The carpet topped the Hill with a last bound and settled roughly to the pavement between the first two bollards. The Ilvar mage sagged, spent and stunned by the tremendous effort he'd put forth. Kirin staggered off the fabric onto gleaming pavement. He caught Terrell as the prince nearly fell in his wake.

"You must offer yourself to it first," Terrell panted to him. "It has to know you before you can try for the Crown. All of the Twenty have been brought here before to meet it. It's your turn."

Kirin stared at the gleaming marble chair. He'd never seen anything as pure white in his life. The silver and amethyst Crown shone quietly on the seat. *I have to touch the throne?*

Open yourself to it first.

Kirin swallowed, his throat tightening. He could see spells wreathing the Throne, the Crown, the whole top of the Hill, a bewildering abundance of spells. The node below rose from an unimaginable depth to a point right beneath the pavement. He'd never been so close to any node before Skyrock, and this one was immeasurably stronger.

His Shadow quailed into a hard ball under his heart, afraid. Not of the power, he understood, but of what ruled it. Something lived inside that marble chair, something that watched him with an enormous concentration.

This is it, he thought, frightened down to his toes. *I either do it, or I don't. And I've got a feeling that whatever-that-is will not let me choose 'don't.'*

The air seemed to ripple in affirmation. The Stone Throne waited.

Kirin took a deep breath, squared his shoulders, and walked towards the snowy marble block. Magic bathed him, threaded through him, cradled him, and his Shadow only curled tighter. He reached the little dais, hesitated, then stretched out his right hand and laid it on the corner of the Throne's left arm. The marble felt cool to the touch and strangely alive.

"I'm Kirin," he began, paused, said, "I mean, I think they named me Ryghar DuRillin DiGwythlo when I was born, but Kirin is the name I'm used to. And I'm here."

The white marble began to glow. First rose, then orange, yellow, through green and turquoise, to blue and violet and finally, the royal purple of the flag flying above the Aretzo Palace. The glow filled the top of the Hill like a giant candle flame. A voice spoke inside his head, sexless and ageless, as scorching as the Suns and as soft as a butterfly wing. It filled him to the skin.

WELCOME, RYGHAR-CALLED-KIRIN. YOU HAVE BEEN KNOWN TO ME SINCE YOUR BIRTH.

"Who," Kirin paused and wet his lips. "Who are you?"

I AM JUDGEMENT.

He swallowed a hundred questions and asked the only important one. "What should I do?"

SHOW ME WHAT YOU ARE.

* * *

Terrell gaped at the sight of the purple glow.

He raised it to purple. I only managed blue. He is judged more worthy than me. All the years I've spent preparing, and Kirin is more acceptable? Acid jealousy scorched his heart. His hands clenched into fists so tight that his fingernails gouged his hard sword-calluses. *He can't possibly be as good a king as I could!*

Then shame flooded him. *Oh no. I'm a fool. This too was a test, and I failed it. Even with all the warnings, I still chose Azerin and Zablock's path. My vanity is more important to me than my service.* He bowed his head and wished that the sky would fall and crush him. *My God, my God, I have failed Thee and my line both. I am truly not worthy.*

* * *

Chisaad leaped up the last steps and burst onto the top of the Hill. His shocked gaze took in Terrell standing head-bowed in front of the second bollard, the passed-out Ilvar mage sprawled on his carpet, and—Kirin? With a hand on the Throne and purple radiance bathing him.

Kirin is royal? Chisaad nearly choked in shock. *He can't be!*

"Get away before it kills you, boy!" He barked in his most commanding voice as he strode closer. Meanwhile his mind keyed his planted spells and activated them all at once.

Kirin turned to face him as the purple glow shrank to a glowing ball above the Throne. "It won't kill me, Magist- No. I'll never call you that again." A cold rage filled the boy's face. "You betrayed me and Terrell both. My father and my wife both died because of you." His hand went to the knife at his belt, drew it and came at him.

Even after months of studying the lad, Chisaad's ingrained habits betrayed him. He threw a lightning bolt at Kirin. It vanished into his Shadow as if it had never been. Then Kirin was on him and raised the knife.

At the last second Chisaad dissolved it to dust. Kirin's fist slammed his chest almost hard enough to crack ribs and the wizard staggered. Half of his spells shattered in a whirl of broken magics.

Kirin swore and flung the handful of dust aside, grabbed Chisaad's robes and dragged his face down to his own. "You murdering bastard," the boy growled, his eyes, black as the pit, staring into Chisaad's.

The wizard's knees gave way and by pure chance he did the right thing; he dropped to the pavement. Kirin lost his grip and tripped over him, the boy's arms windmilling. Fear hammering in his veins, Chisaad scrambled across the pavement toward the Throne and triggered his planted spells. As Kirin recovered, three ghostly shapes erupted from the pavement like sand vipers. Chisaad scrambled between them and staggered to his feet as he ran for the Throne. Behind him Kirin paused, stared at the slithering coils of jet, ruby, and gold while Terrell shouted at him. Then the boy charged through them.

The hesitation had lasted just long enough for Chisaad to make it to the Throne. Kirin caught him on the dias, seized his shoulder with wrenching strength, spun him around and slammed him against the Throne's left arm. A painful jolt shot up and down the wizard's back and for an instant he thought his spine had been broken. Kirin stared into his face and growled like a beast. Terror rippled over Chisaad like a tsunami; he had never been manhandled in his life. Then Kirin drew back a fist and slammed it into his soft belly. Pain exploded.

He can beat me bloody and I cannot stop him, Chisaad knew. He ignored pain and fear both to stretch out his right hand and grasp the Crown.

I RECOGNIZE YOU, CHISAAD DuVAYA DiSILBARI, said a voice in Chisaad's head.

"I am the eldest son of King Tollir!" Chisaad gasped as Kirin punched him again. "You will serve me, Throne! I compel you!" He triggered the strongest of his carefully laid spells.

A purple glow wrapped the crown and flowed up the wizard's forearm. Kirin, stunned, stopped punching him to stare. Chisaad tugged on the Crown.

It didn't move.

YOU CAN CORRUPT THE SPELLS YOUR ANCESTORS LAID IN THIS VESSEL, the voice inside his head calmly informed him. BUT I WHO INHABIT IT CANNOT BE COMPELLED BY ANY MORTAL.

Then the purple glow around his hand turned black and began to flow up his arm.

"No!" Chisaad screeched. He pushed aside pain and fear entirely to push back with every scrap of power at his command. The black tide stopped, wavered, began to reverse.

Kirin ripped his magic from him with a twohanded motion that spun the boy right off the dias. He caught his balance on the pavement, held up triumphant fists roiling with wizardly power, and absorbed it.

Chisaad, bruised, emptied, stared in horrified fascination as his hand melted to black ash, then his arm, and finally his mind.

* * *

Ashes blew away on the breeze. Terrell blinked as the afterimages faded from his eyes. On the Steps, voices were raised in consternation.

Kirin stepped back onto the dias, put his hands upon the crown and lifted it from the Throne. Purple light bathed him.

Terrell stepped forward and knelt before his brother. "My King," he said, his voice choked. *I hope I can be useful to him, help him learn what he needs to know*, he thought in repentance. *Please God, help me to help him to be a good king.*

Then Kirin pressed the Crown down on his head.

The weight was both featherlight and heavy as a mountain. Startled, Terrell shot to his feet as the Ilvar mage sat up and gaped owllike at both of them.

"This is what I am," Kirin declared calmly.

A vast sense of approval answered him; Terrell felt it too. Then they both heard the Throne's voice whisper in their heads. THAT IS A WORTHY DEED FOR A WORTHY MAN.

The overwhelming presence faded out of both their minds.

Terrell's hands crept up to touch the shining silver. "You—you—"

Yes, Kirin answered inside his head. *I know what I am—and what you can be. You'll be a great king, and I'm going back to the Sump to be a great acrobat. Don't tell them about me, please. Let Ryghar stay dead. Just let me be Kirin DiUmbra.*

Terrell stared at him. *But you don't even really know what you can do yet! You have power—*

I know enough. Promise me, please, brother? Keep my secret?

Terrell nodded slowly. *As you wish. I'm not sure it will work, but I promise.*

Kirin turned to look at the Ilvar mage. *Now please, send me home.*

Terrell gestured as Kirin stepped on the carpet. "Take him where he wishes to go, Master of the Air."

The Ilvar bowed and raised his carpet. Kirin crouched easily on the moving fabric, as balanced as if he rode a trapeze. His Shadow stayed tight within him as the carpet slipped over the back of the hill and descended.

Then two panting priestesses and the remaining Twenty swarmed over the top of the Five Hundred Steps, led by the stolidly marching golem. Terrell had to turn his attention away from his disappearing brother.

But not my heart. Oh my dearest brother, what you have done for me!

* * *

The carpet dived down the steep slope, gained speed, and halfway to the bottom it soared out over the crowd. Kirin rode it easily, ignoring the mob of onlookers hundreds of feet below.

The Master of the Air looked at him in more than a little awe. "Where should I take you, My Lord?"

"The roof of the Sulfur Serpent. I'll show you the way. Then forget you ever met me."

The wizard bowed his head.

They flew away as people below shouted and pointed, but the crowd lost track of them soon enough, when a greater spectacle distracted them.

* * *

The Hierarch looked from Terrell to the golem. "Two?" she panted.

"Only one," Terrell told her as he stalked toward his likeness. "That is a false image made by Chisaad, who tried to usurp the Throne."

Dona Seraphina's eyes narrowed and she reached out to send her aura into the golem. "What—"

The golem slapped her hand aside and drew its jeweled belt knife. "I am the true king!" it shouted in Terrell's voice and leaped to meet him, blade poised.

Terrell raised a hand and focused his Light. The golem dissolved into a collapsing mass of wood and wire. The knife clattered on the pavement amid gasps from the Twenty. All eyes went to the silver crown on Terrell's head and the glowing amethyst atop it.

"This is shockingly irregular!" howled DiSolera. "The Choosing must be done where all candidates can see! I protest!"

"I understand your concern, My Lord, and I thank you for it," Terrell told him politely. He lifted the Crown off his head and set it on the Throne once more. "Please, any one of you who is numbered among the Twenty, feel free to test yourselves against the Throne's will. Only pardon Chisaad's ashes there on the seat and floor; he proved too unworthy for the Throne to tolerate."

The next man in line hesitated, thanked Terrell, gently laid a hand on the crown and tugged. He hastily released it when it didn't budge and bowed himself away. Three others tried with similar trepidation, and similar results. DiSolera arrogantly walked up and seized it in both hands—then jumped and fell backward off the dais as sparks flew from the immovable Crown.

"I don't think it likes you, My Lord," Seraphina observed loudly, to a mass chuckle as the shaken noble scrambled to his feet and backed away.

The rest tried it with no more sparks. Terrell picked up the Crown again, put it on his head, and sat on the Throne. A purple light shot from the top of the Hill and burst like the biggest fireworks ever seen in Aretzo, and a great trumpet rang in the minds of all watching.

The crowd roared. The Hierarch, who had observed the whole effort with gimlet-eyed concentration, relaxed and smiled. "We have a new King," she proclaimed, as Penghar pelted up the Steps to announce Ap Marn's arrest.

Brother, Terrell sent out the thought before his people swept him into their embrace and the thousand details of duty. *I'll be here for you, always.*

* * *

Kirin didn't answer with words. The Master of Air let him off on the great humped roof of the Sulfur Serpent as celebration filled the streets and courtyard below. Kirin balanced there on the ridge to look down at it all.

I have to find my son, he thought, exhilaration fading to melancholy. *Mourn Maia; they must have buried her by now. Tell everybody about Pieter and see if we can bring his body home. Clean up, get my clothes patched. And get on with life.*

He climbed down the familiar slates, swung over the edge and dropped onto the top landing of the back stairway, and went inside to startled shouts of joy and welcome.

All the while, his Shadow nestled under his heart, calm and waiting.

OTHER WORKS

For more works by Peter Sartucci, visit
http://www.petersartucci.com/author.html.html

www.ingramcontent.com/pod-product-compliance
Lightning Source LLC
Chambersburg PA
CBHW072300020726
47501CB00002B/329